**As soon as Duke Orsea realized he'd lo
war, and his country's only hope of survival, ne o.
a general retreat. It was the only sensible thing he'd
done all day.**

One hour had made all the difference. An hour ago, when he'd
led the attack, the world had been a very different place. He'd had
an army of twenty-five thousand men, one-tenth of the population
of the Duchy of Eremia. He had a commanding position, a fully
loaded supplies-and-equipment train, a carefully prepared battle
plan, the element of surprise, the love and trust of his people, and
hope. Now, as the horns blared and the ragged lines crumpled and
dissolved into swarms of running dots, he had the miserable job
of getting as many as he could of the fourteen thousand stunned,
bewildered, and resentful survivors away from the enemy cavalry
and back to the relative safety of the mountains.

One hour to change the world; not many men could have done
such a thorough job. It took a particular genius to destroy one's
life so comprehensively in so short a time.

Praise for
K. J. Parker

"A richly textured and emotionally complex fantasy....
Highly recommended."

—*Library Journal* (starred review)

"When so many fantasy sagas are tired, warmed-over affairs,
a writer like K. J. Parker is more of a hurricane than a
breath of fresh air."

—*Dreamwatch*

By K. J. Parker

THE FENCER TRILOGY

Colours in the Steel

The Belly of the Bow

The Proof House

THE SCAVENGER TRILOGY

Shadow

Pattern

Memory

THE ENGINEER TRILOGY

Devices and Desires

Evil for Evil

The Escapement

Devices and Desires

THE ENGINEER TRILOGY
Book One

by K. J. Parker

www.orbitbooks.net
New York London

Copyright © 2005 by K. J. Parker

Orbit
Hachette Book Group USA
237 Park Avenue, New York, NY 10017
Visit our Web site at www.HachetteBookGroupUSA.com

First American Edition, October 2007

First published in Great Britain by Orbit, 2005

Orbit is a trademark of Little, Brown Book Group Ltd.

The characters and events in this book are fictitious. Any similarity to real persons, living or dead, is coincidental and not intended by the author.

Library of Congress Cataloging-in-Publication Data
Parker, K. J.
   Devices and desires / by K. J. Parker. — 1st ed.
      p.   cm. — (The engineer trilogy ; bk. 1)
   ISBN 0-316-00338-7 / 978-0-316-00338-4
   I. Title.
   PR6116.A745D48 2007
   823'.92 — dc22   2007009926

10 9 8 7 6 5 4 3 2 1

Q-FF

Printed in the United States of America

*For Tim Holman, for letting me swim out of my depth,
and for Kester, who I knew before he was infamous*

Devices and Desires

1

"The quickest way to a man's heart," said the instructor, "is proverbially through his stomach. But if you want to get into his brain, I recommend the eye-socket."

Like a whip cracking, he uncurled his languid slouch into the taut, straight lines of the lunge. His forearm launched from the elbow like an arrow as his front leg plunged forward, and the point of the long, slim sword darted, neat as a component in a machine, through the exact center of the finger-ring that dangled from a cord tied to the beam.

It was typical of Valens' father that he insisted on his son learning the new fencing; the stock, the tuck, the small-sword and the rapier. It was elegant, refined, difficult, endlessly time-consuming and, of course, useless. A brigandine or even a thick winter coat would turn one of those exquisite points; if you wanted to have any chance of doing useful work, you had to aim for the holes in the face, targets no bigger than an eight-mark coin. Against a farm worker with a hedging tool, you stood no chance whatsoever. But, for ten years, Valens had flounced and stretched up and down a chalk line in a drafty shed that hadn't been cleaned out since it was still a stable. When he could hit the apple, the instructor had hung up a plum, and then a damson. Now he could get the damson nine times out of ten, and so the ring had taken its place.

Once he'd mastered that, he wondered what he'd be faced with next. The eye of a darning-needle, probably.

"Better," the instructor said, as the point of Valens' sword nicked the ring's edge, making it tinkle like a cow-bell. "Again."

It was typical of Valens that he suffered through his weekly lesson, face frozen and murder in his heart, always striving to do better even though he knew the whole thing was an exercise in fatuity. Fencing was last lesson but one on a Monday; on Wednesday evening, when he actually had an hour free, he paid one of the guardsmen four marks an hour to teach him basic sword and shield, and another two marks to keep the secret from his father. He was actually quite good at proper fencing, or so the guardsman said; but the tuck had no cutting edge, only a point, so he couldn't slice the grin off the instructor's face with a smart backhand wrap, as he longed to do. Instead, he was tethered to this stupid chalk line, like a grazing goat.

"That'll do," the instructor said, two dozen lunges later. "For next week, I want you to practice the hanging guard and the volte."

Valens dipped his head in a perfunctory nod; the instructor scooped up his armful of swords, unhooked his ring and left the room. It was still raining outside, and he had a quarter of an hour before he had to present himself in the west tower for lute and rebec. Awkwardly—it was too small for him at the best of times, and now his fingers were hot and swollen—he eased the ring off his right index finger and cast around for a bit of string.

Usually, he did much better when the instructor wasn't there, when he was on his own. That was fatuous too, since the whole idea of a sword-fight is that there's someone to fight with. Today, though, he was worse solo than he'd been during the lesson. He lunged again, missed, hit the string, which wrapped itself insultingly round the sword-point. Maybe it was simply too difficult for him.

That thought didn't sit comfortably, so he came at the problem

from a different angle. Obviously, he told himself, the reason I can't do it is because it's not difficult *enough*.

Having freed his sword, he stepped back to a length; then he leaned forward just a little and tapped the ring on its edge, setting it swinging. Then he lunged again.

Six times out of six; enough to prove his point. When the ring swung backward and forward, he didn't just have a hole to aim at, he had a line. If he judged the forward allowance right, it was just a simple matter of pointing with the sword as though it was a finger. He steadied the ring until it stopped swinging, stepped back, lunged again and missed. Maybe I should have been a cat, he thought. Cats only lash out at moving objects; if it's still, they can't see it.

He cut the ring off the cord with his small knife and jammed it back on his finger, trapping a little fold of skin. Rebec next; time to stop being a warrior and become an artist. When he was Duke, of course, the finest musicians in the world would bribe his chamberlains for a chance to play while he chatted to his guests or read the day's intelligence reports, ignoring them completely. The son of a powerful, uneducated man has a hard time of it, shouldering the burden of all the advantages his father managed so well without.

An hour of the rebec left his fingertips numb and raw; and then it was time for dinner. That brought back into sharp focus the question he'd been dodging and parrying all day; would she still be there, or had his father sent her back home? If she'd left already—if, while he'd been scanning hexameters and hendeca-syllables, stabbing at dangling jewelry and picking at wire, she'd packed up her bags and walked out of his life, possibly forever—at least he wouldn't have to sit all night at the wrong end of the table, straining to catch a word or two of what she said to someone else. If she was still here.... He cast up his mental accounts, trying to figure out if he was owed a miracle. On balance, he decided, probably not. According to the holy friars, it took three hundred hours of prayer or five hundred of good works to buy a miracle, and he was at least sixty short on either count. All he could afford out of his accrued merit was a revelatory vision of the Divinity, and he wasn't too bothered about that.

If she was still here.

On the off chance, he went back to his room, pulled off his sweaty, dusty shirt and winnowed through his clothes-chest for a replacement. The black, with silver threads and two gold buttons at the neck, made him look like a jackdaw, so he went for the red, with last year's sleeves (but, duke's son or not, he lived in the mountains; if it came in from outside, it came slowly, on a mule), simply because it was relatively clean and free of holes. Shoes; his father chose his shoes for him, and the fashion was still for poulaines, with their ridiculously long pointy toes. He promised himself that she wouldn't be able to see his feet under the table (besides, she wouldn't still be here), and pulled out his good mantle from the bottom of the chest. It was only civet, but it helped mask the disgraceful length of his neck. A glance in the mirror made him wince, but it was the best he could do.

Sixty hours, he told himself; sixty rotten hours I could've made up easily, if only I'd known.

Protocol demanded that he sit on his father's left at dinner. Tonight, the important guest was someone he didn't know, although the man's brown skin and high cheekbones made it easy enough to guess where he was from. An ambassador from Mezentia; no wonder his father was preoccupied, waving his hands and smiling (two generations of courtiers had come to harm trying to point out to the Duke that his smile was infinitely more terrifying than his frown), while the little bald brown man nodded politely and picked at his dinner like a starling. One quick look gave Valens all the information he needed about what was going on there. On his own left, the Chancellor was discussing climbing roses with the controller of the mines. So that was all right; he was free to look round without having to talk to anybody.

She was still here. There was a tiny prickle of guilt mixed in with his relief. She was, after all, a hostage. If she hadn't been sent home, it meant that there'd been some last-minute hitch in the treaty negotiations, and the war between the two dukedoms, two centuries old, was still clinging on to life by a thread. Sooner or later, though, the treaty would be signed: peace would end the fighting and the desperate waste of lives and money, heal the country's wounds and bring the conscript farmers and miners back home; peace would take her away from him before he'd even had a chance to talk to her alone. For now, though, the war was still here and so was she.

(A small diplomatic incident, maybe; if he could contrive it that their ambassador bumped into him on the stairs and knocked him down a flight or two. Would an act of clumsiness toward the heir apparent be enough to disrupt the negotiations for a week or ten days? On the other hand, if he fell awkwardly and broke his neck, might that not constitute an act of war, leading to summary execution of the hostages? And he'd be dead too, of course, for what that was worth.)

Something massive stirred on his right; his father was standing up to say something, and everybody had stopped talking. There was a chance it might be important (Father loved to annoy his advisers by making vital announcements out of the blue at dinner), so Valens tucked in his elbows, looked straight ahead and listened.

But it wasn't anything. The little bald man from Mezentia turned out to be someone terribly important, grand secretary of the Foundrymen's and Machinists' Guild (in Father's court, secretaries were fast-moving, worried-looking men who could write; but apparently they ruled Mezentia, and therefore, by implication, the world), and he was here as an observer to the treaty negotiations, and this was extremely good. Furthermore, as a token of the Republic's respect and esteem, he'd brought an example of cutting-edge Mezentine technology, which they would all have the privilege of seeing demonstrated after dinner.

Distracted as he was by the distant view of the top of her head, Valens couldn't help being slightly curious about that. Everyday

Mezentine technology was so all-pervasive you could scarcely turn round in the castle without knocking some of it over. Every last cup and dish, from the best service reserved for state occasions down to the pewter they ate off when nobody was looking, had come from the Republic's rolling mills; every candle stood in a Mezentine brass candlestick, its light doubled by a Mezentine mirror hanging from a Mezentine nail. But extra-special cutting-edge didn't make it up the mountain passes very often, which meant they had to make do with rumors; the awestruck whispers of traders and commercial travelers, the panicky reports of military intelligence, and the occasional gross slander from a competitor, far from home and desperate. If the little bald man had brought a miracle with him (the ten-thousand-mark kind, rather than the three-hundred-hour variety), Valens reckoned he could spare a little attention for it, though his heart might be broken beyond repair by even the masters of the Solderers' and Braziers' Guild.

The miracle came in a plain wooden crate. It was no more than six feet long by three wide, but it took a man at each corner to move it—a heavy miracle, then. Two Mezentines with grave faces and crowbars prised the crate open; out came a lot of straw, and some curly cedar shavings, and then something which Valens assumed was a suit of armor. It was man-high, man-shaped and shiny, and the four attendants lifted it up and set it down on some kind of stand. Fine, Valens thought. Father'll be happy, he likes armor. But then the attendants did something odd. One of them reached into the bottom of the crate and fished out a steel tube with a ring through one end; a key, but much larger than anything of the kind Valens had seen before. It fitted into a slot in the back of the armor; some kind of specially secure, sword-proof fastening? Apparently not; one of the attendants began turning it over and over again, and each turn produced a clicking sound, like the skittering of mice's feet on a thin ceiling. Meanwhile, two more crates had come in. One of them held nothing more than an ordinary blacksmith's anvil—polished, true, like a silver chalice, but otherwise no big deal. The other was full of tools; hammers, tongs, cold chisels, swages, boring stuff. The anvil came to rest at the suit of armor's feet, and one of the Mezentines prised open the suit's steel fingers and closed them around the stem of a three-pound hammer.

"The operation of the machine..." Valens looked round to see who was talking. It was the short, bald man, the grand secretary. He had a low, rich voice with a fairly mild accent. "The operation of the machine is quite straightforward. A powerful spiral spring, similar to those used in clockwork, is put under tension by winding with a key. Once released, it bears on a flywheel, causing it to spin. A gear train and a series of cams and connecting rods transmits this motion to the machine's main spindle, from which belt-driven takeoffs power the arms. Further cams and trips effect the reciprocating movement, simulating the work of the human arm."

Whatever that was supposed to mean. It didn't look like anybody else understood it either, to judge from the rows of perfectly blank faces around the tables. But then the key-turner stopped turning, pulled out his key and pushed something; and the suit of armor's arm lifted to head height, stopped and fell, and the hammer in its hand rang on the anvil like a silver bell.

Not armor after all; Valens could feel his father's disappointment through the boards of the table. Of course Valens knew what it was, though he'd never seen anything like it. He'd read about it in some book; the citizens of the Perpetual Republic had a childish love of mechanical toys, metal gadgets that did things almost but not quite as well as people could. It was a typically Mezentine touch to send a mechanical blacksmith. Here is a machine, they were saying, that could make another machine just like itself, the way you ordinary humans breed children. Well; it was their proud boast that they had a machine for everything. Mechanizing reproduction, though, was surely cutting off their noses to spite their collective face.

The hammer rang twelve times, then stopped. Figures, Valens

thought. You get a dozen hits at a bit of hot metal before it cools down and needs to go back in the fire. While you're waiting for it to heat up again, you've got time to wind up your mechanical slave. Query whether turning the key is harder work than swinging the hammer yourself would be. In any event, it's just a trip-hammer thinly disguised as a man. Now then; a man convincingly disguised as a trip-hammer, that'd be worth walking a mile to see.

Stunned silence for a moment or so, followed by loud, nervous applause. The little grand secretary stood up, smiled vaguely and sat down again; that concluded the demonstration.

Ten minutes after he got up from the table, Valens couldn't remember what he'd just eaten, or the name of the trade attaché he'd just been introduced to, or the date; as for the explanation of how the heavy miracle worked, it had vanished from his mind completely. That was unfortunate.

"I was wondering," she repeated. "Did you understand what that man said, about how the metal blacksmith worked? I'm afraid I didn't catch any of it, and my father's sure to ask me when I get home."

So she was going home, then. The irony; at last he was talking to her, and tomorrow she was going away. Further irony; it had been his father himself who'd brought them together; *Valens, come over here and talk to the Countess Sirupati.* Father had been towering over her, the way the castle loomed over the village below, all turrets and battlements, and he'd been smiling, which accounted for the look of terror in her eyes. Valens had wanted to reassure her; it's all right, he hasn't actually eaten anybody for weeks. Instead, he'd stood and gawped, and then he'd looked down at his shoes (poulaines, with the ridiculous pointy toes). And then she'd asked him about the mechanical blacksmith.

He pulled himself together, like a boy trying to draw his father's bow. "I'm not really the right person to ask," he said. "I don't know a lot about machines and stuff."

Her expression didn't change, except that it glazed slightly. Of course she didn't give a damn about how the stupid machine worked; she was making conversation. "I think," he went on, "that there's a sort of wheel thing in its chest going round and round, and it's linked to cogs and gears and what have you. Oh, and there's cams, to turn the round and round into up and down."

She blinked at him. "What's a cam?" she asked.

"Ah." What indeed? "Well, it's sort of…" Three hours a week with a specially imported Doctor of Rhetoric, from whom he was supposed to learn how to express himself with clarity, precision and grace. "It's sort of like this," he went on, miming with his hands. "The wheel goes round, you see, and on the edge of the wheel there's like a bit sticking out. Each time it goes round, it kind of bashes on a sort of lever arrangement, like a see-saw; and the lever thing pivots, like it goes down at the bashed end and up at the other end — that's how the arm lifts — and when it's done that, it drops down again under its own weight, nicely in time for the sticky-out bit on the wheel to bash it again. And so on."

"I see," she said. "Yes, I think I understand it now."

"Really?"

"No," she said. "But thank you for trying."

He frowned. "Well, it was probably the worst explanation of anything I've ever heard in my life."

She nodded. "Maybe," she said. "But at least you didn't say, oh, you're only a girl, you wouldn't understand."

He wasn't quite sure what to make of that. Tactically (four hours a week on the Art of War, with General Bozannes) he felt he probably had a slight advantage, a weak point in the line he could probably turn, if he could get his cavalry there in time. Somehow, though, he felt that the usages of the wars didn't apply here, or if they did they shouldn't. Odd; because even before he'd started having formal lessons, he'd run his life like a military campaign, and the usages of war applied to *everything*.

"Well," he said, "I'm a boy and I haven't got a clue. I suppose it's different in Mezentia."

"Oh, it is," she said. "I've been there, actually."

"Really? I mean, what's it like?"

She withdrew into a shell of thought, shutting out him and all the world. "Strange," she said. "Not like anywhere else, really. Oh, it's very grand and big and the buildings are huge and all closely packed together, but that's not what I meant. I can't describe it, really." She paused, and Valens realized he was holding his breath. "We all went there for some diplomatic thing, my father and my sisters and me; it was shortly before my eldest sister's wedding, and I think it was something to do with the negotiations. I was thirteen then, no, twelve. Anyway, I remember there was this enormous banquet in one of the Guild halls. Enormous place, full of statues and tapestries, and there was this amazing painting on the ceiling, a sea-battle or something like that; and all these people were in their fanciest robes, with gold chains round their necks and silks and all kinds of stuff like that. But the food came on these crummy old wooden dishes, and there weren't any knives or forks, just a plain wooden spoon."

Fork? he wondered; what's a farm tool got to do with eating? "Very odd," he agreed. "What was the food like?"

"Horrible. It was very fancy and sort of fussy, the way it was put on the plate, with all sorts of leaves and frills and things to make it look pretty; but really it was just bits of meat and dumplings in slimy sauce."

To the best of his recollection, Valens had never wanted anything in his entire life. Things had come his way, a lot of them; like the loathsome pointy-toed poulaines, the white thoroughbred mare that hated him and tried to bite his feet, the kestrel that wouldn't come back when it was called, the itchy damask pillows, the ivory-handled rapier, all the valuable junk his father kept giving him. He'd been brought up to take care of his possessions, so he treated them with respect until they wore out, broke or died; but he had no love for them, no pride in owning them. He knew that stuff like that mattered to most people; it was a fact about humanity that he accepted without understanding. Other boys his age had wanted a friend; but Valens had always known that the Duke's son didn't make friends; and besides, he preferred thinking to talking, just as he liked to walk on his own. He'd never wanted to be Duke, because that would only happen when his father died. Now, for the first time, he felt what it was like to want something—but, he stopped to consider, is it actually possible to want a person? How? As a pet; to keep in a mews or a stable, to feed twice a day when not in use. It would be possible, of course. You could keep a person, a girl for instance, in a stable or a bower; you could walk her and feed her, dress her and go to bed with her, but.... He didn't want *ownership*. He was the Duke's son, as such he owned everything and nothing. There was a logical paradox here—Doctor Galeazza would be proud of him—but it was so vague and unfamiliar that he didn't know how to begin formulating an equation to solve it. All he could do was be aware of the feeling, which was disturbingly intense.

Not that it mattered. She was going home tomorrow.

"Slimy sauce," he repeated. "Yetch. You had to eat it, I suppose, or risk starting a war."

She smiled, and he looked away, but the smile followed him. "Not all of it," she said. "You've got to leave some if you're a girl, it's ladylike. Not that I minded terribly much."

Valens nodded. "When I was a kid I had to finish everything on my plate, or it'd be served up cold for breakfast and lunch until I ate it. Which was fine," he went on, "I knew where I stood. But when I was nine, we had to go to a reception at the Lorican embassy—"

She giggled. She was way ahead of him. "And they think that if you eat everything on your plate it's a criticism, that they haven't given you enough."

She'd interrupted him and stolen his joke, but he didn't mind. She'd shared his thought. That didn't happen very often.

"Of course," he went on, "nobody bothered telling me, I was just a kid; so I was grimly munching my way through my dinner—"

"Rice," she said. "Plain boiled white rice, with noodles and stuff."

He nodded. "And as soon as I got to the end, someone'd snatch my plate away and dump another heap of the muck on it and hand it back; I thought I'd done something bad and I was being punished. I was so full I could hardly breathe. But Father was busy talking business, and nobody down my end of the table was going to say anything; I'd probably be there still, only—"

He stopped dead.

"Only?"

"I threw up," he confessed; it wasn't a good memory. "All over the tablecloth, and their Lord Chamberlain."

She laughed. He expected to feel hurt, angry. Instead, he laughed too. He had no idea why he should think it was funny, but it was.

"And was there a war?" she asked.

"Nearly," he replied. "God, that rice. I can still taste it if I shut my eyes."

Now she was nodding. "I was there for a whole year," she said. "Lorica, I mean. The rice is what sticks in my mind too. No pun intended."

He thought about that. "You sound like you've been to a lot of places," he said.

"Oh yes." She didn't sound happy about it, which struck him as odd. He'd never been outside the dukedom in his life. "In fact, I've spent more time away than at home."

Well, he had to ask. "Why?"

The question appeared to surprise her. "It's what I'm for," she said. "I guess you could say it's my job."

"Job?"

She nodded again. "Professional hostage. Comes of being the fifth of seven daughters. You see," she went on, "we've got to get married in age order, it's protocol or something, and there's still two of them older than me left; I can't get married till they are. So, the only thing I'm useful for while I'm waiting my turn is being a hostage. Which means, when they're doing a treaty or a settlement or something, off I go on my travels until it's all sorted out."

"That's…" That's barbaric, he was about to say, but he knew better than that. He knew the theory perfectly well (statecraft, two hours a week with Chancellor Vetuarius), but he'd never given it any thought before; like people getting killed in the wars, something that happened but was best not dwelt on. "It must be interesting," he heard himself say. "I've never been abroad."

She paused, considering her reply. "Actually, it's quite dull, mostly. It's not like I get to go out and see things, and one guest wing's pretty like another."

(And, she didn't say, there's always the thought of what might happen if things go wrong.)

"I guess so," he said. "Well, I hope it hasn't been too boring here."

"Boring?" She looked at him. "I wouldn't say that. Going hunting with your father was—"

"Quite." Valens managed not to wince. "I didn't know he'd dragged you out with him. Was it very horrible?"

She shook her head. "I've been before, so the blood and stuff doesn't bother me. It was the standing about waiting for something to happen that got to me."

Valens nodded. "Was it raining?"

"Yes."

"It always rains." He pulled a face. "Whenever I hear about the terrible droughts in the south, and they're asking is it because God's angry with them or something, I know it's just because Dad doesn't go hunting in the south. He could earn a good living as a rainmaker."

She smiled, but he knew his joke hadn't really bitten home. That disconcerted him; usually it had them laughing like drains. Or perhaps they only laughed because he was the Duke's son. "Well," she said, "that was pretty boring. But the rest of it was…" She shrugged. "It was fine."

The shrug hurt. "Any rate," he said briskly, "you'll be home for harvest festival."

"It's not a big thing where I come from," she replied; and then, like an eclipse of the sun that stops the battle while the issue's still in the balance, the chamberlain came out to drive them all into the Great Hall for singing and a recital by the greatest living exponent of the psaltery.

Valens watched her being bustled away with the other women, until an equerry whisked him off to take his place in the front row.

Ironically, the singer sang nothing but love-songs; aubades about young lovers parted by the dawn, razos between the pining youth and the cynical go-between, the bitter complaints of the girl torn from her darling to marry a rich, elderly stranger. All through the endless performance he didn't dare turn round, but the thought that she was somewhere in the rows behind was like an unbearable itch. The greatest living psalterist seemed to linger spitefully over each note, as if he *knew*. The candles were guttering by the time he finally ground to a halt. There would be no more socializing that evening, and in the morning (early, to catch the coolest part of the day) she'd be going home.

(I could start a war, he thought, as he trudged up the stairs to bed. I could conspire with a disaffected faction or send the keys of a frontier post to the enemy; then we'd be at war again, and she could come back as a hostage. Or maybe we could lose, and I could go there; all the same to me, so long as...)

He lay in bed with the lamp flickering, just enough light to see dim shapes by. On the opposite wall, the same boarhounds that had given him nightmares when he was six carried on their endless duel with the boar at bay, trapped in the fibers of the tapestry. He could see them just as well when his eyes were shut; two of them, all neck and almost no head, had their teeth in the boar's front leg, while a third had him by the ear and hung twisting in mid-air, while the enemy's tusks ripped open a fourth from shoulder to tail. Night after night he'd wondered as he lay there which he was, the dogs or the pig, the hunters or the quarry. It was one of the few questions in his life to which he had yet to resolve an answer. It was possible that he was both, a synthesis of the two, made possible by the shared act of ripping and tearing. His father had had the tapestry put there in the hope that it'd inspire him with a love of the chase; but it wasn't a chase, it was a single still moment (perhaps he couldn't see it because it didn't move, like the ring hanging from the rafter); and therefore it represented nothing. Tonight, it made him think of her, standing in the rain while the lymers snuffled up and down false trails, his father bitching at the harborers and the masters of the hounds, the courtiers silent and wet waiting for the violence to begin.

The peace won't last, they said. They gave it three months, then six, then a year; just possibly three years, or five at the very most. Meanwhile, Count Sirupat's third daughter married the Prince of Boha (bad news for the shepherds, the lumber merchants and the dealers in trained falcons, but good for the silver miners and refiners, who were the ones who mattered), and his fourth daughter married her third cousin, Valens' fourth cousin, the Elector of Spalado.

Father celebrated Valens' nineteenth birthday with a hunt; a three-day battue, with the whole army marshaled in the mountains to drive the combes and passes down to the valley, where the long nets were set up like lines of infantry waiting to receive a cavalry charge. On the morning of the third day, they flushed a magnificent mountain boar from the pine woods above the Blue Lake. One look at the monster's tusks sent the master hurrying to find the Duke; it'd be nothing short of treason if it fell to anybody else. But the Duke was right up the other end of the valley; he came as quickly as he could, but when he got there the boar had broken through, slicing open two guardsmen and half a dozen hounds, and was making a run for it across the water-meadows. If it made it to the birch forest on the other side of the water, they'd never find it again, so if the Duke didn't want to miss out on the trophy of a lifetime, he was going to have to address the boar on horseback. As far as Valens' father was concerned, that wasn't a problem; he galloped off after the boar, leaving his escort behind, and caught up with it about three hundred yards from the edge of the forest, in a small dip littered with granite outcrops. The boar didn't want to stop and turn at bay. It could see safety, and all it had to do was run faster than a horse. The Duke managed to slow it up with an arrow in the left shoulder, but the thought of bringing down such a spectacular animal with the bow didn't appeal to him in the least. Anybody could drain its strength with half a dozen snagging hits and then dispatch it tamely, like a farmer slaughtering the family pig. The Duke needed it to still be dangerous when he faced it down the shaft of a number four spear, or else it'd be a waste. So he urged on his horse and managed to overtake it with fifty yards or less to go. The boar was slowing down, favoring its wounded side, as he surged past it and struck with his lance. The strike was good, catching the boar just behind the ear and killing it outright. But in order to get in close he'd pulled his horse in too tight; when the boar dropped, the horse couldn't clear it in time and stumbled, throwing its rider. The Duke fell badly, landing in a nest of granite boulders. His shoulder was smashed and so was his right eye-socket, and when he tried to get up, he found he couldn't move. The dogs had caught up by then and swarmed over him to get to the boar; behind them came the front-riders, who saw what had happened and tried to lift him, until his roars of pain frightened them and they put him down again. It was dark by the time a surgeon arrived from the castle, and the lamps wouldn't stay lit in the rain and wind. Later, they said that if they'd got to him earlier, or if the huntsmen hadn't tried to move him, or if the surgeon had been able to see the full extent of the damage, it might have been different; as it was, there was very little they could do.

Valens wasn't there when it happened. He'd stayed back from the main hunt, pretending he had a headache; then, just after they'd driven the square spinney, he'd been knocked down by an old fat sow nobody had realized was there. As it happened he'd suffered nothing more than a bruised shin and a mild scat on the head; but by then he'd had about as much of his extended birthday as he could take, and lay groaning and clutching his knee until they'd loaded him on the game cart and driven him back to the castle. When they brought Father home, Valens had been lying on his bed reading a book (a twelve-thousand-line didactic poem about beekeeping). Everyone was sure his father was going to die, so Valens was hustled down into the courtyard, where they'd rigged up a tent so they wouldn't have to risk taking the Duke up the narrow spiral stairs of the gatehouse.

"It's not good." The Chancellor's face was streaked with rain, drops of water running off the spikes of hair plastered to his forehead. Like tears, Valens thought, but really only rainwater. "Truth is, the doctor can't say how bad it is, not without a proper examination; but I think we should assume the worst." He looked harassed, like a man late for an appointment who has to stop and chat with someone he daren't offend. "Which means there's a great deal to be done, and not much time. The main thing, of course, is to secure the succession."

It was as though he was talking a different language. "I don't understand," Valens said.

The Chancellor sighed. "No, I don't suppose you do. Listen. You're nineteen, so in law you're still a minor. That means a three-year regency. So, who've we got? There's rules about this sort of thing, obviously, but the fact is that they don't count for all that much when power's at stake. All it takes is a little bit of panic, and all hell's going to break loose."

While he was still talking, Valens' mind had jumped ahead. It wasn't something he'd ever considered—because Father would live forever, naturally—but now that the concept had been planted so violently in his mind, he was bright enough to see the implications. If there was a free-for-all power struggle in the Duchy, there were three obvious contenders: his cousin Count Licinius, commander of the Guards; his step-uncle Vetranio, commissioner of the mines, generally acknowledged as the main representative of the mining lobby; his cousin Count Torquatus, after Father the biggest landowner in the Duchy. Licinius had an army, but he was a cautious, unimaginative man, unlikely to take drastic action unless he felt himself threatened. Torquatus and Vetranio loathed each other, both on a personal level and as representatives of the wool trade and the mines; as such, either of them would be prepared to do whatever was necessary to stop the other getting power, and the easiest way of doing that would of course be to assume it themselves. If Vetranio won the race, Valens wouldn't give much for his chances of seeing his twentieth birthday. Vetranio was third in line of succession after his own nephew Domenicus, a seven-year-old boy that nobody would ever miss. With him and Valens out of the way, Vetranio would be Duke by right. He had thirty thousand silver-miners at his disposal, as against Licinius' six hundred Guards; Torquatus could maybe raise ten thousand men from the mountain pastures, but by the time they were mustered it'd be all over.

"What about you?" Valens asked. "Would you do it? Please?"

The Chancellor looked at him through a curtain of rain. "Me?"

"Yes, you." Valens stepped forward. He was shorter by a head than the older man, and as he looked up the rain stung his eyes. "If Father appoints you as regent before he dies, you'll be able to command the Guards. You can replace Licinius, arrest Vetranio, before they've even heard about this. With both of them out of the game, Torquatus will bide quiet and we'll be home and dry."

"I don't know," the Chancellor said. "I'd be taking a hell of a risk. And besides, what if he won't do it? Appoint me, I mean. Or supposing he doesn't wake up —"

"Listen." Valens caught him by the arm; it was thin and flabby under the heavy wool robe. "You and I go in to see him, with the doctor and a couple of your people you can trust. We come out a minute or so later and make the announcement." I shouldn't have to explain all this, he thought; he's supposed to be the politician. "The doctor and your clerks will be the witnesses. It doesn't matter a damn what actually happens, if we're the only ones who know."

The Chancellor looked away. Valens could see he was on the point of panic, like someone who's afraid of heights stuck up a ladder. Too frightened, he might well decide he'd be safer giving his support to someone with rather more power than a nineteen-year-old kid. "It's all right," Valens said firmly. "This is something that's just got to be done, that's all. If we're quick and firm, there won't be any trouble. Go on; it'll all be fine."

There was a long moment. Valens could see the Chancellor was past thinking rationally; he was waiting to fall, or be pushed, into a decision. "Here's the doctor coming out," Valens said. "Get him, and two of your clerks. Go on now."

The Chancellor nodded and did as he was told. Valens watched him talk to the doctor, saw him nod his agreement—and only then did it occur to Valens to wonder whether the doctor had any news, whether his father was alive, dead or dying. He pushed the thought out of his mind (because there was nothing he could do about that particular issue, but the succession had to be dealt with, and there wasn't anybody else to do it) and watched the Chancellor beckon over a couple of men—Valens knew them by sight, didn't know their names—and whisper to them. One of them looked worried, the other showed nothing. He went to join them.

"Ready?" he said.

The Chancellor nodded; the doctor tried to say something, but nobody was listening. Valens led the way into the tent.

His father was lying on a table; the clever folding table they took out for the after-hunt dinner, on which they laid out the best joints of newly butchered meat. From the doorway he looked like he was asleep; a step or so closer and Valens could see blood, the splintered ends of bones sticking out through incredible red gashes. For just a moment he had to fight to stay in there, with that mess.

"Dad?" he said softly.

"He can't hear you." The doctor's voice, very nervous and strained. "He passed out from the pain a few minutes ago. I don't know if he'll wake up again."

Valens closed his eyes for a moment. "What's the damage?" he said.

The doctor came a little closer. "For a start," he said, "broken skull, collarbone, three ribs, left forearm; but that's not the real problem. He's bleeding heavily, inside, and he's paralyzed, from the neck down. There's several possible causes for that, but I don't yet know which it is."

"You don't know?" Valens repeated.

"I'm sorry." The doctor was afraid, that was it. Understandable; but it would only get in the way. "Until I can do a proper examination..."

"I understand," Valens said. "And I know you're doing everything you can. Meanwhile, we need your help." He turned to look at the Chancellor. "Does he know what he's got to do?"

The Chancellor dipped his head slightly. "They all do," he said.

"Right." Valens looked away from the body on the table. "Then let's get on with it."

In the event, there was no trouble at all. Count Licinius was in bed when a platoon of his own Guards brought him the letter and escorted him, gently but firmly, to a guest-room in the castle; it was perfectly pleasant, but it was on the sixth floor of the tower, and two men stood guard outside it all night. Vetranio made a bit of a fuss when the Guards came for him at his villa on the outskirts of the city. He had guards of his own, and there was an ugly moment when they started to intervene. A sword was drawn, there was a minor scuffle; Vetranio lost his nerve and came quietly, ending up in the room next to Licinius, though neither of them knew it until they were released a week later. By then, the doctors were pleased to be able to announce that the Duke had come through the dangerous phase of his injuries and was conscious again.

For Valens, that week was the longest of his life. Once Licinius and Vetranio were safely locked up and everything was quiet, he forced himself to go back down to the courtyard and into the tent. He freely admitted to himself that he didn't want to go. He had no wish to look at the horrible thing his father had turned into, the disgusting shambles of broken and damaged parts—if it was a cart or a plow, you wouldn't bother trying to mend it, you'd dump it in the hedge and build a new one.

There were many times during his vigil in the tent when he wished his father would die and be done with it. It'd be better for everyone, now that the political situation had been sorted out. He knew, as he sat and stared at his father's closed eyes, that the Duke didn't want to live; somewhere, deep down in his mind, he'd know what had happened to him, the extent of the damage. He'd never hunt again, never walk, never stand up, feed himself; for the rest of his life, he'd shit into a nappy, like a baby. He'd fought more than his share of wars, seen the terror in the eyes of men he'd reduced to nothing as they knelt before him; he'd far rather die than give them this satisfaction. In fact, Valens recognized, he could think of only one person in the world who wanted him not to die, and his reasons were just sentiment, nothing that would survive the brutal interrogation of logic. At some point in the first twenty-four hours he'd fallen asleep in his chair; he'd had a dream, in which he saw Death standing over the table, asking his permission to take his father's life away, like clearing away the dishes after dinner. It seemed such a reasonable request, and refusing it was a foolish, immature thing to do. You know I'm right, Death's voice said softly inside his head, it's the right thing to do and you're being a nuisance. He'd felt guilty when he ordered Death to go away, ashamed of his own petulance; and meanwhile, outside the door, he could hear Licinius and Vetranio and Torquatus and the Chancellor and everybody else in the Duchy muttering about him, how if he couldn't even take a simple decision like this without coming all to pieces, how on earth did he imagine he would ever be fit to govern a country? He felt the leash in his hand, the thin line of rope that tethered his father's life to the tangled mess of bones and wounds on the table. If he let go, it'd all be just fine, it'd be over. He was only hanging on to it out of perversity, contrariness; they should come in, take it away from him and give it to a grown-up...

When he woke up, his father's eyes were open; not looking at him, but out through the tent doorway, at the sunlight. Valens sat up, stifled a yawn; Father's eyes moved and met his, and then he looked away.

I suppose I ought to say something, he thought; but he couldn't think of anything.

(Instead, he thought about his prisoners, Licinius and Vetranio, locked up like dogs shut in on a rainy day. Were they pacing up and down, or lying resigned and still on the bed? Had anybody thought to bring them something to read?)

He was still trying to find some words when the doctor came in; and he carried on trying to find them for the next four years, until his father died, in the middle of the night, on the eve of Valens' twenty-third birthday. But all that time Valens never said a word, so that the last thing he told his father was a lie: *I won't go up to the round wood with you this afternoon, I've got a splitting headache coming on.* Not that it mattered; if he'd been there, his father would still have ridden ahead after the boar, the outcome would have been the same in all material respects.

Someone had thought to have the boar flayed and the hide made into a rug; they draped it over the coffin when they carried it down to the chapel for burial. It was, Valens thought, a loathsome gesture, but Father would've appreciated it.

Valens was duly acclaimed Duke by the representatives of the district assemblies. There was a ceremony in the great hall, followed by a banquet. The Chancellor (Count Licinius, restored to favor; his predecessor had died of a sad combination of ambition and carelessness the previous spring) took him aside for a quiet word before they joined the guests. Now that Valens was officially in charge of the Duchy, there were a few niceties of foreign policy to go through.

"Now?"

"Now," Licinius replied emphatically. "Things are a bit complicated at the moment. There's things you should be aware of, before you go in there and start talking to people."

Badly phrased; Licinius was an intelligent man with a fool's tongue. But Valens was used to that. "You didn't want me to have to bother my pretty little head about them yesterday, I suppose?"

Licinius shrugged. "The situation's been building up gradually for a long time. When it all started, you were still — well, indisposed. By the time you started taking an interest again, it was too involved to explain. You know how it is."

"Sure." Valens nodded. "So now you're going to have to explain it all in five minutes before I go down to dinner."

Licinius waited for a moment, in case Valens wanted to develop this theme. The pause made Valens feel petty. "Go on," he said.

So Licinius told him all about it. Count Sirupat, he said, had kept strictly to the letter of the peace treaty that had been signed when Valens was sixteen. There hadn't been any trouble on the borders, and there was no reason to suppose he wasn't entirely sincere about wanting peace. But things weren't all wine and honey-cakes; Sirupat had seven daughters —

"I know," Valens interrupted, a little abruptly. "I met one of them once; it was when the treaty was signed, she was here as a hostage."

Licinius nodded. "That was the fifth daughter, Veatriz. Anyway, shortly after your father had his accident, my predecessor made a formal approach to Sirupat for a marriage alliance. In his reply, Sirupat —"

"Just a moment," Valens interrupted. "Marriage alliance. Who was supposed to be marrying who?"

Licinius had the grace to look away. "One of Sirupat's daughters. And you, obviously."

"Fine." Valens frowned. "Which one?"

"I'm sorry?"

"Which one of Sirupat's daughters?"

Licinius frowned, as if this fascination with trivial details perplexed him. "The fifth or the sixth," he said. "The older four had already been married off, and there's some interesting implications there, because —"

"The fifth *or* the sixth."

"They're both pleasant enough, so I've heard. Anyway, Sirupat gave his agreement in principle, as you'd expect, because it's the obvious logical move. Before anybody had made any definite proposals, I took over as Chancellor; which shouldn't have made the slightest bit of difference, obviously, but suddenly Sirupat wasn't answering my letters. Next thing we hear, he's negotiating a marriage with his sister's eldest son, Orsea."

"Orsea," Valens repeated. "You don't mean my cousin Orsea, from Scandea?"

"Him," Licinius said. "Well, you can imagine, we were a bit stunned. We all assumed it was just tactical, trying to get us to up our offer, so we decided to take no notice. I mean—"

"I remember when he came to stay, when I was a kid," Valens said. "I suppose he was a hostage too, come to think of it. I just assumed he was here because he's an off-relation. But we got on really well together. I've often wondered what became of him."

"Not much," Licinius said. "He may be related to our lot and their lot, but really he's nothing more than a small-time country squire; spends his time counting his sheep and checking the boundary fences. But if he were to marry Sirupat's daughter, that'd make him the heir presumptive, when Sirupat goes on—"

"Would it? Why?"

Licinius pulled a face. "It's complicated. Actually, I'm not entirely sure why; I think it's because the first three weren't born in the purple, and the fourth came along while the marriage was still nominally morganatic. Anyhow, there's a damn good reason. So in practice, Sirupat was practically appointing him as his successor."

"Assuming the marriage goes ahead," Valens pointed out. "And if it's just a bargaining ploy..."

"Which is what we'd assumed," Licinius said. "But apparently we were wrong. They were married last week."

For a moment, Valens felt as though he'd lost his memory.

Where he was, what he was supposed to be doing, what he was talking about; all of them on the tip of his tongue but he couldn't quite remember. "Last week," he repeated.

"Bolt out of the blue, literally," Licinius said. "No warning, no demands, nothing. Just a report from our ambassador, not even formal notification from the Court—which we're entitled to, incidentally, under the terms of the treaty."

"Which daughter?" Valens said.

"What? Oh, right. I'm not absolutely sure. I think it was number five; which'd make sense, because they've got rules over there about the order princesses get married in. But if it was number six, the effect'd still be the same. Now I'm not saying it was meant as a deliberate provocation or an act of war, but—"

"Can you find out?" Valens said. "Which one it was, I mean."

"Yes, all right. But like I said, it's not really important. What matters is, Sirupat has effectively rejected our claim—some might say the treaty itself—in favor of some nobody who just happens to be a poor relation. In basic diplomatic terms—"

"Find out which one," Valens cut him off. "Quickly as possible, please."

He could see Licinius getting flustered, thinking he hadn't got across the true magnitude of the political situation. "I will, yes. But if you're thinking that's all right, I'll just marry number six, I've got to tell you that'd be a grave miscalculation. You see, under their constitution—"

"Find out," Valens said, raising his voice just a little, "and as soon as you hear, let me know. All right?"

"I've already said yes."

"That's splendid." Valens took a deep breath. "That'll have to do as far as the briefing goes, we can't keep all the guests waiting."

Licinius had his answer within the hour. Yes, it was the fifth daughter, Veatriz, who'd married Count Orsea. Licinius' scribbled note reached Valens at the dinner-table, where he was sandwiched in between the Patriarchal legate (a serene old man who dribbled soup) and a high-ranking Mezentine commercial attaché. Conse-quently, he read the note quickly, tucked it into his sleeve and car-ried on talking to the legate about the best way to blanch chicory.

The next day, for the first time since his father's accident, he an-nounced a hunt. Since everybody was unprepared and out of prac-tice, it would be a simple, perfunctory affair. They would draw the home coverts in the morning, and drive down the millstream in the afternoon. The announcement caused some surprise — people had got the impression from somewhere that the new Duke wasn't keen on hunting — and a great deal of anxious preparation and last-minute dashing about in stables, kennels and tack rooms. Any annoyance, however, was easily outweighed by relief that things were getting back to normal.

2

"The prisoner has suggested," the advocate said, "that his offense is trivial. Let us examine his claim. Let us reflect on what is trivial and what is serious, and see if we can come to a better understanding of these concepts."

He was a nondescript man, by any standards; a little under medium height, bald, with tufts of white hair over each ear; a round man, sedentary, with bright brown eyes. Ziani had known him for years, from committees and receptions and factory visits, had met his wife twice and his daughter once. From those meetings he'd carried away a mental image of a loud, high voice, someone brisk and busy but polite enough, an important man who knew the strategic value of being pleasant to subordinate colleagues. He knew he was some kind of high Guild official, but today was the first time he'd found out what Lodoico Sphrantzes actually did.

"The prisoner, Ziani Vaatzes," the advocate went on, "admits to having created an abomination. He admitted as much to the investigator who inspected it. He signed a deposition confessing that the thing was made by him, and agreeing in detail the departures from Specification. In this court, he has acknowledged his signature on that deposition, and conceded that he said those words to that investigator. But he stands to his defense. He pleads not guilty. His defense..." Advocate Sphrantzes paused to shake his head. "His defense is that his admitted abomination was only a little one, a minor deviation. It was, he tells us, a slight modification, an improvement."

A little buzz of murmuring went round the semicircle of the public gallery, like half a ripple from a stone dropped in water. Sphrantzes let it run its course before he went on.

"Very well then," he said. "Let us consider the details. As regards the construction of automata and mechanical toys, Specification states that the lifting mechanism for the arms shall be powered by a clock-spring seven feet six inches long, one quarter of an inch wide and fifteen thousandths of an inch thick, with a generous permitted tolerance of three percent for length and width, and fifteen percent for thickness. Furthermore, it states that the gear train conveying motive power from the spring to the shoulder assemblies shall comprise five cogs of ratios forty, thirty, twenty-five, twelve and six to one. Furthermore, it lays down that the thickness of such cogs shall be three eighths of an inch, and that each cog shall ride on a brass bushing. I ask the clerk to verify that my summary of Specification is correct."

The clerk stood up, nodded and sat down again.

"So much, then," Phrantzes went on, "for Specification. Let us now turn to the investigator's report concerning the abomination created by the prisoner. Investigator Manin, as you have heard for yourselves, discovered that the spring used by the prisoner was nine feet three inches long, five sixteenths of an inch wide and ten thousandths of an inch thick; that the gear train contained not five but six cogs, the sixth being in ratio of four to one; that the said cogs were seven sixteenths of an inch thick, and their bushings were not brass but bronze. In short, we have unequivocal proof of not one but three distinct and deliberate deviations from Specification."

Advocate Sphrantzes paused for a moment to stare ferociously at the dock; then he continued. "Three distinct deviations; so much, I think we can safely say, for the argument that it was only a little abomination, a trivial departure. Now, if the prisoner had argued that he is an inept metalworker, incapable of observing a tolerance, that might be easier to accept — except, of course, that we know he is no such thing. On the contrary; we know that he holds the rank of supervisor in the Foundrymen's and Machinists' Guild, that he has passed all twelve of the prescribed trade tests and holds no fewer than eleven certificates for exemplary work, one of them for hand-filing a perfect circle to a tolerance of one thousandth of an inch. But he makes no such claim in his defense. No; he admits the work, and accepts the report. He accepts that each deviation bears directly on the others; that the longer, thinner spring affords more power to the gears, in consequence of which a sixth gear is added and the width of the cogs is increased to augment bearing surface, with harder-wearing bushes to handle the additional wear. All this, he claims, he did in order to make a mechanical toy that could raise its arms above its head; in order, members of the committee, to improve on Specification."

No murmurs this time. Absolute silence.

"To improve," Sphrantzes repeated slowly, "on Specification. May I invite you to consider for a moment the implications of that intention.

"When our Guild was first established, fought for by our ancestors and paid for with their very blood, it was agreed that in order to maintain the reputation for excellence enjoyed by our work throughout the world, it was essential that we draw up and rigidly adhere to an agreed specification for everything we make. That specification, represented by the Guild's mark stamped on each piece, has for three hundred years served as an unimpeachable guarantee of quality. It means that anybody who buys Guild work can be categorically assured that the piece is made strictly in accordance with the best possible design, from the best possible materials, using the best possible practices and procedures by the finest craftsmen in the world. It is that guarantee that has made our Guild and our fellow Guilds throughout Mezentia the unrivaled masters of industry and by default given us a monopoly of mass-produced manufactured goods throughout the known world. That, members of the committee, is not a trivial matter.

On the contrary, it is the life blood of our city and our people, and any offense against it, anything that calls it into question, is an act of treason. There can be no exceptions. Even an unwitting slip of the hammer or the file is an abomination and punishable under the law. How much worse, then, is a deliberate and premeditated assault on Specification, such as we have seen in this case? To claim, as the prisoner Vaatzes has done, that his abomination represents an improvement is to assert that Specification is susceptible to being improved upon; that it is fallible, imperfect; that the Guilds and the Eternal Republic are capable of producing and offering for sale imperfect goods. Members of the committee, I tell you that there can be no defense of such a wicked act."

Again Sphrantzes paused; this time, Ziani could feel anger in the silence, and it made the muscles of his stomach bunch together.

"The prisoner has claimed," Sphrantzes went on, "that the abomination was not intended for sale, or even to be taken outside his own house; that it was built as a present for his daughter, on her birthday. We can dispose of this plea very quickly. Surely it is self-evident that once an object leaves its maker's hands, it passes out of his control. At some point in the future, when she is a grown woman perhaps, his daughter might give it away or sell it. At her death, if she retained it till then, it would be sold as an asset of her estate. Or if the prisoner were to default on his taxes or subscriptions, the contents of his house would be seized and auctioned; or it might be stolen from his house by a thief. It takes very little imagination to envisage a score of ways in which the abomination might come to be sold, and its maker's intentions made clear by a cursory examination of its mechanism. The law is absolutely clear, and rightly so. There need be no intention to sell or dispose of an abomination. The mere act of creating it is enough. Members of the committee, in the light of the facts and having in mind the special circumstances of the case — the gross and aggravated nature of the deviation, the deliberate challenge to Specification, above all the prisoner's rank inside the Guild and the high level of trust placed in him, which he has betrayed—I cannot in all conscience call for any lesser penalty than the extreme sanction of the law. It grieves me more than I can say to call for the death of a fellow man, a fellow Guildsman, but I have no choice. Your verdict must be guilty, and your sentence death."

The nondescript little man bowed respectfully to the bench, gathered the tails of his gown and sat down on his stool behind his desk. Ziani noticed that his feet didn't quite reach the floor, and dangled backward and forward, like a small child in a classroom. Somehow, that seemed an appropriate touch. Even now, here in the Guildhall with everybody staring at him, he couldn't help believing that it all had to be some kind of elaborate tease, like the jokes played on apprentices (go and fetch the left-handed screwdriver); an initiation ritual, before he was allowed to eat his dinner at the chargehands' table.

Also at the back of his mind was another question, one that buzzed and buzzed and wouldn't go away: how had they known what he'd done, where to find it, what to look for? As far as he could remember (and he'd thought of little else the past month, in the darkness of his cell) he hadn't mentioned it to anybody, anybody at all. But the investigator had gone straight to his bench, to the box under it where he kept the finished bits of Moritsa's doll; he'd had his callipers and gauges ready, to take the necessary measurements. Ziani hadn't said a word about it at work—even he wasn't that stupid—or mentioned it to his friends or his family. Nobody had known; but here he was. It'd be annoying to die with a loose end like that not tidied away. Perhaps they'd tell him, before it was over.

The committee had stopped whispering; it hadn't taken them long to make up their minds. Ziani didn't know the man who stood up, but that was hardly surprising. Even the foreman of the ordnance factory didn't get to meet the great men of the Guild. The guard caught hold of Ziani's arm and pulled him to his feet. He couldn't look at the great man.

"Ziani Vaatzes," he heard him say, "this tribunal finds you

guilty of abomination. In light of the gravity of your offense, we hereby sentence you to be strangled with the bowstring, and we decree that your head shall be displayed above the gates of the department of ordnance for thirty days, as a warning to others. These proceedings are concluded."

As they led him back to the cells, he sensed something unusual in the way they reacted to him. It wasn't fear, but they were keeping their distance, touching him as little as possible. Disgust, maybe; but if that was what they were feeling, they hid it well. They'd been overtly hostile toward him before the trial, when they brought him his food and water. There wasn't any of that now. Compassion, possibly? No, definitely not.

He'd had his three guesses, it was annoying him, and a condemned man doesn't have to worry about getting into trouble if he annoys his warders. He stopped.

"Look," he said. "What is it? Have I just grown an extra head?"

They looked at each other. They weren't sure what to do. The older man, a northshoreman by the name of Bollo Curiopalates, who'd made a habit of accidentally-on-purpose kicking Ziani on the shins when he brought him his evening meal, pulled a wry face and shrugged.

"No offense, right?" he said. "Just, we never met one of your lot before."

"My lot?"

"Abominators." Bollo shrugged. "It's not like murderers and thieves," he went on, "it's different. Can't understand it, really; what'd make someone do a thing like that."

Curiosity, then; and the diffidence that goes with it, when you're staring at someone and they stare back. He could try and explain, but what would be the point? A man with a cause, now, a true abominator, would seize this chance of converting one last disciple, possibly lighting a candle that would never go out. Ziani had no cause, so he said, "Evil."

The warders looked startled. "You what?"

"Evil," Ziani replied, as blandly as he could. "I was in the market one day, years ago now, and there was this man selling lamps. They were cheap and I needed one, so I bought one. Got it home, unscrewed the cap to fill it up with oil, and this thing came out of it. Like a puff of white smoke, it was. Well, I must've passed out, because the next thing I remember was waking up, and it was pitch dark outside the window; and ever since then I get these terrible uncontrollable urges to do really bad, wicked things. Absolutely nothing I can do about it, can't control it, just have to go with the flow. And look where I've ended up." He sighed. "My life ruined, just like that. Only goes to show, you can't be too careful."

The warders looked at him for rather a long time; then Bollo said, "All right, move along," in a soft, strained voice. At the cell door, he said, "That was all just a joke, right? You were just being funny."

Ziani frowned. "Don't be stupid," he said. "I'm going to die in an hour or so, why the hell would I lie about a thing like that?"

They closed the door on him, and he sat down on the floor. It had been a valid question: what on earth had possessed him to do such a reckless, stupid thing? Unfortunately, he couldn't think of an answer, and he'd been searching for one ever since they arrested him. If they bothered marking the graves of abominators, his headstone would have to read:

SEEMED LIKE A GOOD IDEA AT THE TIME

Wonderful epitaph for a wasted life.

In an hour or so, it wouldn't matter anymore. He'd be out of it; the story would go on, but he wouldn't be in it anymore. He'd be a sad memory in the minds of those who loved him, a wound for time to heal, and of course they'd never mention him to strangers, rarely to each other. A new man would take his place at work, and it'd be pretty uncomfortable there for a week or so until he'd settled in and there was no longer any need for his replacement to ask how the other bloke had done this or that, or where he kept his day-books, or what this funny little shorthand squiggle was supposed to mean. The world would get over him, the way we get over our first ever broken heart, or a bad stomach upset. Somehow, the idea didn't scare him or fill him with rage. It would probably be worse to be remembered and mourned for a long time. There'd be sympathy and condolences, tearing the wound open every time it started to scab over. That was always Ziani's chair; do you remember the time Ziani got his sleeve caught in the lathe chuck; Ziani lent this to me and I never had a chance to give it back.

If it had been a sudden illness, say, or a freak accident; if he'd been stabbed in the street or killed in a war; you could get angry about that, the stuff of tragedy. But to find yourself in the cells waiting to be strangled to death, all on account of a few measurements; it was so bewildering, so impossible to understand, that he could only feel numb. He simply hadn't seen it coming. It was like being beaten at chess by a four-year-old.

The door started to open, and immediately he thought, here it is. But when Bollo came in (still looking decidedly thoughtful), he didn't usher in the man in the black hood, the ends of the bowstring doubled round his gloved hands. The man who was with him was no stranger.

Ziani looked up. "Falier?" he said.

"Me," Falier answered. Bollo glanced at him, nodded, left the cell and bolted the door behind him. "I came…"

"To say goodbye," Ziani helped him out. "It's all right, I'm being really calm about it. Sort of stunned, really. With any luck, by the time the truth hits me I'll have been dead for an hour. Sit down."

His friend looked round. "What on?"

"The floor."

"All right." Falier folded his long legs and rested his bottom tentatively on the flagstones. "It's bloody cold in here, Ziani. You want to ask to see the manager."

"It'll be a damn sight colder where I'm going," Ziani replied.

"Isn't that what they say? Abominators and traitors go to the great ice pool, stand up to their necks in freezing cold water for all eternity?"

Falier frowned. "You believe that?"

"Absolutely," Ziani said. "A chaplain told me, so it must be true." He closed his eyes for a moment. "Gallows humor, you see," he said. "It means I'm either incredibly brave in the face of death, or so hopelessly corrupt I don't even take eternal damnation seriously."

"Right," Falier said, looking at him. "Sorry," he said, "I haven't got a clue what to say."

"Don't worry about it. After all, if you really piss me off and I hold a grudge for the rest of my life, that's—what, three-quarters of an hour? You can handle it."

Falier shook his head. "You always were a kidder, Ziani," he said. "Always Laughing Boy. It was bloody annoying in a foreman, but you make a good martyr."

"Martyr!" Ziani opened his eyes and laughed. "Fine. If someone'd do me a favor and let me know what I'm dying for, I'll try and do it justice."

"Oh, they'll come up with something," Falier said. "Well, I guess this is the bit where I ask you if you've got any messages. For Ariessa, and Moritsa. Sorry," he added.

Ziani shrugged. "Think of something for me, you're good with words. Anything I could come up with would be way short of the mark: I love you, I miss you, I wish this hadn't happened. They deserve better than that."

"Actually." Falier sounded like he was the condemned man. "It's Ariessa and Moritsa I wanted to talk to you about. I'm really sorry to have to bring this up, but it's got to be done. Ziani, you do realize what's going to happen to them, don't you?"

For the first time, a little worm of fear wriggled in Ziani's stomach. "I don't know what you mean," he said.

Falier took a deep breath. "Your pension, Ziani, from the Guild. You're a condemned man, an enemy of the state."

"Yes, but they haven't done anything wrong." The worm was running up his spine now.

"Neither have you, but that doesn't mean…" Falier dried up for a moment. "It's the law, Ziani," he said. "They don't get the pension. Look, obviously I'll do what I can, and the lads at the factory, I'm sure they'll want to help. But—"

"What do you mean, it's the law? I never heard of anything like that."

"I'm sorry," Falier replied, "but it's true. I checked. It's terrible, really wicked if you ask me. I don't know how they can be so cruel."

"But hang on a moment." Ziani tried to rally his scattered thoughts, but they wouldn't come when he called. "Falier, what are they going to do? What're they going to live on, for God's sake?"

Falier looked grave. "Ariessa says she'll try and get work," he said. "But that's not going to be easy; not for the widow of—" He stopped. "I don't think I ought to have told you," he said. "Dying with something like this on your mind. But I was thinking."

Ziani looked up. He knew that tone of voice. "What? There's something I can do, isn't there?"

"You could make a deal," he said.

That made no sense at all. "How? I don't understand."

"You could ask to see the investigator. There's still time. You could say, if they let Ariessa keep your pension, you'll tell them who your accomplices are."

Accomplices. He knew what the word meant, but it made no sense in this context. "No I can't," he said. "There weren't any. I didn't tell anybody about it, even, it was just me."

"They don't know that." Falier paused for a moment, then went on: "It's politics, you see, Ziani. People they don't like, people they'd love an excuse to get rid of. And it wouldn't take much imagination to figure out who they'd be likely to be. If you said the right names, they'd be prepared to listen. In return for a signed deposition—"

"I couldn't do that," Ziani said. "They'd be killed, it'd be murder."

"I know." Falier frowned a little. "But Ariessa, and Moritsa—"

Ziani was silent for a moment. It'd be murder; fine. He could regret it for the rest of his life. But if it meant his wife and daughter would get his pension, what did a few murders matter? Besides, the men he'd be murdering would all be high officials in the Guild.... The thought of revenge had never even crossed his mind before.

"You think they'd go for that?"

"It's got to be worth a try," Falier said. "Face it, Ziani, what else can you do for them, in here, in the time you've got left?"

He considered the idea. A few minutes ago, he'd been clinging to the thought that it didn't matter, any of it. He'd practically erased himself, every trace, from the world. But leaving behind something like this—poverty, misery, destitution—was quite different. The only thing that mattered was Ariessa and Moritsa; if it meant they'd be all right, he would cheerfully burn down the world.

"What's the plan?" he said.

Falier smiled. "Leave it to me," he said. "I can get in to see the secretary of the expediencies committee—"

"How?"

"I got in here, didn't I? Obviously there's not a lot of time. I'd better go."

"All right."

Falier moved to the door, paused. "It's the right thing to do, Ziani," he said. "This whole thing's a bloody mess, but at least there's still something you can do. That's got to be good."

"I suppose."

"I'll be back in an hour." Falier knocked on the door; it opened and he left. Remarkable, Ziani thought; I've known Falier most of my life and I never knew he had magic powers. Always thought he was just ordinary, like me. But he can walk through doors, and I can't.

Hard to measure time in a cell, where you can't see the sunlight.

Pulse; each heartbeat is more or less a second. But counting—sixty sixties is three thousand six hundred—would be too much effort and a waste of his rapidly dwindling supply of life. Ziani looked round; he was an abominator, apparently, but still an engineer. He thought for a moment, then grinned and pulled off his boot, then his sock. With his teeth, he nibbled a small hole; then he scooped a handful of the grimy gray sand off the floor and persuaded it into the sock. That done, he hung the sock from a splinter of wood in the doorframe, with his empty drinking-cup directly underneath. Then he found his pulse, and counted while the sand trickled through the hole in the sock into the cup. When it had all run through, he stopped counting—two hundred and fifty-eight, near as made no odds four minutes. He drew a line in the dirt beside him, and refilled the sock. There; he'd made himself a clock.

Eight fours are thirty-two; half an hour later, the door opened again. Falier was back. He looked excited, and pleased with himself.

"All set up," he said. "The secretary wants to see you in his office." He frowned. "For crying out loud, Ziani, put your boots on."

Ziani smiled. "Are you coming too?" he said.

"No." Falier knocked on the door. "Best of luck, Ziani; but it should be all right. He was definitely intrigued. Have you got a list of good names?"

Ziani nodded. "I'm not too well up in politics, mind," he said. "Any suggestions?"

Falier fired off a dozen or so names, all of whom Ziani had already thought of, as the sand dribbled through into the cup. "That'll probably do," he went on, "but have half a dozen more up your sleeve just in case." The door opened; different warders this time. "Well, so long," Falier said. "It'll be all right, you'll see."

Not all, Ziani thought; but he didn't want to sound ungrateful. "So long," he repeated, and the warders led him out into the corridor.

Three flights of winding stairs brought him to a narrow passage, with heavy oak doors at irregular intervals; quite like the cells, he thought. Outside one of these, the warders stopped and knocked. Someone called out, "Yes, come in." A warder went in first; Ziani followed, and the other warder came in behind him.

He didn't know the secretary's name, or his face; but he was looking at a broad, fat man with huge hands resting on top of a wide, well-polished desk. "This him?" the man asked, and one of the warders nodded.

"Fine." The warder pulled out a chair, and Ziani sat in it. "All right," the man went on, "you two get out. Don't go far, though."

It wasn't easy to make out the man's face; he was sitting with his back to a window, and Ziani had been out of the light for some time. He had a bushy mustache but no beard, and round his neck was a silver chain with a big Guild star hanging from it. "Ziani Vaatzes," he said. "I know all about you. Seventeen years in the ordnance factory, foreman for six of them. Commendations for exceptional work." He yawned. "So, why does a solid type like you go to the bad?"

Ziani shrugged. "I don't know what came over me," he said.

"I do." The man leaned forward a little. The sun edged his dark head with gold, like an icon that's hung too long in the candle smoke. "Thinking you're better than everybody else, that's what did it. Thinking you're so bloody clever and good, the rules don't apply to you. I've seen your kind before."

"I admit I'm guilty," Ziani said. "But that's not what you want to talk to me about. You want to know who else was involved."

"Go on."

Ziani said four names. The secretary, he noticed, had a wax writing-board next to him, but wasn't taking any notes. He tried another four. The secretary yawned.

"You're wasting my time," he said. "You don't even know these people, and you're asking me to believe they all came round to your house, these important men you've never met, to see this mechanical doll you were making for your kid."

"I'm telling you the truth," Ziani said.

"Balls." The man wriggled himself comfortable in his chair. "I don't believe you."

"You agreed to see me."

"So I did. Know why?"

Ziani shrugged. "I'm prepared to sign a deposition," he said. "Or I'll testify in court, if you'd rather."

"No chance. I know for a fact you wouldn't know these people if you met them in the street. You didn't have any accomplices, you were working alone. All I want from you is who put you up to this. Oh, your pal Falier Zenonis, sure; but he's nobody. Who else is in on it?"

Ziani sighed. There was nothing left inside him. "Who would you like it to have been?"

"No." The man shook his head. "If I want to play that sort of game, I decide when and how. You're here because obviously some bugger's been underestimating me."

"All I wanted," Ziani said, "was for my wife to get my pension. That's all that matters to me. I'll say whatever you like, so long as you give me that."

"Not interested." The man sounded bored, maybe a little bit annoyed. "I think you thought the idea up for yourself, all on your own. Trying to be clever with men's lives. You can forget that."

"I see," Ziani said. "So you won't do what I asked, about the pension?"

"No."

"Fine." Ziani jumped to his feet and threw his weight against the edge of the desk, forcing it back. The man tried to get up; the edge of the desk hit the front of his thighs before his legs were straight—a nicely judged piece of timing, though Ziani said it himself—and he staggered. Ziani shoved again, then hopped back to give himself room and scrambled on to the desktop. The man opened his mouth to yell, but Ziani reached out; not for the throat, as the man was expecting, and so Ziani was able to avoid his hands as he lifted them to defend himself. Instead, he grabbed the man's shoulders and pushed back sharply. It was more a folding maneuver than anything else. The man bent at the waist as he went down, and his head, thrown backward, smashed against the stone sill of the window. It worked just as Ziani had seen it in his mind, the angles and the hinges and the moving parts. Seventeen years of looking at blueprints teaches you how to visualize.

He was only mildly stunned, of course, so there was still plenty to do. Ziani had been hoping for a weapon; a dagger slung fashionably at the waist, or something leaning handy in a corner. Nothing like that; but there was a solid-looking iron lampstand, five feet tall, with four branches and four legs at the base to keep it steady. Just the thing; he slid off the desk, caught hold of the lampstand more or less in the middle, and jabbed with it, as though it was a spear. One of the legs hit the man on the forehead, just above the junction of nose and eyebrows. It was the force behind it that got the job done.

The man slid onto the floor; dead or alive, didn't matter, he was no longer relevant. Three flights of stairs, and Ziani had counted the steps, made a fairly accurate assessment of the depth of tread. It would be a long way down from the window and he had no idea what he'd be dropping onto; but he was as good as dead anyway, so what the hell? At the moment when he jumped, entrusting himself to the air without looking at what was underneath, he couldn't stop himself wondering about Falier, who was supposed to be his friend.

It wasn't pavement, which was good; but it was a long way down.

For a moment he couldn't breathe and his legs were numb. I've broken my bloody neck, he thought; but then he felt pain, pretty much everywhere, which suggested the damage was rather less radical. Somewhere, not far away (not far enough), he heard shouts, excitement. It was a fair bet that he was the cause of it. Without knowing how he got there, he found himself on his feet and running. It hurt, but that was the least of his problems.

Because he'd never expected to survive the drop, he hadn't thought ahead any further than this. But here he was, running, in an unplanned and unspecified direction. That was no good. The pity of it was, he had no idea where he should be heading for. He was somewhere in the grounds of the Guildhall; but the grounds, like the building itself, were circular. There was a wall all the way round, he remembered, with two gates in it. The only way out was through a gate. If they were after him, which was pretty much inevitable, the first thing they'd do would be to send runners to the gatehouses.

Every breath and heartbeat is an act of prevarication, a prising open of options. It'd sounded good when the preacher had said it, but did it actually mean anything? Only one way to find out. The gardens were infuriatingly formal, straight lines of foot-high box hedge enclosing neat geometric patterns of flowers, nothing wild and bushy a man could hide in long enough to catch his breath, but there was a sort of trellis arch overgrown with flowery creeper, a bower or arbor or whatever the hell it was called. He headed for it, and collapsed inside just as his legs gave out.

Fine. First place they'll look.

Breathing in was like dragging his heart through brambles. He got to his knees and peered round the edge of the arch. There was the wall, a gray blur behind a curtain of silly little trees. He followed its line until he came to a square shape, almost completely obscured by a lopsided flowering cherry. That would be a gatehouse. He didn't know what time it was and he couldn't see the sun through the arbor roof, so he couldn't tell if it was the north or the south gate. Not that it mattered. He wasn't likely to get that far, and if he did the gatekeepers would be on him like terriers.

He plotted a course. Arbor to the line of trees; using the trees as cover, along the wall to the gatehouse. He could hear shouting coming from several different directions, and he wondered whether they'd catch him and take him back to his cell to be strangled, or just kill him on the spot.

I'll escape, though, if only to be annoying. He stood in the doorway of the arbor for a moment, until he saw two men running toward him. They were wearing helmets and carrying halberds; there goes another option, snapping shut like a mousetrap. He lowered his head and charged in the direction of the trees. They'd get him soon enough, but at least he was making an effort, and he felt it was better to die running toward something, rather than just running away.

It was inevitable that sooner or later he'd trip over something and go sprawling. In the event, it was one of those ridiculous dwarf box hedges that did the damage. He landed on his face in a bed of small orange flowers, and the two warders were on him before he had a chance to move.

"Right." One of them had grabbed his arms and twisted them behind his back. "What's the drill?"

He couldn't see the other warder. "Captain said get him out of sight before we do him. Don't want the Membership seeing a man having his head cut off, it looks bad."

The warder he could see nodded. "Stable block's the nearest," he said.

Between them they hauled him to his feet and dragged him backward across the flowerbeds. He sagged against their arms, letting them do the work; buggered if he was going to walk to his death. He heard a door creak, and a doorframe boxed out the light.

"Block," said the other warder. "Something we can use for a block."

"Log of wood," his colleague suggested.

"How about an upturned bucket?" the first man said.

"Might as well." The unseen warder trod on the backs of Ziani's knees, forcing him down; the other man came forward with a stable bucket, shaking out dusty old grain. Ziani felt the wood under his chin. "Grab his hair," the second warder said, "hold him steady. Halberd's not the right tool for this job."

A simple matter of timing, then. Ziani felt the warder's knuckles against his scalp, then the pain as his hair was pulled, forcing his cheek against the bucket. He heard the cutter's feet crackle in the straw as he stepped up to his mark, in his mind's eye he saw him take a grip on the halberd shaft and raise his arms. A good engineer has the knack of visualization, the ability to orchestrate the concerted action of the mechanism's moving parts. At the moment when he reckoned the cutter's swing had reached its apex and was coming down, he dug his knees into the straw and arched his back, jerking his shoulders and head backward. He felt a handful of his hair pull out, but he was moving, hauling the other warder toward him.

He heard the halberd strike; a flat, solid shearing noise, as its edge bit into the warder's forearms, catching them just right against the base of the iron band that ran round the bottom of the bucket. By the time the warder screamed, he was loose; he hopped up like a frog, located the cutter (standing with a stupid expression on his face, looking at the shorn stub of his mate's left hand) and stamped his foot into the poor fool's kidneys. It wasn't quite enough to put him down; but the other man had obligingly left his halberd leaning up against a partition. All Ziani knew about weapons was how to make them, but he did understand tools— leverage, mechanical advantage—and the principles were more or less the same. With the rear horn of the blade he hooked the cutter's feet out from under him, and finished the job efficiently with the spike. The other man was still kneeling beside the bucket, trying to clamp the gushing stump with his good hand. The hell with finesse, Ziani thought; he pulled the spike clear and shoved it at the wounded man's face. It was more luck than judgment that he stuck him precisely where he'd aimed. In one ear and out the other, like listening to your mother.

His fingers went dead around the halberd shaft; it slipped through, and its weight dragged it down, though the spike was still jammed in that poor bastard's head. It had taken a matter of seconds; two lives ended, one life just possibly reprieved. It was a curious sort of equilibrium, one he wasn't eager to dwell on. Instead he thought: this is a stable, wouldn't it be wonderful if it had horses in it?

Of course, he had no idea how you went about harnessing a

horse. He found a saddle, there was a whole rack of the things; and bridles, and a bewildering selection of straps with buckles on, some or all of which you apparently needed in order to make the horse go. He'd decided on the brown one; it wasn't the biggest, but the other two looked tired (though he had no idea what a tired horse was supposed to look like). Pinching the corners of its mouth got the bit in. He fumbled hopelessly with the bridle straps, sticking the ends in the wrong buckles until eventually he managed to get the proper layout straight in his mind. The saddle went on its back, that was obvious enough. There was some knack or rule of thumb about how tight the girths needed to be. He didn't know it, so he pulled the strap as tight as he could make it go. The horse didn't seem to mind.

That just left getting on. Under better circumstances, he might well have been able to reach the stirrup. As it was, he had to go back and fetch the bucket to stand on. It was slippery, and he nearly fell over. *I wish I knew how to do this*, he thought, and dug his heels into the horse's ribs.

After that it was shamefully simple. The gatekeepers had seen him being caught and so weren't looking for escaped prisoners anymore; besides, he was on a horse, and the prisoner had been on foot. The horse wanted to trot, so the saddle was pounding his bum like a trip-hammer. He passed under the gate, and someone called out, but he couldn't make out the words. Nobody followed him. Two murders, possibly three if he'd killed the secretary of the expediencies committee when he hit him with the lampstand, and he was riding out of there like a prince going hawking. His head ached where the hair had been pulled out.

As soon as he was through the gate, he knew where he was. That tall square building was the bonded warehouse, where he delivered finished arrowheads for export. The superintendent was a friend of his, sometimes on slow days they drank tea and had a game of chess (but today wasn't a slow day). He was in Twenty-Fourth Street, junction with Ninth Avenue.

Three blocks down Ninth Avenue was an alley, leading to the

back gate of a factory. It was quiet and the walls on either side were high; you could stop there for a piss if you were in a hurry. He contrived to get the horse to turn down it, let it amble halfway down, pulled it up and slid awkwardly off its back. It stood there looking at him as he picked himself up. Nevertheless, he said. "Thanks," as he walked away.

The factory gate was bolted on the inside, but he managed to jump up, get his stomach on the top of it and reach over to draw back the bolt. The gate swung open, with him on top of it. He slipped down — bad landing — and shut it behind him, trying to remember what they made here. At any rate, he was back on industrial premises, where the rules were rather closer to what he was used to.

He was in the back yard; and all the back yards of all the factories in the world are more or less identical. The pile of rusting iron scrap might be a foot or so to the left or right; the old tar-barrel full of stagnant rainwater might be in the northeast corner rather than the northwest; the chunky, derelict machine overgrown with brambles might be a brake, a punch, a roller or a shear. The important things, however, are always the same. The big shed with the double doors is always the main workshop. The long shed at right angles to it is always the materials store. The kennel wedged in the corner furthest from the gate is always the office. The tiny hutch in the opposite corner is always the latrine, and you can always be sure of finding it in the dark by the smell.

Ziani ducked behind the scrap pile and quickly took his bearings. Ninth Avenue ran due south, so the gate he'd just climbed over faced east. He glanced up at the sky; it was gray and overcast, but a faint glow seeping through the cloud betrayed the sun, told him it was mid-afternoon. In all factories everywhere, in mid-afternoon the materials store is always deserted. He looked round just in case; nobody to be seen. He scuttled across the yard as fast as he could go.

The geometry of stores is another absolute constant. On the racks that ran its length were the mandatory twenty-foot lengths of various sizes and profiles of iron and brass bar, rod, strip, tube, plate and sheet. Above them was the timber, planked and un-planked, rough and planed. Against the back wall stood the bar-rels and boxes, arranged in order of size; iron rivets (long, medium and short, fifteen different widths), copper rivets, long nails, me-dium nails, short nails, tacks, pins, split pins, washers; drill bits, taps, dies; mills and reamers, long and short series, in increments of one sixty-fourth of an inch; jigs and forms, dogs and faceplates, punches, calipers, rules, squares, scribers, vee-blocks and belts, tool-boats and gauges, broaches and seventeen different weights of ball-peen hammers. At the far end, against the back wall, stood the big shear, bolted to a massive oak bench; three swage-blocks, a grinding-wheel in its bath, two freestanding leg-vices, a pail of grimy water and a three-hundredweight double-bick anvil on a stump. Every surface was slick with oil and filmed with a coating of black dust.

It was the familiarity of it all that cut into him; he'd worked all his life in places like this, but he'd never looked at them; just as, after a while, a blind man can walk round his house without tripping, because he knows where everything is. All his life Ziani had worked hard, anxious to impress and be promoted, until he'd achieved what he most wanted—foreman of the machine room of the Mezentine state ordnance factory, the greatest honor a work-ing engineer could ever attain this side of heaven. Outside Mezen-tia there was nothing like this; the Guilds had seen to that. The Eternal Republic had an absolute monopoly on precision engi-neering; which meant, in practice, that outside the city, in the vast, uncharted world that existed only to buy the products of Mezen-tine industry, there were no foundries or machine shops, no lathes or mills or shapers or planers or gang-drills or surface-grinders; the pinnacle of the metalworker's art was a square stub of iron set in a baked earth floor for an anvil, a goatskin bellows and three hammers. That was how the Republic wanted it to be; and, to keep it that way, there was an absolute prohibition on skilled men leaving the city. Not that any Mezentine in his right mind would want to; but wicked kings of distant, barbarous kingdoms had been known to addle men's minds with vast bribes, luring them away with their heads full of secrets. To deal with such contingencies, the Republic had the Travelers' Company, whose job it was to track down renegades and kill them, as quickly and efficiently as possible. By their efforts, all those clever heads were returned to the city, usually within the week, with their secrets still in place but without their bodies, to be exhibited on pikes above Travelers' Arch as a reassurance to all loyal citizens.

Ziani walked over to the anvil and sat down. The more he thought about it, of course, the worse it got. He couldn't stay in the city—this time tomorrow, they'd be singing out his description in every square, factory and exchange in town—but he couldn't leave and go somewhere else, because it simply wasn't possible to leave unless you went out through one of the seven gates. Even supposing he managed it, by growing wings or perfecting an invisibility charm, there was nowhere he could go. Of course, he'd never get across the plains and the marshes alive; if he did, and made it as far as the mountains, and got through one of the heavily guarded passes without being eaten by bears or shot by sentries, a brown-skinned, black-haired Mezentine couldn't fail to be noticed among the tribes of pale-skinned, yellow-haired savages who lived there. The tribal chiefs knew what happened to anyone foolish enough to harbor renegades. Silly of him; he'd jumped out of check into checkmate, all the while thinking he was getting away.

On the bench beside him he saw a scrap of paper. It was a rough sketch of a mechanism—power source, transmission, crankshaft, flywheel; a few lines and squiggles with a charcoal stub, someone thinking on paper. One glance was enough for him to be able to understand it, as easily as if the squiggles and lines had been letters forming words. Outside the city walls, of course, it'd be meaningless, just hieroglyphics. A mechanism, a machine someone was planning to build in order to achieve an objective. He thought about that. A waterwheel or a treadmill or a windlass turns; that motion is translated into other kinds of motion, circular into linear, horizontal into vertical, by means of artfully shaped components, and when the process is complete one action is turned into something completely different, as if by alchemy. The barbarians, believers in witchcraft and sorcery, never conceived of anything as magical as that.

He thought for a while, lining up components and processes in his mind. Then he slid off the bench, washed his hands and face in the slack-tub and headed across the yard to the office.

As he walked in, a clerk perched on a high stool turned to peer at him.

"Any work going?" Ziani asked.

The clerk looked at him. "Depends on what you can do," he said.

"Not much. Well, I can fetch and carry, sweep floors and stuff."

"Guild member?"

Ziani shook his head. "Left school when I was twelve," he said.

The clerk grinned. "Good answer," he said. "We're all right for skilled men, but we can always use another porter." He shook his head. "Crazy, isn't it? There's Guildsmen sat at home idle for want of a place, and the likes of you can walk in off the street and start immediately."

"Good," Ziani said. "What's the pay?"

The clerk frowned. "Don't push your luck," he said.

Nice clear directions brought Ziani to the shipping bay. The factory made farm machinery—plows, chain and disk harrows, seed drills—for export to the breadbasket countries in the far south. How they got there, very few people knew or cared; the Mezentines sold them to dealers, who took delivery at Lonazep, on the mouth of the estuary. Ziani had never been to Lonazep, but he knew it was outside the walls. After five hours lifting things onto carts, he was asked if he fancied volunteering for carriage duty.

The answer to this question, in every factory in the world, is always no. Carriage duty means sitting on the box of a cart bumping along rutted tracks in the savage wilderness outside the city. It pays time and a half, which isn't nearly enough for the trauma of being Outside; you sleep in a ditch or under the cart, and there are rumored to be spiders whose bite makes your leg swell up like a pumpkin.

"Sure," Ziani said.

(Because the sentries at the gates would be looking for a Guildsman on his own, not a driver's mate on a cart in the long, backed-up queue crawling out of town on the north road. When a particularly dangerous and resourceful fugitive—an abominator, say, or a guard-killer—was on the run, they'd been known to pull the covers off every cart and scrabble about in the packing straw in case there was anyone hiding in there, but they never bothered to look at the unskilled men on the box. Guild thinking.)

God bless the city ordinance that kept annoying heavy traffic off the streets during the day. By its blessed virtue, it was dark when the long line of carts rolled out of the factory gate and merged with the foul-tempered glacier inching its way toward the north gate. Heavy rain was the perfect finishing touch. It turned the streets into glue, but as far as Ziani was concerned it was beautiful, because a sentry who has to stand at his post all night quite reasonably prefers to avoid getting soaked to the skin, and accordingly stays in the guardhouse and peers out through the window. As it turned out, they showed willing and made some sort of effort; a cart six places ahead in the line was pulled over, while the sentries climbed about on it and crawled under it with lanterns. They didn't find anything, of course; and, their point proved, they went back inside in the dry. Ziani guessed the quota was one in ten. Sure enough, looking back over his shoulder once they were through the arch and out the other side, he saw the third cart behind them slow to a halt, and lanterns swinging through the rain.

"You're new, then," said the driver next to him. He hadn't spoken since they left the factory.

"That's right," Ziani said. "Actually, this is my first time out of town."

The driver nodded. "It sucks," he said. "The people smell and the food's shit."

"So I heard," Ziani said.

"So why'd you volunteer?"

"I don't know, really," Ziani replied. "Suppose I always wondered if it's really as bad as they say."

"It is."

"Well, now I know."

The driver grinned. "Maybe next time you'll listen when people tell you things."

A mile out from the north gate the road forked. Half the traffic would stay on the main road, the other half would take the turning that followed the river past the old quarries down to Lonazep. Ziani's original plan had been to try and get himself on a ship going south, maybe even all the way down to the Gulf, as far from the Eternal Republic as you could go without falling off the edge of the world. Seeing the scrap of paper on the bench in the storeroom had changed all that. If he went south, it'd mean he was never coming back. Instead, he waited till they stopped for the night at Seventh Milestone. The driver crawled under the tarpaulin, pointing out that there was only room for one.

"No problem," Ziani said. "I'll be all right under the cart."

As soon as he was satisfied the driver was asleep, Ziani emerged and started to walk. Geography wasn't his strong suit, but as soon as the sun came up he'd be able to see the mountains across the plain, due west. Going west meant he'd be away for a while, maybe a very long time, but sooner or later he'd be back.

3

As soon as Duke Orsea realized he'd lost the battle, the war and his country's only hope of survival, he ordered a general retreat. It was the only sensible thing he'd done all day.

One hour had made all the difference. An hour ago, when he'd led the attack, the world had been a very different place. He'd had an army of twenty-five thousand men, one tenth of the population of the Duchy of Eremia. He had a commanding position, a fully loaded supplies and equipment train, a carefully prepared battle plan, the element of surprise, the love and trust of his people, and hope. Now, as the horns blared and the ragged lines crumpled and dissolved into swarms of running dots, he had the miserable job of getting as many as he could of the fourteen thousand stunned, bewildered and resentful survivors away from the enemy cavalry and back to the relative safety of the mountains. One hour to change the world; not many men could have done such a thorough job. It took a particular genius to destroy one's life so comprehensively in so short a time.

A captain of archers, unrecognizable from a face-wound, ran past him, shouting something he didn't catch. More bad news, or just confirmation of what he already knew; or maybe simple abuse; it didn't greatly matter, because now that he'd given the order, there was precious little he could do about anything. If the soldiers got as far as the thorn-scrub on the edge of the marshes, and if they stopped there and re-formed instead of running blindly into the bog, and if they were still gullible enough to obey his orders after everything he'd let them in for, he might still be relevant. Right now, he was nothing more than a target, and a conspicuous one at that, perched on a stupid white horse and wearing stupid fancy armor.

It hurt him, worse than the blade of the broken-off arrow wedged in his thigh, to turn his back on the dead bodies of his men, scattered on the flat moor like a spoiled child's toys. Once he reined in his horse, turned and rode away, he acknowledged, he'd be breaking a link between himself and his people that he'd never be able to repair. But that was self-indulgence, he knew. He'd forgone the luxury of guilt when he bent his neck to the bait and tripped the snare. The uttermost mortification; his state of mind, his agonized feelings, didn't matter anymore. It was his duty to save himself, and thereby reduce the casualty list by one. He nudged the horse with his heels.

The quickest way to the thorn-hedge was across the place where the center of his line had been. His horse was a dainty stepper, neatly avoiding the tumbled bodies, the carelessly discarded weapons that could cut a delicate hoof to the quick. He saw wounded men, some screaming, some dragging themselves along by their hands, some struggling to draw a few more breaths, as though there was any point. He could get off the stupid white horse, load a wounded man into the saddle and take his chances on foot. Possibly, if there'd only been one, he'd have done it. But there wasn't just one, there were *thousands;* and that made it impossible, for some reason.

Orsea had seen tragedy before, and death. He'd even seen mess, great open slashed wounds, clogged with mud and dust, where a boar had caught a sluggish huntsman, or a careless forester had misjudged the fall of a tree. He'd been there once when a granary had collapsed with fifteen men inside; he'd been one of the first to scrabble through the smashed beams and fallen stone blocks, and he'd pulled two men out of there with his own hands, saved their lives. He'd done it because he couldn't do otherwise; he couldn't turn his back on pain and injury, any more than he could stick his hand in a fire and keep it there. An hour ago, he'd been that kind of man.

A horseman came thundering up behind him. His first thought was that the enemy cavalry was on to him, but the rider slowed and called out his name; his name and his stupid title.

He recognized the voice. "Miel?" he yelled back.

Miel Ducas; he'd never have recognized him. Ten years ago he'd have traded everything he had for Miel Ducas' face, which seemed to have such an irresistible effect on pretty young girls. Now, though, he couldn't see Miel's nose and mouth through a thick splatter of dirt and blood.

"There's another wing," Miel was saying; it took Orsea a heart-beat or so to realize he was talking about the battle. "Another wing of fucking cavalry; reserve, like they need it. They're loop-ing out on the far left, I guess they're planning on cutting us off from the road. I've still got six companies of lancers, but even if we get there in time we won't hold them long, and they'll chew us to buggery."

Orsea sighed. He wanted to shrug his shoulders and ride on — he actually wanted to do that; his own callous indifference shocked him. "Leave it," he heard himself say. "Those lancers are worth more to us than a regiment of infantry. Keep them out of harm's way, and get them off the field as quick as you can."

Miel didn't answer, just pulled his horse's head round and stumbled away. Orsea watched him till he was out of sight over the horizon. It'd be nice to think that over there somewhere, screened by the line of stunted thorns, was that other world of an hour ago, and that Miel would arrive there to find the army, pristine and unbutchered, in time to turn them back.

Orsea still wasn't quite sure what had happened. Last night, camped in the middle of the flat plain, he'd sent out his observ-ers. They started to come back around midnight. The enemy, they said, was more or less where they were supposed to be. At most there were sixteen thousand of them; four thousand cavalry, perched on the wings; between them, ten thousand infantry, and the artillery. The observers knew their trade, what to look for, how to assess numbers by counting camp fires, and as each one reported in, Orsea made a note on his map. Gradually he built up the picture. The units he was most worried about, the Ceftuines and the southern heavy infantry (the whole Mezentine army was made up of foreign mercenaries, apart from the artillery), were camped right in the middle, just as he'd hoped. His plan was to leave them till last; break up the negligible Maderi infantry and light cavalry on either side of the center, forcing the Mezentines to commit their heavy cavalry to a long, grueling charge across the flat, right down the throats of his eight thousand archers. That'd be the end of them, the Bareng heavy dragoons and the lancers. If a tenth of them made it through the arrow-storm, they'd be doing outstandingly well; and then Orsea's own lancers would take them in the flank, drive them back on their own lines as the wholesale roll-up started. In would come the horse-archers from the extreme ends of the line, shepherding the Mezentines in on their own center, where the Ceftuines would've been standing helplessly, watching the world collapse all around them. By the time the fighting reached them, they'd be hemmed in on all sides by their own defeated, outflanked, surrounded comrades. The lancers would close the box, and the grand finale would be a long, one-sided massacre.

It had been that, all right.

A deep, low hum far away to his left; Orsea stood up in his stirrups, trying to get a better view, but all he could see was dust. He couldn't even remember which of his units was over that way now. Every part of his meticulously composed line was out of place. When the disaster struck, he'd tried to fight back, pulling men out of what he thought was the killing zone, only to find he'd sent them somewhere even worse. He didn't understand; that was what made him want to sob with anger. He still didn't know how they were doing it, how the bloody things *worked;* all he'd seen was the effects, the clouds and swarms of steel bolts, three feet long and half an inch thick, shot so fast they flew flat, not looped like an ordinary arrow. He'd been there when a volley struck the seventh lancers. First, a low whistling, like a flock of starlings; next, a black cloud resolving itself into a skyful of tiny needles, hanging in the air for a heartbeat before swooping, following a trajectory that made no sense, broke all the known rules of flight; then pitching, growing bigger so horribly fast (like the savage wild animals that chase you in dreams), then dropping like hailstones all around him; and the shambles, the noise, the suddenness of it all. So many extraordinary images, like a vast painting crammed with incredible detail: a man nailed to the ground by a bolt that hit him in the groin, drove straight through his horse and into the ground, fixing them both so firmly they couldn't even squirm; two men riveted together by the same bolt; a man hit by three bolts simultaneously, each one punched clean through his armor, and still incredibly alive; a great swath of men and horses stamped into the ground, like a careless footstep on a flowerbed full of young seedlings. Just enough time for him to catch fleeting glimpses of these unbelievable sights, and then the next volley fell, two minutes of angle to the left, flattening another section of the line. He couldn't even see where the bolts were coming from, they didn't seem to rise from the surface of the earth, they just materialized or condensed in mid-air, like snow.

As he watched the bolts fall all around him, he couldn't understand why he was the only one left alive, or how they could aim so precisely to kill everybody else and leave him alone. But of course they could. They could do anything.

That was when he'd given his one sensible order, just over an hour ago. A few minutes later, the volleys stopped; there were no coherent bodies of men left to shoot at, and the Mezentine cavalry was surging forward to begin the pursuit and mopping-up. So hard to judge time, when the world has just changed and all the rules are suddenly different, but his best guess was that the disaster had taken ten minutes, twelve at the very most. You couldn't boil a pot of water in that time.

Just a simple steel rod, pointed at one end; he reached out and pulled one out of the ground as he rode. You could use it as a spit; or three of them, tied together at the top, would do to hang a pot from over the fire. They stood up out of the ground, angled, like bristles on an unshaven chin, and there were far too many to count. It'd take weeks just to come round with carts and collect them all up — did the Mezentines do that, or did they leave them, as a monument of victory and a warning to others, till they flaked away into rust? He could imagine them doing that, in this dead, unused plain, which they'd shot full of pins.

I'd have liked just to see one of their machines, he thought, as a sort of consolation prize; but I guess I haven't done anything to deserve that privilege.

He looked back over his shoulder, to see how close the Mezentine cavalry was; but they weren't closing. Instead, they seemed to be pulling back. Well, he could understand that. Why risk the lives of men, even paid servants, when you've got machines to do the work? They'd made their point, and now they were letting him go. So kind of them, so magnanimous. Instead of killing him, they were leaving him to bring the survivors home, to try and find some way of explaining what had become of the dead. (Well, there was this huge cloud of steel pins that came down out of the sky; and the dog ate my homework.) They were too cruel to kill him.

At the thorn hedge, he found what was left of his general staff; twenty out of thirty-six. His first reaction was anger; how could he be expected to organize a coherent retreat without a full staff? (So what are you going to do about it? Write a strongly worded letter?) Then it occurred to him that he wasn't ever going to see those missing faces again, and there was a moment of blind panic when he looked to see who was there and who wasn't. Key personnel — four out of five of the inner circle, but the missing man had to be Faledrin Botaniates; how the *hell* am I going to keep track of duty rosters without Faledrin? The others, the ones who weren't there, were — The shame burned him, he'd just thought *expendable*. He forced himself to go back and repeat the thought. It'd be difficult, a real pain in the bum, to have to cope without them, but a way could be found. Therefore, they were, they'd been, expendable.

There, he'd thought it; the concept he'd promised he'd never let creep into his mind, now that he was the Duke of Eremia. That coped off the day's humiliations, and he was right down there with all the people he despised most. Fine. Now he'd got that over with, it might be an idea to do some work.

They were looking at him; some at his face, some at the blood trickling through the joints of his leg-armor. He'd forgotten all about it.

"What happened to you?" someone said.

The scope of the question appalled him for a moment; then he realized it was just his stupid wound they were talking about. "Friendly fire," he said briskly. "I guess I'm the only man on the field who got hit by one of our arrows." He started to dismount, but something went wrong. His left leg couldn't take any weight, and he ended up in a heap on the ground.

He yelled at them not to fuss as they pulled him to his feet; it was ridiculous, bothering with him when there were thousands of men gradually dying on the other side of the brake. Before he could forbid it, someone sent a runner for the surgeon. Stupid. No time for that.

"We've got to get out of here," someone was saying. "They don't seem to be following up right now, but we've got to assume we'll have their cavalry after us any minute. Does anybody know where anybody is?"

Orsea had views of his own on the subject, but quite suddenly he wasn't feeling too good. Dizziness, like he'd been drinking; and he couldn't think of words. He opened his mouth to say something, but his mind had gone blank. His arms and head seemed to weigh far too much...

When he woke up, the sky had turned to canvas. He looked at it for a moment; he could see the weave, and the lines of stitching at the seams. He realized he was lying on his back, on cushions piled on a heap of empty sacks. His throat was ridiculously dry, and he felt so weak...

"He's coming round," someone said. (Fine; treat me like I'm not here.) "Go and fetch Ducas, and the doctor."

He knew that voice, but while he'd been asleep, someone had burgled his mind and stolen all the names. He tried to lift his head, but his muscles had wilted.

"Lie still," someone else said. "You've lost a hell of a lot of blood."

No I haven't, he wanted to say. He let his head slip back onto the cushion. There were heavy springs bearing on his eyelids, and the light hurt. "Where is this?" he heard himself say, in a tiny little voice.

"God only knows," someone said, just outside his limited circle of vision. "Just to the right of the middle of nowhere. We've rounded up what we can of the army and the Mezentines seem to have lost interest in us, so we've pitched camp. Miel Ducas is running things; I've sent someone to fetch him."

He definitely knew that voice, but it didn't belong here. It was absurdly out of context; it belonged in a garden, a little square patch of green and brown boxed in by mud-brick walls. His father's house. Now he knew who the speaker was; his second oldest friend, after Miel Ducas. Fancy not recognizing someone you'd grown up with.

"Cordea?" he muttered.

"Right here." There was something slightly brittle about Cordea's voice, but that was only to be expected in the circumstances. "They got the arrow out," he was saying, "they had a hell of a job with it. Apparently it was right up against the artery, nicked it but didn't cut into it. The doctor didn't dare draw it out, for fear of the barbs slicing right through. In the end he had to go in from the side, so you're pretty badly cut up. Infection's the biggest risk, of course —"

"Shut up about my stupid leg," Orsea interrupted. "What about the battle? How many...?"

He couldn't bring himself to finish the question. Simple matter of pronouns; *how many of our men did I kill?*

"Nine thousand dead." Cordea's voice was completely flat. "Two thousand badly wounded, another three thousand cut up but on their feet." Cordea paused. "Miel insisted on going back with his lancers and the wagons; he picked up about eight hundred before they started shooting at him. Of course the surgeons can't cope with numbers like that, so we'll lose another two, three hundred just getting home. Actually, it could've been a whole lot worse."

Well, of course it could. But it was plenty bad enough. "Has anybody got any idea what those things were?" Orsea asked.

Cordea nodded. "Tell you about it later," he said. "Look, it was me said that Miel should take charge; only I couldn't think of anybody else. Are you all right with that?"

Orsea tried to laugh. Talk about your stupid questions. "Absolutely fine," he said.

"Only, I know you and he don't always get on..."

"Cordea, that was when we were *twelve*." He wanted to laugh, but apparently he couldn't. "What about moving on?" he said. "We can't just stay here, wherever the hell we are."

"In the morning. They're shattered, we'd lose people if we tried to move out tonight. We've got sentries, in case they attack."

"How far...?" Dizzy again. He gave in and closed his eyes. If he let himself drift back to sleep, maybe he'd wake up to find it had all been taken care of. He'd never wanted to be a duke anyway. "Ask Miel..." he began to say, but the sentence didn't get finished.

"It's a real stroke of luck, him getting wounded."

He'd opened his eyes but it was still dark; there was just a glimmer of lighter blue. He lay still.

"There's going to be hell to pay," Miel's voice went on, "but we'll make out he's at death's door, it'll go down well. No need to tell anybody it was one of our arrows."

"Tell them he was a hero, fighting a desperate rearguard action so the army could escape," someone else said. "I'd rather we were bringing home a victory, but a glorious defeat's not so bad. Better than a bloody good hiding, anyway. How's the water holding out?"

"Not wonderful," Miel answered. "Thank God we were able to save the barrels, or we'd be completely screwed. As it is, we'll probably get to the foothills tomorrow night, and there's plenty of springs coming down off the mountains. You'd better cut the ration, though. The horses should come first, we can't afford to lose any more."

"All right." The second voice was getting further away. "We were right, though, weren't we? I mean, basically it was a good idea."

He heard Miel laugh. "No," he said. "No, it was a bloody stupid idea. Maybe next time when he says, let's not pick a fight with the Mezentine Empire, somebody'll listen."

(But that's wrong, Orsea wanted to say. I was against it to begin with, but then they explained and I realized they were right. It made good sense, it was the bigger, broader view, and the only reason I was against it at the start was fear...)

"Doctor's here," someone else called out. "Is he awake?"

"No," Miel replied. "At least, I don't think so. Tell him to wait, I'll take a look."

They lit a lamp so the doctor could see what he was doing. Not anyone Orsea had ever seen before; he looked drained, as was only to be expected. His eyes were red, and all he said when the examination was over was, "He'll keep. Just don't bounce him up and down too much."

"I'll bear that in mind." Miel turned his head, knelt down beside him, and for the first time since the battle, Orsea saw his face without the thick, obscuring smear of caked blood.

"Hello," Miel said. "How are you doing?"

He was glad he hadn't had to see it before they stitched it up; but Miel wouldn't be getting the sort of stares he was used to from the pretty girls in future. Orsea felt bad about that; he knew how much it meant to him, always being the best-looking, never having to try. Well, that was a thing of the past, too.

"Awful," he replied. "How about you?"

Miel shrugged. "Things are pretty much under control," he said. "One more march should see us off this fucking plain. I don't see them following us up the mountain. I've sent ahead for what we need most."

Orsea closed his eyes. "I was lucky," he said.

"You bet. Another sixteenth of an inch, the doctor said—"

"That's not what I meant. I was lucky I got hurt. It meant I got to sleep through all the worst bits, and you've had to cope. I'm sorry about that."

Miel clicked his tongue. "Forget about it," he said.

"And your face..."

"Forget about that too." Miel's voice tensed up just a little, nonetheless. "It was pretty comical, actually. Ducked out of the way of one of those bolt things, tripped over my feet, laid myself open on a sharp edge. Of course I'll tell all the girlies it was hand-to-hand combat with the Mezentine champion."

"You were standing over the crumpled body of the Duke," Orsea said. "Outnumbered five to one—"

"Seven."

"You're quite right, seven to one; and they were all in full armor, and you'd lost your sword, so all you had was a tent-peg—"

"A broken tent-peg, please."

"Naturally." Orsea sighed. "Actually, that's not so far from the truth. In fact, what you did was rather more important. You see, I wouldn't have been able to—"

"Balls." He heard Miel shift; he was standing up, presumably. A leader's work is never done. "The doctor says you need to rest. I said, it's what he's best at. Try not to die in the night."

Orsea pulled a grim face. "Just to spite you, I will," he said, "and then you'll be left with all my messes to sort out on your own."

Miel frowned at him. "That joke's still funny this time," he said, "but next time it'll just be self-indulgent. While you're in here with nothing to do, you can think of a new one."

"Seriously." Orsea looked at his friend. "I feel really bad about it, you being landed with all of this."

Miel shrugged. "It's my job," he said.

"At least get someone to help you. What about Cordea? He's not the sharpest arrow in the quiver, but he's smarter than me—" He stopped. Miel had turned away, just for a moment.

"Oh," Orsea said.

"Sorry," Miel replied. "My fault, I'd assumed they'd have told you. Blood poisoning, apparently."

"I see." For a moment, Orsea couldn't think; it was as though his mind was completely empty. He ought to say something, but he couldn't remember any suitable words. Miel shook his head.

"Get some sleep," he said. "It's the most useful thing you can do."

"Sleep?" Orsea laughed. "Sorry, but I don't think I can."

But he could; and the next thing he saw was bright daylight through the open tent-flap, and the doctor prodding his leg with his finger.

"You're lucky," the doctor said, "no infection, and it's scarring up nicely. Mind you," he added, with a kind of grim zest, "one wrong move and it'll burst open again, and next time you may not be so fortunate. Try and keep your weight off it for now."

"Thanks," Orsea replied through a mouthful of sleep, "but I've got an army to move up the mountain, so I don't—"

"No you haven't. Miel Ducas is handling all that." He made it sound like the arrangements for a dance. "You can help best by staying put and not causing any trouble."

"Fine. Don't let me keep you."

The doctor grinned. "I was all finished anyway. I'll look at it again this evening. Remember, nothing energetic. They've put together a litter to carry you."

The doctor left before he could argue, which was annoying. He wanted to protest; how could he let himself be carried about on a litter when there were wounded men — *seriously* wounded men — who were going to have to hobble and crawl, and who might well not make it all the way? But, as the tent-flap dropped shut behind the doctor's back, he realized it was pointless. They wouldn't allow it, because he was the Duke and he wasn't allowed to die of impatience and nobility of spirit. If he tried to dismiss the litter-bearers and walk up the mountain, it'd only lead to fuss and delay while Miel and the others told him not to be so bloody stupid; if he protested, he wouldn't impress the doctor, and nobody else would be listening to him. With a sigh, he decided to reclassify himself as a cumbersome but necessary piece of luggage. The galling thing, of course, was that they could manage perfectly well without him; better, probably. After all, he was the one who'd got them all into this appalling situation.

They came and dismantled the tent around him; brisk, efficient men in muddy clothes who seemed to have the knack of not seeing him. They left him on his pile of cushions and sacks under a clear blue sky, in a landscape crowded with activity. He watched them loading the carts with folded tents, barrels, sacks, unused arrows still in their sheaves, boxes of boots, belts and spare side-plates for helmets, trestle tables and wounded men. Finally his litter came. Two Guards captains hauled him onto it; the porters lifted it on their shoulders like a coffin, and joined the queue of slow-moving baggage threading its way onto the narrow path. From his raised and lordly position he could see a long way over the heads of his people (wasn't there an old saying about that, how we're all dwarves on the shoulders of giants; we're lesser men than our fathers, but because we inherit their wisdom and experience, we can see further). First he looked back in case there were any signs of pursuit. It was impossible to make out much on the featureless plain, but he convinced himself he could see the battlefield and the thorn hedge. The gray blur in the air; would that be a huge flock of crows picking at the dead, or smoke from fires where the tidy Mezentines were burning up the litter? He could see the heads of the army, flashes of light on helmets that were beginning to rust, since nobody could be bothered with scouring them down with sand twice a day. On the way out they'd marched in ranks and files, smart and neat as the hedges round formal gardens. Now they trudged in knots and bunches, and the gaps between each group looked like bald patches in a frayed coat.

(Invade Mezentia, they'd told him; clever men who'd chafed at the old Duke's timid caution, because they knew that the longer the job was left, the harder it would be. Attack them now, while there's still time. It's us or them; not aggression but simple, last-ditch self-defense. The old Duke had had the perfect excuse: the long, bitter, unwinnable war against their neighbors, which drained away every spare penny and every fit man. But that war was over now. They'd had to grin and bear painfully humiliating terms—land and water-rights and grazing-rights on the eastern mountains given away instead of fought over to the death—but it had been worth it because it made possible the preemptive strike against the real enemy, and thanks to the last fifty years of relentless campaigning and slaughter they had an army of hardened veterans who'd drive the Mezentine mercenaries into the sea. The alternative, biding still and quiet while the Republic strangled them to death at their leisure, was simply unthinkable. Besides, with an army of twenty-five thousand, how could he possibly lose?)

They were taking the Butter Pass up the mountain. Not through choice. They'd come down into the plain, five days ago, by way of the main cart-road, a relatively gentle gradient and firm going for the horses. But they were a whole day east, thanks to the fear of the Mezentine cavalry, and they didn't have enough water left to go round the foot of the mountain. The Butter Pass was a different proposition altogether. It was adequate for its purpose;

once a month, hundreds of hill-farmers' sons trudged down it with yokes on their shoulders, each carrying a hundredweight of butter and cheese to the cluster of tents where the Mezentine buyers were waiting for them. Going back up the mountain, they had a much lighter load: a few copper pennies or a roll of cotton cloth (third or fourth quality), at most a keg of nails or a rake and a hoe. Taking an army up the Butter Pass was the sort of stupid thing you only did if you had to. It was slow going. To get the carts up without smashing wheels or shearing axles, they had to stop every fifty yards or so to shift boulders, fill in potholes, cut away the rock or improvise embankments to widen the path. Boulders too big to lever aside had to be split, with hammers and wedges or by lighting a fire to heat them up and then quenching them with buckets of precious, scarce water. It was a vast, thankless expenditure of effort and ingenuity—no praise or glory, just a sigh when the obstacle was circumvented and a grim shrug as the next one was addressed—and all Orsea could do was watch, as his bearers lowered him to the ground, glad of the excuse for a rest. It was all wrong; he should be paying off his debt by leading the way. In his mind's eye he saw himself, dusty and bathed in sweat, leaning on a crowbar or swinging a big hammer, exhausted but cheerful, first man to the job and last man off it, and everyone feeling better for knowing he was there with them—instead, he watched, as if this was all a demonstration by the corps of engineers, and he was sitting in a grandstand, waiting to award prizes. Miel Ducas was doing his job for him, and doing it very well. He thought about that, and felt ashamed.

There was still an hour's light left when they gave up for the night, but everybody was too exhausted to carry on. There had already been unnecessary accidents and injuries, and Miel had called a halt. Instead, men stumbled about on a sad excuse for a plateau, struggling to pitch tents on the slope, wedging cartwheels with stones to stop them rolling; the whole tiresome routine of unpacking and setting up, lighting fires without proper kindling, cooking too little food in too little water. They pitched his tent first (were they doing it on purpose to show him up? No, of course they weren't); the doctor came, looked, prodded and failed to announce that the wound had miraculously healed and he'd be fit for duty in the morning. One by one the survivors of his general staff dropped by. They were genuinely anxious about his health, but they didn't want his orders or even his advice. Finally, Miel Ducas came, slow and clumsy with fatigue, squatting on the floor rather than wait for someone to fetch him a chair.

"Slow going," he reported. "I'd sort of counted on making it to the hog's back tonight, so we could get on the southwest road by noon tomorrow. As it is, we might just get there by nightfall; depends on conditions. And if it decides to rain, of course, we're screwed."

Orsea hadn't even considered that. "Who said anything about rain?" he said. "It's been blue skies all day."

Miel nodded. "Talked to a couple of men who make the Butter run," he said. "According to them, it's the time of year for flash storms. Clear sky one minute, and the next you're up to your ankles in muck. That's if you're lucky and you aren't swept away in a mudslide. Cheerful bastards."

Orsea couldn't think of anything to say. "Let's hope it stays dry, then."

"Let's hope." Miel yawned. "Once we reach the hog's back, of course," he went on, "it's all nice and easy till we get to the river; which, needless to say, is probably in spate. I have absolutely no idea how we're going to get across, so I'm relying on inspiration, probably in the form of a dream. My ancestors were always being helped out of pots of shit by obliging and informative dreams, and I'm hoping it runs in the family. How about your lot?"

Orsea smiled. "We don't dream much. Or if we do, it's being chased by bears, or having to give a speech with no clothes on."

"Fascinating." Miel closed his eyes, then opened them again. "Sorry," he said. "Not respectful in the presence of my sovereign. How's the leg?"

"Oh, fine. It's that miserable bloody doctor who's making me lounge around like this."

(Stupid thing to say, of course. The leg wasn't fine; the doctor most likely hadn't had more than a couple of hours' sleep since the battle; and of course the Ducas family received supernatural advice in their dreams, since they were genuine old aristocracy, unlike the jumped-up parvenu Orseoli...)

"Do as he says," Miel replied sternly. "Your trouble is, you don't know a perfectly valid excuse when you see one. You were the same when we were kids. You'd insist on dragging yourself into classes with a raging temperature, and then we'd all catch it off you and be sick as dogs just in time for the recess. You will insist..." He hesitated. "Just for once, stay still and make the most of it. We're all going to have a high old time of it soon as we get home."

Orsea looked away. *You will insist on doing the right thing, even if it's guaranteed to result in misery and mayhem;* or something to that effect. "All right," he said. "It's just so bloody stupid. Getting shot with one of our own arrows."

"At least our side got to draw blood," Miel replied. "Hello, what's all that fuss they're making outside?"

Orsea hadn't noticed; now Miel mentioned it, he could hear shouting. "They've attacked," he said.

"Don't think so, or they'd be doing more than just yelling. Hold still, I'll go and see."

He came back again a moment later, grinning. "Would you believe it," he said, "they caught a spy."

"You're joking."

"I'm not. I saw him. Genuine Mezentine spy, brown face and everything. I told them to string him up."

Orsea frowned. "No, don't do that," he said. "I want to know why they're so interested in us. Maybe they didn't know about this path before. If they're looking for a back way up the mountain, that could be very bad."

Miel shrugged. "It's your treehouse. I'll have him brought in, you can play with him."

The prisoner was a Mezentine, no question about that; with his dark skin and high cheekbones, he couldn't be anything else. But that raised a question in itself. Mezentine officers commanded the army, but the men they gave orders to were all mercenaries; southerners, usually, or people from overseas.

Besides, it was hard to see how a member of the victorious Mezentine expedition, which hadn't come within bowshot or lost a single man as far as Orsea was aware, could have got in such a deplorable state. He could barely stand; the two guards were holding him up rather than restraining him. He had only one shoe; his hair was filthy and full of dust; he had several days' growth of beard (the Mezentines were obsessive about shaving their faces) and he smelled disgusting.

Orsea had never interrogated a prisoner before; of all things, he felt *shy*. "Name," he snapped, because it was as good a starting-point as any.

The man lifted his head, as though his name was the last thing he'd been expecting to be asked. "Ziani Vaatzes," he said, in a feeble whisper.

That didn't need expert interpretation. "Get this man some water," Orsea said, then realized that for once there weren't any attendants or professional bustlers-about on hand. Miel gave him a rather startled, what-me expression, then went outside, returning a little later with a jug and a horn cup, which the prisoner grabbed with both hands. He spilled most of it down his front.

Orsea had thought of another question. "What unit are you with?"

The prisoner had to think about that one. "I'm not a soldier," he said.

"No, you're a spy."

"No, I'm not." The prisoner sounded almost amused. "Is that what you think?"

Miel shifted impatiently. "You sure you want to bother with him?" he asked.

Orsea didn't reply, though he noticed the effect Miel's words had on the prisoner. "Really," the man said. "I'm not a soldier, or a spy or anything." He stopped, looking very unhappy.

"Right," Orsea said. "You're a Mezentine, but you're nothing to do with the army out there on the plain. Excuse me, but your people aren't known for going sightseeing."

"I'm an escaped prisoner," the man said; he made it sound like a profession. "I promise you, it's true. They were going to kill me; I ran away."

Miel laughed. "This one's a comedian," he said. "He's broken out of jail, so naturally he tags along behind the army. Last place they'd look for you, I guess."

The look on the man's face; fear, and disbelief, and sheer fury at not being believed. Any moment now, Orsea thought, he's going to demand to see the manager.

"You must be the enemy, then," the man said.

This time, Miel burst out laughing. "You could say that," he said.

"All right." Orsea was having trouble keeping a straight face. "Yes, we're the enemy. Do you know who we are?"

The man shook his head. "Not a clue, sorry. I don't know where this is or what the hell's going on. I didn't even know there's a war on."

"The army," Miel said softly. "Wasn't that a pretty broad hint?"

Now the man looked embarrassed. "To be honest," he said, "I assumed they were after me."

Orsea looked at him. "Really."

The man nodded. "I thought it was a bit over the top myself," he said. "But we take renegades very seriously. I assumed—"

"Sorry to disappoint you," Miel interrupted. "But your army out there's been fighting us."

"Oh, right." The man frowned. "Who won?"

"You did."

"I'm sorry." Now he looked more bewildered than ever. "Excuse me, but who are you?"

"The Grand Army of Eremia, what's left of it," Orsea replied. "So, if you're not a soldier or a spy, and you didn't know about the war, why were you following the army?"

"I reckoned they must have water," he said. "Or at least they'd lead me to a river or something. I've only been following them for a day. I tried to steal some food, but the sentries spotted me and I had to run. When I stopped running, I realized I was lost. Then I saw your lot, and thought I'd try my luck. Nothing to lose. It was that or lie down and die somewhere. Just my luck I had to run into a war."

Brief silence; then Miel said, "If he's lying, he's very good at it."

"I'm not, I'm telling the truth."

"Cocky with it," Orsea said. "So, you're an escaped convict. What did you do?"

"It's a long story."

"Indulge me."

The man looked at him. "I killed a couple of prison warders," he said. "And maybe the secretary of the tribunal, I'm not sure."

Miel leaned over the man's shoulder. "Are you sure you wouldn't rather be a spy?" he said. "I don't know what they tell you about us in the City, but murder's against the law out here, too."

"Leave him alone, Miel, this is interesting. So," Orsea went on, "if you killed a couple of warders, you were in prison already, yes?"

The man nodded. "I'd just been tried. But I got away and the warders caught me."

"So you'd done something else before you killed the warders?"

"Yes." The man hesitated.

"What?"

"It's complicated."

Orsea raised an eyebrow. Whatever it was, this strange, scruffy man seemed to think it was worse than killing prison officers; he was afraid to say what it was. "I'm game if you are," he said.

The man took a deep breath. "I was charged with mechanical innovation," he said. "It's very serious, in the City."

"Worse than killing people?"

"I suppose so."

"Were you guilty?"

The man nodded. "Apparently," he said.

Miel stood up. "Now can we hang him?" he said. "I mean, he's just confessed to murder."

Orsea frowned. "You still reckon he's a spy?"

"To be honest, I don't care much." Miel yawned. "What it boils down to is we can't very well let him go if he's really a convicted murderer, and I really can't be bothered making the arrangements to send him back. Also, he's seen the Butter Pass, and maybe he's thinking he could do a deal for the information. Either that, or I'm right and he's a spy. No offense, Orsea, but he's running out of play value. Let's pull his neck and get on with what we're supposed to be doing."

That didn't sound much like Miel, Orsea thought; so this must be a ploy to get the prisoner scared and make him confess. On the other hand, the poor devil was unquestionably a Mezentine; lynching one would probably do wonders for the army's morale. Maybe that was why Miel was making such uncharacteristically brutal noises.

He made up his mind, suddenly, without being aware of having thought it through. If Miel was reminding him of his duty toward the army and the country, fine; he still wasn't prepared to string up someone who looked so unspeakably sad. In spite of the battle and the iron pins from the sky and his own unforgivable mistakes, Orsea still had faith in the world; he believed it might still be possible to make it work, somehow or other. The Mezentine, on the other hand, clearly felt that the world was a cruel, nasty place where bad things always happened. Lynching him would only serve to prove him right, and that would be a betrayal; and if Orsea believed in anything, it was loyalty.

"He's not a spy," he said. "And if he's committed crimes in Mezentia, that's really none of our business. I can't go hanging civilians without a trial, in any event. Find him a meal and somewhere to sleep, and in the morning give him three days' rations and a pair of shoes, and let him go. All right?"

Miel nodded. He didn't seem at all put out about having his advice ignored. "I'll get the duty officer to see to it," he said, and went out.

Orsea was about to tell the guards to take the prisoner somewhere else when a thought struck him. He looked at the man and frowned. "Mind if I ask you a question?"

"Go ahead."

"In the battle today," Orsea said, "we did really badly. Your lot slaughtered us, and we never got close enough to see their faces. One minute we were advancing in good order, and then the sky was full of sharp steel bolts, about so long and so thick, and that was that. I was wondering," Orsea went on. "Can you tell me anything about that?"

The man looked at him. "You mean, what sort of weapon was it?"

Orsea nodded. "Obviously it must be a deadly secret; at any rate, it was a complete surprise to us. So I imagine you'd get in all sorts of trouble for disclosing restricted information to the enemy. On the other hand..."

The man smiled. "It's a simple mechanical device. Well," he added, "fairly simple. A powerful steel leaf-spring is drawn back by a ratchet. There's a steel cable fastened to the ends of the spring, just like the string of a conventional bow. When the sear is tripped, the force of the spring acting on the cable shoots the bolt up a groove in the bed. It's called a scorpion."

Orsea raised an eyebrow. "You know a lot about it."

"I should," the man replied. "I used to make them."

There was a long pause. "Is that right?" Orsea said.

"I was the foreman of the machine shop at the ordnance factory," the man said. "I was in charge of production. We've got a building about a hundred yards long by thirty, just for the scorpions. On average we turn out a dozen a day; eighteen if we work three shifts." He looked Orsea in the eye. "Are you going to have me killed now?"

"I'm not sure. Do you want me to?"

He smiled again. "No," he said. "But it's not up to me, and if you're looking for someone to blame—"

"Already got someone, thanks," Orsea said. "Now, there was no need for you to tell me that, and you don't strike me as the sort who blurts things out without thinking."

The man nodded. "Scorpions aren't the only thing we make at the ordnance factory," he said. "And besides, from what little I know about the outside world, I get the impression that you're a long way behind us as far as making things is concerned."

"To put it mildly," Orsea said. "As you very well know."

The man's dirty, battered face was closed, and his eyes were very bright. "I could teach you," he said.

"Teach us what?"

"Everything." His whole body was perfectly still, apart from the slight movements caused by his quick, shallow breathing. "Everything I know; and that's a lot. Basic metallurgy; foundry and forge work; machining and toolmaking; mass production, interchangeable components, gauges and tolerances. It'd take a long time, you'd be starting from scratch and I'd have to train a lot of people. I don't know how you're fixed for raw materials, iron ore and charcoal and coal. We'd probably have to start off by damming a river, to build a race for a decent-sized waterwheel. You'd be lucky to see so much as a nail or a length of wire for at least five years." He shrugged. "And it'd mean a lot of changes, and maybe you're perfectly happy as you are. After all," he added, "I'm hardly the best advertisement for an industrial society."

Orsea frowned. "Leave the bad side to me. You carry on telling me about the advantages."

"You don't need me to do that," the man replied. "You know as well as I do. First, you wouldn't depend on us for pretty well every damned thing you use. Second, you could trade. Undercut the

Mezentines and take over their markets. That's why our government won't let people like me leave the City. You could transform your whole society. You could be like us."

"Really. And why would we want to?"

He raised one dust-caked eyebrow. "As I understand it, you just lost thousands of lives trying to wipe us out, and you never even got close enough to see the color of our eyes. You must've had some reason for wanting to annihilate us. I don't know what it is, but maybe that's the reason why you should turn into us instead."

Orsea tried to think. There was a great deal to think about, great issues of security, prosperity and progress that had to be addressed before taking such a radical decision. Orsea knew what they were, but when he tried to apply his mind to them it was like trying to cut glass with a file. Really he wanted someone to decide for him; but that was a luxury he couldn't afford. He knew it was the wrong approach, but he couldn't help thinking about the battle, the field bristling with the steel pins. It'd be a greater victory than winning the battle; and it'd be the only way of making sure something like that never happened again. But if Miel was here, what would he say? Orsea knew that without having to ask. Of course the Ducas were an old family, you'd expect one of them to have an intuition for this kind of problem, so much more effective than mere intelligence. Miel would know, without having to think, and no amount of convincing arguments would make him change his mind. But Miel (who always got the girls) hadn't married the old Duke's daughter, and so it wasn't up to him. The dreadful thing was, Orsea knew, that nobody could make this choice for him. It was more important that *he* chose than that he made the right decision.

"The men you killed," he said. "Tell me about that."

The man hadn't been expecting that. "How do you mean?" he said. "Do you want to know how I did it?"

"That's not important," Orsea said. "And you did it because you had to escape, or they'd have executed you for whatever it is you did that's too complicated for me to understand. No, what I'm asking is, did you have to kill them or else they'd have killed you on the spot or dragged you off to the scaffold? Or did you have the option of just tying them up or something but you killed them anyway?"

The man seemed to be thinking it over carefully. "The two guards had caught me trying to get out of the Guildhall grounds," he said. "They took me to the stables to kill me. It was two to one, and I was lucky to get away with it. And I was clever," he added, "it wasn't just luck. But it was them or me. The other man, the tribunal secretary—he was the judge, really—I don't know if I killed him or not. I hit him very hard with a lampstand, to get past him so I could jump out of the window. I hit him as hard as I could; but it was so I could escape, not to punish him or get my own back on him for wrecking my life." He paused. "If he was here now, and you said to me, Go ahead, if you want to bash his head in I won't stop you, I'm not sure what I'd do. I mean, he did destroy my life, but killing him wouldn't change anything; and as far as he was concerned, he was doing the right thing." He looked at Orsea. "Does that answer your question?"

"I think so. At any rate, it was what I thought I needed to know; assuming I believe you're telling the truth."

The man shrugged. "That's up to you."

"It's all up to me," Orsea replied. "I wish it wasn't, but it is. There's another thing, too. If I was in your shoes, I don't know how I'd feel about what you're proposing to do. Really, it's betraying your country."

The man nodded, as though showing he understood the point Orsea was making. "Why would I do that," he said, "except out of spite, because of what they did to me? Which means, if I'm capable of spite, maybe I killed the guards and the judge for spite too."

"That thought crossed my mind," Orsea said.

"Naturally." The man was quiet for a while. "I can't be sure," he said, "but I don't think that's the real reason. I think maybe my reason is that if they can order me to be killed when I really didn't do anything wrong, then perhaps the whole system needs to be got rid of, to stop them doing it again. And also," he added, with a slight grin, "there's the fact that I've got a living to make. I need a job, I'm an engineer. Not many openings for someone in my line outside the City, unless I make one for myself. And we hadn't discussed it, but I wasn't really thinking of doing all that work for free."

Orsea laughed. "There's always that," he said. "And I suppose, if you betray your people for money, that's better than doing it for revenge. Actually, I don't think I've ever met an engineer before. Are they all like you?"

"Yes," the man said. "It's a state of mind more than anything. You can't help thinking in mechanisms; always in three dimensions, and always five stages ahead. It takes a little while to learn."

Orsea nodded. "And what about you? Are you married? Children?"

"One daughter," the man replied. "I won't see either of them again, I don't suppose."

"And will anything bad happen to them, if your people find out you've betrayed them?"

"It'll happen anyway, because of what I'm supposed to have done." The man was looking away, and his voice was perfectly flat. "If I was going to take revenge for anything, it'd be that."

"At least you're honest," Orsea said. "Or you come across as honest." He closed his eyes, rubbed them with his thumb and middle finger. "Tell you what," he said. "You come back home with me, stay with me as my guest till I've made my decision. I'm sure we can find something useful for you to do, if you decide you want to stay with us, of course."

"Naturally." The man's face slumped into a long, narrow grin. "You do realize," he said, "I haven't got the faintest idea where your country is, or what it's called, or what you do there, or anything. In the City we have this vague concept of the world as being like a fried egg, with us as the yolk and everywhere else slopped out round the edges."

"Interesting," Orsea said. "Well, my country is called Eremia Montis, and it's basically a big valley cradled by four enormous mountains; we raise sheep and goats and dairy cattle, grow a bit of corn; there's a good-sized forest in the eastern corner, and four rivers run down the mountains and join up to make one big river in the bottom of the valley. There's something like a quarter of a million of us—less now, of course, thanks to me—and till recently we had this ghastly long-standing feud with the duchy on the other side of the northern mountain, but that was all patched up just before I became Duke. We've got loads of fresh air and sky, but not much of anything else. That's about it, really. And I'm Orsea Orseolus, in case you were wondering; and you did tell me your name, but I've forgotten it."

The man nodded. "Ziani Vaatzes," he said. "Just fancy, though; me talking to a real duke. My mother'd be so proud. Not that she'd have known what a duke is. Where I come from, dukes are people in fairy tales who fight dragons and climb pepper-vines up to heaven."

"Oh, I do that all the time," Orsea said. "When I'm not losing battles. So," he went on, "tell me a bit about all these wonderful machines you're going to build for us. You said something just now about a waterwheel. What's that?"

"You're joking, aren't you? You don't know what a waterwheel is?"

Orsea shrugged. "Obviously some kind of wheel that can travel on water. Not much use to us, because the river flows down the mountain, clearly, and there's nowhere in that direction we want to go. Still, it must be terribly clever, so please tell me all about it."

Ziani explained to him about waterwheels, and how the Mezentines used the power of the river Caudene to drive all their great machines. He told him about the vast artificial delta in the middle of the City; scores of deep, straight millraces governed by locks and weirs, lined with rows of giant wheels, undershot and overshot in turn, and the deafening roar of regulated, pent-up water exploited to perfection through the inspired foresight of the Guilds. He explained about the City's seventeen relief aqueducts, which drew off floodwater in the rainy season and circulated reserve current when the pressure was low in summer; about the political dominance of the hydraulic engineers' Guild; about the great plan for building a second delta, worked out to the last detail two centuries ago, still running precisely to schedule and still only a third complete.

"Are you serious?" Orsea interrupted. "There's thousands of your people working on a project that'll never do anybody any good for another four hundred years, but they're happy to spend their whole lives slaving away at it."

"What's so strange about that?" Ziani replied. "When it's finished, it'll double our capacity. We'll be able to build hundreds of new factories, providing tens of thousands of jobs for our people. That means a hundred percent increase in productivity; we'll be able to supply goods to countries we haven't even discovered yet. It's an amazing concept, don't you think?"

Orsea looked at him. "You could say that," he said.

"You don't sound all that impressed."

"Oh, I'm impressed all right," Orsea said. "Stunned would be nearer the mark, actually. You're using up people's lives so that in four hundred years' time you can make a whole lot of unspecified stuff to sell to people who don't even know you exist yet. How do you know they'll want the things you're planning to make for them?"

"Easy," Ziani said. "We'll find out what they need, or what they want, and then we'll make it."

"Supposing they've already got everything they want?"

"We'll persuade them they want something else, or more of the same. We're good at that."

Orsea was quiet for a while. "Strange," he said. "Where I come from, we organize the things to suit the people, or we try to; it doesn't usually work out as well as we'd like, but we do our best. You organize the people to suit the things. By the sound of it you do it very well, but surely it's the wrong way round."

Ziani looked at him. "I guess I'd be more inclined to agree with you," he said, "if you'd won your battle. But you didn't."

There was a long silence. "You're a brave man, Ziani Vaatzes," Orsea said.

"Am I?" Ziani shrugged. "Yes, I suppose I am. I wonder when that happened? Didn't used to be. I suppose it must've been when they took my life away from me. Anyway, that's waterwheels for you. Did you say something a while ago about something to eat?"

That night, when his guest had been fed and clothed and found somewhere to sleep, Orsea expected he'd dream about the great river, squeezed into its man-made channels, turning all those thousands of wheels. Instead, he found himself back in that same old place again, the place he always seemed to end up when he was worried, or things were going on that he didn't understand; and that same man was there waiting for him, the one who'd always been there and who seemed to know him so well. All his life, it seemed to him, the man had been ready for him, a patient listener, a willing provider of sympathy, always glad to give him advice which never seemed to make sense. Tonight the man told him, when he'd finished explaining, that he had in fact won the battle; and he took him to the top of the mountain, to the place where you could see down into the valley on one side, and out as far as the sea on the other, and he'd shown him the city burning, and great clouds of smoke being carried out to sea on the wind. He reached out and caught one of the clouds (he could do that sort of thing; he was very clever); and when he opened his fist, Orsea could see that the cloud was made up of thousands and millions of half-inch steel rods, three feet long and sharpened at one end. So you see, the man said, it turned out all right in the end, just as you designed it. I imagine you're feeling a certain degree of satisfaction, after six hundred years of planning and hard work.

Not really, Orsea replied. All I wanted to do was go home.

The man smiled. Well, of course you did, he said. That's all any of us want; but it's the hardest thing there is, that's why we had to work so hard and be so cunning and resourceful. And you mustn't mind the way he talks to you. Where he comes from, they naturally assume they're better than foreigners, even foreign dukes and princes. But you wanted to see the waterwheels, didn't you? They're just here.

He pointed, and Orsea could see them, but they didn't look quite how he'd imagined them. They were crowded together up close, so that each one touched the one next to it, and the gear-teeth cut into them meshed, so that each one drove its neighbor. All down the riverbank, as far as he could see; but it was the wrong way round, like he'd tried to tell the stranger.

That's not right, he said. The river should be driving the wheels, but it's the other way round.

4

"Orsea said you wanted to learn about the world," Miel said. "Is that right?"

The path was too steep and uneven for horses; even the badly wounded were walking, or being carried. Miel was wearing his riding-boots—he'd brought ordinary shoes, suitable for walking in, but they'd been in a trunk with the rest of his belongings in the supply train, and he didn't fancy going down the mountain and asking the Mezentines if he could have them back. The boots were extremely good for their intended purpose, which wasn't walking; close-fitting, thin-soled and armored with twelve-lame steel sabatons, attached to the leather with rivets. The heads of those rivets were starting to wear through the pigskin lining and chafe his heels and the arches of his feet, and he could feel every pebble and flint through the soles as he walked. As if that wasn't enough to be going on with, he'd been given the job of being nice to the Mezentine he'd done his best to persuade Orsea to lynch. It could be seen as a backhanded compliment, but Miel wasn't in the mood.

"If it's no trouble," the Mezentine said. "I'm afraid I'm rather ignorant about everything outside the City. Most of us are; I think that's a large part of the problem."

Miel shrugged. "Same with us," he said. "We know exactly as much about your people as we care to. Not the best basis on which to start a war."

"I guess not." The Mezentine sounded faintly embarrassed to hear a high officer of state implying a criticism of policy. Quite right, too; but it's always galling to be taught good manners by an enemy.

The Ducas had rules about that sort of thing. *Be specially polite to people who annoy you. True feelings are for true friends.* Miel particularly liked that one because it meant you could convert trying situations into a kind of game; the more you disliked a person, the politer you could be. You knew that each civility was really a rude gesture in disguise, and you could therefore insult the victim like mad without him ever knowing.

"I'm forgetting my manners," Miel said. "You only know me as the bloodthirsty bugger who tried to have you killed. I'm Miel Ducas."

"Ziani Vaatzes."

"Pleased to meet you." Miel thought for a moment, then frowned. "Do all Mezentine names have a z in them?"

The Mezentine—no, at least do him the courtesy of thinking of him by his name; Vaatzes grinned. "It does seem like it sometimes," he said, "but it's not like there's a law or anything. Actually, I believe it's a dialect thing. Back in the country we originally came from, I'd be something like Tiani Badates. A singularly useless piece of information, but there you are."

"Quite so. What was it Orsea said you did, back home? Some kind of blacksmith?"

Vaatzes laughed. "Not really," he said. "I was a foreman at the ordnance factory."

"Fine. What's a foreman?"

"The answer to that," Vaatzes said, "depends on who you ask, but basically, I walk up and down the place all day making sure the workers in each shop are doing the work they're supposed to be doing, and making a proper job of it. A bit like a sergeant in an army, I suppose."

"I see," Miel said. "And have you been doing it long?"

"Six years. Before that, I was a toolmaker."

"Like I said," Miel put in. "A blacksmith."

"If you like. Actually, my job was to make the jigs and fixtures for the machines that made the various products. It was all about knowing how things work, and how to make them do what you want."

"That sounds more like my job," Miel said; and he realized that he wasn't being nearly as polite as he'd intended. "But I'm supposed to be telling you things, not the other way round. What would you like to know?"

"Well." Vaatzes paused. "We could start with geography and put in the history where it's relevant, or the other way round. Whatever suits you."

"Geography. All right, here goes." Miel cast his mind back a long way, to vague recollections of maps he'd paid too little attention to when he was a boy. "Your city stands at the mouth of a gulf, on the east coast of the continent. On the other three sides you've got plains and marshes, where the rivers drain down from these mountains we're walking up. You'll have observed that the eastern plain—where the battle was—separates two distinct mountain ranges, the north and the south. Eremia Montis is a plateau and a bunch of valleys in the heart of the northern mountains; in the southern range live our closest neighbors and traditional enemies, the Vadani. There's not a lot of difference between us, except for one thing; they're lucky enough to have a massive vein of silver running through the middle of their territory. All we've got is some rather thin grass, sheep and the best horses in the world. With me so far?"

"I think so," Vaatzes said. "Go on."

Miel paused for breath; the climb wasn't getting any easier. "South of the Vadani," he said, "is the desert; and it's a wonderful thing and a blessing, because it forms a natural barrier between us and the people who live in the south. If it wasn't for the desert we'd have to build a wall, and it'd have to be a very high one, with big spikes on top. The southerners aren't nice people."

"I see," Vaatzes said. "In what way?"

"Any way you care to name," Miel replied. "They're nomadic, basically they live by stealing each other's sheep; they're barbaric and cruel and there's entirely too many of them. If I tell you we prefer your lot to the southerners, you may get some idea."

"Right," Vaatzes said. "That bad."

"Absolutely. But, like I said, there's a hundred miles of desert between them and us, so that's all right. Now then; above us, that's to the north of Eremia Montis, you've got the Cure Doce. They're no bother to anybody."

"I know about them," Vaatzes interrupted. "That's where most of our food comes from."

"That's right. They trade wheat and beans and wine and God knows what else for your trinkets and stuff. We sell them wool and horses, and buy their barley and their disgusting beer. To the best of my knowledge, they just sort of go on and on into the distance and fade out; the far north of their territory is all snow and ice and what's the word for it, tundra, until you reach the ocean. I have an idea the better quality of falcons come from up there somewhere, but you'd have to ask my cousin Jarnac about that sort of thing. Anyway, that's geography for you."

"Thank you," Vaatzes said. "Can we stop and rest for a minute? We don't have mountains where I come from, just stairs."

"Of course," Miel said; he'd been walking a little bit faster than he'd have liked, so as to wear out the effete City type, and his knees were starting to ache. "We can't stay too long or we'll get left behind, but a minute or two won't hurt. History?"

"Please."

"History," Miel said, "is pretty straightforward. A thousand years ago, or something like that, the mountains were more or less empty, and the ancestors of the Eremians and the Vadani were all one people, living right down south, other side of the desert. When the nomads arrived, they drove us out. It's one of the reasons why we don't like them very much. We crossed the desert — there's lots of good legends about that — and settled in the mountains. Nothing much happened for a while; then there was the most terrific falling-out between us, meaning the Eremians, and the Vadani. Don't ask me what it was all about, but pretty soon it turned into a civil war. We moved into the north mountains and started calling ourselves Eremians, and the civil war stopped being civil and became just plain war. This was long before the silver was discovered, so both sides were pretty evenly matched, and we carried on fighting in a force-of-habit sort of way for generations."

Vaatzes nodded. "Like you do," he said.

"Quite. Then, about three hundred years ago, your lot turned up out of the blue; came over the sea in big ships, as you presumably know better than I do. To begin with, our lot and the Vadani were far too busy beating each other up to notice you were there. It was only when your traders started coming up the mountain and selling us things that we realized you were here to stay. No skin off our noses; we were happy to buy all the things you made, and there was always a chance we could drag you in on our side of the war, if the Vadani didn't beat us to it. Really, it was only—no offense—only when you people started throwing your weight about, trying to push us around and generally acting like you owned the place, that we noticed how big and strong you'd grown. Too late to do anything about it by then, needless to say."

"When you say throwing our weight about…"

Miel stood up. "We'd better be getting along, or they'll be wondering where we've got to. Throwing your weight about; well, it started with little things, the way it always does. For instance: when your traders arrived—they came to us back then, we didn't have to go traipsing down the mountain to get ripped off by middlemen—the first thing they had a big success with was cloth. Beautiful stuff you people make, got to hand it to you; anyhow, we'd say, That's nice, I'll take twelve yards, and the bloke would measure it off with his stick, and we'd go home and find we hadn't got twelve yards, only eleven and a bit. Really screws it up when you're making clothes and there's not quite enough fabric. So we'd go storming back next day in a fine old temper, and the trader would explain that the Mezentine yard is in fact two

and a smidge inches shorter than the Eremian yard, on account
of a yard being a man's stride, and the Eremians have got longer
legs. Put like that, you can't object, it's entirely reasonable. Then
the trader says, Tell you what, to avoid misunderstandings in the
future, how'd it be if you people started using our measurements?
We'd say we weren't sure about that, and the trader would explain
that he buys and sells all over the place, and it'd make life really
tiresome if he had to keep adapting each time he came to a place
that had its own weights and measures; so, being completely practical, it'd be far easier for us to change than it'd be for him; also,
if he's got to spend time consulting conversion charts or cutting
a special stick for Eremian yards, that time'd have to be paid for,
meaning a five or ten percent rise in prices to cover additional
costs and overheads. Naturally we said, Fine, we'll use your yard
instead of ours; and next it was weights, because there's eighteen
ounces in the Eremian pound, and then it was the gallon. Next it
was the calendar, because a couple of our months are a few days
shorter, so we'd arrange to meet your people on such-and-such a
day, and you wouldn't show up. You get the idea, I'm sure.

"Didn't take long before everything was being weighed and
measured in Mezentine units, which meant a whole lot of us didn't
have a clue how much of anything we were buying, or how much it
was really costing us, or even what day of the week it was. Sure, all
just little things, one step at a time, like a man walking to the gallows. But the time came when we stopped making our own cloth
because yours was cheaper and better; same for all the things we
got from you. Then out of the blue the price has shot right up;
we complain, and then it's take it or leave it, we've got plenty of
customers but you've only got one supplier. So we gave in, started
paying the new prices; but when we tried to even things up by asking more for what we had to sell, butter and wool and so forth, it's
a whole different story. Next step, your people are interfering in
every damn thing. The Duke appoints someone to do a job; your
traders turn round and say, We can't work with him, he doesn't
like us, choose someone else; and by the way, here's a list of other

things you do which we don't approve of, if you want to carry on doing business with us, you'd better change your ways. We're about to tell you where you can stick your manufactured goods when suddenly we realize that your people have been quietly buying up chunks of our country; land, live and dead stock, water rights, you name it. Investment, I believe it's called, and by a bizarre coincidence you use the same word for besieging a castle. So there we were, invested on all sides; we can't tell you to go and screw yourselves without getting your permission first. Throwing your weight around."

Vaatzes frowned. "I see," he said. "Honestly, I had no idea. Come to that, before I ran away from the City, I didn't even know you existed."

"Oh, your lot know we exist all right." Miel sighed. "Give you an example. My family, the Ducas, have been landowners and big fish in little ponds and selfless servants of the commonwealth for longer than even we can remember. We've done our bit for our fellow citizens, believe me. About a third of the men in the Ducas over the last five hundred years have died in war, either killed in a battle or gone down with dysentery or infected wounds. We pay more in tax than any other family. In our corner of the country we run the justice system, we're the land and probate registry; we say the magic words at the weddings of our tenants, we're godfathers to their children, we run schools and pay for doctors. We take the view that a tenant deserves to get more for his rent than just a strip of land and a side to be on when there's a feud. That's what I was talking about when I said we do our bit for our fellow citizens; and that's over and above stuff like fighting in wars and being chancellors and ambassadors and commissioners. Do you see what I'm driving at?"

Vaatzes nodded. "You're the government," he said. "But it's different in the City, of course. The big men who do all the top jobs in the Guilds are our government; but they get to make policy, not just carry it out. They can decide what's going to be done, and of course that means they have loads of opportunities to look out for their own Guilds, or their neighbors and families, or themselves. You can only do what the Duke tells you. You've got all the work, but without the privileges and perks."

"That's right," Miel said. "You've certainly got a grasp of politics."

"Like I said, I know how things work. A city or a country is just a kind of machine. It's got a mechanism. I can see mechanisms at a glance, like people who can dowse for water."

"That's quite a gift," Miel said, frowning slightly. "Anyway, the way we've always done things is for the landowning families to be the government, as you call it. But then along come your City people, investors, buying up land and flocks and slices of our lives; and of course, they don't take responsibility, the way we've been brought up to do. They don't think, how will such and such a decision affect the tenants and their shepherds, or the people of the village? They don't live here, and when they make a decision they're guided by what's best for their investment, what'll produce the best profit, or whatever it is that motivates them. So, when two tenants fall out over a boundary or grazing rights on a common or anything like that, they can't do what they've always done, go and see the boss up at the big house and make him sort it out for them. The boss isn't there; and even if they were to go all the way to Mezentia and ask to see the directors of the company, or whatever such people call themselves, and even if those directors could be bothered to see them and listen to them, it wouldn't do any good, because they wouldn't understand a thing about the situation. Not like we would, the Ducas or the Orphanotrophi or the Phocas. See, we're their boss, but we're also their neighbor. They can go out of their front door and look up the mountain and see our houses. You can't see Mezentia's Guildhall from anywhere in Eremia."

Vaatzes nodded. He seemed to be an intelligent man, and quite reasonable. Perhaps that was why they'd put him in prison, Miel decided. "I guess it's a question of attitude," he said. "Perspective. We're concerned mostly with things—making them, selling them. You're concerned with people."

Miel smiled. "That puts it very well," he said. "And maybe you can see why I don't like your City."

"I've gone off it rather myself," Vaatzes said.

"Fine." Miel nodded. "So perhaps you'd care to explain to me why you think it'd be a good idea to turn my country into a copy of it."

It was a neat piece of strategy, Miel couldn't help thinking. He'd have derived more satisfaction from it if he found it easier to dislike the Mezentine; but that was hard going, like running uphill, and the further he went, the harder it got. But he'd laid his trap and sprung it—there was one mechanism the Mezentine hadn't figured out at a glance—and sure enough, for a while Vaatzes seemed to be lost for words.

"It's not quite like that," he said eventually. "Like I told you, I'm an engineer. I know about machines, things." He frowned thoughtfully. "Let's see," he said. "Suppose you come to me and ask me to build you a machine—a loom, say, so you can weave your wool into cloth instead of sending it down the mountain."

"Right," Miel said.

"So I build the machine," Vaatzes went on, "and I deliver it and I get paid. That's my side of the bargain. What you do with it, how you use it and how the use you put it to affects your life and your neighbors'; that's your business. Not my business, and not my fault. It'd be the same if you asked me to build you a scorpion, an arrow-thrower. Once you've taken it from me, it's up to you who you point it at. You can use it to defend your country and your way of life against your worst enemy, or you can set it up on the turret of your castle and shoot your neighbors. All I want to do," he went on, "is make a new life for myself, now the old one's been taken away from me. Now I'm lucky, because I know a secret. It's like I can turn lead into gold. If I can do that, it'd be pretty silly of me to get a job mucking out pigs. From your point of view, I can give you the secrets that make the Mezentines stronger than you are. With that power, you've got a chance of making sure you don't have to go through another horrible disaster, like the one you've just suffered. Now," he went on, stopping for a moment to catch his breath, "if I were to sell you a scorpion without telling you how it works, or how to use it safely without hurting yourself, that'd be no good. But that's not the case. You seem to understand just fine what's wrong with the City and how it works. I can give you the secret, and you know enough not to hurt yourself with it, or spoil all the good things about your way of life. Does that make any sense to you?"

It was a long time before Miel answered. "Yes, actually, it does," he said. "And that's why I'm glad it's not my decision whether we take you up on your offer. If it was up to me, I'd probably say yes, now we've had this conversation, and I have a feeling that'd be a bad thing."

"Oh," Vaatzes said. "Why?"

"Ah, now, if I knew that I'd be all right." Miel smiled suddenly. "I'd be safe, see. But it's all academic, since it's not up to me."

Vaatzes scratched his head. "I don't know," he said. "You're a senior officer of state, if you went to the Duke and said, for God's sake don't let that Mezentine start teaching us his diabolical tricks, he'd listen to you, wouldn't he?"

"You were there when I told him to have you hanged," Miel replied cheerfully. "And here you still are."

"Yes, but you didn't press the point. I was there, remember. It's not like you made any effort to use your influence; and when he said no, let's not, you didn't argue." He lifted his eyes and looked at Miel. "Are you sorry you didn't?"

"Like I said, it wasn't my decision. It never is."

"Would you like it to be?"

Miel shivered, as though he'd just touched a plate he hadn't realized was hot. "We're falling behind," he said. "Come on, don't dawdle."

They walked quickly, past men supporting their wounded

friends on their shoulders, others hauling ropes or pushing the wheels of carts over the rims of potholes. "Of course," Miel said abruptly, "if he decides to let you teach us, common courtesy requires that we teach you something in return."

"Does it?"

"Oh yes. Reciprocity is courtesy, that's an old family rule of the Ducas. We pay our debts in kind."

"Really. We've got money for that."

Miel shook his head. "That's wages," he said. "And wages are a political statement. If I pay you, that makes you my servant, it's a different sort of relationship. Between gentlemen, it's a gift for a gift and a favor for a favor."

"I see," Vaatzes said. "So if you teach me something in return, that's instead of money."

"Of course not, you're missing the point. I'm a nobleman and you're a whatever you said, foreman. Therefore, courtesy demands that I give more than I get."

Vaatzes thought about that. "To show you're better than me."

"That's it. That's what nobility's all about. If you want to be better than someone socially, you've got to be better than them in real terms too; more generous, more forbearing, whatever. Otherwise all the transaction between us proves is that I'm more powerful than you, and that wouldn't say anything about me. Hence the need for me to give more than I get. Simple, really."

There was a pause while Vaatzes thought that one through. "So I get the money and something else?"

"Yes."

"In that case, fine. You have to teach me something."

"That's right."

"Thanks," Vaatzes said. "Thanks very much. So, what do you know that you could teach me?"

"Ah." Miel grinned. "That's a slight problem. Let's see, what do I know? Another thing about nobility," he continued, "is that you don't actually know many things, you just know a few things very well indeed. I could teach you statesmanship."

"Meaning what?"

"How to debate in High Council," Miel said. "How to budget, and cost a project, how to forecast future revenues. Negotiation with foreign ambassadors. Court protocol. That sort of thing."

Vaatzes frowned. "Not a lot of use to me, really."

"I suppose not. So what does that leave? Estate management; no, not particularly relevant. I think we're just left with horsemanship, falconry and fencing."

"Right," Vaatzes said. "All three of which I know nothing about. Which would you say is easiest?"

"None of them."

"In that case, falconry or fencing. Horses give me a rash."

Miel laughed. "Maybe I'll teach you both," he said. "But it'll all depend on what Orsea decides."

Vaatzes nodded. "You've known him a long time, I think."

"All my life. We grew up together, twenty or so of us, hanging round the court. Back then, of course, he was just the Orseoli and I was the Ducas, but we always got on well nonetheless—surprising, since my father was right up the top of the tree and the Orseoli were sort of clinging frantically to the lower branches. But then Orsea married the Countess Sirupati, and she's got no brothers and her sisters aren't eligible for some technical reason, so they got married off outside the duchy; as a result, Orsea was suddenly the heir apparent. Count Sirupat dies, Orsea becomes Duke. Couldn't have happened to a nicer fellow, either."

"So you didn't mind?"

"Mind? Of course not. Oh, I see, you're thinking I might've been resentful because he got to be the Duke. Not a bit of it. The Sirupati would never marry the Ducas."

Vaatzes looked puzzled. "But I thought your family were high-ranking aristocrats."

"We are. Which is the reason. Quite simple, really. The great houses aren't allowed to marry into the ruling family. Otherwise there'd be no end of God-awful power struggles, with all of us trying to get the throne. So we're all excluded; stops us getting dangerous ideas. If the Duke's only got daughters, he has to find his heir from the lesser nobility, people like the Orseoli. It's a good system. But you should've figured that out for yourself, if you've got a special intuition for how things work."

"Well, I know now," Vaatzes said. " I guess I didn't figure it out for myself because it's a good idea, and those don't seem to happen much in politics. Who made the rule, anyhow?"

That struck Miel as a strange question. "We all did," he said. "Gradually, over time. I don't think anybody ever sat down with a piece of paper and wrote the rules out, just so. They grew because everybody could see it made sense."

"An intuitive feel for how things work," Vaatzes said. "Maybe there's hope for you people after all."

That night, they camped in a small valley under a false peak. They didn't start pitching tents until sunset, and most of the work was done by torchlight; tired men doing things they knew by heart, cooperating smoothly and without thinking, like the components of a properly run-in machine. It was probably a good sign that Ziani was given a guest tent all to himself; a small one, with a plain camp bed, a lamp and an old iron brazier, but he didn't have to share and they put it up for him rather than telling him where it was and leaving him to do it. When he was alone, he sat on the bed—he ached all over from the exhaustion of walking uphill all day; his heels and soles were covered in torn blisters and his new shoes were smudged inside with blood—and stared at the boundary where the circle of yellow light touched the white canvas background. Having that sort of mind, he drew up a schedule of resources, a list of materials and components.

First, he had his life. In the Guildhall, and after that on the road, in the plain, on the terrifying outskirts of the battle, he'd recognized the inevitability of his own death without finding any way to reconcile himself to it. For many reasons (but one primarily) he couldn't accept it; death was a part that didn't fit, something that had no place in the scheme of things as they should be; an abomination. He had no illusions about his escape. He didn't believe in destiny, any more than he believed in goblins; if the iron ore was destined to end up as finished products, there'd be no need for an engineer. There had been a certain amount of resourcefulness and clever thinking involved, but mostly it was luck, particularly once he was away from people and under the impersonal, inhuman sky (he'd always hated Nature; it was a machine too big for him to take in, too specialized for him to repair). But he had his life, the essential starting-point. Can't get anything done if you're dead.

Next, he had his knowledge and his trade. Many years ago, he'd come to accept the fact that he was completely and exclusively defined by what he did. Other men were tall or short, strong or weak, kind or cruel, clever or stupid; they were funny, popular, reliable, feckless, miserable; they were lovers or runners or storytellers, bores, growers of prize roses, readers, collectors of antique candlesticks; they were friends, neighbors, enemies, evil bastards, compassionate, selfish, generous. Ziani Vaatzes was an engineer; everything he was, all he was. When he came home in the evening...

Ah yes. Finally, he had his motivation. He had, of course, lied to the Duke and the Duke's pleasant, slow-witted courtier. If it hadn't been for his motivation, he'd have stayed in the prison cell, or curled up in a ball on the moors and died; he certainly wouldn't have killed two men, and he certainly wouldn't be getting ready to betray his City's most precious secrets to the barbarians. He'd considered setting the motivation down in the list of problems and obstacles, since it was such an incredible burden, limiting his actions in so many ways. But in spite of that, it was an asset, and the best facility at his disposal. He saw it, in the blueprint in his mind, as the engine that would power his machine. Certainly nothing else could.

As for that list of problems and obstacles; in the end, it did him a service by putting him to sleep, because it stretched on endlessly, like the sheep you're supposed to count jumping over the gap in the wall. There were so many of them it was almost a relief; so many he didn't have to bother listing them, it couldn't be done. The way to cross a vast, flat plain when you're aching, starving and exhausted is not to resolve to get to the other side, because that's out of the question. You don't look to the mountains, a little gray blip on the bottom edge of the sky. You look ahead and make a bet with yourself: I bet you I'll get as far as that little outcrop of boulders, or that single thorn tree, before I fall over and die. If you win that bet, you double up on the next one, and so on until at last you can't trick yourself into taking another step; at which point, a defeated enemy army which just happens to be passing picks you up and rescues you. Piece of cake, really.

Similarly, he made a point of not looking at the end result he needed to achieve. It was too far away, and there were too many obstacles, he'd never live to reach it. But he might just make it as far as the first step in his design, the second, possibly even the third. Same as a big project in the factory; you know you'll never get it all done in one day, so you plan it out: today we'll cut the material, tomorrow we'll face off and mark out, the next day we'll turn the diameter, cut the threads, and so on. It complicated things a little that his motivation and his objective were so closely linked, because they were so simple (but it's good design to make one part carry out two functions); if he couldn't let himself believe in it, he couldn't very well rely on it to drive him forward across the heather and the tussocks of couch-grass. Fortunately, he found he could turn a blind eye to the inconsistency. The motivation was strong enough to keep him going, even though the objective was so ridiculously far-fetched. All he had to do — it was so simple, to a man who lived by and for complexities — all he had to do was close his eyes and think of her, and he was like the flywheel driven by the belt, whether it likes it or not.

The next day was all uphill, and Miel was needed to supervise the carts, and the wounded, and various other things that had got slightly worse overnight. It didn't help that Orsea was insisting he was strong enough to ride; it wasn't fair on the doctor, for one thing. The wretched man had enough to do with several hundred critical cases (who weren't dukes, but who did what they were told) without having to stay within earshot of His Highness in case the partially healed wound burst and the idiot needed to be seen to straight away before he bled to death.

"I can manage, really," Miel told his oldest friend.

"I know that," Orsea replied, shifting painfully in his saddle, "but you shouldn't have to. This is my responsibility. You look like death warmed up."

"Thank you so much." Miel winced, as though he wanted to ride away in a huff but knew he wasn't allowed to, because it would be discourteous. "Look, it's no big deal. If I can just get a few tangles straightened out, we can be on our way and it'll be fine. It'll be much quicker for me to deal with the problems myself than explain what they are so you can handle them. And," he added, with the air of a general committing his last reserves in a final reckless charge, "the doctor says you won't be fit to ride for another three days."

Orsea made a remark about the doctor that was both vulgar and inaccurate. "Besides," he went on, "if it's my health you're all worried about, you ought to realize that if I've got to spend another day alone in a cart brooding about what a fuck-up I've made of everything, it's absolutely guaranteed I'll die of guilt and frustration. So telling me what the doctor said isn't just annoying and high treason, it's counterproductive."

Miel sighed melodramatically. "Not up to me," he said. "If you want to risk a massive hematoma—"

"You mean hemorrhage," Orsea pointed out. "Hematoma is bruises. Trust me, all right? Now let's talk about something else. How's that cousin of yours getting on, Jarnac—" He stopped himself abruptly; Miel smiled.

"It's all right," he said, "Jarnac wasn't killed in the battle. In fact, he didn't join the army at all. Stayed at home."

"Sensible chap."

Miel frowned. "No, actually. Cousin Jarnac doesn't approve of the war. He thinks it's wrong. And I don't mean wrong as in liable to end up a complete fiasco; wrong as in morally bad. All wars, not just this one."

Orsea nodded. "There's a word for that, isn't there?"

"I can think of several."

"No, I mean it's a known-about thing, an ism. Pacifism."

"Is that right?" Miel yawned. "There's times when my cousin gets so far up my nose he's practically poking out of my ear. Why did you mention him, all of a sudden?"

"Don't know," Orsea said. "Or rather, yes I do. I was lying there awake in the early hours, and for some reason I was remembering that sparrowhawk he had when we were kids. Mad keen on falconry he was, back then."

"Still is. Why, do you fancy going hawking when we get home? I'm sure he'd be glad of the excuse to show off."

"It might be fun," Orsea said. "Though God knows, I shouldn't even be thinking of swanning about enjoying myself when there's so much work to be done. Besides, what would people think?"

"There goes the Duke, having a day off," Miel replied. "You aren't the first man in history who's lost a battle. And it wasn't your fault. No, really. You weren't to know about those scorpion things. If it hadn't been for them—"

"Which is like saying if it wasn't for the rain, it'd be a dry day." Orsea scowled. "Sooner or later, you'll have to admit it, Miel. I screwed up. I led thousands of our people to their death."

Miel sighed loudly. "All right, yes. It's very bad. And it's going to be very tense for a while back home, until people come to terms with it. But these things happen; and you know what? It's not you they're going to hate, it's the Mezentines, because they're the ones who killed our people. Now, do you want me to organize a day with the birds when we get home, or not?"

Orsea shook his head. "Best not," he said. "At least, not for a while. Now, what can I do to help?"

Eventually, Miel let him organize the reconnaissance parties. That was all right, he was happy with that. They were, he knew, in sensitive territory. Not far away (nobody was entirely sure where; that was the problem) was the border between the two mountain dukedoms. He felt confident that the Vadani wouldn't make trouble unless they felt they were provoked. Straying inadvertently onto their land with an army, however, even if that army was a chewed-up remnant, would probably constitute provocation, particularly to some of the old-school Vadani commanders who were still having trouble coming to terms with the peace. Vital, therefore, to keep a sharp eye open for routine border patrols, and to keep well out of their way. The scout captains duly set off, and he settled down in the vanguard to wait for the first reports.

The Vadani, he thought; that's probably what made me think about falcons, and Jarnac Ducas. It had been years since he'd seen his cousin Valens; the last time, come to think of it, was before he—before either of them—had come to the throne; before his wedding, even. He tried to picture Valens in his mind, and saw a thin, sharp-nosed, sullen boy who never spoke first. He remembered feeling sorry for him, watching him riding to the hunt with his outrageous father. It had been a cold, miserable occasion; a state visit, reception and grand battue to celebrate a truce in the unending, insoluble war. It was obvious that nobody on either side believed in the truce—they were all proved right a few months later, when it collapsed into bloody shambles—and hardly anybody made any effort to mask his skepticism; but they'd attended the reception, watched the dancers, listened to the musicians, gone through the motions with fixed smiles, and then that dreadful day's hunting, in the cold mist, everybody getting muddled about the directions, not hearing the horns, getting to their pegs too early or too late; the old Duke in a raging temper because the beaters had gone in before they were supposed to, and the deer had been flushed and had gone on long before the guests were in position. Not that any of the Eremian contingent cared a damn; but the Duke did, because he actually cared whether they caught anything or not—some of the Eremians reckoned the visit and the whole truce business was just a pretext he'd cooked up for a full-scale battue at the beginning of the season. As a result, the Duke spent the day charging backward and forward across the field yelling at huntsmen and line-captains, and young Valens had charged with him, grimly wretched but keeping up, so as not to get lost and add to the day's problems. It was painfully obvious that he didn't want to be there; obvious that his father knew it, and didn't care. He took his son with him the way you'd wear a brooch or a belt you hated, but which a relative had given you, so you had to wear it so as not to hurt their feelings. That day, he'd felt very sorry for Valens, and it was still the mental image his mind defaulted to, when his advisers debated the Vadani question in council, or when his wife talked about Valens to him. It's hard to hate someone who, in your mind, is forever a sad twelve-year-old, soaking wet on a horse far too big for him. Orsea, of course, made a point of never hating anybody unless it was absolutely unavoidable.

The first party of scouts hadn't seen anything. The second party reported a body of horsemen, apparently shadowing the army on the other side of a hog's back; somewhere between seventy-five and a hundred and twenty of them, a third- or half-squadron, therefore quite possibly a routine patrol. The third party were late, and when they came in they had a shamefaced look about them; they'd been intercepted by Vadani cavalry who'd apparently materialized out of thin air in front of them on the road, and given them a message to take back. Duke Valens sent his greetings and sympathy on their unfortunate experience. It occurred to him that the army might be short of food, clothes, doctors, whatever. If there was anything they needed, anything the Vadani could do to help (except, of course, military action of any kind), all they had to do was ask.

Orsea's first instinct was to refuse. While he was trying to come up with a sufficiently polite form of words, he found himself wondering why; true, it would be galling to be in Valens' debt, but food, at least a dozen more doctors, best of all a guide or two to show them the easiest way—that could be enough to save lives.

He sent a reply thanking Valens very much indeed, and listing everything he could think of. The offer wasn't kindly meant, he had no illusions on that score, but he was in no position to take account of intentions.

The Vadani doctors came with the supply-wagons, perched among sacks and barrels and wearing bemused, scared expressions, like helpless peasants abducted by the fairies. Maybe the Vadani told the same sort of stories about the Eremians as Orsea had heard about them, during the war—they can't be trusted, don't take prisoners, they string you up by the ankles and use you for javelin practice; at any rate, they seemed anxious to help and please, and the Vadani had always had a good reputation for medicine. Orsea amused himself by wondering where they'd been press-ganged from; they'd arrived so fast, they could hardly have been given time to grab their boots and their bags. They asked permission to take some of the worst cases away with them (these men need proper care in a hospital, and so forth), but he couldn't allow that. If there was one thing the Vadani were better at than curing people, it was taking hostages.

Once or twice as the day wore on, he caught himself thinking about the Mezentine fugitive, and his extraordinary offer. But that would have to wait until he got home; the decision would have to be taken in the proper way, with the opinions of the council guiding him. Better, therefore, that he kept his mind open and didn't think about it at all until then.

They stopped for the night an hour before sunset, a long way short of where they'd hoped they'd reach. This journey was taking forever. Orsea was tired but not exhausted, and his wound hadn't burst like everybody had said it would; there was a little blood showing through the bandage, but nothing spectacular. A Vadani doctor came to examine and dress it; a short, stout man with a fringe of straight white hair round a glowing bald head, very quiet, as though each word was costing him thirty shillings. Orsea guessed that it was the first time he'd had anything to do with the effects of a battle. Some people reacted like that, shutting the

doors and windows of their minds to keep the intrusive information out. He said the wound was knitting very well, tutted to himself at the cack-handed Eremian way of winding a bandage, and
left quickly. When he'd gone, Orsea poured himself a small drink
and opened the book he'd brought along to read, and hadn't yet
looked at—Pescennia Alastro's sonnets, the latest rescension, an
anniversary present from his wife. He opened it at the first page,
laid it carefully face down on his knee, and burst into tears.

5

Unlike his father, the young Duke hunted three days a week, always following the same pattern. On Tuesdays he rode parforce, with the full pack, drawing the upland coverts for roe (in season), boar, bear and wolf. On Thursdays the hunt was bow-and-stable, the hunters on foot and stationary while the pack flushed the valley plantations and the moors on the forest perimeter. Saturday was for hawking, unless the weather was too wet and cold, in which case they'd work the warrens with terriers, or try their luck walking up rabbits around the orchards. The great battues were a thing of the past now; the young Duke didn't hold with the disturbance they caused, or the scattering of game from their regular beats.

Duke Valens took the hunt very seriously. The rule was, no business on a hunt day unless it's a genuine emergency; and even then, the court knew better than to expect him to be good-tempered about it. Accordingly, Chancellor Delmatius was in two minds, possibly three, about passing on the message from the northeastern frontier. He spent a couple of tormented hours contemplating the true meaning of the words *genuine emergency*, evaluated the risks to a hair's weight, and was just in time to intercept Valens before he left for the stables.

"It's probably nothing," he said, pausing to catch his breath.

"I thought I'd mention it, but I don't think we need do anything about it."

Valens wasn't looking at him; he was scowling at a square of blue sky beyond the window. "Shit," he said (Valens very rarely swore). "And I was hoping we'd work through the long drive this morning. Pranno reckons there's a twelve-pointer just moved in there."

Delmatius didn't sigh with relief, but only because he'd learned how not to. "Do you want to see the messengers first, or should I call the council?"

"I suppose I'd better see the messengers," Valens answered, looking thoughtfully at the gloves in his hand. "I don't need you to sit in, I'll get Strepho to take notes for you. You get on and call the meeting. We'll use the side-chamber off the east hall."

Delmatius scuttled away like a mouse who's left half his tail in the cat's mouth; as soon as he'd gone, Valens relaxed his scowl and perched on the edge of the table. It was a pity; if there really was a twelve-pointer in the narrow wood, it'd be long gone by next week, most likely heading downhill toward the lusher grass. Either the Natho clan would get it, or some poacher who'd take the meat and bury the rest, and that superb trophy would go to waste.

Even a twelve-pointer, however, didn't justify spitting in the face of opportunity. He'd already heard about the battle itself, of course. The scouts (his personal unit, not the regulars who reported to the chiefs of staff) had brought him the news a fraction less than twenty-four hours after the last scorpion-bolt pitched. By the time the joint chiefs and the council knew about it, Valens had already read the casualty reports (both sides' versions, naturally). Predictably, they were split into two irreconcilable factions: attack now, kill them all, worry about the treaty later; or leave well alone and hope the wolves tidy up the stragglers.

Instead, Valens had given orders for a modest relief column: food, blankets, doctors of course. The council were used to him adopting the one course of action they were sure he wouldn't take, and listened meekly to their assignments. As usual when he gave an incomprehensible order, Valens didn't stop to explain the rationale behind it. The most favored theory was that he wanted the doctors to bring him back extremely detailed reports of what state the Eremians were in, the exact strength of the vanguard and rearguard, so he could make the attack, when it came, as effective as possible. Other theories included an unannounced illness, a sudden conversion to some new religion that preached non-violence, or that old catch-all, lulling the enemy into a false sense of security.

In fact, he was allowing himself the luxury of savoring the moment. It had been a long time coming; but now, at last, his proper enemy and natural prey had made the mistake of bolting from cover at the first horn-call, so to speak. It'd be fatally easy to take the obvious course of action and lay into them, kill as many as possible and scatter the rest. Any fool could do that. Valens, on the other hand, knew the value of waiting just a little longer and doing a proper job. He'd heard a saying once; maybe it was from a Mezentine diplomat, boasting insufferably about how wonderful his people were at making things. *The easiest way to do something is properly.* When he'd heard it first, he'd been unable to make up his mind whether it was terribly profound or utterly banal. The moment of revelation had been when he realized it was both.

He knew what the people said about him, of course; he was the best Duke in living memory, he was a bastard but a clever bastard, he was ten times the ruler his father had been. Well, he knew the third one was lies. The second one he was prepared to acknowledge, if put to it. The first one he dismissed as unlikely. It was good that they said it, however. If they admired him, they were likely to do as they were told, just so long as he stayed successful. But there was no reason why he shouldn't. If the hunt had taught him anything, it was the inestimable value of thinking in three dimensions. To hunt successfully, you must know your ground, your pack and your quarry. You must learn, by fieldwork and reconnaissance, where the quarry is likely to be and what it's liable to do once disturbed. You must know the capacities and weaknesses of the resources—men, dogs, equipment—at your disposal. You must be able to visualize at all times where everybody is, once you've sent them to their stations to do their assigned tasks. You must be aware of the interplay of time and distance, so you can be sure that the stops and the beaters are in position when you loose the pack. You must be able to judge allowances—the angle to off-set a drive so as to head off the quarry from its customary line of escape, how far ahead of a running stag to shoot so as to pitch your arrow where it's going, not where it's just been. Above all, at all times you must be in perfect control, regardless of whether things are going well or badly. A brilliant mind is not required; nor is genius, intuition, inspiration. Clarity and concentration are helpful; but the main thing is vision, the ability to draw invisible lines with the mind's eye, to see round corners and through walls. It's a knack that can be learned fairly readily; slightly harder than swimming, rather easier than juggling or playing the flute.

Well; if he wasn't going to hunt today, he'd better go to the council meeting. Nothing useful would be achieved there—he would do all the work himself, it'd take him just under half an hour—but it was necessary in order to keep his leading men, his pack, alert and obedient. He'd been at pains to train them over the last few years, encouraging, rewarding, culling as needed, and they were shaping well; but time had to be spent with them, or they'd grow restive and willful. He swung his legs off the table onto the ground, a brisk, almost boyish movement that he certainly wouldn't have made had anybody been watching, and walked quickly across the yard, composing the agenda for the meeting as he went. On the stairs he met the master cutler, who told him the new case of rapiers had finally arrived from the City. He thanked the man and told him to bring them along to his study an hour after dinner.

The meeting lived down to his expectations. The council had wanted to debate whether or not to launch an attack on the Eremi-ans while they were vulnerable and desperate. When he told them he'd already sent food and doctors, they had nothing left to say;

they hadn't thought ahead, and so the buck had slipped through the cordon and left them standing. As it should be; it was easier to tell people what to do if they didn't interrupt. He delegated to them the simple, unimportant matters that he hadn't already provided for, and sent them away with a sense of bewildered purpose.

To his study next, where he had a map of the mountains. It was big, covering the whole of the north wall (there was a hole for the window in the middle of the Horsehead Ridge, but that didn't matter; the ridge was sheer rock capped with snow, and you needed ropes and winches to get there); it was a tapestry, so that he could mark positions with pins and tapes if he chose to, but that was rarely necessary. He fixed his eye on the place where Orsea's army had last been seen, and calculated where they were likely to be now.

An attack would be feasible—not straight away, there were two possible escape routes and he couldn't get his forces in place to block both of them before the Eremians moved on; tomorrow evening or the morning of the next day would be the right time. He could bottle them up in the long pass between Horn Cross and Finis Montium, and it ought to be possible to wipe them out to the last man without incurring unacceptable losses. It could be done; now he had to decide whether he wanted to do it.

That was a much bigger question, involving a complex interplay of imperatives. His father, or his grandfather, great-grandfather and so back four degrees, wouldn't have thought twice: kill the men, absorb the women and children, annex the land. They'd been trying to do just that, through war, for two hundred years. The hunt had, however, moved on; thanks to the long war, and the recent short interval of peace, Valens knew he didn't have the resources, human or material, to control the aftermath of victory to his satisfaction. He'd be occupying a bitterly hostile country, through which his lines of communication would be stretched and brittle. Facts duly faced, there wasn't actually anything in Eremia that he hadn't already got an adequate sufficiency of. Get rid of the Eremians and take their land, and he'd find himself with two frontiers abutting the desert instead of just one; two doors the nomad tribes might one day be able to prise open. A preemptive massacre would cause more problems than it solved.

He considered a few peripheral options. He could secure Orsea himself and keep him as a hostage. The advantages of that were obvious enough, but they didn't convince him. Sooner or later he'd either have to kill his cousin or let him go; at which point he could expect reprisals, and the Eremians had just proved themselves capable of gross overreaction. They would send an army; which he could defeat, of course, but then he'd be left with heavy casualties and the same undesirable situation he'd have faced if he'd taken this opportunity to wipe the Eremians out in the Butter Pass. Forget that, then; forget also bottling them up in the pass and extorting concessions. A republic or a democracy might do that, trading a vote-winning triumph in the short term against a nasty mess at some time in the future (hopefully when the other lot were in government). Valens was grateful he didn't have to do that sort of thing.

Decided, then; if he wasn't going to slaughter them, he must either ignore them or help them. Ignoring them would be a neutral act, and Valens found neutrality frustrating. Helping them would create an obligation, along with gratitude and goodwill. He who has his enemy's love and trust is in a far better position to attack, later, when the time is right. The cost would be negligible, and in any event he could make it a loan. It would send the right signals to the Mezentines (mountain solidarity, the truce is working); if he made a show of siding with the Eremians against them, it'd incline them to make a better offer when they came to buy his allegiance.

He sat down and wrote seven letters. As anticipated, it took him just under half an hour — admirably efficient, but not quick enough. It was far too late for hunting today, and the twelve-pointer would be three quarters of the way to the river valley by now. Best not to dwell on wasted chances.

(And then there was the real reason. If he sent food and blankets and doctors, she'd be pleased. If he sent cavalry, she'd hate him. So; he had no choice in the matter, none whatsoever.)

He spent the rest of the day in the small, windowless room at the top of the north tower, reading reports and petitions, checking accounts, writing obstreperous notes to exchequer clerks and procurement officers. Then there was a thick stack of pleadings for a substantial mercantile lawsuit that he'd been putting off reading for weeks; but today, having been cheated of his day in the fresh air, he was resigned and miserable enough to face anything, even that. After the snakelike meanderings of the legal documents, the diplomatic mail was positively refreshing in its clarity and brevity: a letter of introduction for the new ambassador from the Cure Doce, and a brusque note from a Mezentine government department he'd never heard of requiring him (arrogant bastards!) to arrest and extradite a criminal fugitive with a difficult name, should he attempt to cross the border. Neither of them needed a reply, so he marked each of them with a cross in the left-hand corner, to tell his clerk to send a formal acknowledgment. Dinner came up on a tray while he was making notes for a meeting with the merchant adventurers (tariffs, again); when at last he'd dealt with that, it was time to see the new rapiers. Not much of a reward for a long, tedious day, but better than nothing at all.

The rapiers had come in their own dear little case, oak with brass hinges and catches. They were superb examples of Mezentine craftsmanship—the finest steel, beautifully finished and polished, not a filemark or an uncrowned edge—but the balance was hopeless and the side-rings chafed his forefinger. He told the armorer to pay for them and hang them on a wall somewhere where he wouldn't have to look at them. Then he went to bed.

The next day was better; in fact, it was as good as a day could be, because, after the servants had taken away his bath and he was drying his hair, a page came to tell him that a woman was waiting to see him; a middle-aged woman in a huge red dress with sleeves, the page said, and pearls in her hair. Valens didn't smile, but it cost him an effort. "Show her into the study," he said.

He hadn't met this one before, but it didn't matter; the huge red dress was practically a uniform with the Merchant Adventurers these days, and the delicate, obscenely expensive pearl headdress told him all he needed to know about her status within the company. He gave her a pleasant smile.

"You've brought a letter," he said.

She started to apologize; it was late, because she'd been held up at the Duty & Diligence waiting for a consignment of five gross of sheep's grease that hadn't arrived, and by the time it finally showed up it was too late to go on that night so she cut her losses and took her twenty-six barrels of white butter to Lonazep instead, because in this heat they wouldn't keep as far as the Compassion & Grace, and of course that meant it was just as quick to go on up the mountain to Pericordia where she'd made an appointment to see some bone needles, two hundred gross at a good price but the quality wasn't there, so rather than go back down the mountain empty-handed she nipped across to Mandiritto to buy more of that nine-point lace, and that was when it decided to rain—

"That's quite all right," Valens said. "You're here now. Can I have the letter, please?"

She looked blank for a moment, then nodded briskly. "Of course, yes." From her satchel (particularly magnificent; tapestry, with golden lions sitting under a flat-looking tree) she took out a stiff packet of parchment about the size of her hand, and laid it down on the table.

"Thank you," Valens said, and waited.

She smiled at him. "My pleasure, of course," she said. "Now, I don't suppose you've got a moment, I know how terribly busy you must be..."

He wanted to say yes straight away and save having to listen, but that wouldn't do at all; his hands were itching to get hold of the letter—not open it, not straight away, just hold it and know it was there—but he folded them in a dignified manner on the table and listened for a very long time, until she finally got to what she wanted. It turned out to be nothing much, a license to import

Eremian rawhide single bends, theoretically still restricted by the embargo but nobody took any notice anymore; he got the feeling she was only asking so as to have a favor for him to grant. He said yes, had to repeat it five times before she finally accepted it, and once more to get her out of the door without physical violence. He managed not to shout, and kept smiling until she'd finally gone. Then he sat down and looked at the letter.

It had started eighteen months ago, pretty much by accident. A trader had been caught at the frontier with contraband (trivial stuff; silver earrings and a set of fine decorated jesses for a sparrowhawk); instead of paying the fine, however, she'd claimed Eremian diplomatic immunity and pleaded the peace treaty, claiming she was a special envoy of the Duchess, and the trinkets were privileged diplomatic mail. Probably, it was her ingenuity that impressed the excise inspector. Instead of smiling and dropping hints for the usual bribe, he decided to call her bluff; he impounded the goods and sent to the Duke for verification through the proper diplomatic channels. Valens' clerk wrote to the proper officer in Eremia Montis, and in due course received a reply from the keeper of the wardrobe, enclosing a notarized set of diplomatic credentials and a promise that it wouldn't happen again. It wasn't the sort of thing Valens would normally expect to see, even though the original request had been written in his name, and he supposed he must have signed the thing, along with a batch of other stuff. But the reply was brought for him to see by a nervous-looking clerk, because there was something written in at the bottom, just under the seal.

The handwriting was different; it was, in fact, practically illegible, all spikes and cramped squiggles, not the fluent, graceful hand of a clerk. It was a brief note, an unaccountable impulse frozen in ink, like a fly trapped in amber; are you, it asked, that boy who used to stare at me every evening when I was a hostage in Civitas Vadanis? I've often wondered what became of you; please write to me. And then her name; or he assumed it was her name, rather than two superimposed clawmarks.

It had taken him a long time to reply, during which he considered a wide range of issues: the possibility of a trap designed to create a diplomatic incident, the real reason he'd never married, the paradox of the atrocious handwriting. Mostly, however, he hesitated because he didn't know the answer to the question. He remembered the boy she'd referred to, but the memory brought him little except embarrassment. He thought of the boy's strange, willful isolation, his refusal to do what was expected of him, his reluctance to ride to the hunt with his father; he resented all the opportunities the boy had wasted, which would never come again.

So; the correct answer would be no, and the proper course of action would be to ignore the scribbled note and the breach of protocol it represented, and forget the whole matter. That would have been the right thing to do. Luckily, he had the sense to do the wrong thing. The only problem now was to decide what he was going to say.

He could think of a lot of things, enough for a book; he could write for a week and only set out the general headings. Curiously, the things he wanted to write about weren't anything to do with her. They were about him; things he'd never told anybody, because there was nobody qualified to listen. None of those things, he knew, would be suitable for a letter from one duke to another duke's wife. So instead he sat down one morning in the upper room with no windows, and tried to picture the view from the battlement above the gatehouse, looking west over the water-meadows toward the long covert and the river. Once he'd caught the picture, flushed it from his mind and driven it into the nets of his mind's eye, he thought carefully about the best way to turn it into words. The task took him all morning. In the afternoon he had meetings, a lawsuit to hear, a session of the greater council postponed from the previous month. That evening he tore up what he'd written and started again. He had no possible reason to believe that she'd be interested in what he could see from his front door, but he worked through four or five drafts until he had something he was satisfied with, made a fair copy, folded it and sent for the president of the Company of Merchant Adventurers. To make his point, he entrusted the request for a meeting to six guards, suggesting they deliver it some time around midnight.

The wretched woman came, fully expecting to die, and he asked her, as sweetly as he could manage, to do him a favor. Members of her company were forever popping (good choice of word) to and fro across the border—yes, of course there was an embargo, but there wasn't any need to dwell on it; would it be possible, did she think, for one of them to pass on a letter to one of her Eremian colleagues? It was no big deal (he said, looking over her head toward the door, outside which the armed guards were waiting) but on balance it'd probably be just as well if the whole business could be treated with a certain amount of the businesslike discretion for which the company was so justly famous. And so on.

The woman went away again, white with fear and secretly hugging herself with joy at securing a royal mandate to smuggle at will across the border; a month later, she came back with a letter. She was, she stressed, only too pleased to be able to help; while she was there, however, there were one or two silly little things she'd like to mention, if he could spare the time. Luckily, she had the sense not to push her luck too far. He agreed; the mechanism was set up.

He never knew when she was going to write. He always replied at once, the same day, canceling or forgetting about all other commitments. Letter days were long and busy. First, he would read it, six or seven times, methodically; the first reading took in the general tone and impression, each subsequent reading going deeper. Next, he would think carefully about everything she'd said, with a view to planning the outline of his reply. The actual writing of it generally took the afternoon and most of the evening, with two pauses in which he'd read her letter again, to make sure he'd got the facts and issues straight. Last thing at night, he'd read the letter and his reply over once more, and make the fair copy. From start to finish, sixteen hours. It was just as well he was used to long periods of intense concentration.

Valens reached out slowly toward the letter on the table, like the fencer in First advancing on an opponent of unknown capacity. This might, after all, be the letter that said there would be no more letters, and until he'd looked and seen that it wasn't, he daren't lower his guard to Third and engage with the actual text. His fingers made contact, gentle as the first pressure of blade on blade as the fencers gauge each other by feel at the narrow distance. Applying a minute amount of force through the pad of his middle finger, he drew it toward him until his hand could close around it. Then he paused, because the next movement would draw him into an irrevocable moment. He was a brave man (he wasn't proud of his courage; he simply acknowledged it) and he was afraid. Gentle and progressive as the clean loose of an arrow, he slid his finger under the fold and prised upward against the seal until the brittle wax burst. The parchment slowly relaxed, the way a body does the moment after death. He unfolded the letter.

Veatriz Longamen Sirupati to Valens Valentinianus, greetings.

You were right, of course. It was Meruina; fifty-third sonnet, line six. I was so sure I was right, so I looked it up, and now you can gloat if you want to. It's simply infuriating; you're supposed to know all about hounds and tiercels and tracking, and how to tell a stag's age from his footprints; how was I meant to guess you'd be an expert on early Mannerist poetry as well? I'm sure there must be something you haven't got the first idea about, but I don't suppose you'll ever tell me. I'll find out by pure chance one of these days, and then we'll see.

I sat at my window yesterday watching two of the men saw a big log into planks. They'd dug a hole so one of them could be underneath the log (you know all this); and the man on top couldn't see the other one, because the log was in the way. But they pulled the saw backward and forward between them so smoothly, without talking to each other (I wonder if they'd had a quarrel); it was like the pendulum of a clock, each movement exactly the same as the last; I timed them by my pulse, and they were perfect. I suppose it was just practice, they were so used to each other that they didn't have to think or anything, one would pull and then the other. How strange, to know someone so well, over something so mundane as sawing wood. I don't think I know anybody that well over anything.

Coridan — he's one of Orsea's friends from school — came to stay. After dinner one evening, he was telling us about a machine he'd seen once; either it was in Mezentia itself, or it was made there, it doesn't really matter which. Apparently, you light a fire under an enormous brass kettle; and the steam rises from the spout up a complicated series of pipes and tubes into a sort of brass barrel, where it blows on a thing like a wheel with paddles attached, sort of like a water-mill; and the wheel drives something else round and round and it all gets horribly complicated; and at the end, what actually happens is that a little brass model of a nightingale pops up out of a little box and twirls slowly round and round on a little table, making a sound just like a real nightingale singing. At least, that's the idea, according to Coridan, and if you listen closely you can hear it tweeting and warbling away; but you need to be right up close, or else its singing is drowned out by all the whirrings and clankings of the machine.

Talking of birds; we had to go somewhere recently, and we rode down the side of an enormous field, Orsea said it was beans and I'm sure he was right. As we rode by a big flock of pigeons got up and flew off; when we were safely out of the way, they started coming back in ones and twos and landing to carry on feeding; and I noticed how they come swooping in with their wings tight to their bodies, like swimmers; then they glide for a bit, and turn; and what they're doing is turning into the wind, and their wings are like sails, and it slows them down so they can come in gently to land. As they curled down, it made me think of dead leaves in autumn, the way they drift and spin. Odd, isn't it, how many quite different things move in similar ways; as if nature's lazy and can't be bothered to think up something different for each one.

Another curious thing: they always fly up to perch, instead of dropping down. I suppose it's easier for them to stop that way. It reminds me of a man running to get on a moving cart.

I know we promised each other we wouldn't talk about work and things in these letters; but Orsea has to go away quite soon, with the army, and I think there's going to be a war. I hate it when he goes away, but usually he's quite cheerful about it; this time he was very quiet, like a small boy who knows he's done something wrong. That's so unlike him. If there really is to be a war, I know he'll worry about whether he'll know the right things to do — he's so frightened of making mistakes, I think it's because he never expected to be made Duke or anything like that. I don't know about such things, but I should think it's like what they say about riding a horse; if you let it see you're afraid of it, you can guarantee it'll play you up.

Ladence has been much better lately; whether it's anything to do with the new doctor I don't know, he's tried to explain what he's doing but none of it makes any sense to me. It starts off sounding perfectly reasonable — the human body is like a clock, or a newly sown field, or some such thing — but after a bit he says things that sound like they're perfectly logical and reasonable, but when you stop and think it's like a couple of steps have been missed out, so you can't see the connection between what he says the problem is, and what he's proposing to do about it. At any rate, it seems to be working, or else Ladence is getting better in spite of it. I don't care, so long as it carries on like this. I really don't think I could stand another winter like the last one.

When you reply, be sure to tell me some more about the sparrowhawks; did the new one fit in like you hoped, or did the others gang up on her and peck her on the roosting-perch? They remind me of my eldest sister and her friends — Maiaut sends her best wishes, by the way; I suppose that means they want something else, from one of us, or both. I do hope it won't cause you any problems (I feel very guilty about it all). I suppose I'm lucky; there's not really very much I can do for them, so they don't usually ask anything of me. I know it must be different for you; are they an awful nuisance? Sometimes I wonder if all this is necessary. After all, you're Orsea's cousin, so you're family, why shouldn't we write to each other? But it's better not to risk it, just in case Orsea did get upset. I don't imagine for one moment that he would, but you never know.

That's about all I can get on this silly bit of parchment. I have to beg bits of offcut from the clerks (I pretend I want them for household accounts, or patching windows). I wish I could write very small, like the men who draw maps and write in the place-names.

Please tell me something interesting when you write. I love the way you explain things. It seems to me that you must see the whole world as a fascinating puzzle, you're dying to observe it and take it apart to see how it works; you always seem to know the details of everything. When we saw the pigeons I had this picture of you in my mind; you stood there for hours watching them, trying to figure out if there was a pattern to the way they landed and walked about. You seem to have the knack of noticing things the rest of us miss (how do you ever find time to rule a country?). So please, think of something fascinating, and tell me what I should be looking out for. Must stop now — no more room.

True enough; the last seven words tapered away into the edge of the parchment, using up all the remaining space; a top-flight

calligrapher might just have been able to squeeze in two more letters, but no more.

This isn't love, Valens told himself. He knew about love, having
seen it at work among his friends and people around him. Love
was altogether more predatory. It was concerned with pursuit,
capture, enjoyment; it was caused by beauty, the way raw red skin
is caused by the sun; it was an appetite, like hunger or thirst, a
physical discomfort that tortured you until it was satisfied. That,
he knew from her letters, was how she felt about Orsea—how
they felt about each other—and so this couldn't be love, in which
case it could only be friendship; shared interests, an instructive
comparison of perspectives, a meeting of minds, a pooling of resources. (She'd said in a letter that he seemed to go through life
like one of the agents sent by the trading companies to observe
foreign countries and report back, with details of manners and
customs, geography and society, that might come in handy for future operations; who did he report to? she wondered. He'd been
surprised at that. Surely she would have guessed.) Not love, obviously. Different. Better...

He read the letter through three more times; on the second and
third readings he made notes on a piece of paper. That in itself
was more evidence, because who makes notes for a love letter?
He'd seen plenty of them and they were all the same, all earth, air,
fire and water; was it his imagination, or could nobody, no matter
how clever, write a love letter without coming across as slightly ridiculous? No, you made notes for a meeting, a lecture, an essay, a
sermon, a dissertation. That was more like it; he and she were the
only two members of a learned society, a college of philosophers
and scientists observing the world, publishing their results to each
other, occasionally discussing a disputed conclusion in the interests of pure truth. He'd met people like that; they wrote letters
to colleagues they'd never met, or once only for a few minutes at
some function, and often their shared correspondence would last
for years, a lifetime, until one day some acquaintance mentioned
that so-and-so had died (in his sleep, advanced old age), thereby

explaining a longer than usual interval between letter and reply. If it was love, he'd long ago have sent for his marshals and generals, invaded Eremia, stuck Orsea's head up on a pike and brought her back home as a great and marvelous prize; or he'd have climbed the castle wall in the middle of the night and stolen her away with rope ladders and relays of horses ready and waiting at carefully planned stages; or, having considered the strategic position and reached the conclusion that the venture was impractical, he'd have given it up and fallen in love with someone else.

He stood up, crossed the room, pulled a book off the shelf and opened it. The book was rather a shameful possession, because it was only a collection of drawings of various animals and birds, with a rather unreliable commentary under each one, and it had cost as much as eight good horses or a small farm. He'd had it made after he received the third letter; he'd sent his three best clerks over the mountain to the Cure Doce, whose holy men collected books of all kinds; they'd gone from monastery to monastery looking for the sort of thing he wanted; found this one and copied the whole thing in a week, working three shifts round the clock (and, because the Cure Doce didn't share their scriptures, they'd had to smuggle the copied pages out of the country packed in a crate between layers of dried apricots; the smell still lingered, and he was sick of it). He turned the pages slowly, searching for a half-remembered paragraph about the feeding patterns of geese. This wasn't, he told himself, something a lover would do.

He found what he was after (geese turn their heads into the wind to feed; was that right? He didn't think so, and he'd be prepared to bet he'd seen more geese than whoever wrote the book), put the book away and made his note. He was thinking about his cousin, that clown Orsea. If he was in love, he'd know precisely what he ought to do right now. He'd sit down at the desk and write an order to the chiefs of staff. They'd be ready in six hours; by the time they reached the Butter Pass, they'd be in perfect position to bottle Orsea's convoy of stragglers up in Horn Canyon. Losses would be five percent, seven at most; there would be no enemy survivors. He would then write an official complaint to the Mezentines, chiding them for pursuing the Eremians into his territory and massacring them there; the Mezentines would deny responsibility, nobody would believe them; she would never know, or even suspect (he'd have to sacrifice the chiefs of staff, some of the senior officers too, so that if word ever did leak out, it could be their crime, excessive zeal in the pursuit of duty). That was what a true lover would do. Instead, he took a fresh sheet of paper and wrote to the officer commanding the relief column he'd already sent, increasing his authority to indent for food, clothing, blankets, transport, personnel, medical supplies. His first priority, Valens wrote, was to put the Eremians in a position to get home without further loss of life. Also (added as an afterthought, under the seal) would he please convey to Duke Orsea Duke Valens' personal sympathy and good wishes at this most difficult time.

How stupid could Orsea be, anyway? (He took down another book, Patellus' *Concerning Animals;* nothing in the index under geese, so he checked under waterfowl.) If his advisers came to him suggesting he launch a preemptive strike against Mezentia, the first thing he'd do would be put them under house arrest until he'd figured out how many of them were in on the conspiracy; if it turned out there wasn't one, he'd sack the whole lot of them for gross incompetence; he'd have them paraded through the streets of the capital sitting back-to-front on donkeys, with IDIOT branded on their foreheads. Needless to say, the contingency would never arise. He opened the door and called for a page to take the letter to the commander of the relief column.

It was just as well he and the Eremian Duchess were just good friends, when you thought of all the damage a lover could do in the world.

When at last the letter was finished (written, written out and fit to send; Valens had beautiful handwriting, learned on his father's insistence at the rod's end), he sent for the president of the Merchant Adventurers, with instructions to show her into the smaller audience room and keep her waiting twenty minutes. The commission cost him two small but annoying concessions on revenue procedure; he'd been expecting worse, and perhaps gave in a little too easily. Just as she was about to leave, he stopped her.

"Writing paper," he said.

She looked at him. "Yes?"

"I want some." He frowned. "First-quality parchment; sheepskin, not goat. Say twenty sheets, about so big." He indicated with his hands. "Can you get some for me?"

"Of course." Behind her smile he could see a web of future transactions being frantically woven; a maze, with a ream of writing paper at the center. "When would you be —?"

"Straight away," Valens said. "To go with the letter."

"Ah." The web dissolved and a new one formed in its place. "That oughtn't to be a problem. Yes, I think we can —"

"How much?"

"Let me see." She could do long multiplication in her head without moving her lips. In spite of himself, Valens was impressed. "Of course, if it's for immediate delivery..."

"That's right. How much?"

She quoted a figure which would have outfitted a squadron of cavalry, including horses and harness. She was good at her job and put it over well; unfortunately for her, Valens could do mental long multiplication too. They agreed on a third of the original quote — still way over the odds, but he wasn't just buying parchment. "Would you like to see a sample first?" she asked.

"Yes."

"I'll have it sent over in an hour."

"Bring it yourself," Valens replied. He noticed she was wearing a new diamond on the third finger of her right hand; *I paid for that,* he thought resentfully. Of course it should have been a ruby, to match her dress, but diamonds were worth twice as much, scruple for scruple, and she had appearances to think of. Thank God for the silver mines, he thought.

"Certainly," she said. "Now, while I'm here, there was just one other tiny thing…"

They were a force of nature, these traders. Even his father had had to give them best, more than once. This time he put up a bit more of a fight (the hunter likes quarry with a bit of devil in it) and she met him halfway; most likely she was only trying it on for wickedness' sake, and never expected to get anything. Of course, he told himself, it's good business all round for them to have a way of manipulating me; otherwise they'd push me too far and I'd have to slap them down, and that'd be bad for the economy. He was delighted to see the blood-red back of her.

Once she'd gone, however, the world changed. The brief flurry of activity, the tremendous draining effort of concentration, the feeling of being alive, all faded away so quickly that he wondered if it had been a dream. But he knew the feeling too well for that. It was the same at bow-and-stable, or the lowly off-season hunts, where you sit and wait, and nothing happens; where you perch in your high-seat or cower in your hide, waiting for the wild and elusive quarry that is under no obligation to come to you, until it's too dark or too wet, and you go home. While you wait there, impatient and resigned as a lover waiting for a letter, your mind detaches, you can for a little while be someone completely different, and believe that the stranger is really you. It's only when you see the flicker of movement or hear the muffled, inhuman cough that the real you comes skittering back, panicked and eager and suddenly wide awake, and at once the bow is back in your hands, the arrow is notched, cockfeather out, and the world is small and sharp once again.

(Hunters will tell you that patience is their greatest virtue, but it's the other way about. If they were capable of true patience, they could never be hunters, because the desire for the capture wouldn't be enough to motivate them through the boredom, the suffering and the cramp. They would be content without the capture, and so would stay at home. The hunter's virtue lies in being able to endure the desperate, agonizing impatience for the sake of the moment when it comes, if it comes, like an unreliable letter smuggled by a greedy trader in a crate of nectarines.)

One of the doctors, his tour of duty completed, reported in on his return. The Eremians, he said, were a mess. It was a miracle they'd lost as few people as they had, what with exhaustion and exposure and neglect of the wounded, and starvation. For a while the second-in-command, Miel Ducas, had managed to hold things together by sheer tenacity, but he was shattered, on his knees with fatigue and worry, and with him out of action there wasn't anybody else fit to be trusted with a pony-chaise, let alone an army. Duke Orsea? The doctor smiled grimly. It had been a real stroke of luck for the Eremians, he said, Orsea getting carved up in the battle and put out of action during the crisis that followed. If he'd been in command on the way up the Butter Pass... The doctor remembered who he was talking to and apologized. No disrespect intended; but since Ducas' collapse, Duke Orsea had taken back command; one had to make allowances for a sick man, but even so.

Now, though; now, the doctor was pleased to report, things were practically under control. The Eremians had been fed, they had tents and blankets and firewood. As for the wounded, they were safe in an improvised mobile hospital (twenty huge tents requisitioned from markets, the military, and traveling actors) and nine-tenths of them would probably make some sort of recovery. It was all, of course, thanks to Valens; if he hadn't intervened, if he'd been content to let the Eremians stumble by on their side of the border, it was more than likely that they'd all be dead by now. It had been, the doctor said in bewildered admiration, a magnificent humanitarian act.

"Is that right?" Valens interrupted. "They'd really have died? All of them?"

The doctor shrugged. "Maybe a few dozen might've made it home, no more than that," he said. "Duke Orsea would've been dead for sure. One of my colleagues got to him just in time, before blood-poisoning set in." The doctor frowned. "Excuse me for asking," he went on, "but they're saying that they didn't even ask us for help. You authorized the relief entirely off your own bat. Is that really true?"

Valens nodded.

"I see," the doctor said. "Because there's terms in the treaty that mean we've got to go to each other's assistance if formally asked to do so; I'd sort of assumed they'd sent an official request, and so we had no choice. I didn't realize…"

Valens shrugged. "To start with, all I was concerned about was the frontier. I thought that if they were in a bad way for food, they might start raiding our territory, which would've meant war whether we wanted it or not. I didn't want to risk that, obviously."

"Ah," the doctor said. "Because I was wondering. After all, it's not so long ago we were fighting them, and if they hadn't made a request and we'd just let well alone…" He sighed. "My son fought in the war, you know. He was killed. But if it was to safeguard our border, of course, that's a different matter entirely."

Valens shook his head. "Just, what's the phrase, enlightened self-interest. I haven't gone soft in my old age, or anything like that."

The doctor smiled weakly. "That's all right, then," he said.

Other reports came in. The Eremians were on the move again; Valens' scouts had put them back on the right road, and they were well clear of the border. The mobile hospital had been disbanded, the serious cases taken down the mountain to a good Vadani hospital, the rest judged fit to rejoin the column and go home. Miel Ducas was back in charge; the Vadani doctors had warned Duke Orsea in the strongest possible terms of the ghastly consequences that would follow if he stirred from his litter at all before they reached the capital—not strictly true, but essential to keep him out of mischief. Details of what had actually happened in the battle were proving hard to come by. Some of the Eremians were tight-lipped in the company of their old enemy;

the vast majority would've told the Vadani anything they wanted but simply didn't have any idea what had hit them out of a clear blue sky. They hadn't known about the scorpions, still didn't; but (said a few of them) that'll all change soon enough, now that we've got the defector.

The what?

Well, it was supposed to be a dark and deadly secret; still, obviously we're all friends together now, so it can't do any harm. The defector was a Mezentine — some said he was an important government official, others said he was just a blacksmith — and he was going to teach them all the Mezentines' diabolical tricks, especially the scorpions, because he used to be something to do with making them. He was either a prisoner taken during the battle or a refugee claiming political asylum, or both; the main thing was, he was why the whole expedition had been worthwhile after all; getting their hands on him was as good as if they'd won the battle, or at least that was what they were going to tell the people back home, to keep from getting lynched.

Valens, meticulous with details and blessed with a good memory, turned up the relevant letter in the files and deduced that the defector was the Ziani Vaaztes whom he was required to send to Mezentia. The old resentment flared up again when he saw that fatal word; but he thought about it and saw the slight potential advantage. He wrote to the Mezentine authorities, telling them that the man they were looking for was now a guest of their new best enemy, should they wish to take the matter further; he wished to remain, and so forth.

And then there were the hunt days; days when he drove the woods and covers, reading the subtle verses written on the woodland floor by the feet of his quarry better than any paid huntsman, always diligent, always searching for the buck, the doe, the boar, the bear, the wolf that for an hour or two suddenly became the most important thing in the world. Once it was caught and killed it was meat for the larder or one less hazard to agriculture, no more or less — but there; the fact that he'd caught it proved that it couldn't have been the one he was really looking for. He'd been brought up on the folk tales; a prince out hunting comes across a milk-white doe with silver hoofs, and a gold collar around its neck, which leads him to the castle hidden in the depths of the greenwood, where the princess is held captive; or he flies his peregrine at a white dove that carries in its beak a golden flower, and follows it to the seashore, where the enchanted, crewless ship waits to carry him to the Beautiful Island. He'd been in no doubt at all when he was a boy; the white doe and the white dove were somewhere close at hand, in the long covert or the rough moor between the big wood and the hog's back, and it was just a matter of finding them. But his father had never found them and neither had he, yet. Each time the lymers put up a doe or the spaniels found in the reeds he raised his head to look, and many times he'd been quite certain he'd seen it, the flash of white, the glow of the gold. Sometimes he wondered if it was all a vast conspiracy of willing martyrs; each time he came close to the one true quarry, some humble volunteer would dart out across the ride to run interference, while the genuine article slipped away unobserved.

6

Duke Valens' letter rode with an official courier as far as Forza; there it was transferred to a pack-train carrying silver ingots and mountain-goat skins (half-tanned, for the luxury footwear trade), as far as Lonazep. It waited there a day or so until a shipment of copper and tin ore came in from the Cure Doce, and hitched a ride with the wagons to Mezentia. There it lay forgotten in a canvas satchel, along with reports from the Foundrymen's Guild's commercial resident in Doria-Voce and one side of a fractious correspondence about delivery dates and penalty clauses in the wholesale rope trade, until someone woke it up and carried it to the Guildhall, where it was opened in error by a clerk from the wrong department, sent on a long tour of the building, and finally washed up on the desk of the proper official like a beached whale.

The proper official immediately convened an emergency meeting. This should have been held in the grand chamber; but the Social & Benevolent Association had booked the chamber for the day and it was too short notice to cancel, so the committee was forced to cram itself into the smaller of the two chapter-houses, on the seventh floor.

It was a beautiful room, needless to say. Perfectly circular, with a vaulted roof and gilded traces supported by twelve impossibly slender gray stone columns, it was decorated with frescos in the grand manner, briefly popular a hundred and twenty years earlier, when allegory was regarded as the height of sophisticated taste. Accordingly, the committee huddled, three men to a two-man bench, between the feet and in the shadows of vast, plump nude giants and giantesses, all delicately poised in attitudes of refined emotion—Authority, in a monstrous gold helmet like a cooper's bucket, accepted the world's scepter from the hands of Wisdom and Obedience, while a flight of stocky angels, their heads all turned full-face in accordance with the prevailing convention, floated serenely by on dumplings of white cloud.

At ground level, they were way past serenity. Lucao Psellus, chairman of the compliance directorate, had just read out the Vadanis' letter. For once, nobody appreciated the exquisite acoustics of the chapter-house; the wretched words rang out clear as bells and chased each other round and round the cupped belly of the dome, when they should have been whispered and quickly hushed away.

"In fact," Psellus concluded, "it's hard to see how things could possibly be any worse. We take a man, a hard-working, loyal Guild officer who happens to have made one stupid mistake, and in trying to make an example of him, we coerce him into violence and murder, and drive him into the arms of our current worst enemy; a man whose technical knowledge and practical ability gives him the capability of betraying at least thirty-seven restricted techniques and scores of other trade secrets. Result: it's imperative that he's caught and disposed of as quickly as possible, but now he's in pretty much the hardest place in the world for us to winkle him out of. I'm not saying it can't be done—"

"I don't see a problem," someone interrupted. "We know the Eremians've got him, surely that's more than half the battle. It's when you don't have a clue where to start looking that it's difficult to process a job. Meanwhile, I'm prepared to bet, after what's just happened I don't see this Duke Orsea giving us much trouble, provided we put the wind up him forcefully enough. He's just had a crash course in what happens to people who mess with us. And besides, what actual harm can he do? The Eremians are primitives; if Vaatzes was minded to betray Guild secrets, how's he going to go about it? They're in no position to exploit anything he tells them, they've got no manufacturing capacity, no infrastructure. They can barely make a horseshoe up there in the mountains; Vaatzes would have to teach them to start from scratch."

Psellus scowled in the direction the voice had come from; because of the annoying echo he couldn't quite place the voice, and the speaker's face had been lost against a background of primary colors and pale apricot. "For a start," he said, "that's entirely beside the point. If we don't deal with this Vaatzes straight away, it sets a dangerous precedent. Troublemakers and malcontents will see that here's a man who broke the rules and got away with it. Furthermore, you know as well as I do, a trade secret is a negotiable commodity. The Eremians may not be able to use it, but there's nothing to stop them selling it on to someone who can. No, we have to face facts, this is a crisis and we've got to take it seriously. This is exactly the sort of situation we were put here for. The question is, how do we go about it?"

There was a brief silence, just long enough for his words to come to rest in the vaulting, like bees settling in a tree full of blossom.

"Well," someone said, "it's obviously not a job we can tackle ourselves, not directly. Any one of our people'd stick out a mile among the tribesmen. I say we put a tender out to the traders. It wouldn't be the first time, and they'll do anything for money."

That was simply stating the obvious, but at least they were getting somewhere; no small achievement, in a committee of political appointees. Psellus nodded. "The Merchant Adventurers are clearly the place to start," he said. "We've got a reasonable network of contacts in place now; at the very least they can do the fieldwork and gather the necessary intelligence: where he is exactly, the sort of security measures we'll have to face, his daily routine, the attitude of the Duke and his people. As regards the actual capture, I'm not sure we can rely on people like that; but let's take it one step at a time. Now, who's in charge of running our contacts in the company?"

Manuo Crisestem stood up; six feet of idiot in a purple brocaded gown. Psellus managed not to groan. "I have the file here," Crisestem said, brandishing a parchment folder. "Anticipating this discussion, I took the trouble to read it through before we convened. There is a problem."

There was a grin behind his words. Crisestem (Tailors' and Clothiers') had only joined the committee a few months ago, replacing one of Psellus' fellow Foundrymen as controller of intelligence. If there was a problem, it'd be the Foundrymen's fault, and Crisestem would be only too delighted to make a full confession and abject apology on their behalf. "I regret to have to inform this committee," he said, "that our resources in Eremia Montis are unsatisfactory. We have agents in the cheese, butter and leather trades and among the horse-breeders, but at relatively low levels. Furthermore, our resources are such that, after the recent incursion, they can no longer be relied on. It won't take the Duke long to figure out who gave us advance warning of his adventure; those agents will be exposed and presumably dealt with, and it will be exceedingly difficult to recruit replacements as a result. The fact is that all our people in Eremia have been used up—in a good cause, needless to say; but now that they're gone, we have nothing worth mentioning in reserve."

Muttering, slightly exaggerated, from the Stonemasons' and Wainwrights' delegates. Political committees. Psellus ground on: "I take it you have something positive to propose."

"As a matter of fact, I have." Crisestem smiled amiably. "It seems to me that, since we cannot handle this matter directly, we must take a more oblique approach." He opened his folder and took out a piece of paper, holding it close to his body, as if it was a candle in a stiff breeze. "This came in today, from one of my observers in Forza. Apparently, Duke Valens has taken a hand in the Eremian crisis; he's sent significant aid to the survivors of Orsea's army — food, doctors, transport. It would appear that the alliance between Eremia and the Vadani is by no means as brittle as we had assumed."

Eyebrows were raised at that; typical of the Tailors to keep back genuinely important news just to gain a brief tactical advantage.

"That's an interesting development," Psellus said.

"Certainly. Let's confine ouselves, however, to its relevance to the matter in hand. A closer relationship between the two duchies will inevitably lead to closer commercial ties. We have excellent resources inside the Vadani mercantile. I suggest we use them. We won't be needing them for anything else; the Vadani will never be a threat to us, they have too much sense. Furthermore, we can place our own people in the Vadani court, to supervise and coordinate operations. No doubt the foreign affairs directorate will be sending diplomats to Duke Valens to find out what lies behind this remarkable display of neighborly feeling. The actual transaction can be managed very well from Civitas Vadanis; if we manage to get Vaatzes out alive, it will be much simpler to bring him home from there. I imagine Valens will be eager to propitiate us, if he's up to something with his cousin, so we can be confident we won't be unduly hampered by interference from that quarter. It would appear to be the logical approach."

Psellus had, of course, hated the Tailors and Clothiers from birth; they were Consolidationists, the Foundrymen were Didactics, there could be no common ground, no compromise on anything, ever. Even if Manuo Crisestem had been a Foundryman, however, Psellus would still have loathed him with every cell, hair and drop of moisture in his body. "Agreed," he said. "Do we need to take a formal vote on this? Objections from the floor? Very well, I propose that we minute that and move on to appropriations." He gazed into Crisestem's unspeakably smug face and continued: "When do you think you can let us have a draft budget for approval?"

Crisestem hesitated; he was apprehensive, but didn't know why. Confused, presumably, by his easy victory — which was understandable, since the Foundrymen had beaten the Tailors to a pulp in every major confrontation that century. "Depends on how much detail you want me to go into at this stage," he replied. "Obviously, since we've only just agreed this, I haven't done any proper costings; haven't got a plan I can cost yet, not till I sit down and work it all out."

"I think we can all appreciate that," Psellus said—he knew Crisestem was floundering—"but it goes without saying, time is of the essence. If we reconvened here at, say, this time tomorrow, do you think you could have an outline plan of action with an appropriations schedule for us by then?"

"I should think so," Crisestem replied, at the very moment when both he and Psellus realized what had happened. It hadn't been intentional (if it had been, Crisestem told himself, I'd have seen it coming, read it in his weaselly little face), but it was a good, bold counterattack, what the fencers would call a riposte in straight time. Without formal proposal or debate, Manuo Crisestem had been put in charge of the whole wretched business. If he succeeded, nobody outside this room would ever know who deserved the credit. If he failed, he'd be finished in Guild politics.

It took a little longer, maybe the time it takes to eat an apple, for the rest of the committee to realize what had just happened. Nobody said anything, of course. It wasn't the sort of thing you discussed, except in private, two or three close colleagues talking together behind locked doors. In politics, it's what isn't said that matters. The fencers say that you never see the move that kills you; in politics also. It appears out of nowhere, like goblins in a fairy tale, but once it's happened you start to smell of failure. People who used to look at you and see the next director of finance or foreign affairs start turning their speculations elsewhere, and the brief hush when you enter a room has a different, rather more bitter flavor. Of course, Crisestem might succeed. It was more likely than not that he would. But until the job was done and the file was closed, he was a man marked by the possibility of failure, someone who might not be there anymore in six months' time. In a game played so many moves ahead, someone like that was at best on suspension. He might succeed, at which time he'd be eligible to start again at the foot of the ladder. Meanwhile, he had to face life as a liability in waiting.

Not such a bad day after all, Psellus thought.

Any other business; no other business. He confirmed tomorrow's meeting—they'd be back in the great hall, where they belonged—and closed. The committee stood up slowly, like the audience at the end of a particularly powerful and moving play, taking time to adjust to being back in the real world. Crisestem indulged in the luxury of one swift, ferocious stare. Psellus returned it with a gentle smile, and returned to his chambers.

Back in his favorite chair, facing the wall with the tarnished but glorious mosaic (Mezentine Destiny as a knight in armor riding down the twin evils of Chaos and Doubt), he reflected on the changed state of play. A fool would still be able to turn this fortuitous victory into a total defeat. A fool would try and take advantage by sabotaging the operation, in the hope of guaranteeing Crisestem's downfall. It was a sore temptation—he was almost certain it could be done, efficiently and discreetly, one hundred percent success—but it was also the only way he could lose, and losing in this instance would mean disaster. The obvious alternative was to be as helpful and supportive as possible and trust Crisestem to destroy himself. Psellus thought about that. If he had true faith, in the Foundrymen, in the Didactic movement itself, he wouldn't doubt for a moment that Crisestem would fail (because Didacticism was right, Consolidation was wrong, and good always triumphs over evil). It'd be easy to glide down into that belief; Crisestem was an idiot, no question about that. But he was cunning; his clever encircling maneuver had demonstrated that, even if he had turned his victory into a desperate wire for his own feet.

Psellus yawned. So what if Crisestem did succeed? He'd get no thanks for it outside the committee because nobody would know it had been him. Inside—well, you never could tell. Psellus was more inclined to believe that they'd remember him walking blithely into the pitfall long after he'd dug his way out clutching a fistful of rubies, but you couldn't build a policy on a vague intuition. Instead, he considered the worst likely outcome. Crisestem succeeded, thereby increasing his personal prestige inside the committee out of all recognition. So what? Just so long as Psellus kept his nerve and played his moves on the merits rather than through anger or fear, the position at the end would still be pretty much the same as it was right now. Psellus would still have the actual, procedural authority; he'd still see the minutes in draft before each meeting, and be able to make subtle, deft changes to key words under the pretext of proofreading. As for Crisestem, the higher he rose, the further he had to come down when finally he did make a mistake. Tranquility, serenity and patience.

To take his mind off the problem, Psellus reached for his copy of Vaatzes' dossier. Age: thirty-four. Guild: Foundrymen's and Machinists' (Psellus sighed; one in every barrel). Physical description: he read the details, tried to compile a mental image, but failed. Nondescript, then (except for his height; a tall man, six feet three inches, so among the hill-tribes he'd be a giant). Family: neither parent living—father had been a convener at the bloom mills for thirty years; a wife, Ariessa, age twenty-four, and a daughter, Moritsa, age six—so assuming she was seventeen when they married, he'd have been, what, ten years older. Psellus frowned. Was there a story behind that? He turned back to the wife's details. Father, Taudor Connenus, a toolmaker in the ordnance factory. Psellus compared his works number with Vaatzes' service history. Connenus had worked on Vaatzes' floor at the time of the marriage, therefore had been his subordinate. And Connenus was no longer a toolmaker but a junior supervisor; likewise Zan Connenus, the wife's brother, promoted at the same time as his father.

Psellus closed his eyes and thought about that. A hundred and fifty years ago, yes; it had been quite common back then for men to marry girls much younger than themselves, particularly where the marriage was part of some greater chain of transactions. There had been trouble—he struggled to remember his ancient history—there had been trouble in the Tinsmiths' Guild over a marriage and the practice had been disapproved (not denounced; it was still perfectly legal, but you weren't supposed to do it). There had been thirty years or so of compliance, a reaction, a counter-reaction, and then it had ceased to be an issue. At best, then, it was an eccentricity. He made a note to interview the two Con-neni, and returned to the dossier.

Details of the offense: he read the technical data—straight-forward enough—and the investigating officer's notes. The back-ground was pathetic, really; a man wanted to make a nice present for his daughter and allowed his own cleverness to tempt him into disaster. The rest of the section was unremarkable enough, except for one thing that made Psellus raise his eyebrows in surprise.

Next in the dossier were copies of supervisors' annual assess-ment reports, going back twenty years. Psellus sighed, poured himself a small glass of brandy, and made himself concentrate. The picture that began to emerge was of a willing, serious ap-prentice, a reliable and careful machinist, a good supervisor; resourceful (and look where that had got him), intelligent, a plan-ner; content to do his work to the best of his ability; a quiet man, a family man—rarely took part in social activities except where his status required it; a man who worked late when it was necessary, but preferred to go home on time. There had been no petty thefts of offcuts of material or discarded tools, no reports of private work done on the side; respected by his equals and his subordinates, few friends but no enemies—all those years as a supervisor and nobody hated him; now that was really rather remarkable. A mild man, but he'd married a subordinate's daughter when she was little more than a child, and promotions had followed. Query: do quiet and mild always necessarily mean the same thing?

Several pages of details, headed *restricted*, of his work on ord-nance development projects. Psellus nodded to himself; a question which had been nagging him like mild toothache would appear to have answered itself. There were, of course, no Guild specifi-cations for military equipment. It was the only area not covered by specifications, the only area in which innovation and improvement were permitted. Vaatzes, apparently, had been responsible for no fewer than three amendments to approved designs, all to do with the scorpions: an improved ratchet stop, upgrading of the thread on the sear nut axle pin from five eighths coarse to three quarters fine, addition of an oil nipple to the slider housing to facilitate lubrication of the slider on active service. That wasn't all; he'd proposed a further four amendments which had been rejected by the standing committee on ordnance design. Psellus sighed. Allow a man to get the taste for innovation and you put his very soul at risk. The compliance directorate had considered the issue on several occasions and had recommended a program of advanced doctrinal training to make sure that workers exposed to the danger had a proper understanding of the issues involved; the recommendation had been approved years ago but was still held up in committee. A tragedy. A small voice inside his head reminded him that the training idea had been a Foundrymen's proposal, and that the subcommittee obstructing it was dominated by the Tailors and the Joiners. He stowed the fact carefully away in his mental quiver for future use.

Three approved amendments; he thought some more about that. Three amendments by a serving officer. Usually an amendment was held to be the glorious culmination of a long and distinguished career; it was something you held back until it was time for you to retire, and there'd be a little ceremony, the chief inspector of ordnance would shake you by the hand in front of the assembled workforce and present you with your letter of patent at the same time as your long-service certificate. It wasn't a perfect system, because a man might have to wait fifteen years before submitting his amendment, all that time churning out a product he knew could be improved; but it was worthwhile because it limited exposure to the innovation bug. Only a very few men proposed amendments while they were still working, and nearly all such applications were rejected on principle, regardless of merit. *Three*, for God's sake. Why hadn't he heard about this man years ago? And why, when the facts were here in the file for anyone to see, hadn't he been put under level six supervision after the first proposal?

In a sense, Psellus thought, we failed him. He was reminded of the old story about the man who kept a baby manticore for the eggs, until at last one day the manticore, fully grown and reverting to its basic nature, killed him. We let Vaatzes walk this highly dangerous path alone because the amendments were all good, sound engineering, allowing us to improve the performance of the product. Credit for that improvement would've gone primarily to the chief inspector of ordnance, and from him to the members of the departmental steering committee. Manticore eggs.

One last page caught his eye: schedule of items seized by investigators from the prisoner's house, after his arrest. It was a short list. Usually, when a man came to no good, there'd be pages of this sort of thing — tools and equipment stolen from the factory; the usual depressing catalog of pornographic or subversive literature (always the same titles; the circulating repertoire of both categories was reassuringly small in Mezentia); forbidden articles of clothing, proscribed food and drink, religious fetishes. In this case, however, there were only a handful of items, and none of them was strictly illegal, though they were all disapproved. A portfolio of drawings of yet more amendments to the scorpion (a note in the margin pointing out that the drawings numbered seven, twenty-six and forty-one should be forwarded to the standing committee for assessment, since they appeared to have considerable merit); a book, *The True Mirror of Defense* — a fencing manual, copied in Civitas Vadanis (private ownership of weapons was, of course, strictly forbidden; whether it was also illegal to read books about them was something of a gray area); another book, *The Art of Venery*, about hunting and falconry. Psellus smiled; he was prepared to bet that Vaatzes had thought the word *venery* meant something quite different. Another book: *A General Discourse of Bodily Ailments and the Complete Herbal*, together with some pots of dried leaves and a pestle and mortar. Psellus frowned. He'd have to check, but he had an idea that the *General Discourse* was still a permitted text in the Physicians', so it was against the law for a Foundryman to have a copy. How had he come by it? Did that mean that somewhere there was a doctor with a complete set of engineer's thread and drilling tables? If so, why?

He closed the file, feeling vaguely uncomfortable, as though he'd been handling something dirty. A case like this was, of course, an effective remedy for incipient complacency. It was easy to forget how perilously fine was the line between normality and aberration. How simple and straightforward life would be if all the deviants were wild-eyed, unkempt and slobbering, and all the honest men upright and clean-shaven. There wasn't really anything disturbing about a thoroughgoing deviant; it was inevitable that, from time to time, nature would throw up the occasional monster, easy to identify and quickly disposed of. Far more disquieting the man who's almost normal but not quite; he looks and sounds rational, you can work beside him for years and never hear anything to give you cause for concern, until one day he's not at his post, and investigators are interviewing the whole department. Truly disquieting, because there's always the possibility (orthodox doctrine denies it categorically, but you can't help wondering) that anybody, everybody, might be capable of just one small aberration, if circumstances conspired to put an opportunity in their path. *If the temptation was strong enough, perhaps even me* — Psellus shuddered at the thought, and dismissed it from his mind as moral hypochondria (look at the list of symptoms long enough, you can convince yourself you've got *everything*). It was just as well, he decided, that he wasn't an investigator working in the field. You'd need to have nerves of steel or no imagination whatsoever to survive in that job.

He leaned back in his chair, closed his eyes and waited to see if an image of Vaatzes would form in his mind—he thought of the process as something like what happens to an egg when it's broken into the frying pan—but all he got was a vague shape, a cutout in a black backcloth through which you could catch glimpses of what lay behind. His best hope of understanding the man, he decided, lay in interviewing the wife. If there was a key to the mystery, either she'd be it or have an idea of where it was to be found. Strictly speaking, of course, none of this was necessary. They weren't being asked to understand the man, just hunt him down and kill him. Probably just as well. Even so; the pathology of aberration was worth studying, in spite of the obvious danger to the student, or else how could further outbreaks be prevented in the future? Definitely the wife, Psellus decided. She was the anomaly he kept coming back to.

He stood up, shook himself like a wet dog to get rid of unwelcome burrs of thought. A man could lose himself in work like this, and in his case that would be a sad waste. There were other letters waiting for him; he'd seen them when he came in but forgotten about them while his mind was full of Vaatzes and that dreadful man Crisestem. As was his custom, he broke the seals of all of them before he started to read.

Two circular memoranda about dead issues; minutes of meetings of committees he wasn't a member of, for information only; a letter from his cousin, attached to the diplomatic mission to the Cure Doce, asking him to look something up in the *Absolute Concordance*—some nonsense about the structure of leaves and the diseases of oak-trees; notice of a lecture on early Mannerist poetry; an invitation to speak, from a learned society he no longer belonged to. The sad thing was, if he didn't get letters like these he'd feel left out, worried that he might be slipping gradually out of favor. He made a note to tell his clerk to check the oak-disease reference; he'd take the speaking engagement; standard acknowledgments to all the rest. So much for the day's mail—the world bringing him new challenges to revel in, like a cat that will insist on presenting you with its freshly slain mice. Another glass of brandy was a virtual necessity, if he didn't want to lie awake all night thinking about Vaatzes, and deviance in general. One last note to his clerk: set up meetings with Vaatzes' wife, father- and brother-in-law. Yes, that was where the answer lay, he was almost certain of that. It would help him make sense of it all if she turned out to be pretty, but he wasn't inclined to hold his breath.

In the event he slept soundly, dreaming of Manuo Crisestem being eaten alive by monkeys, so that he woke early with a smile on his face, ready for his breakfast. His clerk had already come and gone, so he took his time shaving and dressing — it was always pleasant not to have to rush in the mornings; he even had time to trim his nails and pumice yesterday's ink stains from his fingertips. That made him smile — subconsciously, was he preening himself just in case the deviant's wife did turn out to be pretty? — and he back-combed his hair in gentle self-mockery; then he thought about his wife, spending the off season at the lodge, out at Blachen with the rest of the committee wives, and that took the feather off his clean, sharp mood. Still, he wouldn't have to join her for a month at least, which was something.

The first three hours of every working day were eaten up by letters; from the morals and ethics directorate, the assessment board, the treasurer's office, the performance standards commission (twenty years in the service and he still didn't know what they actually did), the general auditors of requisitions, the foreign affairs committee. Three of them he answered himself; two he left for his clerk to deal with; one went to one side for filing in the box he privately thought of as the Coal Seam. The process left him feeling drained and irritable, as though he'd been cooped up in a small room with a lot of people all talking at once. To restore his equilibrium he spent half an hour tinkering with the third draft of his address to the apprentices' conference, at which he would be the keynote speaker for the fourth year running ("Doctrine: A Living Legacy"). He was contemplating the best way to give a Didactic spin to the proceedings of the Third Rescensionist Council when his clerk arrived to tell him that the abominator's wife would be arriving at a quarter past noon.

He'd forgotten all about her, and his first reaction was irritation—he had a deskful of more important things to do than talk to criminals' wives—but as the day wore on he found himself looking forward to the break in his routine. His clerk, he suspected, was getting to know him a little too well; the hour between noon and resumption was his least productive time, the part of the day when he was most likely to make mistakes. Far better to use it for something restful and quiet, where a momentary lapse in concentration wasn't likely to involve the state in embarrassment and ruin.

There were five interrogation rooms on the seventh floor of the Guildhall. He chose the smallest, and left instructions that he wasn't to be disturbed. The woman was punctual; she turned up half an hour early. Psellus left her to wait, on the bench in the front corridor. A little apprehension, forced on like chicory by solitude and confinement, would do no harm at all, and he'd have time to read another couple of letters.

He'd been right; she was pretty enough, in a small, wide-eyed sort of a way. He had the dossier's conclusive evidence that she was twenty-four; without it, he'd have put her at somewhere between nineteen and twenty-one, so what she must have looked like when she was seventeen and the subject of negotiations between her father and the abominator, he wouldn't have liked to say. She sat on the low, backless chair in the corner of the room quite still, reminding him of something he couldn't place for a long time, until it suddenly dawned on him; he'd seen a mewed falcon once, jessed and hooded, standing motionless on a perch shaped like a bent bow. An incongruous comparison, he told himself; she certainly didn't come across as a predator, quite the opposite. You couldn't imagine such a delicate creature eating anything, let alone prey that had once been alive.

He sat down in the big, high-backed chair and rested his hands on the armrests, wrists upward (he'd seen judges do that, and it had stuck in his mind). "Your name," he said.

Her voice was surprisingly deep. "Ariessa Vaatzes Connena,"

she said. There was no bashful hesitation, but her eyes were big and round and deep (so are a hawk's, he thought). "Why am I here?"

"There are some questions," he said, and left it at that. "You were married young, I gather."

She frowned. "Not really," she said. "At least, I was seventeen. But five of the fifteen girls in my class got married before I did."

She was right, of course; he'd misplaced the emphasis. It wasn't her youth that was unusual, but her husband's age. "You married a man ten years older than yourself," he said.

She nodded. "That's right."

"Why?"

What a curious question, her eyes said. "My father thought it was a good match," she said.

"Was it?"

"Well, clearly not."

"You were unhappy with the idea?"

"Not at the time," she said firmly.

"Of course," Psellus said gravely, "you weren't to know how things would turn out."

"No."

"At the time," he said, "did you find the marriage agreeable?"

A faint trace of a smile. There are some faces that light up in smiling; this wasn't one. "That's a curious word to use," she said. "I loved my husband, from the first time I saw him."

"Do you still love him?"

"Yes."

She said the word crisply, like someone breaking a stick. He thought for a moment. Another comparison was lurking in the back of his mind, but he couldn't place it. "You're aware of the law regarding the wives of abominators."

She nodded, said nothing. She didn't seem unduly frightened.

"There is, of course, a discretion in such cases," he said slowly.

"I see."

She was watching him, the way one animal watches another:

wary, cautious, but no fear beyond the permanent, all-encompassing fear of creatures who live all the time surrounded by predators, and prey. "The discretion," he went on, "vests in the proper compliance officer of the offender's Guild."

"That would be you, then."

"That's right."

"I imagine," she said, "there's something I can help you with."

(In her dossier, which he'd glanced through before the interview, there was a certificate from the investigators; the wife, they said, had not been party to the offense and was not to be proceeded against; her father and brother were Guildsmen of good standing and had cooperated unreservedly in the investigation on the understanding that she should be spared. It was, of course, a condition of this arrangement that she should not know of it; nor had she been made aware of the fact that clemency had been extended in her case.)

"Yes," Psellus said. "There are a few questions, as I think I mentioned."

"You want me to betray him, don't you?"

Psellus moved a little in his chair; the back and arms seemed to be restricting him, like guards holding a prisoner. "I shall expect you to cooperate with my inquiries," he said. "You know who I am, what I do."

She nodded. "There's nothing I can tell you," she said. "I don't know where he's gone, or anything like that."

"I do," Psellus said.

Her eyes opened wide; no other movement, and no sound.

"We have reports," he went on, "that place him in the company of Duke Orsea of Eremia Montis. Do you know who he is?"

"Of course I do," she said. "How did he—?"

Psellus ignored her. "Clearly," he said, "this raises new questions. For example: do you think it possible that your husband had been in contact with the Eremians at any time before his arrest?"

"You mean, spying for them or something?" She raised an eyebrow. "Well, if he was, he can't have done a very good job."

He'd seen a fencing-match once; an exhibition bout between two foreigners, Vadani or Cure Doce or something of the sort. He remembered the look on the face of one of them, when he'd lunged forward ferociously to run his enemy through; but when he reached forward full stretch the other man wasn't there anymore. He'd sidestepped, and as his opponent surged past him, he'd given him a neat little prod in the ribs, and down he'd gone. Psellus had an uncomfortable feeling that the expression on his face wasn't so different to the look he'd seen on the dying fencer's.

"You didn't answer my question," he said.

"No," she said. "I don't think he was spying for Eremia. I don't think he'd have known where Eremia is. I didn't," she added, "not until the other day. A lot of people don't."

"You sound very certain," he said quietly.

"Yes," she said. A pause, then: "I know that what my husband did was wrong. One of your colleagues explained it all to me, and I understand. But that was all he did, I'm absolutely positive. He just did it for our little girl, for her birthday. I suppose he thought nobody'd ever find out."

Psellus looked at her for a while. She ought to be frightened, he thought. At the very least, she ought to be frightened. Maybe her father or her brother broke the terms of the deal and told her; but then she'd know that if we found out, the deal would be off, and she ought to be frightened about that. I don't think she likes me very much.

He thought about that. I don't like her very much either, he thought.

"So," he went on, "you don't think your husband took any interest in politics, foreign affairs, things like that."

"Good Lord, no. He couldn't care less."

He nodded. "What did he care about?"

"Us," she said, quick as a parry. "Me and our daughter. Our family."

Psellus nodded. "His work?"

"Yes," she said—it was a concession. "But he didn't talk about it much at home. He tried to keep it separate, home and work. I could never understand about machinery and things."

"But he did work at home sometimes?"

She shrugged. "In the evenings," she said, "sometimes he'd be in the back room or the cellar, making things. He liked doing it. But I don't know if it was work or things he made for himself, or us."

Psellus nodded again. "It's customary for an engineer to make some of his own tools—specialized tools, not the sort of thing you'd find hanging on the rack—in his own time. Do you think it's likely that that's what he was doing?"

She shrugged; no words.

"We found quite a few such tools," he went on, "in the house, and at his bench in the factory. The quality of the work was very high."

She looked at him. "He was a clever man," she said.

"Too clever," Psellus said; but it wasn't like the fencer's ambush. Leaden-footed, and a blind man could have seen it coming. Nevertheless, she must parry it or else be hit. He waited to see what form her defense would take; he anticipated a good defense, from a fencer of such skill and mettle. Not a mere block; he was hoping for a maneuver combining defense and counterattack in the same move, what Vaatzes' illegal fencing manual would call a riposte in narrow time. He made a mental note to requisition the book and read it, when he had a moment.

"Yes," she said.

Oh, Psellus thought. (Well, it was a riposte, of a sort; stand still and let your opponent skewer you, and die, leaving the enemy to feel wretched and guilty ever after. Probably the most damaging riposte of all, if all you cared about was hurting the opponent.)

I had a point once, he told himself. I was making it. But I can't remember what it was.

"So that's the picture, is it?" he said. "In the evenings, after dinner, while you wash the dishes, he retreats to his private bench with his files and hacksaws and bow-drills, and makes things for the pure pleasure of it. Is that how it was?"

She frowned. "Well, sometimes," she said.

"Sometimes," Psellus repeated. "You'd have thought he'd had enough of it at work, measuring and marking out and cutting metal and finishing and burnishing and polishing and so on."

"He liked that sort of thing," she said, and her voice was almost bored. "It was what he did when we were first married, but then he got promoted, supervisor and then foreman, and he was telling other people what to do, instead of doing it himself." She shrugged. "He was glad of the promotion, obviously, but I think he missed actually making things, with his hands. Or maybe he wanted to keep himself in practice. I don't know about that kind of stuff, but maybe if you stop doing it for a while you forget how to do it. You'd know more about that than me."

Psellus nodded. "You think he wanted to keep his hand in?"

She shrugged again. Her slim shoulders were perfectly suited to the gesture, which was probably why she favored it so much.

"Do you think he'll want to keep his hand in now he's with Duke Orsea?"

To his surprise, she nodded; as though she was a colleague rather than a subject brought in for interrogation. "I know," she said, "they explained it to me before. You're afraid he'll teach all sorts of trade secrets to the enemy."

"Do you think he's liable to do that?"

"I don't know," she said.

"You don't know," he repeated.

"That's right," she said. "I suppose it'd depend on what he's got to do to stay alive. I mean, the people you say he's with, they're our enemies. We just wiped out their army, isn't that right? Well, maybe they caught him, wandering about on the moors, and thought he was a spy or something."

Psellus frowned. "Possibly."

"Well then. If you were him and that's what'd happened to you, what would you do?"

Psellus leaned back a little in his chair; he felt a need to increase the distance between them. "I hope," he said, "that I would die rather than betray my country."

It sounded completely ridiculous, of course, and she didn't bother to react. She didn't need to; she didn't have to point out what Vaatzes' country had done to him in the first place. This wasn't getting anywhere, Psellus decided. He was here to get information, not defend himself.

"Fine," she said. "I'm glad to hear it."

(She was letting him off lightly, though; she was past his guard, controlling the bind, in a strong position to shrug off his defense and strike home. Which is what you'd do, surely, if your husband had just been driven into exile; you'd be *angry*. But she was no more angry than frightened. Curious hawk; doesn't strike or bate. It dawned on him suddenly why he felt so confused. It was as though he didn't matter.) "I take it," he persevered, though he knew he was achieving nothing by it, "that you feel the same about treachery."

She looked at him. "You mean, about betraying the Republic? Well, of course."

He frowned at her, trying to be intimidating, failing. I'm not concentrating, he realized; there's something wrong, like one of those tiny splinters that get right in under your skin, too small to see but you can feel them. "The circumstances," he said slowly, "of your marriage. Let's go back to that, shall we?"

"If you want."

He made a show of making himself comfortable in his chair. "When was the first time he became aware of you? How did you meet?"

She was looking at him as though he was standing in front of something she wanted to see, blocking her view. "Which one do you want me to answer first?" she said.

"Why did he want to marry you?"

Another beautiful shrug. "I think he wanted to get married," she said. "Men do. And my dad wanted to find me a husband."

"At seventeen? A bit quick off the mark."

"We never got on," she said. "I wasn't happy at home."

"He wanted you off his hands?"

"Yes."

Psellus winced. She's good, he noted ruefully, at that defense. Probably one hell of a cardplayer, if women play cards. Do they? He had to admit he didn't know. "So your father became aware that his supervisor was looking for a wife, and thought, here's a fine opportunity, two birds with one stone. Is that how it was?"

"Pretty much."

He hesitated. It was like when he'd been a boy, fighting in the playground. He'd been a good fighter; he had the reach, and good reflexes, and he was older than most of the other boys. He threw a good punch, to the nose, chin or mouth. But he was too scared to fight, because he hated the pain — jarring his elbow as he bashed in their faces, skinning his knuckles as he broke their teeth — until the pleasure of inflicting pain ceased to outweigh the discomfort of receiving it. Even hitting them with sticks hurt his hands more than he was prepared to accept. "Was it a deal, then?" he persevered. "Your father and your brother's promotions, in exchange for you?"

"Yes."

"I see. And how about the terms of the transaction? Was he buying sight unseen?"

"What does that mean?"

"Did he come and inspect you first, before the deal was finalized? Or wasn't he bothered?"

She frowned, as though she was having trouble understanding. "He came to dinner at our house," she said.

"And?"

"He sat next to me. We talked about birds."

"Birds."

She nodded. "I don't know how we got on to the subject. I wasn't particularly interested in birds, nor was he."

"But you'd already fallen in love at first sight."

"Yes."

More gashed knuckles. "And presumably he decided you would fit the bill."

"Yes."

"So everybody was happy."

"Yes. We were all happy."

The hell with this, Psellus thought; there was a time, long ago, when I used to be a decent human being. "I see," he said. "Well, I don't think I need detain you further. You may go."

She stood up; no hurry, no delay. "Your discretion," she said. She made it sound like an illness or something.

"Provided you undertake to let us know immediately if you hear anything from him, if he tries to get in touch with you in any way. Do you understand?"

She nodded. "Hardly likely, though, is it?"

"Nonetheless." He made his face stern and fierce. "Make no mistake," he said. "You're being discharged under license, which we can revoke at any time. The obligation is on you to come to us with any information which might be of use to us. If you fail to do so..."

"I understand."

"Very well, then. You may leave." He thought of something; too little too late, but it would be a small victory, he'd at least have drawn blood, even if it was just a scratch. "You may return to the matrimonial home for the time being," he said. "Long enough to collect your possessions, the things that belong to you exclusively—clothing and the like. After that, you'll be returned to your father's house."

She rode the strike well, but he'd touched home. There was a degree of satisfaction in the hit, rather less than he'd anticipated. "I see," she said.

"An offender's property," he went on, "reverts to his Guild. An official confiscator will be appointed shortly; until he's made his inspection and compiled an inventory, you may not remove anything from the house."

"Fine. Can I empty the chamber-pot?"

(Interesting; that's the first sign of anger she's shown.)

"The confiscator," he went on, "will issue a certificate specifying which items are your exclusive property; that means the things you'll be allowed to take away with you. If you disagree with his decision, you may make representations to him in writing. Is that clear?"

She nodded. "How about my daughter's things?" she said. "Can she keep them, or does the Guild want them too?"

"The same rules apply," Psellus said. "The confiscator will decide what she can keep. The adjudication process usually takes about six weeks."

"I see," she said. "Can I leave now, please?"

Psellus raised his hand in a vague gesture of manumission. "Thank you for your time," he said. "And remember, if you hear anything at all from your husband…"

After she'd gone, Psellus sat for a while, watching the lamp burn down. Had he achieved what he'd set out to do, or anything at all? He had no idea. The objective was to catch Ziani Vaatzes and bring him home to die, or kill him wherever he happened to be; that job had been given to Manuo Crisestem, and was therefore effectively out of Psellus' hands, for the time being. The purpose of this interview—he tried to remember what it was. Something about motivation, trying to understand; he'd been intrigued by the marriage, the difference in ages. Well, he had an explanation, of sorts: Vaatzes had wanted a wife, the man Connenus had wanted to get his stroppy daughter off his hands, and apparently the daughter had been obliging enough to fall in love with Vaatzes, who was in a position to square the deal with promotions for his new in-laws. There; everything accounted for neat and tidy; and he, Lucao Psellus, was sitting in the dark as the point flew high over his head like a skein of geese going home for the winter.

No. He'd learned something important today, and he had no idea what it was.

When the lamp finally failed, he stood up and tracked his way to the door by feel. Outside it was still broad daylight; as he stood in the corridor facing the open window, the light stunned him, like an unexpected punch. It'd be vexing, he told himself, if Crisestem succeeded; as for Vaatzes, Psellus found it very hard to recapture the cold, pure burn of anger against him for his however-many-it-was offenses against Specification. But he stood facing the light and made a wish, like he used to do on the first of the month when he was a boy, that Crisestem would bring Vaatzes' head home in a bag, soon, and that this case would very quickly be over.

7

The road to Civitas Eremiae, capital and only city of Eremia Montis, encircles the stony peg of mountain on which it sits in long, slow, regular loops, like a screw-thread. From the river valley, it looks as if the city can be reached in two hours at the very most; but it's a long day's climb, assuming you start at dawn; if not, you face the unattractive choice of camping overnight on the narrow ledge of road or walking up it in the dark. At the crown of the mountain, the road funnels through a low, narrow gate in the curtain-wall; three more turns of the thread brings it to the city wall proper, where it ducks through a gateway under two high, thin towers built on massive spurs of rock. From the city gate to the citadel is another eight turns, through streets wide enough for a donkey or an economically fed horse. Chastra Eremiae, the Duke's castle, was chiseled and scooped out of the yellow stone four hundred years ago, and is protected by an encircling ditch twenty-six feet deep and a thirty-foot wall studded with squat round towers; a third of the interior is derelict through neglect. The Eremians proudly boast that nobody has ever taken the citadel by storm. It's hard to imagine why anybody should want to.

Most of the population of the city turned out in the morning to see the remains of the army come home; by nightfall, however, when Orsea rode his weary horse through the gate, the crowd had long since given up and drifted away. That in itself was encouraging; maybe they weren't going to lynch him after all.

Miel Ducas was looking after all the important stuff; accommodation for the wounded and so forth. There was no good reason why Orsea shouldn't just go home and go to bed. It was what he wanted to do, more than anything else in the world. Tomorrow, of course, he'd have to do the things he'd been dreading all the way up the Butter Pass. At the very least, he'd have to convene the general council, tell them about the battle and everything that had happened—the extraordinary kindness of the Vadani; the Mezentine defector and his offer. Probably he ought to stand out on the balcony that overlooked the market square and address the people. That was only reasonable, and he knew he had to do it. Tomorrow.

He clattered through the citadel gate, and there was a group of people waiting for him: a doctor whom he recognized, some people whose names he knew, some strangers. The doctor pounced on him as soon as his feet hit the cobbles. He'd had a detailed letter from one of the Vadani medics, he explained, full details of the injury, description of treatment to date, prognosis, recommendations. It was imperative that the Duke get some rest as soon as possible. For once, Orsea didn't argue.

Remarkably soon he was in his bedroom on the fourth floor of the South Tower. He sat on the bed and tugged at his boots (if they were this tight, how had he ever managed to get them on?), gave up and flopped on his back with his hands behind his head. He was home; that made him one of the lucky ones. Tomorrow...

Tomorrow, he told himself, I'll deal with everything. First I'll have a meeting with Miel, he'll brief me on everything he's done, getting the army home, and everything that happened on the way. Then I'll have to go to the council, and make my speech on the balcony (he made a mental note: think of something to say). Right; I'll do that, and the rest of the day's your own.

Veatriz, he thought. I'll see her tomorrow. She's not here tonight because she knows I need to be alone, but tomorrow I'll see them both again, and that'll make things better. It occurred to him that he hadn't thought much about her over the last few days; he felt ashamed, because really she was everything, the whole world. But there'd be time for her tomorrow, and things could slowly start to get back to normal.

Things would never be normal again, he knew that really. But he was tired, and there wasn't anything he could do tonight; and besides, the doctor had told him, rest...

He fell asleep. Below in the castle yard, Miel Ducas was still trying to find billets for wounded men, water and fuel for cooking, hay and oats for horses, somewhere for the carts to turn so the road wouldn't get jammed, somewhere to put the Mezentine until he had time to deal with him. He didn't resent the fact that Orsea had left him with all the arrangements; he was too busy, standing out of the way by the stable door so that the stretcher-bearers could get in and out, and women with bedding. He was trying to carry on four conversations at once—the garrison captain, the chief steward, Orsea's doctor and a representative of the Merchant Adventurers, who was trying to gouge him over the price of twenty gross of plain wool bandages. He kept going because there wasn't anybody else. It would, of course, be just as bad tomorrow.

Ziani Vaatzes sat in a stationary cart for an hour, and then some men came. They didn't seem to know whether they were welcoming a guest or guarding a prisoner, but they made a fair job of hedging their bets. They took him up a long spiral staircase with no handrail—it was dark and the steps were worn smooth—to a landing with a thick black door. If there was anything he wanted, they said, all he had to do was ask. Then they opened the door for him and vanished, leaving him completely alone.

There was a candle burning in the room—one candle—and a jug of water and a plate of bread and cheese on a table. It was a large room, though the darkness around the candle-flame made it look bigger than it really was. He found the fireplace; a basket of logs, some twigs and moss for kindling. He laid a fire, lit a spill (very carefully, so as not to snuff the candle out), found a small hand-bellows hanging on a nail in the wall. It hadn't occurred to him that the mountains would be so cold. The bed was huge, musty, slightly damp. He took his boots off but kept his clothes on. He couldn't sleep, needless to say; so he lay on his back staring at the extraordinarily high ceiling (he could just make out shapes of vaulting on the extreme edge of the disk of candlelight), and soon his mind was full of details as he worked on the mechanism that was gradually beginning to take shape. Somewhere below, a dog was barking, and he could hear heavily shod cartwheels grinding the cobbles, like a mill crushing wheat. For some reason it comforted him, like rain on the roof or the soft swish of the sea.

"This Mezentine."

Zanferenc Iraclido (Orsea had always felt overawed by him; not by his intellect or his commanding presence or his strength of purpose, but by the sonorous beauty of his name) reached across the table and took the last honey-cake from the plate. He'd had six already. None of the other members of the council appeared to have noticed.

"His name's Vaatzes," Miel Ducas said. "I had a long talk with him on the way home, and I'm fairly sure he's genuine — not a spy or anything. But that's just my intuition."

Iraclido made a gesture, a quick opening and closing of the hand. "Let's say for the sake of argument that he is. Let's also assume he can actually deliver on this promise to teach us all the stuff he claims he knows. The question is, would it actually do us any good?"

Heads nodded, turned to look down the table. "I think so," Orsea said. "But it'd be a huge step. What do you reckon, Ferenc?"

"Me?" Iraclido raised his eyebrows. "Not up to me."

"Yes, but suppose it was. What would you do?"

Iraclido paused before answering. "On balance," he said, "I think I'd have his head cut off and stuck up on a pike in the market square, and I'll tell you why. Yes, it'd be just grand if we could learn how to build these spear-throwing machines—though I don't suppose you'd approve of the direction I'd be inclined to point them in once they were finished. But we won't go into that."

"Good," someone else said; mild ripple of laughter.

"It'd be just grand," Iraclido repeated. "And when this Mezentine says he knows how to build them, I believe him. But it's no good giving a shepherd a box of tools and a drawing and telling him to build you a clock, or a threshing machine. My point is, we can't make use of this knowledge, we aren't..." He waved his hands again. "We aren't set up to start building machines. Might as well give a ninety-pound bow to a kid. It works, it's a bloody good weapon, but he's simply not strong enough to draw it. And you know what happens next. The kid can't use it so he puts it somewhere; then along comes his big brother, picks it up and shoots you with it. Not smart."

"Slow down," someone said. "You just lost me."

"Then use your brain," Iraclido said. "I said I'd have the Mezentine executed. Here's why. We can't afford to let him live, not with all that stuff in his head; because we can't use it, we aren't strong enough. But we all know who is."

Brief silence; then Miel said, "Let me translate, since Ferenc here's decided to be all elliptical. He's afraid the Mezentine's knowledge would fall into the hands of the Vadani. They're no smarter than us, but they've got pots more money; they might be able to use the knowledge, presumably against us. Right?"

"More or less," Iraclido said. "So the only safe thing to do is get rid of the information. Now, while it's still in the box, so to speak."

"It's a point of view," Orsea said after a moment. "Anyone like to comment?"

"Under normal circumstances," (the voice came from the other end of the table; a thin elderly man Orsea didn't know particularly well; Simbulo or some name like that) "I'd agree with the senator; we can't easily use this knowledge, and there's times when a head on a pike is worth two in the bush; we could make out he's a spy—which could be true, for all we know—and it'd go down well with the market crowd. But we have a problem. We've just had our guts ripped out by the Republic, like a cat on a fence; people need to see a miracle cure, or they're going to get nervous. Basically, we need a secret weapon."

Iraclido leaned forward and glared down the table. "So you want to build these machines?"

The thin man shook his head. "I want to tell the people we're going to build these machines," he said, "and I want to parade this Mezentine in front of them and say, here, look what we've found, here's a Mezentine traitor who's going to show us how to build them, and a whole lot of other stuff too. Now," he went on with a shrug, "whether we actually build any machines, now or at some indeterminate point in the future, is a subject for another day. What concerns me is what we're going to do tomorrow." He paused, as though inviting interruptions. There were none, so he went on: "Same goes for our friends and allies over the mountain. We won't get started on all that now; but I don't suppose I'm the only one who'd love to know what all that loving-kindness stuff was really in aid of. I'd also like to know who the genius was who thought it'd be a good idea to take the army home over the Butter Pass, right under Valens' nose. The fact we got away with it doesn't mean it wasn't a bloody stupid thing to do."

Orsea saw Miel take a deep breath and say nothing. He was proud of his friend.

"But anyway," the thin man went on. "Valens has made his point; he had us in the palm of his hand, and for reasons best known to himself he let us go. Fact remains, we've just lost a big slice of our military capability; if Valens wants to break the treaty, as things stand we can't give him a good game. In other words, we're at his mercy; and I don't know about you gentlemen, but that makes my teeth ache. I'd feel a whole lot happier if Valens was under the impression we had the secret of the spear-throwing machines."

"It'd give him something to think about," someone said.

"Too right," Iraclido said. "And if I was in his shoes and I heard that we were planning on arming ourselves with those things, I know what I'd do. I'd invade straight away, before we had a chance to build them."

"What about that, though?" A short, round man with curly hair; Bassamontis, from the west valleys. "What do you think he's playing at?"

"Good question," Miel said. "And I don't think we can reasonably make any decisions about this or anything else until we know the answer."

"You were there," the thin man said. "What did you make of it?"

"Beats me," Miel admitted. "They just appeared out of nowhere and started helping. No explanations, they weren't even patronizing about it. Just got on with it, and a bloody good job they made of it too." He frowned. "One thing that did strike me," he said, "was how very well prepared they were: food, blankets, medical stuff, it all just sort of materialized, like it was magic. Either Valens has got them very well organized indeed, or they had some idea what'd be needed well in advance." He shook his head. "Which still doesn't make any sense," he added. "It's a puzzle all right."

"Like the Ducas says," said the thin man, "it's a puzzle. And, like he says, I don't think we can make a decision until we've got some idea what actually happened there. The problem is, how do we find out?"

Silence. Then Miel said: "We could ask them."

Puzzled frowns. "I don't follow," someone said.

"I suggest we send a delegation," Miel said. "To say thank you very much for helping us. Only polite, after all. While they're there, if they keep their ears open and their mouths shut—"

"That's not a bad idea," Bassamontis said. "The Ducas is right, we owe them a bread-and-butter letter; we might as well combine it with a fishing trip."

"And what do we tell them," Iraclido interrupted, "about the Mezentine? We've got to assume they know about him already."

"Nothing," the thin man said firmly. "Let them fret about it for a while, it'll do them good."

"If Valens wanted to attack us," someone else said, "he had his chance. I can't see how it benefits him, lulling us into a true sense of security."

"We don't know what kind of issues he's involved with," Bassamontis said. "We're not the only ones with borders, or neighbors. Which is why I'd like to get some sort of idea of what's going on over there; and the best way to find out is to go and see for ourselves."

"Well?" Miel turned to look at Iraclido. "Are you still in favor of putting the Mezentine's head up on a pike?"

Iraclido smiled. "I never expected you'd go along with that," he said. "I was just telling you my opinion. By all means go ahead, send the delegation. As you say, it's simple good manners. And on balance, I'm inclined to agree with Simbulo here; we can't really do anything until we've got some idea of what's going on next door. So, for the time being, we'll just have to keep the Mezentine on a short leash and see what happens."

"Wouldn't do any harm," someone suggested, "to start finding out what he can do for us; assuming we decide to go down that road, I mean. So far, we've had some big promises. I propose we see the Mezentine for ourselves."

"Orsea?" Miel said.

Orsea nodded. "By all means," he said. "I've told you the gist of what he told me, but I'm no engineer, I don't know if what he said's possible, or what it'd involve. The trouble is, there's not many of us who do. We need some experts of our own to listen to this man."

There was a short silence, as if he'd said something embarrassing. Then Iraclido said: "All due respect, but isn't that the point? We don't have any experts of our own. If we'd got anybody who could understand what the hell the Mezentine's talking about, we wouldn't need the Mezentine."

Miel lifted his head sharply. "I don't think it's as black and white as all that," he said; and Orsea thought: actually, Iraclido's right and Miel knows it, but he's upset with him for being clever at my expense, and he's too well-mannered to say so. "My father used to say," Miel went on, "that so long as you've got ears and a tongue, you can learn anything. What'd be helpful is if we had someone who's halfway there."

Iraclido looked at him. "You mean like a blacksmith, or a wheelwright?"

"Yes, why not?" Orsea winced; he knew how much Miel disliked being wrong, and how stubborn he could be when circumstances had betrayed him into being wrong in public. "A bright man with an inquiring mind, that's what we need. That can't be impossible, surely."

"Maybe they were all killed in the war," someone muttered, down the far end of the table. Orsea was glad he hadn't seen who said it.

"Well." Iraclido was enjoying himself, in a languid sort of way. "If the Ducas can find someone who fits the bill, I suppose it can't do any harm. As for bringing the Mezentine before this council, I'm afraid I can't see what useful purpose that would serve. But if anyone else has strong feelings on the subject—"

"Boca Cantacusene," Orsea said briskly. Several heads turned to stare blankly at him; under other circumstances, he'd have found the looks on their faces amusing. "The armorer," he explained. "Come on, some of you must have heard of him, he's the warrant-holder. I gather he runs the best-equipped workshop in town. I don't suppose it's a patch on anything they've got in Mezentia, but at least he ought to be able to tell us if the Mezentine's genuine, or whether he's just making stuff up out of his head to con us out of money."

Iraclido shrugged. "Fine," he said. "By all means have your blacksmith interview the Mezentine, I'd be interested to hear what he thinks. Meanwhile, we need to agree a course of action in respect of Duke Valens."

"With respect..." (Orsea looked round; Miel was only this polite and soft-spoken when he was furiously angry.) "With respect, I suggest we need rather more to go on before we decide anything in that regard. All we have to go on is a magnificent, though possibly uncharacteristic, act of generosity. I say a little research—"

"Absolutely," Orsea broke in, mainly to head off his friend before he lost his temper. "We need some reliable information about what's going on, what Valens and the Vadani are up to."

Someone down the table stifled a yawn. "In that case," whoever it was said, "how about the Merchant Adventurers? They're good at intuition, picking up trends; got to be able to sense which way the wind's blowing in business."

Mumbled approval all round the table; predictably, Orsea decided, since it was precisely the sort of compromise that satisfied committees and nobody else: if you can't reach a decision, find a pretext for postponing it. "You can never have too much information," he said. "It's highly unlikely we'd get a straight answer through normal diplomatic channels. Who's got a tame merchant who owes him a favor?"

Two ducal summonses, neatly written on crisp new parchment (the first of the new batch, from the slaughter of the winter sheep) in oak-apple ink. One to Boca Cantacusene at his workshop in the lower town, requiring him to call on Count Ducas at his earliest convenience; one in similar terms to Belha Severina of the Weavers' Company.

Of course, Miel Ducas had met Boca Cantacusene before; had been measured by him—across the shoulders, under the armpits, from armpit to thighbone, thigh to knee, knee to ankle, an anatomy so complete that you could have built a perfect replica of the Ducas with nothing to go on except the armorer's notes and drawings. Miel tried to remember if he'd paid the man's latest bill.

Cantacusene arrived in his best clothes, stiffer and more unnatural-looking on him than any suit of armor. He was a short man of around fifty, with massive forearms tapering down into thin wrists and small, short-fingered hands. He was nervous and bumped into furniture.

"Do you think you could help?" Miel said, after he'd explained the situation and extracted a dreadful oath of discretion. "I mean, I wouldn't understand a word he said, it'd be like a foreign language."

Cantacusene frowned, as if trying to picture a thirty-second of an inch in abstract. "It'd take a long time," he said. "I'd have to get him to explain a whole lot of things before I started understanding, if you see what I mean."

"Of course," Miel said. "But you'd at least be able to understand the explanations."

Another frown; a nod. "Yes, I think I could do that."

"Splendid." Miel was fidgeting with his hands, something he didn't usually do. "At this stage," he said, "all we really need to know is whether he's really a high-class Mezentine engineer, or whether he's just pretending to be one—because he's a spy, or just a vagrant looking to cheat us out of money. You could ask him questions, I suppose; like a quiz. Metalworking stuff."

Cantacusene shook his head. "I don't think that would help a lot," he said. "Me testing him, it'd be like testing a doctor on surgery by asking him how to cut toenails. But I think I can see my way, if you know what I mean."

"Of course," Miel said. "You're the expert, I'll leave it up to you how to proceed." He paused, looked away. "One other thing," he said. "I haven't discussed this with the Duke, but I thought I'd sound you out first. It was him who suggested you, by the way."

"Honored," Cantacusene said.

"Well." Miel stopped, as if he'd forgotten what he was going to say. "If we do decide to go along with this, try and set up factories and such, like they've got in Mezentia, obviously we're going to need skilled men for the Mezentine to teach his stuff to; and then they'll go away and run the factories."

"Like foremen," Cantacusene said.

"Exactly, that's right. Well, since the Duke himself suggested you, I guess you're at the top of my list of candidates."

"I see." Cantacusene had a knack of saying things with no perceptible intonation; completely neutral, like clean water.

"Would you want to do that?"

Another pause for thought. "Yes," Cantacusene replied.

"Good. I mean," Miel went on, "it's all hypothetical, assuming we decide to go ahead—and obviously, to a certain extent that'll depend on what you make of the man when you see him. But I thought I'd mention it."

"I see."

This time, Miel stood up. "Excellent," he said, in a slightly strained voice. "Well, in that case we'll send for you when we're ready for the interview with the Mezentine, and we'll take it from there. Meanwhile, thank you for your time."

Cantacusene nodded politely, got up and left. Why was that so difficult? Miel asked himself; then he rang the bell and told the usher he was ready for the merchant.

She was younger than he'd expected; a year or so either side of forty, thin-faced, sharp-chinned, dressed in a tent of red velvet with seed-pearl trim, her hair short and staked down with combs and gold filigree pins. He had an idea she was some sort of off-relation—the Severinus was distantly connected to the Philargyrus, who trailed in and out of the Ducas family tree like ivy.

(He'd seen a remarkable thing once; an oak sapling had tried to grow next to a vigorous, bushy willow, on the warm southern slopes of the Ducas winter grazing; but the willow grew quicker, and it had twined its withies through the young oak's branches for ten years or so, and then put on a spurt in its trunk, gradually ripping it out of the ground, until its dead roots drooped in mid-air like a hung man's feet. He'd come back with men and axes, because the Ducas had always stood for justice on their lands, but he hadn't been able to find the place again.)

She'd listened carefully as he explained, rather awkwardly,

what he wanted her to do. She didn't seem surprised at all. "Do you think you can help us?" he'd asked.

"It should be possible," she replied. "My sister Teano's just joined a consortium with a contract for green sand—"

"I'm sorry," Miel interrupted. "Green sand?"

"Casting sand." She almost smiled. "For making molds," she said. "You know, melting metal and casting. You need a special kind of sand, very fine and even. The Vadani used to get it from the Lonazep cartels, who got it from the Cure Hardy; so obviously, it wasn't cheap. But Teano's consortium have found a deposit of the stuff in the Red River valley. They can undercut Lonazep by a third and still clear three hundred percent."

"Good heavens," said Miel, assuming it was expected of him. "So, your sister's likely to be going back and forth across the mountains quite a bit from now on?"

She nodded; actually it was more of a peck, like a woodpecker in a dead tree. "The contract is with the Vadani silver board. That'll put Teano right in the center of the Vadani government. It oughtn't to be impossible to get the information you want."

"But it won't be cheap," Miel said. "Will it?"

There was a trace of disapproval in her expression. "No," she said. "At least, Teano will want a lot of money—if they figure out what she's up to, the very best she can hope for is losing a very lucrative deal. She'll want an indemnity in case that happens, and a substantial retainer; and then there's my fee, of course."

Miel pursed his lips. "I see."

"Ten percent," she went on. "Paid by the customer."

"You make it sound like, I don't know, a lawyer's bill or something. Broken down into items, and each one with a fancy name."

"Quite," she said, unmoved. "Professional expenses. If you're in business, you have to be businesslike."

"Fine. So what does an indemnity plus a retainer plus a fee come to? In round numbers?"

"Does it matter?" She was frowning slightly. "You need this

information. I don't imagine Duke Orsea has given you a specific budget."

"No. He leaves things like that to me." Miel shrugged. "We won't quibble about it now."

"I should think not." She was scolding him, he thought. "The security of the Duchy is at stake. And, as I hope I've made clear, my sister will be running a substantial risk."

The Ducas charm didn't seem to be working as well as it usually did — the scar, Miel thought, maybe it's as simple as that. If so, it's a damned nuisance. You get used to having your own way on the strength of a smile and a softly spoken word. If the charm's gone, I suppose I'll have to learn some new skills; eloquence, or maybe even sincerity. "Quite," he said. "Well, I think we've covered everything. I'll look forward to getting your first report in due course. Thank you very much for your time."

As he showed her out and closed the door behind her, Miel was left with the depressing feeling of having done a bad job. Not that it mattered; he was paying money for a service to a professional specialist, there was no requirement that she should like him. Even so — *I guess I've got used to being able to make people like me; it makes things easier, and they try harder. I'll have to think about that.*

He yawned. What he wanted to do most in all the world was to go home to his fine house on the east face, send down to the cellars for a few bottles of something better than usual, and spend an hour or two after dinner relaxing; a few games of chess, some music. Instead, he had reports to read, letters to write, meetings to prepare for. There was a big marble pillar in the middle cloister of the Ducas house, on which were inscribed the various public offices held by members of the family over the past two and a half centuries. His father had four inches, narrowly beating his grandfather (three and two thirds). As a boy, when Father had been away from home so often, he'd sat on the neatly trimmed grass and stared up at the pillar, wondering what the unfamiliar words meant: *six times elected Excubitor of the Chamber.* Was that a good thing to be?

What did an Excubitor do? Was Dad never at home because he was away somewhere Excubiting? For years he'd played secret, violent games in which he'd been Orphanotrophus Ducas, Grand Excubitor, fighting two dragons simultaneously or facing down a hundred Cure Hardy armed only with a garden rake. Six months ago, when Heleret Phocas had died and Orsea had given him his old job, he'd not been able to keep from bursting out laughing when he heard what the job title was. (No dragons so far, and no Cure Hardy; the Excubitor of the Chamber, Grand or just plain ordinary, was nominally in charge of the castle laundry.) Now he already had two inches of his own on the pillar; gradually, day by day and step by painful step, he was turning into somebody else.

Reports, letters, minutes, agendas; he left the South Tower, where the interview rooms were, and headed across the middle cloister to the north wing and his office. The quickest route took him past the mews, and he noticed that the door was open. He paused; at this time of day, there'd be hawks loose, the door should be kept shut. He frowned, and went to close it, but there was a woman sitting in the outer list. He didn't recognize her till she turned her head and smiled at him.

"Hello, Miel," she said.

"Veatriz." He relaxed slightly. "You left the door open."

"It's all right," she replied, "Hanno's put the birds away early. I've been watching him fly the new tiercel."

"Ah, right. What new tiercel?"

She laughed. "The one you gave Orsea, silly. The peregrine."

"Yes, of course." She was right, of course; it had been Orsea's birthday present. His cousin had chosen it, since Miel didn't really know about hawks; it had been expensive, a passager from the Cure Doce country. It'd been that word *new* that had thrown him, because Orsea's birthday had been a month ago, just before they set off for the war, and anything that had happened back then belonged to a time so remote as to be practically legendary. "Is it any good?" he asked.

"Hanno thinks so," she said. "He says it'll be ready for the start of the season, whenever that is. It'll do Orsea good to get out and enjoy himself, after everything that's happened."

"We were talking about going out with the hawks just the other day. Is that a new brooch you're wearing?"

"Do you like it?"

"Yes," he lied. "Lonazep?"

She shook her head. "Vadani. I got it from a merchant. Fancy you noticing, though. Men aren't supposed to notice jewelry and things."

She had a box on the bench beside her; a small, flat rosewood case. He recognized it as something he'd given her; a writing set. Her wedding present from the Ducas. "I know," he said. "That's why I've trained myself in observation. Women think I'm sensitive and considerate."

She was looking at his face. "You look tired," she said.

"Too many late nights," he said. "And tomorrow I've got to take the Mezentine to see a blacksmith."

"What?"

"Doesn't matter." He yawned again. "Do excuse me," he said. "I'd better be getting on. Would you tell Orsea I've seen the Severina woman? He knows what it's about."

"Severina. Do you mean the trader? I think I've met her." She nodded. "Yes, all right. What did you need to see her about, then?"

Miel grinned. "Sand."

"Sand?"

He nodded. "Green sand, to be precise."

"Serves me right for asking."

As he climbed the stairs to the North Tower, he wondered why Veatriz would take her writing set with her when she went to see the falcons. Not that it mattered. That was the trouble with noticing things; you got cluttered up, like a hedgehog in dry leaves.

Meetings. He made a note in his day-book about Belha Severina, not that there was a great deal to say; *agreed to arrange inquiries through her sister; terms unspecified.* Was that all? He pondered for a while, but couldn't think of anything else to add.

It was close; the shape, the structure. He could almost see it, but not quite.

Once, not long after he married Ariessa, he'd designed a clock. He had no idea why he'd done it; it was something he wanted to do, because a clock is a challenge. There's the problem of turning linear into rotary movement. There are issues of gearing, timing, calibration. Anything that diverts or dissipates the energy transmitted from the power source to the components is an open wound. Those in themselves were vast issues; but they'd been settled long ago by the Clockmakers' Guild, and their triumph was frozen forever in the Seventy-Third Specification. There'd be no point torturing himself, two hundred components moving in his mind like maggots, unless he could add something, unless he could improve on the perfection the Specification represented. He'd done it in the end; he'd redefined the concept of the escapement, leaping over perfection like a chessboard knight; he'd reduced the friction on the bearing surfaces by a quarter, using lines and angles that only he could see. Slowly and with infinite care, he'd drawn out his design, working late at night when there was no risk of being discovered, until he had a complete set of working drawings, perfectly to scale and annotated with all the relevant data, from the gauge of the brass plate from which the parts were to be cut, to the pitch and major and minor diameters of the screw-threads. When it was complete, perfect, he'd laid the sheets of crisp, hard drawing paper out on the cellar floor and checked them through thoroughly, just in case he'd missed something. Then he'd set light to them and watched them shrivel up into light-gray ash, curled like the petals of a rose.

Now he was designing without pens, dividers, straight edge, square, calipers or books of tables. It would be his finest work, even though the objective, the job this machine would be built to do, was so simple as to be utterly mundane. It was like damming a river to run a flywheel to drive a gear-train to operate a camshaft to move a piston to power a reciprocating blade to sharpen a pencil. Ridiculous, to go to such absurd lengths, needing such ingenuity, such a desperate and destructive use of resources, for something he ought to be able to do empty-handed with his eyes shut. But he couldn't. Misguided but powerful men wouldn't let him do it the easy way, and so he was forced to this ludicrously elaborate expedient. It was like having to move the earth in order to slide the table close enough to reach a hairbrush, because he was forbidden to stand up and walk across the room.

I didn't start it, he reminded himself. *They did that. All I can do is finish it.*

He had no idea, even with the shape coming into existence in his mind, how many components the machine would have, in the end: thousands, hundreds of thousands — someone probably had the resources to calculate the exact figure; he didn't, but it wasn't necessary.

He stood up. It was taking him a long time to come to terms with this room. If it was a prison, it was pointlessly elegant. Looking at the fit of the paneling, the depth of relief of the carved friezes, all he could see was the infinity of work and care that had gone into making them. You wouldn't waste that sort of time and effort on a prison cell. If it was a guest room in a fine house, on the other hand, the door would open when he tried the handle, and there wouldn't be guards on the other side of it. The room chafed him like a tight shoe; every moment he spent in it was uncomfortable, because it wasn't right. It wasn't suited to the purpose for which it was being used. That, surely, was an abomination.

I hate these people, he thought. *They work by eye and feel, there's no precision here.*

Decisively, as though closing a big folio of drawings, he put the design away in the back of his mind, and turned his attention to domestic trivia. There was water in the jug; it tasted odd, probably because it was pure, not like the partly filtered sewage they drank at home. Not long ago they'd brought him food on a tray.

He'd eaten it because he was hungry and he needed to keep his strength up, but he missed the taste of grit. With every second that passed, it became more and more likely that they'd let him live. At least he had that.

His elbow twinged. He rubbed it with the palm of his other hand until both patches of skin were warm. The elbow, the whole arm were excellent machines, and so wickedly versatile; you could brush a cheek or swing a hammer or push in a knife, using a wide redundancy of different approaches and techniques. So many different things a man can do...

I could stay here and make myself useful. I could teach these people, who are no better than children, how to improve themselves. A man could be happy doing that. Instead...

There's so many things I could have done, if I'd been allowed.

The door opened, and the man he'd started to get to know— names, names; Miel Ducas—came in. Ziani noticed he was looking tired. Here's someone who's a great lord among these people, he thought, but he chases around running errands for his master like a servant. Using the wrong tool for the job, he thought; they don't know anything.

"How are you settling in?" Ducas said.

It was, of course, an absurd question. *Fine, except I'm not allowed to leave this horrible room.* "Fine," Ziani said. "The room's very comfortable."

"Good." Ducas looked guilty; he was thinking, we don't know yet if this man's a prisoner or a guest, so we're hedging our bets. No wonder the poor man was embarrassed. "I thought I'd better drop in, see how you're getting on."

Ziani nodded. "Has the Duke decided yet if he wants to accept my offer?"

"That's what I wanted to talk to you about." Ducas hesitated before he sat down; maybe he's wondering whether he ought to ask me first, since if I'm a guest that would be the polite thing to do. "The thing is," he went on, "we can't really make that decision, because none of us really understands what it'd mean. So we'd like you to explain a bit more, to one of our experts. He'd be better placed to advise than me, for instance."

"That's fine by me," Ziani replied. "I'm happy to cooperate, any way I can."

"Thank you," Ducas said. "That'll be a great help. You see, this expert knows what we're capable of, from a technical point of view. He can tell me if we'd actually be able to make use of what you've got to offer, how much it'd cost, how long it'd take; that sort of thing. You must appreciate, things are difficult for us right now, because of the war and everything. And it'd be a huge step for us, obviously."

"I quite understand," Ziani said. "Actually, I've been thinking a lot about what would have to be done. It'd be a long haul, no doubt about that, but I'm absolutely certain it'd be worth it in the end."

Ducas looked even more uncomfortable, if that was possible; clearly he didn't want to get caught up in a discussion. He's a simple man, Ziani thought, and he's had to learn to be versatile. Like using the back of a wrench as a hammer.

"Sorry we've had to leave you cooped up like this," Ducas went on. "Only we've all been very busy, as you'll appreciate. I expect you could do with a bit of fresh air and exercise."

No, not really. "Yes, that'd be good," Ziani said. "But I don't want to put you to any trouble on my account."

"That's all right," Ducas said. "Anyway, I'd better be going. I'll call for you tomorrow morning, and we'll go and see the expert."

"I'll look forward to it," Ziani said gravely, though he wanted to laugh. "Thank you for stopping by."

Ducas went away, and Ziani sat down on the bed, frowning. This man Ducas; how versatile could he be? What was he exactly: a spring, a gearwheel, a lever, a cam, a sear? It would be delightfully efficient if he could be made to be all of them, but as yet he couldn't be sure of the qualities of his material—tensile strength, shearing point, ductility, brittleness. How much load could he bear, and how far could he distort before he broke? (But all these people are so fragile, he thought; even I can't do good work with rubbish.)

In the event, he slept reasonably well. Happiness, beauty, love, the usual bad dreams came to visit him, like dutiful children paying their respects, but on this occasion there was no development, merely the same again—he was back home, it had all been a dreadful mistake, he'd committed no crimes, killed nobody. After his favorite dinner and an hour beside the lamp with an interesting book, he'd gone to bed, to sleep, and woken up to find his wife lying next to him, dead, shrunken, her skin like coarse parchment, her hair white cobwebs, her fingernails curled and brittle, her body as light as rotten wood, her eyes dried up into pebbles, her lips shriveled away from her teeth, one hand (the bones standing out through the skin like the veins of a leaf) closed tenderly on his arm.

8

To his surprise, Valens was curious. He'd expected to feel scared, horrified or revolted, as though he was getting ready to meet an embassy of goblins. Maybe I don't scare so easily these days, he thought; but he knew he was missing the point.

"Well," he said, "we'd better not keep them waiting."

He nudged his horse forward; it started to move, its head still down, its mouth full of fat green spring grass. It was a singularly graceless, slovenly animal, but it had a wonderful turn of speed.

"I've never met one before, what are they like?" Young Gabbaeus on his left, trying to look calm; Valens noticed that he was wearing a heavy wool cloak over his armor, and the sleeves of a double-weight gambeson poked out from under the steel vambraces on his forearms. Curious, since Gabbaeus had always insisted he despised the heat; then Valens realized he'd dressed up extra warm to make sure he wouldn't shiver.

"I don't know," Valens replied, "it's hard to say, really. I guess the key word is different."

"Different," Gabbaeus repeated. "Different in what way?"

"Pretty much every way, I suppose," Valens replied. "They don't look anything like us. Their clothes are nothing like ours. Their horses—either bloody great big things you'd happily plow with, or little thin ponies. Like everything; you expect one thing, you get another. The difficulty is, there's so many of them—

different tribes and sects and splinter-groups and all—you can't generalize till you know exactly which lot you're dealing with."

"I see," Gabbaeus said nervously. "So you can't really know what to expect when they come at you."

Valens grinned. "Trouble," he said. "That's a constant. It's the details that vary."

According to the herald, Skeddanlothi and his raiding party were waiting for them on the edge of the wood, where the river vanished into the trees. Valens knew very little about the enemy leader; little more than what he'd learned from a couple of stragglers his scouts had brought in the day before. According to them, Skeddanlothi was the second or third son of the High King's elder brother. He'd brought a raiding party into Vadani territory in order to get plunder; he wanted to marry, apparently, and his half of the takings was to be the dowry. The men with him presumably had similar motives. If they were offered enough money, they'd probably go away without the need for bloodshed.

"Beats me," Gabbaeus went on, "how they got here at all. I thought it was impossible to get across the desert. No water."

Valens nodded. "That's the story," he said. "And fortunately for us, most of the Cure Hardy believe it; with good reason, because raiding parties go out every few years, and none of them ever come back. They assume, naturally enough, that the raiders die in the desert." He yawned; it was a habit of his when he was nervous. "But there is a way. Some clown of a trader found it a few years ago. Being a trader, of course, she didn't tell anybody, apart from the people in her company; then one of their caravans got itself intercepted by one of the Cure Hardy sects."

"Wonderful," Gabbaeus said.

"Actually, not as bad as all that." Valens yawned again. It was a mannerism he made no effort to rid himself of, since it made him look fearless. "The Cure Hardy are worse than the traders for keeping secrets from each other. I think it was the Lauzeta who first got hold of it; they'd rather be buried alive in anthills than share a good thing with the Auzeil or the Flos Glaia. Even within a particular sect, they don't talk to each other. Something like a safe way across the desert is an opportunity for one faction to get rich and powerful at the expense of the others. Sooner or later, of course, the High King or one of his loathsome relations will get hold of it, and then we'll be in real trouble. Meanwhile, we have to deal with minor infestations, like this one. It's never much fun, but it could be worse; sort of like the difference between a wasps' nest in the roof and a plague of locusts."

Gabbaeus had gone quiet. Valens made an effort not to smile. A first encounter with the Cure Hardy was rather like your first time after boar on foot in the woods. Most people survived it, but some didn't.

Valens had done it before, six or seven times; so he wasn't too disconcerted when their escort turned up. How they did it he had no idea; they seemed to materialize out of thin air. One moment the Vadani had been alone on a flat moor; the next, they were surrounded by armored horsemen. Valens made no effort to stifle a third yawn. He knew from experience that it impressed the Cure Hardy, too.

Not Lauzeta, he decided. Maybe that was a good thing, maybe not. The Lauzeta, who wore long coats of hardened leather scale and conical helmets with nasals and aventails, were clever, imaginative fighters; tremendous speed and flexibility based on innate horsemanship and constant practice. This lot, on the other hand, wore coats of plates over fine mail, and their rounded helmets had cheek-pieces and articulated neck-guards. At a guess, that made them Partetz or Aram Chantat; he knew nothing about either sect beyond the basics of fashions in armor, and he didn't want to think about how the secret of the safe passage had penetrated right down to the far south. At least they'd be one or the other, rather than both. The Partetz and the Aram Chantat hated each other even more than the Auzeil, the Cler Votz, the Rosinholet or the Flos Glaia. On balance, he decided, he'd rather they were the Partetz.

They were, of course, the Aram Chantat. Their demands were simple: four hundred thousand gold thalers, or two million in silver, and five hundred horses, at least half of them brood mares. Delivery (their interpreter spoke tolerably clear Mezentine, with a firm grasp of the specialist vocabulary of the extortion business) within three days, during which time the raiding party would be left to forage at will; once payment had been made, they undertook to leave Vadani territory within a week, causing no further damage (provided that they were kept supplied with food, wine and fodder for the horses). Nobody said anything about what would happen if the demands weren't met. No need to go into all that.

Valens replied that he'd think it over and send his answer before daybreak. The horsemen watched him go, then vanished.

"So," Gabbaeus asked, after they'd ridden halfway back to the camp, "what are you going to do?"

"I'm not sure yet," Valens answered.

Back at his camp, he sent for the people he wanted to see, and put guards on the tent door so he wouldn't be disturbed. Just after midnight, most of the staff officers left. Two riders were sent back on the road to Civitas Vadanis. Their departure wasn't lost on the Aram Chantat scouts, who reported back to their leaders. Around three in the morning, they saw a great number of watch-fires being lit on the far side of the camp, where the horse-pens were, and sent word back to Skeddanlothi to prepare for a sneak attack at first light.

The messengers never got there. They were intercepted by the Vadani light cavalry, dismounted and covering the left flank, and efficiently disposed of. An hour later, the scouts sent another message to say that the heavy cavalry had mounted up and ridden due west, which they took to mean a wide encircling movement. Valens let them through. They reached Skeddanlothi an hour and a half before dawn. He drew up his forces in dead ground below his camp, facing west, to surprise the heavy cavalry when they arrived.

They never did, of course. What the scouts had seen was the horses being led away by their grooms. The heavy cavalry, also dismounted, came up on the east side of the camp and launched a sudden, noisy attack that took the Aram Chantat reserves completely by surprise. Someone had the presence of mind to send riders to the main army on the west side, who came scrambling back just in time to be taken in flank and rear by the light cavalry and the infantry.

It was still a tricky business. The Cure Hardy were on horseback, Valens' men were on foot; it was still too dark for accurate shooting, and the coats of plates and mail took some piercing. Valens told his archers to aim for the horses rather than the men, and sent up his infantry to engage Skeddanlothi's personal guard.

If the Cure Hardy had been huntsmen, they'd have understood what Valens was up to; let the dogs face the boar, while the hunters come at it from the side. Valens led the infantry himself, because they were going to have to face the boar's tusks. As always on these occasions, as soon as he'd given the word to move up he found he was almost paralyzed with fear; his stomach muscles twisted like ropes and he wet himself. But it was his job to stay three paces ahead of the line; if you don't keep your place, nobody knows where you are, and you're liable to come to harm. At the same time as he was forcing his legs to move, he was struggling to hold the full picture in his mind: movements of men and horses, timings, closures and avoidances. Forty yards across open ground in the pale, thick light, and then someone stood out in front of him, a man who wanted to kill him. He let go of the grand design and concentrated on the job in hand.

Fighting six hundred enemies in four dimensions over thirty-five acres is one thing; fighting one man within arm's length is something else entirely. Someone had told him once, the first thing to do is always look at the other man's face, see who you're up against; once you've done that, keep your eyes glued to his hands. Whether it was good advice or not Valens wasn't sure, but he followed it anyway, because it was the only method he knew. On this occasion, the other man was big and broad, but the look on his face and the puckering of his eyes told Valens that he'd been asleep and wasn't quite awake yet. He had a spear in his right hand and a round shield on his left arm; he was maybe inclined to hide behind the shield, conceding distance and therefore time. It was therefore essential that the other man should attack first; this, however, he was annoyingly reluctant to do, and a whole second passed while the two of them stood and looked at each other. That wasn't right; so Valens took a half-step forward, just inside the other man's reach; he recognized the mistake, but he wasn't watching where Valens put his feet. He lunged, spear and shield thrust forward together in a semi-ferocious hedging of bets. Valens stepped forward and to the right with his back foot—a fencing move he'd learned from the tiresome instructor when he was a boy—grabbed the back rim of the shield with his left hand and twisted as hard as he could from the waist. His enemy was a stronger man but he hadn't been expecting anything like that; he stumbled forward, and Valens stabbed him in the hollow just below the ear, where the earflap of the helmet left a half-finger-width of gap. The whole performance took less time than sneezing, and not much more effort. The dead man's forward momentum pulled him obligingly off Valens' sword, so that a half-turn brought him neatly back on guard.

That would've been a good place to finish; a well-planned, controlled encounter, practically textbook. Instead, he found himself facing two men with spears, at precisely the moment when someone else way off to his right shot him in the shoulder with an arrow.

It skidded off, needless to say, without piercing the steel of the pauldron. But he wasn't expecting the impact—about the same as being kicked by a bullock—and it made him drop his sword. His first thought was to get his feet out of the way of the falling sharp thing; he skipped, found he was off balance from the impact of the arrow, and staggered like a drunk. One of the two Cure Hardy stabbed him in the pit of the stomach with his spear. Again the armor held good, but he lost his footing altogether and fell over backward, landing badly. All the breath jarred out of his lungs, like air from a bellows, and he saw his enemy take a step forward;

he could visualize the next stage, the foot planted on his chest and the spearpoint driven down through the eyeslot of his helmet, but instead the other man stepped over him and went away. Some time later, thinking it through for the hundred-and-somethingth time, he realized that his opponent had assumed the spear-thrust had killed him.

He lay still and quiet while men, enemies and friends, walked and ran around and over him; someone trod on his elbow, someone else stepped on his cheek, but his helmet took the weight. He knew he was too terrified to move. He'd seen animals behave in exactly the same way: a hare surrounded by four hounds, crouching absolutely still; a partridge with a broken wing, dropped by the hawk after an awkward swoop, lying in the snow with its eye two perfect concentric circles. Someone had told him once that predatory animals can only see movement; if the quarry stays still, they lose sight of it. He hoped it was true, because he had no other option.

Some time later, a hand reached down and pulled him up. His legs weren't working and he slumped, but someone caught him and asked if he was all right. The voice was Vadani, not the intonation of someone addressing his Duke; he muttered, "Thanks, I'm fine," and whoever it was let go of him and went away.

He shook his head like a wet dog and looked up. Directly in front of him the sun was rising; in front of it he could see a smaller, thinner fire rising from a Cure Hardy tent. There were many men in front of him, only a few behind, and most of the bodies on the ground, still or moving slightly, were Cure Hardy. Valens wasn't a man who jumped to conclusions, but the first indications were hopeful. Probably, they'd won.

In which case—he scrabbled in his memory for the shape of the battle—in that case, the dismounted cavalry should by now have stove in the enemy flank, allowing his infantry to roll them up on to their camp, where the heavy cavalry should have been waiting to take them in rear. That would be satisfactory, on the higher level. More immediately relevant, the enemy survivors and stragglers would tend to be squeezed out at either end, and once they were clear of the slaughter they'd turn east, which was the direction he was facing. He turned round, but he couldn't see anybody coming toward him. That was all right, then.

Someone—a Vadani infantryman in a hurry—shouted at him, but he didn't catch what the man had said. Immediate dangers; mostly from Cure Hardy knocked down or wounded, if he got in their way. His people would, of course, notice sooner or later that he wasn't where he was supposed to be. Battles had been lost at the last moment because a general had been killed, or was believed to be dead. Wearily, and worried about the pain and weakness in his ankle (he'd turned it over when he fell), he started to run after the main body of his men. He went about five yards, then slowed to an energetic hobble.

It was just as well that someone recognized him. There was shouting, men turning round and running toward him, like the surge of well-wishers who greet an athlete as he crosses the finishing line; as though he'd done something wonderful, just by still being alive. "What happened to you?" someone roared in his ear, as overprotective hands grabbed and mauled him. "Are you all right? We thought—"

"I'm not. What's happening?"

"Like a bloody charm. Rolled them up like a carpet."

Suddenly, Valens found that he no longer cared terribly much. "That's good," he said. "What's the full picture? I've been out of it."

Someone made a proper report; someone else kept interrupting, with conflicting but mostly trivial information. Valens tried to summon the clear diagram back into his mind, but it was crumpled and torn, he couldn't put it all together. For some reason, that ruined any feeling of accomplishment he might have had. Not like a hunt, where you have the tangible proof of success, dead meat stretched out on the grass. There were plenty of dead bodies, but in war they aren't the point. Success is vaguer, more metaphysical. Perhaps for the first time, Valens admitted to himself that he found the whole business revolting, even a relatively clean victory, as this appeared to be. His mind slipped on the idea, because war was his trade, as the Duke of the Vadani; but he felt a phrase coalesce in his mind: *given the choice between killing animals and killing people, I'd rather kill animals.*

The fighting was still going on, bits and pieces, scraps of unfinished business; but that could all be left to sergeants and captains. He allowed information to slide off him, like water off feathers. Then someone said: "And we got the chief, Skeddanwhatsit."

Valens looked up; he was being escorted back to the camp by half a dozen men whose names he ought to know but couldn't remember offhand. "Fine," he said.

"He's back at the camp."

It took Valens a moment to realize that they meant the man was still alive. Now that was interesting. "Good," he said. "I'll see him in an hour. Find an interpreter."

"He speaks Mezentine," someone said. "Quite well, actually."

Catching them alive; that was an interesting idea. Worth the effort, because you could talk to them, and learn from them. He remembered the conversation he'd had the previous day, riding to the parley. "Find that young clown Gabbaeus and fetch him along," he said. "He was dead keen to meet a real Cure Hardy."

Nobody said anything for long enough to make words unnecessary. Pity; the boy was a second cousin, and he remembered him from years back (from before It happened, before Father died and everything changed; why is it, Valens wondered, that I tend to think of that time as real life, and everything that's happened since I became Duke as some sort of dream or pretense?). He made a resolution to have Skeddanlothi's throat cut, after he'd finished chatting with him. Barbaric and unfair, but so was his second cousin getting killed in a stupid little show like this.

Once they'd brought him to his tent, they left him alone for a while (he had to shout at them a bit, but they got the message). Slowly, taking his time over each buckle and tightly knotted point, he took off his armor. It was a ritual; he had no idea what it meant or why he found it useful. As usual, it had taken a degree of abuse. The middle lame on the pauldron that had turned the arrow was bent, so that the unit no longer flexed smoothly; if he'd tried to strike a blow, it'd probably have jammed up. The armorer would fix it, of course, and he'd have a word or two to say about the fit. There was a small dent in the placket of the breastplate where that man had stuck him with his spear. A couple of rivets had torn through on the left cuisse. It pleased him to be able to shed his bruised steel skin, like a snake, and have his smooth, soft, unmarked skin underneath. The simple act of taking off forty pounds of steel is as refreshing as a good night's sleep, inevitably makes you feel livelier; each limb weighs less, takes less effort to move; it's like being in water, or suddenly being much younger, fitter and stronger. Each shedding of the skin marks a stage in growth, even if it's only death avoided one more time; each time I get away with it, he thought, I really ought to come out of it a deeper, wiser, better person. Shame about that.

A page came in, properly diffident, and left behind a plate of bread and cheese and a big jug of water. He'd forgotten the cup, but Valens grinned and drank from the jug, putting the spout in his mouth and swallowing. He ate the cheese and most of the bread, instinctively moved his hand to sweep the leftovers onto the floor for the dogs—but there weren't any, not here—and put the plate down on the bed. His ankle was throbbing, but he knew it was just a minor wrench, something that'd sort itself out in a day or so. His shoulder and arm would be painful tomorrow, but they hadn't stiffened up yet. He got to his feet and went to find the prisoner.

They had him in a small tent in the middle of the camp; he was sitting on a big log, which Valens thought was odd until he saw the chain; a steel collar round the poor bastard's neck, and the end of the chain attached to the log by a big staple. Someone brought him one of those folding chairs; he gauged the length of the chain and added to it the fullest extent of the prisoner's reach, put the chair down and sat on it. Two guards stood behind him.

"Hello," he said. "I'm Valens."

Skeddanlothi looked at him.

"My people tell me," Valens went on, "that I won the battle, and that your lot have been wiped out to the last man." He paused. The other man was looking at him as though he was the ugliest thing in the world. "I don't suppose that's strictly true, there'll be one or two stragglers who'll have slipped outside the net, but they won't get far, I don't suppose. If it'd help, we've counted" — he took out a slip of paper he'd been given — "let's see, five hundred and twenty-three dead, seventy-two captured; if you're fond of round numbers, I make that five unaccounted for. If you like, you could tell me how many you started the day with, and then I'd know for sure."

Skeddanlothi didn't like, apparently. Valens hadn't expected him to.

"We rounded up a few of your scouts the other day," he went on, "and they said you came out here to steal enough to get married on. Is that right?"

No reply; so he leaned back a little in his chair and gave one of the guards some instructions. The guard moved forward; Skeddanlothi jumped up, but the guard knelt smoothly down, grabbed a handful of the chain and yanked hard. Skeddanlothi went down on his face, and the guard pressed his boot on his neck.

"Keep going till he says something," Valens called out. "He's no bloody use if he just sits there staring."

It was quite some time before Skeddanlothi screamed. Valens had the guard apply a few extra pounds of pressure, just to convince him that he couldn't stand pain. Then he asked the guard to help him back onto his log, and repeated the question.

"Yes," Skeddanlothi said; he was rubbing his neck, not surprisingly. "It's the custom of our people."

"To win honor and respect, I suppose," Valens said.

"Yes."

"Presumably," Valens went on, "most of the time you raid each other — the Aram Chantat against the Partetz, the Doce Votz against the Rosinholet, and so forth."

This time, Skeddanlothi nodded.

"That's interesting," Valens said. "To most of us, you're all just Cure Hardy. We don't think of you as a lot of little tribes beating each other up. To us, you're hundreds of thousands of savages, penned in by a desert." He paused. "Why do you fight each other like that?"

Skeddanlothi frowned, as though the question didn't make sense. "They are our enemies," he said.

"Why?"

It took Skeddanlothi a moment to answer. "They always have been. We fight over grazing, water, cattle. Everything."

Valens raised his eyebrows. "Why?" he said. "By all accounts, it's a huge country south of the desert. Can't you just move out of each other's way or something?"

Skeddanlothi shook his head. "Most of the land is bad," he said. "The cattle graze a valley for three years, the grass stops growing. So we have to move away until it comes right."

"On to somebody else's land," Valens said.

"Land doesn't belong to anybody," Skeddanlothi said, "it's just there. We drive them off it, they have to go somewhere else. When it's all eaten up, we have to move again. Everybody moves."

Valens thought for a moment. "You all move round, like the chair dance."

Skeddanlothi scowled. "Dance?"

"We have this children's game," Valens explained. "The dancers dance round in a ring, and in the middle there's a row of chairs, one for each dancer. When the music stops, everyone grabs a chair. Then one chair gets taken out, and the dance starts again. Next time the music stops, everyone dives for a chair, but obviously one of them doesn't get one, so he's out. And so on, till there's just one chair left, and two dancers."

Skeddanlothi shrugged. "We move around," he said. "If we win, we get good grazing for two years, three maybe. If we lose, we have to go into the bad land, where the grass is thin and there's very little water. But that makes us fight harder the next time we go to war."

Valens stood up. He was disappointed. "These people are stupid," he said. "Make him tell you where this secret way across the desert is. Do what it takes; I don't want him for anything else."

He made a point of not looking back as he left the tent; he didn't want to see terror in the prisoner's eyes, if it was there, and if there was something else there instead he knew it wouldn't interest him. He went back to his tent, drank some more water and called a staff meeting in two hours.

My own fault, he thought. I wanted them to be more than just savages. I wanted him to tell me that the girl's father had sent him on a quest for something—her weight in gold, or five hundred milk-white horses, or even the head of the Vadani Duke in a silver casket; I could have forgiven him for that. But instead they're just barbarians, and they killed my poor cousin. I can't put that in a letter, it's just crude and ugly.

He put his feet up on the bed, closed his eyes. Useful information: a map, or the nearest thing to it that could be wrung out of the savage on the log; a map marked with the name and territory of each sect—no, that wouldn't be any use, not if they moved round all the time. All right; a list, then, the names of all the sects; he was sure there wasn't a definitive list anywhere, just a collation from various scrappy and unreliable sources. What else; what else, for pity's sake? He had a specimen, for study; if he had a talking roebuck or boar or partridge he could interrogate for information likely to be useful to the hunter—he could think of a great many things he'd like to ask a roebuck: why do you lie up in the upland woods at night and come down the hill to feed just before dawn? When do you leave the winter grazing and head up to the outer woods for the first sweet buds? But torturing data out of a savage was a chore he was pleased to leave to others, even though he knew they wouldn't get the best, choicest facts, because they didn't have the understanding. The truth is, Valens realized, you can only hunt what you love. Chasing and killing what bores or disgusts you is just slaughter, because you don't want to understand it, get into its mind.

(My father never understood that, he thought; he hunted, and made war, because he liked to win. I'm better at both than he ever was.)

He sent orders, hustling out the intrusive thoughts. Soon he'd be on duty again, holding the full picture in his mind. Wasn't there some tribe or sect somewhere who believed that the world was an image in the mind of God; that He thought, or dreamed, the whole world, and things only existed so long as He held them in mind? There were, of course, no gods; but you could see how a busy man might like to believe in something like that.

An hour later a doctor came bothering him about his ankle. He managed to be polite, because the man was only doing his job; besides, there was something on his mind that wouldn't go away. It took him a long time to realize what it was; the problem buzzed quietly like a trapped fly in his mind all through the staff meeting, disrupting the pattern he was trying to build there like a bored dog in a room full of ornaments. In fact, it was the constant barrage of names (people, places) that finally showed him where it was.

After the staff had dispersed, he called for two guards and went to the tent where the prisoner was being held. Skeddanlothi was in a sorry state. He lay on his face on the ground, his back messy with lash-cuts, his hair slicked with blood. He didn't look up when Valens came in.

"We got the list," said one of the guards. "At least, we got *a* list, if you see what I mean. Could be a load of shit he thought up out of his head, just to be ornery."

Valens had forgotten about the list; which seemed rather reprehensible, since so much pain and effort had gone into procuring it.

"Difficult bastard," the guard went on—was he making conversation, like someone at a diplomatic reception? "He really doesn't like it when it hurts, but each time you've got to start all over again, if you follow me. We've had to bust him up quite a bit."

"That's all right," Valens said. "You cut along and get some rest, write up your report."

They left; changing shifts, quite usual. Valens went over and sat on the log. The prisoner didn't move, so he tugged on the chain once or twice.

"I wanted to ask you," he said. "What does your name mean?"

He hadn't expected a reply straight away, so a guard had to apply a little pressure. He repeated the question. It took three tries before the prisoner spoke.

"What the hell do you want to know that for?"

"Curious," Valens said. "I'm looking for—I don't know, some little glimmer of light. A chink in the wall I can peep in through. What does your name mean? Come on, it can't hurt you to tell me."

"I can't."

Valens sighed. "There's some taboo on saying your name to outsiders. Once they know your name, they can steal your soul or something."

The other man laughed. "No, that's stupid," he said. "But there's no word for it."

"Ah." Valens nodded to a guard. "You know," he said, "I believe this man hasn't had anything to drink for several hours. Get him some water."

He took the cup, which was nearly full; he emptied a third onto the ground. "Paraphrase," he said.

"What?"

"Well," Valens said, "what's the closest you can get, in our language?"

Skeddanlothi was looking at the dark brown dust, where the water had soaked away. "It's a kind of bird," he said. "But they don't live north of the desert."

"Describe it."

Hesitation. Valens poured away a little more water.

"It's small," the man said. "Bigger than a thrush but smaller than a partridge."

"You mean a pigeon."

"No, not a pigeon." The prisoner, as well as being in agony and despair, was also annoyed. "It's a wading bird, with a long beak. Brown. It feeds in the mud."

"I see," Valens said. "Pardon me saying so, but it sounds an odd creature to name a great warrior after. I assume your parents wanted you to grow up to be a great warrior."

"It's the bird of our family," Skeddanlothi said. "All the families have a bird."

"I see. Like heraldry."

"No." Almost petulant. "We follow a bird. Each family follows a different one."

"Follow," Valens repeated. "You mean, you choose one as a favorite."

"No, *follow*." Petulant to angry now. "When the grazing is used up and goes bad, we follow our family's bird, the first one we see. We follow it for a day, from dawn to sunset, and where it stops to roost is where we move to."

"Good heavens," Valens said. "But supposing it just flies round in circles."

"If it stops, we drive it on."

"Makes sense," Valens said. "And a wader would always fly to water, of course. Do all the families follow water-birds?"

But that was all; even pouring away the last of the water and the guard's best efforts earned him nothing more, which was frustrating, and by then there wasn't enough left to justify further expense of time and energy. It was the glimmer of light he'd been looking for, but it had gone out. He drew his finger across his throat; the guard nodded. Valens went back to his tent and gave orders to break camp and move out.

"It's not an interrogation," Miel Ducas said, "or anything like that."

The Mezentine still looked apprehensive. "But you want him to ask me questions?"

"Let's say we want you to talk to someone who speaks your own language." They'd reached the gate. Like all forge gates everywhere, it was almost derelict; the latch had long since gone, re-placed by a length of frayed rope, and the pintles of the hinges on one side had come halfway out of the wood. There was probably a knack to opening it without pulling several muscles, but Miel wasn't a regular visitor. "Basically, so you can see how much we know about, well, metalworking and things; and the other way about."

The Mezentine shrugged. "If you think it'll help," he said.

"The key is always to establish"—Miel grunted as he heaved at the gate—"communication. No point talking if you can't un-derstand."

All forge gates open on to identical yards. There must have been a time, two or three hundred years ago, when all the blacksmiths in the world decided it would be a splendid thing to pave their yards with handsome, square-cut flagstones. Once this had been done, a great decline of resources and enthusiasm must have set in—you'll search in vain in the history books for any reference to the cause of it, but the evidence is there, plain as day; those proud, confi-dent flags are all cracked up now. Grass and young trees push up through the fissures, kept in check only by the seepage of temper-ing oil and a very occasional, resented assault with the hook. Ivy and various creepers grow up through the scrap pile, their hairy tendrils taking an uncertain grip in the rust. Worn-out and bro-ken tools and equipment wait patiently through the generations for someone to find time to fix them. There's always a tall water-butt with moss on one side, close to the smithy door, which has scraped a permanent furrow where it drags. There's always a mound of perfectly good coal, inexplicably left out in the wet to spoil.

Cantacusene came out when he heard the yard gate scritch. He was almost unnaturally clean (blacksmiths aren't called that for nothing) and he looked painfully nervous, as if he'd been chosen to be a human sacrifice. His greeting was splendidly formal, and he was wearing his best apron.

"This is the man I was telling you about," Miel said. "I hope you've thought up some good questions."

Cantacusene looked as though someone had just walked up to him and yanked out one of his teeth. "I'll do my best," he said. "Please, come in. There's wine and cakes."

Indeed there were, and Miel tried to be polite about fishing a flake of dark gray scale out of his cup before drinking from it. It tasted like eggs beaten in vinegar.

The place looked pretty much the same as it had the last time he'd been there; as though it had been burgled by someone with a grudge against the owner. There were tools lying about on the benches and the floor, a hopeless jumble of hammers, stakes, tongs, setts, fullers. On the floor were chalked patterns for various pieces of armor, their meticulously drawn details scuffed by feet passing in a hurry. Every surface was thick with black grime; everything glistened with spilled drops of water and new rust. Here, Miel said to himself, our guest will feel at home.

But he didn't, by the looks of it. He had the air of a man who is trying hard not to give offense by showing disapproval. Cantacusene picked up on that straight away; the poor man was in pain, obviously. Miel felt bad about torturing him like this, but it had to be done, apparently.

"What I thought," Cantacusene said, mumbling, "was that we could start off…" His words dwindled away as he looked at the expression on Vaatzes' face. "Sort of like a trade test," he said. "If you think that'd be in order."

Miel waited for a response from the Mezentine, who just stood registering distaste. "That sounds like a good idea," he said. "What did you have in mind?"

Cantacusene's test would be to make a perfect circle, precisely one foot in diameter, out of quarter-inch plate. "Feel free to use whatever you like," he added nervously. "If you think that'd be—"

"Fine," Vaatzes said. "Material?"

Cantacusene picked up a three-foot square of steel and offered it to him. It didn't mean anything to Miel, of course (except he noticed that someone had recently made a job of scrubbing the rust off it with a wire brush; like a woman being visited by her mother-in-law, he thought), but Vaatzes studied it for some time, turning it over in his hands and pinching at the edges with his fingers.

"Have you got calipers?" he asked.

"Calipers," Cantacusene repeated. "Yes, of course."

He dug a pair of calipers out of a pile of junk and handed them over. Vaatzes took three or four measurements and handed them back. "Dividers," he said, "or a bit of string and a nail, if you haven't got any."

Cantacusene had some dividers; also files, a chest-drill and bits, a rule (Vaatzes stared at it in horror for a couple of seconds) and various other things Miel had never heard of. Vaatzes took them and laid them out on the floor, like a huntsman displaying the day's bag; the files in order of length, and so on. With the dividers he measured a foot off the rule, then knelt on the floor and scribed his circle on the plate — he did it three times, but Miel could only see one scribed mark. Next he stood up, clamped the plate upright in the leg-vice, and started to drill holes all round the circle with the chest-drill. This took a very long time. Miel soon lost interest and sat down to read the book he'd had the wit to bring with him. Each time he looked up, he saw Cantacusene rooted to the spot, watching like a dog at a rabbit-hole.

When Vaatzes had finished drilling the ring of holes, he laid the plate on the bed of the anvil and cut through the web between the holes with a small cold chisel. This freed something that looked like a gear-wheel. Next he wiped his finger through the nearest accumulation of soot, rubbing black into the thin graven line left by the dividers; then he fixed the gear-wheel thing in the vice and picked up a file. Miel went back to his book.

He'd almost finished it when he heard Vaatzes say: "I'm sorry." He looked up. Vaatzes was holding up what looked to him like a steel platter. He handed it to Cantacusene as if it was something revolting and dead.

"I did the best I could," he said. "But the drill-bits are blunt, the files are soft as butter, there's no light in here and the plate isn't an even thickness. And," he went on, "I made a botch of it. It's twenty years since I did any serious hand-filing, so I guess I'm out of practice."

"It's perfect," Cantacusene said.

Miel looked at him. He had the expression of someone who's just seen a miracle, a revelation of the divine.

"It bloody well isn't," Vaatzes said. "I can't measure it, of course, but I'd say the tolerance is no better than two thousandths, if that. And if you call that a square edge, I don't."

Miel saw Cantacusene staring at him; he looked utterly miserable. "It's better than I could do, anyway," Cantacusene said. "Look, I'll show you."

He took the drill and made a hole in the middle of the platter, passed a length of steel rod through it and clamped the rod in the vice; then he laid his fingers on the edge and set it spinning. "Perfect," he repeated. Miel looked at it; it was as though the spinning disk was absolutely still.

"I'll try again if you like," Vaatzes said. "Maybe if I took it outside, where I could see better…"

Miel had seen more than enough pain in his life, but rarely such suffering as Cantacusene went through as the day wore on. Next he asked Vaatzes to make a square; then to draw out a round bar on the forge into a triangular section; then to make six identical square pegs, to fit perfectly into the square hole on the back of the anvil. Each time, the outstanding quality of the result seemed to hurt him like a stab-wound, and Vaatzes' escalating self-reproaches were even worse. Miel excused himself at one point, went up the hill to a friend's house and borrowed another book; it was going to be a long day. He got the impression that Cantacusene had set himself the task of finding something the foreigner couldn't do better than he could, and that he knew he was going to fail, and that his whole world was coming apart. Miel enjoyed reading and listening to tragedy, but only when it came with the author's guarantee that it wasn't real.

An hour before sunset he decided to call a halt to the butchery. By that point, Cantacusene had the Mezentine doing sheet-work, which was, of course, Cantacusene's speciality in his capacity as Armorer Royal. There had been a note of desperation close to hysteria in his voice when he gave Vaatzes the specifications: a left-hand shell gauntlet, fluted in the Mezentine style, with four articulated lames over the fingers, the cuff moving on sliding rivets. Here at least Miel could understand some of the technical language; he had a pair of gauntlets to exactly that specification, for which Cantacusene had charged him nine silver thalers. He remembered thinking what a bargain they were at that price, when he took delivery. Accordingly, he marked his place, closed the book and shuffled discreetly close to watch.

Vaatzes started with a sheet of steel plate — not the one Cantacusene provided him with, because he looked at it and said it wasn't even; too thick at the top, too thin in the middle. So instead he scrabbled about in the scrap pile like a terrier, until he found a rusty offcut he reckoned would just about do, at a pinch. He traced the pattern onto it with chalk, cut it out on the shear, stopped cutting to take the shear to bits, make and fit a new pivot pin, clout the frame with a hammer, walk round it several times, stooping down and squinting, clout it a few more times, put it back together again (because he couldn't be expected to do accurate work on a shear that was completely out of line); next he formed the component parts on the anvil and the swage block (it was impossible, he declared, to do anything at all with either of them; if only he had a lathe, he could at least make a decent ball stake. Cantacusene went white as a sheet and stood opening and closing his hands) and punched the holes, having first stripped down and reworked the punch; then he did the fluting, half an hour of tiny woodpecker taps, quick as the patter of falling rain, his left hand constantly moving the work while his right hand fluttered like a hummingbird's wing (it was worthless, he declared as he held up the finished shell, because the flutes were uneven in depth and spacing, and the ridges weren't sharply defined); he cut the slots for the sliding rivets with the blunt drill and the butter-soft files; finally, more in sorrow than anger, he adjusted the fit of the moving parts, peened the rivets so that everything glided perfectly, declared it was hopeless, cut the rivets off with a chisel and did them again. Then he handed the gauntlet to Cantacusene, who took it as though it was his own heart, torn out with tongs through his smashed ribs.

"I'll polish it if you want," Vaatzes said, "but it'd be a waste of soap. Useless."

Cantacusene turned it over a few times, slipped it onto his left hand, flexed his fingers, turned his wrist; the five wood-louse sections moved up and down like the skin of a breathing animal. He took it off and gave it to Miel, who could hardly bear to touch it. He'd seen more than enough for one day.

"Well," he said. The gauntlet was still on his hand; somehow he didn't want to take it off. He could hardly feel it. Part of him was thinking, *nine thalers;* he had the grace, catching sight of Cantacusene's face, to feel ashamed of himself for that.

Getting out of the forge wasn't something that could be achieved gracefully; he thanked Cantacusene as best he could and walked away, leaving the gate open because he couldn't face fussing with it. All he wanted to do was leave behind the worst embarrassment he'd ever had to endure.

They'd been walking for ten minutes, up through the winding alleys, before he felt safe to say anything to the Mezentine.

"Was that necessary?" he said.

"How do you mean?"

Perhaps the man simply didn't understand; but that wasn't very likely. He might be all sorts of things, but he wasn't a fool. The whole thing had been deliberate, from start to finish. "You might as well have cut his throat or bashed his head in."

"What?" Vaatzes frowned. "Did I do something wrong?"

More than anything he'd ever wanted in his life, Miel wanted to hit the Mezentine. Nothing else would do but to smash his face until the cheekbones and jaws and teeth were beyond recognition as human. But if he did that, he'd have lost.

"You had to make your point," he said. "But did you have to be so bloody cruel about it?"

"You wanted to see some metalwork."

Miel looked at him. "Were you getting your own back?" he asked.

Slowly, Vaatzes shook his head. "You needed to be convinced," he said. "That I'm what I claim to be, and I can do what I say I can. Now you are. I'm sorry if your blacksmith got caught up in the machinery, but I didn't start it. Besides," he went on, "his whole setup was a joke."

"Not to him," Miel said.

Vaatzes waved the objection away. "It's not a subjective issue," he said. "There's a right way to do things and a wrong way, and his was wrong. Everything was wrong about it. Tools useless and jumbled up all over the place; no decent work space; nothing calibrated or even straight, every single thing out of true." He shook his head. "If I hurt him, he deserved it. It was his shop, so it must be his fault. It's an abomination."

Miel was silent for a moment. Then he said, "Oh."

Vaatzes laughed. "You think that word's a bit odd, coming from me."

"I wouldn't have imagined you'd think in those terms."

Vaatzes stopped walking and looked at him. "The thing you need to understand," he said, "if you want to understand what I have to offer—if you want to understand *me*, even; the one thing that matters is the principle of tolerance."

The word didn't fit at all. Miel repeated it. "Tolerance."

Vaatzes nodded. "That's right. Do you know what it means, to an engineer?"

Miel shrugged. "I thought I did, but maybe I don't."

"Tolerance," Vaatzes said, "is the degree something can differ from perfection and still be acceptable. It's not always the same. For one job, it could be three thousandths of an inch, and for something else it could be half a thousandth. The point is, if you want to make something that's good, you need your tolerance to be as small as possible. That's the key, to everything. It's what the Guilds are built on, it's everything Mezentia stands for. Precision; tolerance. We try and get as close to perfection as we possibly can, and we don't tolerate anything less than that." He smiled. "Your man back there," he said, "I don't suppose he even thinks in those terms. If it just about works and it sort of fits, it's good enough." Miel thought about his gauntlets, which had saved his hands in half a dozen battles. "We don't tolerate the word *enough*," Vaatzes went on. "Either it's good or it isn't. Either a line is straight and a right angle's a right angle, or it's not; it's true, or out of true. True or false, no gray areas. Do you see what I mean?"

"Fine," Miel said. "Which are you?"

Vaatzes laughed. "Oh, I'm all right," he said. "I've never had any doubts on that score. You mean, if I believe so strongly in the Mezentine way, how come they were going to kill me for abomination?"

Miel didn't say anything.

"The trouble is," Vaatzes went on, "the Guilds have lost their way. They've become..." He made a vague gesture. "I'm not quite sure how to put it. I suppose you could say they've become too tolerant."

"What did you say?"

"They tolerate a lie," Vaatzes said. "The lie is that their specifications, which are written down in the books and can't be changed, ever, are perfect and can't be improved on. And that's wrong. Obviously it's wrong. We can do better, if only we're allowed to. That's what I mean; their tolerances are too great. They make it an article of faith that you can't cut this line closer than one thousandth, when it's actually possible to shave that by half. *That's* the real abomination, don't you think?"

Miel didn't say anything for a while. "And that makes it all right for you to humiliate perfect strangers."

Vaatzes shrugged. "Either he'll learn from it and be a better craftsman, now he's seen there's a better way; or else he won't, in which case he isn't fit to be in the trade. I remember my trade test, when I was an apprentice. Actually, it was the same as your man back there set me, to file a perfect circle. But it had to be *right*. The tolerance was one thousandth of an inch, which is the thickness of a line scribed with a Guild specification dogleg caliper. The material was half-inch plate, and the edge had to be chamfered to exactly forty-five degrees, in accordance with a Guild half-corner square. If you got it right, you passed and got your Guild membership."

Miel nodded. "What happened if you got it wrong? Did they burn you at the stake or something?"

Vaatzes shook his head. "The finished piece is measured with the Guild's prescribed gauges; basically, a hole the right size cut into a big half-inch sheet. It has to be an exact fit—they test it with a candle. If light shows through, or if a speck of soot finds its way into the join, you fail. If that happens, there's a sort of ceremony. They put you in a cart, with your work hung round your neck on a bit of string, and on Guild meeting day, when everybody goes to the Guildhall to hear the speeches, they drive you round and round the town square from noon to sunset. People don't jeer or throw things at you, it's worse than that. It's dead quiet. Nobody says anything, they just stare. For that half a day, you're completely—I don't know what the right word is. You're completely separate, apart; you're up there and they're down below looking at you, like you're everything that's wrong in the world, captured and brought out so they can all have a good look at you and see what evil looks like, so they'll know it if they meet it again. Then, at sunset, they get you down off the cart in front of everybody, and Guild officers take your piece of work and they kill it; they bash it with hammers, they bend it and fold it over stakes, and finally they heat it up white hot in a furnace until it melts, and they pour the melted metal into sand, so it can't ever be made into anything else ever again."

It took Miel a moment to find his voice. "And that happened to you?"

"Good God, no," Vaatzes said. "I passed. It's incredibly rare, someone not passing; I think it's happened two or three times in my lifetime. Which goes to show, the system works. It's a bit harsh, but it makes for good workmanship."

"And what happens to people who fail? Do they get thrown out of the City?"

"Of course not. They learn their lesson, and the next year, they take the test again. Nobody's ever failed twice."

"Fine," Miel said. "I wouldn't recommend you trying to introduce that system here. I don't think that sort of thing would go down well."

"Of course not. You've got a long way to go, I can see that."

Miel took Vaatzes back to his room. He had to make his report to the Duke, he said, and then the decision would be made about whether to accept his offer. "We'll try not to keep you in suspense any longer than necessary," he told him. Then he went to find Orsea, thinking long thoughts about the nature of perfection.

The Duke in council considered his report, together with a written submission from the Armorer Royal, who gave his opinion that the Mezentine possessed skills far in advance of anything known to the Vadani, and recommended in the strongest possible terms that his offer should be accepted. Further submissions were heard from the exchequer, the trade commissioners, the Merchant Adventurers and other concerned parties, after which the meeting debated the issue, with special reference to the effects of the aftermath of the recent war, the manpower position, the need to remodel the Duchy's defenses and other pertinent factors. At the conclusion of the debate, the Duke and his special adviser Miel Ducas retired to consider their decision. After a brief recess, the Duke announced that the Mezentine's offer was rejected.

9

Commissioner Lucao Psellus had seen many strange sights in his time, and it was a tribute to his flawless orthodoxy that he had survived each disturbing experience without allowing a single one of them to damage him in any way. He had, reluctantly, read heresy and listened to abomination, both the forced confessions of the man broken up by torture and the proud ranting of the unrepentant martyr. He had seen things that nobody ought to have to see, every imaginable permutation of the aberrant and the false. He had endured.

The spectacle he was presented with on this occasion was different, if no less taxing, and he found it extremely difficult to cope with. It took the form of a very large foreign woman, dressed in painfully bright patterned red velvet, with pearls in her hair and rings on all ten fingers. Even her boots were red, he noticed. Compared to the woman herself, the news she brought was trivial.

"Of course," she was saying, "they haven't made a formal decision yet. It'll have to go before the council. They'll call for reports and evidence and what have you, and then there'll be a meeting, and then the Duke will finally make up what he pleases to call his mind. They're like that in Eremia, since that young Orsea took over. He's the worst thing that ever happened to the Duchy; can't take a decision on his own, always terrified he'll do the wrong thing, no confidence in his own judgment."

Psellus made an effort to pull himself together. "You're not Eremian, are you?"

She laughed. It was an extraordinary noise. "I suppose we all look alike to you," she said. "No, I'm Vadani, I'm delighted to say."

"No offense," Psellus said weakly.

"None taken." She laughed again. "I know that you people in the City don't get to see foreigners very often. Besides, it's actually quite an easy mistake to make. The Adventurers are pretty much a breed apart on both sides of the border; we're more merchant than Vadani or Eremian. I suppose I've got more in common with my colleagues in Eremia than with the silver-miners or the horse-breeders back home. It comes with travel, I always think; you can't be parochial if you're constantly moving about. And you don't get more parochial than backcountry Vadani."

Psellus frowned. "Since we're talking about that sort of thing," he said, "I might as well ask you now. Why is it that all you merchants are women?"

She raised both eyebrows. "Blunt, aren't you?" she said. "But it's a fair question, I suppose, and if you don't ask, you won't ever know. It's a social thing, I suppose you could say. You see, where I come from — I know it's different here, but so's everything — we don't like waste. Mountains, you see; you don't waste anything if you live in the mountains, because anything you can't actually grow up there, or catch, or dig out of the ground, has got to come all the way up the mountain, usually on someone's back. So we have this mindset, I guess you could say: make best use of everything you've got, and don't squander your resources. And if there's something you can't use, you apply your mind and find a use for it."

"That makes sense," Psellus conceded.

"Well," she continued. "people are a resource, just like everything else. And mostly, it's obvious what use most people should be put to. Men work outside, in the pastures or mining; men of good family run things, naturally. Women work inside, running the home, bringing up children. But there's one group of people who don't immediately seem to be much good for anything. People like me."

She paused, clearly waiting for a rebuttal or at least a protest. Psellus wasn't minded to indulge her, so she went on: "Unmarried middle-aged women of good family. Completely useless, wouldn't you say? No homes to run or families to look after; obviously we can't go out herding goats or spinning wool. All we've got is a bit of capital of our own and a bit of education. So, when you think about it, it's obvious, isn't it?"

"I suppose so," Psellus replied. That made her laugh again.

"You don't see it, I can tell. And that's understandable, you don't have the problem. You've got people at the top—all men, of course—and people at the bottom, and nothing in between. I imagine you think it's perfect, like everything else here."

Psellus tried not to frown. He wished he hadn't raised the subject. Some of his colleagues claimed that they actually enjoyed foreigners, their appallingly quaint lack of civilization, but he couldn't see it himself. "As you say," he replied, "we don't have the problem. Please forgive me if the question was offensive."

She shook her head. "It's pretty hard to offend an Adventurer," she said. "You get to learn quite quickly, people are different wherever you go. Wouldn't do if we were all the same."

"Ziani Vaatzes," Psellus said.

"Ah yes. Him. Well, I think I've told you everything I know. Seems to me," she added cheerfully, "like all your nightmares have come true. One of your top people has got away and taken all your secrets with him, and he's offered to give the whole lot to your deadly enemies, who you just stomped on hard in a war. Couldn't really be any worse, from your point of view. Of course," she added, "there's not a lot to worry about really. The Eremians are poor as dirt, it'd take them a hundred years to get to the point where they could be a threat to you, even if you left them alone and let them get on with it. It'd be different if this Vaatzes of yours had gone to the Vadani, of course, because we may be ignorant hill folk just like the Eremians, but we've got all that lovely silver, not to mention a duke who knows his own mind and gets things done. And I wouldn't be surprised if this Vaatzes isn't wishing he'd gone the other way up the mountain, if you follow me."

It took him another quarter of an hour and a certain sum of money to get rid of her; then he crawled away to his office at the top of the Foundrymen's tower, to pick the meat off what he'd just heard. A cup of strong willowbark tea helped him clear his head, and as the fog dispersed and he was able to give his full mind to the facts, he started to worry.

No doubt the woman was right. The Perpetual Republic wasn't scared of Eremia Montis. The whole Eremian army, hell-bent on razing the city to the ground, hadn't constituted enough of a threat to warrant a meeting of the full executive council; and where was that army now? If you took the broad view, there really wasn't anything to worry about.

But he didn't have that luxury. Another thing the wretched woman had been right about: from the point of view of the commissioner of the compliance directorate, this was the worst day in the history of the world. A convicted abominator had escaped justice, killed two jailers, seriously injured an officer of the tribunal, walked out of the Guildhall in broad daylight, fled the country and run straight to the court of an actively hostile enemy, begging them to accept all the most closely guarded secrets of the Foundrymen's and Machinists' Guild. Yes, Eremia was negligible. So, come to that, were the Vadani, for all their wealth. But that wasn't the point. Once the secrets were outside the Guild's control, there was no way of knowing who would get hold of them, or where they'd end up. Geography wasn't his strong suit, but he knew there was an inhabited world beyond the Cure Doce and the Cure Hardy, not to mention beyond the sea (his colleagues in the Cartographers' Guild would know about that; except, of course, he daren't ask them, because they'd want to know the reason for his unusual curiosity). And besides; even if there was no risk at all, that was entirely beside the point. His directorate had been created on the assumption that there was a risk, and the sole justification for his existence was that that risk had to be guarded against at any expense. In those terms, which were all that mattered, he'd failed.

He thought about it for a while, just in case he'd overlooked something, but he knew there was nothing to overlook. It was perfectly clear and perfectly simple. Crisestem and his assassination squad weren't relevant anymore. Killing Vaatzes would be a desirable end in itself, of course, but it would no longer be enough. The whole of Eremia—

He wanted to laugh, because it was absurd. Here he sat, one man, chairman of a committee, in a tower above a small formal garden, and he'd just taken the decision to wipe out an entire nation. Ludicrous; because even if Vaatzes had already betrayed the secrets; even if he'd written them all out in a book, with notes and explanatory diagrams and a glossary and index in the back, there wasn't a single soul in Eremia, or Vadanis, or among the Cure Doce or (God help us all) the Cure Hardy who could understand a word of it. But he was going to have to go down the stairs, through the cloister, across the small formal garden into the Great Hall and recommend that the army of the Perpetual Republic be mobilized and sent to kill every man, woman and child in a place he knew virtually nothing about, just in case; better safe than sorry, after all. It was *stupid;* and of course his recommendation would be accepted, and once the resolution had been passed in Guild chapter and the order had been given to the military, it would happen, and nothing on earth could stop it. Even if, by some extraordinary freak of chance, the army was resisted, defeated, massacred in a narrow mountain pass or drowned by a river in spate, another army would be raised and dispatched, and another, and another after that (because the Republic daren't ever say it was going to do something and then back down; gods must be seen to be omnipotent, or the sky will fall). Even if the world was emptied of expendable people and the Mezentines themselves had to be conscripted, they'd keep sending armies, until the job was done. As soon as he left this room, the machine would be set in motion and the outcome would inevitably follow.

Not that he cared about savages; not that it mattered particularly if the whole lot of them were wiped out—there was a body of opinion among the more radical Consolidationist factions that held that the Eremians and the Vadani formed a necessary buffer between the Republic and the human ocean of the Cure Hardy, but that was fatuous. The real barrier was the desert, and there was no way an army could cross it. Therefore the Eremians and the Vadani were irrelevant, and it wouldn't matter if they all died tomorrow.

But for hundreds of thousands of people, even savages, to die simply because he got up out of this chair and walked across that stretch of floor to that door and opened it... The reluctance was like a weight on his shoulders, pinning him to his seat. It was simply too big an act for one man. It was (he grinned as the thought crossed his mind; why? It wasn't funny) an abomination.

But if it was that, how could it be happening? This act, this extraordinary thing, was nothing more than the Republic conducting business in the prescribed manner. It wasn't as though he was some king or duke among the savages, acting on a whim. He was a component, an operation of a machine. That was more like it, he thought. The Republic is a vast and complex machine, powered by constitution and specification, with hundreds of thousands of human cogs, gears, cams, spindles, shafts, beams, arms, pawls, hands, keys, axles, cotters, manifolds, bearings, sears, pins, latches, flies, pistons, links, quills, leads, screws, drums and escapements, each performing in turn its specific operation. He was the last operation before the army was engaged, but he was a component of the whole; ordinances and directives drove him, his office and his duties were the keyway he traveled in. It wasn't as though he had any choice in the matter.

But if he stood up, he would walk to the door and open it, and the Eremians would all be killed. It occurred to him that although sooner or later he would have to stand up, he didn't have to do it quite yet. He could pour himself another cup of the willowbark tea (it was cold now, but there), pick up a letter or a memorandum, answer some correspondence, sharpen his pen. If he really tried, using every trick of prevarication he could think of, maybe he could buy the Eremians a whole half-hour—

He stood up.

"I'm sorry," Ducas said.

Ziani lifted his head and looked at him. "That's all right," he said. "It was just a suggestion." He waited for the Eremian to leave, but he didn't seem to be in any hurry. Ziani wondered if he was going to apologize; maybe he'd confess he was the one who talked the Duke out of accepting his offer—he was sure that was what had happened. A strange man, Ducas. But that made him complex, and a complex component can be made to perform several operations at once. Over the last few days, Ziani had come to value him.

"So," he said, "have they decided what's going to happen to me?"

Ducas left the doorway, came in; he stood over the chair but hesitated before sitting down. The instinctive good manners of the aristocrat (it's more important to be polite to your inferiors than your equals). Ziani nodded, and Ducas sat down.

"That's pretty much up to you," he said. "Well, strictly speaking it's up to me, since you've been bailed into my charge; but that's just a formality, since in theory you're an enemy alien and all that."

"I see."

Ducas shook his head. "Don't worry about that," he said. "You're free to go, if that's what you want. You can go wherever you like. Or," he added with a slight frown; probably he didn't realize he was betraying himself with that frown, "you can stay here, whichever you like. You don't need me to tell you, you could set up shop as a smith or an armorer or pretty much anything you like, and you'd be guaranteed a damn good living."

Ziani raised an eyebrow. "People would be prepared to have dealings with a Mezentine?"

"Of course." Ducas grinned. "Even if you were no good, they'd flock to you for the novelty value. But according to Cantacusene, you're the best craftsman who ever set foot in the Duchy, so..."

Ziani nodded. "I'd need capital," he said. "A workshop, tools, materials..."

"That wouldn't be a problem, I'm sure. You'll have no trouble finding a backer. The whole city's talking about you, you know."

"I'd have thought they'd have other things on their minds right now."

"Yes," Ducas admitted. "But life goes on. We're a resilient lot. A great many people died in the Vadani war; it's not the first time we've had to cope with a national disaster. And as far as you're concerned, they won't blame you just because of where you're from or the color of your skin. We aren't like that here. And everybody knows you've suffered just as much at the hands of the Republic as they have."

Everybody knows that, do they? What exactly do they know, Ziani wondered, about anything? He kept his face blank. "Well," he said, "at first sight that'd seem like the logical thing to do. At least until I find my feet and decide what's the best use I can put my life to. It's a strange feeling, you know," he went on, watching Ducas out of the corner of his eye. "Suddenly finding yourself in a new place, with nothing at all except yourself. I mean, from what you've just told me, it could be the making of me."

"Perfectly true," Ducas said. "A man like you, with your skills and talents. How old are you, if you don't mind me asking?"

"Thirty-four."

"Well, there you are, then." Ducas was smiling. "You've got plenty of time to start again. Settle down, build up a business, start a family. You can do anything you like."

I could so easily hate you for saying that, Ziani thought; but you're too valuable to hate. "Clouds and silver linings," he said. "Or I could move on. If I were to do that, where could I go?"

Ducas shrugged. "Well," he said, "if you're dead set on this business of teaching people the Mezentine way, you'd probably be better off across the border, in Vadanis. They'd be more likely to listen to you there. Of course," he added quickly, "there's no hurry, you can take your time and decide. Really, in spite of everything, I guess you're in a good position—I know that's hard to believe, seeing what you've been through, but..." He paused, rebuking himself for crassness. Really, it would be easy to like this man. "What I mean is, you're a free agent; no ties, no responsibilities. You can make a fresh start, wherever you want."

Ducas went away shortly after that. There was, he'd stressed again before he left, no hurry at all. Vaatzes could stay here in the castle for a bit, it was entirely up to him. No pressure. Everything very relaxed, very tranquil. Quite.

Ziani looked round the room to see if there was anything that might come in handy, but there wasn't. They'd given him clothes, respectable, what passed for good quality among these tribesmen; clothes and shoes were all he'd take when he left in the morning, and that would do fine. He'd got over the sudden spurt of violent anger that had made him want to grab Ducas by the throat and dig his thumbs into the hollow between the collarbones, thus quickly and efficiently stopping the mechanism. He thought about that impulse for a moment, and wondered what was happening to him. He'd been alive for thirty-four blameless years, he could remember, and count on the fingers of one hand, all the times when he'd lost his temper and committed or even contemplated violence. It was, he'd always prided himself, completely foreign to his nature. He'd seen fights at the factory, once or twice in the street (drunks, of course), and he'd acknowledged the existence of the violent impulse without being able or wanting to understand it. There were bad things in the world, and that was one of them. Since then, he'd killed two men, possibly three, but he'd been forced to it. The acts had been neutral, since they'd been imposed on him by forces outside his control. This time, though...

He analyzed the moment. Ducas had said something unbearable, and it had provoked him; he couldn't stand the idea that the words would go unanswered, as though unless they were challenged and avenged, they'd be minuted forever in some sort of metaphysical transcript, the proceedings of his life. But he knew perfectly well that Ducas hadn't meant to torture him, or even give offense. He'd been trying to be helpful. True, he had his own clumsy motivations. Ducas, he knew, was afraid of him, which was understandable. He wanted him to go away. Because of his breeding and upbringing and the mess of jumbled principles and ethics his poor brain was stuffed with, he'd found himself urging this foreigner whose presence disturbed him so much to do the opposite of what he wanted him to; because he was ashamed of his fear, presumably, and because he felt he was offending his duty of hospitality. Accordingly, because he wanted Ziani to go away, he'd made a great song and dance about how easy and profitable it'd be for him to stay. It would be dangerously easy to like these people.

That was beside the point. There had been a moment when he'd wanted to kill Ducas, or at least hurt him very badly, just for a tactless word. He wondered: have I been quiet and harmless all my life because that's who I am, or just because I've never before run into anything more than trivial provocation? It was, he recognized, an important issue. It was essential that he should know his own properties, tensile strength and breaking strain, before he started work.

A little later they brought him up some food (it was a depressing thought that the garbage on his plate probably counted as the best this country could offer); he ate it, lay down on the bed and stared at the ceiling until he fell asleep.

Veatriz Sirupati to Valens Valentinianus; greetings.
     Trying to understand people is like trying to catch flies in
a net; just when you think you've got them and you pounce,

they flit out through the holes in the mesh and leave you feeling baffled and stupid.

When Orsea got back from the war, I thought everything was going to be dreadful; and so it has been, but not in anything like the way I thought. I was sure everybody would be angry and bitter and hysterical, there'd be riots and mobs throwing stones and ferocious speeches in the streets, everybody blaming Orsea and the court, everything out in the open. But it hasn't been like that at all. It's been quiet; and I think that's much, much worse. It's like a married couple, I suppose. If they quarrel and shout at each other and throw things, obviously it's pretty bad; but when they just don't talk at all, you know it's hopeless. That's the sort of quiet there's been here, ever since the news broke about the disaster; except I don't get the feeling anybody blames us for what happened (which is ridiculous, isn't it? Surely it was all our fault, when you come right down to it). They don't hate us; I don't even think they particularly hate the Mezentines, either. It's like there's no point getting angry with what's happened, the way you don't get angry with death. It's something that happens and there's absolutely nothing you can do about it. All I can think of is that people here are so used to war and slaughter and armies not coming back that they don't get angry anymore. Do you know that, over the last two hundred years, among men over the age of twenty-five, one in three has been killed in wars? No wonder they all marry young here. I can't understand how people can live like this.

(I'm not thinking, of course. Since most of that time we've been at war with you, presumably it's pretty much the same with your people; so you understand it better than I can. I hate the fact that I spent so much time living away from here when I was young. This might as well be a foreign country, for all I understand it.)

The biggest thing that's been happening lately is the

business with the Mezentine exile. It's all been a complete mystery to me, I'm afraid. As far as I was concerned, there simply wasn't an issue. He was offering to teach us how to be just like the Republic: all working in factories, making things to sell abroad with those amazing Mezentine machines and so forth. But it would've been completely impossible; we're nothing like the Mezentines—by their standards, I suppose we're unspeakably primitive; and besides, if we were to start making all these things to sell, who on earth are we supposed to sell them to? But Orsea and the court had a long debate about it. I think Orsea really liked the idea; it would've been a new future for the Duchy, he thought, at a time when he'd just brought about a total disaster; it would've been a way of putting things right, and he's so completely heartbroken and torn up with guilt. But Miel Ducas talked him out of it, and of course he listened to Miel. He listens to everybody except himself. It's stupid, really; it's not just that Orsea's his own worst enemy, he's his only enemy. But he puts so much work into it, to make up the shortfall.

This is turning into a very bad letter. It's full of politics and news and personal stuff and all the things we agreed we wouldn't write to each other about; I'm being very boring and no fun. I really don't mean to dump all my problems on you like this. Let's talk about something interesting instead.

I've left some lines blank to indicate me sitting here trying to think of something interesting to say. If I could draw, I'd put in a little sketch of me, baffled (but I can't, as you know; all my faces end up long and thin and pointy, like goblins). The truth is, I'm so worried about Orsea and there's absolutely nothing I can do to help him. He's wandering about the place all numb—it's the way he is first thing in the morning, when he blunders about still asleep for an hour, except that it lasts all day. He's not trying to be horrible or anything like that. I think he's trying so hard not to think about the disaster and everything, and the only way he can manage it is not to think about anything. It's like when you've got a little scrap of a tune going round and round in your head, and the only way you can make it shut up is to think a kind of low, monotonous hum.

I've left some more lines blank, because I really am trying to think of something cheerful and interesting, because I imagine you need cheering up, too. Your last letter — here I go again — it was so intensely bright and clever and full of fascinating things that I got the distinct feeling you've got an annoying tune in your head as well; but you don't hum, you sing something else to get rid of it. Which is not to say that it wasn't a wonderful letter, and it kept me going for ages; I rationed it, a paragraph a day for a week, like a besieged city. Look, I can't leave any more lines, because this is all the paper I've got, and it's got to fit inside a little carved soapstone box that that dreadful Adventurer woman is taking to sell in Avadoce, so I can't waste any more space; but I've got to tell you something interesting, or you won't want to bother with me anymore.

Here's something I've just thought of. It's not new, I'm afraid. I've been saving it up. Apparently — this is from one of the merchant women, so believe it or not as you like — somewhere in the desert there's an underground river. It's a long way down under the sand, and the only way they know it's there is because there's a certain kind of flower that puts down incredibly long roots, and it can tap into the river and that's how it survives. Apparently there was this man lost in the desert one time, and he was wandering around convinced he was going to die, and suddenly he saw the most amazing thing: a long, straight line of bright red flowers, like a fence beside a road. At first he thought it was some kind of vision, and if he followed the flowers it'd lead him to Paradise; so, he thought, I might as well, just in case; and he followed the line, and just when he couldn't go a step further, he literally stepped into a pool of water and very nearly drowned. Anyway, he was all right after that; the thing is (according to this merchant woman) that these flowers only bloom for one week a year, and then they die off completely and shrink back into their roots, and you could tread on them and never know they were there.

Thinking about it, I'm pretty much positive it isn't true; but it's a bit more cheerful than me moaning on about how sad everything is. You never know; tomorrow Orsea might tread on an unexpected flower, and we'll find our way out of here.

Write soon.

Walking out of the castle felt strangely familiar. It took Ziani a moment or so to work out what it reminded him of; passing under the gateway arch and into the narrow street, he remembered leaving the Guildhall in Mezentia. He tried to think how long ago that had been, but he couldn't. It was a notable failure in calibration. Perhaps he was losing his fine judgment.

There was one distinct difference from the last time. Then, he'd walked out alone and nobody had seen him. This time, there was someone waiting for him.

A tall man in a long cloak had been leaning against the gatepost; he straightened up and hurried after Ziani. "Excuse me," he called out. Obviously Ziani didn't recognize him, but the voice was easily classified; another feature of the nobility is how similar they all sound. Since it was unlikely that an Eremian aristocrat would be acting as a paid assassin for the Republic, Ziani allowed himself to breathe again.

Ziani stopped and waited for him.

"You're the Mezentine," the man said.

No point trying to deny it, even if he wanted to. "That's right," he said.

"Vaatzes," the man said. He pronounced it slightly wrong; one long A instead of two short ones. "The Ducas told me about you. My name is Sorit Calaphates."

He paused, as if waiting for some reaction; then he realized he was talking to someone who couldn't be expected to know who he was. "Pleased to meet you," Ziani said.

Calaphates seemed a little nervous, but most likely only because he was talking to someone he hadn't been formally introduced to. "I understand from the Ducas," he went on, "that you may be considering setting up in business here in the city. Would that be correct?"

"I'm not sure," Ziani said. "I haven't made up my mind, to be honest with you."

Calaphates shifted a little; he didn't seem happy standing still in public. "If you've got nothing better to do," he said, "I wonder if you'd care to come and share a glass of wine with me, and perhaps we could talk about that."

Ziani considered him, as a commodity. He was somewhere between forty and sixty; a long man, thin arms and legs, a slight potbelly and the makings of a spare chin under a patchy beard. He had very small hands, Ziani noticed, with short fingers. He didn't look like he was any use for anything, but Ziani knew you couldn't judge the nobility by appearances. His shoes were badly blocked and stitched, but they had heavy silver buckles.

"Thank you," Ziani said.

Calaphates led him across the square to a small doorway in a bare, crumbling wall; he produced a large key and opened it. "Follow me," he said quietly (there was something rather comic about the way he said it).

The door opened into a garden. Apart from the Guildhall grounds and a few similar spaces in the cloisters of other Guild buildings, there were no gardens in Mezentia. Ziani certainly hadn't expected to find one here, not in a city perched on top of a mountain. His knowledge of the subject was more or less exactly matched by his interest in it, but he knew gardens needed a lot of water, and he still hadn't quite figured out how the city's water supply worked. It stood to reason that, however it got there, water wasn't something that could be wasted. But here was this garden; a lush green lawn, beautifully even, edged with terraced beds blazing with extremes of color. There were green and brown and silver and purple trees, cut and restrained into unnaturally symmetrical shapes. The beds were edged with low hedges of green and blue-gray shrubs — he recognized lavender by its smell, though he'd never seen it growing; the whole place stank of flowers, like the soap factory in Mezentia. There were tall, smooth stone pillars with flowering vines trained up them, and huge stone urns with still more flowers spilling over the edges, like overfilled tankards. Ziani looked round but he couldn't see anything he recognized as edible; the obvious conclusion was that all this effort and ingenuity and expense was simply to look nice. Strange people, Ziani thought.

In the middle of the lawn was a round stone table, with two small throne-like chairs. Calaphates gestured to him to sit in one of them, and took the other for himself. By the time he'd lowered himself into the thing (it was designed for appearance rather than comfort) a woman had appeared from nowhere holding a silver tray with a jug and two silver cups. She poured him a drink. It tasted horrible.

"Your good health," Calaphates said.

Ziani smiled awkwardly at him. "What can I do for you?" he said.

Calaphates took a moment before answering. (Is he afraid of me in some way, Ziani wondered; or is it just diffidence, or embarrassment?) "I should tell you," he said, "that I'm a member of the Duke's council. Yesterday we debated your offer—"

"Turned me down, yes," Ziani interrupted.

"That was the Duke's decision," Calaphates said. "It's not what

I'd have chosen to do myself. However, the decision has been taken, and, to put it bluntly, that leaves you at rather a loose end."

Ziani nodded.

"If you intend to stay here and set up in business" — Ziani could feel the effort it was costing Calaphates to talk to him; is it because I'm Mezentine, Ziani wondered, or just because he doesn't know what to make of me? — "you will obviously need capital; a workshop, tools, supplies. I won't pretend I understand the technical aspects. But I flatter myself I know a good investment when I see one."

Ziani allowed himself to smile. "You want to invest in me?"

"Exactly."

"Doing what?"

Calaphates shrugged. "That's not for me to say," he said. "All I know is that the Armorer Royal has given you the most extraordinary endorsement. According to him — and I know the man well, of course — there's practically nothing you can't do, in the way of making things. I wouldn't presume to tell you what to make, because I don't know the first thing about such matters. What I've got in mind is a partnership. Quite straightforward."

Ziani nodded. "Equal shares."

Calaphates looked at him, and Ziani realized he'd have settled for rather less. Not that it mattered. "Quite," he said. "All profits split straight down the middle, and that way we both know exactly where we stand."

"Fine," Ziani said. "I'll be quite happy with that."

"Excellent." He could feel a distinct release of tension; for some reason, Calaphates hadn't been expecting things to go so smoothly. No doubt he assumed all Mezentines were ruthless chiselers, cunning and subtle in matters of business. "Now, it's entirely up to you, of course, but as it happens I own a site here in the city that might suit you; it used to be a tanner's yard, but the man who used to rent it from me died — actually, he was killed in the war — and since he was relatively young, he had no children or apprentices to carry on the business, so the place is standing empty, apart from his vats and some stock in hand, which of course belongs to his family. Naturally, it'll be up to you entirely, how you want the place done up. You must do it properly, of course: forges and furnaces and sheds and anything else in the way of permanent fixtures."

"It'll be expensive," Ziani said.

He caught a faint flicker in Calaphates' eyes. "Well, I'm sure it'll be worth it. The main thing is to get started as soon as possible. The sooner we start, the sooner we'll be ready."

"It'll take some time, I'm afraid," Ziani replied. "Mostly I'm thinking about housing for the heavy machinery."

"I..." Now the poor man was looking worried. "That's your side of things," he said.

"Yes," Ziani went on, "but the point is, there are some pieces of equipment that I'll have to build first before we can raise the sheds to house them. A proper cupola foundry, for instance, for casting in iron; a machine shop, for the lathe and the mill."

Calaphates was being terribly brave. "Whatever it takes," he said. "If you think the premises will be suitable — we'll go there right now so you can see for yourself — I'll tell my overseer to take his orders direct from you, and you can get on with it exactly as you wish. Don't worry," he added with a very slight effort, "about the money side. I'll handle that."

Ziani shrugged. "Good," he said. "It'd be difficult for me to cost the whole thing out from scratch, because I don't know how much things cost here, or what'll need to be brought in from outside and what I'll have to build for myself. Also," he added, "I'll need men. Otherwise, if I've got to do everything myself, it'll take a lot longer."

Calaphates looked at him. "Certainly," he said. "Of course, there may be difficulty finding enough sufficiently skilled labor —"

"I was thinking of your friend Cantacusene," Ziani said. "I expect he could be persuaded. Really, what I need is people who'll do as they're told and don't need to be supervised all the time. And teaching apprentices the basics wouldn't leave me much time to do the more complicated work."

(He's wondering what the hell he's got himself into, Ziani thought; but it'll be all right. He's strong enough to take the load. I think I've got my second component.)

The tannery was in the lower city, out on the east side, where the prevailing wind could be relied on to carry the stench away from the houses. "Handy for the gate," Calaphates pointed out. "You won't have so much trouble getting carts in and out through the streets."

Ziani had been wondering about that. In Mezentia, all the streets were the same width, everywhere; wide enough for two standard wagons to pass axle to axle without touching. Civitas Eremiae wasn't like that at all. A wide boulevard would pass under an arch and suddenly dwindle into a narrow snicket, where the eaves of the houses on either side almost touched. A hundred yards further down, there'd be a flight of narrow stairs, leading to a street as broad as a ropewalk; two hundred yards further on, a wall and a sharp right-hand turn, and a maze of little winding alleys culminating in a dead end. Because of the gradient, the buildings were often five stories high on one side and two on the other, and most of them sported a turret or a tower; it was like being in an old, neglected forest where the trees are too close together and have grown up tall and spindly, fighting to get at the light. In places, the thoroughfares jumped over the tangle of buildings on narrow, high-arched bridges, like a deer leaping in dense cover. Every hundred yards or so there was an arch, a gateway, a covered portico, a cloister. The people he saw in the streets had a knack of scuttling sideways like crabs, so as not to crash into each other with their shoulders in the bottlenecks. It took a long time to get anywhere, what with steps up and steps down, waiting to let other people pass (good manners would be essential in a place like this, if you didn't want to spend your whole life fighting impromptu duels); even when the way was relatively straight and flat, it wound backward and forward up the steep incline, so that a hundred yards up the slope cost you a mile in actual distance covered. It would be a nightmare to get a steel-cart from the gate to the castle square.

You'd probably have to have a system of portages, like carrying barges round waterfalls—stop, unload the cart, carry the stuff through the obstruction, load it on to another cart on the other side. No wonder these people had rejected his offer. It amazed him that humans could live under such conditions.

"Something that's been puzzling me," he said to Calaphates, as they passed through a tunnel. "I'm sure you can tell me the answer. What on earth do you do for water here?"

Calaphates smiled. "We manage," he said. "In fact, we manage quite well. We're rather proud of our arrangement, actually. We have a network of underground cisterns, a long way down inside the mountain. Originally, I believe, they were natural caves. Every roof and gutter and downpipe feeds into them, so basically not a single drop of rain that falls here is wasted. We get quite ferocious storms in the late winter and early spring; it rains for days at a time, sometimes weeks. The cisterns fill up, and we have our year's supply. To draw it up again we have a large number of public wells—there's one, look." He pointed at a door on the opposite side of the street. As far as Ziani could tell, it was just a small door in a long, blank wall; you had to know where they were, presumably. "Anyone can go in, let down the bucket, take as much as he can carry home. We don't waste the stuff, obviously; it costs too much effort to carry it about. But there's more than enough for everyone. In fact, once every ten years or so the cisterns get so full we have to drain off the surplus."

"Impressive," Ziani said. "Has anyone ever done a proper survey of these cisterns?"

"How do you mean?" Calaphates asked.

"A survey," Ziani repeated. "Like a map."

"I don't think so."

Ziani nodded. "Well," he said, "thank you. I was wondering how you coped."

"The project was begun by the fourth Duke, about two hundred years ago," Calaphates said; and he talked about history for a quarter of an hour, while Ziani pretended to listen. A survey would've been too much to hope for, he realized, but it shouldn't present too much of a problem to make one of his own. Simply plotting the well-houses on a map would be a good start.

"Here we are." Calaphates sounded relieved. They'd stopped outside another plain door in another blank wall. "Now, so you can get your bearings; the city gate is about three hundred yards over there, behind that tower. The castle is northwest, straight up the slope. The yard has its own well, of course."

The door opened into a wide, bare, sloping yard with five rows of big, low-sided stone tanks. Beyond them was a long two-story stone shed. The yard walls were high, with a catwalk running round the top, and two watchtowers. It felt more like a military camp than a factory.

"What are those for?" Ziani asked.

"The towers?" Calaphates smiled. "It's an eccentricity of Eremian architecture. We like towers. Most of the buildings have them. I suppose it comes from being on top of the mountain; we like a good view. I think the tanner used one as his office and countinghouse, and the men liked to go up into the other for their meals, to get away from the smell."

Ziani frowned. "I'd have thought they'd be used to it after a few months."

"Possibly. Now, through this arch here, we've got another yard."

The same as the first one, but a bit smaller. No shed. "These tanks," Ziani said. "Is there any reason we can't use them as footings for buildings?"

Calaphates shrugged. "Don't ask me," he said. "I'm not a builder. My overseer would be able to tell you about how they were built. He's been with me a long time."

"Show me the well-house," Ziani said.

As he'd hoped, it was on the higher side of the slope; not much of a gradient to work with, but anything would be better than nothing. "You said you're allowed to draw as much water as you want from these wells," he said. "Is that right, or are there limits?"

The question seemed to puzzle Calaphates. "Not that I'm

aware of," he said. "It's not a problem that's ever arisen, if you see what I mean."

"Fine." Ziani looked round; shapes were starting to form in his mind. "Is that it?"

Calaphates nodded. "There are cellars, of course, under the main shed. Another feature of Civitas Eremiae. Because we're short on space for building sideways, we've become very inventive about going up and down. Hence, towers and cellars."

The toolmarks on the cellar walls showed that it had been excavated the hard way, chip by chip with straight drills and hammers. "There'd be no objection to extending this?" Ziani asked.

"I don't see why not," Calaphates said. "If necessary."

"And we can use the spoil for building above ground," Ziani went on, "instead of having to lug blocks of stone through the streets."

For the first time, Calaphates allowed his anxiety to show in his face. "You've got something quite extensive in mind, then."

Ziani turned and looked at him. "There's an old saying in the Guild," he said. "The quickest, easiest and cheapest way to do a thing properly is the first time. If you're having second thoughts about this..."

Calaphates assured him that he wasn't. He was almost convincing.

"I'll have to spend a few days here," Ziani said, as they climbed the cellar steps into the light, "drawing up plans, taking measurements. I'll need a few things for that, but I'm sure your overseer can deal with it. I might as well camp out in the shed for the time being."

Calaphates looked at him. "It'll do, then?"

"It'll do fine," Ziani replied. "I feel at home here already."

When Calaphates had gone and he had the place to himself, Ziani made a proper inspection, pacing out distances, getting a feel for the space and how it worked. The biggest problem, water, might not be such an insurmountable obstacle after all (but if he sidestepped the water issue, it would make the fuel problem worse;

if only you could burn stone...). Time would be difficult, because this Calaphates would have to be managed carefully; he was flexible and fairly resilient, like a good spring, but if bent too far he'd probably prove brittle. He would need to be allowed for, but such allowance wouldn't necessarily compromise the tolerances Ziani was hoping to achieve.

He was concentrating so intensely on the shape of the mechanism slowly consolidating in his mind that he didn't notice the passing of the day, until the sun set and it was too dark to see. He lay down on a pile of half-tanned hides in the long shed, but he couldn't settle; so, after one final tour of the site (he found his way in the dark mostly by memory, like a blind man; already he knew most of it by heart, not by what was there already but by what would be there, when the work was done) he climbed up one of the towers and looked down over the city. There were few lights to be seen, because of the angle, but lamps burned in some of the towers that perked up over the rooftops like the heads of fledgling birds in a nest, enough of them that he could make out a pattern, a first rough working sketch for a city. He felt — he paused to analyze what he felt, since the properties of materials change according to the stresses imposed on them by each operation. There was guilt, inevitably, and generic sorrow, the unavoidable compassion of one human for others. There was a place for such feelings. In an ideal world, a machine running smoothly, they were the coolants and lubricants that stopped the components from jamming and seizing under load; it would be difficult, perhaps impossible, for a functional society to work without them. At this stage, however, they were swarf and waste, and he needed to control them. The top of a tower was a good place for perspectives, particularly at night, when you're spared the sight of the greater context. He didn't need to see it, since its outline was drawn out clearly in his mind. The detail, yet to be resolved, could wait until the time was right.

10

A satisfactory meeting, in many respects; no significant disagreements between factions, for once, no disruptive intrusion of party agendas. How pleasant, to be able to get useful work done without anything getting in the way.

Commissioner Psellus' report was well received, and the debate on his recommendations was perfunctory, since nobody really disagreed. Commissioner Crisestem, whose nose might have been put out of joint now that his own role had been largely superseded, was one of the first to welcome the initiative, while Psellus made a point of stressing that Crisestem's contribution was still entirely relevant, and should be carried through as a matter of priority. Crisestem in turn advised the committee that he'd made substantial progress in recruiting and briefing agents, and was confident that he'd be in a position to report a successful outcome at the next meeting.

The motion was put to a formal vote and carried unanimously. In view of the possible leakage of restricted Guild secrets, it stated, the Eremians posed an unacceptable threat to the security of the Perpetual Republic, and should be wiped out. A memorandum was composed by the appropriate subcommittee and dispatched to the Commissioners of War, with copies to the General Council, the Guild Assemblies, the Finance Department, the foreign and manpower directorates and the managing councils of the individual Guilds. No further business arising, the meeting was adjourned.

Psellus went back to his office. The chair was still there, and the desk, and the empty cup and plate. It made no sense, but he didn't want to sit in that chair again just yet; he perched in the window-seat instead, and looked out at his view (the back end of the glass factory; a blank brick wall with three doors in it). About an hour later, a clerk came to tell him that he was wanted at the War Commission.

I should have prepared better for this meeting, he rebuked himself, as he followed the clerk across the quadrangle to the west cloister, where the commission's offices were. *They'll want all the specifics about Vaatzes, and I haven't brought the file.* He considered going back for it, but decided not to bother. Most of it he had by heart, and they'd all be getting copies of the relevant documents in due course.

The War Commission liked to refer to themselves as the Department of Necessary Evil (there were other names for them around the Guildhall, none of which were used to their faces). As befitted an anomaly in an otherwise standardized world, they cultivated a slightly eccentric manner; accordingly, it was their custom when the weather permitted to meet in the open air, in the cloister garden. It was an undeniably pleasant spot: a square garden enclosed by the cloister walls, with a fountain in the center of the lawn, and raised flowerbeds at the edges. Grapevines and wisteria were trained on the walls, and a quincunx of elderly fig trees provided shade in the middle. According to people who knew about such things, the garden was one of the oldest parts of the Guildhall complex, dating back to before the Reformation. That made sense; it had a distinctly effete feel about it. You could picture the nobles and scribes of the old Republic strutting on the lawn, waited on by obsequious footmen in extravagant livery.

Necessary Evil didn't indulge itself to quite that extent; there were no brocade coats or powdered wigs, no string quartet scratching out incidental music in the background. Instead, the fourteen commissioners sat in a semicircle of ornately carved chairs facing the fountain. Secretaries and clerks hovered around them, setting up folding desks, topping up inkwells, sharpening pens. Two flustered-looking men were trying to stand up an easel for a large framed map; two more were struggling with a huge brass lectern that must have weighed four hundredweight. There was a pleasant hum of chatter, like distant bees.

The only member of Necessary Evil that Psellus knew by sight was the assistant secretary, who was also vice-chairman of the Foundrymen's standing committee on doctrine and specifications. He was easy to spot from a distance by his perfectly bald, slightly pointed head. In the event, he saw Psellus first and beckoned him over. His name was Zanipulo Staurachus, and Psellus had disliked him for thirty years.

"Well," Staurachus said, in a loud whisper, "a fine state of affairs you've landed us in."

Ever since they were apprentices together, Psellus had been trying to figure out a way of coping with Staurachus. Being an optimist at heart, he still hadn't given up hope.

"Presumably I've got to brief you about Vaatzes," he said.

"Formality, really. We need to be able to minute having interviewed you. But tell me, why did the bloody fool do it? I've read his assessments, and I'm pretty sure I met him once. Wouldn't have thought he was the type."

Psellus thought for a moment. "I'm not entirely sure there is a type," he replied. "I think that what people do depends a lot on what's done to them first."

"I'm not talking about the defection," Staurachus said. "Really, that's our fault for letting him get away. But what possessed him to go fooling about building stupid mechanical toys in the first place? If he was that way inclined, someone should've picked up on it years ago, and we could've done something about it, and all this nonsense would've been avoided. You realize this war business is playing right into the Consolidationists' hands, just when there's three seats on General Council up for grabs."

Psellus frowned. "I didn't know that," he said.

"Of course you didn't. It's not the sort of thing someone like you ought to know. But I'm telling you now, because obviously this stupid war is going to change everything, and I need all our people to focus on the issues. I mean, Eremia doesn't matter, in the long run, but if Consolidation manages to get an overall majority on General Council, that's a disaster."

Psellus hated having to agree with Staurachus; insult to injury. "But assuming we win the war—" he said.

"Of course we'll win," Staurachus interrupted. "It's *how* we win that matters. Frankly, it couldn't have come at a worse time, with me being the only Foundryman on this commission. Which," he added, scowling, "is where you come in."

"Me?"

Staurachus nodded. "I know you won't have figured it out for yourself, because you've only got ten fingers for counting on; but the rules say there should be sixteen commissioners in time of war, and we're two short. I'm proposing we co-opt you for the duration."

"Me?" Psellus repeated. "Why?"

"Well, because you're Foundry, obviously. And you know the background, you've researched the Eremians, specialized local knowledge and so forth. That's what I'll tell the others, anyhow. There shouldn't be any bother. The other co-optee will probably be either Ropemakers' or Linen Armorers', and we've got to be seen to be evenhanded in appointments."

"It's a great honor," Psellus said flatly. "But I don't think… What about Curiatzes? Or Crisestem," he added, in a burst of happy inspiration. "He's got the background, and he's ambitious."

"Exactly. So I chose you instead. Because," Staurachus explained, "you're not bright enough to be a nuisance, and you generally do as you're told. Now get over there and make your presentation. Try and make it good; I want something decent from you, if I'm going to get them to accept you."

Up to that point, Psellus hadn't really hated Ziani Vaatzes, except in an objective way. The abominator had inspired in him more curiosity than hatred. Now, though...

Mostly through force of habit, he made the best job he could of presenting the facts to the commission and fielding their awkward questions. There wasn't anything he couldn't handle, and the only overt hostility came from a Ropemaker and was therefore to be expected. He disarmed the annoying man by admitting that Compliance had indeed made several reprehensible errors of judgment in their handling of the case. Since this wasn't true and everybody knew it, the Ropemaker wasn't in any position to make capital out of it; he accepted the admission with a grunt and sat down again. As soon as Psellus had been dismissed and had sat down in the chair set out for him next to the fountain (a fine spray, deflected off the marble rim, fell on his collar, but he managed to ignore it), Staurachus got up and proposed that he be co-opted. The motion was seconded by a Carpenter and passed, twelve to one with a Shipwright abstaining. Duly elected, Psellus was led by a clerk across the lawn to a fortuitously empty chair next to Staurachus, on the left wing of the semicircle. The chief commissioner got up and recited a formal welcome. It was all as smooth and quick as slipping on ice.

Psellus spent his evening clearing out his old office and moving to his new one, which was just off the main gallery of the cloister, and about a third smaller than the one he'd just vacated. That meant there wasn't room for his old desk and chair, but somehow he wasn't heartbroken about that. It was a ghastly mess, of course; inevitably, Crisestem would get his old job at Compliance, at least until this ridiculous war was over. He tried to focus on the fact that his promotion was good for the Foundrymen and for Didacticism in general; somewhat marginal, once you'd balanced a seat gained on Necessary Evil against control of Compliance lost to the Tailors and Consolidation. If the war went wrong, needless to say, he'd be finished (which was rather like saying that if the sun failed to rise one morning, the world would be very dark. The Republic's wars never went wrong. Hadn't ever gone wrong yet).

It was just after midnight by the time he'd finished arranging his books and sorting his files, and it occurred to him that he hadn't had anything to eat for a very long time — not since he was in Compliance, in fact, and that was easily a lifetime ago. He wasn't in the least hungry, but he knew what missing meals did to his digestion. The dining room would be closed by now, but the buttery over in Foundrymen's Hall stayed open all night; stale bread, thick, slightly translucent yellow cheese and a small soft apple if he was lucky. Probably Necessary Evil had its own private, secret canteen where you could get plovers' eggs and mashed artichoke at three in the morning, but nobody had mentioned it at the meeting. Presumably you had to serve a probationary period before you were trusted with a map reference and a key.

Foundrymen's Hall was two quadrangles down and one across. It was twenty-five years since he'd first walked under its modest arch, knees weak and guts twisted into a knot. He'd got used to it since then; now it was just a building, ever so slightly shabby if you knew where to look. He didn't get lost in the corridors anymore, and when nervous young men asked him the way, he answered clearly and immediately without having to think, the way you move your hand. A day would come when his name would be written up on one of the honors boards in the downstairs lobby — he'd never see it, of course, because he'd be dead — and some terrified youth waiting to be collected and shown to his new desk would stare up at it and wonder without really caring who the hell he'd been, and what he'd done. When that day came, he'd be the sixth Psellus on the boards, and of course the last. There were no annotations beside those gilded names, so nobody would ever know, unless they had occasion to delve back through ancient minute-books and cross-reference with the archives of memoranda, that he was the man who destroyed Eremia Montis by getting up out of a chair; a neat trick, though he wasn't quite sure how he'd come to achieve it. It's something to ensure that your name will live forever, even if the reason why gets lost along the way.

There were half a dozen men in the buttery when he got there;

he recognized the faces of two sessions clerks but couldn't remember their names, and the other four were strangers. He declined the vegetable soup (twenty-five years, and he'd never seen or heard of anybody having the vegetable soup; it was universally shunned, like leprosy, but all day every day there was a black cauldron full of it, simmering like a dormant volcano over the fire) and risked a pear instead of an apple.

"Congratulations," someone said in his ear. He looked round.

"Thank you," he said gravely. "You're having the salt pork."

"I always do when I come in here. It's disgusting, but I'm too set in my ways to change."

They sat down at a table in the corner furthest from the hatch. "What are you doing up at this hour, Stali?" Psellus asked. "You're never up late."

"It's all your fault," replied Stali Maniacis, his oldest and only friend. "You get it into your head to declare war on some tribe nobody knows anything about, so naturally they send for the treasurer, and he sends for me. I've spent the last eight hours shuffling jetons around, trying to find some money for you to hire your soldiers with."

"Ah," Psellus replied. "Any luck?"

Maniacis nodded. "Pots of money," he said. "It's there, you can go down the cellars with a lamp and look at it, all heaped up on the floor. The problem's finding it on paper. Backdated appropriations and contingency reserves and five-year retentions and God only knows what. Your best bet, if you really want this war of yours, is to hire a bunch of pirates to break in and steal it. Cut through all the formalities, and we can write it off as hostile action, make our lives a whole lot easier. So," he went on, "rank and power at last. How did you manage it?"

Psellus shrugged. "I didn't get out of the way quick enough, I suppose."

"Balls. The lightness of the foot deceives the eye. One moment you were the failure responsible for a fuck-up in Compliance, next thing you're magically transfigured into a god of war, and nothing will be your fault ever again. Don't tell me you haven't been cooking this up for months."

"If only," Psellus said. "It was nothing to do with me."

"All right. So who, then?"

"Staurachus."

"Oh." Maniacis pulled a face. "Him. Fine. So presumably this is all part of some magnificently intricate maneuver on behalf of the greater glory of Didacticism." He shook his head. "Don't see it myself, but then I wouldn't expect to. What's your new office like?"

"Small."

"View?"

"You can just about see a corner of the cloister garden, if you lean out and crane your neck a bit."

"Better than the glassworks, though."

"True."

Maniacis frowned. "You really aren't very happy about this, are you? What's the problem? Feeling out of your depth?"

"I'm used to that," Psellus said. "I've been a politician now for fifteen years, I wouldn't know my depth if I fell in it. But I'm sure there's something I've missed, and I don't know where."

"You always were a worrier."

"Yes," Psellus said. "But it probably doesn't matter. That's what's so good about war, it papers over all the cracks. If we scrape Eremia Montis off the map, none of the fiddling little details will matter anymore." He yawned. "I think I'll go to bed," he said. "I expect tomorrow is going to be a long and interesting day."

"Going home?"

Psellus shook his head. "I'll sleep in the lodge," he said. "I can't face all those flights of stairs at this time of night."

"Count yourself lucky," Maniacis grumbled. "I've still got three projections to do. I don't imagine I'll be finished much before dawn. Next time you declare war, do you think you could do it around nine in the morning? Some of us have to work for a living, you know."

"If you call shuffling brass disks round a checkerboard work," Psellus replied. It was, of course, an old debate between them, as thoroughly rehearsed as a wedding dance. It could be started with a word, or stopped immediately and put on one side, bookmarked, to be continued later at some more opportune time. "Now I suppose you're going to say it's all my fault that you've got to go scrabbling about trying to find the money to pay for all of this."

Maniacis frowned. "All of what?"

"The war, of course."

"Oh." Somehow Psellus felt he'd said something unexpected. "No, we're used to that," Maniacis went on. "You politicals say the word, all we've got to do is click our fingers and the money appears out of thin air. I mean, it's not like we've got anything else to do."

It was synthetic, because it was always synthetic between them, like an exhibition bout between prizefighters; this time, though, he noticed a certain edge in his friend's voice, a slight reluctance to look him in the eye. But that was strange, since Stali wouldn't ever be genuinely upset with him because of work. Something he'd said was rattling about in his mind loose, but he couldn't place it. Because he was so tired, probably.

"Bed for me," he said, standing up. "Have fun with your projections."

Maniacis said something vulgar, and he left. All the way down the stairs and across the back courtyard he tried to work out what it was that didn't fit. Something was wrong; something small and trivial, of course.

The lodge porter opened up a guest room for him; slightly smaller than a prison cell, with a plain unaired bed, a washstand, an empty water jug, one elderly shoe left behind by a previous visitor. He undressed, snuffed the lamp and lay down on top of the threadbare coverlet, his hands folded on his chest like a corpse laid out for embalming. Directly overhead was the old dorter, a survival from the days when the Guildhall was still a religious house; in consequence, the ceilings of these rooms were all vaulted, though of course you couldn't see anything in the dark. One of the rooms still had traces of the old painted stucco, devotional scenes from a religion nobody remembered anymore. Probably not this one; Psellus had seen them once, years ago, but they were just people standing about in the flat, stylized poses of pre-Reformation religious painting. Authentic but entirely lacking in artistic merit; it'd probably be kinder to chip them off and whitewash over the top. It'd be miserable, he reckoned, to be the ghost of a god, pinned to the mortal world by one crumbling and indistinct fresco.

(And in Eremia shortly . . . Did the Eremians have any gods? He had an idea they'd believed in something once, but they'd grown out of it. Just as well, probably. If you eradicated a religious people, would their gods survive even with nobody to pray to them? And if so, what would they find to do all day?)

He closed his eyes, like a fencer moving from First guard to Third.

"Civitas Eremiae," said the expert, "is the highest city in the known world. It's built on the peak of a mountain; the walls are founded on solid rock, so you can forget about sapping, undermining or tunneling your way in. They have an excellent system of underground cisterns, with never less than six months' supply of water. There's also a substantial communal granary, likewise underground. That means a siege would present us with enormous difficulties as regards supply. They have plenty of water and food in store at all times; if we wanted to lay siege to them and starve or parch them out, we'd have to carry water and food for our men up the mountain. There's just the one road, narrow and winding back and forth. Even if we kept up a continual relay, we couldn't shift enough supplies in one day along that road for more than seven thousand men, way too few to maintain an effective blockade. To be blunt: we'd be dead of hunger and thirst long before them, and we'd also be outnumbered two to one. Unless someone can think of a way round those problems, a siege is out of the question. If you want to take Civitas Eremiae, it'll have to be by way of direct assault; and the longest an army capable of doing that could last up there would be forty-eight hours. Talking of which; the very least number of defenders we'd be likely to come up against would be fifteen thousand infantry on the walls. The city has never been taken, either by siege or storm. If you contrived somehow to get through the gate or over the wall, that's where the fun would start. The whole place is a tangle of poxy little alleys and snickets; from our point of view, one bottleneck and ambush after another. There are some thatched roofs, a handful of wooden buildings; not enough for a decent fire to get a foothold on. Artillery isn't going to be much help to you. In order to get it up the approach road, you'd have to break it down completely and rebuild it once you're in position, but you'd be wasting a lot of sweat and effort for nothing. The slope's so aggressive, you'd be hard put to it to find a level footprint for anything bigger than a series five scorpion; but nothing less than a full-size torsion catapult's going to make any kind of a mark on those walls. The same goes for battering rams and siege towers — and maybe this is an appropriate moment to point out that the main strength of the Eremian military is archers. Put the picture together and I think you'll agree, you've set yourself a difficult job."

Thoughtful silence. After a nicely judged pause, the expert went on: "Maybe you're wondering why a poor and relatively primitive bunch like the Eremians have gone to such extraordinary lengths to fortify their city. It's worth dwelling on that for a moment. Consider the drain on national resources, both material and manpower, involved in building something like that. The Eremians keep a few slaves, true. Not many, though; all that work was mostly done by free Eremian citizens, in between their daily chores and the seasonal demands of the sheep and goats. Why bother? you're asking yourselves. They must've been afraid of somebody, but it wasn't us."

Another pause, and everything so quiet you could hear the patter of water-drops from the fountain. "The answer," the expert said, "is of course their neighbors, the Vadani. Eremia Montis has just emerged from a long and particularly nasty border war with the Vadani; and that's the direction I'm asking you to look in for help in cracking this nut. There may be peace right now, but the Eremians and the Vadani hate each other to bits, always have and always will. If you want the Eremians, you're going to have to get the Vadani on your side first. At the very least, they've got generations of experience of fighting the Eremians. They also have money, from the silver mines. The first stage, therefore, will have to be diplomacy rather than straightforward military action. Everything will depend on the Vadani; and the only way you can do business with them is through their chief, Duke Valens. He's your first objective." The expert relaxed slightly, aware that he'd done his job and not left anything out. "To brief you on him, I'd like to call Maris Boioannes of the diplomatic service."

Psellus sat up a little straighter. He knew Boioannes, or had known him a long time ago. A man stood up in the front row of seats, but he could only see his back; he had to wait until he'd made his way up to the lectern before he could get a look at his face.

Curious, how the changes of age surprise us. The Maris Boioannes he remembered had mostly been objectionable on account of his appearance: a tall man, with a perfect profile, a strong chin and thick black hair, a revoltingly charming smile, deep and flashing brown eyes. You knew you never stood a chance when Boioannes was around. This man—oddly enough, the smile was still there, although the chin had melted and the hair was thin, palpably flicked sideways to cover a bald summit as prominent as Civitas Eremia as described by the previous speaker. Deprived of its natural setting, however, the smile was weak and silly. You could easily despise this man, which would make you tend to underestimate him. Probably why he'd done well in the diplomatic service.

"Duke Valens Valentinianus," Boioannes said (his voice was the same; still rich and warm. He looked different once he'd started to speak), "is almost certainly the most capable duke to rule the Vadani in two centuries. He's intelligent, he's firm, decisive; he's a good leader, highly respected; still very young, only in his early twenties, but that's not so uncommon among the mountain tribes, where life expectancy is short and prominent men tend to die young. He's well educated, by Vadani standards, with a firm grasp of practical economics; he reads books for pleasure—we know what he reads, of course, because his books all come from the Republic; we've compiled a list from the ledgers of his book-seller, and it'll be worth your while to take a look at it. He has an inquiring mind, maybe even a soul. He's not, however, an effete intellectual. We're still working on a complete schedule of all the men he's had executed or assassinated since he came to power, but I can tell you now, he's quite ruthless in that way. Not a story-book bloodthirsty tyrant, shouting 'off with his head' every five minutes; there are several well-authenticated instances where he spared someone he really ought to have disposed of, gave him a second and even a third chance. It's notable, however, that in each of these cases he took full precautions to make sure that the of-fender couldn't do any serious harm while on license, so to speak. He's an excellent judge of character, and he has great confidence in his own judgment. He believes in himself, and the people be-lieve in him too. All in all, a most efficient and practical ruler for a nation like the Vadani."

Boioannes paused and drank a little water. He still had that mannerism of using only his index and middle fingers to grip the cup. "As far as weaknesses go," he went on, "we haven't found any yet, though of course we're working on it. He's depressingly temperate as far as wine and women are concerned; his only in-dulgence appears to be hunting, which is a big thing among both of the mountain nations. Buying him isn't really an option, since the revenue from the silver mines is more than a tribal chief would know what to do with; also, he doesn't seem to show any interest in conspicuous expenditure—no solid gold dinner services, price-less tapestries, jewel-encrusted sword-hilts. He draws only a very moderate sum from the profits of the silver mines, and lives well within his means. Currently, therefore, the most productive line of approach would seem to be intimidation; but we have an uncomfortable feeling that it could go badly wrong, and force him into a genuine alliance with his neighbor. What we need to find, therefore, is a crack in the armor. We're confident that there is one—there always is—and given time we know we can find it. Much depends, therefore, on how much time we have available. That's for you to tell us. What we're fairly certain we can't do is simply rely on his instinctive hatred for the Eremians. Common sense would seem to be the keynote of this man's character, and an ability to ignore or override emotional impulses that conflict with what his brain tells him is the sensible thing to do. He'll know straight away that if we come to him and propose an alliance against Eremia, the whole balance of power in the region will be irrevocably changed. Remember, his father started the peace process with Eremia and he saw it through; not through fear, or because he doesn't hold with war on principle, but because he realized that peace was the sensible thing, in the circumstances."

Psellus' attention started to wander; he wasn't really interested in the Vadani Duke. Instead, he opened his mind to a picture of a mountaintop (he'd never seen a mountain, except as a vague fringe at the edge of a landscape, hardly distinguishable from banks of cloud) with all those impossible defenses—the walls, the narrow spaces, above all the desperate gradient. He knew that Civitas Eremia would fall, because the Republic had promised that it would, but as an engineer he could only see the problems, not the solution to them. He felt as if he'd heard the beginning of a story, and the end, but not the middle. Not by assault; not by siege; if they wanted to get inside the gates, they'd have to persuade someone in the city to open them for them.

He allowed himself a little smile. Of course, how silly of him not to see it earlier. The old saying: no city, however massively fortified, is impregnable to a mule carrying chests of gold coins. Treachery, that old faithful, would see them through.

Boioannes had stopped talking; people were standing up and chatting, so the meeting must be over. He wished he knew a bit more about Necessary Evil protocols; at the end of a meeting, were you supposed to hurry straight back to work, or did you linger, mix and network? He wished he was back somewhere where he knew the rules.

"Good briefing, don't you think?" Staurachus had materialized next to him, like a genie in a fairy tale popping up out of a bottle.

He nodded. "I've certainly learned quite a bit," he said.

Staurachus rubbed his eyes. Of course, he wasn't getting any younger, and all this extra work would be tiring to a man of his age. Somehow you don't expect frailty in your enemies, only your friends; you imagine that their malice makes them immune. "So how do you think we should proceed?"

"Get hold of someone inside the city and pay them a lot of money."

Staurachus smiled. "Very good," he said. "And who do you think would be a good prospect?"

Psellus shrugged. "I don't know a lot about them," he said, "but from what I've heard, I'd say the Merchant Adventurers. Mind you," he added quickly, "that's just off the top of my head. I'd need to know a bit more in the way of background. I mean, do the Eremians allow their women to go wandering about the place at night on their own?"

"Who knows?" Staurachus raised his hands in a vague, all-purpose gesture of dismissal. "We have people working on that side of things, cultural issues and what have you. It's standard operating procedure to compile a complete profile in these cases."

Reassuring, Psellus thought; we'll wipe them out, but the file will be preserved forever somewhere in the archives. A kind of immortality for them, every aspect of their culture scientifically recorded in the specified manner. "That's good," he heard himself say. "At any rate, we've got to try it before we risk an assault against those defenses."

Staurachus shrugged. "If it comes to that, I don't think it'll prove to be beyond our resources. We're blessed with advantages that few other nations have in war; we have the best engineers in the world, and our armies are made up of well-paid foreigners. Arguably, the harder the assault proves to be, the better the demonstration to the rest of the world."

"I suppose so," Psellus said. "But it'd probably be better to try treachery first. For one thing, we could forget all that business about having to get the Vadani on our side."

"Ah yes." Staurachus smiled a little. "You knew Boioannes at school, didn't you? Or was it later, in vocational training?"

"Both."

"The diplomatic service see things from a slightly different angle," Staurachus said tolerantly. "They have their pride, same as the rest of us. They like to believe they're useful. We listen to what they can tell us, but we don't usually tend to follow their recommendations."

At the end of his first day in Necessary Evil, Psellus felt an overwhelming need for a bath. As a Guild officer of senior executive rank, he was entitled to use the private bath in the main cistern house, instead of having to pitch in at the public bathhouse on the other side of the square. It was a privilege he valued more than any other, since he'd always been diffident about taking his clothes off in front of other people (I have so much, he often told himself, to be diffident about: so much, and a little more each year); and besides, the water in the cistern house was always pleasantly warm, instead of ice-cold or scaldingly hot.

His luck was in; nobody else was using it, and quite soon he was lying on his back lapped in soothing warmth, gazing up at the severely geometrical pattern of the ceiling tiles. As he relaxed, he mused on treachery. Staurachus had sounded as though he already had a plan for the betrayal of Civitas Eremiae; probably involving the Merchant Adventurers, either directly or indirectly. His question, therefore, had been by way of a test; fair enough, since Staurachus was his sponsor, and one likes to reassure oneself that one's protégé is worth putting one's name to. But there'd been something about his old enemy's manner that raised the hairs on the back of his neck, and it referred back, he was sure, to the big question: why had Staurachus chosen him, of all people?

There was a saying—Cure Hardy, he rather thought—that when making a sacrifice to the gods, you should offer the best animal in the herd, preferably someone else's. He paused his train of thought, and tried to work out which herds he belonged to. Foundrymen's; Didactics; no enlightenment there. Compliance; yes, but he wasn't Compliance anymore. What else? Who would his failure and disgrace reflect badly on? When he failed—

But how could he possibly fail? He couldn't, because the Republic couldn't lose a war. It might just conceivably lose a battle. It might even, under circumstances too far-fetched to be readily imagined, lose an army. The war might drag on for a year, or twenty years. The Republic would, however, inevitably win. Furthermore, as Staurachus had said himself, a military disaster wasn't necessarily a failure. A nation that wins a great victory frightens its neighbors; a nation that suffers a devastating defeat and then goes on to win the war, hardly noticing its losses, terrifies them to the point where both aggression and resistance are unthinkable. It wouldn't matter to the Republic if it lost fifty thousand men in one engagement, since all its armies were made up of hired foreigners. Indeed, the simple fact that dead men don't need to be paid had helped the Republic on several occasions in the past to regard bloody defeats with a measure of equanimity. No, failure wasn't possible. No matter how hard one tried, it simply couldn't be done.

After he'd finished his bath, Psellus went to his room. He slumped on the bed (his calves and knees ached pitifully, because of all the unaccustomed standing and walking) and put his hands behind his head. Normally he'd read a little before going to sleep; a few pages of early Mannerist poetry, perhaps, or Pogonas' *On Details;* something wholesome, orthodox, approved and gently soothing in its familiarity. Tonight, anything like that would be too bland to have any effect. He sat up again, scanned the titles on the shelf that stood against the wall and, on a whim, pulled down a very old, fat, squat book he hadn't looked at in years.

He made up for that now with a brief inspection. The covers, bound in plain off-white vellum gradually losing its translucence with age, were about the size of his palm; width, the length of his thumb. On the spine a previous owner had written, in ink now brown and faded with light and age, *Orphanotrophus, concerning the measurement of small things,* between the first and second backstraps of the binding. It was, he reflected, an accurate but misleading description. He let the book sit in his palm. The binding, still tight after four hundred years, nevertheless allowed a slight gap between the pages about a third of the way in. He opened it at that point, and stared for a moment at the tiny, precise handwriting. He'd forgotten that the book was written in what he believed was called copy minuscule — perfect, but very, very small, so that although he could read it without difficulty it made him feel dizzy, as if gazing too long at something a very long way away. He read:

In considering this same virtue which we call tolerance, namely the virtue that seeks ever to diminish and make small its own substance, we should most diligently consider wherein lies the true end of an endeavor: whether it be the perfection of the act of making, or of the thing made. For to value and cherish fine small work in the making of a worthless thing were folly, and but little to be regarded against the making of an useful thing, though basely and roughly done, save that in such act of making there is an effect of making fine worked upon the maker: so that each thing made small and fine by such making refines the hand that wrought it. Thus a man of great arts continually exercising his skill upon the perfection of fine things, though they be but idle and nothing worth, gains therefrom, besides material trash, a prize of great value, namely that same art of making small and fine, or rather the augmentation thereof by practice and perfection. Let a man therefore turn his hand to all manner of vain and foolish toys, so that thereby he shall make good his skill for when he shall require of it to serve a nobler purpose.

Psellus lifted his head and rubbed his eyes. Thirty-five years ago, he remembered, he'd sat in a badly lit room the size of an apple-crate, staring dumbly at this very same page on the eve of his Theory of Doctrine exam. Addled with too much concentration and too little sleep, he'd read it over three or four times before he finally got a toehold in a crevice between its slabs of verbiage, and hauled himself painfully into understanding. Not long afterward he'd dozed off, woken to see the sun in the sky, and run like a madman to the examination halls just in time to take his place... But the great force of providence that looks after idle students in the hour of their trial had been with him that day. Out of the whole of that fat, dense book, which he'd been meaning to get around to reading for two years and opened for the first time the previous evening, the learned examiners had seen fit to set for construction and comment the one and only paragraph he'd managed to look at before sleep ambushed him. Accordingly, he scored ninety marks out of a hundred, thereby earning his degree and with it the chance of a career in Guild politics.

Maybe that was why the book had fallen open at that page. He frowned, as a tiny spark flared in his memory. Vaatzes the abominator had owned a copy of this book, and had, apparently, misunderstood it. In spite of everything, he leaned his head back and grinned like a dog. *Let a man therefore turn his hand to all manner of vain and foolish toys,* the book said, and the poor literal-minded fool, striving to improve his mind to the level of his betters by reading the classics, had gone away and done as he'd been told, and got caught at it into the bargain. As a result, he'd earn himself a footnote in history as the man who brought about the eradication of an entire tribe by his failure to construe an archaic usage in a set text. It'd make a good joke, if it wasn't for all the deaths it would cause.

He put the book back in its place and took down Azotes' *Flowers of Didacticism* instead.

The next morning there was another meeting in the cloister garden. It wasn't on the schedule, which was posted every week on the chapterhouse door; half a dozen pages had spent a nervous hour just after dawn scurrying through the Guildhall rounding up Necessary Evil and shepherding them here, puzzled and irritable and speculating about the nature of this urgent new development.

When the stipulated quorum had gathered, Maris Boioannes of the diplomatic service asked leave to address the meeting. Before he started to speak, however, he picked a sack up off the ground, balanced it on the ledge of the rostrum while he opened it, and took out of it something the size and shape of a large melon, wrapped in dark brown sailcloth. It wasn't a melon.

"This," he said, letting the thing dangle from his hand by the hair, "used to be Auzida Razo, our chief of section among the Merchant Adventurers in Eremia." He paused. The thing was dripping onto the neat, short grass. "I have reason to believe," he went on, "that the covert stage of this operation is over."

11

"Auzida Razo," Orsea repeated. "I know the name."

One of the drawbacks to sending your enemy a head by way of a gesture is that you're left with the rest of the body. Orsea had insisted on seeing it. Miel wasn't sure why; he believed it was because Orsea had always had a tendency to be squeamish. Since he'd ordered the wretched woman's execution, he felt he should punish himself by viewing her decapitated trunk. If that was the reason, it was confused, irrational, hard for anyone else to understand and quite in character.

"You've met her," Miel said. "Several times. You'd remember her if—" He stopped.

Orsea grinned; he was white as milk and shaking a bit. "Of course," he said. "That's me all over. Not so good with names, but an excellent memory for faces. In this case, however..."

Miel frowned. "Can we go now?" he said.

"Yes, why not?" Orsea turned away abruptly. He'd seen worse, to Miel's certain knowledge, but the fact that he was directly responsible, having given the order, presumably made it more immediate. Of course Orsea would argue that he'd also given the order to attack Mezentia. "I've never had anybody put to death before," he said, all false-casual. "What's the procedure? Can it just be buried quietly somewhere, or does it have to be nailed to a door or strung up off a gateway somewhere?"

Miel nearly said, *Well, that's up to you,* but stopped himself just in time. "I'd leave it to the guard commander if I were you," he said. "There's no set protocol, if that's what you mean."

They walked through the arch into the main courtyard of the guardhouse. "So," Orsea said, "I met her a couple of times. When and where?"

"She used to call at the palace," Miel said, carefully looking ahead.

"Call," Orsea repeated, as though it was an abtruse foreign loanword. "What, on business, you mean?"

"That's right," Miel said. "She mostly dealt in luxury stationery—ivory writing sets, antique Mezentine ink bottles, signet rings, that kind of stuff. Come to think of it, I bought a silver sand-shaker from her myself last spring."

"She did a lot of business with the court, then?"

"Like I said, luxury goods. Not the sort of thing most people can afford."

"Yes," Orsea said, as though Miel was being obtuse, "but what I mean is, she knew people here in the palace, and she was spying for the Republic. Aren't you worried about that?"

Only Orsea could ask such a question. "Of course I'm worried," Miel said. Just not surprised, like you, he didn't add. "Obviously there's a serious problem."

"Glad you can see that," Orsea snapped. "What are you proposing to do about it?"

Miel stopped, frowning. "Thank you," he said.

"What are you thanking me for?"

"The promotion. Apparently I'm head of security now, or captain of the palace guard, or something. I'm honored, but you might have told me earlier."

"I'm sorry." And he was, too; sincerely sorry for being nasty to his friend. That was why Miel loved him, and why he was such a bad duke. "It's because I've come to rely on you so much since—well, since the battle. I got wounded and you had to get us all out of that ghastly mess; and since then I've turned to you first for everything, loaded it all on your shoulders without even asking if you minded, and now I automatically assume you're dealing with it all, like a one-man cabinet." He sighed. Miel felt embarrassed. "You should be doing this job, Miel, not me. I just can't manage it."

Miel forced a laugh. "Only if you wanted a civil war on your hands," he said. "A Ducas on the throne; think about it. Half the people in this country would rather see Duke Valens get the crown than me."

Orsea turned his head slightly, looked him in the eye. "You wouldn't have invaded Mezentia, though."

"You don't know that." Miel shrugged. "This isn't getting us anywhere. In answer to your question—"

"What question? Oh, yes. Slipped my mind."

"What do we do about the spy," Miel said. They started walking again. "Well," he said, "you don't need to be a doctor of logic to figure out that the likeliest place to find spies is the Merchant Adventurers. They go everywhere, know people here and abroad, they haven't got the same loyalties as us. Nobody else has the opportunities or the motive like they have."

Orsea frowned. "So what are you saying?" he said. "Round them all up and have them all killed?"

Miel clicked his tongue. "No, of course not," he said. "But we're looking at this the wrong way. Asking ourselves the wrong questions."

"Such as?"

"Such as why," Miel said. "Think about it for a moment. Why is Mezentia spying on us, *after* they've just beaten us so hard we won't be a threat to them again for a hundred years? Before, now, that'd make sense. But after?"

Orsea was quiet for a moment. "I don't know," he said.

"Nor me," Miel said. "I mean, there could be several reasons."

"Such as?"

"Well." Miel ordered his thoughts. "It could be that this Razo woman had been spying for them for years, and we only just found out. Like, she was a fixture, permanently stationed here as part of a standing intelligence network."

"You think that's what she was doing?"

"It's a possibility. There's others. For instance, they could've been alarmed because they didn't have as much advance notice of the invasion as they'd have liked—"

"Didn't seem to trouble them much."

"Yes, but they're a nation of perfectionists," Miel said, slightly wearily. "So they decided to set up a long-term spy ring here, to give them more warning next time."

Orsea looked worried. "So that's what you reckon..."

Miel succeeded in keeping the irritation out of his face. No point in setting up a string of straw men if Orsea took them all seriously. "Another possibility," he said, "is that they're planning to invade us."

This time Orsea just looked bewildered. "Why would they want to do that?" he said.

Miel shrugged. "To save face," he said. "To punish us for daring to attack them. To make sure we never pose a threat again. There's all sorts of possible reasons. Most likely, it'd be internal politics inside the Republic—"

"Do they have politics?" Orsea interrupted. "I thought they were above all that sort of thing."

Miel actually laughed. "Do they have politics?" he said. "Yes, they do. Quite apart from ordinary backstabbing and dead-men's-shoes-filling and infighting for who gets the top jobs, they have a number of factions; started as ideological differences over doctrine, nowadays it's just force of habit and an excuse for taking sides. It's not politics *about* anything; just politics."

"Oh." Orsea looked mildly shocked. "Is that good or bad?"

"For us?" Miel made a vague gesture with his hands. "Depends on the circumstances. Bad for us if someone wants a quick, easy war to gain popular support; good for us if the opposing faction outplays them. It'd be really nice if we could find a way of influencing them, playing off one faction against another. But we can't."

"Why not?"

"We haven't got anything any of them could conceivably want," Miel replied. "Except," he added, "if the Didactics or the Consolidationists want a war for the approval ratings, we're a handy target."

Orsea pulled a face. "Bad, then."

"Probably."

"You know all this stuff." There was bitterness in Orsea's voice, and guilt, and other things too complex to bother with. "I feel so stupid."

"I'm an adviser," Miel said, trying not to sound awkward. "It's an adviser's job to know stuff, so you don't have to."

Orsea laughed. "Yes, but look at me. Clueless. What did I ever do to deserve to be a duke, except marry someone's daughter?"

Miel frowned, ever so slightly. "Orsea, this isn't helping. You wanted to know the implications of this Razo woman being a spy."

"I'm sorry," Orsea said. "Go on, you were saying."

"That's right." Miel pulled a face. "Forgotten where I'd got to. Right; we know she was spying for the Republic, because she admitted it. We can guess why, but that's about all. To go back to your original question: what are we going to do about it?"

"Yes?"

Miel rubbed his eyes. He'd been up all night, and he felt suddenly tired. "I don't know what to suggest, right now," he said. "That was all we managed to get out of her, that she was spying for the Mezentines. We tried to get names of other spies, contacts, the usual stuff, but she died on us. Weak heart, apparently."

Orsea nodded. "So really," he said, "we need to find out some more background before we make any decisions."

"I think so. I mean, we've sent a pretty clear message to the Republic that we know what they were up to and there won't be any more reports from that particular source; so that's probably the immediate problem taken care of. Next priority, I would suggest, is finding out who else was in on the spy ring, and making our peace with the Merchant Adventurers. After that, it depends on what we come up with."

Orsea was satisfied with that, and they parted at the lodge gate. Miel went away with mixed feelings; a large part of them guilt, for having misled his friend. It wasn't a significant act of deception. All he'd done was steer the conversation away from one particular topic, and the amount of effort he'd had to put into it, given Orsea's naïveté, was practically nil. Still, he felt uneasy, guilty. Must be catching, he thought.

He went back to the turret room in the west court that he'd appropriated for an office (*me*, he thought, *needing an office. If cousin Jarnac ever finds out I've got an office, he'll wet himself laughing*). He shut the door and bolted it, then pulled out a key on a chain from under his shirt. The key opened a strong oak chest bound with heavy iron straps and hasps. All it contained was one very small piece of paper, folded many times to make it small. He unfolded it, for the tenth or eleventh time since it had come into his possession. As he did so, he read the words, tiny but superbly elegant, on the outside fold:

Valens Valentinianus to Veatriz Sirupati, greetings.

"Shouldn't we wait," Ziani said, "until your husband gets here?"

The woman in the red dress looked at him. "You'll be waiting a long time," she said. "I'm not married."

"You're..." Ziani could feel the brick fall. "I'm sorry," he said. "Only it's different where I come from."

"Oh yes." There was a grim ring to her voice. "But you're not in the Republic anymore."

"I'm beginning to see that," Ziani said. "Look, I didn't mean anything by it. Can we forget—?"

"Sure," the woman replied, her tone making it clear that she had no intention of doing so. "So, you're the new great white hope—well, you know what I mean—of Eremian trade. Everybody's talking about you."

"Are they?" Ziani said. "Well, there's not much to see yet, but I can take you round and give you an idea of what we're going to be doing here, once we're up and running."

She looked at him again. She seemed to find him fascinating; he wondered, has she ever seen a Mezentine before? He'd have expected her to, being a merchant and an Adventurer, but it was possible she hadn't. Not that it mattered.

"Fine," she said. "I'll try and use my imagination."

"Right," Ziani said. He put her out of his mind—not easy to ignore something quite so large and so very red; it was like failing to notice a battle in your wardrobe—and engaged the plan. It had grown inside his head to the point where he could see it, quite clearly, with his eyes open, superimposed over the dusty, weed-grown yard like a cutter's template. "Well, where we're stood now, this is where the foundry's going to be."

"I see."

"The plan is to do all our own casting," Ziani went on. "Mostly it'll be just small components, but I'm going to build a fair-sized drop-bottom cupola so we can pour substantial lost-wax castings as well as the usual sandbox stuff. It sounds like a big undertaking, but really it's just four walls, a hearth, ventilation and a clay-lined pit. Next to it, so we can share some of the pipework, I want to have the puddling mill—"

"Excuse me?"

Ziani smiled. "For smelting direct from ore," he said. "Back home we can get sufficient heat to melt iron into a pourable liquid, but it'll be a while before I'm ready to do that here. Until then, we'll have to do it the old-fashioned labor-intensive way. The best we'll be able to do is get the iron out of the ore and into a soft, malleable lump—that's called puddling. Then it's got to be bashed on with big hammers to draw it out into the sections we want: sheet, plate, square bar, round bar and so on. Quite high on the list of priorities is a big trip-hammer, so we won't actually have to do the bashing by hand, but we can't do that until we've got the water to drive it. Three months, maybe, assuming everything runs to schedule."

"Water?" the woman said.

"That's right. Like a water-mill for grinding flour. The first big mechanical project will need to be a pump—wind-driven, God help us—to get water up in a tower to a sufficient height. Once we've done that, life will be a lot easier."

She stared at him for a moment, then shrugged. "Right," she said. "Go on."

"Over here," Ziani continued, "I want the main machine shop—it makes sense to have the shop right next to the foundry and the smelting area, it saves on time and labor hauling big, heavy chunks of material about the place. So basically we'll have a big open square area, for fabrication and assembly; the machine shop on the north side, foundry and smelter on the south side, main forge on the east, I thought, because we don't need the light there so much . . ."

He knew it was all passing her by, soaring over her head like the white-fronted geese in spring. He was a little surprised by that; a trader ought to be able to understand technical matters, well enough at least to grasp the implications: that this was an enterprise on an unprecedented scale, never seen outside the Republic; an astounding opportunity, therefore, for anybody with an instinct for business. She didn't seem to have picked up on that. She was bored. She looked as if she was being introduced to his large, tiresome family, none of whom she'd ever meet again, not if she could help it. Annoying, he thought; can she really be the person in charge, or had they just sent down a junior?

But he didn't mind giving her the tour of his hidden realm (wasn't there a fairy tale about a magical land that only the pure in heart could see?); saying it out loud helped him make it ever more solid in his own mind, gave him another chance to pick up any flaws or omissions that had slipped past him. He was, as usual, talking to himself for the benefit of an eavesdropper.

"And that," he concluded, "is all there is to it, more or less. So, what do you think?"

She was silent, frowning. Then she said, "Fine. Just one thing."

"What's that?"

"You haven't actually said what you're planning on making here."

"But—" Stupid woman, hadn't she been listening? No, he realized, she hadn't. He'd assumed she'd be able to work that out for herself. Apparently not. "Pretty much anything, really," he said. "If it's made of metal, of course. Anything from a siege catapult to an earring back."

"Really." The look in her eyes said, *You still haven't answered my question.*

"Furthermore," Ziani went on, "and this is the real point of it, we can make machines that'll make anything at all: pottery, cloth, furniture, glass, you name it. What's more, it'll be made to Mezentine standards, faster and cheaper than anywhere else in the world, and every single item will be exactly the same as all the others. Can you begin to understand what that'll mean?"

He had an idea that she was struggling to keep her temper. "That's fine," she said. "I'm impressed, truly I am. But you haven't told me what you're planning to *make*. I need something I can load in the back of a cart and sell. All you've shown me is a derelict yard with thistles growing in it."

Ziani took a deep breath. "You don't quite understand," he said. "Here's the idea. You tell me what you want; what you think you can sell a thousand of, at a good profit. Anything you like. Then you go away and come back a bit later, and there it'll be. Anything you like."

The look she was giving him now was quite different. She'd stopped thinking he was boring. Now she thought he was mad. If only, he thought, I had something I could actually show her, some little piece of Mezentine magic like a lathe or a drill, so she could see for herself. But it didn't work like that.

She was saying something; he pulled himself together and paid attention.

"When you were back in Mezentia," she said. "That place where you used to work. What did you make there?"

Ziani grinned. "Weapons," he said.

She looked at him. The final straw, obviously. "Like those machines they killed our army with?"

He nodded. "The scorpion," he said. "Lightweight, mobile field artillery. We built twelve hundred units while I was at the ordnance factory. They used to leave the production line at the rate of a dozen a day." He couldn't read the expression on her face, which was unusual. "Quite a straightforward item, in engineering terms," he went on, filling time. "Tempering the spring was the only tricky bit, and we figured out a quick, easy way of doing that. Machining the winding mechanism—"

"Why don't you make them?" she asked, and he thought she was probably thinking aloud. "Orsea'd buy them from you, no doubt about that."

Ziani shrugged. "If he could afford them," he said. "It's a question of setting up. It'd take a long time before the first one was finished, and in the meantime there'd be workers and material to pay for. I was thinking of something nice and simple to begin with. Spoons, maybe, or dungforks. We'd have to start off doing a lot of the operations by hand, till we'd made enough money to pay for building the more advanced machines."

She shook her head. "Orsea doesn't want spoons," she said. "And nobody else in this country's got any money—not the sort of money you're thinking of. These are poor people, by your standards."

"I know," Ziani said. "That's—" He stopped. She wasn't invited into that part of the plan; it wasn't in a fit state to receive visitors yet. "What would you suggest?" he said.

"Make weapons," she told him, without hesitation. "Orsea would buy them, he'd give you the money, if you could show him a finished—what's the word?"

"Prototype."

"That's it. If you had one he could see. He'd feel he had to buy them, to make up for losing the war and putting us all in danger." She hesitated, then went on. "We'd put up the money to make the first one, in return for a share in the profits."

"You're forgetting," Ziani said. "I offered to work for him. He turned me down."

She shook her head. "I know all about that," she said. "You just went at it from the wrong angle; head on, bull-at-a-gate. You've got to be more like twiddling a bit of string under a cat's nose. You get Orsea up here and show him one of these scorpion machines, tell him, this is what wiped out your army, how many of them do you want; he wouldn't be able to refuse." She frowned thoughtfully. "Then you could give him your speech, the one you gave me: furnaces and trip-hammers and piddling mills—"

"Puddling."

"Whatever. He wouldn't be listening, of course. He'd be looking at the war machine. And then he'd say yes."

Ziani nodded slowly. "And you, your Merchant Adventurers, would put up the money."

"Yes. Within reason," she added quickly. "For just one. You can make just one without all the machinery and everything?"

"I could," Ziani said. "Hand forging and filing, it'd be a bit of a bodge-up. But I don't suppose your Duke Orsea would know what he was looking at."

"So long as it worked," she replied. She took a deep breath. "So," she went on, "roughly how much are we talking about?"

She couldn't hear it, of course, the soft click of the component dropping into place. Ziani kept the smile off his face, and answered her question. As he'd expected, she looked rather unwell for a moment; then she said, "All right." After that, they talked about timescales and materials and money for a while; then she went away. She was looking tired, Ziani reckoned, as though she was carrying a heavy weight.

He went back to the tower after she'd gone. There was something about it that appealed to him; the view, perhaps, or the confined nature of the space, maybe just the fact that it was a comfortable temperature in the fierce midday heat. In an hour or so, when it was cool enough for work, the builders would be arriving to start work on the footings for the foundry house. Something tangible, even if it was only a hole in the flagstones, a pile of sand, a stack of bricks: something he could see with his eyes rather than just his mind, to confirm that the design was starting to take shape.

Starting; there was still a long way to go. The factory, the Duke's involvement, making scorpions, all the individual components that were also intricate mechanisms in themselves; if only, he couldn't help thinking, all this inventiveness and ingenuity could be spent on something truly worthwhile, such as a modified dividing head for the vertical mills at the ordnance factory in Mezentia; if only his talent could be used for something other than abomination.

He'd heard a story once; about the old days, the very early days of the Guilds, before the Specifications were drawn up and the world was made fixed. Once, according to the story, there lived in the City a great engineer, who worked in the first of the new-style factories as a toolmaker. One day there was a terrible accident with one of the machines, and he lost both his hands. It happened that he was much afflicted by an itch in the middle of his back, something he'd lived with for years. Without hands, he couldn't scratch; so he summoned his two ablest assistants and with their help designed and built a machine, operated by the feet, which would scratch his back for him. It was frighteningly complicated, and in the process of getting it to work he thought up and perfected a number of mechanical innovations (the universal joint, according to some versions of the story; or the ratchet and escapement). When it was finished, all the cleverest designers in the Guild came to look at it. They were filled with admiration, and praised him for his skill and cunning. "Yes," he replied sadly, "that's all very well; but I'd much rather use my hand, like I did before."

All that invention and application, to make a machine to do a task a small child could do without thinking; there was undoubtedly a lesson there (all stories from the old days had morals, it was practically a legal requirement) but he'd never been sure till quite recently what it was. Now of course he knew, but that wasn't really much comfort to him.

When the men eventually showed up—the Eremian nation had many virtues, of which punctuality wasn't one—he went down to show them what to do and where to do it, then escaped back to his tower, the shade and the coolness of the massive stone blocks it was built from. He should have been down below—he had work to do, a machine to build, he ought by rights to be alive again, not a ghost haunting himself—but there were issues to be resolved before he could apply an uncluttered mind to the serious business of cutting and bending steel. He summoned a general parliament of his thoughts, and put the motion to be debated.

It could be argued (he opened, for the prosecution) that he'd come a long way—away from the ordnance factory, the City, his home. Now he was in a place that was in many respects unsatisfactory, but which he could survive in, more or less. It might be hard to live here, but he could work, which was what really mattered. So long as he could work, he could exist. In a tenuous sort of a way (but the only one that mattered) he could be happy. A proverb says that the beating of the heart and the action of the lungs are a useful prevarication, keeping all options open. He'd lost everything he'd ever had, but he was still on his feet, able to move, able to scribe a line and hold a file. The world hadn't ended, the day they came for him—Compliance, with their writ and their investigating officer and the armed men from the Guildhall. Now he was here, and there wasn't any real need (was there?) to build and set in motion the enormous machine that so far existed only in his mind. He was here; he could stay here, settle down, start a business. A lot of people did that, lesser men than himself. So could he.

But (replied the defense) he could only do this if he was still, at heart, the man he'd been the day before they came for him. If leaving there and coming here had changed him, *damaged* him (that was what he was getting at, surely), then the absolute priority must be to put the damage right; and only the machine could do that.

Query (the prosecution rejoined) the motivation behind the machine. Consider the man in the story; did he build his machine just to scratch his back, or because he was an engineer, because he *could?* Consider himself; was the purpose of the machine as simple, small and pure as he wanted this court to believe, or was it something darker and vaguer? An inevitable result of engaging the machine would be the end of the world; he'd admitted and regretted it as an unavoidable piece of collateral damage, but what if it was really his principal motive? What if he was building the machine out of a desire to punish them, or (punishment sublimated) to destroy an evil? What if the real reason for the machine was just revenge?

What nonsense (the defense replied). He could only desire revenge against the Republic if he hated it, and he didn't; nor did he want to change it, except in one very small way. He had no quarrel with the Guilds, or Specification, or anything big and important; the constitution, operating procedures and internal structures were as near perfect as they could be, given that the Republic was built from fallible human flesh rather than reliable materials like stone and steel. One small adjustment was all he was after; a little thing, a trifle, something a fourth-level clerk in Central Office could grant with a pen-stroke. It was only because he was out here, outside, unable to follow the ordained procedure, that he had need to resort to the machine. Since his exclusion wasn't his fault, the damage the machine would do wouldn't be his fault either. It was a shame that it had to be done this way, but that one little adjustment wasn't negotiable. He had to have it; and if it meant the end of the world, that wasn't his problem.

I've changed, he recognized. *Something has happened to me. I never used to be like this. On the other hand, I was never in this situation before. Maybe I've simply grown to fit, rather than changed.*

Nevertheless; the machine, the overthrow of nations, the deaths of thousands, hundreds of thousands of people, just so I can scratch my itching back; I have to ask myself whether it's justified.

He thought about it, and the little thing he wanted to achieve; and he realized that the debate was irrelevant. He had no choice, as far as the little thing was concerned. He could no more turn his back on it than a stone dropped from a tower could refrain from falling. Most men, desiring this thing, wouldn't build the machine, but only because they wouldn't know how to. He knew; so he had to build it. He couldn't pretend it was beyond him, because he knew it wasn't. The little thing—the most powerful, destructive force in the world, the cause of all true suffering, the one thing everybody wants most of all—was pulling on him like the force that pulls the falling stone, and there was nothing he could do to resist it.

Debate adjourned.

He stood up; his back was slightly stiff, from leaning up against the wall as he squatted on the tower floor. He narrowed the focus of his mind, crowding out the bigger picture until all he could see was the frame, cycle parts and mechanism of a scorpion. First, he said to himself, I'll need thirty-two feet of half-inch square section steel bar...

Valens Valentinianus to Veatriz Sirupati, greetings.

I have read your letter.

I know what you want; you want me to tell you how sympathetic I feel, how I know how difficult it must be for you, how brave you're being, how awful it is, you poor thing. I'd really like to be able to oblige, but that's not how my mind works, unfortunately. I read your letter, and at once I start thinking about ways and means; things you could do, things I could do, things to be taken account of in deciding what's the best thing to be done. Only a few lines in, and already I have a mind full of things.

Which is the difference between you and me. You live in a world of people, I live in a world of things. To you, what

matters is thoughts, feelings, love and hurt and pain and distress, with joy squeezing in wherever it can, in little cracks,
like light; in small observations, which you are kind enough
to share with me. I, on the other hand, was brought up by
my vicious bastard of a father to play chess with my life; a
piece, a thing, manipulated here and there to bring about a
desired result; an action taken, a move made, and I get what
I want—the wolf driven into the net, the boar enfiladed by
archers in covert, the enemy driven off with heavy losses,
the famine averted, the nation saved. When I was a boy—
when all men were boys, they lived from one toy to the next,
their lives were charted out by a relay of things longed for (a
new bow, a new horse, a new doublet, a new girl, an education, enlightenment, a crown), laid out alongside the desert
road like way-stations to get you home at last to wherever it is
you're supposed to be going.

I've always lived for things; some of them I can touch,
some of them are abstracts (glory, honor, justice, prosperity, peace); all of them are beads on a wire with which to
tally the score. I have, of course, never married; and it's a
very long time now since I was last in love. Accordingly, I've
never brutalized myself by turning love into another thing-
to-be-acquired (I've brutalized myself in lots of other ways,
mind you, but not that one); so there's a sort of virginal innocence about me when I read your letter, and instantly start
translating your feelings into my list-of-things-to-be-done,
the way bankers convert one currency into another.

Put it another way. Having read your letter, I'm bursting like a cracked dam with suggestions about how to make
things better. But, because I am more than the sum of my
upbringing and environment, I am managing, just about,
not to. Congratulate me.

You poor thing. It sounds absolutely awful. I feel for you.

The trouble is, when I write that, I mean it; buggered if
I know how to say it so it sounds sincere. When I was a boy

I learned hunting, fencing and how to rule a small country. Self-expression was optional, and I took self-pity instead. It was more boring, but I liked the teacher better.

Poor Orsea. I wish he and I weren't enemies; in fact, I have an idea that we'd have got on well together, if we'd met many years ago, and all the things had been different. He and I are very different; opposites, in most respects. I think I would have liked him. I believe he can see beyond things to people; it's a blessing to him, and a curse. If he plays chess and sacrifices a knight to gain a winning advantage, I expect he can hear the knight scream as it dies. There are many wonderful uses in this world for a man like him; it's a pity he was forced into the wrong one.

We took out the new lymers today; we found in the long cover, ran the boar out onto the downs, finally killed in a little spinney, where he turned at bay. I ran in as soon as he stopped running and turned his head; I was so concerned about the dogs not getting hurt (because I've only just got them; they're my newest things, you see) that I went at the boar front-on, just me; staring into his eyes, with nothing between us except eight feet of ash pole with a spike on the end. As he charged, he hated me; because he hated me, he charged; because he charged, he lost. I'm not strong enough to drive a spearblade through all that hide, muscle and bone, but he is. His hate was his undoing, so it served him right. The hunter never hates his quarry; it's a thing which he wants to get, to reduce into possession, so how could he hate it? The boar only hated me because he recognized he'd been manipulated into an impossible situation, where he couldn't win or survive. I can understand that. I made him hate me; but hate is unforgivable, so it served him right. It was my fault that he was brought to bay, but he was responsible for his own undoing. I think. It's hard to be sure. I think it's the gray areas that I find most satisfying.

(Molyttus, too, used the hunt as an allegory for human

passions and feelings. Strictly speaking, he was more a neo-
Mannerist than a Romantic, I feel, but that's a largely subjective judgment.)

Poor Orsea. I feel for him, too. If there's anything you'd
like me to do, just say.

That made the tenth time he'd read it, and it still said the same.

Miel folded the letter up again and put it back in the chest; he
turned the key, took it out, put it away. There, now; nobody but
he knew where it was, or even that it existed (but he could feel
it, through an inch of oak, as though it was watching him and
grinning).

A sensible man would burn it, he told himself. Get rid of it, pretend he'd never seen it, wipe it out of his life and hope it'd go away
forever. That was what a sensible man would do.

He went down the stairs and walked briskly to the long solar,
where Orsea would be waiting for him. His clothes felt clammy
against his skin, and his hands itched where he'd touched the
parchment.

"Miel." Orsea was sitting in a big chair with broad, flat arms;
he had his feet up on a table, and he was reading a book.

"Sorry I'm late."

"You aren't." Orsea put the book face down on his knee.
"Against an unarmored opponent, the common pitchfork is a
more effective weapon than a conventional spear; discuss."

Miel raised both eyebrows. "Good heavens," he said, "let me
think. Well, you've got the advantage of the bit in the middle, I
suppose, where the two arms of the fork join; you can use it for
blocking against a sword or an axe, or binding and jamming a
spear or a halberd. Or you could use it to trap the other man
by the neck without injuring him." He paused; Orsea was still
looking at him. "You can't overpenetrate, because the fork stops
you going too far in, so you can disengage quicker. How'm I
doing?"

Orsea nodded. "This man here," he said, waggling the book,

"reckons the pitchfork is the ideal weapon for hastily levied troops in time of emergency. Actually, he's full of bright ideas; for instance, there's the triple-armed man."

"A man with three arms?"

"No." Orsea shook his head. "It's like this. You've got your bow and arrow, right? Strapped to your left wrist—which is extended holding the bow—you've got your pike. Finally, you've got your sword at your side, if all else fails. Or there's a really good one here; you've got your heavy siege catapults drawn up behind your infantry line, and instead of rocks you load them with poisonous snakes. As soon as the enemy charge, you let go, and down come the snakes like a heavy shower."

Miel frowned. "Who is this clown?"

Orsea lifted the book so Miel could see the spine. "His name," Orsea said, "isn't actually recorded; it just says, *A Treatise on the National Defense, by a Patriot.*" He held the book out at arm's length and let it fall to the floor. "The snake idea is particularly silly," he said. "I can see it now; you spend a year poking round under rocks to find all these snakes, you pack them up in jars or wicker baskets or whatever you keep snakes in; you've got special snake-wardens, hired at fabulous expense, and a separate wagon train to carry them, plus all their food and fresh water and God knows what else; somehow or other you get them to the battle, along with two dozen huge great catapults, which you've somehow contrived to lug through the mountain passes without smashing them to splinters; you wind back the catapults and you're all ready, the enemy's about to charge, so you give the order, break out the snakes; so they open up the jars, and find all the snakes have died in the night, just to spite you." He sighed. "I won't tell you what he said about the military uses of honey. It's one of those things that gets inside your head and lies dormant for a while, and then you go mad."

Miel shrugged. "Why are you wasting your time with this stuff?" he said.

"Desperation, I think," Orsea replied. "I asked the librarian to look out anything he could find that looked like a military manual or textbook. So far, that was the pick of the bunch."

Miel frowned. "The spy business," he said. "You're worried they're planning to invade."

"Yes," Orsea said. "It's the only explanation that makes any sense. Say what you like about the Republic, they don't waste money. If they're spying on us, it must mean they're planning an attack. And when it comes, we don't stand a chance."

Miel shifted slightly. "There are other explanations," he said. "We've been through all this."

Orsea slid his face between his hands. "There ought to be something we could do," he said. "I know this sounds really stupid, but I've got this horrible picture in my mind; one of those fancy illuminated histories, where you get charts of kings and queens; and there's one that says, 'The Dukes of Eremia,' and there's all the names, with dates and who they married, and right at the bottom, there's me: Orsea Orseolus, and nothing to follow. I hate the thought that it's all going to end with me, and all because—"

"Pull yourself together, for God's sake," Miel said. He hadn't meant to say it so loud. Orsea looked up at him. "I'm sorry," he said.

"Don't worry about it," Orsea said wearily. "Maybe you're right. Maybe we can still get out of this in one piece. But if we don't, whose fault will it be? I can't seem to get past that, somehow."

Miel took a deep breath, and let it go slowly. "Think about it, will you?" he said. "Like you said yourself, the Mezentines don't waste money. We aren't a threat to them, not now; it'd take a fortune in money and God knows how many lives to take the city. They aren't going to do it. What would it achieve for them, apart from wiping out thousands of customers for all that useless junk they churn out?"

But Orsea shook his head. "This isn't what we were going to talk about," he said.

"No, it isn't." Miel tried to recall what the meeting was supposed to deal with. "Ambassadors from the Cure Hardy," he remembered. "Arriving some time next week."

"Yes," Orsea replied. "Well, they're early. Turned up this morning. Suddenly appeared out of nowhere, according to Cerba."

"Who?"

Slight frown. "Cerba Phocas, the warden of the southern zone. Your second cousin."

Miel shrugged. Practically everybody above the rank of captain was his second cousin. "Right," he said. "Sorry, you were saying. Hang on, though—"

"In fact," Orsea continued, "one of his patrols took them for bandits and arrested them, which is a great way to start a diplomatic relationship."

Don't laugh, Miel ordered himself. "Well, at least it shows our border security's up to scratch," he said. "But what were they doing on Cerba's patch? I thought they'd be coming up the Lonazep road."

"Don't ask me," Orsea said, standing up. "I suppose they must've wandered off the road and got lost. I don't think it'd be tactful to ask them. Anyhow, I've rescheduled the meeting for just after early vespers; we can go straight in to dinner as soon as it's over. God knows what we're going to give them to eat."

They discussed the agenda for the meeting for a while. Miel did his best without being too obvious about it, but Orsea refused to cheer up. A pity; establishing proper grown-up diplomatic relations with the Cure Hardy was easily the biggest success of Orsea's reign so far, and he'd mostly brought it about by his own efforts; choosing and sending presents, writing letters, refusing to be put off by the lack of a reply or even the disappearance of his messengers. Also, Miel couldn't help thinking (though he'd made himself promise not to entertain such thoughts), if the Republic actually was considering an invasion of Eremia, a rapprochement with their barbarous southern neighbors couldn't come at a better time. Given the Mezentines' paranoia about the Cure Hardy, it wouldn't take much in the way of dark hints and artful suggestion to persuade them that Orsea had concluded an offensive and defensive alliance with the savages, and that war with Eremia would open the door to limitless hordes of Cure Hardy tribesmen, poised to flood down out of the mountains like volcanic lava. That alone might be enough to avert an invasion, provided that the Mezentines didn't think too long or too hard about how such hordes might be expected to cross the uncrossable desert.

As soon as he could get away without being rude, Miel left the long solar and crossed the quadrangle to the east apartments. At least, he thought, the Cure Hardy had taken his mind off the letter for a while.

"It's all right," Miel whispered to Orsea, as they took their seats in the lesser day-chamber, behind a table the size of a castle door. "I sent the kitchen steward to the market, and he bought up all the game he could find: venison, boar, hare, mountain goat, you name it. Also, he's doing roast mutton, guinea fowl, peahen and rabbit in cider. There's got to be something in that lot they'll eat."

"Marvelous," Orsea said. "And plenty of booze too, I hope."

Miel shuddered slightly. "Enough to float a coal barge. Wine, beer, porter, mead, cider…"

"Then we should be all right," Orsea said, with a faint sigh of relief. "At least something'll go right. Are you nervous?"

"Petrified."

"Same here. Right, we'd better have them in and take a look at them."

Miel nodded to the chamberlain, who slid noiselessly away and returned with the fascinating, exotic guests. Miel and Orsea stood up; Miel bowed slightly, Orsea nodded.

There were five of them. Miel's first impression was simple surprise. He'd been expecting—what, savages in animal skins with rings through their eyebrows, something like that. Instead, he saw five old men in identical plain brown robes, loose at the neck and full in the sleeve, some kind of coarse wool; they had sandals on their feet, and rather splendid silk sashes round their waists. Their faces reminded him irresistibly of hawks, on the bow-perch in a mews; the same bright, round eyes, the stillness of the head, the set expression. All five of their faces were tanned and deeply lined; they all wore short white beards, and their hair was cropped close; one of them was bald, with a slightly pointed head. They bowed too; if pressed, Miel would have said they were trying to copy their hosts' manner of greeting.

Translator, he thought. *We need a translator, or how the hell are we going to understand each other?*

While he was cursing himself for overlooking this vital point, the bald man cleared his throat with a soft cough and said, "Thank you for agreeing to see us." His pronunciation was excellent received Mezentine; his voice deep, his accent noticeable but not in the least intrusive. He had a little stub of a nose and small, almost translucent ears. "We apologize," he went on, "for arriving early; we had already embarked on our journey when our guide pointed out to us a more direct road, which we followed. We hope we have not inconvenienced you."

"Not at all." Orsea was sounding nervously cheerful; at least, Miel could construe nerves in his tone of voice. He'd known Orsea too long to be able to judge whether anybody else would pick up on it. The savages didn't seem at all apprehensive, as though they did this sort of thing every day before breakfast. "We're delighted to meet you, and thank you for coming. My name is Orsea Orseolus, and this is my adviser Miel Ducas."

The bald man dipped his head, and recited his name and those of his colleagues. They slipped through Miel's mind like eels, but he'd never been good with names; he fancied the bald man was called something like Carlaregion; he didn't have a clue what it'd look like written down.

Orsea bowed again; they bowed back. Orsea tried some vague gestures to get them to sit down, which eventually they did. Something about the chairs bothered them, but they didn't say anything.

"Perhaps," the bald man said, "we should get down to business. You would like to establish a formal diplomatic mission to the Biau Votz."

Miel blinked. Surely they hadn't got the wrong savages, after all? Or was Biau whatsit the name of their capital city; except nomads don't have cities. In that case, what was the whatever he'd just said? Some name they called their leader?

Orsea said, "Yes, absolutely." Miel knew he was confused too, and trying hard not to show it. Was one of the savages smiling?

"We would, of course, be happy to forge this historic link," the bald man went on. "However, there are various issues that we should perhaps address at this stage; matters you may not be aware of, which might influence your decision. If you have already considered these points, please forgive us."

He paused. Really, Miel thought, they're far more polite than I expected. "Please go on," Orsea said. The bald man nodded, then looked at the man on his left, who said: "We must confess, we are a little puzzled why you should have chosen us, rather than, say, the Flos Glaia or the Lauzeta. Not that we do not appreciate the honor of being the first sect of the Cure Hardy to open a dialogue with your people; but our circuit brings us to the edge of the desert only once every twenty years, and in the interim we spend most of our time in the Culomb and Rosinholet valleys—by our calculations, some eight hundred miles from the nearest point on your border. With the best will in the world, communications between us and yourselves would be difficult. We should point out that the sects through whose circuits your envoys would need to pass are nearly all hostile to us, and accordingly we would not be able to guarantee their safety outside our own circuit. Furthermore," the man went on, frowning slightly, "although naturally we have only a sketchy and incomplete knowledge of your economic position, we have to ask whether any regular trade between yourselves and us would be worth the effort. The cost of transporting bulk foodstuffs, for example, would be prohibitive; likewise heavy goods such as metal ores or timber. As for luxury goods..."

Sects, Miel thought; he must mean tribes, something like that. We thought the Cure Hardy were all one tribe, but maybe there's loads of them, all different; and we've picked the wrong one.

"Your points are well made," Orsea was saying; the savage had stopped talking, there had been a brief, brittle silence. "However, I must confess, we hadn't really thought as far ahead as trade and so on. Really, all we're trying to do at this stage is, well, get to know each other. One step at a time is what I'm getting at."

"Of course." The savage nodded very slightly. "Forgive us if we were unduly forward. Naturally, we welcome any overtures of friendship, and of course our two nations have much to offer each other above and beyond mere material commerce. In any event, we have clarified the position as far as we are concerned."

As the afternoon wore on, Miel found it increasingly hard to concentrate. Reading between the lines, he was fairly certain that his earlier guess had been right; there were any number of different tribes of Cure Hardy, and they'd somehow managed to get in touch with the wrong one. That was annoying, to say the least, but the thing needn't be a complete disaster. If they were tactful and managed not to give too much away, they ought at the very least to be able to get some useful background information, enough to help them figure out which tribe they really wanted to talk to. From what he'd managed to glean so far, Miel thought either the Lauzeta or the Aram Chantat—although, confusingly, the Lauzeta were apparently mortal enemies of the Biau Votz, the Aram Chantat hated the Lauzeta like poison (not, as far as he could make out, vice versa), and both the Biau Votz and the Aram Chantat were best friends with the Rosinholet, who hated everybody else in the whole world. It might, Miel decided, be a good idea to find out a whole lot more before venturing on any serious diplomatic initiatives.

At least the invitation to dinner went down well. At the mention of food, the savages became quite animated, and one of them even smiled. A good feed and a few drinks might liven them up a bit, Miel thought, loosen their tongues and get them to relax a little. So far they'd been so stiff and formal that he wondered if they were really savages at all.

"May we venture to ask," one of them was saying as they made their way to the great hall, "how matters stand between yourselves and the Republic of Mezentia? Our own relations with the Mezentines have been few and perfunctory, but cordial nonetheless."

Miel didn't manage to hear Orsea's reply to that, because at that moment the bald man asked him something about Eremian horse-breeding. Apparently, the horses he'd seen since he crossed the border were quite like the ones back home, which were different from the horses raised by most of the other sects. Miel answered as best he could, but he didn't know the technical stuff the bald man seemed to be after. He tried to remember if his cousin Jarnac had been invited to the dinner; he'd know all about it, if he was there. Meanwhile, the bald man was telling him a lot of stuff he didn't really want to know about horse-breeding back home; he let his attention wander as they crossed the front courtyard, until the bald man said, "Of course, we are only a small sect, we muster barely nine hundred thousand men-at-arms, and so our pool of brood mares is far smaller than that of the larger sects, such as the Lauzeta or the Doce Votz—"

"Excuse me," Miel said. "Did you say nine hundred thousand?"

The bald man nodded. "It is our small size that enables us to follow such a wide circuit. The larger sects are confined to more circumscribed areas, since they need to graze eight, even ten times that number. We can subsist, therefore, where they cannot, and they are not tempted to appropriate our grazing, since it would be of no use to them. Accordingly—"

"This is the great hall," Orsea interrupted. "If you'd like to follow me."

There was something vaguely comic about the savages' reaction to being inside it; from time to time, when they thought no one was looking, they'd crane their necks and snatch a quick look at the roof-beams, as if they were worried it was all about to come crashing down on their heads. Fair enough, Miel reckoned, if they lived their entire lives in tents. If anything else about their surroundings impressed them, they gave no sign of it, and that made Miel wonder if their ingenuous remarks about their few but cordial contacts with the Republic were the truth and the whole truth. They'd be forgiven for regarding the great hall of the castle as no big deal if they were familiar with the interior of the Guild-hall...

Before Miel took his place at the table, he made a show of beck-oning to the hall steward. When the man came over to him, he leaned in close and whispered, "Get me something to write on." Luckily, the steward knew him well enough not to argue; he dis-appeared and came back a moment later with a dripping pen and a scrap of parchment, hastily cut from the wrapping of a Low-land cheese. Resting against the wall, Miel scribbled, *Orsea, there are millions of them.* "Give this to the Duke when the guests aren't looking," he muttered to the steward; then he sat down next to the bald man.

"This is a most impressive building," the bald man said, with-out much sincerity. "Are the cross-pieces of the roof each made from a single tree, or are they spliced together in some way?"

Miel had no idea, but he said, "A single tree, they were brought in specially from the north," because he reckoned that was what the man would want to hear. Maybe it was; he didn't pursue the subject further. Instead, he asked what sort of timber the table was made out of. Miel didn't know that either, so he said it was oak; at which point, the servers started bringing in the food.

"We have a serious shortage of timber," the bald man said. "Traditionally, we cut lumber from the forests of the Culomb val-ley in the seventh year of our circuit. Recently, however, the Doce Votz have laid claim to that part of the valley and forbidden us to fell any standing timber. This leaves us in an unfortunate position. Dogwood, hazel and ash, in particular..."

Miel nodded politely, while scanning the incoming dishes. The steward had done a good job at short notice. As well as the veni-son, boar, hare, mountain goat, roast mutton, guinea fowl, peahen and rabbit in cider, there was partridge, rock grouse (just coming into season), collar dove and whole roast goose. He nodded to the steward, who nodded to the servers.

"Excuse me," said the bald man. He looked embarrassed. So did his colleagues. "Excuse me," he repeated, "but we do not eat meat."

"But—" Orsea said; then he checked himself, and went on: "What can we get for you?"

"Some cheese, perhaps." The bald man stressed the word, as if he wasn't sure his hosts had ever heard of it. "And some plain bread and fruit, if possible."

"Of course." Credit where it was due, Orsea was taking it in his stride. "What would you like to drink? We've got wine, beer—"

Just a trace of a frown. "We do not drink intoxicants," the bald man said. "Plain water would suit us very well."

"Plain water," Orsea repeated. "Fine." He waved to the steward, and said, "Take all this away, fetch us some bread and cheese, apples and some jugs of water."

"Certainly, sir," the steward said, and handed him the scrap of parchment. Miel wasn't sure, because the bald man partly obstructed his view, but he had an idea that Orsea flinched when he read it. He dropped it beside his plate. Some time later, Miel noticed, while Orsea was talking to the man on his other side, the savage quietly picked it up, glanced at it and tucked it into his sleeve.

The dinner didn't last long, since there wasn't much to eat and the visitors didn't care for music or dancing, either. Orsea himself took them to their quarters, allowing Miel to escape from the great hall and beat a hasty retreat to the security of his office, the main attraction of which was a tall stone bottle of the distilled liquor the Vadani made from mountain oats. It went by the curious name of Living Death, and Miel reckoned it was probably the only thing in the world that might do some good.

He'd swallowed three fingers of the stuff and was nerving himself for another dose when Orsea came in, without knocking; he crossed to the empty chair, dropped into it like a headshot doe, and groaned.

"Come in," Miel said. "Take a seat."

"Thanks," Orsea replied. "Miel, have you still got any of that disgusting Vadani stuff that tastes like etching acid?"

Miel pushed the small horn cup across the table; he was a loyal subject, and could drink straight from the bottle when he had to.

"I'm fairly sure," Orsea said slowly, after he'd taken his medicine, "that there wasn't anything else we could've got wrong; I mean, as far as I can see, we've got the complete set. If I missed anything, though, we could have a stab at it tomorrow morning early, before they set off."

Miel thought for a moment. "We didn't actually kill any of them," he said, "or set fire to their hair."

"True." Orsea leaned forward and reached for the bottle. "But that'd just be gilding the lily. We did enough, I reckon."

"It didn't go well."

"Not really." Orsea passed the bottle back, and they sat in silence for a while.

"What bugs me, though," Miel said, "is why they came up from the south, instead of down the Lonazep road." He had a certain amount of trouble with the word Lonazep. "It's all very well saying they got lost, but they were early. If they'd got lost, they should've been late."

"Wish they had got lost," Orsea said. "Permanently."

Another silence; then Miel said: "Well, now we know what the Cure Hardy look like."

"Miserable lot," Orsea said. "Always complaining. Didn't like their rooms much, either. Oh, they didn't say anything, but I could tell."

Miel suggested various things they could do. "And besides," he went on, "it doesn't actually matter, does it? You heard them. Won't be back this way for another twenty years. By which time," he added brightly, "we'll all've been massacred by the Mezentines."

"There's that," Orsea conceded. "No, I won't, thanks," he said, as Miel threatened him with the bottle. "Got to be up early to-morrow to see 'em off, don't forget, and I'd hate for us to give a bad impression."

"One thing," Miel remembered. "That bald man. He asked me if we could sell them some wood."

Orsea frowned, as if the concept was unfamiliar to him. "Wood."

"That's right. For immediate delivery, before they move out of range. Dogwood, cornel wood, ash, hazel. Willing to pay top thaler for quality merchandise."

"Well, he's out of luck," Orsea said. "Besides, after the way they behaved, I wouldn't sell them wood if they were the last men on earth. Screw them, in fact."

"Absolutely." Miel thought for a bit, but all the edges were getting blurred. "What's dogwood?" he asked.

"No idea."

"Doesn't matter." Miel waved away dogwood in perpetuity. "Sure you won't have another?"

"Revolting stuff. Just a taste, then."

Just a taste was all that was left in the bottle; odd, Miel thought, because it was nearly full a moment ago. Evaporation, maybe. "I'll say this for them," he said, "if I hadn't known they were savages, I'd never have guessed."

Orsea concentrated. "Insidious," he said. "Get under your guard pretending to be not savage." He looked at the tips of his fingers for a long minute, then said: "So let's get this straight. Nearest to our border are the Doce Votz. Next to them are the Rosinholet."

Miel shook his head; an interesting experience. "No, you're wrong," he said. "Next to the Doce Votz you've got the Lauzeta. Next to them's the Aram Chantat."

"The Aram Chantat? You sure?"

Miel shrugged. "Something like that. Anyhow, now we know what they're like, these barbarians—"

"No meat. And no drink."

"Exactly. Now we know what they're like, we can talk to them. Bloody useful initiative. Good men to have on your side in a fight, I bet."

For some reason, Orsea thought that was terribly funny. So, after a moment, did Miel. "No, but seriously," Miel went on. "If only we knew why they didn't come up the Lonzanep road—"

"Lonazep."

"That too. Can't figure that out. Bloody great big desert in the way if you're coming from that direction. Should've starved and parched ten times over before they got here."

"Oh, I don't know," Orsea objected. "I mean, they don't eat a lot, or drink." He reached for the bottle, just in case there was a drop lurking inside it somewhere, and knocked it off the table onto the floor. "Bloody Vadani," he said. "Can't even make a bottle that stands upright."

Not long after that he fell asleep. Miel, who knew about protocol, struggled to his feet, called a page and had him carried back to his apartments; then he flopped back into his chair and closed his eyes. That was one of the good things about not being a duke: he could grab forty winks in his chair without having to be carried home like a drunk.

Someone he didn't know woke him up in his chair the next morning with a message from Orsea. The Cure Hardy had gone home, the message said (Miel asked the stranger what time it was; just after noon, the man replied); the Duke's compliments, and it would've been nice if Miel could have been there to see them on their way. A little later, he found Orsea in the small rose garden and apologized. His head hurt and his digestion wasn't quite right—that was what came of eating bread and cheese for dinner, Orsea said—which probably explained why he forgot to tell Orsea about the letter. He considered mentioning it then and there, but decided not to.

Since he wasn't feeling his best, he reckoned he might as well go home. On his way, he ran into Sorit Calaphates, who thanked him for inviting him to meet the Cure Hardy at dinner. It was news to Miel that he'd done so, but he accepted the thanks in the spirit in which they were given.

"So," Miel said, "haven't seen you around much lately. Been busy?"

Calaphates nodded. "My new business venture," he said with a slight roll of the eyes. "I'm starting to wonder what I've got myself into."

"Remind me," Miel said.

"The Mezentine," Calaphates said. "You suggested it, remember?"

"Oh yes," Miel said. "Him. Going well?"

"You could say that," Calaphates muttered. "Going to cost me an absolute fortune by the time he's done. Still, clever man, can't deny that. This morning he was on about some new way of smelting iron ore; reckons it'll be better than how it's done in Mezentia, even. Anyway, that's what I need to talk to you about sometime. Not now," he added, because he was a reasonably perceptive man. "Later, when you've got a moment. I'll send my clerk, and he can fix up a time."

"Splendid," Miel said. "I'll look forward to that. So, what did you think of the savages?"

"Not what I'd been expecting," Calaphates admitted. "Quiet. Can't say I took to them."

"They've gone now," Miel said. "Still, we had some useful discussions."

Calaphates nodded. "Wonder what they'll make of the Merchant Adventurers," he said. "Don't suppose they've got anything like them back where they come from."

"Merchant Adventurers?" Miel repeated. "What've they got to do with anything?"

"The man I was talking to last night said they were meeting them this morning, on their way home. Didn't they mention it?"

"Possibly," Miel said. "Can't think why, though, they live too far away." He shrugged. He'd had enough of the Cure Hardy. "Can't do any harm," he said.

"Probably want to sell them something," Calaphates said, reasonably enough. "In which case, bloody good luck. Strange people, though. All those different tribes."

"Sects," Miel corrected.

"As you say, sects. The man I was talking to did try and explain, but I'm afraid I lost the thread. Apparently they're all descended from one tribe, but they split up hundreds of years ago over religious differences; they stopped believing in the religion long since, but they still keep up the differences. Charming, though, about the names."

"What about the names?" Miel asked.

"The names of the sects. Let's see." Calaphates' narrow forehead crinkled in thought. "Their lot, the Biau Votz; that means Beautiful Voice in their language. The Rosinholet are the Nightingales, the Aram Chantat are the Voices Raised in Song, the Flos Glaia are the Meadow Flowers or something of the sort, and so on. Apparently they believe that when they die, they're reborn as songbirds."

"Good heavens," Miel said, mildly stunned.

Calaphates nodded. "People are curious, aren't they? Well, I won't keep you." He dipped his head in formal salutation and scuttled away.

The Beautiful Voice and the Meadow Flowers . . . Miel gave that a great deal of thought on the way home, but in spite of his best endeavors he was unable to arrive at any meaningful conclusion.

12

"This," the foreman said, "is the main transmission house. Power for the whole machine shop comes from this one flywheel, which is driven by direct gearing from the big overshot waterwheel out back. This here is the main takeoff"—he pointed with his stick—"and that's the gear train that supplies the overhead shafts in the long gallery, where all the heavy lathes and mills are."

Falier Zenonis nodded and muttered, "Ah" for the twentieth time that morning. He knew it all already, of course, though he'd never actually seen it. But he'd spent a week laboriously working through the notes poor Ziani had made; notes, drawings, sketches, detail sketches, you couldn't fault Ziani on his thoroughness when it came to mechanisms. As a result, he knew his way round the machine shop better than his guide; like a blind man who's lived in the same house all his life. But even if Ziani's notes were strictly legal (which he doubted) he didn't want to draw attention to the fact that he'd read them, or known Ziani at all. So, "What does that thing there do?" he asked, though he knew perfectly well.

"That?" The foreman pointed. "That's clever. You just knock back the handle—there, look—and that disengages the main drive. It's a safety thing, mostly; someone gets his arm caught in a belt, you call up to the transmission house and they throw this lever, and the whole lot stops dead."

"I see," Falier replied, remembering to sound suitably impressed. "Do we get a lot of accidents?"

"Not really," the foreman replied. "Not when you consider how many people work here, and how much machinery we've got running. Obviously, from time to time someone's going to get careless, there's nothing anybody can do to stop it happening. But you can cut down the risk with the right shift rotations, so nobody's working the dangerous machines long enough to get tired, and only properly trained men use the really big, heavy stuff. That sort of thing's going to be a large part of your job: duty rosters, choosing the right men for each machine, all that stuff."

Before his disgrace, Ziani had written out frameworks for duty rosters for the next eighteen months; all Falier would need to do would be to fill in the names and copy them out in his own handwriting. Involuntarily, he wondered where Ziani was at that precise moment, and what he was doing.

"Tell me about the man who used to do this," he said, as casually as he could. "Didn't he get into some kind of trouble?"

"You could say that," the foreman replied with a grin. "You must've heard, it was really big news, just before the Eremian invasion."

"Hold on," Falier said. "That's right, I remember now. Abomination, wasn't it?"

The foreman scowled as he nodded. "We were stunned, I can tell you. Gutted. I mean, he always came across as, you know, an ordinary kind of bloke. A bit keen, maybe, inclined to shave the rules a bit to get on top of a schedule; but sometimes you've got to be like that to get things done around here. Within reason," he added quickly. "I mean, what he did, there's no excuse for that."

No excuse. Well. A picture of Ziani as he'd last seen him flooded uninvited into Falier's mind; dazed, he'd seemed, wondering what was going on, in the prison cell in the Guildhall basement, clutching trustingly to the tiny fragment of hope Falier had given him—not for himself, but for his wife and daughter. No excuse; reading the notes and the rosters, page after page covered in neat, ugly, small writing—Ziani always wrote quickly, but he'd never mastered the art of joined-up letters, so he'd invented a method all his own (which was also an abomination, strictly speaking), he remembered the times he'd borrowed Ziani's notes for revision in school, because he'd lost his own, or he'd been playing truant that day. You looked at the page and you thought it was illegible scrawl, but when you looked closer it was as easy to follow as the best clerk's copy-hand.

"It's always the quiet ones," he heard himself say.

The foreman nodded briskly. "He was that all right," he said. "Always kept himself to himself. I mean, he talked to the lads, but he was never one of them, if you see what I mean. Standoffish, I guess you could call it—not like he thought he was better than us, just sort of like he didn't want to join in. Like his mind was always somewhere else. And now," he added grimly, "we know all about it, don't we?"

"Well, I'm not like that," Falier said, and he gave him one of his trust-me smiles. "I expect I'm going to have to rely on all of you quite a lot, till I'm up to speed."

The foreman shrugged his concerns away. "Place more or less runs itself," he said, thereby damning himself forever in Falier's judgment. "Let the lads get on with it, they know what to do. I mean, you've got the Specifications, what else do you need?"

Down the iron spiral stairs into the main shop; a huge place, bare walls like horizons enclosing a vast stone-flagged plain, on which stood rows and rows of machines. Falier had never seen an orchard, though he'd seen pictures and heard descriptions, and had imagined the straight, bare rides between the rows of trees. There was something like that about the shop floor, the same sense of order firmly imposed. There was far more than he could take in; the noise, an amalgam of dozens of different sounds forming a buzzing, intrusive composite; the smell of cutting oil, sheep's grease, steel filings, sweat and hot metal; the crunch of swarf under his feet, the taste in his mouth of thick, wet air and carborundum powder. He knew that Ziani had loved it here, that there was only one place on earth he'd rather be. Himself, he found it too hot, too noisy and too crowded. It had cost him a great deal of effort to get here, but he wasn't planning on staying any longer than he had to.

"This," the foreman was saying, "is your standard production center lathe; it's what we use for general turning, dressing up castings, turning down diameters, facing off, all that. Driven off the overhead shaft by a two-inch leather belt; four speeds on the box plus two sizes of flywheel, so you've got eight running speeds straight away, before you need to start adding changewheels. Spindle bore diameter one and a half inches; center height above the bed twelve inches; length between centers…"

Falier smiled appreciatively. It was just a machine. He'd seen loads of them, spent hours standing beside them turning the little wheels, reading off the scribed lines of the dials, dodging the vicious, sharp, hot blue spirals of swarf flying out from the axis of rotation like poisoned arrows. Ziani, now, he'd loved the big machines, the way a rider loves his horse or a falconer his falcons. To him, backlash in the leadscrew was a tragedy, like a child with a terminal illness; a snapped tap or a badly ground parting tool was the remorseless savagery of the world directed at him personally. There was a certain manic quality about the way Ziani had loved his work which Falier had always found vaguely disturbing. A Guildsman should be a part of his machine—the bit on the end of the handle that turned it a specified number of turns. Passion had no part in it. Looking back, you could see he was likely to come to a bad end.

"And over here," the foreman went on, "you've got your millers; verticals that side, horizontals this side. Tool racks here; you can see they're all arranged in size order, slot drills on the top row, end-mills next row down, bull-noses and dovetail cutters, flycutters, side-and-face, gang-mills, slotting saws. Collets and tee-nuts here, look, vee-blocks, couple of rotary tables…" Falier kept himself from yawning; a lesser man would've given in, because the foreman wasn't looking at him. He felt like a prospective son-in-law meeting the whole family, right down to the last seven-year-old third cousin.

"Anyhow," the foreman said, "that's about it, the grand tour. If there's anything I can help you with, anything you want to know, just ask."

"Thanks," Falier said—his mouth had almost forgotten how to shape words during the long, slow circuit. "It's going to be a pleasure working here."

The foreman smirked. Falier decided he loathed him, and that he'd need to be got rid of, sooner rather than later. No big deal. "That just leaves your office," the foreman said. "This way, up the stairs."

The ordnance factory was an old building—ever since Falier could remember they'd been on the point of pulling it down and rebuilding it from scratch, but the moment never quite came. Before the Reformation it had been a religious building of some kind, a temple or a monastery. It had been gutted two centuries earlier, all the internal walls demolished to make the long, high halls and galleries for the rows of machines, but four towers still remained, one at each corner. Bell-towers, Falier had heard them called. Three of them housed cranes and winches, for lifting oversized sections of material. The fourth one was the senior foreman's office. Falier had been here once, to see Ziani. It was empty now, apart from a single chair and a bare table (not the ones that had been there the last time he'd seen it; every last trace of Ziani had been purged). There was no door; you looked out and down onto the factory floor, spread out in front of you like a vast, complex mechanism.

The foreman went away, leaving Falier sitting in the chair looking at the table. He was wondering what he was supposed to do next when a boy, about twelve years old, appeared in the archway and asked if there was anything he wanted.

Falier frowned. "Who are you?"

"Bosc," the boy replied.

"Right. What do you do around here?"

The boy thought for a moment. "What I'm told."

"Good. In that case, get me fifty sheets of writing paper, a bottle of ink and a pen."

That was all it took, apparently; Bosc came back in a surprisingly short time with everything he'd asked for. "Thanks," Falier said. "How do I find you when I need you for something?"

"Yell," said Bosc, and went away.

Fine, Falier thought. He spread out a sheet of paper, and began writing down the things he knew he'd need to remember, before they slipped his mind. He'd covered three sheets and was crowding the foot of a fourth when a shadow cut out his light. He looked up. Bosc was back.

"Letter for you," he said, and he brandished a small, folded square of parchment, presumably in case Falier wasn't inclined to believe him without tangible proof.

"Thanks," Falier said. "You can go."

Bosc went. There was nothing written on the outside, so he unfolded it. He saw writing, and folded it back up again. He yelled.

Bosc came back, almost instantaneously. Presumably he sat on the stairs when not in use, like an end-mill on its rack.

"Who brought this?" Falier asked.

"Woman," Bosc replied. "Odd-looking."

Falier felt muscles tighten in his stomach and chest. "Odd-looking how?"

"She was big and old and fat, her face was sort of pale pink, and she was wearing a big red dress like a tent," Bosc said. "She talked funny."

"Thanks," Falier said. "Go away."

He counted up to twenty before unfolding the letter again. That handwriting; at first sight, you thought you'd never be able to read it.

Falier—
    The woman I've given this to reckons she can get it to you discreetly. Apparently, they're good at it, years of practice. For your sake, I hope it's true.

In case she's lying or overconfident: to whom it may concern. Be it known that I, Ziani Vaatzes, am writing to Falier Zenonis for the first time since my escape from the Guildhall. He has not been in touch with me since he visited me in prison, and he had nothing to do with my escape or subsequent defection. I'm writing to him because he's my oldest friend in the world, and about the only person in Mezentia who might just read this, rather than throw it straight on the nearest fire. I have information that will prove of great value to the Republic, but what good is it if nobody'll listen to me?

There; I hope that'll help, if they intercept this. If not, I'm very sorry for getting you into trouble. I don't suppose you'll be able to forgive me if that's happened, but you're the only one I could think of. If you've read this far, thanks, Falier.

I'm a realist. I know I can't buy my way back home, not after what's happened. I know that even if what I've found out turns out to be as useful as I know it is, and the Republic's saved huge quantities of money and lives, it won't do me any good. But just because I'm here and I did what I did to stay alive, that doesn't change everything about me. I still believe in the important things: the Republic, the Guild, all the really big stuff. Also, I'm hoping there's still a chance that if I can do something for the Republic, it might make things easier for Ariessa and Moritsa. If there's anything I can do, that way, it's worth it, no matter what. And if that's out of the question, Falier, maybe you could use it to do yourself a bit of good; you couldn't let on you'd got it from me, of course, but I'm sure you can think of something. You always were a smart lad.

Falier, I don't know how much you know about diplomacy and foreign affairs and stuff, but it looks like there's going to be a war soon between Eremia Montis (that's where I am now) and the Republic. Naturally, the Republic will win. But the problem will be storming the capital city. City; it's more like a gigantic castle right on top of a mountain, really hard to get to at the best of times. Trying to attack this place head on would cost millions of thalers and thousands of lives, and it'd take years; but I know a better way, quick, easy and cheap. Piece of cake. It's like this...

Falier read the rest of the letter slowly, trying to visualize what Ziani was talking about. He wasn't very good at that sort of thing; he preferred it all down on paper, diagrams and charts and plans, with someone to talk him through them and explain what he couldn't understand. The general principle was simple enough, though, and someone who knew about this sort of thing would be able to follow it. His instincts told him that Ziani's system would work, considered as a piece of engineering; assuming, of course, that the whole thing wasn't false — a trap, a mechanism designed to inflict harm at long range, a weapon. He was, of course, the only man in Mezentia who knew Ziani well enough to form an opinion about that.

There was no fireplace in the office. To burn the letter, he'd have to go down the stairs (past Bosc, presumably) and walk into the west gallery, where the forges were. He'd have to go up close to one of the forge hearths — only authorized personnel allowed within ten feet — and lean across and drop it into the flames, with the smith and his hammermen watching. Or he could take it home with him (that'd mean either hiding it somewhere, or carrying it around in his pocket all the rest of the day) and burn it there. Or he could keep it.

He looked down at the folded paper in his hands, just in case it had all been a hallucination; but it was still there.

The woman; *big and old and fat, her face was sort of pale pink.* He knew enough to guess that she must've been a merchant, Eremian or Vadani. If she'd opened the letter and read it (no seal, of course, to tell if she had or not; that'd have been too much to hope for) — even if she was discreet, suppose she was caught and questioned. It'd all come out, and if he burned the letter it'd probably be worse, because he'd have disposed of Ziani's pathetic attempt to protect him—pretty well worthless, of course, but better than nothing, perhaps. Or Bosc; had he read it? Could he read? Fucking Ziani, might as well have stuck a knife in his neck. Or maybe, just maybe, this wodge of paper was a magic carpet that could carry him to places he'd never even dreamed of reaching. That was the cruelest part; not the despair, but the hope.

No door on his office. Cursing, he sat down and pulled off his left boot, trying to keep his movements slow and casual. In this place, people must be forever getting swarf and filings in their boots, having to take them off and put them on again. He slipped the letter into it and replaced it, lacing it up a little tighter than usual. If ever I see Ziani again, he promised himself, I'll make him wish Compliance had caught up with him first; even if it's power and wealth and glory, I'll skin him alive.

He stood up. He would have to spend the rest of the day walking round with the sharp corners of the letter digging into the sole of his foot, not daring to limp or wince. He felt like a dead man; heir to an incredible fortune, maybe, but too dead to enjoy it. Screw Ziani for trying to do the right thing. No surer recipe for a killer of men and sacker of cities than a subtle blend of altruism and stupidity.

All day, he felt as if people were staring at him. Which of course they were, since he was the new boss, and he was stalking round the place as though his knee-joints had been soldered up.

The first dozen ships docked at Lonazep early on a cold, gray morning, before the sea-frets had cleared. Nobody was expecting them; they were early, or the memo had got lost on someone's desk. They slid into existence out of the wet mist and cast anchor. Only a few old-timers had seen anything like them before.

For one thing, they weren't built of wood, like the honest fishing boats and merchantmen of Lonazep. Instead, they looked to have been contrived out of long strips of thick yellow rope, twisted out of straw and stitched together. They shifted, stretched and sagged like living things with every movement of the water. It was hard to see how they stayed afloat at all.

Furthermore, they were enormous. An ordinary trading coaster could have sailed under the prow of any one of them without fouling its mast-head. They were so tall that nobody on the quay could see beyond the chunky rope rails, and this gave the impression that there might not be anybody on board them at all; that they were ghost ships, or curious sea-monsters pretending to be ships in order to get close enough to attack.

After an unusually long time, they started lowering boats, which were crammed dangerously full of men. They were all wearing round steel helmets painted black, with tall horsehair plumes that nodded and swayed, grossly exaggerating the movements of the heads inside them. The boats were twice the size of the Lonazep herring and tuna boats, not much shorter than the whalers, and substantially broader in the beam; they too were made of rope, but they were powered by oars rather than sails, and they moved across the water alarmingly fast, like spiders climbing a wall.

A group of men bustled out of the customs house, trotting down the cob so as to get there before the first boat landed. In front was the harbormaster, followed by his inspectors and clerks, with four anxious-looking guards in no great hurry to keep up. As he scuttled, the harbormaster kept glancing down at a sheet of paper in his hand, as if he was on his way to an exam. He made it to the top of the steps with seconds to spare, as the first horsehair plume came up to meet him.

The face under the helmet was the same brown color as the Mezentines', but it was bearded, long and thin. The top of the harbormaster's head came up to its chin.

The harbormaster was apologizing (communications breakdown, wasn't expecting you for another fortnight, please forgive the apparent lack of respect) but the man in the plumed helmet didn't seem to be paying much attention. He was looking about him, at the square stone buildings and the beached ships, as if to say that this wasn't up to the standard he'd come to expect.

"We're the advance party," he said, in good Mezentine. "We caught the morning breeze. The rest'll be along later today."

The rest... The harbormaster's face sagged, as though his jaw had just melted. The dozen rope ships all but filled the available space. "The rest," he repeated. "Excuse me, how many would that—"

"Fifty-two," the plumed man replied. "That's the first squadron. We staggered it, so you'd be able to cope. The remaining squadron will be arriving over the next six days."

The harbormaster's clerk was counting on his fingers; sixty-four times six. Nobody else was bothered about the exact number.

"I think there may have been a misunderstanding," the harbormaster said. "All those ships—and your men, too. I mean, arrangements will have to be made..."

The plumed man dipped his head very slightly. "You'd better go away and make them," he said.

Shortly after noon, when the rope boats had made their last crossing, and the town square was crammed to bursting with plumed men, the wagons started to arrive. The road was solid with them, the horses' noses snuffling in the back of the cart in front, and none of them could turn until they got off the causeway through the marshes. It was impossible to imagine how the mess would ever be sorted out; the town stuffed with men, the road paved with carts, and the men's food was in the carts, and the men were getting hungry. The harbormaster, who hadn't known anything about it but whose fault it all apparently was, made an excuse and vanished into the customs house, where he proved impossible to find. Responsibility accordingly devolved on the clerk.

The remaining fifty-two ships arrived in mid-afternoon.

Their arrival prompted the leader of the plumed men to take charge. He sent the clerk scuttling away in fear of his life, then started shouting orders in a language the townspeople couldn't understand. The effect was remarkable. Carts were picked up, ten men a side, lifted up and carried off the road, plundered of their loads and turned round to face the other way; human chains passed the jars of flour and barrels of salt pork and cheese back down the road into the town square, where men formed orderly queues. Meanwhile, the strangers chased away the Lonazep pilots and brought the fifty-two ships in themselves. There was room, just about. A line of boats roped together formed floating gang-planks linking each ship to the shore, and thousands more plumed men swarmed along them; officers and NCOs formed them up and marched them off, fitting each company neatly into the available space in the square, like pieces in a wooden puzzle. Carts were still arriving, but plumed men had laid a makeshift causeway of uprooted fenceposts and joists from dismantled roofs across the salt flats, so that the emptied, departing carts bypassed the start of the jam, and the lifting-plundering-turning-around details worked in precisely timed shifts to process each new arrival. The plumed men's leader organized the whole operation from the little watch-tower on the roof of the customs house, with relays of runners pounding up and down the narrow spiral stone staircase, taking turns to go up and down since there wasn't room for two people to pass.

At dawn, the harbormaster emerged from his hiding place, in time to see the empty ships sailing out of the harbor to make room for the next squadron. The carts were all gone; instead, the road was solid with an unbroken column of marching men, each one with his heavy pack covered by his gray wool cloak, his two spears sloped over his shoulder, his helmet-plume nodding in time to the quick march, so that from a distance the whole line of plumes, as far as the eye could see, all swayed together, forward and back.

Since everything seemed to be under control, the harbormaster risked climbing the tower. There was something he needed to know, and his curiosity had finally got the better of his bewilderment and terror.

"Excuse me," he said to the plumed leader, who turned his head and looked at him. "But who are you?"

The plumed man looked at him some more and turned back to the battlement without answering, and the harbormaster went away again without repeating the question.

At noon on the fourth day, the advance guard marched into the City, having made better time than anticipated. In Mezentia itself, however, arrangements had been made. Barracks were waiting for them—the Foundrymen and Machinists, the Clothiers, the Carpenters and Joiners, and the Stonemasons had each emptied a warehouse, so there was plenty of room; the staff officers, of course, were directed to the Guildhall, where Necessary Evil had laid on private quarters, hot baths and a reception with a buffet lunch and musicians in the Old Cloister; they'd taken a gamble that it wouldn't rain, but in all other respects nothing had been left to chance.

"Allow me to present Colonel Dezenansa," Staurachus said. "Colonel, this is my colleague Lucao Psellus, formerly of the compliance directorate."

The foreigner had taken off his plumed helmet but he was still wearing his gray cloak and under it his fish-scale armor, steel plates the size of beech leaves and painted black. They clinked slightly every time he moved; *if I had to wear something like that and it made that noise all the time,* Psellus thought, *I'd go mad.* "Pleased to meet you," he said; he started to extend his hand but the foreigner didn't move. "Commissioner Psellus," the foreigner said.

"The Colonel is in charge of the first six squadrons," Staurachus went on, "comprising sixteen thousand men. Their job will be to enter Eremian territory and secure the road known as the Butter Pass. This will enable the main army, under General Dejauzida—"

"The Butter Pass," Psellus interrupted. "But surely that's the long way round. And it leads you very close to the Vadani border. Surely—"

"Quite right," Staurachus said, with a little scowl. "Apparently

Boioannes believes that there's a risk the Vadani may misinterpret our intentions and get drawn into the war, unless we neutralize them at the outset with a suitable show of strength. Accordingly, the Colonel will position a thousand men at the Silvergate crossroads, thereby effectively blocking the road the Vadani would have to take if they wanted to reach Civitas Eremiae before our army. There will, of course, be a slight loss of time in reaching Civitas, but that hardly matters, we'll be setting a siege when we get there, and the hold-up won't be long enough for the Eremians to bring in any appreciable quantities of supplies. After all," he added with a smile, "where would they bring them in from?"

It took Psellus an hour to get away from the reception without being too obvious about it. He went straight to the Clock Court, where Maniacis' office was.

"Who the hell are all these men in armor," he demanded, "and what are they doing here?"

His friend looked up from his counting frame and grinned. "You should know," he said. "You're the warrior, I'm just an accountant."

Psellus breathed in sharply; Maniacis raised his hands in supplication.

"They're your new army," he said. "From the old country, across the water. Jazyges, mostly, with some Bretavians and a couple of divisions of Solatz sappers and engineers. They cost twice as much as Cure Doce, that's without transport costs, but apparently your old friend Boioannes reckons they're worth it. We, of course, have to find the extra money without appearing to break into Contingency funds. We thought we might announce a little pretend earthquake somewhere, and siphon it out through Disaster Relief."

"Boioannes," Psellus repeated. "What's he got to do with it? He's a diplomat."

Maniacis raised both eyebrows. "Either you've been cutting briefings or they're keeping things from you," he said. "Boioannes is now Necessary Evil. In fact, not to put too fine a point on it, he's running the show. Don't ask me why," he preempted, "there's some things even I don't know. In fact," he added with a smirk, "I was going to ask you."

Psellus sat down. "I give up," he said. "Ever since I joined this ludicrous department I've been kicking my heels waiting to be given something to do, and meanwhile they've imported an army from the old country and they're planning to take it up the Butter Pass. I might as well go home and stay there till it's all over."

"The Butter Pass," Maniacis said. "You're kidding."

Psellus shrugged. "That's what Staurachus just told me, him and the colonel-in-chief or whatever he was. I didn't catch his name—"

"Colonel Dezenansa," Maniacis said promptly. "Quite a distinguished service record, we were lucky to get him. More an administrator than a front-line fighter, but—I'm sorry, you were saying."

"Perhaps," Psellus said wearily, "you could fill me in on what you know about all this."

Maniacis laughed. "I just did," he said. "That's about it. Boioannes has been maneuvering and pulling strings for months to get his hands on Necessary Evil; all these arrangements were made for the invasion—you know, when the Eremians were invading us, rather than the other way round—but some fool of a soldier went and cut him out by sending the scorpions. They massacred the Eremians in about ten minutes flat, leaving Boioannes without a war to fight. He was livid, naturally; and then this abominator of yours conveniently escapes, and the war's back on again. Fortuitous, wouldn't you say? Hardly interfered with the original timetable at all."

Psellus thought about that a lot over the next few days. He had little else to do; he'd retreated into his office (like the Eremians, he told himself, taking refuge behind the walls of their fortified mountaintop) and was waiting for the war to come to him. The war, however, was busy with other things and couldn't be bothered with him. Two or three times a day, a memo came round. It was always the same memo, very slightly amended:

Owing to unforeseen operational and administrative factors, the initial advance into Eremian territory has been rescheduled. There will be a delay. You will be informed as soon as a new schedule has been agreed.

Sometimes the memo said "further delay" or "once again been rescheduled"; sometimes not. The name at the top was usually Boioannes, though sometimes it was Staurachus, just occasionally Ostin Tropaeas (Psellus had never heard of him). Once it started off, "By order of Colonel Dezenansa," but the variation wasn't repeated. Psellus wondered if such a divergence from the approved text constituted an abomination.

His duty as a member of Necessary Evil was to stay in his office till called for, so that was what he did, with all his might. To help pass the time, he read; and since there were only two books on his shelf (*Approved Specifications of the Guild of Foundrymen and Machinists* and *Collected Poetical Works of Arnaut Pegilannes*) he went back over his files on the Vaatzes case; in particular the documents in the abominator's own handwriting, recovered by the investigating officers from his desk in the ordnance factory. There was no point in doing this, but he did it anyway, because he was bored.

Mostly they were technical stuff: tables of screw thread pitches, tapping drill sizes, major and minor diameters of the standard ordnance coarse and fine threads, material codes, tables of feeds and speeds for each class of lathe and mill. Every qualified Guildsman was expected to have his own copy, taken with infinite care from the master copy on the wall of the Guild chapterhouse. Just for fun, Psellus dug out his own copy and compared it with Ziani's; there were only two differences, and when he went down to chapter he checked them and found that he was the one who'd made the mistakes, twenty-odd years ago.

There was also a small book; homemade out of offcuts of paper

(crate lining, possibly) stitched together with thick waxed thread
and glued down the spine to a leather hinge that joined two covers,
cut out of scrap wooden veneer. It was a neat job, but why bother;
why go to the trouble of making such a thing when you could buy
a proper one from a stationer's stall in the market for a quarter
thaler? Psellus checked himself; quite possibly, Ziani hadn't had a
quarter thaler to spare.

He opened it. The same handwriting, precisely laid out on the
unruled page — on a whim he measured the spaces between the
lines with a pair of calipers, and was impressed to find that they
never varied by more than thirty thousandths of an inch; close
tolerances, for a man writing freehand; writing *poetry*...

Psellus frowned. Poetry.

He read a few lines, to see if it was just something Ziani had
copied out. He didn't recognize it, and he was fairly sure it was
as homemade as the book it was written in. It was *bad* poetry. It
scanned pretty well, as you'd expect from an engineer, and the
rhymes were close enough for export, as the saying went, but it
was unmistakably drivel. Psellus smiled.

Her cheek is as soft as a rose's petal
Her eyes are as dark as night
Her smile is as bright as polished metal
She is a lovely sight.

Which explained, he thought, why Ziani never quit the day job.
He imagined him, sitting in his office in the old bell-tower (he'd
been to see it during the initial investigation; he'd taken this book
from the desk drawer himself, and slipped it into his pocket) on
a slow day, nothing much happening; he saw him slide open the
drawer and take out the book; a quick glance round to make sure
he's alone, a dip in the ink, a furrowing of the brow; then he starts
writing, beautifully even lines through invincible force of habit;
secretly, deep down, everybody on earth believes they can write
poetry, apart from the members of the Poets' Guild, who know

they can't. He hesitates, running down the alphabet for a rhyme for night (blight, cite, fight, height), and when he reaches S a smile spreads over his face, as the finished line forms in his mind like an egg inside a chicken.

Psellus rested the book on his desk. So what? Right across the known world, in every country with some degree of literacy, there are millions of otherwise sane, normal, harmless people who are guilty of poetry. Maybe Vaatzes thought he was good at it (if those long-haired layabouts can do it, it can't be so very hard), maybe he thought he could make money at it, easier than cutting and measuring metal all day; maybe there was a voice in his head, bees making honey in his throat, and he had no choice but to write it down before he burst. Maybe it was a code, and really it was all secret messages from Eremian intelligence.

He opened the book again and read on. It didn't get better; if anything, Ziani had put his best stuff at the front, like a woman running a fruit stall. It ran in loops; the same rhymes repeated over and over (he'd been particularly taken with *cold/gold* and *heart/apart*; sometimes he stacked them in a different order — *apart/heart* — but that was the limit of his avant-garde tendencies), the same bland sentiments stuffed into the same trite conceits, like sliced meat into flat bread; if original thinking had been Ziani's besetting sin, there wasn't much sign of it in his poetry:

> *My love is like the nightingale*
> *Who sings her soft and tender tale*
> *My love is like the hyacinth*
> *That blossoms on its marble plinth*

He frowned again. Would it be useful, he wondered, if he knew who this terrible stuff was addressed to? Anybody in particular? A sort of picture emerged from internal evidence; she had a soft face and wavy hair, and Ziani seemed to think she was nice-looking. That wasn't much help in narrowing down the list of candidates. Maybe her name didn't rhyme with anything. Maybe—anything's possible—the lady in question was his wife.

(What was her name again? Ariessa. Ariessa, confessor, dresser, guesser...)

Well, Psellus thought, the world is full of strange things, and an engineer who writes bad poetry isn't the strangest. He closed the book again, tagging it in his mind as a piquant and mildly amusing curiosity. On a spurt of inspiration, he opened it again and read down the first letters of each line. Gibberish; no acrostics. What you see is all there is. Sad, in a way. Certainly, there was a bittersweet irony in the fact that the man who would soon be bringing annihilation on the Eremian people was someone who thought *prove* was a legitimate rhyme for *love*.

Query: was there any more of this stuff among the papers found at the house, or was this a vice he only indulged while he was at work? Further query: now that Eremia was going to be destroyed and the whole question of Ziani Vaatzes' crime was thus redundant, could he really be bothered to go down to the file archive and look? Answer to both: probably not.

With an effort, he evicted Ziani's poetry from his mind and turned his thoughts to Boioannes, and various issues to do with timing. It did rather look as though Boioannes had contrived the war, just so that he could sidestep the ladder of dead men's shoes (he paused at that particular image; Ziani, he felt, would've reckoned it was really good) and gratify his ambition to join and lead Necessary Evil. Sure, Boioannes would be capable of it, but was that what had actually happened? He could probably ascertain the truth by working out timetables, cross-referencing, looking in the files, assuming he was allowed access at that security level. Did it matter? No. It mattered even less than Ziani Vaatzes' poetry. The simple fact was that the Eremian Duke (Orseus? Orseo? Whatever) had been right—them or us—but the scorpions had done for him. The strongest always wins, and who on earth was stronger than the Perpetual Republic?

Going round in little circles, like a mouse in a box. Psellus yawned, and put the Vaatzes papers away where he wouldn't have to look at them. If Boioannes was responsible for the wiping out of Eremia, Vaatzes was only a pretext, of little importance; if Vaatzes wasn't really to blame, neither was Lucao Psellus. He didn't smile at that thought, because things had moved beyond smiling, but he felt a little happier with himself; like a drunk carter who runs someone over in the dark, and then finds he was already dead.

He stood up. True, he was supposed to wait there until he was sent for. On the other hand, he was bored stiff and his back hurt from too much sitting. He wanted to get out of his office and go somewhere. He left the tower, and the Guildhall campus.

Psellus had lived in the City all his life, but there were huge parts of it he'd never been to (like a good archer, who only uses a very small part of the target). He didn't even know where Sixty-Seventh Street was, so he stopped at the Guildhall lodge and asked the duty porter, who explained that Sixty-Seventh Street was between Sixty-Sixth Street and Sixty-Eighth Street. Psellus thanked him and started to walk.

It took him the best part of an hour to find the building; a seven-story block, what the people who lived in this part of town called an island. According to the file, the Vaatzes family lived on the sixth floor, west side. They had four rooms, as befitted their status as supervisory grade. As an act of extreme clemency, Ariessa Vaatzes had been allowed to stay there after her husband's disgrace, at least until the child came of age; her rent was paid out of the Benevolent Fund, and she received half the standard widow's pension.

Psellus climbed the stairs. Islands weren't like the Guildhall, which was a pre-Reformation building, beautiful and impractical. Island Seventeen, Sixty-Seventh Street, was built of yellow mud brick; it was ugly but the stairs were straight and wide, and hadn't yet been worn glass-smooth by generations of boot-soles. The stairwell was lit by tall, thin, unglazed windows blocked in by iron bars. There was a smell of damp, and various other smells he couldn't quite identify.

Apartment Twenty-Seven had a plain plank door with external flat hinges. He knocked and waited. Nothing. He knocked again. Across the landing, the door of number twenty-nine opened a crack and a head poked out; an old man with deep eye-sockets and a big, round-ended nose.

"Excuse me," Psellus said. "I'm looking for the Vaatzes family. Have I got the right place?"

The man looked at him. "Gone away," he said.

Psellus frowned. "Are you sure?" he said. "The Guild register says they're still here."

The man shook his head. "Been gone three weeks now," he said. "Her and the little girl. *He* went on before them, of course."

"I see," Psellus said. "Would you happen to know where they went? The wife and the daughter, I mean."

"Couldn't say," the old man said. "Men came by to shift the furniture — wasn't a lot of it left, mind, the soldiers took on most of it when they came for Him. Wasn't anything good, anyhow," the man added sourly, "just a few chairs and tables, and some boxes, and the beds. She had her clothes, in a bag. Place is empty now. Don't reckon they're in any hurry to move a new lot in. People don't like living where something bad happened."

Psellus hesitated; then he said, "Do you think it'd be all right if I went in and had a look? I'm from the Guild, there were some things —"

"Nothing to do with me," the old man said. "You do what you like."

Psellus tried the door, pressing down the plain tongue latch. Of course, he noticed, there's no outside lock; just bolts on the inside, probably. "Thanks," he said. The old man stepped back and closed the door, then opened it again, just a crack.

He'd been right; someone had stripped the place bare, even wrenched out the nails where pictures had hung on the wall. The windows were shuttered but the shutters had been left open; a few stray leaves had been blown in by the wind, and in places the floor was spattered with white bird droppings. In the main room a floorboard had been levered up and not replaced. Maybe that's where Vaatzes used to hide his poetry, Psellus thought.

Plain walls, washed with off-white pipeclay distemper; clean and unmarked, which would've been impossible if people had been living there. Someone had seen the need to whitewash the place since the family left. From the bedroom window you could see the roof of the ordnance factory.

So, Psellus thought, why would Ariessa Vaatzes move out, after so much mercy had been expended to let her stay here? Several possibilities. Unhappy memories, that'd do it; hostility from the neighbors; she'd gone back to live with her father now she was on her own. Fine; but regardless of what'd happened to her, she was obliged to register her address with the Guild, same as everybody else, and the address in the file was this one. Another possibility: she was dead, and the old man across the way was lying about having seen her take her clothes away in a bag. But if she'd died lawfully, that'd be registered on her file; and who would want to murder her?

Not that it mattered. Sheer idle curiosity was all that had brought him here; he'd wanted to look at her again, to see if she was the sort of woman who'd inspire a man to rhyme *love* and *prove* in a homemade book. What if an important memo arrived while he was out of the office?

He shut the apartment door behind him. The old man wasn't the Vaatzes' only neighbor. There was bound to be a perfectly simple explanation for her absence, and once he'd found it out he could go back and stare at his wall some more.

Nobody at home at number twenty-eight, but the woman at number thirty seemed positively delighted to talk to him. No, he wouldn't come in, thanks all the same; she was short, almost circular, with long hair and a bald patch on top, neatly dressed in a faded, carefully pressed blue dress and sandals that looked like they'd belonged to her mother. Ariessa Vaatzes; yes, she went on three weeks ago, took all her things. Three men came to help her, they took all the furniture that was left. A youngish man, and two middle-aged ones; the young man gave orders and the other two did as they were told. They were quick about it, like they were in a hurry. No, no idea where she'd gone. Always kept themselves to themselves, and the little girl was such a sweetheart, it's always the kids that suffer most when bad things happen.

"Did you see the little girl leave?" Psellus asked.

"Oh yes," she told him. "Went on with her mother. She didn't seem upset or anything, of course they don't realize at that age, bless them."

"Did Ariessa Vaatzes seem upset at all?"

"Not really," she replied. "A bit on edge, that's all. Didn't say anything to the men, but she left with them. But she never did say much. Quiet little thing, she was. Must've been dreadful for her, him turning out like he did."

Psellus thought for a moment. "Did you talk to him much?" he asked.

"Him?" She looked at him as though he'd insulted her. "No, hardly at all. Oh, he wasn't rude or anything, just never had anything to say. Always the quiet ones, isn't it?"

"Did they have any friends in the island? Anybody they got on particularly well with?"

Apparently not. "They did have a few callers, though," she added, "from time to time. Friends of his from work, I think, and her family, once or twice. Never met any of them to talk to, though, so I can't tell you much about them. There was a very tall man with gray hair, and a young woman with a baby who came round in the daytime."

He thanked her and left, walking fast to get back to the office, just in case. No memo; apparently, the war didn't need him just yet. *When was it,* he asked himself, *that I stopped doing work that was actually of any use to anybody? Was it round about the time I was given a degree of power and authority over my fellow citizens?* In the filtered light of his office he wasn't even sure what time of day it was; time passed unevenly there, dragging or flying depending on how close he was able to come to a state of mental detachment. Had he only just got back from his trip to the outside world, or had he been sitting staring at the wall for hours? Not that it mattered. Like all good Guildsmen, he lived only to serve the Republic. If it could afford to leave him idle for a while, it wasn't his place to complain, just as he would have no right to object if it required him to work three days and nights without food or sleep. *When was it that I stopped believing that?*

Some time later, a memo arrived. A tall, thin boy brought it; he knocked at the door, pushed it at him and walked away. Psellus scraped the seal off with his thumbnail.

From Maris Boioannes:

In consequence of various matters, it has been decided to postpone the proposed military action against Eremia Montis for the time being. A document will be issued in due course. Personnel should resume their ordinary duties until further notice. You are required to refrain from discussing any aspect of the proposed military action with unauthorized personnel. Members of the Viability & Effects subcommittee will meet in the lesser chapterhouse at noon tomorrow to consider various issues arising from the above. None of the above affects the status of the mercenary troops currently billeted in the Crescent district of the city, who will be remaining until further notice. Commissioner Lucao Psellus is required to consult with the compliance directorate as soon as possible regarding the detention or elimination of the abominator Ziani Vaatzes, who is still at large.

By order &c.

13

Abominations, Ziani thought, looking down at his work. If I wasn't an abominator before, I'm definitely one now.

It was horrible; no other word for it. Instead of square-section steel the frame was built out of wood. The lockwork wasn't machined but pressed and bashed out of plate. The slider was no more than a square of thin steel sheet hammered into a folded box over a square mandrel. The spring had been wound by hand and eye out of junk—scrap pitchfork tines, of all things, drawn down and forge-welded together. Just looking at it made Ziani feel sick.

But it had taken him just three days to put together, and it worked: the first functional scorpion ever built outside the Mezentine ordnance factory. And he could make more of them, very quickly, which was all that mattered.

True, the timber frame would shake itself to bits under the savage force of the recoiling spring. The lock clunked and twanged into battery rather than purring and softly clicking. The slider rattled about in its slot, wasting precious energy. The spring wouldn't last, but that hardly mattered, since the frame would unquestionably disintegrate first. Without destruct-testing it he couldn't be sure, but his best guess was that it would last two thousand shots. Which would be enough.

(Enough; it was a word in Mezentine, but people tried not to use it if they could help it. It stood for the admission of defeat, the recognition of the inevitability of inaccuracy, breakdown and failure. Enough was an abomination. In the perfect world to which Specification was a gateway, there would be no more enough. Eremia, however, was about as far as you could get from the perfect world without supernatural help, and the prototype scorpion would be enough for Eremia.)

He sighed. When he shut his eyes, he could see the ratchet mechanism—a blank cut with a shear, teeth filed by eye to lines scribed with a nail, pivot-holes punched on an anvil, sear bent over a stake; it haunted his conscience like a murder. He hated it. But an Eremian blacksmith could make twenty of them in a day, during which time two Eremian carpenters could make a frame out of a log, an Eremian armorer could make ten sliders or a dozen locks, any bloody fool with another bloody fool to do the striking could make ten springs, and the garrison of Civitas Eremiae could drive the Mezentine army away from the walls with horrendous losses. That would be enough.

Someone called his name; that fool Calaphates, whose money had made all this possible. He looked up and there was the fool himself, leading a gaggle of suspicious-looking men across the yard. Ziani found a smile somewhere in his mental lumber-room.

"Gentlemen," Calaphates was saying, "allow me to present Ziani Vaatzes, until recently the foreman of the Mezentine state armory. Ziani, I'd like to introduce you to..."

(The names slipped in and out of his mind like elvers through a coarse net. That level of detail—being able to tell one Eremian nobleman from another—was not required at this stage. All that mattered was that these six worried-looking men were here to see the scorpion; if they liked it, they would go to Duke Orsea and tell him he ought to buy as many of them as Ziani could make. A smile was a lot to ask of him, but on balance it was worth it.)

One of the men cleared his throat. He was trying to look skeptical, but he just looked nervous. "So," he said, "this is it, is it?"

Ziani could have smiled at that free of charge, but he refrained. "We call them scorpions," he said. "Of course, this is a very crude copy of the ones they make in the Republic, but it works just as well. I'll give you a demonstration in a moment."

The man recoiled slightly. Probably he wasn't used to being spoken to so freely by someone whose grandfather hadn't known his grandfather. Unimportant; the machine would speak for itself. "So this is what they used against us…" The man's nerves got the better of him and he fell silent. Ziani nodded.

"More or less," he said. "The Mezentine ordnance factory makes these at the rate of twenty a day when they're running flat out. I think we can match that, if we really want to. It'll cost a lot of money, but I think you'll agree it's worth it."

One of the others was frowning, as though the subject was somehow obscene. "You said you'd show us how it works," he said.

"Of course." Ziani took a breath, then pointed. "Over there, see that lump of steel sheet set up on a stand? The distance is fifty yards, and the sheet is sixteen gauge, roughly one sixteenth of an inch; it's what the Mezentines use to make armor. Now," he went on, "if you'd all care to stand behind me."

They were happy to do that; eager, even. He took the ratchet handle, fitted it into the square slot, and began to wind the winch. To show off, he used one finger to turn it; a mistake, because the ratchet wasn't beautifully engineered like the ones he was used to, and he had to use rather more pressure than he'd have liked, but it was too late to stop without losing the effect. The winch cable drew back the slider, compressing the spring, until the catch dropped into its detent. Ziani picked up the three-foot-long, half-inch-diameter steel pin that was leaning against the side of the frame and laid it in the loading groove, its butt end resting on the nose of the slider. He'd already set up the sights (if you could call them that; a small rectangular plate with a hole in it, mounted on two crude set screws for windage and elevation; a post on a bent-nail gate at the front end to line it up by). He paused, to check they were all watching, and flipped the catch that released the sear. The spring shot the slider forward until it slammed into the stop, the noise coinciding with the hollow clang of the pin against the target.

"My God," someone said.

"Let's go and have a look, shall we?" Calaphates said in a rather embarrassed voice, as though he wanted everybody to know that this really wasn't his fault.

As Ziani had known it would, the steel spike had gone clean through the steel sheet; and the one behind it, and the two behind that; it was buried deep in the brickwork of the wall. He asked if anybody wanted to try and pull it out; no takers.

"Anyhow," he said, "that's what it does. The differences between this one and the ones they make in the Republic are mostly about durability; this one won't last nearly as long, it's more likely to break apart or get out of true, you can't aim it as precisely; it's heavier, too, and because it jumps about rather more when you let it off, you'll need to check the alignment after every fourth or fifth shot. On the other hand, it's a bloody sight better than what you've got at the moment, which is nothing at all."

Calaphates looked like he wanted to crawl down a hole and die, but Ziani couldn't help that. His job was to create a strong impression, and he was doing just fine. "You can make twenty of these a day?" one of them asked. Ziani nodded.

"I don't see why not," he said, "provided I can hire the workers I need. I've got a list of suitably skilled men who've agreed to join me. All I need now is a firm order and some money."

"Money," one of them repeated. "How much are we talking about?"

Ziani looked at him, and then at the plate, with the steel pin stuck in it. "Does it matter?" he said.

They didn't have anything to say to that. "Of course," Ziani went on, "as and when I've got the time and the resources, I can make a far better machine. I can make pretty much anything you like, as cheaply or as well as you want. For now, though, what you need is a lot of these things mounted on the city wall and pointed down the road. As soon as you tell me I can get started, I'll have the first batch of twenty for you inside a week; twenty a day after that until you tell me to stop. How does that sound?"

They were looking at him again, their eyes bright and feverish with an uneasy blend of hope and fear. On one level, he could understand why. Here was a Mezentine, by his own admission the man who'd made the machines that had butchered their army only a very short time ago; a Mezentine, offering to build them machines with which to massacre his fellow citizens in return for an unspecified but presumably vast sum of money. They wanted the weapons, but having them would change everything and they weren't the sort of men who held with huge, irrevocable changes, particularly ones involving slaughter. Paying out money bothered them, too. They were simple but weak components and he wished he didn't have to rely on them, on his estimate of their tensile strength. But they would do what he wanted, because they had no choice, not even if he spat in their faces or cut off their beards with a sharp knife.

He felt mildly guilty when he saw the look on Calaphates' face; after all, Calaphates had done nothing except give him money and support, and now Ziani was dragging him into the world-changing business, which wasn't quite what he'd believed he was putting his money into. But he hardened his heart. Calaphates would get his money back, along with an enormous profit—it'd do him no good, but it was what he wanted, and Ziani would get it for him, no question about that. As to the larger scope of the mechanism; already been into that, not his fault. It'd be like feeling guilty about an earthquake or a tidal wave.

They went away eventually, and Ziani got back to some proper work. The angle of the ratchet sear, the diameter of the spring link retaining bolt, the depth of engagement of the slider lock pin; real issues, soluble and precise. Every step away from chaos toward perfection accrues merit, no matter what the context, and the line between them is straight. When you can devote yourself to one problem, with everything else subsidiary to it, you begin to understand.

"There you are," she said, walking in across the polished threshold. "I've been looking for you."

Miel caught his breath; it was a sensation remarkably like fear in its symptoms and effects. He turned round slowly and smiled.

"What can I do for you?" he asked.

"Well." She sat down on the window-seat, right next to the chest in which he'd imprisoned her letter. "This is a bit awkward," she said.

"Go on."

"It's Orsea," she said. "I don't know. Ever since he came back from the war. It's like..." She frowned. She had the most precise face he'd ever seen; not sharp or pointy, but perfectly defined, as though it had been carefully designed by an architect. He knew it by heart, of course; it was there when he closed his eyes, it ambushed him when his mind wandered. He had learned it years ago, when they were both little more than children; he'd learned it the way a schoolboy prepares his lesson, because it was virtually inevitable that, sooner or later, they'd get married, thereby linking the Sirupat to the Ducas, with a view to breeding a superlative strain of nobleman. It hadn't turned out that way in the end. By a highly unlikely freak of chance, the Sirupat had suddenly been elevated from minor royalty to heirs to the Duchy; infelicity of timing had made her the carrier of the succession (as though it was some painful disease, passed down the female line to afflict the male) and the banalities of political expediency had made Orsea the only possible husband for her—Orsea his best friend, from back when they were safely outside the golden circle, married to the girl he'd never felt the need to fall in love with, because she'd been his practically from the cradle...

"It's like," she said, "that old fairy story, where the prince is kidnapped by goblins, and the goblin king turns himself into an identical copy and goes away to rule the kingdom, and everybody's fooled except the girl the prince is going to marry. It's like he hasn't come home yet, I don't know. It's awkward."

Awkward, Miel thought; and he could almost see the letter, through an inch of oak board. "I know," he heard himself say. "He's going through a rough patch. What happened in the war really smashed him up."

She was looking at him; he knew, though he was looking the other way. He always knew when she was watching him. "He seems quite his old self when he's with you," she said.

Miel shrugged. "Well," he said, "that's different. For one thing, I was there with him; also, we only ever talk about work—you know, affairs of state, all that." He grinned; had he really said *affairs of state?* She was grinning too. She knew him too well. "Boys' stuff," he said. "Things you can talk about on the surface without having to go to the bad places. I know he's tearing himself into little bits inside, but that's not..." He hesitated. She couldn't understand how his oldest friend could talk to him and not to her; it was, of course, because Orsea loved her. That single fact made everything different. Love, Miel had known for some time, is the most destructive force in the world, doing more harm than war and famine put together. "Look," he said. "Have you actually talked to him about it? About what happened?"

She shook her head. "I've hardly said two words to him about anything," she said. "And that's not how it used to be." He could feel her come to the stop, the point beyond which she couldn't go with someone else. It was murderously frustrating; the two most important people in Orsea's life, and they couldn't talk about him beyond that point. "I was wondering," she said, "if there's something we could do to—I don't know, snap him out of it. Which is why I thought of you."

"Like?"

"He needs—I don't know, he needs to do something *fun* for a change, so he can forget about this terrible thing that's smothering him for a while; something frivolous and outdoors and energetic, nothing to do with the war or politics or—"

"Affairs of state."

"Absolutely." She'd slipped into that mock scowl, with the furrowed eyebrows and the exaggerated pout. No matter how much her face changed as time passed, that expression always stayed the same, and when she wore it she was fourteen again, and so was he. "So I thought, your cousin Jarec—"

"You mean Jarnac. Jarec was my uncle."

"As though it mattered," she said pleasantly. "Your cousin, the great big tall one with the big shoulders and the impossible manners. Him. I think you should get him to take Orsea out hunting. Or hawking. Orsea used to love hawking, a few years ago, and your cousin whatever-his-name-is has got lots and lots of hawks. He showed them to me once," she added. "I've never been so bored in my life. But Orsea was sick with jealousy for a week."

Miel frowned. "It's not the season yet," he said. "Hawking doesn't start till the middle of next month."

"Oh for heaven's sake." She waved away a thousand years of immutable law with a wave of the fingers. "Nobody's going to mind, and it'd do him so much good, I'm sure of it."

"Will you come?" Miel said. "If I can arrange it?"

She nodded. "And I'll make it look like I'm enjoying myself," she said. "Just so long as I don't have to give bits of dead animal to anybody. There are limits."

He smiled. "That's boar-hunting," he said, "not hawking. And besides, it's a great honor to preside over the unmaking. You should be thrilled to be asked."

"Should I really? I'll try to bear that in mind. Meanwhile, will you do it? Ask your cousin, I mean. I'm convinced it'd help."

Miel shook his head. "Jarnac won't fly his precious hawks out of season," he said. "Not for anybody. If I asked him, he'd just look down his nose at me and quote bits out of King Fashion and Queen Reason."

She stared at him. "Out of what?"

"*The Venerable Dialogue of King Fashion and Queen Reason, Concern-*

ing the Proper Exercise of Huntsmanship," Miel said. "Good God, you mean you weren't made to read it as a child?"

"Never heard of it."

"You lucky—" Miel shook his head. "I had to learn the whole thing off by heart when I was nine."

"Is it ghastly?"

"It's long," Miel replied, with feeling. "And the bit about how to tell the age of a roebuck by the shape and texture of its droppings is just a bit too graphic for my taste. Jarnac lives by it, you'd never get him to break the rules."

"How about if I—?"

"But," Miel went on briskly, "Jarnac also keeps an excellent kennel, and it's still boar season, so we can go boar-hunting instead, and that'll do just as well, if you really think it'd help."

"You aren't sure about that, are you?"

Miel shrugged. "I don't think Orsea'd let himself have a good time, not the mood he's in at the moment. The trouble is, he's torturing himself because he believes the disaster was his fault, and to a certain extent he's right. Someone like him can't get round something like that."

"I know." She stood up, kicking at the hem of her dress. "And it's so stupid, because nobody else would carry on like that, and people really don't blame him. They're so used to things like that happening, it's just a fact of life to them. That's something I don't understand," she went on. "I guess it's because I spent most of my childhood abroad, being a hostage. I can't see how you'd get to a state where thousands of people suddenly aren't there anymore, and yet you carry on like nothing's happened. How can people live like that?"

Miel sighed. "It was very bad in the war—the proper war, I mean, between us and the Vadani. We were within an inch of bleeding each other to death. That's why your father and Valentinian had to patch it up at all costs." That, he didn't add, is why you had to marry Orsea instead of me. "Anyhow," he went on, "back in those days—you weren't here—it was one hideous massacre after another, except when we were butchering them, and that wasn't often. Or often enough, anyhow." He shook his head. "That's where the trouble lay with this war," he went on. "We simply hadn't realized how weak we'd become, not till we'd committed to the invasion and it was too late to go back. We knew before we left the city, deep down, that the whole thing was a complete joke—us, fighting the Mezentines—but we didn't dare face up to it. Orsea should've, but everybody wanted to go, so we could feel good about ourselves, and he went along with it because he always does. It's remarkable the truly stupid things people can do just because it's expected of them, or they think it's expected of them."

She gave him a look he didn't like. It said, *You could have stopped him.* He shook his head to say, no, I couldn't. He believed that was true, as an article of faith.

"I'll go and see Cousin Jarnac," he said. "There won't be any trouble about getting up a boar-hunt; any excuse, as far as he's concerned." Miel clicked his tongue. "And who knows," he said. "Maybe someone can get into a tight spot and Orsea can be terribly brave and save his life. That'd do him the world of good; it's a sort of blind spot with him, he's got no sense of perspective. So long as he does well and helps someone and does the right thing, it doesn't really matter whether it's something big and important, like saving the city, or something small and trivial, like rescuing an old woman's dog from drowning." He paused. "Did he ever tell you about that?"

"About what?"

Miel smiled broadly. "You should get him to tell you, it's glorious."

"You tell me. He's not talking to me, remember."

Miel frowned, then went on: "We were out walking once, when we were kids—playing rovers, I think, or something like that. Anyway, there's this river, and there's this old woman kneeling on the bank, and two or three puppies splashing about in the water. Orsea immediately assumes they've fallen in by accident, so he hurls himself into the water to save them, forgetting in the excitement of the moment that he can't swim—well he can, but only a sort of feeble frogs'-legs-and-otters'-paws swimming, which is no good at all in a fast-flowing river. Luckily we've got a couple of my father's men along with us—thinking about it, I think we were shooting wild duck, not playing rovers; anyhow, they jump in and fish him out, and he makes them go back and rescue the puppies; they get two of them but not the third. He takes them to the old woman, and she looks at him like he's gone off his head: what did you want to go and do that for? she says. Turns out, of course, that they were the leftovers from the litter and she was drowning them on purpose. I'd figured that out pretty early on, of course, but Orsea had real trouble with the whole idea, he couldn't believe someone'd actually do that. Anyway, he caught one hell of a cold, and his father gave him a dreadful shouting-at for nearly getting drowned making a fool of himself. And he hasn't changed. I think he'd still do exactly the same thing if we walked in on some old woman and a dog in the water; just in case, if you see what I mean."

She looked at him, and he wondered what she could see. "Tell you what," she said. "Go somewhere where there's no rivers. For my sake."

"No rivers," he said solemnly. "Right. I'll tell Jarnac." A thought flitted across his mind, like a woodcock crossing a ride. "It'll be good practice for him, hosting a ducal function and all that."

"Will it?"

He nodded. "Sooner or later the Vadani are going to want to celebrate the peace with a state visit, something grand with all the trimmings. We'll have to lay on a hunt for them, and Jarnac's our resident expert on all that stuff—the right way of doing things, you know. Their Duke's mad keen on hunting, I gather."

"That's right," she said. "Which surprises me. I met him once, years ago when I was living there, and practically the first thing he said to me was how much he hated it. Hunting, I mean."

"Oh," Miel said. "You've met him. What's he like?"

She shrugged. "What he's like now I have no idea. Back then he was just a boy, of course. Shy, quiet, a bit introverted. Hardly surprising; his father was the big, noisy type. I suppose he was quite sweet, in a dozy sort of way."

Miel raised an eyebrow. "He's not quite so sweet these days, by all accounts."

"People change," she said. "And I suppose he's gone through a lot in a short time, losing his father and having to take control of the government and everything. That'd be enough to change anyone."

"I don't know," Miel said. "Look at Orsea. He was made Duke at an early age, and he seems pretty much the same now as he was back when we were kids. A bit gilded round the edges, of course, but under the surface he hasn't changed a lot."

"Well, I don't know," she said. "Like I said, I only met Valens once, and we were both very young."

"Anyway." Miel moved away abruptly. "I'll certainly talk to Jarnac if you think it'll help."

"Thanks," she said, and smiled. The smile hit him unexpectedly, like a drunk in a tavern, and for a moment he was unable to think. *Does she know?* he wondered. All this time he'd assumed she didn't; he clung to that belief as an article of faith. It'd be too hard to bear if she knew and still treated him as though nothing had changed since they were children. (But of course, faith comes in different tempers: there's the hard, brittle faith that shatters when it meets an obstacle it can't cut through, and the tough, springy faith that bounces off unchipped.)

Just for once, Miel didn't go to his office, or a meeting, or Orsea's apartments; just for once, he went home. Not proper home, of course; proper home was a castle on top of a mountain in the Sabens, seventy miles away along narrow cliffside roads. Home in Civitas Eremiae meant the Ducas house down by the Essenhatz gate; a tall, thin house cut into the rock, with the finest Mannerist fresco ceilings in the city and virtually no windows. All there was to see from the street was a small, very old double gate, grainy gray wood worn smooth and shiny, studded with heavy nails, in a solid slab wall. Beyond the gate was the famous Ducas knot garden; a square courtyard with a formal garden in the middle, divided into twelve segments by low box and lavender hedges radiating out from a central fountain like wheel-spokes. Each segment was planted out with seventeen different types of white and yellow rose, all of them unique to this one garden (for centuries, kings, emperors and Mezentine Guild masters had pleaded and plotted in vain for cuttings; the Ducas gardeners were better paid than most goldsmiths and entirely incorruptible). Around the court-yard was the equally famous painted cloister, on whose ceiling the finest artists had recorded the glorious deeds of the thirty-seven Ducas, from Amadea I down to Garsio IV, Miel's father; there was still the underside of an arch and a portico left bare for Miel, as and when he ever got around to achieving anything. If he did well, and one day married and had a son who lived up to the fami-ly's glorious traditions, they'd either have to scrape off Amadea I's wedding for him, or build a covered walkway to the fountain.

At the left-hand corner of the north side of the cloister was the family door (as opposed to the visitors' door, which was twelve feet high, bronze-embossed with scenes of warfare and the chase), which opened directly on to the back stair, which in turn led up to the first-floor back landing. Only the Ducas and their inner servants ever permeated through the various filters to this part of the house, which was plain black oak floorboards and paneling, with not so much as a painted architrave in sight. Fifth door off the landing was the writing room (according to family tradition, the first sixteen Ducas hadn't known how to write and hadn't wanted to), where the head of the family could finally turn at bay like a hunted boar and be safe for a while from his guests, his dependents and his responsibilities. It wasn't a spectacular interior—the fire-place was plain and unadorned, apart from the monogram of the ninth Ducas cut into the upper panel, and the plasterwork on the ceiling was positively restrained by the standards of the time—but it had become sanctified over the centuries by its function, as the only place on earth where the Ducas could be sure of being alone.

Miel dropped into the chair—there was only one in the writing room—and stretched out his legs toward the cold fireplace. What had possessed him, he wondered, to raise the subject? He'd not so much dropped a hint as bombarded her with it, like the Mezentines with their scorpions; she must have guessed that he'd intercepted the letter and read it, and that could only make everything worse. He supposed he'd wanted to know how she felt about the man she was writing to, and he'd hoped she'd betray her emotions to his mercilessly perceptive eye. That'd be in character; he'd always been prone to doing stupid things on the spur of the moment. Now, of course, the next time he encountered her, the gates would be shut and the walls lined with archers; he'd never get past her calm stare again, or her smile. It had been a double betrayal too, because he should have gone to Orsea as soon as he saw her name on the little folded-up parchment square. All in all, he reckoned, he'd just reached a new pinnacle of achievement in a lifetime of making bad situations worse by getting involved.

He sat until it was too dark to see; then he crossed the landing to the lesser hall. He found a footman there, messing about with the flower arrangement on the long table.

"I need to send a letter to my cousin Jarnac," he said.

The footman bowed and left, came back a few minutes later with a writing-slope, a pen (in its ivory box, with spare nibs), a sand-shaker, a penknife (blued Mezentine steel blade, silver handle in the shape of a heron), a small square gold ink-pot with lid, the Ducas private seal, sealing-wax, candle in a silver holder and twelve sheets of the finest newly scraped parchment. The Ducas did not scribble notes on scraps with feathers.

> Miel to Jarnac
> I need you to do me a favor. The Duke—

The Duke? Orsea? No; Jarnac was third in succession to the minor title in the collateral line.

The Duke would like to go hunting; he's been working very hard, as you can imagine, and he wants a day off. Could you organize something? Nothing too formal, please; bow-and-stable, maybe, rather than a full parforce day. I expect you know where there's a nice, gentle, slow-witted boar who's tired of life. Obviously we'll have to liaise with the chamberlain's office as regards dates. There's no tearing hurry, any time in the next ten days ought to do.

He waggled the sand-shaker over the page, blew, folded the sheet twice and sealed it. The footman, who didn't seem to have moved at all while he'd been writing, put all the bits and pieces back into the slope, took the letter and glided away, swift and silent as a cloud riding a strong wind.

An hour later, Miel was in the small library, painfully refreshing his childhood memories of King Fashion and Queen Reason, when the reply came. Cousin Jarnac's handwriting had always annoyed Miel intensely; Jarnac was a great big tall, broad man with fingers like peasant sausages, but he had the most elegant, almost dainty handwriting.

Jarnac to Miel

Delighted. Leave everything to me. Will sort dates out direct with chamberlain. Can offer trophy four-year-old abnormal in the Farthings, or possible record six-year-old feral cross in the Collamel valley; advise. Could do both in same day, but would involve early start and long ride in between; up to you.

Miel sighed. King Fashion had just reminded him that abnormal meant a boar with unusual-shaped tusks, but he had no idea what a feral cross was.

PS What's the name of that Mezentine character who's just set up shop in town? I seem to remember you had something to do with him. If we're hosting the Duke, better get the kit overhauled, don't you think?

The footman brought back the writing-slope, the pen, the sand-shaker and all the rest of the panoply. Miel wrote:

Miel to Jarnac

Leave it all to your discretion. The Mezentine is called Ziani Vaatzes; care of Sorit Calaphates ought to find him — they're in partnership. Don't know if he's actually trading yet, but you can try. Say I sent you if you think it'll help.

On second thoughts, not the one in the Collamel valley. I'm under strict orders: no rivers.

Sealed, handed over to the footman; done. That should have been that, but Miel found he couldn't keep still. It was like an insect-bite or nettle-rash, the letter, a speck of grit lodged in his mind's eye. All of his illustrious line had been fretters, prone to waking up in the early hours of the morning and scaring themselves to death with perilous thoughts. What if someone else got hold of it? Unlikely (his better self, fighting a doomed rearguard action), because it was locked up in his trunk in his office, and the trunk had a genuine Mezentine three-lever lock — his great-grandfather had brought it back from the City sixty-two years ago, the first Mezentine lock ever seen in Eremia — not to mention sides of inch-thick oak board and massive steel bands, hardened and tempered like a sword-blade. Yes, but three men with axes would take a quarter of an hour to get through that, and there the letter would be, nestling inside like a scorpion in a bouquet of roses. Suppose she'd realized he'd got it — how couldn't she, since he'd been so stupid? — and was feeling desperate; what would she do, she'd get her secretary or her maid's lover to hire some thugs from the marketplace to go and get it (she'd know where he'd keep it; she knew him too well); they'd make a botch of the job and get caught, be searched, the letter would be in Orsea's hands by morning, with full details of where it had been found. Leaving it there was next thing to pinning it up on the castle gate. Or maybe she'd already decided to cut her losses by going to Orsea, telling him about it—an innocent letter, I knew him years ago when we were just children, but Miel got hold of it and I think he means to make trouble, I thought you ought to know; and Orsea would know about the trunk—they'd tried to pick the lock together when they were kids, failed, of course; the world-famous Ducas chest with its legendary lock; he'd send his men with axes and big hammers, and God only knew what the upshot would be.

I've got to get rid of it, he thought, it's the only way out of this. No letter, no proof, no risk. But he knew he couldn't do that— because it was important, because he wasn't at all sure why it was important; because it was something of hers, and he had so very little of her, it'd be murder to kill something that had been made for her. So, can't burn it or bury it; he'd have to find a better place to keep it, which shouldn't be hard, surely. The Ducas house was full of places where a letter could be kept hidden. He'd spent enough weary, frustrating hours looking for things he'd put in a safe place over the years to know that the house guarded its secrets with grim efficiency. There were all sorts of places that only he knew about: the crack where the paneling was lifting away from the wall in the old chapel, the false front over the boarded-up fireplace in the flower still. At least it'd be here, under his eye. It'd be far more awkward for Orsea, or a bunch of hired muscle, to come looking for it here than in his office in the castle; there'd have to be explanations, scenes, offense given and umbrage taken, writs and warrants, enough delay that he'd have time to nip in, recover it and put it on the fire while the search party was still outside in the courtyard arguing the toss with the porters.

It was getting late, but the household was used to him slipping out to the castle at all hours. He let himself out through the postern, a small, secret door that led directly into the Essenhatz watch-tower. The duty sergeant knew him by sight, of course, and nodded respectfully as he hurried past, down the smooth spiral staircase into Essenhatz Street; across the Blind Bridge into Lepers' Court, down the twenty-seven steps of Cutlers' Stair into Desirat, across the open square with its seven orange trees into Farriers' Path and then Miraval, leading to the Ducas' private sally-port into the castle yard; across four quadrangles and down the west cloister to the foot of the stairs that led to his office, on whose floor rested the Ducas trunk with its famous but ultimately unreliable imported lock.

He'd remembered to bring the key with him, which was a blessing.

It was still there, where he'd left it, tucked into a report on waste and inefficiency in charcoal procurement. For a moment he weakened; wasn't he worrying unnecesarily, wouldn't it be safer to leave it where it was, the strongest box in Eremia Montis (apart from the other Ducas trunk in the treasury of Sabens Guard; it had not one but three Mezentine locks, and the head keeper's wolfhound liked to sleep on top of it; but of course that'd be the first place anybody'd think of looking)? His fingertips were slick with damp as he picked it up. Not for the first time, he wished he'd been born to a simpler life.

After a long and painful bout of indecision, he stuffed it into his left sleeve and buttoned the cuff down tight around it. There was nobody about — nobody he could see, at any rate — in the cloister, he heard no footsteps echoing his own across the quadrangles and the yard. He fumbled with the key to the sally-port, nearly dropped it as he locked up behind him. He went back home a different way, just in case.

Ziani was tempering a spring in the lead bath when the odd-job boy found him; he opened the door at precisely the wrong moment, when Ziani's concentration was fixed on the faint bloom of color in the hot metal, visible only in the concentrated beam of light slanting through the narrow window into the darkened gallery. When the door opened, light flooded in like the sea overrunning the polder at Lonazep.

"Get out," Ziani snapped.

But by then it was too late; the job would have to be done all over again (reheat to bright orange, quench in salt water, dry thoroughly, dip in molten lead till the blue smudge shows) and yelling at the workforce wouldn't help. It wasn't as if the boy had done it on purpose.

"Sorry," he said, straightening up and lifting the tongs clear of the tank. "Not your fault. What is it?"

The boy looked at him nervously. "Man here to see you," he replied. "Said it's dead urgent. I told him you're busy but it's life and death, he said."

Ziani frowned. "Did he say his name?"

"Ducas."

"Oh." Ziani shrugged. "Better show him in, then." He banked the fire up with fresh coal to keep it alight, in case the emergency took more than a few minutes.

The man who pushed past the boy and strode in (not many people can genuinely stride; it's part breeding, part knack) was easily the biggest human being Ziani had ever seen. It was hard to gauge his height with any precision, because the breadth of his shoulders and the thickness of his neck skewed the proportions; at a guess, Ziani reckoned six and a half feet, a foot taller than the average Mezentine. It was only his size that made his head seem small; he had a clean-cut face, strong chin, high cheekbones, bright blue eyes, hair cropped very short; if he carried enough fat to fry a pigeon's egg, Ziani would've been most surprised. His fingers were huge but his hands were long, his forearms widening from a slim wrist to a massive swell of muscle above the elbow. He was smiling.

"You're Ziani Vaatzes," the man said.

Well-informed, too. "That's right," Ziani said, letting the bad pronunciation go by. "The boy said there's an emergency."

"You can say that again," the man said. "I'm Jarnac Ducas, by the way. You know my cousin Miel."

Ziani nodded. "The emergency?" he said.

Jarnac Ducas sat on the table of the big anvil, his knee hooked over the horn. He looked like a hero on his day off. "Pretty desperate," he said, and his eyes actually twinkled as he smiled. "I've been told to organize a hunt for the Duke and party in ten days' time and you should see the state the gear's in. Spear-blades blunt, rusty and bent, loose on the stem, hanging by their langets, some of them. Question is, will it be quicker to fettle the old ones or make, say, a dozen from scratch? You tell me," he added, before Ziani could say anything, "you're the expert."

"Spear-blades," Ziani repeated.

"That's right," said Jarnac. "You know the pattern, of course: broad leaf shape with a strong middle rib, flowing into a square shank with a slot for the stem, crossbar, langets on two sides. Don't get me wrong, the old ones are good bits of kit, been in the family since God knows when, but it's the look of the thing more than anything. I don't want any fancy engraving or anything, just a really good, strong tool that'll get the job done. Actually," he added, "better make it fourteen. Couple of spares won't hurt, and I'm not absolutely sure yet who'll be coming."

Ziani looked at him for a moment before answering. "I'm sorry," he said, "but I'm rather busy at the moment, and it's not really the sort of thing I do. I'm sure there's plenty of other smiths who'll do a much better job than I could."

The wrong answer, evidently; Jarnac Ducas gave him a well-bred look and went on: "Obviously, since it's a rush job, that'll have to be reflected in the price. I don't mind paying over the odds for the best. The main thing is to have them ready in time without skimping on quality. I'm sure you understand."

Then Ziani realized he was being stupid, allowing his irritation to cloud his perception. He looked at Jarnac Ducas again and this time saw him for what he was. "Of course," he said. "I think the best thing would be if you could have the old spears brought here, so I can have a look at them and decide whether they can be spruced up, or whether we'll need to make new ones. Would that be all right?"

"Of course. I'll see to it straight away."

"That would be most helpful," Ziani said.

Jarnac beamed at him; he'd forgiven and forgotten the earlier misunderstanding, where Ziani had misinterpreted his request as something capable of being refused, and now they understood each other. "Oh, and another thing," he said.

Half an hour later, Ziani crossed the yard to the materials store, where Cantacusene was marking out timber for scorpion frames. Cantacusene had joined him straight away, as soon as he asked; he'd left his workshop, locking the door behind him, and vowing never to return. It was like a religious conversion, a disciple following the master.

"What do you know," Ziani asked him, "about boiled leatherwork?"

"Ah." Cantacusene nodded. "You don't do that in Mezentia, then."

Ziani shook his head. "Not that I ever heard. But it'd presumably come under the Shoemakers', or maybe the Saddlers'. You know about it, then."

Cantacusene nodded again. "You take your leather," he said, "sole bends are best but it depends on what you're making. You cut it out a third bigger than you want it to be, nail it to a wooden former, and dip it in boiling water for as long as it takes to count fifty. Pull it out, it'll have shrunk to size and gone hard as oak. They use it for armor mostly. Why?"

Ziani frowned. "Why not use steel?" he said.

"Steel's dear, leather's cheap. Also, for hunting armor, it doesn't clank or rattle. If you want to be really fancy, you can dip it in melted beeswax instead of boiling water; makes it even harder, but you got to be careful on a hot day."

"You've done it, then?"

"Loads of times," Cantacusene said. "Very popular line with the gentry, specially those who can't run to a full set of steel. I got all the formers back at my place."

"Fine," Ziani said. "Some clown called Jarnac Ducas wants a dozen sets of hunting armor in ten days: vambraces, couters, rere-braces, pauldrons, gorgets, plackets, cuirasses, taces, cuisses, cops and greaves. Plain, he said, not fancy, whatever that means."

Cantacusene was staring at him. "Ten *days?*"

"That's right. Problem?"

"I can't do all that. Not on my own."

Ziani smiled; at least his lips parted, like a crack in an old post. "Well of course not," he said. "You show me what to do and I'll help you. Doesn't sound like it'd be too hard, not if you've already got the formers."

Cantacusene had that worried look; there was something dog-like about it, Ziani thought. "Me teach you?" he said.

"That's right. Now, presumably you know where we can get the material from, and you've got all the tools and stuff. The material won't be a problem, will it?"

Cantacusene shook his head. "Sole bends," he said. "Got to be a quarter inch thick, good clean hides without scars or fly-bites. I always used to get them from—"

"I'll leave all that to you, then," Ziani said. "Let me know when you're ready to start. And, I nearly forgot, we'll need a thirteenth set, but I'll be making that one all myself."

"For his lordship, is it?"

"No," Ziani said. "For me." He smiled again; private joke. "I'm going on this hunt as well."

Cantacusene couldn't have been more surprised if Ziani had pushed him down a well. "You're going hunting with the Ducas?"

"That's right. Jarnac invited me."

"Invited you?"

"After I asked him, yes. I said I'd never done it, nothing like it where I come from. He was very pleasant about it; of course I could come along, he said. I suppose he's hoping for a good deal on the armor. Oh yes, and a dozen boar-spears as well, but I'll see to them."

That was obviously as much as Cantacusene could take. He mumbled something about going to see the leather merchant, and stumbled away as though he'd been in a fight.

Ziani shrugged, and went back to tempering his spring. It came out well enough in the end; half as much power again as the Mezentine standard for a scorpion spring, with a modified hook linkage that should help with the awkward problem of stress fracture that the Guild had given up on two hundred years ago. It would increase the strain on the wooden frame, of course, reducing the machine's working life still further, but that hardly mattered. No point building anything to last, given who his customers would be.

Cantacusene came back two hours later; the material would be delivered early in the morning (he started to tell Ziani the price, but Ziani wasn't interested), and the carrier would pick up the tools and formers from his workshop later that evening; they could start work tomorrow, if that suited. Ziani thanked him and went back to his bench, where he was clearing up a few minor problems with a redesigned ratchet axis. He would have liked to have given it more thought, made a few more changes, but there wouldn't be time now. His mind drifted; he was contemplating a two-piece fabricated spear-blade socket, square section box drawn down so the tang of the blade could simply slot in (interference fit) and be retained by the crossbar —

"Are you busy? Could you spare a moment?"

It was the Ducas voice, but not Jarnac this time; quieter, politer. Which meant it had to be the more important one, Miel Ducas. Ziani put down his calipers, looked up and smiled.

"Of course," he said. "What can I do for you?"

Miel Ducas looked different; tired, that would account for some of it, but he'd also been worrying about something recently. His face wasn't exactly hard to read. "I've got a message for you, from the Duke's council. They'll be writing, but I thought I'd come and tell you myself."

There could be no doubt as to what the message would be;

even so, Ziani found that his lungs were locked and he couldn't breathe. "That was very kind of you," he said. "This is about the scorpions."

Miel nodded. "The council would like to place an order," he said, in a guarded, level voice. "Basically, as many as you can make, as soon as possible."

Ziani nodded. He was afraid it'd look offhand, but he wasn't able to speak. Miel Ducas was having difficulties, too; he started to say something, hesitated, and started again.

"About the price—" he said.

"That's all right," Ziani interrupted. "I've decided I'll do it at cost—materials and what I'll have to pay my men. Calaphates doesn't know yet, but I'll talk to him."

"That's—" Miel stopped; he reminded Ziani of someone searching for a word in a foreign language. "That's very generous of you," he said.

"Least I can do," Ziani replied. "After all, I owe you people my life. My way of saying thank you."

A long moment, with neither of them knowing quite how to say what was in their minds. Then Ziani went on: "We'll start straight away. I've been doing some preliminary work, a few improvements to the design. Nothing you'd notice, unless you knew what you were looking for. I've taken on twenty men so far, and there's fifteen more I'm waiting to hear from."

"That's a lot," Miel said, though he knew he was wrong as soon as he said it. "I thought you were on your own here, actually."

Ziani smiled. "That wouldn't be any good, not for a job like this. Actually, I won't be involved at all, once everything's up and running. In fact, I'll be busy with a job for your cousin."

"Jarnac?" Miel scowled. "Look, no offense, but this is far more important. I'll talk to Jarnac, tell him he'll have to find someone else."

"It's all right," Ziani said. "Once everything's set up, I'm just another pair of hands. Besides, your cousin's job'll only take a week, and then I'll be free to muck in with the rest of the men.

You'll have the first half-dozen scorpions finished and ready in three days, you've got my word on that."

When the Ducas had gone and he was alone, Ziani allowed his knees to buckle, as they'd been wanting to do ever since he'd heard the words he knew he'd hear. He leaned against the wall and slid down it, until he was sitting on the floor. Strange; it was simply the moving into engagement of a component of known qualities, sliding along its keyway and coming to rest against its stop. Perhaps it was the scale of what this development meant that affected him so powerfully: the expenditure of lives and resources, the men killed (they were alive, presumably walking about, eating, talking somewhere, but they were already as good as dead, and Ziani had seen to all that); the destruction, the laying waste, the burning and breaking of well-made goods, the sheer effort he'd unleashed; like the man in the story who was given all the four winds tied up in a sack, and some fool untied it and let them go. There would be so much noise, and movement, and pain. A man with a keen imagination would have trouble with the thought of it.

But not yet. Before all that, he had a lot of work to do, a great deal to think about; and he had the hunt to look forward to. As yet, that was still a separate piece, little more than an unfinished casting waiting to be fettled, machined, drilled to accept moving parts. He would have to design a mechanism for it, once he knew what it was going to be for. A pity; the man was a clown, but he'd quite liked Jarnac Ducas. There was a straightforwardness about him that he shared with his cousin. Ziani had arrived in Eremia expecting to find the aristocracy difficult to work with — brittle like cast iron, or soft and sticky to cut, like copper — but so far at least they'd proved to be quality material, a pleasure to use. It had all come together very sweetly, though of course it was the easy bit; and making the parts was one thing, assembling them was something else entirely.

This is no time to be sitting on floors, he told himself, and stood up. As he put the finishing touches to the axis pin, he called Miel Ducas back into his mind, considering and analyzing his manner, his appearance. Tired, a little nervous, and worried about something beyond the awkwardness of his mission; what would worry the Ducas, the second most important man in Eremia, to the point that it showed in his face to a stranger?

Of course he couldn't answer that, or even know where to begin speculating. You can't take the back off a man's head and examine the works for signs of damage and wear. The most you can do is make a note of where the visible flaws run, the line along which the material will eventually break once it's been flexed a few times too often.

14

The unmaking *[he read]* is the crown, the very flower of the hunt; therefore it follows that it must be conducted solemnly, seriously and with respect. There are two parts thereof, namely the abay and the undoing. First, let the carcass be turned on its back and the skin of the throat cut open most carefully up the length of the neck, and let cuts be made through the flesh to the bone. Let the master of the hunt approach then, with his sleeves rolled to the elbow, and let the huntsmen sound the death on their horns; thereafter let the hounds first and then the lymers be loosed so that they might tear at the neck before they are coupled up, that the taste thereof might quicken them to the chase thereafter. Then let a forked stick with one arm longer than the other be set up in the earth beside the carcass, and let the master with his garniture split the skin from throat to vent...

Valens frowned. The book, with its brightly colored pictures and carefully pumiced margins, had cost him the price of a small farm; but all they'd done was loosely paraphrase Cadentius, leaving a few bits out and dressing up other bits in fancy prose. For a start, the lengthwise cut was part of the undoing, not the abay; and whoever wrote this had no idea what a garniture was.

He sighed, closed the book and stood up. The woman in the red dress had sworn blind that it was the last known surviving copy of a rare early text attributed to Polinus Rex, but Polinus was three hundred years earlier than Cadentius, who'd been the first to have the master roll up his sleeves. He'd been had; twenty good-weight thalers he'd never see again, and still the woman in the red dress hadn't brought a letter...

Through the window he could see the raindrops dripping from the pine-branches. It was a hunting day, but there wasn't any point going out in this; there'd be no scent in the wet, the mud would make the going treacherous, the deer would be holding in the high wood where there'd be precious little chance of finding them. The sharpness of his disappointment surprised him; the rain would stop soon, there would be other days, the deer would still be there next week, but every day lost was a precious thing stolen from him, a treat held just out of reach to tease him. Instead, he'd have to read letters, convene the council, do work. He smiled; he could hear his eight-year-old self saying it, *not fair.* To which one of many voices replies: *life isn't fair, the sooner you learn that, the better.*

It wasn't fair that she hadn't written back; it had never been this long before, and it was no good saying there hadn't been a suitable courier, because five women in red dresses had been and gone (a velvet cloak, a set of rosewood and whalebone chessmen, a pair of pointy-toed shoes, very latest style, a marquetry box to keep things in, and finally the bloody useless book), all from Eremia, all without a letter. And on top of that, it was raining.

On a table beside the window lay a pile of documents; routine reports, mostly, from his prefects, agents and observers, making sure he knew the facts before anybody else did. He sat down and picked one off the top of the heap. The handwriting was steep and cramped, and he recognized it—his man in Lonazep, with a full account of the landing of the Mezentine mercenary army. He'd had the gist already, but there would be a great deal to be gleaned from the details, from the descriptions of the staff officers to the number of barrels of arrows. He read it, then read it again; the information was good and solid, but he couldn't get his mind to bite on it. He smiled, because he could picture his father sitting at this very table (back then, of course, it was downstairs in the small anteroom off the great solar; but the daylight lasted longer here in the West Tower), wading through his paperwork with palpable growing impatience, until he jumped up from his chair and stormed out of the room to go and look at the horses or the dogs. Somehow he'd always managed to absorb just enough from his reports to stay sharp, but he'd always lived in and for the present, content or resigned to react to each development as it came. He'd been the same when playing chess, too; he'd never quite come to terms with the idea that the point of the game was to trap the enemy king, rather than slaughter the opponent's pieces like sheep. That thought brought back the first time Valens had ever beaten him. It was an ambiguous memory, because even now he couldn't call it to mind without an automatic smirk of pride; he'd used his father's aggression against him, lured him into checkmate with the offer of a gaggle of defenseless pawns, pinned him in a corner with his only two surviving capital pieces, while his father's queen, bishops and knights stood by, unused and impotent. But he also remembered the disbelief, followed by the hurt, followed by the anger. They hadn't spoken to each other for two days afterward.

A report from Boton about a meeting between Duke Orsea and representatives of the Cure Hardy. Well; he knew about that. Orsea had picked the wrong sect to make eyes at, and the whole thing had been a waste of time. A report from Civitas Eremiae about the Mezentine defector, Vaatzes; what he was up to was still unclear, but he'd got money from somewhere to set up a factory, and was buying up bloom iron, old horseshoes, farm scrap iron of all kinds; also, he'd hired half the blacksmiths and carpenters in the city. Valens raised an eyebrow at that. If he'd heard about it, he was pretty sure the Mezentines had too, and surely such reports would confirm their worst fears about defectors betraying their precious trade secrets. If this Vaatzes had deliberately set out to antagonize the Republic, he couldn't have gone about it better. Valens went back a line: broken scythe blades, rakes, pitch-fork tines, hooks, hammers, any kind of scrap made of hardening steel; also charcoal in enormous quantities, planed and unplaned lumber. The steel suggested weapons; the lumber sounded more like building works. He folded down a corner of the dispatch and moved on.

Petitions; he groaned aloud, allowing himself the indulgence of a little melodrama, since there was nobody else there to see. Not just petitions; appeals, from the general assizes and the marches assizes and the levy sessions; appeals on points of law and points of fact, procedural irregularities (the original summons recited in the presence of eight witnesses rather than the prescribed seven; how that could possibly invalidate a man's case he had no idea, but that was the law), limitations and claims out of time. He could just about have endured a morning in court, with a couple of clever speakers to entertain him, but the thought of sitting at a table and fighting his way through a two-inch wedge of the stuff made him wince.

Nevertheless, he told himself; I am the Duke, and therefore duty's slave. Never mind. He broke the seal on the first one and tried to concentrate.

Alleged: that Marcianus Lolliotes of Ascra in the Dalmatic ward beginning in the time of Duke Valentinius on occasions too numerous to particularize entered upon the demesne land of Aetius Cassinus with the intention of cutting hay, the property of the said Cassinus. Defended: that the said land was not the demesne land of the said Cassinus, having been charged by the said Cassinus' grandfather in the time of Duke Valentius with payment to the great-grandfather of the said Lolliotes of heriot and customary mortmain, which payments were duly made but without the interest thereto pertaining; accordingly, the said Lolliotes having an interest in the said land, there was no trespass; further or in the alternative...

It took him a long time, and he had to check many cross-references in many books before he managed to get it all straight in his mind, but he got there in the end. As usual, it was nobody's fault, both of them were sort of right and slightly wrong, and there wasn't a clear-cut or obvious solution, because the law was outdated, contradictory and sloppily drawn, made up on the spot by his great-great-grandfather, probably because he was bored and wanted to go outside in the fresh air and kill something rather than sitting indoors. Wearily, Valens uncapped his ink-well, dipped the nib and started to write. It didn't have to be fair copy; he had secretaries to do the bland, beautiful, cursive law-hand that needed to stay legible for centuries. But the sheer effort of writing made his wrist and forearm ache, and although he knew what he wanted to say, it was hard to keep everything in order; the points, facts and conclusions strayed like willful sheep and had to be chased back into the fold. He lost his way twice, had to cross out and go back; the pen dropped a big fat blot and he'd swept his sleeve across it before he noticed. When finally it was done he read it through twice (once silently, once aloud) for errors and ambiguities; made three corrections; read it through again and realized one correction was actually a mistake; corrected the correction, read it through one more time, sprinkled and blew off sand, put it on the corner of the desk for the copyist to deal with later. Last step: he made a note in the margin of the relevant page of his copy of the *Consolidated Digest,* in his smallest writing (*can't charge for heriot in 3d generation, statute barred after 2d, but reliefs apply in equity*), to save himself the effort of doing all the research if the point happened to come up ever again. It was a good practice, recommended by several authors on jurisprudence, and he'd wasted more time looking for notes he'd made eighteen months ago but forgotten exactly where or under what than he'd have spent looking it all up from scratch.

(*Just think,* he told himself; *men scheme and betray and murder so as to get to be kings and dukes, and this is what they end up doing all day long. Serves them right, really.*)

Mercifully, the next three petitions weren't nearly so bad. Two of them were points he knew, and there was already an annotation on the relevant page of the book for the third—not his writing, or his father's; his grandfather, maybe, or his great-uncle, during his father's short but disastrous regency. Possibly on a better day he'd have checked for himself rather than take the unknown writer's word for it; possibly not. The fifth petition made up for the three easy ones; it was something to do with uses on lives in being and the perpetuity rules, which he'd never been able to understand, and there was a barred entail, a claim of adverse possession and the hedge-and-ditch rule thrown in for good measure. He could have been outside in the fresh air killing something (wry smile for his earlier self-righteousness) but he fought his way through to the end, realized he still couldn't make head or tail of it, and decided to split the difference: farmer Mazaninus could have the north end of the field and farmer Ischinus could have the south end, and they could share the bloody water and like it. Enough justice for one day. Too much fun is bad for the soul.

Perhaps, he thought (the ink-bottle was still uncapped, he had plenty of paper left), he should write to her again—no mention of the fact that she hadn't replied to his last letter, just something bright and witty and entertaining, the sort of thing he could do well, for some reason he'd never been able to grasp. If what he'd said the last time had offended her, maybe it'd be the right thing to pretend that letter had never been written; they could start again, talking about Mannerist poetry, observations on birds and flowers, the weather. But if he knew her (he'd only talked to her once, but how could there be anybody in the world he knew better?) she wouldn't sulk if he'd offended her, or break off entirely; she'd tell him he was wrong, stupid, insensitive, horrible, but she'd write back, if she possibly could. So maybe she couldn't.

The hell with this, he thought. He frowned, took a new sheet of paper, and started to write: to Lelius Lelianus, alias Nustea Cordatzes, timber merchant in Civitas Eremiae and his best spy in Eremia. Query: any rumors circulating anywhere about the Duchess, ructions in the Duke's household, society scandals, unexplained disappearances of Merchant Adventurers. Urgent. That one he wrote out himself, rather than adding it to the pile for copying.

Outside, the rain had slowed to a fine drizzle. He went down two flights to his wardrobe, quickly put on an oilskin cloak, big hat and waxed boots, collected a bow and quiver from the ascham (an old self-bow that wouldn't come apart in the wet) and left the castle by the north-end postern, heading for the dew-ponds. There might be duck there, though strictly speaking ducks didn't start for a month (but what's the point in being supreme and final judge of appeals if you can't bend the rules in an emergency?), and he hadn't shot for weeks.

The air smelled wet. It had been an unusually dry summer, so the rain hadn't sunk in to what passed for soil in the high marches. Water trickled down from his hair into his eyes, like tears, and he mopped it away with the back of his hand. Nobody had been this way for several days; the footprints in the softened dirt of the track had baked into puddled cups, filling with rain. He brushed past a low branch, spraying water. A drop landed on his tongue, and he spared some attention to taste it. *I'm a different man outside,* he thought; *not better, but different.*

The path down to the ponds was steep, slicked with dust turned to mud; he had to dig his heels in to keep upright, and the soles of his boots were too smooth (some hobnails would deal with that, if he remembered later). The light below the treeline was gray and faintly misty, and he could smell the leaves and the wet leaf-mold. He was aware of the silence, until something crashed away twenty yards or so to his left; a pricket buck, probably (he'll keep, he thought, and made an entry in his mental register). There weren't any duck, which was probably just as well for his conscience. He stood under a crooked beech tree for half an hour, listening to the rain and watching for ducks flighting in for the evening feed, but nothing showed; so he shot a big old crow out of the upper branches and went home.

They had told her that Orsea was in the arbor behind the chestnut tree. She called his name a few times, but he didn't reply, so she assumed he'd gone back inside. Then she caught sight of a flash of blue through the curtain of trailing vine. He hadn't answered her because he was asleep.

Like an old man, she thought, snoozing in the afternoon. Orsea never slept during the day; indeed, he resented sleep on principle, the way people resent paying taxes. It wasn't fair, he'd told her once, that nature only gave you a very short time on earth, and then saw fit to steal a third of it back from you. At one time he'd tried to train himself to make do with less of it—like a devious banker, he'd said, clipping little bits off the edges of coins. If he learned how to get by on seven hours a night instead of eight, he'd told her, at the end of a year he'd have gained fifteen days. Suppose he lived another forty years; that'd be over eighteen months, absolutely free. But it hadn't lasted, of course. He struggled through six weeks of the new regime, yawning and drifting off into daydreams, and then issued a revised opinion. Scrounging extra time by neglecting a vital function like sleep was counterproductive. For every waking hour gained you sacrificed two or three spent in a daze halfway between concussion and a bad hangover. In fact, eight hours wasn't really enough. Nine hours, on the other hand; nine hours would lose you eighteen months, theoretically speaking, but the extra energy and zest you'd get from being properly rested would mean you'd fit more activity into your voluntarily truncated life than you'd manage to wring out of your unnaturally extended one.

He was asleep now, though; dead to the world, with his head cradled on his arms, his face buried in the extravagant sleeves of his blue slash-cut doublet. Men say that the sight of a man asleep touches a woman's maternal instinct; for once, she thought, men might have a point. He looked about twelve years old, his hair scrambled, the tip of his nose visible in the crook of his elbow. She felt a deep-seated urge to tuck a blanket round him.

"Orsea," she said. He didn't stir, so she came closer. "Orsea."

At least he didn't snore. She could never have endured a snorer. Her brother had snored so badly, all through her early years, when he slept at her end of the great solar, no barrier to the excruciating noise except a tapestry screen, that her first thought when they told her he was dead was that now she'd be able to sleep at night. False optimism; by the time she'd driven his face out of her dreams, her father's had replaced it. Lately, she'd dreamed about Orsea, dead on the battlefield or hanging by his hair from the low branches of a tree.

"Orsea," she said. He twitched a little, like a pig. She smiled, and sat down beside him. When he was so fast asleep that her voice didn't stir him, it meant he'd wake up of his own accord quite soon. She could wait. She could sit and read the letter from Maiaut, and get that particular chore out of the way.

Maiaut to Veatriz: greetings.

Or not. It was a warm, mellow autumn day, too pleasant to spoil with echoes of the most annoying of all her sisters. There was something about Maiaut, even on paper, that made her want to break things. That was, of course, unreasonable. It wasn't Maiaut's fault that she was a widow; and there was nothing inherently wrong with a noblewoman in reduced circumstances putting on the red dress and trekking around the world buying and selling things. It had taken her away from home, and it meant that her visits to Civitas Eremiae were pleasantly infrequent, though not nearly infrequent enough. She made enough money at it, God only knew (there were times, black times in the middle of the night when her dreams stabbed her awake, when she suspected that Maiaut had considerably more money than she did; and wouldn't that count as high treason, being richer than your Duchess?), and it gave her plenty of scope for her exceptional gift for whining.

Maiaut to Veatriz, greetings.

Well, here I am in Caervox. It's a nasty, smelly place. The water in the public reservoir is green on top and there are green squiggly things living in it; probably explains why the people here don't wash. The food tastes like armpit. I'm stuck here for another three days at least, probably more like five, because I'm waiting for a mule-train from Corsus, and the Cure Doce muleteers are the laziest people on earth. Also the most careless, so they may not arrive at all, or else they'll turn up without the cargo, having dropped it down a crevasse or lost it crossing a river. If by some miracle they do eventually show up, I'll be taking fifteen hundred rolls of gaudy, stringy carpet with me south to Herulia; sell enough of it there for a grubstake, and move on to Civitas Vadanis by slow, easy stages. At least the Vadani pay in silver and I won't be lumbered with anything bulky or heavy, though of course the western passes are swarming with bandits.

"Orsea," Veatriz said loudly, and still he didn't move. She resented him for not waking up and saving her from Maiaut's letter.

Mind you, bandits are likely to be the least of my troubles crossing the border, if the latest rumors are true. They were saying in Durodrice that there could be a war, Eremia against the Republic. I told them don't be silly, the war's been and gone, but they reckon there's going to be another one. I asked them, how could they possibly know that? Of course, you can't get a straight answer out of these people. It makes doing business with them very trying indeed. They just smile at you and look dumb and innocent, or gabble away among themselves.

"Triz," said a voice beside her. "Where did you appear from? I didn't see you come."

There were times when she'd wondered if she really loved him;

because if she did, why did she feel hot and panicky when she saw Valens' name on the top line of a letter? And there were times like this, when it was so obvious she loved him, it was surprising how passers-by could see them together and not grin. She'd never doubted him like that. She knew exactly what and how Orsea felt, as though there was a little window in the side of his head and she could read all his thoughts written up on a blackboard.

"You were fast asleep," she said.

He groaned. "What's the time? I only came out here so I could concentrate on this wretched report. I tried reading it indoors but people kept coming up and talking to me, so I slipped out here."

"About an hour after noon," she said. "Hungry?"

He shook his head. He was never hungry when he'd just woken up. "I'll have something later. I'll need to see Miel about this purchase order business; we can have something together."

She nodded, hurt; but he was looking dozy and creased, and she knew he hadn't meant it to sound the way it came out. "What's the report about?" she asked. "Something important?"

"Unfortunately," he said. "Those horrible machines the Mezentines used on us. The exile, that chap we found, he reckons he can build them for us, loads of them and quickly. The committee's agreed and placed an order."

"Can they do that?" she asked. "Without you agreeing, I mean?"

He smiled. "No they can't," he said, "which is why I've got to read their report and then sign it. Then they'll be able to. In practice I leave them to it, they know all about this sort of stuff, far more than I do, so I'd be stupid not to do as they say. So the decision's been made already, but I've still got to plow my way through it."

"Can't you just sign it and pretend you've read it?"

He laughed, as though she'd meant it as a joke. "He offered me something like it before," he said, "the day we found him, in fact. I turned him down. To listen to him talk, he was going to turn the whole of Civitas into one huge factory. Now he's back again, apparently, and he's got Sorit Calaphates putting up the money and an old tanner's yard, which he's—"

"Sorit Calaphates?" she interrupted. "Lycaena's father?"

Orsea thought for a moment. "That's right," he said. "I'd forgotten you knew the family. How is Lycaena, by the way?"

"Haven't seen her for a while." She hesitated, but the hesitation was too obvious; he'd noticed it. "Careo was wounded in the war," she said. "He lost an arm, and he was in pretty bad shape for a while. But last time I heard he was on the mend; they've gone back to his uncle's place out on the Green River while he gets his strength back."

"Ah," Orsea said, and for a moment she saw that terrible look in his eyes; something new to feel guilty about, ambushing him in his safe place, like the hunters in bow-and-stable. "Anyway," he went on, "that's what this report's about; and even if I could say no now that the council's approved it, I wouldn't." He shook his head, like a horse plagued with flies in summer. "I hate the thought of those machines, after what they did to us. I can't get those pictures out of my head, all those dead men pinned to the ground, and the ones who weren't dead yet... But if there's going to be an invasion—"

"Which there won't be," she said.

"If there's going to be an invasion, and if this wretched man can make them for us, so we can put them up on the ramparts and shoot down at the road; just think, Triz, it could be the difference between surviving and being wiped out. So of course we've got to have them, even if it's an evil, wicked thing." He turned his head away so he wasn't looking at her; as if he could pass on the infection through his eyes. "People used to think," he said, "that there were gods who punished you if you did bad things, and sometimes I wonder if they're not still up there, in the clouds or on top of Crane Mountain or wherever it was they were supposed to live. It'd be a joke if they were, don't you think? But if they really are still there, it'd be better if they only had me to pick on for arming the city with scorpions, rather than all of us. It all comes from my mistake, so——"

"You should hear yourself," she said. "Really, Orsea. This is so stupid."

He shook his head again. "I keep having these dreams," he said. "I'm at this place my uncle Achima took me to once, when I was a kid. It's on a hilltop in the Lanceta; there's a river winding round the bottom of the hill, really peaceful and quiet, you can see for miles but you won't see another human being. But years ago——a thousand years, Uncle Ach said——it was a great castle; you can still make out ditches and ramparts and gateways, just dips and humps in the ground now, with grass growing. In my dream, I'm climbing up this hill and I'm asking my uncle who built it, and he says nobody knows, they all died out so long ago we don't know a thing about them; and when I get to the top and look down, it's not the Lanceta any more, it's here; and then I realize that I'm seeing where Civitas used to be, before the Mezentines came and killed us all, till there weren't any of us left; and they only came because of me——"

"That's ridiculous," she said. "It's just a dream."

He turned a little more; his back was to her. "Anyhow," he said, "that's why I've got to read the stupid report."

"I see," she said. "I'm sorry. I wouldn't have woken you up if I'd known."

"Triz..." He was still looking away, so she couldn't see. "If I abdicated, do you think Miel would make a good Duke?"

"You can't abdicate," she said. "You know that."

"I'm the Duke because I'm married to you," he said.

"I think it's a stupid question," she said. "And there won't be an invasion, because they've got no reason to invade. It won't make money for them if we're all dead. And as long as you're like this, you're no good to anybody."

She didn't wait to see if he turned round. She crossed the lawn to the arch that led back into the cloister, straight up the stairs to the little solar. Most of all, she hated Valens, because he hadn't answered her letter, and instead she had to reply to her insufferable sister, who thought there was going to be an invasion, because that was what they were saying in the market at Durodrice, wherever the hell that was. (If there was an invasion, she thought, could they escape to Durodrice, among the peaceful, cowlike Cure Doce? Would they take them in, or would they be afraid of the Mezentines?) She had a good mind to sit down right now and write to Valens, telling him she didn't want to hear from him anymore. It was wrong, anyway, this secret correspondence; she ought to put an end to it before it was found out, and people got the wrong idea. Would Valens protect them? Protect them both? The boy she'd spoken to would, but he wasn't the man who wrote to her about Mannerist poetry and the hover of the peregrine and the blind carter whose dog opened gates for him. She knew him too well. He'd protect both of them, just as he'd rescued Orsea in the Butter Pass, even if it brought the Mezentines down on him and lost him his duchy. He'd do it, for her, but she'd lose him; and if she lost him, she'd have nothing; except Orsea.

I love Orsea, and I could never love anybody else. But would that be enough? If I had nothing else?

Ziani was tired; he felt like he hadn't had a good night's sleep for a year, though in fact it was only a few days; only since Jarnac Ducas had placed his order. Since then he'd been up at first light each day, cutting sixteen-ounce leather on the saddler's shear, ready for when Cantacusene arrived. He cut out the pieces, Cantacusene nailed them to the formers, did the boiling, shaping and tempering; when Cantacusene went home in the evening, Ziani did the riveting, assembly and fitting. They were getting on well, ahead of schedule. When he'd finished work for the day on the hunting armors, he went round the main shop, checking the men's progress on the first batch of scorpions—they were turning out well, too, even the lockwork and the springs. After that, he'd sit in the tower and read—either *King Fashion*, or the equally seminal and tedious *Mirror of the Chase;* he couldn't make up his mind which of them he hated more, but he now knew two thirds of both of them by heart—before finishing up the day with an hour's archery practice in the cellar.

He was doing well with the archery. This was perhaps the most surprising thing of all, since he'd never held a bow in his life before he left Mezentia. Because he had no money to buy one with and didn't know how to make one, he'd had to re-invent the bow from scratch. A bow, he realized, is just a spring. He knew how to make springs, so that was all right. He had no idea whether there was such a thing as a steel bow; but he went across to the forge after the men had gone home, drew down a length of broken cart-spring into a long, elongated diamond, worked each end down to a gentle distal taper, shaped it till it looked like pictures he'd seen in books, and tempered it to a deep blue. His first attempt at a string was three strands of fine wire, which cut his fingertips like cheese. Luckily, King Fashion had a bit to say about bowstrings; they should be linen, he reckoned, rather than hemp. He made his second string out of twelve strands of strong linen serving thread; and when it broke, the top limb of the bow smacked him so hard under the chin he blacked out for quite some time. His next attempt, eighteen strands, seemed to be strong enough, and hadn't broken yet.

Whether or not the thing he practiced with was a bow in any conventional sense of the term, it did seem to work. He was using three-eighths cedar dowel for arrows; he knew you were meant to tie or glue bits of feather on the ends, but he didn't have any feathers, and the arrows seemed to go through the air quite happily without them. He cut his arrows at thirty inches, because that was as far as he could draw them without them falling off the bow.

For a target he had a sack, lying on its side, stuffed with rags, straw and general rubbish. He'd painted a circle on it with white-wash, and at fifteen yards (which was as far back as you could go in the cellar before you bumped up against a wall) he could hit the circle four times out of six, thanks to the *Mirror,* a picture he'd seen in a book many years ago, dogged perseverance and a certain degree of common sense. One time in five that he loosed the arrow, the string would come back and lash the inside of his left forearm. He had a huge purple bruise there, which meant he had to keep his sleeve buttoned all day in case one of the men noticed. He'd made up a guard for it out of offcuts of leather, but it still hurt. Meanwhile, the inside of his right forefinger tip was red and raw, and there wasn't much he could do about that.

But nevertheless; progress was being made, and if he could get to the stage where he hit the whitewash circle six times out of six, that'd be good enough (that word again) for his purposes. Whether or not the opportunity would present itself when the time came was, of course, entirely outside his control. It depended on the whim of a hunted animal and the choices and decisions of an unascertained number of hunters, beaters and other unknowns, following rules he was struggling to learn out of a book and didn't really understand. It'd be sheer luck; he hated that. But if he got the chance, at least he'd be prepared to make the most of it. Hence King Fashion, the *Mirror*, the steel bow and archery practice.

Yesterday he'd forgotten to eat anything. Stupid; there was plenty of food, a woman brought it in a basket every morning and left it in the lodge. Calaphates had seen to that — a curious thing to do, almost as if he was concerned about Ziani's well-being. And he'd asked about it, the last two times he'd visited: *are you sure you're eating properly*, as though he was Ziani's mother.

Just looking after his investment, Ziani told himself as he lined up the leather in the shear. All these people care about is how much money I can make for them. If I don't eat and I get sick, I can't work. That explains it all.

He fed the edge of the hide in under the top blade of the shear, making sure it was in line. He'd drawn the shape onto the leather with a stick of charcoal because that was all he had to mark up with. Because of that, the lines were far too thick, allowing too great a margin of error, so he had to concentrate hard to see the true line he needed to follow. There was far too much play in the shear for his liking (he'd had to buy a shear, because there hadn't been time to make one; it was Mezentine-made, but very old and bent by years of brutal mishandling). He hated every part of this sloppy, inaccurate work, but it had to be done, just in case the opportunity arose.

"You there?"

Cantacusene. He glanced up at the high, narrow window, but he was kidding himself. Back home, there were clocks to tell the time by. Here, they seemed to be able to manage it by looking at the sun; but the slim section of gray and blue framed by the window had no sun in it. He had an idea that Cantacusene was early this morning, but he couldn't verify it. God, what a country.

"Yes, come through." He smiled. By unspoken agreement, they didn't use each other's names. Cantacusene couldn't very well call him Ziani, and Master Vaatzes would've been ridiculous coming from a man who'd been peening rivets and curling lames for the nobility when Ziani was still learning to walk; for his part, he didn't understand Eremian industrial etiquette and couldn't be bothered to learn. With goodwill and understanding on both sides and a certain degree of imagination, they'd so far managed to bypass the issue completely.

"Are you early?" he asked, as Cantacusene shuffled in.

"A bit. We need to get a move on. We've still got half the greaves and cuisses and all the gorgets to do."

Ziani shrugged. "I've cut out the gorget lames, they're ready for you. I'll have the greaves and the cuisses by dinnertime."

Cantacusene looked at him; a curious blend of admiration, devotion and hatred. He could more or less understand it. A few days ago, Ziani had known nothing about the subtle art of making boiled leather armor, and Cantacusene had been back on his familiar ground, where he knew the rules. He hadn't presumed on that superiority, but it was pretty clear he'd relished it while it lasted. Now, here was Ziani cutting out a thick stack of lames before breakfast, as well or better than Cantacusene could have done it. A god would feel unsettled, Ziani thought, if a mortal learned in a week how to make rain and raise the dead.

"That's all right, then," Cantacusene said. "I'll get a fire laid in."

"Already done," Ziani said. "You can get on with nailing up while the water boils."

The shear was even more sluggish today than usual. It munched the leather rather than slicing it, chewing ragged, hairy edges instead of crisp, square-sided cuts. Ziani quickly diagnosed the problem as drift and slippage in the jaw alignment. He could fix it, but he'd have to take the shear apart, heat the frame and bend it a little. A sloppy cut, on the other hand, was no big deal in this line of work, since the shrinkage turned even a perfectly square-shorn edge into a rounded burr in need of facing off with a rasp. There was something infuriating about seeing poor work come out indistinguishable from good work. Tolerating it was practically collaborating with evil.

The greaves were one big piece rather than lots of small lames put together, but their profile was all curves; a misery to cut, even when the shear had still been working properly. He knew how to design and build a throatless rotary shear, Mezentine pattern, that would handle the curved profiles effortlessly, but there wasn't time. It was horribly frustrating, and he felt ashamed of himself. But it was better work than the Duchy's foremost armorer could've done. That was no consolation whatsoever.

The men were turning up for the start of their day. They would be cutting and joining wood to make scorpion frames, forging the joining bands, filing and shaping the lockwork. *Other hands than mine,* he thought, and he wasn't sure whether that was a good thing or not. They would be doing his work, while he was wasting his time cutting and riveting leather to protect an aristocrat and his hangers-on from pigs with big teeth. It was hard to relate that to the invisible machine. Faith was needed, and he'd never really believed in anything much, apart from the two things he'd lost, and which were all that mattered.

Cantacusene was whistling. He did it very badly; so badly, in fact, that Ziani stopped work to listen. If there was a tune involved, he couldn't detect it. He found he was grinning. Cantacusene and music, even horribly mutilated music, didn't seem to go together.

"You're in a good mood," he said, when Cantacusene came in to collect the next batch of cut-out pieces.

"What makes you say that?"

Ziani shrugged. "I don't know," he said.

Cantacusene hesitated; apparently he had something on his mind, but was uncertain as to whether he could or should talk about it. Ziani turned back to the shear. It would have been quicker to take it to bits and straighten it after all. He hated the shear, and everything it stood for; at that moment, all the evil in the world resided in its bent and misused frame. There's a certain comfort in knowing who your enemies are.

"If you must know," Cantacusene said, "my wife's coming home today."

"Is that right?" Ziani said to the shear. "She's been away, then?"

"Yes." He couldn't see Cantacusene's face, and the word was just a word. "She's in service, see. Ladies' maid. The family's been away out east for three months."

"Ah," Ziani said. "So that's why you're in a good mood."

"Well, yes." There was obviously something in his manner that was annoying Cantacusene, keeping him there talking when he should be next door, nailing bits of leather to bits of wood. "I missed her, see. I don't like it when she's got to go away. But she doesn't want to leave the family. Been with them fifteen years."

"Well," Ziani said, "if you don't like her going away, you should tell her to pack it in. I should think you could do without her wages, now you're working here."

"Like I said, she wouldn't want to let the family down."

Ziani didn't answer, and he hunched his shoulders a little to show that it was none of his business. But Cantacusene didn't seem to be able to read body language. "You married?" he asked.

"Yes."

"Kids?"

"A daughter," Ziani replied.

Silence; then Cantacusene said: "Must be hard on you, then."

"Yes," Ziani said. "And I don't suppose I'll ever see them again."

"I couldn't handle that," Cantacusene said.

"No." Ziani let go of the shear handle. It was important that the line be cut straight, since the lame had to sit true. "Nor me." He turned round slowly. "It's difficult," he said. "It's fortunate I'm an engineer, really. Otherwise . . ." He shrugged. "What time's she due back?"

"Not till this evening," Cantacusene said. "Look, I'm sorry. Didn't mean to upset you or anything."

"No, of course." Ziani smiled, though his face felt numb. "If you want to knock off early, you go ahead."

"That's all right. Like I said, she's not back till late."

"Suit yourself." It felt like all the poison in his blood was sinking into his toes and fingers. "If you change your mind, go on anyway."

"Thanks." Cantacusene frowned, as if considering a puzzle. "I'd better be getting on," he continued. "If we lay into it, we can have the greaves finished today."

"Fine." Ziani turned his back on him, laid his hand on the shear handle. He heard footsteps, and then the whistling, far away and still terrible. He drew the handle toward him, feeling the slight spring in the leather as the blade cut it.

It was like an abcess: full of poison, under the skin, swelling, ready to burst. It was a disease lying latent in his blood, breeding and eating him. It was the worst thing in the world. It was love, and that idiot Cantacusene had reminded him of it, after he'd done so well to put it away where he couldn't see it.

Almost certainly, he knew, Cantacusene would die because of him; and his wife, the ladies' maid who spent so much precious time away, not knowing how little there was of it left. Each nail the poor fool drove through the leather into the wood brought his own death a little nearer. That wasn't so bad, Ziani reflected.

Only a coward is afraid of dying for himself; the true terror in death, the fear that crawls into the mind and stays there forever, comes from the lethal mixture of death and love, the knowledge that dying will bring unbearable pain to those we love, those who love us. Death is to be feared because of the pain and loss it inflicts through love, and for no other reason.

Not the shear, after all. Reaching down to turn the half-cut lame, Ziani admitted to himself the preeminently obvious fact that he'd been denying ever since Compliance came for him in the early hours of the morning when everything went wrong. All the evil in the world, all the harm and suffering it's possible to come to, are concentrated in one place; in love. If there was no love, there'd be no fear in death, no pain in loss, no suffering anywhere. If he could string his steel bow and nock an arrow and kill love with a single shot to the head, it'd go down in history as the day mankind was rescued from all its torments and miseries; if he could meet love face to face down the narrow shaft of a spear, like a hunter standing up to the charging boar, wolf or bear, if he could kill the monster and set the people free from all evil, then the Eremians wouldn't have to die, or the Mezentines, or the Vadani or the Cure Hardy or the Cure Doce or all the other nations of victims whose names he didn't even know yet. In old stories there are dragons who burn cities, gigantic bulls from the sea and boars with steel tusks, terrible birds with the heads of women and the bodies of lions, and a hero kills them; it's so simple in stories, because once the monster is dead the pain is over and done with. The monster has a heart or a brain or lungs that can be pierced, it's a simple mechanical problem of how to get a length of sharp steel through the hide and the scales and the armor. But love hovers over the dying, it lies coiled waiting to strike at the exile, the lover betrayed or unrequited, it chains men to the places where they can't bear to be, forces them to endure all tyrannies, injustices and humiliations rather than run away and leave the ones they love, the ones who love them; it baits its trap with everything good in the world and arms it with everything bad; and it survives, thriving on its own poisons, growing where nothing else can live; an infestation, a parasite, a disease.

Cantacusene misses his wife, he thought; me too. And it's likely I'll never see her again, but because of love I'm building a machine that'll smash cities and slaughter nations and bring to an end the magnificent, glorious, holy Perpetual Republic of Mezentia; all simply so that one day I might be able to go home and see her again, see them both, my wife and my daughter. Such a little thing to ask, such a simple operation for a machine to perform. Every day in cities, towns, villages all over the world, men come home to their wives and children. A simple thing, it's nothing at all, for everybody else but not for me. I've got to breach the city wall, bash through the gates, pick my way over the dead bodies of millions, just to reach my own front door and get home. So much easier and more sensible to give up, start again, stay here in Civitas Eremiae and get a job; but I don't have that choice, because of love. Instead, I have the machine, and faith that love will prevail, because love conquers all.

Someone came in and asked him to go and look at the scorpion frames. Ziani followed him, not really aware of who he was or what he wanted. He saw them, squat and ugly and botched, inherently flawed, abominations in every sense of the word. He measured a few of them at random with the yard and the inside calipers and the dogleg calipers. They were sloppy and only fitted where they touched, but they were within tolerance (because he was working on a completely different set of tolerances now). He looked at them, drawn up like a squad of newly levied troops, awkward, horrible. In his mind's eye he gave them locks, springs, sliders, winches, and saw that they were abominations, but they would do what had to be done. He loved them, because they would slaughter the hireling Mezentine army by the tens of thousands, they would defend the citadel of Eremia for a time, and then they would fail.

15

They were saying in chapter that the war had gone to sleep. They were saying that paying, feeding and sheltering forty thousand men, keeping them away from the shops and the women, was a horrendous waste of effort, energy and money if they weren't going to be set loose against anybody any time soon. They were saying that Necessary Evil had lost its nerve, and its grip.

Psellus still hadn't found out why everything had suddenly ground to a halt. The soldiers had arrived, Vaatzes was in Eremia (up to no good there, by all accounts), and there was no earthly reason he could see why the war shouldn't be over and done with inside a month, if only they'd get it started. Some of the voices around the Guildhall were saying it was because there were another forty thousand on the way (Psellus happened to know this was true); others that the enemy capital was impregnable; that Eremia had signed a secret treaty with the Vadani, the Cure Doce, the Cure Hardy, all three simultaneously; that someone in Ways and Means had made a mistake and there was only just enough food left in the country to feed the soldiers for a week; that the real object of the war wasn't Eremia after all; that the Carpenters and Joiners were planning a military coup, and that's what the army was really for; that the soldiers had found out about the defenses of Civitas Eremiae and were striking for double pay and death benefit. Necessary Evil's response was to look smug and stay quiet. As one of its members, trying to guess which of the rumors was true, Psellus found this attitude extremely annoying.

Mostly, though, he was bored. He had nothing to do. Even the memos had stopped coming. There were no meetings. For a while he'd sat in his office, afraid to leave it in case he missed a message ordering him to a briefing where everything would be explained. Then he'd tried writing to his colleagues and superiors, asking what was going on, but they never answered him. He tried a series of surprise visits to their offices, but they were never there. Finally he'd taken to wandering about the Guildhall on the off chance of running into one of them. That was a waste of time, too. Nobody had seen them recently, or knew anything about what they were up to. When he went out to the camp where the soldiers were billeted, he was turned away at the gate by the sentries. Over their shoulders he could see the peaks of thousands of tents, thin wisps of smoke rising straight up into the windless sky. He could smell the soldiers from two hundred yards away, but he couldn't see them. It was like a party to which all the other children in his class had been invited.

It wouldn't have been so bad if the war wasn't his fault.

After a while (he'd lost track of time rather) he decided to alter his perspective. He resolved to look at it all from a different angle. After years of stress and overwork, he told himself, he was having a holiday. He still had his office, his rank, all the things he'd fought for over the years — better still, he'd been promoted, from Compliance to Necessary Evil. If they needed him, they'd find him. Meanwhile, until the call came, he was at liberty to indulge himself.

With what, though? He hadn't had more than an hour's continuous free time since he was twenty-one, and pleasure is something you can easily lose the knack of, if you allow yourself to get out of practice. Not that he'd exactly been a libertine in his remote youth; you didn't get to be a Guild official by drinking and chasing girls, so he hadn't ever done any of that; and it was simple realism to admit that it was probably too late to start now. He applied his mind, sitting in his office one cold gray morning. What did people do for pleasure, apart from drinking and being obnoxious to women?

What indeed. In Mezentia, not much that he could think of. Abroad, in less favored countries, they rode to hounds, flew falcons, jousted, fenced; but the Perpetual Republic had outgrown that sort of thing. What else? They read books, looked at works of art, listened to music. That sounded somewhat more promising. There were works of art, he was pretty sure; the Sculptors and Painters produced them, and (a quick glance at the relevant memo) their productivity had risen last year by an admirable six-point-three percent. But (he remembered) four fifths of their output went for export, mostly to the Vadani and the Cure Doce, and wherever the remaining one fifth ended up, it wasn't anywhere he was allowed to go. Music: the Musicians amalgamated with the Ancillary & Allied Trades a century ago. Their harp was still just about visible among the quarterings on the Guild's coat of arms, but he couldn't remember ever having met a Guild musician. There were people who played pipes and fiddles and little drums at private functions, but they were strictly amateurs, and the practice was officially frowned upon. That left literature, by default. For literature, you had to apply to the Stationers and Copyists. Like the Sculptors, they catered mostly for the export market, but the Guild had a retail outlet in a small alley off Progress Square. It was where you went to buy copies of Guild decrees and regulations, set books for the further examinations, commentaries and cribs to the more complex specifications; and, occasionally (usually as the result of a canceled export order), literature. He'd been there himself half a dozen times over the years, most recently to look for a wedding present for a mildly eccentric cousin who liked poetry — it was very much the sort of place where you went to buy things for other people, not for yourself.

His cousin had got married seven years ago, but the shop was exactly as he remembered it. The front part was given over to stationery, both export and domestic quality. There were ink-wells in gold, silver, silver plate, brass and pewter; writing-sets, plain, fancy and presentation grade, loose or boxed. There was paper in staggering quantities, all types and qualities, from pads of four-times scraped scraps sewn up with sacking twine, to virgin linen-pulp contract-and-conveyance paper, to the very best mutton and calf vellum. He counted thirty different inks before he lost interest and gave up; and if you didn't like any of them you could buy loose ingredients to make your own: oak-apple gall ready dried and powdered; finest quality soot, candle not chimney, and any number of specialist pigments for emphasizing the operative words in legal documents or illuminating capitals. There were trays of twenty different cuts of pen nib (types one to six export only; seven to thirteen restricted to copyists only, on proof of good standing; the rest available to the public at large); goose-quills in gray, black, barred or white and dainty little bronze knives to cut them with; sand-shakers, seals, wax-holders, seal-edge-smooth-ers (to round off splodged edges), bookmarks, erasing pumice in three grades and four handy sizes, binding needles and the fin-est flax thread, roll-covers in solid brass or tinplate with brass es-cutcheons for engraving book titles on. A few surreptitious glances at the price-tickets showed that nearly all this stuff was not for domestic consumption, but then, very little of what the Guilds produced was.

And in the back quarter of the shop there were books. Last time there had been five bookcases, but one of them had been taken out to make way for a display of chains and hasps for chained libraries. Three of the shelves were Guild publications, carefully divided up into numbered and coded categories. The fourth was marked *Clearance*, and half its shelves were empty.

A quick look round just in case somebody he knew was watch-ing him; then Psellus began to browse. *The Mirror of Fair Ladies, newly and copiously illustrated;* tempting, but how would he explain it away if someone caught him with it? *A Dialogue of King Fashion and Queen Reason* caught his attention, mostly because of the pictures of animals being slaughtered in various improbable ways, but the text was in a language he didn't understand. *A Garland of Violets* turned out to be an anthology of inspirational verse by or about great Guildsmen from history; so did *A Calendar of Heroes* and *Line, Rule and Calipers*, but without illuminations or pictures. He was tempted by *Early Mannerist Lyric Poetry*, a parallel text in Mezentine and Luzanesc, but a previous owner had paved the Mezentine side of each page with clouds of notes and extracts from the commentaries, presumably for some exam, so that it was barely legible. He was considering the practicalities of re-covering *The Mirror of Fair Ladies* in plain brown paper when he caught sight of a name, and held his breath.

Elements of Chess, by Galazo Vaatzes.

It was an ancient, tatty book, perhaps as much as thirty years old. The lettering on the spine wasn't Guild cursive or italic, and the binding was rough and uneven: pitched canvas stuck onto thin wood (packing-crate lath, maybe) with rabbitskin size, the sort they used in the plaster works. A homemade book, rather like one he'd seen recently. It fell open at the flyleaf: *Elements of Chess: being a memorial of various innovations and strategies collected or invented by Me, Galazo Vaatzes; herein recorded for the benefit of my son Ziani, on the occasion of his fourth birthday.* Followed by a date; he'd been out by a year. The book was thirty-one years old.

Back in his office he laid the two books on his desk, side by side: two acts of love, one by a father to his son, the other (he assumed) by a husband to his wife. Between them they were trying to tell him something (the purpose of a book is to communicate) but he wasn't quite sure what it was.

One of them, the abominator's awkward and labored love poetry, had a nice, clean provenance, but how had the other one got here? Someone had brought it in, on its own or together with other books, and sold it. His first thought was the liquidator of confiscated assets; but there had been a specific order against confiscation in the Vaatzes case (why was that?), and all the chattels at the Vaatzes house had reverted to the wife as her unencumbered property. So; maybe Ziani Vaatzes had sold it himself at some point, when he needed money, as so many people did from time to time. Entirely plausible, but he doubted it (unless Ziani hadn't got on with his father, and therefore had no qualms about getting rid of the book). He could have given it to a friend as a present, and the friend disposed of it.

He looked again. The younger Vaatzes was a better craftsman than his father, but at least the old man hadn't purported to write poetry. Just for curiosity's sake, he played out one or two of Galazo Vaatzes' gambits in his mind (memories of playing chess with his own father, who never managed to grasp the simple fact that children need to win occasionally) and found them unexpectedly ingenious. After the first four or so, they became too complicated for him to follow without a board and a set of pieces in front of him, but he was prepared to take their merits on trust. The seventh gambit was annotated, in handwriting he knew. At some point, Ziani had found a flaw in his father's strategy and made a note of it to remind himself.

Do engineers usually make good chess-players? He thought about that. He could think of one or two—his father, his uncle—but he'd never been any great shakes at the game himself; the data was inconclusive. The effort involved in making the book; there was something in that, he felt sure. Was it a family tradition, the making of books out of scrounged and liberated materials? Interesting if it was (and had the person who sold this one also disposed of further generations of the tradition; only one shop in Mezentia, but perhaps all the rest had already been bought by the time he got there). He found himself back at that strange moment of disposal. Who had sold the book, and why?

Wherever I go, he thought, he follows me; like a ghost haunting me, trying to tell me something. As to why he would choose me to confide in; mystifying, but perhaps simply because there's nobody else with the inclination—and, of course, the leisure—to listen. He closed his eyes, and found himself watching a chess game, father against son; father winning, unable to defy his principles and lose on purpose, angry that his son is such a weak opponent; he wants his son to beat him, but refuses to give anything away. The father is, of course, Matao Psellus, and the son is poor disappointing Lucao, who never really liked the game anyway (and so he applied himself to a different but similar game, whose gambits and ploys have brought him here).

Matao Psellus never wrote a book for his son. It would never have occurred to him to do anything of the sort. Yet here were two books, two acts of stifled love, like water bursting through a cracked pipe and soaking away into the dirt. As he studied them, Psellus felt sure he could sense the presence of a third, whereby the chess-book had come into his hands, but he couldn't quite make it out—he could see the end result, but not the workings of the mechanism by which that result was achieved.

Ariessa Vaatzes; she needed money, and she knows he's never coming back. Even so, he thought, even so. She might have sold his clothes, which were replaceable, or the furniture, or anything else. What would she have got for it? He'd paid two doubles and a turner, the price of three spring cabbages; suppose she'd got half of that, or a third. You can eat cabbages but not a book, said a small, starved voice in his mind. It had a point, he was prepared to concede, but he was sure there was more to it than that.

It was all beside the point, since Vaatzes would be dead soon, along with all the Eremians and quite a few of those invisible soldiers he wasn't allowed to see. He put one book away, opened the other, put his feet up on the desk (holiday, remember) and tried to visualize a chessboard.

"Lucao." The voice came from above and behind. "I'm glad to see we're not working you to death."

He sat up sharply, dragging his feet off the desk. The book shot onto the floor, and the spine burst. "Zanipulo," he said. "There you are at last. I've been trying to talk to you for ages."

"Quite," Staurachus replied. "Well, here I am. Meeting in ten minutes, in the cloister. Perhaps you didn't get the memo."

"Memo?" Psellus looked up at him stupidly, as though he'd never heard the expression before. "No, I haven't seen any memos." As he said it, he caught sight of a piece of paper on the desk that hadn't been there when he left to go shopping. It said MEMORANDUM at the top in big square letters. "Sorry, I—"

"Just as well I checked," Staurachus said, and left.

Psellus snatched at the paper; his sleeve fanned up a breeze that wafted it just beyond the reach of his fingers, off the desk onto the floor. He sighed, stooped and retrieved it.

The war had woken up, apparently. No explanation, just as there'd been none when it was canceled, or adjourned. He read the memo again, just in case he'd missed something. Ten minutes; he could just about reach the cloister if he ran.

"Splendid," said Jarnac Ducas. A big smile split his handsome, suntanned face, curling the ends of his mustache down over the corners of his mouth. He tapped the lower plate of a gorget with his knuckle; it sounded like someone knocking at a door.

"There's still two sets of cuisses to do," Ziani said, watching him, "but they'll be ready in plenty of time. I'll bring them with me on the day, shall I?"

Just the faintest of frowns, until Jarnac remembered that Ziani was invited to the hunt. "Yes, why not? That'll be fine. Excellent work. You must let me know how much I owe you."

Behind him, Cantacusene was standing awkwardly, shifting his weight from one foot to the other, as though being in the presence of a scion of the Ducas was more honor than he could endure. Extraordinary, the attitude of these people. What puzzled Ziani was the fact that he himself had never shown the slightest degree of deference or respect to any of them, not even Miel Ducas or the Duke, and nobody had seemed to notice. Because he was a foreigner, presumably.

"I've been reading the books you lent me," Ziani went on— another slight frown; Jarnac had forgotten he'd sent round copies of *King Fashion* and the *Mirror.* "Fascinating stuff. I'm looking forward to it."

"Splendid." Jarnac's smile widened. It was entirely possible that he genuinely enjoyed giving pleasure to others less fortunate than himself, provided it was one of his own pleasures, and he wouldn't have to go without in order to do so. "So we may make a huntsman of you yet, then." He looked away, back at the sets of newly buffed and polished armor laid out on the long table. He really did seem pleased (why am I surprised? Ziani thought).

"I'll have it sent round this evening, if that's convenient," he said. "Obviously there may need to be a few adjustments for fit and so forth."

Jarnac nodded; probably he wasn't listening. It was difficult being in the presence of somebody this large. He wasn't just taller and broader than anyone Ziani had ever seen before; it was as though he used space in a different way, as though he was used to a much bigger world and hadn't quite adjusted to living among midgets. "Excellent work," he said, "first rate. And I'll be seeing you on the day, of course. Can't promise anything—you never can, in hunting—but I've been setting aside the beeches up above the long lake, we haven't been in there with the lymers or the wolfhounds, and the farmers reckon there's been at least one big boar rootling about round there. I'll be sending someone up to feed the outer covers, see if we can't draw a hog or two out from the thick stuff in the middle. They won't stick around during the day, of course, but at least there'll be a trail for the dogs to follow."

Ziani smiled pleasantly. He had an idea that Jarnac talked mostly to himself, through the medium of his listeners. It would be nice, however, if he could make him go away, so he could get on with his work. "Would you like to see round the factory?" he said. "We've just finished putting in a new treadle saw; I believe it's the only one of its kind outside Mezentia."

Infallible. It's a curious fact that boring people seem to have a mortal fear of being bored by others. Jarnac thanked and congratulated him once again, reminded him to send in his bill as soon as possible, and strode away, ducking to avoid the beams and the doorframe.

"Pleasant enough man," Ziani observed. "But I prefer his cousin, the other Ducas. Doesn't talk quite so much."

Cantacusene looked at him. "He's the cadet branch," he said. "Jarnac Ducas, I mean."

"Ah," Ziani said. "Is that a good thing? I don't understand about nobility."

"Means Jarnac won't ever be in line to be head of the family, not unless all the other branch get wiped out before he does."

"I see. So really, Jarnac isn't anyone special."

A look of disgust and horror flitted across Cantacusene's face, and Ziani realized he'd committed yet another abomination. He wasn't all that interested, anyway. He wanted to get the last few bits of leather cut out, so he could go and look at the scorpion locks. Cantacusene walked away, clearly not trusting himself to speak.

In the main shop, they were cutting quarter-inch plate on the big shear. It was, if anything, worse than the leather shear he'd been using himself. It wasn't even Mezentine-made, and the handle was a broken-off stub with a length of bent iron pipe peened over it. Luckily, the tolerances for the lock plates were broad. He didn't recognize any of the faces around him, but they'd all know who he was, the only brown-skinned man in Eremia. Some of them looked up, others looked in the opposite direction. All in all, he'd met with far less resentment and hatred than he'd expected, given that his people had only recently massacred the flower of the Eremian army. An Eremian wouldn't last a day in the ordnance factory at home.

He left them to it and wandered over to the filing bench, where two men were cutting teeth into gear-wheels. They were better at it than he'd expected. They were standing right, weight on both feet equally, square to the bench, holding the file level and true. He'd marked out the pattern piece himself; all they had to do was scribe round it onto each wheel, then follow the scribed lines as closely as they could. Back home, of course, a machine would be doing this job, a hundred times faster and much more accurately.

One of the men was old. His thin, wiry forearms ended in broad, clenched hands with huge knuckles, and he bent close over his work to be able to see the scratched line. Ziani saw that he'd rubbed the piece over with candle-soot mixed with spit, to make the line show up better. At home they used a special dark blue paste.

"How's it going?" he asked. He noticed that he was speaking a bit louder than usual; either because he assumed the old man must be deaf, or because subconsciously he was imitating Jarnac Ducas.

The man didn't look up. "This file's no good," he said. "Blunt."

"Chalk it," Ziani said.

"Done that," the old man said. "And carded it. No good. It's not clogged, it's blunt."

"Let me see," Ziani said. It was a Mezentine three-square file, with a Guild mark; the letter next to the stamped lion's head told him it was no more than a year old. He ran the pad of his forefinger over the teeth. "You're right," he said. "Funny. Have you been cutting hardening steel with it?"

The old man shook his head. "My best file," he said. "Only ever used it for brass and latten."

For some reason, Ziani couldn't help taking it personally; his Guild had made the file, to Specification, so it ought to be perfect; but it had failed before its time, and that was wrong. The foreman of the tool works ought to be on charges for something like that. "I'll get you a new one," Ziani said and went to go, but the old man grabbed his arm.

"Where are you going with my file?" he said.

"But it's no good," Ziani said. "You said so yourself."

"It's my file. Give it back."

Ziani put it down on the bench, went to the tool chest in the corner and found a three-square file, brand new, still in its grease. "Here," he said to the old man. "Yours to keep."

The old man scowled at it, took it, rubbed his fingertip over the base of the tang, where the Guild marks were. "Needs a handle," he said.

Ziani picked a file at random off the bench, knocked the handle off against the bench-leg and handed it to him. He tapped it into place, then put the file carefully away in his apron pocket.

"Fine," Ziani said. "Apart from the blunt file, how's it going?"

The old man shrugged. "Foreman said file out the notches in these wheels, so that's what I'm doing. Don't ask me what they're for, I don't know."

"How many have you managed to get done today?" Ziani asked; but either the old man hadn't heard him, or the question was too offensive to be answered. "Carry on," Ziani said, and moved away.

On the next bench they were bending ratchet sears over formers in a vice. Nice simple work (at home, the sears would be machined from solid and case-hardened in bonemeal and leather dust) and the three men who were doing it had filled one box with finished pieces and half-filled another. He watched them open the vice, clamp a strip of shear-cut plate between the former and the jaw, tighten up the vice and bend the piece with thumps from a hide mallet until it lay flat against the former. At the end of the bench, another man worked a long-lever punch, drifting out the pivot holes. The punch was pretty deplorable too, but he had only himself to blame for it; he'd made it himself, in a tearing hurry, and he knew it'd break soon and the hinge-pin would need replacing. It wounded him to think that something he'd made himself would inevitably fail.

The day wore on. For the first time since he'd escaped from Mezentia, Ziani was aware of being very tired. Everything he did cost him effort, and he couldn't settle to anything. He remembered, just as the men were leaving for the day, that he hadn't made arrangements for taking the finished pieces of armor to Jarnac's house. By then, he and Cantacusene were the only people left in the building. Fine.

"Do me a favor," he said, leaning against the doorpost of the small foundry, where Cantacusene had set up his leather-boiling cauldron.

Cantacusene was sitting cross-legged on the floor, a chunky oak log gripped between his knees. Over it he was hammering a cuisse, stretching the leather back into shape where it had crinkled slightly in the boiling water. "What?" he said.

"Give me a hand delivering this lot," Ziani replied.

He hadn't been expecting it, but Cantacusene nodded without argument, or even face-pulling. "All right," he said. "Just let me finish this before it cools down."

So Ziani watched for a while as Cantacusene tapped and poked and wheedled, then dunked the cuisse into a bucket of cold water to set it. It came out dripping; he wiped it over with his sleeve and stood it against the wall to dry off. "Nearly all done," he said. "Should finish off tomorrow."

Together they packed the armor in straw and loaded it into six barrels, which they lugged out into the yard and dumped in the cart they used for fetching iron stock and charcoal. Cantacusene harnessed up the two mules while Ziani locked up; then they set out. They had to go a very long way round, because the straight way was too narrow for the cart and there were stairs and bridges. They rode in silence most of the way, but Ziani could sense that Cantacusene was winding himself up to ask something. When it came, it came in a rush.

"You didn't tell me you were going on this hunt."

"Yes I did," Ziani replied. "You remember, when this Jarnac character came round to order the stuff."

Cantacusene frowned. "Why?"

"I don't know," Ziani said. "I guess I thought it'd be good to see how it's done. If there's a market for hunting gear, it's a good idea to see for myself what goes on. And I'm curious," he added. "There's nothing like it at home."

"Did he invite you?"

"Sort of." Ziani grinned. "I dropped some heavy hints. You ever been?"

Cantacusene shook his head. "Strictly for the gentry," he said. "Except if you're beating or carrying or picking up and stuff.

Mostly, though, the household does all that, they only hire in casuals for the really big meets. And it's country people that tend to get hired, not anyone from the city."

"Right," Ziani said. "I think this is going to be a big occasion, with the Duke going."

"You can be sure of that," Cantacusene said. "Orsea's not a great one for hunting, mind; he likes it, but they reckon he never finds the time. His father Orseola was big on the falcons but not riding to hounds, but of course they never had the money for a decent pack, or good horses. Costs a fair bit, see."

Ziani nodded. "But Jarnac can afford it, obviously."

"Well, the Ducas," Cantacusene said, with a subtle mixture of respect and contempt, "they got all the money you can think of, even the cadet line. Though they reckon that with what Jarnac spends, he cuts it a bit close sometimes."

It was amusing, Ziani thought, how Cantacusene the dour and silent became so animated when he got onto the subject of the nobility. It wasn't anything like the attitude he'd have expected. Resentment, he'd have thought, maybe even downright hatred—after all, the nobles did no work and lived off the sweated labor of others, wasting enough on their idle and vicious pleasures in a month to feed fifty working families for a year. He'd have expected someone like Cantacusene to froth at the mouth when talking about such people. Apparently not. The closest thing in his experience was the way people back home talked about the dog-racing or handball teams they supported. Get a Mezentine Guildsman started on his team and he'd tell you every minute detail—life histories and career statistics of every player, arcane details of rules and form, which tracks favored which pitchers, more than any rational man could possibly want to know about anything. In the same way Cantacusene seemed to come alive talking about the Ducas, with whom he had nothing in common except occasional commissions and a wedge of unpaid invoices for work delivered. It was touching and revolting at the same time, this vicarious enjoyment of the gentry's lifestyle. For some reason Cantacusene supported the Ducas (and the Phocas and the Stratiotes, and up to a point the Callinicas), which somehow gave him the right to refer to them by their first names, as though they were his own family, and to preen himself on their ridiculous achievements (hunting, politicking, marrying and giving in marriage, bickering over land and dabbling disdainfully and half-competently in trade). For a long time, all the way from Lantern Street to Wallgate via Shave Cross, he gabbled about genealogies and lawsuits, trophy stags and champion destriers, with a counterpoint of scandals, infidelities and indiscretions in which he seemed to take an equal pride. By the time they came out into Fountain Street and started to climb the long, cobbled ride up to the old lists, where the cadet Ducas had their town house, Ziani reckoned he'd learned enough about the family to fill two epic poems and nine books of commentaries.

"The only other one of them I've actually met," he broke in, during a brief lull, "is Miel Ducas. He's the head of the family, isn't he?"

Cantacusene nodded vigorously. "Ever since his uncle died, old Acer Ducas. Mind, he was only head because his first cousin Celat died young—bust his neck riding in the forest, the bloody fool. If it hadn't been for that, Acer wouldn't have been nobody. 'Course, he was seventy if he was a day when he came into the honor; up till then he'd just been collateral in the main line, and everybody expected him to peg out and Celat to take over when Jiraut died. But Celat died, what, seven years back; Jiraut went on the year after that, which meant Acer took over, and he only lasted six months, and then it was Miel. Youngest Ducas this century."

Ziani frowned. "So Miel wasn't really anybody important till six years ago."

"Oh, he was *important*," Cantacusene snapped, as though Ziani had just insulted his mother. "Leading collateral heir, he'd have copped for the minor honor in the main line when Acer died. But actually being the Ducas, that's something else entirely. I don't suppose you can understand that, not being from here."

Ziani shrugged. "He's always come across to me as a pleasant enough man," he said. "Quite quiet, very polite. I'm starting to see that that's what I should have expected, but I'd been assuming the head of the family would be more like Jarnac, and the also-ran would've been like Miel. But really, it's got to be the other way round, hasn't it?"

Cantacusene was torn, he could see, between two powerful forces: on the one hand, extreme discomfort at Ziani's disrespectful attitude; on the other, the glorious opportunity to tell an ignorant foreigner all about the Ducas. Luckily, the opportunity won the day. "It's something you got to understand about the good families," Cantacusene said. "What they live by is duty. Duty to the family, traditions and stuff; duty to the Duke and the country. Nothing means more to them than that. So, the higher up they are, the more the duty sort of weighs on them, if you see what I mean. Really, all Jarnac's got to do is keep up to what's expected of him; like, he's got to dress well, he's got to hold big fancy banquets and dinners, he's got to have the best stables and hounds and hawks — this is in peace-time, of course — and generally have the best of everything and be the best at everything, if you get me. It's not his place to be getting into politics and government and all, or being a counselor or a minister or anything. Cadet branch, see. But Miel, it's different for him. If he was to go putting on a big show, talking loud and that stuff, it wouldn't be suitable, it'd be out of place. Not the right way for a senior man in the state to go on. He's got to be a serious man, you see. Polite, quiet, all that, like you said."

"I see," Ziani said. "Part of the job, then. Well, he's very good at it."

Cantacusene laughed. "Didn't use to be," he said. "Of course, he got that scat in the face, which spoiled his looks. But before he got the honor, when he was more like Jarnac is now, if you follow me, he was a real bright spark. Specially with the girls."

Ziani frowned. "Because it was expected of him."

"Got to be the best at everything," Cantacusene said. "And

I suppose you could say he was, back then. Oh, I could tell you stories."

"I'm sure," Ziani said.

It was dark by the time they arrived at the list gate. They were directly under the shadow of the highest point of the keep wall. Being the cadet branch, the lesser Ducas lived outside the inner castle; being Ducas, they lived as close to it as they could possibly get. Cantacusene turned off the paved highway down a narrow alley — the wheel-hubs fouled the brickwork on both sides simultaneously as they turned a corner — that twisted to and fro up a slope between high walls until it came to a small door in a dark stone frontage. If it hadn't been a dead end, Ziani wouldn't have noticed it. Cantacusene jumped down and clubbed on the planking with the heel of his fist.

"You've been here before, then?" Ziani said.

"Been here delivering. Never gone inside, of course."

The door opened, just enough to give them sight of a pale blue eye and a wisp of gray hair. "Ziani Vaatzes," Ziani said. "Delivery."

The owner of the eye and the hair came out and looked at him for a moment. "You're to fetch it into the Great Hall," he said. "He's in his bath, but he'll be down soon as he's ready."

For a moment Ziani was sure Cantacusene would refuse to pass the door, like a horse shying at a jump. Curiosity must've got the better of awe for once; he shuffled along after Ziani, holding up one end of the first barrel and muttering something under his breath.

The courtyard that separated them from the inner gate was laid out as a formal garden, with neatly trimmed knee-high hedges of lavender and box surrounding square or diamond-shaped beds, where closely mustered ranks of roses quartered with lilies and some kind of blue flower they didn't have in Mezentia filled out the shape of the Ducas family arms. The effect wasn't immediately obvious from the ground, but if a god happened to look down from the clouds, he'd be left in no doubt as to who lived there. A fountain dribbled quietly and unheeded in the exact center of the arrangement, feeding a small pond that probably housed small, inedible fish.

While Ziani and Cantacusene were manhandling the barrel along the gravel path, someone had opened the inner gate, which led into a cloister; a roofed-over hollow square enclosing a larger garden, with a lawn and an almond tree. The cloister itself was paved with polished limestone slabs; the walls were painted with scenes of Ducas family history, including one involving a small, pig-like dragon (up against a huge, bearded Ducas cap-à-pie in armor, it didn't stand a chance). Ziani and Cantacusene toiled round three sides of the cloister, and arrived at a set of broad, shallow steps leading up to a massive studded oak door, which opened inward as they approached it.

The hall they found themselves in was smaller than the Guildhall, or the main gallery of the ordnance factory; it was the height of the roof that set Ziani's head swimming. He couldn't begin to guess how far up the sheer walls went, until they sprouted a jungle of beams, plates and purlins (all painted and gilded, carved and embossed with flowers, animals, birds, gargoyles, severely frowning heads of the ancient Ducas, stars, suns and moons). He might have been able to cope with the sheer size, if it hadn't been for the fact that every available square foot of wall was adorned with trophies of the hunt. There were forests of antlers, dense as an orchard; heads, skulls, escutcheons of boar-tusks, bear-claws and wolf-fangs arranged in circles, half-circles and spirals; claws, paws, tails, hoofs, enough spare parts to build a herd of composite monsters. Stuffed herons, partridges, rock-grouse, pigeons swung overhead on wires suspended from rafters, frozen in perpetuity in desperate flight from stuffed peregrines, goshawks, merlins and buzzards, their shadows huge and dramatic in the yellow glare of twelve-hundred-candle chandeliers. At the far end of the hall, flanking the high table on its raised platform, stood two enormous bears reared up on their hind legs, their forepaws raised to strike. Directly behind the massive, high-backed chair in the dead center

of the table hung a wooden shield, on which the skull of an absurdly large wolf bared its fangs at all comers. Underneath each
trophy, in lettering too small to read, was an inscription, painted
on a billowing scroll.

"Leave it here," someone said; a short, bald man with a gold
chain round his neck, some kind of steward. "More to come?"

Ziani nodded. "Five more," he replied. The steward nodded,
as if to say he'd feared as much. "No, you stay there," he added,
as Ziani turned to go back out the way he'd just come. "I'll send
a couple of the men to get them. You sit down, I'll get someone to
fetch you a drink."

He went away (hospitality, service, disdain; the Ducas for you).
Cantacusene sat down on the nearest bench, but Ziani strolled
across the floor to get a better look at some of the trophies. Closest to him was a group of roebuck skulls, and he noticed that their
antlers were all malformed; one horn normal, the other looking
as if it had been melted, squashed or worn away. King Fashion
had prepared him for that; abnormals, the King called them, and
they were far more highly prized as trophies than larger, regular specimens. The Ducas clearly had an outstanding collection;
every conceivable irregularity, deformation and variation from
the orthodox was represented, from great splayed fans of horn to
pathetic little needles. He grinned in spite of himself, because here
(honored and treasured in death) was a glorious gallery of abominations, enough to make the whole Compliance directorate die of
revulsion. It reminded him of the fairy-stories about lovely women
pursued by amorous gods, rescued and set among the stars as
constellations; just as dead as any other mortal, but on show forever, trophies of the hunt. That in turn made him think of Miel
Ducas (a great chaser of women in his day, according to what he'd
heard).

He owed that mental leap, he knew, to King Fashion's insufferably arch consort, Queen Reason, whose job it was to point
up each of the King's pithy hints with a parallel from the world
of courtly love. To Queen Reason, the fleeing doe was the coy

maiden, glancing back over her shoulder as she fled, no doubt, and the hunter was the amorous youth, armed with sighs and tears and vows everlasting, his nets and snares and arrows. Ziani had skipped most of her side of the dialogue, on the grounds that life was too short, but occasionally the Queen had succeeded in ambushing him; the hunter lying in wait in bow-and-stable is the young lover lurking in the rose arbor, sonnet properly braced, its blade smeared with honey; the boar at bay among the hounds is the nymph beset by eligible suitors (reaching somewhat there, he felt); the partridge circling to avoid the swooping goshawk is the minx playing hard to get; and so on, interminably, while her husband the King politely ignores her and lectures earnestly on the shape of droppings. The only explanation Ziani could think of was that Reason was a mistranslation of the wretched woman's name.

Sullen-looking men lugged in the other barrels, and there was no longer any reason for Ziani to stay. He stood up—the drink had never arrived, but he hadn't been expecting it to; in a week's time, he imagined, a footman would approach the bench with two cups on a tray, and find nobody there to take them—and nodded to Cantacusene to follow him like a dog.

"So," he said, as they got back into the cart, "what did you make of it?"

"What?"

Ziani frowned. "Jarnac's house. Was it as magnificent as you'd imagined?"

Cantacusene shrugged. "It was very nice," he said.

He dropped Cantacusene off on the way, and drove home alone; he was starting to get the hang of managing horses, and luckily they knew the way. He managed to get the harness off them without drawing blood, threw them some hay, and went back to his cellar. He didn't feel so tired now. Maybe it was the fresh air, or the melodrama of the lesser Ducas. The steel bow was leaning against the wall where he'd left it, and he practiced for over an hour, until the scars on his fingers were raw again. Then he climbed the stairs to the tower and put in a session with *The Mirror of the Chase,* which was slightly less turgid than *King Fashion,* but which also had a love interest. It put him to sleep until just before first light. He woke up with a crick in his neck, and went down the stairs to look at the scorpions.

A day and a half, and the first batch would be finished. They were drawn up in rows, like vines in a vineyard, and he walked up and down between them. All that was left was basic assembly and fitting, and although he hated them for being crude, he loved them for being there at all, against the odds; like a farmer who's raised a thin crop in dry stony soil where by rights nothing should grow at all.

The night before the hunt, after he'd tried on the leather armor made by the foreigner, looked in on the kennels and the stables, given a final briefing to the huntsmen, heard the most recent reports from the harborers concerning the last known movements of the quarry, Jarnac Ducas left the main hall by a small door in the top left corner of the room, climbed a long circular stair, walked down a narrow corridor and eventually came out on the rampart of the castle wall. When he was a boy, he'd loved the thrill of this genuine secret passage (only male Ducas over the age of twelve knew about it) that linked the house with the castle itself. He'd imagined himself escaping down it while savage enemies looted below, fighting every step of the way until he reached the narrow sally-port and safety. He must've killed a dozen imaginary goblins or Vadani for every yard. Now he was older and the house belonged to him, he valued it as a means of getting some air, peace and quiet without the risk of meeting anybody.

The sentry on duty knew him by sight, of course. Officially the passage wasn't there, so the soldier looked straight through him, as though he didn't exist either. At this time of night, he knew he'd have this stretch of rampart to himself. It was a valuable privilege, one of many, and naturally he knew better than to abuse it by overuse. He turned his back on the castle, leaned his forearms on the battlements and stared out over the city toward the mountains. All he could see of them was a ridge of shadow against the paler darkness of the night sky, but he knew they were there.

He heard someone behind him; a boot-heel scuffing the stone. Whoever it was seemed not to have noticed him, standing still in the dark. The steps moved away, then stopped. Not the sentry, then. He stepped away from the battlement.

"Jarnac?"

The voice was easily recognized. Duke Orsea had always had a tendency to be a little high-pitched when he was surprised or nervous. Understandable that he should be slightly apprehensive, coming across someone lurking in the shadows on a wall where nobody was supposed to be. Of course he knew about the non-existent secret passage; he'd been led down it when he was an unimportant boy, a tag-along, allowed to join in because he was cousin Miel's friend. Now, however, Jarnac considered protocol. "My lord" would be inappropriate here, since they were alone and Orsea had greeted him by his private name.

"Hello, Orsea," he replied. "Sorry, did I make you jump?"

Orsea came a step closer; still wary, like a dog approaching an unidentified object. When he was close enough for his face to be visible, Jarnac saw the worried frown relax, though not completely.

"Came up for a breath of air," Jarnac explained. "Hope you don't mind."

"No, of course not." Orsea had never been more than a moderately competent liar at best. "It's just that I wasn't expecting anybody to be up here, that's all."

"Me too," Jarnac replied with a grin. "So, looking forward to tomorrow?"

Orsea smiled. "I expect you've got something special lined up."

"You can't line up wild animals," Jarnac replied. "All you can do is hope they'll be there. No promises, but we'll see."

Orsea nodded gravely. "Thanks for arranging it all," he said.

"Veatriz has been keeping on about me needing a day in the fresh air."

"Quite right," Jarnac said. "You're looking a bit peaky. Too many council meetings and state receptions and not enough healthy exercise." He saw Orsea stiffen slightly, and remembered that he'd always been quick to take offense. Probably, too, he was thinking about a certain occasion fifteen years ago when Jarnac and Juifrez Phocas had pushed him into the old disused cesspit behind the Lesser Phocas stables. Offhand Jarnac couldn't recall the reason, but he was sure there'd been one.

"That's right," Orsea said, maintaining his smile with a degree of effort. "It's what comes of getting mixed up in politics, you know."

Jarnac nodded. "Glad I stayed clear of it, then," he said. "Always struck me as a mug's game. Glad to leave it to you and cousin Miel. He's coming tomorrow, isn't he? Only I hadn't heard back from him."

"Oh yes, he's coming." Orsea reinforced the statement with a brisk nod, just to clear up any ambiguity. "And Ferens Bardanes and your cousin Erec, apparently. I haven't seen either of them for ages."

Now Orsea mentioned it, Ferens had also been present during the cesspit incident. Not Erec, though; he'd been off snogging with Sospiria Miletas out behind the old lime-kilns. Orsea had been rather keen on Sospiria round about that time, he fancied; wasting his time, of course.

"If Miel's coming we'll be a field of thirty," Jarnac said. "No, scrub that, thirty-one. I invited that Mezentine, the blacksmith. He kept dropping hints, so I thought, why not?"

Orsea shrugged.

"I believe you've met him," Jarnac went on.

"A couple of times, yes."

"Strange man," Jarnac said. "Very much the oily tradesman one minute, cold as a snake the next. That's Mezentines for you, I suppose. How's Veatriz?"

"What? Oh, she's fine."

"Is she coming?"

"No."

"Didn't think she would be," Jarnac said. "Not really her thing. I remember, she did come out with us once, years ago." That would be when everybody expected her to marry Miel, of course; not long after she came back from playing hostage with the Vadani.

"Oh," Orsea said.

"She didn't like it much," Jarnac said. "Well, it was a foul day, lashed down with rain; we didn't find all morning, lunch went to the wrong place so she didn't get anything to eat, and then we had a long, hard chase in the afternoon, and I think she was with the party that went the wrong way. Don't blame her for thinking it's an over-rated pastime, really."

Orsea laughed, a sound like the last drops gurgling out of a bottle. "She thought about coming, actually," he said. "But she decided she'd rather stay at home and catch up with writing letters or something." He looked away. Something bothering him, Jarnac thought. Just for a split second, he caught himself remembering Veatriz Sirupati as she'd been when she was sixteen; definitely worth stopping to look at back then, though in his opinion she'd gone off quite a bit since she married Orsea. Not that he'd ever looked too closely, since she'd always been earmarked for Miel. They'd have gone well together, he'd always thought, Miel and Veatriz Sirupati, if it hadn't been for the politics.

He decided it'd be a good idea to change the subject. "So," he said, "do you think there's going to be a war?"

Orsea looked at him as though he'd let slip a deadly secret. "I hope not," he said. "We're still picking up the pieces after the last one. And the one before that."

Jarnac shrugged. "Some of us were talking about it the other day," he said. "About Duke Valens just happening to be there on his side of the Butter Pass when you were on your way back from Mezentia. Bit of a coincidence, we thought."

For a moment, Orsea looked like he didn't follow, and Jarnac realized he'd misunderstood; he'd been thinking about a possible war right enough, but not against the Vadani. Well, that was interesting in itself. "I think that's all it was," Orsea said, sounding a little bit awkward. "And very lucky for us, the way things turned out."

"Oh, quite right. And they helped us out, no question about it." Jarnac paused. Probably not a good idea to be harping on about the disastrous Mezentia expedition, given that he hadn't been there. The stupid part of it was, he'd really wanted to go, he'd been furious about missing it. But people got funny about that sort of thing, after a disaster. "Well, I'm glad to hear you don't think there's a danger," Jarnac said. "We could do without any major excitements for a while."

"I think I'll go and get some sleep," Orsea said, "if I'm getting up early in the morning. First light, I think Miel said, in the stable yard."

"A bit before, if you can manage it," Jarnac corrected him. "I want to be up on the mountain while the dew's still on the grass."

"Right," Orsea said, with an obvious lack of enthusiasm. "Bright and early. I'll say goodnight, then."

"Sleep well," Jarnac replied. "Wish I could. But I get a bit wound up before a big day."

Back down the secret passage into the long corridor; halfway down the circular stair, Jarnac remembered that it hadn't been Sospiria Miletas that Erec was with that time, but Sospiria Poliorcetes. Not that it made any odds; Orsea had fancied her, too.

He didn't bother going to bed; instead, he called for a lamp and sat alone in the great hall, under Uncle Dara's record wolf, with a big cup of hot milk and cinnamon and a copy of Isoitz's *The Complete Record of the Hunt,* where there was something about mid-season three-year-old boars and how you could track them on stony ground, except that he couldn't recall offhand where it came in the book. He found what he was looking for two hours before dawn, when the first light blue stain was starting to soak through, but it was just the same old stuff out of Varrano rehashed.

He stood up, yawned and stretched. It was tomorrow already, and his big day had begun.

Ziani rolled off his mattress, got up and ate the crust of the stale bread. Not, he decided, a civilized hour of the morning. But he'd feel stronger once he'd washed his face and put on a fresh shirt.

He hadn't slept well. Partly nerves; partly because a bad dream had woken him up in the small hours, and he'd found it hard to get back to sleep again; or he'd been afraid to, because he always reacted badly to nightmares.

It wasn't a new dream, by any means. Originally, it had been his grandfather's fault, because the old fool was one of those people who believed that children enjoy being scared out of their wits. Accordingly, when Ziani was six or seven, he'd told him the legend of the storm-hunt, and the horrible thing had lodged in the back of his mind ever since. Easy enough to guess why it had come back out of the shadows tonight, when his mind was stuffed with *King Fashion* and the *Mirror* and similar garbage, all that stuff about hounds and lymers and brachets, the baying of the pack and the horn-calls. In Grandad's story, of course, the hounds were red-eyed and black as coal, the horns were blown by dead men riding on dead horses, and the hunt was led by King Utan the Terrible, who'd rode away to hounds five hundred years before and never came back, except on dark nights, when the wind was high and the wild geese were flying low. Ever since then, in his dream, King Utan had worn a deep black hood and ridden a huge black horse; and sometimes Ziani had been running away from him, and sometimes he'd been riding beside him, so close that the cloak's hem flicked his face, and he could smell the rain-soaked cloth. The end was always the same: horns blowing wildly, rain stinging in his eyes, the hounds pressing round in a circle over something lying on the ground, while the King reached up with his old, swollen hands and started to lift the cowl away from his face.

16

The Ducas rides to the hunt on a white palfrey. He wears a quilted pourpoint of white or gray silk over a white linen shirt, cord breeches and arming boots with points for his sabatons; the only weapon he carries is a slightly curved, single-edged hanger as long as his arm from shoulder to fingertips. He may wear a hat if rain is actually falling. He is followed by four huntsmen on barbs or jennets, who carry his armor, his great spear, his light spears, his bow and his close sword, which can be either a falchion or a tuck, depending on the likely quarry. A page on an ambler or a mule follows with the wet-weather gear—a hooded mantle, a surcoat, chaps and spats—and the horn.

On arriving at the meet, the Ducas dismounts, and is accomplished for the hunt in the following order, which differs slightly from the proper order for war: first the sabatons, laced tightly at the toes and under the instep; next the greaves, followed by the leg-harness of demi-greaves, poleyns and cuisses (gamboised cuisses are considered excessive except where the quarry is exclusively bear or wolf)—these are secured by points to the hem of the pourpoint, and the usual straps and buckles around the thigh, the calf and the inside of the knee. Since the cuirass and placket are not worn for the hunt, the upper points are secured to the kidney-belt, after which the faulds are added to protect the buttocks, thighs and groin. The arm-harness is fitted next; in the hunting harness, the vambraces close on the outside of the forearm with buckles, and the half-rerebrace is worn, secured at the shoulder with a single point. Spaudlers are preferred to pauldrons for the protection of the shoulder, and a simple one-lame gorget suffices for the neck. Finally, the Ducas puts on his gauntlets (the finger type is preferred to the clamshell or mitten varieties) and his baldric, from which hang his close sword and his horn. He carries his great spear in his right hand. The four huntsmen carry the rest of the gear between them; the page stays behind at the meet to hold the horses.

Miel couldn't stop yawning. He'd gone to bed early and slept well; in spite of which, he'd woken up with a slight headache (in his temples, just behind his eyes). If it hadn't been for the fact that this was Orsea's special treat and Veatriz had asked him to go, he'd have stayed in bed.

The sky was black with a few silver cracks and he could smell rain in the air. The Ducas never takes any notice of the weather, in the same way as a king can decline to recognize a government of which he doesn't approve; accordingly, he was bare-headed, and the damp made his head throb. A day or so before, Jarnac had muttered something about working down the high pastures in the hope of flushing a good boar in the open; that meant a lot of walking, most of it uphill. What joy.

Long practice made it possible for him to greet his fellow hunters with a reasonable show of affability, in spite of the pain behind his eyes. Jarnac hadn't arrived yet, of course; neither had Orsea, who had to make his entrance immediately after his host. Miel looked round for unfamiliar faces: a thin, spotty young man with the unfortunate Poliorcetes nose (two possible candidates, Gacher or Dester; he hadn't seen either of them for five years); a stout, flat-faced man in the Phocas livery (he'd heard someone say that old Eston had retired and his son had taken over as whipper-in for the Phocas pack); everyone else he knew. Including—he frowned—a dark-skinned man, shorter than everyone else, unarmored and carrying a long cloth bag made of sacking.

"Hello," Miel said, squeezing out a little more affability from somewhere. "I'd forgotten, Jarnac mentioned you were coming along today."

Ziani Vaatzes turned his head and looked at him for a heartbeat before answering. "I'm afraid I sort of bullied him into inviting me," he said. "Only, I've never seen anything like this before."

Miel smiled. "Anybody who can bully Jarnac has my sincere admiration," he said. "I'd have thought it couldn't be done. So, what do you make of it all?"

"Impressive," Vaatzes replied; not that it mattered, since Miel wasn't particularly interested in the truth. "I had no idea it'd be so formal. I expect I look ridiculous."

"Not at all," Miel said (it wasn't a good day for truth generally). "What've you got there, in the bag?"

Vaatzes looked sheepish. "I didn't know what to bring, so I fetched along my bow. I hope that's all right."

"Very good," Miel said. "Is it one you made yourself?" he added, as a way of filling the silence.

Vaatzes nodded, loosed the knot and pulled something out of the bag. It would have looked quite like a bow if it hadn't been made of metal. He was holding it out for Miel to examine, like a cat that insists on bringing small dead birds into the house.

"Steel?" Miel guessed. Actually, he was impressed. It was very light and thin, but extremely stiff. Hard to guess the draw weight while it was unstrung, but Miel figured something around eighty to eighty-five pounds.

Vaatzes nodded again, as Miel noticed the groove stamped down the middle. Clever; it added strength while conserving mass, like the fuller in a sword-blade. "I've never seen a bow like this before," Miel said. Vaatzes shrugged. "It's the standard pattern back home," he said. Miel guessed from a slight trace of color in his voice that he was lying, but he couldn't imagine why.

A clatter of hoofs and the yapping of dogs announced the arrival of Jarnac. He looked tired, tense, if possible even larger than usual. As Master, he was wearing his surcoat over his armor, so that everybody would be able to recognize him even at a distance. Today (only today) he could wear the Ducas arms proper, free from the quarterings of the cadet branch. Somehow they seemed to sit more naturally on Jarnac's massive chest than they'd ever done on Miel. Life is crammed with little ironies, if you know where to look. It was probably Miel's imagination, but he thought he noticed Vaatzes flinch a little when he saw Jarnac on his horse, and maybe he relaxed a bit when he dismounted.

To business straight away. On his own ground, Jarnac could explain a complicated plan of action clearly and quickly. The basic idea was to get up on the high pasture to the west of the big wood, approaching downwind from the east while the dew was still on the grass, in hopes of putting up one of a group of four particularly fine mature boars that had been consistently sighted in the area over the last ten days. Normally they'd stay in the wood during the hours of daylight, but there was a chance of catching them out at this time of year, when dawn came early and the wet, lush grass was particularly tempting. Being realistic, they had precious little chance of bringing a boar to bay in the pasture, even if they put one up there; they'd have to follow it into the wood and drive it out the other side—down into the river, ideally—but at least there would be a clear scent for the dogs to follow, which would save the uncertainty and frustration of crashing about in the underwood hoping they'd be lucky enough to tread on one's tail, which was the only sure way of finding a boar in deep cover. If they drew a blank in the pasture, they'd have to fall back on that anyway; but the result as far as the standing party was concerned would be more or less the same. Wherever they found it, Jarnac and the hounds would be looking to drive the boar through the wood east-west, down the hill, aiming to bring it to bay either in the river or in the furze on the far bank. The standing party, accordingly, should make its way up the old carters' drove until they drew level with the lower edge of the wood; they should then follow the edge round, making as little noise as possible, and line out in a circle on the southwestern side, twenty-five yards inside the wood, ten yards apart. No shots to be taken eastward, of course, for fear of an arrow skipping on a branch and hitting the beaters or the dogs; one horn-call meant the boar was in sight, two if it was on the move, three for at bay, four for the death, five to signal mortal peril requiring immediate assistance, and had everybody brought a horn?

Miel nudged Ziani in the ribs. "No," Ziani said (his voice rather squeaky). "Sorry, I didn't realize..."

Someone handed him one. "Do you know how to sound it?" Jarnac asked. "In that case, you'd better have a practice now. Doesn't matter a damn if it sounds like a mule farting, but it's essential everybody knows where everybody else is, otherwise things can go wrong very quickly."

That was exactly what it sounded like; but after four tries Jarnac nodded and said, "That'll do," and Ziani was able to sink back into the obscurity of the circle. The huntsmen were starting to collect the dogs, while the pages led the horses away to wooden mangers filled with oats. Ziani remembered that he'd forgotten to bring the last pieces of armor, but either Jarnac had forgotten too or he had other things on his mind.

The beating party were almost ready to leave. Ziani noticed that Miel Ducas was still standing next to him; odd, because he'd have thought that the Ducas would be circulating, chatting to his fellow nobles. Then he realized: good manners ordained that, since Ziani was a stranger and didn't know anybody else here, Miel had to stay with him and put him at his ease. For a moment he was touched; but the Ducas is considerate of his inferiors in the same way a cat slashes at trailing string, because instinct gives him no choice.

"Where's the Duke?" he asked. "They aren't going to leave without him, are they?"

Miel grinned. "Not likely. But it's not polite for the guest of honor to be there for the briefing. Don't ask me why, it's just one of those things. He shows up—well, any minute now, and I fill him in on the plan of campaign."

Ziani was about to ask, "Why you?," but he guessed in time. Miel was senior nobleman in the standing party, so passing on the Master's orders was his job. Come to think of it, there'd been something about it in one of the books.

Orsea arrived, at last. His clothes, armor and escort had been set down immutably by King Fashion back when the Mezentines were still living in the old country, but the Duke of Eremia Montis traditionally defied tradition when hunting informally with close friends. Accordingly he was wearing an old, comfortable arming coat under distinctly scruffy leathers, and he had his hat on, even though it wasn't raining. He looked more cheerful than Miel could remember seeing him since before the Mezentine expedition. Veatriz was with him.

But she didn't dismount when he did; she leaned forward in the saddle to kiss him, then pulled her horse's head round and rode back down the path. Orsea turned back to watch her go, then strode forward to greet Miel.

"Don't tell me," he said. "Jarnac's found us a pig the size of an ox, with tusks like parsnips, and it's sitting waiting for us just over there in the bushes."

"In a sense," Miel replied. "There's supposed to be half a dozen feeding in the fat grass up top, and the idea is to pick them up in the open and drive them through the wood and out the other side." He shrugged. "Don't quite see it myself, but Jarnac's the expert, or so he keeps telling me."

Orsea grinned. "That's your cousin for you," he said. "I remember one time we were out after geese, years ago, and he'd cooked up this incredibly elaborate plan whereby the geese came in here, saw the decoys, turned through sixty-five degrees over one hide, got shot at, turned another thirty-two degrees which took them over another hide, and so on. Absolutely crazy, the whole thing, and everybody was saying, bloody Jarnac, why can't he just keep it simple? Except it worked, and we got twenty-seven geese in one night." He shrugged. "Disastrous, of course," he went on, "because after that, every time Jarnac said the geese were coming in on the stubbles and he had a clever plan, we all trudged out over the mudflats and sat in flooded ditches half the night expecting another miracle, and of course we'd have seen more geese staying at home and hiding in the clothes-press."

Miel smiled broadly. He'd heard the story many times before, and it had been much closer to the truth the first time; but it pleased him to see his friend happy, though of course the reason for it was nothing to do with the prospects for the day's hunt, or fresh air, or anything like that. He was happy because Veatriz had come out to the meet with him; because Orsea loved Veatriz more than anyone else in the world, more than being Duke, more than anything (one more thing he had in common with his old friend, his liege lord). How it had come about that he'd managed to persuade himself that she didn't love him, Miel couldn't say, but it was obvious to everyone but Orsea, and possibly Veatriz herself. He wished, for a variety of reasons, that she hadn't gone straight back home just now.

She sat down on the slim, brittle-looking chair and opened her writing-box. As she took out the ink-bottle, she hesitated, scowled; then she stood up, went to the door, and wedged it shut with the handle of a broom some maid had carelessly left behind.

Pen, ink, the little square of scraped parchment; she'd cut it from the inside of the binding of a book, and cleaned it up herself with pumice. Maybe she'd been a bit too enthusiastic about it; there were a few places where she'd scrubbed it too thin and made a small hole, or else worn down into the soft inside, so that any ink applied there would soak away into the fibers and make a ghastly mess.

Veatriz Sirupati to Valens Valentinianus, greetings.

Orsea, she thought. She hoped he was having a wonderful day. For a moment or so she'd persuaded herself that she'd go with him, at least for the morning. If they'd have been hunting parforce and she could have ridden instead of walking, probably she would have stayed. But she'd never liked walking much, especially not up hills or through dense, tangled forests. Besides, if she'd gone she'd probably have spoiled the day for him; he'd have had to hang back with her, being thoughtful and considerate, when really he wanted to be up at the front with the harborers, or crouched in the underbrush waiting to shoot.

You never replied to my last letter. I suppose there could be several different reasons. I offended you; I was putting pressure on you, breaking the rules of our friendship; I brought Orsea into it, when this has always been just you and me. Or perhaps you're just tired of me and bored by my letters. If it's any one of those, I'd understand. Going too far: that's always been my biggest failing.

Well; if I've offended you, I'm sorry. I'm not going to plead or anything; if you can forgive me, please do. If not—well, I'm sorry. It's my fault.

This is a very bad day for thinking about you, because Orsea is out hunting, and so of course you've been in my mind all the time he's been fussing around, looking for his old felt hat and the belt for his surcoat, telling me over and over again that he doesn't really want to go but everybody's been to so much trouble. Of course he wants to go really, but he automatically assumes I don't want him to, precisely because he's been looking forward to it so much. I don't know why he does that; it's like secretly, deep down inside, he wants me to come between him and happiness. All I want is for him to be happy; that's all, quite simple. It puzzles me how he can love me as much as he does and still know so little about me. It makes me wonder why he loves me, if it's not for who I really am.

And I'm doing it again, bringing Orsea in, like insisting my mother comes along on my honeymoon. But, if that's the reason you didn't answer my last letter, you won't have read this far; which means I can say what I like, but you won't read it.

Actually, I do quite like hunting; or at least, the only reason I don't like it's because it's usually tiresome and boring and either too hot or too cold and wet, and I'm lazy about walking. Orsea thinks I'm squeamish about animals being killed. A couple of times I've been when we were riding all the time, and I quite enjoyed it. At least it made a change from sewing and arranging flowers and listening to the house minstrels playing the same seven tunes all day. He can't seem to tell the difference between when I'm desperately sad and unhappy, and when I'm just bored and fed up.

Anyway; I'm prattling on, hoping you're reading. Sometimes I wonder if writing to you is just a clever way of talking to myself, because things suddenly get much clearer in my mind when I'm trying to tell you about them. I'm not sure about that. Partly I think it's true, but also I think that knowing you're reading what I'm writing makes me be honest with myself. I can lie to myself, if I've got to or I really want to, but I don't think I could lie to you.

No sign of a boar in the high pasture; no tracks, droppings, wallows or trampled grass. Jarnac had sent the dogs through five times, and all they'd done was stick their heads up and stare at him, as though he was trying to be funny.

It was a strange characteristic of Jarnac Ducas—a strength as often as it was a weakness—that he could be absolutely sure that something was going to happen and simultaneously know beyond a shadow of a doubt that it wasn't. This curious ability of his led him to make a lot of mistakes, but also meant that even while he was making them, he was also hard at work on putting them right. Half of him had known the long grass would be a complete waste of time, so he was fully prepared with a backup plan, which he lost no time in putting into effect. The main thing was that the standing party wouldn't know he'd screwed up till he told them so himself.

The backup plan involved sweeping the whole of the long cover, in one carefully coordinated drive. Such an approach was fraught with the most appalling difficulties — keeping the line level, so that one wing didn't get ahead of the other, or start drifting downhill, or overcompensate and go too far uphill and come out on the top, driving the quarry ahead of them and into perfect safety. That sort of thing didn't worry him in the least. He knew his huntsmen were the best trained and led beaters in the world, and of course they'd keep the line; at the same time, he could foresee exactly where the problems were going to be, and dealt with them in advance by posting stops at regular intervals all round the top and bottom boundaries — he'd sent them to get into position an hour before the main party set off, just in case.

In the event, they found quite easily, by the simple expedient of assuming that the boar would be in the densest, remotest, least accessible part of the cover, the last place they'd want it to be.

The first find was no more than a hundred yards in, but it turned out to be a false alarm; plenty big enough, but its bristles were still brown across the shoulders and back, not the dusty black of a full-grown animal. They let it run back, so it'd be out of the way and wouldn't confuse the hounds.

Twenty minutes later, they found again. A tall, spindly sweet chestnut had blown down, pulling its roots up; the shallow pit thereby formed had grown over with young holly, and the lymers picked up a scent leading straight to it. This time it was a full-grown boar, but for some reason it didn't want to run; instead, it wedged its back against the butt of the fallen tree and stood at bay, as the hounds surged around it. If Jarnac had been out for his own enjoyment he'd have gone straight in, but not today; it'd be shocking manners to kill in the wood while the guests were waiting outside. He called off the dogs and left the boar for another day.

Almost immediately after that, the hounds picked up a scent which seemed promising enough, but it turned out to be a milky old sow instead of a boar, no good to anybody at this time of the year. What it was doing out on its own, lying up in the deep, he had no idea, and no time to stop and find out.

He hadn't been expecting any of these finds to come to anything, of course; he knew that the boar they were looking for would inevitably be found in the dense mass of holly, briars and general impenetrable rubbish just north of the old charcoal-burners' camp, a little southeast of the dead center of the wood. There, sure enough, it was: a record trophy, without a doubt (tusks at least eight inches, a double abnormal, and the carcass not far short of eight hundredweight undressed), hunkered down in a natural fortress that the whole Eremian army would've had a job to take by assault.

Its lair was, in fact, an overgrown old burn site — the ash from the charcoal fires had sweetened the ground to perfection, hence the astonishingly abundant growth of briars, thorns and the like.

Presumably it had managed to get in there somehow or other, but Jarnac couldn't see how or where, unless it had a secret tunnel or had been lowered in on ropes.

"We could go in with hooks," one of the huntsmen suggested, "cut a way in through the brush."

Jarnac shook his head. "Too dangerous," he said. "I'm not risking men or dogs in that."

"Smoke it out?" someone else said, and Jarnac didn't even bother to reply. He stood looking at the boar for a while, then shook his head and gave the order to move on.

Not going to plan; that was definitely the boar he'd seen in his mind's eye, but apparently he'd overlooked its context. The chances of finding another one half as good were negligible; there might be a brown yearling or two, but that wouldn't be any use. Being realistic, the only course open to him would be to push straight on to the next likely cover, on the other side of the river. If they got a move on, they could be there in a couple of hours; then allow an hour for the standing party to get into position, an hour and a half (optimistic) for driving through and finding. By then, it'd be mid-afternoon, too late to try anywhere else. The infuriating thing was, the boar had been there, exactly where he knew it would be. Tiresome bloody creature.

The harborers weren't keeping up. He stopped and looked back. His own dogs and men were moving along, as he'd told them to do, but the Phocas pack (his heart had sunk when he saw them at the meet; useless, the lot of them, disobedient, reckless, forever getting ahead or chasing off after rabbits) were hanging back, and he could hear a lymer yelping. Stupid creature; it could see the boar and couldn't understand why it couldn't get at it.

"Maritz," he called out, "nip back and tell the Phocas lads to move their bloody dogs. We haven't got time for stragglers."

The huntsman ran off and didn't come back. For a moment, Jarnac wasn't sure what to do, a very rare experience for him. Properly speaking, he should press on and leave the Phocas pack to their own devices—it was what King Fashion would've done—but he couldn't quite bring himself to abandon them, thereby tacitly accusing the Phocas of incompetence. It'd be fair comment, but bad diplomacy. With a sigh, aware he was doing the wrong thing, he turned back and went to see what the problem was.

Easy enough. One of the Phocas lymers had managed to force itself about halfway through the briar tangle before getting completely laid up. It was yelping in panic and frustration, tugging at the brambles tangled in its ears, snarling at the boar; two more of the Phocas dogs were struggling to join it; a third had been intercepted by Maritz and one of the Phocas people, but was putting up a very convincing fight, dragging on its collar, scrabbling for traction with all four paws. The boar, meanwhile, was looking very unhappy. The stuck lymer's muzzle was only about a foot and a half away from its snout; there was a solid fuzz of grown-in bramble in the way, enough to keep three men with staffhooks busy for an hour, but that didn't seem to count for very much as far as the boar was concerned. It could smell enemy, right up close.

Its instincts were telling it: attack, run away, but do something instead of just standing there. All in all, Jarnac reflected, I couldn't have designed a worse mess if I'd had a month to think about it and half a dozen clerks to help out with the geometry.

King Fashion would've left the Phocas to sort out their own mess, but never mind. The priority was to get the dog out of the briars without it or anybody else getting ripped up by the boar. There was one obvious answer, but he kept dodging away from it like a nervous fencer. It was a fine boar, a trophy animal; it was beautiful, and he didn't want to have to murder it just to rescue someone else's stupid, badly trained dog. It would be on his conscience. But then, so would the dog, and anyone or anything else that got mangled or killed because of his scruples. He swore, then called over his shoulder for his heavy bow.

In Jarnac's terms, this meant the hundred-and-fifty-pounder, a monstrous deflexed recurve made of laminated buffalo horn, rock maple and boar backstrap sinew. Bending it involved crouching like a frog and springing up into the draw, so as to use every last scrap of back and thigh muscle to supplement the force of the arms and chest. They'd strung it for him before they left the house, using the big press in the tack room (when unstrung, it bent back on itself the wrong way, like a horseshoe). He nocked an arrow, looked the boar in the eyes, wound himself up, drew and loosed.

At five yards, there wasn't much danger that he'd miss. The arrow caught the boar in the fold of skin where the throat met the chest; at a guess, he'd say it went in a good handspan. The boar looked at him, blinked—he noticed the fine, long eyelashes, like a girl's—and folded up like a traveling chair. First it sank to its knees, its backside pointing up in the air. Then the strength in its joints evaporated and it rolled slowly onto its side, its feet lifting off the ground. Two muscle spasms stretched its back, and then it was perfectly still.

He lowered the bow. "Get that fucking dog out of there," he said.

They approached with staffhooks, but he yelled at them; no point in killing the boar if they mutilated the dog with a missed slash. He told them to put their gloves on and pull the briars apart. Then he walked away. He felt utterly miserable, and he wanted not to be there.

As soon as they'd rescued the dogs, they cut the boar out, hocked it and slung it on a pole. Maritz tried to tell him the weight, but Jarnac shut him up; he didn't want to know. It had been a trophy boar, and now it was just pork; fine, it'd make good dinners for the farm workers, who didn't see meat very often, and it wouldn't be trampling any more growing crops. He didn't want to think about it, or what he'd just done. He wanted to go home.

"Right," he said aloud.

Maritz scampered up beside him, anticipating new instructions. Jarnac's mind was a blank, but he said, "Get the line back together, we'll push through anyhow. You never know, there may be something." He hoped there wouldn't be. He'd just broken the contract between hunter and quarry, so that nothing could go right for him from now on, all for the sake of the stupid Phocas' useless dog.

He wasn't really taking notice as they drove the rest of the wood. Usually, when beating out a cover, he was aware of everything; he heard every snapped twig, saw every movement, every gradation of color and texture, every detail of bark, lichen and moss. The slightest thing snagged his attention — the call of a jay, sunlight in a water-drop hanging from a leaf, the smell of leaf mold, the taste of sweat running down his face. When the hunt was on and the next pace forward might bring him to the quarry, he felt so alive he could hardly bear it. All that had gone, though, and there was nothing left in it except a long walk over rough ground.

They dragged themselves through a dense tangle of holly, out onto the third lateral ride. As soon as he was on the path, in the open, he realized that the line had gone to hell. There were dogs in front, dogs behind, men everywhere, chaos. Under normal circumstances he'd have been beside himself with rage. He grinned. Like it mattered.

Behind him, somebody shouted; then someone else shouted back, a dog yelped, high and frightened, other dogs joined in. Something was crashing through thick cover. Immediately, Jarnac snapped out of his self-indulgent sulk. Everything was going wrong at once. Somehow, against all the odds and all the rules, they'd found another boar — a big one, by the sound of it — right on top of the one he'd murdered. That was impossible, of course, because you didn't get two fully grown boars this close together, but apparently it had happened, and his line was all screwed up. Disaster; there were men and dogs in front of a bolted boar, right in the danger zone. It was the worst thing that could happen. Without stopping to think, he hurled himself at the source of the noise, tugging at his sword-hilt (but the stupid thing was binding in the scabbard and wouldn't come out). All he could see in his mind's eye was the boar coming up behind the men who'd strayed ahead. They wouldn't know what was happening, they wouldn't have time to turn round, let alone get out of the way. He couldn't think of anything to do, except get to the boar before it hurt anybody, and kill it.

Pelhaz and Garsio were shouting, dead ahead; dogs were barking all round. He charged straight into trees, branches bashed him across the face, clubbed his shoulders. He couldn't see more than five yards in front, and he suspected he was losing his sense of direction (so easily done in thick cover, no matter how experienced you were). He tried to pull himself together, plot the boar's likely course from the sounds around him, but there didn't seem to be a pattern. One moment he was sure he could hear it crashing about on his left; then it was behind him, then over on the right. For one crazy, horrifying moment he wondered if there were half a dozen of them, not just one. And then he saw it.

Not for long. A black shape slipped past him, glimpsed between the trunks of two skinny oaks. He saw enough to identify it: a six-year-old, but huge for its age, running flat out (that rather ludicrous straight-backed seesaw run, like a lame man sprinting). He hadn't seen the tusks, but he didn't care about stuff like that right now. Desperately he tried to reassemble the positions of men and dogs in his mind, and adjust for straying. If he was right and not just thinking wishfully, the boar was on a slanting course that led it away from the end of the line that had got ahead of itself; in which case, the men would be safe and probably the dogs too.

It occurred to him to blow a dead stop, which was what he should have done as soon as the wretched animal broke cover. Better late than never; he sounded his horn, caught his breath, and tried to think.

Horn-calls answered him, and at last he was able to plot the positions of his men. The Phocas were well behind (out of harm's way; good); his own men were in front, but over on the right, away from the boar. The dogs could be anywhere, thanks to the panic and the confusion, but he could hear the huntsmen calling them back. With any luck, none of them were so hot on the scent that they'd disobey the calls. Jarnac closed his eyes and thanked whoever was in charge of destiny that day. He didn't deserve it, but he seemed to have got away with it.

More horn-calls, some shouting; the line was pulling itself together. Garsio was calling for him; he shouted back, to give his position. Another shout; he recognized the captain of the Phocas contingent. He made sure the line was re-formed and perfect before he called out instructions for Maritz and Pelhaz to pass on to the under-captains. By now, the boar could be well in front, but from what he'd seen of it he was pretty sure it wouldn't veer off the line it'd been on, not unless it found a new source of danger or an unpassable obstacle. Suddenly he laughed. Everything possible had gone wrong, he'd fucked it all up worse than he'd ever done in his entire life, and even so he'd found a cracking good pig for the Duke, and every prospect of presenting it, on time, exactly where it was supposed to be. It was enough to make you die of despair; if the universe could reward such gross incompetence with success, how could he ever trust it again?

Ziani was feeling cold.

He wouldn't have noticed the chill, or the clamminess of his wet clothes, if he hadn't been so bored; but he had nothing else to occupy his mind except his misfortunes, so inevitably he dwelt on them. This wasn't how he'd imagined it'd be.

For the first few minutes he'd stood completely still in his assigned spot, poised like a fencer waiting for his enemy's initial strike. But those first few minutes had passed and large animals hadn't come streaming at him out of every bush. He'd familiarized himself with the terrain; then he'd looked up at the treetops, then down at the mush of rotting leaves under his feet; then he'd counted all the trees he could see. Nothing had happened. He was bored. If this was hunting, they could shove it.

Mostly, he was unhappy because he was completely out of his depth (he stooped down, picked up a bit of twig, and started breaking it up into little bits). He didn't understand the rules or the procedures, he couldn't see the pattern, and he didn't like being outdoors. None of any of this, he realized, had anything to do with him. That was where he'd made his mistake; believing he could incorporate this mechanism into his own. But it wasn't compatible. It was all about something else (What? Getting food? Controlling dangerous pests? Having fun?) and he couldn't get a handle on it. He should be in the factory, making things.

He took an arrow out of his homemade, sadly unorthodox quiver, and played with it for a while. It was a wretched artifact by any standards: thirty inches of unevenly planed cedarwood dowel, with a crudely forged and excessively heavy spike socketed on one end. He'd underestimated arrow-making; he'd assumed that if the Eremians could do it, it must be easy. Not so. The dowel was rubbish to start with, but his sad blob of iron made it worse. He fitted it to the bowstring anyway, for something to do.

In his imagination, it had been quite different. He'd pictured all of them hurrying along together, shoulder to shoulder down a trail of smashed branches and scuffed earth, following the pig. That was how it was supposed to be in the books—except, he realized, there were two distinct methods of hunting, and he'd assumed they'd be doing parforce and instead they were doing the other one, bow-and-stable. His plan wouldn't work doing it this way. He was wasting his time.

Nothing he could do about it now, though. He made a wish that there wouldn't be any pigs in the wood, and that they could all go home soon. From there, he set to worrying—what if he didn't hear them calling the whole thing off, or they forgot about him, left him standing in the middle of all these ridiculous trees, without the faintest idea where he was? Easily done, he would imagine; he was a stranger, a foreigner, a gatecrasher who'd invited himself along. Why should they remember him, or bother to let him know it was time to move on?

Noise, somewhere sort of close. He'd learned that noises in a forest are deceptive, and you can't accurately judge distance or direction by them. The forest was full of noisy things. Apart from the humans and their horrible savage dogs, there were animals— deer, badgers, God knows what else—and birds, not to mention creaking and groaning trees. He'd heard stories, back home, about the dangers of forests; how the tops of tall, thin trees can snap off in the wind and get laid up in the branches of their neighbors thirty feet or so up in the air, held only by tangles of twig and creeper, so that any damn thing (a breeze, a careless movement, a shout, even) might be enough to dislodge them and bring them crashing down, entirely without warning. Foresters called them widow-makers, he remembered, and sometimes they were so deceptively hidden that even the canniest and most wary lumberjack was caught out and flattened. He peered upward again, just in case. All he could see was branches and an untidy mess of foliage. There could be wagons, ships, even houses up there, masked by the leafy swathes, and he'd never see them till it was too late.

He was concentrating so hard on scanning the treetops for hidden terrors that he nearly missed it all.

First, the noise. It sounded comical, high-pitched, a furious squealing, mingled with the desperate yapping of dogs, and it seemed to be coming from all around him. He'd heard pigs before: pigs in sties in alleys and entries and snickets (pig-rearing in the City fell in that uncomfortable debatable zone between forbidden and disapproved of); pigs snuffling, grunting, complaining and being killed. This noise was similar but somehow wrong— because it was out of place, he realized; pigs lived in cities, not out in the wilderness, among the stupid trees—and the dog noises confused the issue hopelessly. His best guess, however, was that the pig was about seventy yards distant and heading away from him at speed.

The boar burst out at him through the twisted branches of a blown-sideways mountain ash; an enormous blurred monstrosity, a cruel parody of the useful, harmless Mezentine pig. Its way of running was hopelessly inefficient, a seesaw motion (it didn't seem able to bend its back, so it didn't so much run as bounce), but horribly quick. It had the flat, wet, soppy nose of a proper pig, but there was coarse black hair all over its face, and four huge yellow teeth.

It's going to kill me, Ziani told himself—it wasn't an upsetting thought, somehow—but instead the boar jackknifed past him (bounce-bounce, like a leather ball), crushing bushes and briars as it went by like a ship plowing through a heavy sea. It passed him no further than six feet away; as it departed, Ziani could see its jaws chomping up and down, the absurdly oversize teeth rubbing furiously together like someone trying to start a fire with dry sticks. It looked lethal and ridiculous, and it sounded like an outraged customer demanding to see the manager.

It was almost out of Ziani's little patch of clearing when the dogs showed up. They were running so fast he could barely make out their shapes, beyond an impression of long, flexible bodies contorted by extraordinary effort; and when they jumped at the boar they seemed to flow, like water poured at a height. His eye and brain weren't sharp enough to register how many of them there were; they were too quick for that. But one of them had sprung onto the boar's table-wide back; another was being dragged along underneath it by its teeth clamped in its venerable dewlap; another was curled round the boar's front legs like ivy, skittering frantically backward as it tried to bite into a ham much wider than the full gape of its long, pointed jaws. Ziani had seen hate occasionally, and if anyone had asked him, he'd have stated confidently that it was a uniquely human emotion; but he'd never seen anything like the way the dogs hated the boar. There was a diabolical agility to it that almost amounted to grace, but the absolute commitment of their fury was terrifying.

Compared to the dogs, the boar was slow, rigid and oafish; but it was strong. With a short, apparently slight movement of its neck and shoulders, it lifted up one of the dogs and threw it straight up in the air, like a man spinning himself a catch with an apple. The dog's back arched, all four legs scrambled at empty air; it came down in a tangle of holly laced with briars and ground elder, sprang up again and shot itself like an arrow or a scorpion bolt at the boar's head. Another dog was tearing at the boar's ear, and yet another was trying to bite its nose. The boar made another of those short movements, and one of the dogs yelped—it was shriller than any human scream—and fell sprawling on its back, its belly ripped open like a burst seam.

The dogs were losing, but they didn't seem to care. They were too light to slow the boar's momentum, and their weapons were too slight to penetrate its armor. The boar dragged them, four of them with their jaws locked in it, through the middle of a holly-clump, like someone wiping mud off his shoes in long grass. One of them was pulled off, but rolled over, jumped, vaulted over the boar's back and disappeared underneath it again, all in one movement. Such a degree of recklessness was almost beyond Ziani's capacity to believe; until that moment, he'd have said he was the only living thing in the world capable of it.

Which reminded him. It wasn't perfect, but it might do. He only had this moment, which wouldn't come again. He bent the bow, pushing with his left arm and pulling with his right, and stared down the arrow.

Miel Ducas had run into a tree. It was an unspeakably stupid thing to do and until a moment ago he'd have sworn it wasn't physically possible for a grown man with adequate eyesight not to notice a big, broad sweet chestnut dead ahead of him on a reasonably clear path. But he'd managed it, somehow.

After a dazed moment when he couldn't remember anything, he picked himself up off the ground, yelled angrily at the pain in his shins and jaw, and tried to sell himself on the idea that it hadn't happened. At least nobody had seen him.

One consequence of his deplorable lapse was that he'd lost the bloody boar. It had been there right in front of him, a black hairy bum heaving obscenely up and down on the edge of his vision, just slow enough that he could keep pace with it if he ran like a lunatic. Wasted effort that had turned out to be. He leaned against his enemy the tree and listened.

Not too far away, he could hear squealing, and the furious yelping of dogs. If he ran fast, he could probably catch up (except that he couldn't run fast, because his leg hurt); or he could walk, or hobble, following the trail, and hear about the outcome from somebody else.

He decided his leg didn't hurt so much after all, and started to run.

The pitch and intensity of the yelping had changed. Jarnac could've interpreted it without thinking; Miel wasn't nearly as good, but he reckoned the dogs had caught up to the boar, but the boar hadn't yet turned at bay. That was bad. A boar in that mood could easily gut or trample a dog, and God help any human who got in its way. What should've happened, if King Fashion had been running the show, was that the dogs should've chased the boar without catching up with it, until they were outside the forest and in the open. From the edge of the wood the ground fell away in a long, gentle slope all the way to the river. The boar would head for the river-bed, wade deep into the water and there turn at bay—a stupid thing to do, since it could be quickly and safely dispatched, but they all did it, bless them. That was how Jarnac had planned it, no question, but something must've gone wrong.

A very unpleasant picture formed in his mind: Orsea, with sword drawn, diving into the mêlée to rescue the dogs. It was one of the classic heroic deeds in boar-hunting. Jarnac had done it loads of times (but Jarnac knew what he was doing). If the opportunity presented itself, Orsea wouldn't hesitate for an instant.

(Years ago, when he was a boy nagging to be allowed to go on his first hunt, Miel had been taken to see an old man who worked in the stables. The old man had opened his shirt and showed off a long pink scar that ran from his neck to his navel; to this day, they'd told him afterward, nobody could explain how the man had survived. He'd been the lucky one, that day.)

Perhaps, Miel told himself as he ran, perhaps someone with a cool head, common sense and a good eye will put an arrow in the stupid pig before Orsea gets there. Disappointing for poor Orsea, but at least he'll still be alive this evening, and I won't have to tell Veatriz.

Another sound: a man's voice, high and very scared, yelling for help. Miel swore and tried to run faster, but this would be a very bad time to collide with another tree. He made himself slow down, just as his spear caught in a low branch and was ripped out of his hand.

Very bad, because he couldn't stop and go back for it. He had his falchion, of course. He'd never killed a boar with a close sword, though he'd seen it done twice. Mostly when he went hunting, they didn't find anything. Hell of a time for his luck to change.

He saw the dog first. It was almost but not quite dead, shivering. He managed to jump over it without slowing down, and that was when he saw the boar.

Now it had turned at bay, and he could see why. Some fool, some criminal incompetent, had contrived to stick an arrow in its hind leg. Worst possible thing you could do. The front leg, fine; a boar goes down like a sack of turnips if you nail its front leg, you can stroll up to it and kill it at your ease. An arrow in the back leg stops it running, so it has to turn at bay, but the motive force for its attack is the forequarters and chest. Whoever had shot that arrow had made the boar as dangerous as it could possibly get.

He might have known. Lying on his side, with nothing between him and the boar but a screen of twisting, snapping dogs, was the stupid bastard foreigner. He didn't seem to be hurt, no blood; Miel had seen total blind panic often enough in circumstances like these to know he'd simply frozen. He'd done it himself, once. A bow, lying just out of arm's reach, completed the evidence for the prosecution.

Just as well I'm here, Miel thought sadly.

"It was extraordinary," Jarnac was saying. "Never seen anything like it in my life."

Miel scowled at him. "It was bloody stupid," he said, "that's all. Half an inch out and you'd have brought me home hanging off a long stick, along with the boar."

Jarnac shook his head. "Ignore him," he said, "he's being modest. When I say it was the neatest bit of work I've seen in the hunting field for ten years, you know I'm not exaggerating. It was bloody stupid as well, of course, but that's Miel for you. Never could resist showing off."

Miel tried to shift, but a sharp spike of pain stopped him. "How could I have been showing off?" he said. "I didn't know you two were there watching. I thought it was just me and him, or else I'd have left it to you to deal with the stupid animal."

"Where is he?" Veatriz interrupted. "The foreigner, I mean."

Miel sighed. "Upstairs," he said, "in the Oak Room. Well," he went on unhappily, "I couldn't very well leave him to fend for himself, when he'd just come that close to being ripped up. From what I gather, he lives on his own in that factory place of his, and he's in no fit state to look after himself."

"It was his own stupid fault," Orsea put in, helping himself to another drink. "Would've served him right, at that. Jarnac, whatever possessed you to invite him in the first place?"

Jarnac shrugged. "He seemed to want to come," he replied. "I mean, he spun this yarn about how he needed to see what hunting's actually like if he was going to be making hunting armor; which is drivel, of course; Cantacusene and his father and his father before him have been fitting our family out every year for a century, and none of them ever came within a mile of a boar or a buck unless it was sausages. But he really did seem fearfully keen, and I couldn't see any harm in it..."

Miel groaned. "Next time you're inclined to yield to a generous impulse, resist," he said. "I'm not made of ankles, you know."

Veatriz laughed; he wasn't looking at her, deliberately, but he could picture her face. Instead, he saw Orsea grin. Jarnac clicked his tongue and said: "I don't know what you're complaining about. You know the old saying: pain's temporary, glory is forever, and the girls dig the scars. You'll be fighting them off with a pitchfork once word gets around. Honestly," he said to Veatriz, ignoring Miel's miserable protests, "you should have seen him. He comes charging out of the bushes, sword in hand; he sees the foreigner lying there on the deck wetting himself, frozen stiff with fear; he sees the boar. He knows the dogs are getting tired, they can't hold it back much longer. He's still running flat out; he jumps, lands on the boar's back if you please, launches himself off again, and in passing, damn near chops the boar's head off with a downward backhand slash —"

"And lands in a clump of fuzz that turns out to be a coppiced stump and twists his stupid ankle," Miel said. "Actually, Triz, you should've seen it. Must've been the most comical sight since the farmer chucked his dog down the well and threw a stick for the bucket."

"You be quiet," Jarnac said ferociously. "By your own admission you couldn't see what was going on round you, so clearly you're the last person to comment. Also, the self-deprecating modesty is just fishing for compliments. This isn't the first time, you see," he added, as Veatriz giggled. "When he was younger, with some girl in tow — there was always a girl in tow —"

"Look," Miel protested.

"Used to be a positive menace," Jarnac went on. "Very disruptive to the smooth running of the hunt, having someone forever committing acts of gratuitous valor every time the girl happened to be looking in his direction. I had to stop taking him along in the end. I should have known better, but I'd assumed he'd grown out of it."

"True," Orsea put in (traitor, Miel thought). "It got so that you couldn't take a quiet stroll in the park if he'd got a girl along with him. I remember, there was a goat in a paddock. I swear he used to sneak out and kick this goat whenever he had the chance, just so it'd hate him and go for him on sight; and it was quite an elderly goat, not much of a threat to life and limb, but of course the girl wouldn't know that —"

"Complete and utter lies," Miel growled, though of course Orsea was telling the truth. Miel tried to remember if he'd ever taken Veatriz for a stroll past the goat's paddock.

"I remember," Jarnac butted in. "It was on a chain, so it couldn't actually get at him if he judged the distance right; but then one day the goat charged him so ferociously that the chain broke —"

Veatriz burst out laughing; Miel winced, jarred his ankle, and yelped with pain. He wished they'd shut up now. The joke was wearing thin, as far as he was concerned.

"Anyway," Veatriz said, "it was very brave of you, Miel, and I'm sure that this time your motives were impeccable." She was teasing him, he didn't like that. He almost wanted to explain what his true motive had been; to get there, at all costs, before Orsea could do what he was being accused of, because if Orsea had tried a stunt like that he'd have been killed, and then there wouldn't be all this merriment. He managed to keep that sentiment where it belonged, though.

"I think it's time you all pushed off and let me get some rest," he said. "It's not fair, picking on me when I can't move."

Jarnac frowned, and Miel realized there was something bothering him, which he hadn't told them about. Knowing Jarnac, it'd be some aspect of the hunt, some transgression of the rules on his part that he felt bad about, though nobody else would be inclined to make a fuss about it. "Let's leave him alone with his glory, then," Jarnac said, and he stood up to leave. "I suppose I'd better look in on the foreigner before I go."

"I wouldn't bother," Miel said, with a touch of bitterness. "Unless you want to yell at him for managing to prick the boar in the back leg like that. But I don't suppose he'd understand the significance of it, so there wouldn't be much point."

"Actually," Orsea said, "I need to talk to him myself—not about this," he added, with a slight nod in Miel's direction. "Business."

Miel remembered. He'd been thinking of the foreigner as simply an embarrassing fool who'd done a stupid thing; he'd forgotten who the man actually was. He nodded back. "That's right," he said. "Don't worry, he's not really damaged, just a bit shaken. He'll be up and about again in the morning."

"Good," Orsea said. "But I still need to talk to him. Don't worry about that now, Miel. You keep still and let that ankle heal. I'll deal with the other business."

"What other business?" Jarnac asked, as he and Orsea climbed the stairs. "I hadn't realized you knew the man."

Orsea pulled a wry grin. "Oh yes," he said. "He's the Mezentine we picked up on the way back from—well, you remember, I'm sure."

Jarnac frowned. "The one who wanted to turn us all into little pseudo-Mezentines, working in factories," he said. "I thought you'd said no to all that."

"I did. But he talked the Calaphates into putting up the money for this factory."

"Ah, right. They make good armor, I'll say that for them, and sensibly priced, too."

"It's not just armor," Orsea said quietly. "Anyhow, I don't want to be rude or anything, but — is this the room here?"

"The Oak Room." Jarnac nodded. "Would you like me to wait outside?"

"I'll find my own way back," Orsea replied.

Jarnac nodded and went away; Orsea could hear the firm clump of his boots on the stairs. Nobody could call Jarnac clumsy, but his enormous size made the staircase shake all the way up to the landing. He raised his hand to knock, then remembered who he was and lifted the latch.

The foreigner was lying on the bed, arms by his side, staring up at the ceiling; he sat up as Orsea walked in. "It's all right," Orsea said, as he started to get to his feet. "You stay where you are. How are you feeling?"

"Stupid," Vaatzes replied.

Orsea nodded. "Quite right," he said. "But of course, you didn't know. Or else you're a rotten shot. Neither of them's a criminal offense in this country."

Vaatzes shook his head. "I shouldn't even have been there," he said. "I suppose I hadn't realized what sort of occasion it'd be. Did I ruin everything?"

Orsea thought before answering. "Depends," he said. "You caused a very nasty incident which could've got somebody killed. On the other hand, you gave Miel Ducas an opportunity to be terribly brave and clever, so he's happy; propped up on pillows downstairs pretending he's not loving every bit of the attention, he's like that. So he's happy, and he's my oldest friend, so I'm happy too. Jarnac Ducas is going to have the boar's tusks mounted in a gorget for him, with a little silver plate inscribed, *For saving the life of another*. In a year's time, everybody'll remember it as the hunt where the Ducas pulled off the most amazing flying cut, and you'll be bored sick of telling people the story when they ask you. Jarnac's the only one who's really upset, because three of his dogs were killed. He wouldn't dream of showing it, but he's heartbroken. Still, all in all, not a complete disaster."

Vaatzes drew in a deep breath. "You're all being extremely kind," he said. "Which makes me feel terrible. I'm sorry."

"Forget it," Orsea said. "And promise me, if anybody invites you to go hunting again, refuse."

"I promise."

"Fine. Now," Orsea went on, "I need to talk to you about the scorpions."

17

On the morning after the Duke's hunt, a tall stocky middle-aged woman whose florid complexion matched her loud red dress left Civitas Eremiae by the east gate, riding a light-boned skewbald horse in the middle of a caravan. With her were her escort, nine riders in armor who doubtless made up for in experience what they lacked in youth; three muleteers on elderly dog's-meat palfreys; a pale, thin young woman with a bad cold; and twenty-seven well-laden mules.

It was necessarily slow going down the mountain. The thin young woman looked nervous as she leaned back in the saddle, as if she expected to vanish backward over the horse's tail at any moment. Her aunt, the woman in the red dress, spread her ample seat comfortably, as though her knees were stitched tight to the girths. She yawned once or twice, not bothering to cover her mouth.

At the crossroads the party turned east along the rutted, dusty track that followed the top of the ridge until it joined the Edgeway, which in turn led to the Butter Pass. The guards, riding in front and somewhat close together, talked for a while about cockfighting, horse-racing and the chances of war with Mezentia, which they decided was most unlikely. The muleteers were busy keeping the mules moving. The merchant and her niece rode side by side most of the time, but didn't talk to each other. They rested for an hour at noon, in the shade of a knot of canted, scrubby thorn trees that marked the point where the Butter Pass began. They picked the pace up gradually in the afternoon, and by nightfall they were close enough to the border to see the lights of the Vadani frontier post. Shortly after midnight they crossed into Vadani territory, following a narrow path along the bed of a steep-sided gully that kept them well out of sight of the border guards. It would have been an awkward ride in the dark, except that they and their horses knew the way very well indeed, and didn't need to see the hazards in order to avoid them.

At some point in the small hours they rejoined the road, a little way beyond a village by the name of Gueritz, and spent the rest of the night there, recovering from the stresses of their prosaic little adventure. At first light they rode on as far as Schantz, where they stopped at the inn for breakfast, and to have one of the guards' horses reshod. Two of the muleteers entertained the Schantz ostlers and grooms with an account of Duke Orsea's hunt, which they'd heard from one of Jarnac's men in an inn in Civitas Eremiae the night before they left. Such parts of the account as were not invented were greatly exaggerated: Miel Ducas had been savagely mauled by the boar and it was uncertain whether he'd recover; the Mezentine exile Vaatzes was also hovering at death's door, having been picked up bodily on the boar's snout and hurled down a rock-lined goyle into a riverbed; the Ducas had killed the boar that mangled him, after wrestling it to the ground and cutting its throat with his short knife.

The road from Schantz to Pasador was broad, flat and easy; they had the river on their right all the way, and they stopped several times to water the horses. Even so, they made Pasador by noon and sat in out of the heat in a ruined barn, while two muleteers who wanted to stretch their legs walked into the village and bought bread, cheese, figs and white wheat beer for the midday meal. When the edge had gone off the sun, they carried on briskly and peacefully as far as the crossroads, where they picked up the Silver Pass, leading direct to Civitas Vadanis. It was only the delay caused by having the guard's horse shod that stopped them reaching the city gate before dark; as it was, they had to ride the last hour and a half by moonlight, which was no great hardship. In fact, they were happy to enter the city in the dark, since it made them less conspicuous. Since the sheep-driving season was over for the year, they were able to pen the mules in a small paddock in the main stockyard, handy for the inns. The guards and the muleteers limped off to go drinking; the merchant and her niece washed up in the back yard of the Convention before setting off for Duke Valens' castle, in the northeast corner of the city.

The story of Orsea's hunt was told many times that evening in the stockyard inns, each containing a slight development on its predecessor. By the time it was recited in the Gold & Silvermen's Hall, a large and popular inn on the edge of the assay court, both the Ducas and Vaatzes had been killed, though not before the Ducas had given the boar its death-wound with the shattered truncheon of his spear.

One of Valens' austringers left the Gold & Silver shortly after that and headed up the hill to the castle. He was aware that he'd had rather more to drink than he'd have liked, since his duty was to seek an immediate audience with the Duke himself. The news of the Mezentine exile's death, however, shouldn't really be left till morning, and besides, he knew a couple of other people who'd want to hear about it straight away. He had to tell the Duke first, of course, he realized that; but afterward, time would be of the essence with his other customers, who wouldn't want to pay him if they'd already heard the news from someone else.

"He's dead," Psellus announced at the general staff meeting. He paused, then added: "Apparently, he was killed by a pig."

There was an element of shock in the silence that followed; also the tension of strong, serious men trying not to laugh. Eventually, a senior officer of the Coppersmiths' said, "A pig?"

"A wild pig," Psellus said. "It appears that he was invited to go hunting with the Duke and his courtiers. A wild pig killed him—

apparently they are quite ferocious animals, capable of inflicting serious injury. One of the courtiers was killed also."

A different kind of silence; thoughtful, reticent. The Coppersmith broke it to say: "This changes nothing. But I am surprised to hear that he was invited to hunt with the Duke and his court. My understanding is that only persons of high social standing attend on these occasions."

Psellus nodded. "As participants," he said. "But please bear in mind that the hunters are accompanied by a substantial number of assistants. There are men who look after the dogs, others who drive the animals out of hiding by making a noise, and of course there are porters, to carry equipment and the carcasses. My understanding is that the hunters usually hire casual labor for some of these tasks. It's highly possible that he was there in that capacity, rather than as a guest." Psellus hesitated. "Unfortunately, my sources—I must stress, these are preliminary reports only—my sources weren't able to furnish any details, so the theory remains uncorroborated. Nevertheless..." He hesitated again. "If these reports are accurate, Vaatzes is dead. I think we can safely assume that, contrary to what my colleague has just said, the position has changed significantly. In fact, I would ask the commission to consider whether the war is still necessary."

"On what grounds?" Tropaeus, needless to say, defending the infant war as though it was his cub. "If there has been a change," he went on, "it's for the worse. Let us put your theory on one side for a moment and assume that Vaatzes was there as a guest. In that case, logic suggests that he was on good terms with the Eremian aristocracy—a Mezentine, a representative of the nation that wiped out the flower of their army. There can only be one explanation, just as Vaatzes had only one commodity to sell in order to buy their favor. In other words, we must conclude that Vaatzes had already betrayed the technical secrets entrusted to him by virtue of his position at the ordnance factory, or was preparing to do so."

Psellus coughed mildly. "Assuming," he said, "the wretched

man was there as a guest. If not, if he was simply a day-laborer, surely it implies the opposite; that he was destitute, or at least forced by necessity to take any work he could get, and therefore that either he made no attempt to sell our secrets, or he had tried and failed. I should add," he went on before Tropaeus could interrupt, "that I have seen minutes of a meeting of the Eremian council at which an offer to introduce new skills and methods of metalworking were offered to the Duke by an unnamed Mezentine, and refused. Unless our security is even worse than we've been supposing, I can only assume that the man refused by the council must be Vaatzes."

"We've all seen that report," someone objected—he was sitting too far back for Psellus to see his face; he thought the voice was familiar but he couldn't put a name to it. "But you're missing the point, both of you. It doesn't matter. So Vaatzes is dead; so we have evidence to suggest that the Eremians refused to listen to him. What are you suggesting? Are you trying to argue that we shouldn't go on with the invasion?"

Psellus stiffened. "I don't recall proposing that," he said. "And I fully accept the argument that we need to make sure there's no possibility of leakage of restricted Guild knowledge."

"Which means the Eremians must be wiped out," the unseen man broke in. "We've discussed all this. So, unless you're saying we should reopen that decision—which, personally, I'm not inclined to do unless you can produce some pretty strong new arguments that we haven't considered previously—I don't see what difference Vaatzes' death makes to anything. We've got the soldiers, right here, kicking their heels and waiting to go. I won't remind you how much they're costing us per day. I'm not aware of any significant strategic or tactical considerations which would keep us from launching the invasion immediately. Gentlemen, we're wasting time and money. Let's get on and do what we've already agreed has to be done."

Loud rumble of approval. Very unwillingly, Psellus got to his feet once more. "I'm not opposing that view," he said, "or arguing against the invasion. All I'm trying to ask is whether it's quite so urgent now that Vaatzes himself is dead—"

"If he *is* dead," someone else put in. "A moment ago you said it was unconfirmed."

"It is," Psellus said raggedly. "But let's assume it's right. If Vaatzes is dead, he won't be giving away any more secrets. We know from the Eremian council minutes that they turned him down. So we're left with any secrets he passed on to someone else, private citizens rather than the Eremian government, before his death. And I can't help wondering—"

"It changes nothing," said another voice, off to his left. "Even if Vaatzes said nothing, or nobody listened to him, it's all beside the point. We've got to be sure; and the only way we can be sure is to invade. It's how we've managed to keep our total monopoly for well over a hundred years; and if it means we have to go to war, then we've got to do it. I propose that Commissioner Psellus receive our thanks for updating us on these new developments; I further propose that we set a definite date for the launch of the invasion, namely ten days from now. Do I have a seconder for that?"

Motion carried; orders issued to the commander in chief, requisitions to the Treasurer's office and other parties concerned; vote of thanks to Commissioner Psellus, as minuted.

What was I doing, Psellus asked himself, as he climbed the stairs back to his office; was I trying to stop the war? Somebody thought so, and now we've got a firm date. I didn't think that was what I was trying to do. I don't know anymore. It's as though this war's alive now. It's crawled in from wherever wars come from, like bees getting in through a thin place in the thatch, and already it's too big and too clever to be stopped.

The sooner it starts, the sooner it'll be over and I won't have to think about it anymore.

"Where the hell have you been?" Cantacusene said, as Ziani limped through the factory gate. He'd been measuring out timber for the scorpion frames; a boxwood rule in one hand, a nail in the other. "They've been saying you're dead."

"Don't you believe it," Ziani replied, and Cantacusene wondered what'd made him so cheerful. "If you think a wild pig could succeed where the Guild tribunal and the compliance directorate failed, you're a bigger fool than I took you for. How's it going? Did they get that problem with the sear-plate bolts sorted out?"

Cantacusene nodded. "We're ahead of the book," he said, with more than a hint of pride. "You said run four shifts, so I've been keeping them going flat out. Haven't been home since you've been away."

"Fine. Good." Ziani wished he'd put a bit more sincerity into that, but too late now. "The good news is, the Duke has just doubled the order. He wants a hundred."

"That's all right," Cantacusene said. "At this rate, he can have them in a week."

"At this rate maybe," Ziani said, and he set off for the long gallery. Cantacusene dropped the rule and dashed after him. "But this rate's too bloody slow. Day after tomorrow at the very latest, he'll be back asking for two hundred in a fortnight. I'm planning for two hundred and fifty in ten days."

Cantacusene stopped. He had a stitch and he was out of breath. "Impossible."

"No." Ziani hadn't stopped. Cantacusene set off again. "Perfectly possible. We just need more men. I stopped off at Calaphates' place and told him to get his men out recruiting. Also, he's seeing to materials; we're all right for timber, but we'll need more quarter-inch iron plate. It can be done, you'll see."

"Why two hundred and fifty?"

"Because that's what it'll take to defend this city," Ziani replied, as though it was perfectly obvious. "Two hunded and fifty is the minimum number, we should have seventy-five more but I've got an idea about that. If only we'd had time to build a rolling mill, I wouldn't be relying on bloody merchants for my quarter plate."

He shook his head. "Everything's going quite well," he said. "You never know, we might just get there."

He left Cantacusene at the gallery door, and headed straight for the forge, where the springs were being tempered. It was the stage in the process where things were most likely to go wrong, he knew perfectly well; ideally, that was where he needed to be for the next week or so, judging each spring by eye as it lifted orange off the fire. The lead-baths took all the skill out of drawing the temper, but he was still obliged to trust Eremians for the hardening pass. The thought of that worried and annoyed him, but he had no choice.

The heat in the forge was overwhelming. As instructed, they'd laid in an extra half-dozen double-action bellows, which meant ten fires were running on a hearth designed for five. There was water all over the floor, and a pall of black smoke from the tempering oil wreathed the roof-beams like summer morning mist in a forest. He watched them for quarter of an hour; one man on each fire worked the bellows, another splashed water from a ladle around the hearth-bed and tue-iron to keep them from overheating, while the third used tongs to draw the spring slowly backward and forward through the tunnel of ash and clinker that covered the roaring red heart of the fire. When the orange heat had soaked all the way through the whole spring, so that it seemed to glow from the inside, the tong-worker fished it out like an angler landing a fish and dipped it full-length in the upright oil-filled pipe. The oil lit, raising a sheet of flame as long as a man's arm, and almost immediately put itself out; as soon as the oil had stopped bubbling, out it came; a rod up through the middle of the coil to carry it by, and across the room it went to the great iron trough full of molten lead, where another man picked it off the rod with tongs and dunked it under the scum of the lead-bath to temper.

Not bad, Ziani thought, though he was a little concerned that the oil in the quenching tubes was running a bit too hot. He watched a man pause to wipe his face on his sleeve, dragging a white furrow through the smear of wet soot. Sweating near the lead-bath was asking for trouble; a spot of water on the molten lead would make it spit, enough to blind you if your luck was out. They were learning quickly, which was what he needed. Another man was coughing through the quench-smoke. One of the bellows had a slight leak, and whistled as it drew. It wasn't the ordnance factory, of course; it resembled the real thing like a child's drawing. But all he needed was two hundred and fifty scorpions by the time the Mezentines arrived. That was all. Anything else would be mere finish and ornament. They were going to make it; which meant that the design had moved on from here, and now everything depended on his colleague and dear friend Falier back in Mezentia; so far away, so hard to control at such distance, so fragile and governed by so tenuous a connection. But he knew Falier, in ways he could never know the Eremians; he trusted him to do the job he'd given him. After that, the weight of the design would pull everything into shape, just as it is its own weight that brings down a felled tree, and all the woodsmen do with their ropes and wedges is guide the lie.

He left the forge and headed for the fitting room, to see the fitting of the lockplates into the frames. So he was dead, was he? If only. He thought of the boar, dragging the dogs along with it. He remembered Miel Ducas stooping in mid-leap to slash a hinge in its spine with his falchion. It had been, he recognized, a moment of glorious, extraordinary grace, forced on an unwilling and unlikely man by honor, fear, courage and duty. That was Ducas' problem: his life was too complicated, and all his actions were stained with a contradictory mixture of motives. If only he'd had a simple job to do, he could've been a productive and efficient man, for an Eremian. As it was, he'd be useful, and that was all that mattered. Ziani considered for a moment the slender connecting rod that joined the Ducas and Falier and Duke Orsea and his Duchess and all the other little parts of the mechanism, and smiled to think that so many disparate people had something so vital in common. Almost he wished he could tell them; but that, of course...

When he had time, after he'd done his rounds and made sure everything was running smoothly, he took a quarter of an hour to do a few calculations, see how close his estimate would be. The variables were, of course, only rough reckonings, in some cases little more than guesses; nevertheless, he felt reasonably sure that by the time the Mezentines arrived to assault the city, he should have enough scorpions available to allow them to be placed at sixteen-yard intervals right along the city wall; that meant he could put just under twenty thousand bolts in the air every hour (ordinary fence-palings and vine-props with a folded sheet-iron tip; all in hand). Only a third of what the Eremians had faced in the battle, but precisely the right number for his purposes.

He smiled to himself, and thought of Falier.

He'd had to buy two tablecloths, two sets of matching napkins, two dozen pillowcases embroidered with songbirds, a dozen tapestry cushions and a rug. He hated them all at first sight, and as soon as she'd gone, he sent for his chamberlain and ordered him to take them away.

"Give them to somebody," he said.

"Very good," the chamberlain replied. "Who?"

Valens considered. "Who don't you like?"

"Sir?"

"Think of somebody you hate very much."

The chamberlain's turn to consider. "My wife's mother's sister," he said. "She's got a small white dog she's trained to walk on its hind legs. It's got its own little silver drinking bowl and everything."

"Perfect," Valens said, with grim satisfaction. "Tell her they're from me, and hint I may be coming to dinner."

He'd never seen his chamberlain grin before. Well, it was good to make somebody happy.

It was nearly mid-morning. The sun had burned the last of the dew off the grass, but the wind was rising. It would've been a good day to fly the goshawks, or try for duck on the long lake. He had something else to do, however, and he wanted to make the most of it.

Each time he opened a letter from her, he was afraid, in case it was the last. *I can't write to you anymore*—he'd seen those words in his mind's eye a thousand times, he knew the shape of the letters by heart. When the day came and he saw them traced for real on parchment, it'd be like coming back to a familiar place; a runaway slave recaptured and dragged home, a criminal brought to the town gallows. This time he was stiff with fear, because it'd been so long since she'd written, because she'd missed a letter. Staring at the small, squat packet in the exact center of his reading table, he felt like he was walking up to a wounded boar in dense briars, waiting for it to charge. He thought of all the risks he chose to take, in the hunt, in war, knowing that the worst that could happen was that he'd be killed. There are circumstances where staying alive could be worse than that.

With the tips of his forefingers, he prised apart the fold until the seal split neatly down the middle. A few crumbs of broken wax fell away as he bent the stiff parchment back on itself (like the unmaking of the quarry, he thought). Her handwriting was even smaller than usual, and for a moment he wasn't sure he'd be able to read it—now that would be a devilish refinement of torture, worthy of the stories of the punishments reserved for damned souls in hell, to have a letter from her and not to be able to make out what it said.

Veatriz Sirupati to Valens Valentinianus, greetings.

Well, he'd found; the wolf, the bear, the boar were here, ready for him. It'd be churlish to keep them waiting.

You never replied to my last letter.

He frowned. "Yes I did," he said aloud. "You're the one who didn't write back."

I suppose there could be several different reasons. I offended you; I was putting pressure on you, breaking the rules of our friendship; I brought Orsea into it, when this has always been just you and me. Or perhaps you're just tired of me and bored by my letters. If it's any one of those, I'd understand.

For a moment he felt as if he'd lost his balance and was about to fall. Then he realized: fear had made him stupid, and it was perfectly obvious what had happened. His letter to her, or her reply, had gone astray. Somebody, some fat woman in a red dress, had lost it or forgotten about it or used it to start a fire or pad a shoe where it rubbed her heel. For a moment he wanted to do something about that; send his guard to arrest every woman in a red dress in the country and have them all thrown in a snake-pit, to teach them respect. *But I haven't got a snake-pit,* he reminded himself, *and it'd take too long to build one and collect enough snakes to fill it.*

He read the rest of the letter. It felt cold, because it was all based on error. It irritated him, as though he'd corrected her mistake but she carried on regardless, missing the point, refusing to listen to him. That was wrong; in fact, she was saying things he'd never thought she'd ever say, things that changed the world forever, but he found it very difficult to get past the frustration. He made an effort and cleared his mind of it; but the damage had been done. A letter from her had been wasted because of a misunderstanding, and all the things she could have said in it would have to wait till next time, or the time after that. He felt cheated, and had to remind himself that it wasn't her fault.

Someone was standing in the doorway. "Go away," he snapped, then pulled a face. "No," he said, "it's all right, take no notice. What is it?"

Stellachus, his chief of intelligence. "You sent for me," he said apologetically.

"Did I? Yes, I did. Come in and close the door."

Valens put his hand over the letter. If Stellachus noticed, he didn't show it.

"The Mezentine defector," Valens said. "The one who went to Eremia. Apparently he's dead."

Stellachus frowned. "I see," he said. "May I ask...?"

Valens told him about the austringer's report of what he'd heard in the inn. "Find out if it's true," Valens went on. "It sounds a bit unlikely, but I expect there's something behind it. Also, I don't seem to have seen anything recently about what's going on in Mezentia. Last I heard, they'd got a bloody great big army sitting around doing nothing, and that's not the way they like to do business. If you can get me accurate numbers, that'd be very good; also, they must be feeding them on something, and I want to know where all those supplies are coming from. And when you've done that," he added with a grin, "I'd better see the chiefs of staff. Get someone to round them up for mid-afternoon, all right?"

Stellachus bowed formally and went away, leaving him with the letter. His mind was clogged up with distractions (troop movements, supply routes, frontiers and lines on maps) and he felt as though the field had gone on ahead and left him behind. The world was tightening around him, he could feel it; it was a bad time not to be able to concentrate.

He straightened his mind. He had the rest of the morning and the first half of the afternoon to reply to her letter — not long enough, but the first priority was to get a reply on its way as soon as possible, to make sure she wasn't fretting. *It's all right; my previous letter didn't reach you* would probably be enough, but he couldn't quite leave it at that, though perhaps he should. Then he'd need to think hard about the Mezentines — he'd let that slip, worrying about not having heard from her — but he needed the intelligence reports first, so it could wait a little while. Then there were other considerations, basic housekeeping: money, for one thing, and stocks of flour and oil and honey and the like, duty rosters and mobilization times, musters and resources. It'd be nice if he didn't have to see to every last detail himself...

Rain again, and he couldn't help smiling as he remembered what she'd written.

For some reason, summer rain falling on oak leaves always makes me think of you. I have no idea why, since the one time I saw you (that I can remember), we were both indoors and it was quite unbearably hot. Maybe I went out with the hunt one time, and we sheltered from the rain under an oak tree, but if so, I can't remember that, either. To put this observation in context, the sound of horses on a hot day puts me in mind of my father, and I can't smell onions without thinking of my mother. The last example can have no possible significance whatsoever. My mother hated onions, except when cooked for a long time in a stew.

There was going to be a war, and she was going to be caught up in it. The realization made him stop dead, as though he'd walked into a wall. If the Mezentines laid siege to Civitas Eremiae there'd be no more women in red dresses bringing him letters; and she . . . He scowled. The Mezentines were strange, cold people but they weren't savages. They didn't butcher civilians, or sell them into slavery. Nevertheless, there was going to be a war, and there wasn't anything he could do about it. What he could do (had to do) was keep the war from seeping through into his own territory, because it was a simple fact of life that nobody ever beat the Mezentines at anything. If half of what he'd heard about the army mustering outside Mezentia was true, this was more than a punitive expedition or a judicious redefining of buffer zones and frontiers. The one aspect of the matter he wasn't quite clear about was the reason behind it; but the Mezentines were under no obligation to explain to anybody, before or after the fact.

Even so . . .

Predictably, Stellachus was in the old library. He'd annexed the two small rooms at the back—nobody could remember what they'd been built for, and Valens' father had used them to store and display his collection of hoods and jesses—and he spent most of his time there, when he wasn't out trying to look busy. He glanced up in surprise as Valens walked in, and just possibly (his reactions were quick, as befitted a fencer) he pushed a small book he'd been reading under a sheaf of worthy-looking papers.

"Sorry to barge in," Valens said, with a slight grin. "Just a quick thought, before the meeting. You passed the word round, I take it."

Stellachus nodded twice. "They're all on notice to attend," he said.

"Splendid." Valens sat down, reached across the table, lifted the papers. *The Garden of Love in Idleness,* according to the small book's spine. He covered it up again. "The Mezentines," he said. "We both know that army's headed for Eremia. What's bothering me rather is why."

Stellachus did his best to look wise. "Retribution, presumably. Duke Orsea's unprovoked attack."

Valens shrugged. "Hardly necessary," he said. "It was a massacre, and if the Mezentines lost any men, I haven't heard about it. That army they've put together must be costing them a fortune. They don't spend money for fun."

"To make sure nothing of the sort ever happens again," Stellachus said. "Last time, the Mezentines won an easy victory because of their war machines. They had plenty of time to deploy them, and the machines came as a complete surprise to Orsea and his people. Next time, they won't walk so obligingly into the trap."

"Possibly," Valens said, rubbing his palms together slowly. "And from their point of view, the Eremians are irrational, stupid; it's only been five minutes since they got out of that crippling war with us, and what do they do? They pick on the most powerful nation in the world. People that stupid are capable of anything, and next time they might get incredibly lucky." He frowned. "They might be thinking that way if they were us," he said. "I mean, if they had a king or a duke who could make decisions on a whim. But they aren't like that. Everything's got to be debated in committees and sub-committees and special assemblies and general assemblies. For which we should be eternally grateful, since it means they move slowly and cautiously. Everything's political with them, unless it goes right down deep under the politics to something really fundamental. If it was just a good-idea-at-the-time thing, it'd never get through. One party'd be in favor, all the other parties would be against, and you'd be able to hear them debating it from halfway across the desert." He shrugged. "Don't you agree?"

"I hear what you're saying," Stellachus replied cautiously. "But it's the party politics that makes them do a lot of apparently pointless or inexplicable things—inexplicable to outsiders, who don't know the finer points of their infighting."

There was a degree of truth in that, Valens conceded. "Still," he went on, "it seems a strange way to carry on, because surely it's to their disadvantage to stamp on the Eremians too hard."

"You mean the Cure Hardy," Stellachus said.

"Exactly. They need Eremia as a buffer. That's why they helped broker the peace between us and the Eremians, because they need both of us as a first line of defense. Weaken the Eremians too much, or wipe them out completely, and that just leaves us between them and the people they're most afraid of. Now, how can that possibly make any sense?"

Stellachus got up, poured two cups of wine, put one in front of Valens, sat down again. Valens sipped his cup, to be polite. "I don't know," Stellachus said. "All I can do is theorize. Would that help?"

Valens lifted his hands. "Go ahead."

"Well." Stellachus took a long pull at his wine (*I must watch that,* Valens thought; *I guess he's been under pressure recently*). "Two possibilities come to mind. First, it's like you say, something to do with Mezentine politics. Actually," he added with a slight frown, "make that three possibilities. As I was saying; Mezentine politics. There's a power struggle between two factions, and for some reason one of them wants a big war, to help with whatever their agenda may be. They're looking round for someone to hit; Eremia's the best target, because they're unpunished aggressors and they're small. That's the first possibility. Number two. Let's consider the size of this army of theirs." He hesitated. "Now we can't do that properly,

because I haven't got you the full data yet; but we'll forgive me
for that and move on. It's a very large army, costing them a lot of
money, causing them all sorts of logistical problems which presumably they've figured out how to handle. Query: is this the biggest army Mezentia's ever put in the field? Don't know, but we'll
find out. Anyway, it's big; and the Mezentine policy's always been
to defend themselves with clever machines rather than big armies.
A defensive strategy, in other words."

Valens dipped his head in acknowledgment of a valid point.
"They've changed, then," he said. "From machines to men; from
defensive to offensive."

"It's a hypothesis," Stellachus said, "but no proof. Possibility two is that they've been taking a long-term approach to the
Cure Hardy problem, and this invasion of Eremia's just a prelude
to them taking the offensive against the Cure Hardy. Now why
they'd want to do that is another issue; the Cure Hardy live a long
way away and have never caused the Mezentines any bother—
which isn't to say they wouldn't if they could, and through sheer
force of numbers they're the only power we know of that could
give the Mezentines a bad time. The way they think—if I'm right
about that—a threat in being simply isn't acceptable. As long as
the Cure Hardy exist, the Mezentines can't sleep at night. You'd
have to look at all sorts of factors—economics, cash reserves,
manpower levels—and see if there's a pattern that'd suggest that
the Mezentines have been working toward this point for some
time, where they're strong enough to go on the offensive against
the Cure Hardy. If so, crushing Eremia might make sense as a
preparatory move. Personally, in their shoes, I'd want them as
allies—us, too—if I was considering something like that, but the
Mezentines' minds work differently to ours. Quite possibly they'd
see wiping out the Eremians as a necessary preliminary chore;
clearing away the brushwood, if you like, before you start felling."

Valens nodded again. "And number three?"

"Number three," Stellachus repeated. "You said earlier that
sometimes they do things because of reasons that go right down

under the politics to something absolutely basic, something that's so deeply ingrained in their mindset that even they won't bicker and bitch about it. In which case," he went on, "I don't suppose they'd stop to consider the effects on the balance of power or regional stability; not if it's — well, a matter of principle. Actually, of the three this one fits best what we know about this business."

"Which isn't as much as we should," Valens said quietly.

"Granted." Stellachus looked away. "But we'll put that right, I promise. It seems to me, though, that the Mezentines have moved very quickly, very *decisively,* on this; by their standards, I mean. And what I'm getting at isn't what we've heard but what we haven't heard. I mean, normally we'd expect to be hearing reports and rumors about major ructions and debates in the Guilds long before any armies landed. Instead, practically the first thing we know about it is soldiers getting off ships. Therefore, I suggest, we've got a cause of war that doesn't need to be endlessly argued over and politicked about; and I think I know what it might be."

Valens smiled. "The defector," he said.

Really, it was a shame to disappoint him, after he'd worked toward his grand finale so artfully. "Yes," Stellachus said, "the one they wanted information about."

"The one who's just died," Valens pointed out.

"Indeed. Now we know how the Republic thinks about defectors; it's legendary, they're hunted down and killed, no messing. But this particular one, who was not only a defector but a murderer and possibly a political dissident as well; and a big wheel at one of their factories, so he must've known a lot of sensitive stuff about engineering—"

"Foreman at the ordnance factory," Valens said. "You should read your own reports."

Stellachus didn't wince visibly; he was growing a thick hide, Valens noted with approval. "This one's obviously worse than usual," he said. "And as soon as he escaped he headed straight for Eremia and Duke Orsea. Like, let's say, a homing pigeon."

Valens smiled. "Nicely put," he said. "So Orsea's implicated, in their minds at least. Hence open war rather than the usual covert assassination."

"Mezentine defectors traditionally don't get very far," Stellachus said. "The price on their heads is too tempting, and of course a brown face is pretty hard to overlook. Nobody wants anything to do with them, because it's too dangerous. But this one—"

"Ziani Vaatzes."

"Vaatzes," Stellachus said, "makes a clean getaway and goes straight to Duke Orsea, who takes him back to Eremia on his way home from having the shit kicked out of him by the Mezentine war engines. Vaatzes used to work in the factory where those engines were made. Now, some of it may be coincidence, but—"

Valens held up a hand. "The Eremians couldn't make copies of the war engines," he said. "You'd have to start from scratch, build the machines that make the machines that make the special steel, and all that. It'd mean years of expensive investment. And besides," he added, "I happen to know, Vaatzes suggested it and Orsea turned him down. And if I know that, the Mezentines do too."

"Doesn't signify," Stellachus said emphatically. "It creates a possibility, you see; something else besides the Cure Hardy for the Mezentines to lie awake worrying about. If I'm right, the moment Orsea and Vaatzes met, under those rather special circumstances, this invasion was inevitable. In which case," he went on, "it won't just be an invasion."

For a moment, Valens was silent. "That's a rather large undertaking," he said.

"Hence," Stellachus replied, "the rather large army. We know they don't do things by halves. No skin off their noses, of course; that's the charm of using mercenaries. Every casualty's a saving on the wage bill rather than a dead citizen."

It was Valens' turn to look away. "Have you ever been to Civitas Eremiae? Me neither. But by all accounts it's the perfect defensive position, massively fortified—"

"War engines," Stellachus said. "Why send a man where you

can send a large rock, or a big steel spike? Probably just the sort of technical challenge your red-blooded Mezentine engineer relishes."

The Mezentines aren't savages, Valens reminded himself, but it didn't sound so reassuring this time. "Storming Civitas Eremiae," he said slowly, "would be an impressive achievement."

"The Cure Hardy."

"Quite." Valens frowned. "Assuming it's possible to impress them, or that they care. But I can see how the Mezentines would view it as a pleasant fringe benefit, to scare the wits out of the Cure Hardy."

"And it'd make a first-class frontier post," Stellachus added, "assuming they don't level it to the ground in the process. Anyway," he said briskly, "that's three possibilities. There could well be others; those were just the first things that came to mind."

Valens grinned. It'd be wise to keep an eye on Stellachus' drinking, and he was as lazy as a fat dog, but he was still most likely the best man for his job. "Think about it some more," he said. "Meanwhile, I'll let you get back to your paperwork."

Stellachus inclined his head, like a fencer admitting a touch. "I'll have the stuff you need about the Mezentine army as soon as possible," he said.

"Good. See you later, at the meeting."

As he retraced his steps back to his reading room, Valens wondered how on earth he was going to reply to her letter now, with his mind full of what Stellachus had suggested. Perhaps she didn't know there was going to be a war; perhaps Orsea didn't know...He lifted his head and stared blankly out of the window, at the billowing curtain of thin, slanted rain. If the defector was dead, surely the problem had solved itself; no Vaatzes, no risk to the Republic, no war. Somehow, he knew it wouldn't work like that.

I'm not in control of this situation, he told himself suddenly. *I wonder who is.*

He sat down, laid his sheet of parchment flat on the tabletop, looked at it. At that moment it put him in mind of the very best tempered steel armor; warranted impossible to make a mark on it, no matter how hard you tried.

Valens Valentinianus to Veatriz Sirupati, greetings.

He put the pen down, lined it up carefully with the edge of the desk. Precision in all things, like a Mezentine.

(I'll have to tell her, he thought. Maybe, if I can make her understand, I can get her to promise; as soon as the Mezentines get too close, she'll come here—she can bring him too, if she likes, just so long as she's safe, here, with me...)

He closed his eyes. I might as well soak the palace in lamp-oil and set light to it, he told himself. I've just been thinking how stupid Orsea is, and I've proved I'm worse than him. To bring the war *here;* unforgivable. I shouldn't even think it, in case they can read minds; they seem to be able to do pretty much everything else.

He sighed. No point hating the Mezentines; you might as well hate the winter, or lightning, or disease, or death. As far as he knew—he actually paused and thought about it for a moment—he didn't hate anybody; not even Orsea, though at times he came quite close. Hate, like love, was an indulgence he didn't need and refused to waste lifespan on—

(Correction, he admitted; I hated Father sometimes. But that was inevitable, and besides, I should be proud of myself for the elegant economy of effort. Hatred and love only once, and both for the same person.)

In any event; hate and anger wouldn't make anything better. His fencing instructor had taught him that; they make the hand shake, they spoil your concentration. The most you can ever feel for your opponent, if you want to defeat and kill him, is a certain mild dislike.

He picked the pen up.

You never got my last letter *[he wrote]*. So that settles that, and we needn't discuss it.

I don't know where the wet oak leaves business comes from; can't have been anything I said. As a matter of fact, I despise getting wet, particularly in the morning. The smell of damp cloth drying out depresses me and gives me a headache. I like bright sunlight, cool breezes, tidy blue skies without piles of cloud left scattered about, moonlit nights—I like to be able to see for miles in every direction. Not quite sure where I stand on the issue of forests; I like them because that's where the quarry tends to be, and every bush could be hiding the record buck or the boar the farmers have been telling me about for weeks. But I don't like the tangle, or the obstruction. You can't go fast in a forest, and you can't see. I like to flush my quarry out into the open. Unfortunately, it doesn't always work like that.

Veatriz, I need to ask you something. Do you think there's going to be a war? I don't know how much Orsea's told you, or even how much he knows himself; but the Mezentines have raised a large army, and it looks horribly like they mean to use it against Eremia. I'd like to say don't be scared, but I can't. If you haven't talked to Orsea about it, maybe you should. And—I'm going to have to be obnoxious for a bit, so bite your tongue and don't yell at me—the truth is, I have my doubts about how Orsea's likely to handle this. I think Orsea is a good man, from what I've heard about him. He's brave, and conscientious, he cares very much about doing his job and not letting his people down. That's why I'm worried. You see, I believe that if the Mezentines invade, Orsea would rather die than run away and desert his people; which is all very well, and I'd like to think I'd do the same in his shoes, though I wouldn't bet money on it. I'm not a good, noble man, like he is. If I'd been good and noble, I'd be dead by now.

I'm still writing this letter; you haven't read it yet; so the waves of furious anger and resentment I can feel coming back at me off the paper must just be my imagination. Yes,

I know. How dare I criticize Orsea, or suggest...We both know what you're thinking. But listen to me, please. Your place is at your husband's side, yes, right. But

Valens stopped writing. He knew that if he finished the sentence, he could be condemning the Vadani to war and death. Why would he want to do something like that?

I want you to know that, if things go badly—you don't know the Mezentines like I do, once they start something, they don't give up—if things go badly, I can protect you, both of you, if you come here. I don't know how, exactly, but you can leave that to me. I can do it, and I will. Piece of cake.

There; now you see what I mean about getting the quarry out in the open. You do it by bursting in, making a noise, waving your arms, yelling, making a complete exhibition of yourself, being as loud and as scary as you possibly can.

This is going very badly. I'm not thinking. For a start, even if you're prepared to do as I say, how are you going to persuade Orsea? He doesn't know you and I are

(Valens hesitated for a very long time.)

friends; so why on earth would he want to come here, to the lair of his traditional enemy and all that? I can see him, he's looking at you as though you've gone soft in the head. He's asking himself, why's she saying this, what on earth makes her think we'd be safer with the bloody Vadani than we are here? And besides, I couldn't ever do that, it'd be betraying my people.

Veatriz, I'm worried. I'm scared, and I can't make the fear go away. Please, at least think about it. The Mezentines aren't savages, but they're very different from us, they think in a completely different way.

I have no right to make this sort of proposition to you; it's worse than making a pass at you, in some ways. Most ways, actually. But if you think I've been wicked and hateful and manipulative, you just wait and see what I"m going to say next. Namely: I know you love Orsea, and your place is with him, and you'd never do anything to hurt him. But which do you think is the better option: Orsea good and brave and keeping faith with his people and dead, or Orsea ashamed, dishonored and alive?

I'm your friend. I want to keep you safe. If, when, if the Mezentines get to Palicuro (in case you don't know it, it's a small village on the main east-west road, about seventeen miles from Civitas; inn, smithy, little village square with an old almond tree in the middle), I want to ask you to think very carefully about what I've suggested. It's the only thing I'll ever ask you to do for me. Please.

A short, round woman whose red dress didn't suit her complexion at all was half-killing her elderly gray palfrey, making it lug her not insignificant weight all the way up the long uphill road to Civitas Eremiae. She'd come to sell perfumes, flower essences and herbal remedies to the Duchess at extortionate prices. She came away smirking.

In the heel of her shoe was a little piece of folded parchment. It was sharp-edged and it chafed like hell, but she didn't mind; she was riding rather than walking, and besides, it would make it possible for her to sell perfumes, flower essences and herbal remedies to the Duke of the Vadani for an absurdly large sum of money. Her feet hurt anyway, because of the corns.

The Duchess had asked her to wait while she wrote the reply, and she'd been expecting to be kept hanging about for a long time; she'd made a little nest of cushions for herself in the handsome window-seat in the small gallery (such a good view down across the valley) and she'd brought a book—*The Garden of Love in Idleness;* very hard to get hold of a copy, especially one with quality pictures—but she'd hardly had time to open it when the Duchess came back again. She'd looked tense and unhappy, but that was her business.

The woman in the red dress didn't take her shoe off until she reached the inn at Palicuro (miserable little place, and some clown had cut down the almond tree). She was a thoughtful woman, careful and attentive to detail, so she packed her shoes with lavender overnight. The Vadani Duke was reckoned to be a good mark and a cash customer; he wouldn't want his letter smelling of hot feet.

An hour or so after the woman in the red dress reached the bottom of the mountain, a team of carpenters, stonemasons and guardsmen set about installing the first batch of the new war engines on the ramparts of Civitas Eremiae.

It was a bitch of a job. The stupid things were heavy, but their wooden frames weren't robust enough to allow them to be hauled about on ropes and cranes (the little Mezentine had been very fussy about that) so they had to be manhandled up the stairs, and they were an awkward shape. There wasn't anywhere you could hold on to them easily, and unless you shuffled along a few inches at a time, you barked your shins on the legs of the stand. It was the general consensus of opinion that if the little Mezentine had had to install the things himself, he'd have given a bit more thought to stuff like that; also, that the engines themselves were a complete waste of public money, since nobody in their right mind would ever dream of attacking Civitas, which was universally acknowledged to be impregnable; and only a born idiot like Duke Orsea would've been gullible enough to buy such a load of old junk in the first place. Still, what could you expect from someone who spent all his time pig-hunting when he should be running the country?

Forty-seven of the things—they'd been delivered fifty, but there was simply no way of fitting fifty onto the top platform of the old gate tower, there just wasn't room, and if only people would take the time to measure up for a job before starting, it'd make life so much easier for the poor sods who had to do the actual work—

eventually sat in their cradles overlooking the road, like elderly wooden vultures waiting for something to die. In theory they were adjustable for windage and elevation — you made the adjustments by knocking in a series of little wedges until you'd got the angle, but you just had to look at it to know it wouldn't actually work in practice — and the range was supposedly up to three hundred yards. Word was that the Duke had upped the order to two hundred, proving the old saying about fools and their money, not that it was actually his money, when you stopped and thought about it.

The installation crews finished their work, stood shaking their heads sadly for a while, and went away. Tomorrow they had the equally rotten job of fetching up the arrow things to shoot out of them. Stupid. It wasn't like there was going to be a war anyway, not now that this Valens character was in charge of the Vadani. Another rich bastard who spent all his time chasing pigs. What they all saw in it was a mystery.

Just as it was beginning to get dark, Ziani Vaatzes climbed up the long stair and stood on the top platform for a while. He'd come to inspect the scorpions, set his mind at rest, but instead he looked down at the road, dropping steeply away into the valley.

It was a great pity, he thought, and if there had been any other way he'd have taken it. But he'd had no choice, no more than a dropped stone has a choice about falling. He hadn't started it. It wasn't his fault.

18

Captain Beltista Eiconodoulus of the First Republican Engineers—the title was, he felt, meaningless, since the unit had been arbitrarily formed only three days ago—was afraid of maps. Something inside him went cold when a superior officer summoned him and unrolled one. *We're here, the enemy is over here, this is the road, here are the mountains, bit of rough ground between here and here;* he would stand rather awkwardly and try and look eager and intelligent, but the fear would start to grow in his mind like an abscess under a tooth, until he could feel it with every heartbeat. The diagram became the focus of all the terrible possibilities that inevitably arise in a war—the mistakes, the enemy's superior knowledge or ability, the unforeseen and the negligently omitted, the things left undone and the things done to hurt and deceive. He felt as though he was looking at a sketch, such as artists make before they mix their paint and trim their brushes, a study for what was about to happen. Somewhere (that mess of brown rings representing mountains, that stipple of short lines signifying marshes, that bridge, that apparent plain) was the place where he would meet the contingency he hadn't prepared for or couldn't prepare for, and when he arrived there, as and when, there'd be confusion, terror, pain and death.

"You'll take this road to begin with," he was told. "They call it the Butter Pass, for some reason. Follow it up as far as this ridge here, then branch off along this track—it's a bit rough, apparently, but they assure me it's fit for wheeled traffic; you might want to take bridging and road-building equipment just in case—and follow it round all the way up to here. You can then double back along this pass here, which'll bring you out north of the city. By then, our main expeditionary force will be here, Palicuro, and we'll be able to establish a line of communication and put you in the picture. That's about it for now. Questions?"

He'd asked one or two, just to show he was smart and had been listening; but the map told him everything he needed to know.

He went back to his tent, summoned his lieutenants, fired off a string of orders while the key points were still fresh in his mind. He hardly knew the men he gave the orders to, but if the recruiters back home and the Mezentines had confidence in them, he supposed they must be all right. He'd find out soon enough, in any case.

Really, he told himself, *I'm just a wagon-master, delivering goods. And there's the enemy to consider, of course, but we'll cross that bridge when we come to it.* He steadied his mind with a series of tried and tested departure rituals. He carefully packed up his writing-desk, checking to make sure the paper-box was full and that there was a good supply of soot and oak-gall for making ink (running out of materials to write orders with in the middle of a battle would be a singularly stupid way to die, he'd always felt). He loaded his clothes, spare boots, books of tables and tolerances, food, bandages and medicines methodically into his pack. He checked his armor, joint by joint and strap by strap. Finally, he moved everything to the middle of the floor of his tent, in a neat pile, ready for the muleteers to collect and load. Twenty-seven years of soldiering and he was still alive and he hadn't caused a defeat or a disaster yet; if there was a reason for that (it was a question he remained openminded about) it was probably attention to detail and the methodical approach.

As soon as they were under way (he didn't like the look of the road; it was dusty, which obscured visibility, and the ruts and potholes were already beginning to gnaw away at the temper of his cart axles), he made a start on the next step in his customary procedure: to consider the purpose of his mission, and to make it as simple as possible, so he'd be able to keep sight of it. Fortunately, in this instance that was straightforward enough. All he had to do was deliver his cargo, one hundred and fifty Mezentine war machines, to the place on the map marked with an X. There was other stuff once he'd got there—unpack the machines, assemble them, tune them, assemble the carriages and the mobile platforms and install the machines on them—but he had a bunch of Mezentine civilians along to do all that, so his involvement would be limited, in effect, to nodding to them and saying, "Go." Once he'd done that, of course, there'd be new orders, but that'd be another day.

The next step was, of course, to plan a daily routine. He'd found that if you broke the day up into small pieces, it was easier to control (hardly a startlingly new discovery, but as far as he was concerned, it was one of the great truths of human existence); accordingly, he preferred his days dismantled into units of one hour. He could hold an hour comfortably in his mind without straining. Sometimes he wondered who'd invented the hour. A genius, whoever it was; the hour was a perfect tool for handling and controlling the world, ranking alongside fire, the wheel and the axe.

These exercises kept his mind engaged and unavailable for worry and panic as far as the first night's stop, at which point he was able to hand over to fatigue, which put him gently to sleep until an hour before first light, when his day began. That first hour of the day was essential, as far as he was concerned. It bore the weight of the rest of the day like an arch. In it, he woke up, drew up his duty rosters and assignment schedules, studied his map and his intelligence reports; all the components of the armor that would protect him against chaos and failure.

The final stage of his early-morning procedure, and the one that always caused the most amusement to his subordinates, involved the rolling of two densely woven rush mats around a green half-inch stick, which fitted upright into a slot in a heavy piece of board. Mats and stick together simulated perfectly, so he'd been reliably informed, the human neck, viewed as an objective for the swordsman. If he performed the cut neatly and accurately each time, he could get three days' cutting practice out of each mat, but he was a realist and always made sure he had a plentiful supply. He was, after all, a soldier; which is a euphemism for a man who kills other men by slashing at them with a sharp edge.

Because his men didn't know him well yet, he didn't attract an audience for cutting practice on the first morning. Information travels quickly through an army, however; by the third morning, he performed a distinctly botched cut in the presence of two lieutenants, two sergeants, half a dozen enlisted engineers and the captain of muleteers, all of whom had managed to find legitimate reasons for calling on him a quarter of an hour before the scheduled start of the daily briefing. He no longer minded. He didn't object to being laughed at behind his back, so long as he had control of the subject matter.

"You should try it," he chided a young lieutenant whose face he didn't like, although he was probably the most competent of the junior staff. "Warms up the muscles, helps concentration, good mental and physical discipline. In fact, I'd make it compulsory if we could source enough mats."

The lieutenant had the inherent good sense not to reply, and Eiconodoulus wished he could remember what the man was called. He was razor-sharp when it came to faces, but a martyr to names. He hoped there'd be time to learn them all.

It was a rather fraught meeting; mostly his own fault, because they'd reached the point where they had to turn off (according to the map) but there was no sign of the track they were meant to follow. Everything else was there, as duly and faithfully recorded: a slight horn in the mountain wall, and under it a gully, the perfect place for a track, except there wasn't one.

"Maybe it's an old map and the road's just got a bit worn away," suggested one of the lieutenants (big, square man with a short beard, too old to be a lieutenant, too ineffectual to be promoted, but reasonably bright nevertheless). "It's surprising how quickly a track can heal up, if you see what I mean. But—"

Eiconodoulus shook his head. "I've been and looked," he said. "While you were still asleep," he added, unnecessarily and untruthfully. "There never was a track there, which means either the map's wrong or we're in the wrong place. You," he went on—not being able to remember names meant he'd got a reputation for brusqueness in all his previous commands; mostly, he'd found it helped. "Take a dozen men on horses and go and have a look. Ride on about five miles, see if you can see any sign of this bloody track. You, take half a dozen on foot, go and see if your friend here's right and there was a track there. Don't take too long about it."

Oddly enough, both scouting parties reported back within minutes of each other. No, there wasn't a turning further up the main road. No, there hadn't ever been a track in the gully under the horn. Eiconodoulus could feel the world tightening around his head like a sawyer's clamp, but at least it wasn't totally unexpected.

"Fine," he said, as the scouts waited for the miracle they obviously expected him to be able to perform. "My guess is, whoever made the map looked at that gully and assumed there'd be a track down it. In any case, that's the direction we've got to go in, and we don't have any choice. Lucky we brought the road-building stuff."

Hardly luck; he'd been ordered to bring it. But they needn't know that. Let them assume it was his own resourcefulness and foresight. They seemed happy enough. They had confidence in him. Probably they'd asked around when they heard who they were being assigned to, and men who'd served with him in other campaigns had told them, you'll be all right, he's eccentric and a bit of a bastard, but he'll get you home again. He'd worked hard for that reputation, so that over the years the lie had gradually started to come true. Anyway, he knew how to lay a road quickly and with the minimum of materials. Just to cover himself, he sent a messenger back to headquarters: *No sign of track, am building road, anticipate three-day delay, will advise.* That put it rather well, he felt.

Mostly it was digging, with pickaxes, crowbars, mattocks and shovels; get the big rocks out of the way and use them to fill the big holes. The further he went, the more certain he became that there was indeed a track, probably just over the lip of the first rise up ahead, somewhere in that basin of dead ground. As he stared at the hillside beyond he was sure he could see the line of it, a very slight contrast in color, like an old scar. In which case, what had happened was that the map-makers knew there was a track around here somewhere—maybe they were coming along it from the other direction—but through sloppiness or lack of time they didn't bother to survey the link from it to the Butter Pass, just assumed that it followed the convenient gully. It annoyed him to think that they were probably dead by now (it was an old map) and so they'd never be officially found out and reprimanded.

He was right. They found the track a day and a half later. Just out of curiosity, he sent scouts back along it, and they reported back that it did indeed come out on the Butter Pass, about ten miles before the mouth of the gully. They'd probably have seen it quite easily if they hadn't been relying on the map. Eiconodoulus tucked the thought of that away in the back of his mind, in his private store of other people's notable failures, to be relished properly at leisure.

It wasn't much of a track, after all that fuss. At times, Eiconodoulus wondered if he'd have been better off cutting his own, because there was a much more suitable lie about a hundred yards further up the slope. Clearly these hills had never been grazed—sheep are much better surveyors than humans when it comes to finding the easiest path—and whoever had laid this track in the first place must've been blind, or at any rate short-sighted. Every time a cart bottomed out in a hole or a hub graunched against a half-buried rock he winced, expecting to hear the crisp crack of failing wood or the brittle note of snapping iron. There would be worse places to be laid up mending a busted cart—it was open enough to allow him to see an approaching enemy in good time—but he had food and water to consider. They were going to be several days later than anticipated, and this wasn't land you could live off. He knew better than even to consider ditching the carts and going back, leaving Mezentine war engines lying about for the enemy to find. If the worst came to the worst...Now he came to consider it, he didn't know what he should do. Nobody had told him; destroy the engines before the enemy could get hold of them, yes, but the wretched things were made of steel, so they wouldn't burn, and he didn't have the tools to cut them up. The most he could do was bend them out of shape, but that'd take a long time and a lot of effort. He should have been briefed on that point. More negligence.

Well, he'd just have to complete the mission successfully, then. So much clearer when you simplify.

On the fourth day, young Lieutenant Stesimbracus—the one he didn't like, the competent one—came back from scouting looking unusually cheerful. He'd found, he said, the other track marked on the map, the one which had been supposed to cross the one they were on at a place marked as "cairn," except there were no cairns. Not being able to find it was more than a trivial annoyance. The missing track was a link between their path and another running parallel to it, which happened to be the frontier between Eremian and Vadani territory. Obviously it was important not to cross the border inadvertently. Likewise, they could reasonably assume that they wouldn't be attacked from that direction, since the Eremians wouldn't dare trespass on Vadani land. The last thing the Eremians would want would be a war on two fronts.

"It's annoying, though," Stesimbracus said. "The path on the Vadani side's a much better road; straighter, and properly made up. We could save a day, and cut back here"—he jabbed a finger at the map—"and precious little chance of getting found out, because we're a long way away from any of their manned outposts. Also, there's a river down in a goyle on the other side."

Eiconodoulus scowled. Neither of the streams marked on the map had been there, and although they'd found one that wasn't marked, that had been two days ago, when they weren't so worried about the water running out. They'd been relying on the imaginary streams believed in by the map-makers.

"You know better than that," he said. "If we go blundering about down there and run into a Vadani unit, you don't need me to tell you what could happen. In fact, you'd better pass the word around: nobody is to cross into Vadani territory for any reason whatsoever. Got that?"

"Sir." Stesimbracus was wearing that kicked-puppy look he found so intensely annoying. "May I ask, what *are* we going to do about water?"

"Use it sensibly," Eiconodoulus answered briskly. "We've got enough, so long as we don't waste it. You'd better talk to the quartermaster about that."

It got worse. Just after noon on the fifth day they reached the top of a low ridge, only to find a completely unexpected combe dropping away at their feet. Eiconodoulus' first reaction was fury; competent scouts should've found it and told him, it should've been on the bloody map. He got off his horse, walked up to the lip and looked at it as though it was a personal affront.

You couldn't get a cart down there. The other side perhaps, going up again; but going down would be suicide. He turned his head left and right. The bloody thing seemed to go on forever, it'd take days to go round it, assuming there actually was a way round. Combe; canyon, more like. The downward slope was studded with boulders, and he was prepared to bet that the dust and gravel wouldn't give a firm footing. Final mockery: there was a substantial stream, practically a river, gurgling cheerfully away at the bottom of it. All the water in the world, but he couldn't get at it.

He sulked for an hour, pretending to study the map, while scouts went out to see if there was a way round. Of course not. On one side the canyon went away straight until it faded out of sight, a very long way away. The other side wasn't even worth exploring. He was fairly sure there would be a crossing-point quite close, a trail zigzagging down, or a hole in the wall. It had to be possible to get through on the other side, because that was where the Vadani road ran, and of course he couldn't go there.

Nothing for it. They'd have to cut a road of their own, just enough to let them take the carts down, unloaded, without the horses; then back up to the top, collect the dismantled war engines and carry them down on their backs. Three days? Be realistic, four. Plenty of water, of course, but food was going to be a serious problem. Half-rations; the men were going to love that. Finally, just in case that wasn't enough to be going on with, he'd lost his precious visibility. Standing on the lip and looking round, he could see at least a dozen places where an enemy unit could sneak up on him and attack with little more than a quarter of an hour's notice.

He thought about manpower. Building a road, then unloading, then carrying the machines; he needed sentries on those vulnerable approaches, and a fighting reserve in case he was attacked. He didn't have nearly enough men (which was just as well, given the food situation) and he was already horribly late. It didn't take much imagination to visualize the main expeditionary force pushing on to its assigned position, confident of artillery cover that wouldn't be there. The map had done for him, just as he knew it would one day.

He sent Stesimbracus away with the sentries, mostly because he was getting to the point where he couldn't stand the sight of him anymore. That meant he had to put stolid, stupid Lieutenant Ariophrantzes in charge of the road party, while he perched on the edge of the combe doing nothing with the fighting reserve. That looked bad, he knew. The men would think he was skiving, when he ought to be down on the slope, digging or lugging baskets. But Ariophrantzes couldn't be trusted to command the reserve if there was an attack; it was a tactical nightmare in any case, because any enemy with a functional brain would use the terrain to attack in front and at the side, possibly from the rear as well if there were other gullies and ravines he hadn't spotted yet. One thing he could do: he gave orders for two dozen of the war engines to be assembled, fitted to their field carriages, and set up on the highest point of the lip. If he had to carry the wretched things, he might as well use them.

As four days dragged on into six, and half-rations had to be further reduced, and the road party's progress gradually slowed, he became convinced that there'd be an attack. It was obvious, the logical thing. It went without saying that the Eremians must have scouts out, watching every single thing he did. They'd know that he'd be at his most vulnerable when the road party were almost at the bottom of the canyon. First they'd attack the reserve, kill them or drive them off. The road party, practically defenseless, could then be slaughtered at leisure, the engines brought down the road Eiconodoulus had so obligingly built and carried off in triumph to Eremia. Anybody, some nobleman's idiot nephew, could devise an effective strategy for that. Defending against it, on the other hand...At the back of his mind, Eiconodoulus knew it was possible, but he also knew that he wasn't a good enough tactician to do it. Probably they'd write up the disaster in the military textbooks—his place in history—and cadets would be taught what he should have done (blindingly obvious, no doubt, with hindsight) as an awful warning against overconfidence. It amused him that he didn't even know the name of this place, though he'd be remembered in the same breath as it forever. Meanwhile, the Eremians would be inspired by their miraculous victory, the Mezentines would be stunned by the worst defeat in their history, and all because some fool couldn't draw a decent map, though nobody would remember *that* in two hundred years' time.

The digging party reached the bottom of the combe, and no sign of any enemy. Eiconodoulus merely found that insulting; as well as building the road for them, he had to lug the stupid machines down it just to save them the effort. He thought about that for a while; and yes, it was blindingly obvious. They wanted the two dozen engines dismantled and out of action before they committed themselves. Very sensible. He obliged, and gave the order.

They didn't attack while the unloaded carts were led down, but of course they had more sense. Then it was time to carry the dismantled engines; the men were very unhappy about doing that, but they'd be even unhappier when the Eremian arrows started dropping down on them. Apparently, however, Eiconodoulus hadn't quite judged their plan right, because no arrows flew and the engines reached the river, eventually, after the hardest day's work Eiconodoulus could remember. By now he was very worried indeed. If the Eremians were content to pass up such a glorious opportunity as the one he'd just given them, it could only be because they had something even more deadly in mind, which he was too stupid to perceive. The engines went back on the carts, the water-barrels were filled, the horses spanned in; gradually it dawned on Eiconodoulus that there wasn't going to be an attack after all. They'd blundered; they'd passed up the most wonderful opportunity to give the Republic a bloody nose, through laziness, negligence, cowardice or stupidity. For the first time since they left the Butter Pass, Eiconodoulus laughed out loud. He'd beaten the map, after all.

On the other side of the canyon, there was no sign of any path; but there was gloriously even ground, better than the pitted and rutted surface of a track. Heather had probably grown there once, but the wind had scoured off the thin layer of topsoil and ground away the bumps and tussocks, leaving a layer of shingle and small stones that would've compared favorably with a nobleman's carefully tended gravel drive. The ground fell slowly away to the blurred gray seam of land and sky, where mists rose from the Lasenia river valley. Two days, or a day and a half if they could force the pace, and they'd be bypassing the foot of the mountain on which the city perched, on their way to where they were supposed to be. Eiconodoulus was a cautious man when it came to interpreting the actions of Providence, but he reckoned it wouldn't be presumptuous to assume that he was getting his reward for the tribulations he'd recently endured.

The final confirmation for this view came in the shape of a flock of wild sheep sheltering from the wind in a small dish-shaped combe; the scouts who found them managed to creep away without startling them, and Eiconodoulus quickly convened a tactical meeting. He listened to various suggestions (the oaf Ariophrantzes had been a hunter in his youth, and prattled on about nets and drives and beaters until ordered to shut up) and gave his orders.

His strategy was basic and simple. On three sides of the combe he drew up his spearmen, creating a hedge of sharp points about a hundred yards shy of the skyline. On the fourth side he sent in his strike force in two ranks; in front, the archers, and behind them the rest of the men, shouting, banging rocks and pans and helmets, waving their arms, generally making themselves as obnoxious as possible. As soon as they advanced over the rim of the combe the sheep bolted in the opposite direction. Running into the spearmen they veered off to the sides, round the inside of the encircling hedge, back to where the advancing line had closed the ring. Forced back into the hollow of the combe, they could then be shot down by the archers without risk to the spearmen.

It went perfectly, smooth as a carefully designed machine. At the precise moment he'd specified, the panic-stricken sheep galloped straight into his enfilade. About forty-seven went down in the first volley, whereupon the survivors bolted down into the belly of the combe, giving the archers the backstop they needed. There wasn't any need for skill. The archers simply loosed volleys until there was nothing left moving; then they strolled down into the combe to pick up their arrows and collect the carcasses for dressing. None of the sheep escaped. It was, Eiconodoulus couldn't help thinking, a rather encouraging omen for the war at large.

After days on half-rations, the men were happy again, and the excitement of it (Eiconodoulus wasn't sure if it had been a hunt or a battle) had done wonders for their morale; there were even volunteers for the chores of skinning, paunching and butchering. The only man who seemed unhappy was the fool Ariophrantzes; he scowled when he thought nobody was looking, and tried to stay out of the proceedings as much as possible. Eiconodoulus was inclined to put that down to pique (Ariophrantzes had put himself forward at the tactical meeting as a mighty hunter, his learned advice had been ignored, and still they'd got the lot) and he decided that such an attitude needed to be nipped in the bud. "What's the matter with you?" he asked him.

Eventually he got a straight answer. "It's nothing really, sir," the oaf replied. "Honestly. We had to get some food from somewhere, and it all worked out pretty well."

Big of you, Eiconodoulus thought. "So what's bugging you?"

"I don't know." The oaf made a vague, helpless gesture. "It's just that—well, like I told you earlier, my people hunted a lot when I was a kid, and I suppose I've still got their way of looking at things. Killing the whole lot like that—"

He couldn't be bothered to argue. "If that's all," he said, "you can get on with your work. This is a military expedition, Lieutenant, not a day out with the hounds."

"Very good, sir. One thing, though, if I might ask. What were you proposing to cook the meat with?"

The world is full of annoyances; none more infuriating than a fool with a valid point. In the end they had to unload a cart and trash it for firewood, having distributed its load between the others. Being best-quality Mezentine treated timber, it burned with a foul smell and a thick cloud of dark gray smoke, which made the meat taste of pitch. It was still a distinct improvement on nothing at all, but it wasn't the glorious feast of roast mutton that Eiconodoulus had been anticipating as a due reward for his achievement. Then it rained in the night, putting out the fires and drenching the remaining firewood with half the carcasses still raw. There was no point burdening themselves with uncooked meat that'd spoil by the time they reached anywhere they might expect to find more fuel, so the remaining carcasses had to be abandoned. It was just an unfortunate mishap, but somehow Eiconodoulus couldn't help feeling that the oaf Ariophrantzes had somehow been vindicated.

They made up time the next day, and by nightfall they reached the river. For once, the map was accurate; the river was shallow enough to wade across, although they had to unload the carts yet again (the second time in two days; they'd had to unload to redistribute the load from the firewood wagon). By now, Eiconodoulus was having to think and calculate in order to work out how many days they were behind schedule. Obviously he had no idea what had become of the main army, or how his tardiness was affecting the war. It wouldn't be good, he knew, but the scope of his contribution was still mercifully vague, although that didn't keep him from speculating about it endlessly. They wouldn't court-martial him or cut off his head, but they wouldn't listen to his excuses either. Somewhat perversely, he responded to that inevitability by refusing to hurry unduly; he was late already but he was making steady progress, and undue haste would probably lead to negligence and disaster. The next morning, as the sutlers filled the water-barrels from the river, he used up the last of his cutting-practice mats. No way of knowing when or where he'd be able to get hold of any more; another of the girders holding his life in shape had quietly failed. His victory over the sheep was beginning to fade from his mind, and the empty space it left quickly silted up with anxiety. More than anything, he wanted to be rid of this assignment and back with the rest of the army. He wasn't at his best in isolation, as he well knew.

From the top of the ridge overlooking the river, he was able to see the city for the first time. It was mid-afternoon by then, and the morning mist had burned away; there was nothing to soften the steepness of the mountain, and the sight horrified him. He'd been in assaults and sieges, he knew about such things; and if ever a city was impregnable, this one was. For a while he could do nothing but stand and gawp, like a rabbit faced with a stoat. It seemed bitterly unfair that he should have been sent here, set such a difficult task which he'd somehow managed to achieve, simply in order to participate in an impossible venture, an inevitable disaster. There aren't many heroic ballads about men who strive against insuperable odds, surmount unthinkable obstacles and then die in the final act of abject failure. It wasn't his fault, but nobody would remember that, or ever get to hear about the criminally negligent map, the crossing of the great canyon or the flawlessly conceived and executed campaign against the sheep. He'd remain as anonymous as the waves smashing themselves into foam against a rock.

With an effort he pulled himself together. It was an extraordinary city, yes, but it remained no more than a problem in engineering, and the Mezentines were the finest engineers in the world. No doubt they'd already worked out how to deal with it; all he needed to do was deliver his cargo to the appointed place with as little further delay as possible; at which point he could hand the problem over to somebody else who was properly qualified to deal with it. They were welcome to the glory, provided he could unload the blame along with the dismantled war engines, mountings and carriages.

"So that's it, sir," said a voice at his side — Stesimbracus, the good young officer he couldn't stand. "Where we're headed."

He nodded without looking round. "Impressive, isn't it?"

Stesimbracus laughed. "As a monument to short-sightedness, maybe," he said. "Personally, sir, I'm just grateful to be on our side. I'd hate to have the job of defending that."

Which was probably, Eiconodoulus told himself, why he detested Stesimbracus so much. "You don't see any problems, then?"

"Well, no, not really. It's a nice piece of construction work, but there's that obvious flaw. You'd have thought someone would've pointed it out while they were actually building the thing, but I suppose everybody thought somebody else would do it."

Obvious flaw? Not that obvious, Lieutenant. "So," he said, "tell me how you'd go about it."

And Stesimbracus told him; and as soon as he'd finished, he couldn't help but agree. It was vividly, painfully, humiliatingly obvious. Maybe that was what genius was: the knack of seeing the obvious through its obscure curtain of irrelevancies. "Well," he said quietly, "no doubt that's what Central Command intends to do. All we need to concern ourselves with is getting these carts up into the hills behind it."

Stesimbracus nodded. "Though you can't help wondering, sir, why they're bothering. I mean, why bother to put the catapult things up there? They won't be contributing anything. Diversion, I suppose; make them think we're planning a direct frontal assault."

For some time after that, Eiconodoulus was plagued by that last thought. Suppose the boy was right about the plan—he very much hoped he was right, for the sake of the war and the hope of survival and victory—and that he was also right about the purpose of the war engines: a diversion. In which case, the engines weren't going to be loosed in anger; he'd carried them, and their stock of eighty thousand bolts, over the mountains and up and down the canyon and across the river, all for nothing, for show. Thin wooden cut-out silhouettes would've done just as well. All his efforts, his defeats and small victories and indelible humiliations, just to be part of a dirty great lie...

Next morning, at first light, they set off on what Eiconodoulus hoped would be the last stage of the journey. This time (perversely, he thought) the map was accurate; there was a road, a good one, skirting the city and going where they wanted it to. They made good progress, forcing the pace wherever possible; they had a superb view of the valley below, and the hills above them were too steep to allow an attack, so there was no chance of an ambush. Eiconodoulus was finally able to send messengers to the main army at Palicuro, so that was another weight off his conscience, although that hadn't troubled him quite so much once Stesimbracus had pointed out what the true strategy was. If he was a little late, so what? He was, after all, just the decoy.

As far as he could tell from observing traffic in and out of the city, the Eremians either didn't know they were being invaded or didn't care. Neither explanation was credible, but he was past caring about matters of high strategy. All that mattered was to get to the end of the journey and deliver the war engines. If they kept up their current rate of progress, they could be there by noon tomorrow, and history would have no further use for them. Simple carriers' motivation: deliver the load and go home.

The Eremians attacked them on the open hillside, at the junction of the road they were on and a small, straight track leading up from the city. The first that Eiconodoulus knew of it was yelling and the neighing of horses, from somewhere at the back of the train. He'd heard that sound in his mind many times; an axle had finally given way, a cart had foundered, other carts were swerving to avoid it, there'd be chaos in a matter of minutes. He swung his horse round, and saw what looked at first sight like a swarm of flies; small black dots in the air above him. But flies don't usually fly slanting down, and they don't grow as you watch them. Arrows, he thought; but they were too high up.

He heard himself shouting, and was faintly impressed to hear what he was saying: get out of the way, get off the carts, take cover. But he was too preoccupied to take his own advice. A small black dot turned into a falling pole, suddenly growing enormous as it bent its trajectory toward him. He realized, through innate mathematical ability or sheer intuition, that it was going to hit him. It was a curious idea, and while it was forming he felt no fear; a small voice in the back of his mind suggested that it'd be worth trying to get out of the way if that was possible, but there wouldn't be time to make the horse move. But if he rolled out of the saddle—yes, why not?

He landed on his elbows and knees, and the pain knocked everything out of his mind for a moment. The first thought to return was a mild anxiety—have I broken anything?—and he wriggled a bit to see if anything wasn't working. The pain gave place to the sharp protests of jarred bone and tendon, and he stifled a yell. Then a terrible weight flopped onto him, crushing his thigh, jamming his lower leg against the ground so that all the force of impact fell on the joint of his right knee. He felt something fail—it

was like listening to a single note on the harp, if pain was music—
and his mind registered and accepted that there was something
badly wrong before everything was washed away in a surging tide
of agony.

That lasted three or four seconds, an intolerably long time, and
then it stopped. Vaguely he was aware of human voices, a voice,
someone shouting, someone shouting at him. He couldn't think
why, he hadn't done anything wrong; then he was moving, being
pulled. Very bad, because his knee and leg were still trapped
under the heavy thing. He screamed. The movement stopped, the
pain swelled to bursting point, and the world went away.

When it came back—how long had it been away? Not terribly
long; he remembered he'd been more or less here, and the voice
was still shouting. He forced himself to concentrate. The voice
was Lieutenant Stesimbracus', and the weight that had crunched
his leg was his own horse. It was lying a few feet away, its back legs
twitching, its head perfectly still, and there was something like
a clothesline prop sticking out of it, at the point where the neck
meets the shoulder. It occurred to him, in an abstract, detached
sort of a way, that Stesimbracus must have pulled him out from
under the horse; very kind of him, because the weight was ripping
his knee tendons off the bone, but he still wasn't prepared to like
the man.

"Are you all right?" Stesimbracus was roaring in his ear, and
he really wanted to laugh, because he obviously wasn't, a dead
horse had just fallen on his leg—

"What's happening?" he heard himself say; but before Stesimbracus could answer, another of the clothesline prop things
dropped out of nowhere and hit him. The point went in on the left
side of his collarbone and came out through the small of his back,
pinning him upright to the ground.

War engines, Eiconodoulus thought; and then he realized
what must be happening. He tried to move, then remembered he
couldn't; and that was the point at which panic hit him, and fear,

and all the physical effects that go with them. He could feel his stomach muscles twist, his bladder loosen, his arms tremble and ache; he could hardly breathe, as though something even heavier than the dead horse was pressing down on his chest. But he knew those feelings, and he knew he could make them go away for a while by concentrating.

Unbelievably, Stesimbracus was still alive, because he saw him blink, and then his lips moved. He stared for a moment, as much from curiosity as horror or compassion; but a running man chose that moment to trip over him, and pain took over for a while.

When it let him go again, he saw the fallen runner scrabbling to his feet and leaving; he'd never seen a man run so fast, it was no wonder he'd tripped. He remembered Stesimbracus and looked back. His lips were still moving a little, but his eyes had the empty look that Eiconodoulus had seen before. He felt very bad about having disliked him so much, but it was too late to do anything about it now.

Experiments showed that he could still move everything apart from the wrecked knee. If he could get to his feet and find something to use as a crutch, he'd be able to stand, possibly even get about. That would probably be a wise course of action. He realized that everything had changed, and until he'd found out exactly how things stood, he couldn't rely on any of the information or the plans of action that had applied a minute ago. That hurt almost worse than the crushed knee. He realized he needed somebody who could tell him what was happening (but that would've been Stesimbracus' job). He was, of course, still the most significant man in this action; everything would depend on how he dealt with it, but he couldn't even stand up.

Ludicrous, he thought, someone's got to come and find me, I'm needed—Another clothes-prop dropped very close, kicking up dust that blinded him for a moment and reminding him that the bombardment, the source of the damage, was still going on. For a second or two he experimented with various ways of pushing, squirming or bouncing himself to his feet, but they all failed painfully. But he was a resourceful man, he knew it perfectly well, and this wasn't a time to go all to pieces.

He saw the solution to the problem; it was standing, literally, in front of him. If he grabbed hold of Stesimbracus, he could pull himself up that way, assuming the spike that had transfixed him was firmly enough in the ground. Unfortunately, the poor fellow was still just faintly alive, and for a moment he was too... Eiconodoulus analyzed the cause. He was too embarrassed to reach out and grab a handful of a dying man's trouser leg, while the dying man was watching. That seemed to make some sort of sense, but he forced himself to do it nevertheless.

It worked, just about; he got himself upright, though in the process he dragged the spike out of the ground and it toppled slowly, with its grotesque burden, to the ground. Never mind; he fought to find stability, because nothing mattered more than staying on his feet, his foot, and not crashing back to the ground again. He balanced self-consciously for a second or so. He'd made it.

He lifted his head and, for the first time since it all started, looked to see what was happening. It didn't look hopeful. There was now a forest of the clothes-prop things, planted slanting in the ground like a spindly crop of beans. Rather too many of them were planted in dead or dying bodies, and there didn't seem to be many living people about. He rationalized: that'd be because they were taking cover, as he'd ordered them to do. He thought about trying to move from where he was. Another spike pitched about three feet away. He looked up; the sky was still full of them, like a distant flock of rooks. This is hopeless, he thought, there's nothing I can do. I might as well let myself fall over, because it'd take less effort and I've got no strength left.

But he didn't do that. Instead, he took a step forward. Mistake; badly thought out. The ground hit him in the face, and pain took over again. Hopeless. Even if he could stand up and find someone to give orders to, his mind was so blurred and sodden with pain that he couldn't think straight. It was as bad as being drunk (it was the loss of clarity that had put him off drinking, many years ago); that awful sense of knowing what needed to be done, but not being able to order and express the thoughts. He was no use to anybody anymore. Best thing would be to lie still and quiet. If he insisted on moving, find a cart and crawl under it, wait for the attack to stop and for someone to come and rescue him.

(But somehow he knew, as a positive certainty, like someone remembering the past, that none of the spikes were actually going to hit him, not *him;* it was quite likely that he was going to die — thirst, starvation, heat, throat cut by looters — but it wouldn't be from a clothes-prop dropping out of the sky. Strange, that this comforting but strictly qualified revelation should have been granted to him, because he didn't have any sense of being needed, by destiny, the powers that be, whatever. It was just a fact, a piece of information.)

One more go at it, he promised himself; I'll have one more try, and if that fails I'll have done my best. He contrived to bounce himself up onto his good knee, and found that if he let the ruined leg drag, like a travois behind a mule, he could haul himself along after a fashion by his elbows. It was a ludicrous way for a grown man to act; it was the sort of thing you'd expect of a child playing a game, pretending to be a snail or a caterpillar. He wouldn't get very far like this, but he could go a little way, just to show willing. So he crawled five yards (the small stones and gravel flayed the points of his elbows, even through the padded sleeves of his aketon) and stopped. A little later, he crawled another five yards. He realized he wasn't actually achieving anything, but he knew he'd just get restless if he lay still and quiet waiting to die.

Ten distinct stages, five yards at a time, brought him to the shade of a cart. There was somebody else under it. He called out, "I need help, I can't walk"; the man under the cart didn't move. Eiconodoulus called again, but still no answer. Fine, he thought, he's dead; so he heaved himself forward, banging his forehead on one of the chassis timbers. Only then did the man seem to notice him; he leaned forward, grabbed Eiconodoulus' arm and pulled him under the cart.

"Thanks," Eiconodoulus said. The man was staring at him as though he'd never seen a human before. "What's happening?"

The man shook his head. "We're getting slaughtered," he said, and laughed.

Shock; takes different people in different ways. "The mounted escort," Eiconodoulus said. "Have you seen them?"

"All dead," the man answered. "I saw it. One shower of bolts, nobody left. All gone."

That was a blow. "Who are you?" he asked. "Engineer?"

The man shook his head again. "Carter," he replied. "Soon as I saw what was happening, I dived under here. Fucking waste of time. Those bolts'd go through the woodwork like it's not there."

"Are you hurt?"

"No." He said it with a wry grin, as though there was something funny about it; then he added, "You know what's happening, don't you? You know who's shooting at us?"

Eiconodoulus opened his mouth to answer, then hesitated.

"It's our own bloody side, that's who," the man said, his voice rising in anger. "Got to be. Because those are scorpion bolts, and only the Mezentines have got scorpions. It's our own fucking side shooting at us."

Eiconodoulus froze. It was as though the thought was too big to fit in his mind, and had jammed up the opening, making it impossible for him to think at all. "Can't be," he said. "Why? Why would they do that?"

The man shrugged. "Don't ask me," he said. "I mean, obviously they think we're the enemy."

"But..." With an effort, Eiconodoulus forced his mind clear. It was, in fact, entirely possible. He was days later than scheduled, and maybe his messages hadn't reached the main army; they'd assumed he was dead or captured, so they'd sent up more scorpions; they'd arrived and been installed to guard the road, and somehow their observers hadn't recognized his column, had assumed that it must be the enemy. It was possible; in which case...

He thought about it for a moment. Scorpion bolts; and the Mezentines had a ferociously guarded monopoly on field artillery. It was the only possible explanation.

"In that case," he said slowly, "we've got to tell them, and then they'll stop."

"Fine," the other man snapped. "You go."

"I can't," Eiconodoulus said, quiet and reasonable. "My knee's all broken up. I can just about crawl a couple of yards, that's all."

The other man was scowling at him; he had a thin, dry face and he spoke with an eastern accent. "Fucked if I'm going out there," he said.

"Why not?" Eiconodoulus said. "You just told me it's not safe under here. The only way we'll be safe is if someone goes and finds the battery and tells them to stop shooting. I can't do it." He paused, watching the man's face. "I wouldn't get fifty yards."

He could see the other man doing the mathematics; only two of us, he can't go... "I'm not going out there," he said, as though Eiconodoulus had made an indecent suggestion. "No, you can forget that."

Best not to say anything; so he shrugged and kept quiet. The man protested a few more times, then slowly crawled out from under the cart, straightened up—cramp, probably—and began to run, wobbling like a baby calf. Eiconodoulus could only see his legs from the knee down; he followed him until he was out of sight. Well, he thought; it's my job to give orders.

He lay on his back, and the pleasure of being still and quiet surged through him like a wave. He closed his eyes to rest them, knowing it was impossible to go to sleep, here in the middle of so much danger. He tried to rally his thoughts, but it was too much effort. There wasn't anything he could do anyway. The responsibility was slipping away from him; he wasn't in charge anymore, because he had the perfect excuse.

Light, movement, the sound of voices. His body was awake

before he was; he woke up in the act of shrinking away, dragging himself backward with his elbows. As his eyes opened, he found himself staring at an extraordinary human being. The spectacle reminded him of something he'd read about or heard, maybe in a briefing; the man's face and hands were the most remarkable color: pale, bone-white tinged with pink. At the back of his mind he was sure he knew about this, but the only explanations that occurred to him were that the man had been rolling in white slip, the thin clay wash potters paint on the outsides of big jars, or he'd managed to get himself covered in flour.

Then he remembered; where he was, what had happened, his wrecked knee, the fact that the enemy, the Eremians, were a white-skinned race.

"Got one," the man was shouting. "Over here." Eiconodoulus wondered what had become of the cart, but he didn't dare take his eyes off the white man. He couldn't see a weapon, but he was under no illusions about what would happen next. The Eremians (a casual aside in a briefing, months ago) don't take prisoners.

That was that, then.

(All his adult life, he'd wondered about this moment, which he'd long since accepted as inevitable; the moment when he faced the enemy who would kill him. He'd assumed that it would be a spasm of blind, hurting, thrashing pain and terror—he'd seen wounded animals being dispatched, men being executed, victims of accident and artillery—and it had bothered him, because he'd die a wriggling, squirming, convulsing thing, and the weapon tearing into his body would hurt unbearably. The thought had almost been enough to make him quit the profession, but there had always been good, sensible reasons to hang on for another six months, another year. Now that he faced it, he felt like an explorer or a philosopher finally arriving at the place he'd searched all his life to find; the great question, *what will it be like,* was finally going to be answered, and he found himself considering the situation objectively, as though he'd have the opportunity to report back to a commission of inquiry. He'd tell them, I felt sick, very wide awake, completely aware of everything everywhere apart from my own body, and calm.)

Other white men were standing over him; one on each side, maybe two behind. Out of the corner of his eye he could see a spearhead—so it'd be a stab rather than a cut, he noted; good, because puncture wounds kill quickly, by organ damage, whereas slashes tend to kill by shock and loss of blood. A small part of his mind that was still interested in collecting information noted that the white men spoke good Mezentine but with a strong, rather comical accent.

"What do you want to do?" one of them asked.

"Take him back with the wagons," said another, a disembodied voice over his head. The others mumbled agreement, and arms came down out of the air and dragged him up. He stood for a moment, then collapsed.

"Fuck," someone said. "Look at his knee."

They don't know I can understand them, he realized. Not that it mattered; he had nothing to say to them. It occurred to him that if he revealed the fact that he could communicate with them, they might torture him for information before they killed him. That thought made him horribly aware of how painful and sensitive his knee was; anything would be better than being hurt by them, death would be much better. Suddenly he felt fear take over; he was shaking, and he couldn't make it stop. His body felt loose, as though all the joints had slipped and come unstrung; all his strength had evaporated, he was hanging from their hands, a dead weight. Why couldn't they just kill him and be done with it?

"He's in pretty bad shape," someone said. "Put him in the wagon and let's get out of here."

They carried him, gently. As he was moved along he could see dozens of the white men, busily at work. Some of them were getting the carts ready to drive off, others were plucking up the clothes-props, carrying them in bundles, like men harvesting maize. At that moment, he realized that the Eremians had war engines too (not that it mattered to him, of course) and he'd blundered into a carefully laid ambush. At another time he'd be furious with himself for letting it happen; it was somehow pleasant to be released from the obligation to feel shame and self-reproach.

They put him carefully in the back of one of his own carts; they laid out blankets for him to lie on, and tried not to jar his knee as they put him down. They made a bad job of it, but he was bewildered by their concern. He'd braced himself for a different kind of pain, the being-dropped, slamming kind, and instead it was the awkward, clumsy sort. A white man sat next to him in the cart, and when it started to move Eiconodoulus nearly screamed, as a jolt twisted his knee the wrong way. The white man frowned at him, then looked away; his hands were clamped tight on the side of the cart.

Not dead yet, he thought, as the cart pitched and jostled over the ruts and stones; not dead yet, but don't go getting your hopes up. Look at it logically; things can really only get worse. Are hours or days of pain really worth staying alive for? Of course not. Then let's hope they kill me quickly, before this numb feeling wears off and I go to pieces. He tried to calculate in his mind the distance from the ambush site to the city (presumably where they were headed) but he couldn't quite get the map into his mind. It was as if it was part of a dream, in which he'd been a career officer of engineers in charge of a routine convoy, and it was swiftly fading away, as dreams tend to do in the light.

Ludicrous (he told himself when he woke up) that I should have wasted my last few hours of life in sleep; but then, I probably wouldn't have enjoyed them anyway. He opened his eyes and saw blue sky overhead; the jolting underneath him told him he was still on the cart. He realized that he felt unbearably impatient— why can't they just kill me now, instead of making me live through this interminable cart ride?—and while he'd been asleep his knee had locked up stiff and hurt worse than ever. If it hadn't been for the thought of how ridiculous it would sound, he'd have started demanding to be killed immediately; he grinned as he heard his own high, querulous voice in his mind, insisting...

Suddenly a great gray stone shape appeared overhead, like a swooping hawk; he was passing under an arch. The blue sky was edged with gray walls and red roof tiles, and the jolting was the multiple taps of steel-rimmed wheels on cobblestones. Here we are, then — at which point, a desperate feeling of reluctance swept over him, so that if he'd been able to move at all he'd have tried to jump off the cart and run. As it was, all he could do was lever himself up a little way on the points of his elbows. The white man next to him looked down, his face registering no interest. Eiconodoulus' strength ran out and he slipped back to rest.

Bouncing on cobbles for a very long time; then the cart stopped and the white man jumped up, calling to someone he couldn't see. Four or five of them appeared over him; they lifted him up (that hurt) and put him carefully on something long and flat, possibly a door or a hurdle. He couldn't make out what they were saying; there were unfamiliar words, possibly names. They moved him quickly; he had to close his eyes to keep from getting dizzy.

For a while after that, things blurred, like drops of water on a painting. He was carried about on the flat thing, then put down, then picked up again and carried some more. There were apparently long periods of lying still, sometimes voices overhead. Occasionally he made out one or two words, but they were meaningless out of context. Then came a long, bad patch; someone was digging about in his damaged knee, twisting it and stabbing into it with a knife or a tool. He opened his eyes and tried to sit up, but hands pushed him down flat. He could see white men standing over him, but he couldn't see the torturer himself. He waited impatiently for the questions to start — why the hell torture someone if you don't ask questions, where's the point? — but all he could hear was the men murmuring to each other. They aren't torturers, they're doctors, he realized; he laughed out loud, and then the pain blotted out everything. He wasn't aware of trying to move, but the men were having trouble keeping him still. At some point, the world went out like a snuffed candle.

A voice was murmuring overhead. It was talking. It was talking to him. "How are you feeling?" it said.

He didn't know, of course. He took a moment to gather the necessary information, then he opened his eyes.

The white man didn't seem to want an answer after all, because he went on, "My name is Miel Ducas. What's yours?"

Excellent question; don't know. He went to the very back of his mind and dragged it out. "Captain Beltista Eiconodoulus," he said. He shouldn't have told them that, of course.

"You're going to be all right," the man called Miel Ducas told him. "I'm afraid they couldn't save the leg, though. I'm sorry."

Save the leg? What was he talking about? His leg was still hurting, of course, but what did it matter, since they were going to kill him? He felt confusion pressing on him like a pillow over his face.

"As soon as you're fit to travel we're sending you back," Miel Ducas went on. "We'd like you to take a message to your commanding officer. We won't bother with that now. You get some sleep, if you can."

All the confusion welled up into a bubble, a blister; he tried to sit up, failed, and heard himself say, "What happened?"

Miel Ducas sort of grinned. "You got ambushed," he said. "You very nearly didn't, mind. We had scouts out tracking you up the Butter Pass, but then you went diving off the road into the shale and they lost you completely. We only managed to pick you up later, when you lit some fires."

Fires. Ah yes, roasting the wild sheep. But we had no choice, we were starving.

"Anyhow," Miel Ducas went on, "you were obliging enough to come to the lure in the end, and thank you very much for the scorpions. With those and what we've already got, we reckon we can defend this city against anything you can throw at us. We'd have liked a bit more in the way of ammunition, of course, but, well; gift horses' teeth, and all that."

He didn't understand what that meant, but he couldn't be bothered to ask. Instead, he took a moment to look at his surroundings. The bed he was lying on was in the middle of the floor of a circular room—where do you get those? In the turrets of castles. There was a straight-backed, carved oak chair, dark with age and assiduous polishing, and a door, and a narrow window. Miel Ducas looked at him for a moment, then went on: "You've been out of it for a week, believe it or not. During that time we used your scorpions, with their sweet little carriages, to attack the main column you were supposed to meet up with. We ran out of bolts before we were able to get them all, but the latest reports say we cleared about seven thousand men, which isn't bad going for a race of backward mountain savages, don't you think? Anyhow, what's left of them have scuttled back down the pass; they took their wounded but left the scorpion bolts, which shows your people have no idea about priorities. Anyway," he went on, leaning back in his chair a little, "that's enough for now. You get some rest, and I'll be back to give you our message later on."

When Miel Ducas had gone, he stretched out full length and shut his eyes; he felt dizzy and uncomfortable, and his head was aching. Apparently he wasn't going to die after all. It should have been a moment of sheer joy but it wasn't. He was going to live; they were sending him back to Mezentia. They'd cut off his leg.

Carefully he sat up. There was a blanket over him, which he twitched away; it fell on the floor, where he wouldn't be able to retrieve it. He hadn't realized before that he had no clothes on. He could see his thigh, down to the knee. It was wrapped in bandages, and there was nothing beyond it. Extraordinary.

Instinctively, he tried to wiggle his toes. The left side worked fine. He frowned. It was like when he'd been lying awkwardly and woken up with his leg completely numb; unless he grabbed it with his hand, he couldn't move it. There was actually nothing there. It was a bizarre feeling, like something out of a dream.

Now what? He tried to imagine what it was going to be like, but he couldn't. Soon his leg would stop being numb and he'd have a ferocious attack of pins and needles. He concentrated. Well, for one thing, he wouldn't be able to walk.

Fear choked him like hands tight around his throat. He curled up in a ball and for a long time all he could do was try and fight off the waves of terror and despair. If only they'd killed him; he was ready for that, it would've been no big deal. This kind of mutilation, though, that was far worse. Better death than life as a cripple. (He was making gestures, striking poses; even while he raged and cringed against the horror of it, a calm voice in the back of his mind was making lists—things I can still do, things I can't—and figuring out ways of coping. Meanwhile, the rest of him relaxed into the comfort of despair: *as soon as I'm out of here, I'll get hold of some poison, or I'll just refuse to eat.* Thinking about killing himself helped him calm down, because it was one thing he knew he'd never do.)

He was lost in these thoughts when the door opened again. He froze, suddenly aware that he hadn't got any clothes on. The newcomer came in and looked down at him. He wasn't white, like the others; his skin was the normal color. An ambassador maybe, or someone who'd been sent to negotiate for his release, or supervise a prisoner exchange? Highly unlikely that he'd be here on his own; he'd be escorted, there'd be guards with him.

"Who are you?" he heard himself say.

The newcomer smiled. "I'm Ziani Vaatzes," he said.

Eiconodoulus knew who he was. "They told us you're dead," he said.

Vaatzes raised an eyebrow. "Is that right?" he said. "Well, I'm not. In fact, I'd be grateful if you would set the record straight when you go back to the City. I'm most definitely still alive. Furthermore, the scorpions that shot up your column were built by me. Maybe you'd be kind enough to emphasize that when you make your report."

"All right," Eiconodoulus said.

"Thank you." Vaatzes dipped his head in mock courtesy. "Was

that one of my bolts?" he asked, nodding toward the bandaged stump.

Eiconodoulus shook his head. "My horse fell on me," he said.

"Really? What dreadful bad luck. Infection, I suppose. When you get back to the City, ask to be taken to the Coppersmiths' Guild. Don't ask me why, but the artificial limb-makers count as coppersmiths for the purposes of registration. Anyhow, they'll fix you up. It's amazing, the quality of their work. I wouldn't be surprised if they had you walking again, eventually. One model they make, for above-the-knee cases like yours, it's got a joint so it bends just like the real thing; and there's a really neat little spring-and-catch arrangement that locks the joint up when you put weight on it, and releases it when you take the weight off again. Once you've learned to sort of throw the false leg forward as you move, you can actually get along at close on normal walking speed, though I understand it can't be used on stairs or anything like that."

"I'll do that," Eiconodoulus said. He nearly added, "Thank you," but decided against it. Instead he asked, "Is it true? What they told me, about the attack on the main column."

Vaatzes nodded. "At least seven thousand killed," he said. "They ran out of bolts. Unfortunately, the ones I made don't work with the genuine article. But they're interchangeable the other way round—my scorpions can loose genuine ordnance bolts—so I'm changing the pattern a little. By the time you attack again, we'll have a good supply."

Eiconodoulus frowned. "Do you want me to tell them that too?"

"You can if you like," Vaatzes replied. "But that's not why I'm here. I want you to take a message for me, a private message, for a friend of mine. He's bound to be in close contact with the main army, he's foreman of the ordnance factory, so someone'll take it to him. Falier, his name is."

"Falier," Eiconodoulus repeated.

"You've got it. And by the way, it'll be well worth your while, trust me. It'll make it possible for your side to win the war."

Eiconodoulus was sure he hadn't heard that right. "What did you just say?"

"This message," Vaatzes said, "to my friend Falier. It'll tell him how to get past our defenses." He grinned. "It's called treachery," he said. "It's frowned on in some quarters, but it saves lives and gets results. Now, I want you to listen very carefully, because this is important." He paused and furrowed his brow. "You're looking at me strangely," he said. "You do want your side to win the war, don't you? I mean, it'll be good for you, not to mention getting your own back, for the leg and everything."

"I don't understand," Eiconodoulus said. "I thought you're on their side."

"I am," Vaatzes replied, "for the moment. But listen, you've got to get the message to Falier. It won't be any good unless he gets it, so don't go telling it to your superior officer or the commander in chief or the Guild Assembly; it'd just be meaningless drivel to them, and they'd think you're up to something or loose in the head. It's only valuable if Falier gets it, do you understand?"

Eiconodoulus nodded, because it wasn't really a lie if he didn't actually say the word. "What's the message?" he asked.

He thought about it a lot, after Vaatzes had gone away, and later, on the long cart-ride back to Mezentia, but it made no sense at all. Several times he made up his mind that he wouldn't deliver it—why should he, after all? It was bound to be a trick or a trap, but so crude that the Mezentines would never fall for it. He'd only make a fool of himself; maybe the whole thing was Vaatzes' idea of a joke. It was unthinkable that the same man who'd betrayed the Republic by defecting to its worst enemy and building them war engines that could wipe out seven thousand men could also give away the key to breaching the unassailable walls of Civitas Eremiae. It made no sense. You'd have to be born stupid to fall for something like that.

The Mezentines were very considerate, in their way. After he'd been debriefed and questioned, by his own people and the Mezentine authorities and representatives from their war cabinet, he was sent to the Coppersmiths' Hall, where he was measured in two dozen places with tapes and rules and calipers. They showed him an example of what they were planning to make for him, and sure enough, it had a cunning little mechanism to lock it when you put your weight on it, just as Vaatzes had said. For some reason (he couldn't detect any logic to it), that was what made him decide to pass on Vaatzes' message to Falier after all. He asked one of the false-leg people to do it for him; apparently, the man knew someone who knew someone else who was an off-relation of Falier's new wife. Once he'd done that, he put it out of his mind. After all, it was meaningless, and he had other matters to think about now.

19

The worst defeat in the history of the Perpetual Republic was properly debated and acknowledged by an extraordinary general meeting of the Guilds in the great chapterhouse. After the defense committee had made their report, a motion proposed by the Wool, Cotton and Allied Trades that it was not, in fact, the worst ever defeat was rejected on the grounds that, although sixty-two more men were lost at the battle of Curoneia, eighty-seven years earlier, the loss of the war engines was far more significant than the human cost, comprised in both cases only of mercenaries. On the motion of the Foundrymen and Machinists, an emergency subcommittee of the general assembly with full powers was appointed to consider the immediate future conduct of the war, in concert with the defense committee, and the ordnance factory was given an unlimited budget and ordered to move to maximum productivity of scorpions. Inventory revealed a stock of five hundred and seventy-three completed scorpions standing at the factory, and these were appropriated to the use of Colonel Polydama Cersebleptes, who was confirmed as commander in chief of the expeditionary army. Colonel Cersebleptes then addressed the meeting, stating his opinion that with the forces at his disposal and the five hundred and seventy-three scorpions, he was confident of taking Civitas Eremiae within six weeks. Votes of confidence were then taken in favor of the Colonel, the defense committee and the

Guiding Committee itself. A motion of thanks to Captain Beltista Eiconodoulus was proposed by the Silversmiths, but rejected.

After a long day on the walls, Miel Ducas came home and yelled for a bath. He knew he was being inconsiderate—a bath in the Ducas house required the services of twelve people to carry water and fuel, and disrupted the work of the kitchens and the house-keeper's room for an hour—but he didn't care. He was exhausted and his back ached from lifting (he'd led by example, which had seemed like a good idea at the time). He'd stayed until the last scorpion was installed, aligned and bolted down. He'd made Orsea go home two hours before the finish, since it wasn't good for the men to see their Duke making stupid mistakes out of fatigue; besides, he'd been in the way, and Miel's patience had worn thin.

Even in the Ducas house, water takes its time coming to the boil. He undressed, struggled into a bathrobe, and sat on the window-seat of the butler's pantry waiting for the hot water to be carried in. It was a breach of decorum for the Ducas' naked feet to be seen by the chambermaids, so he put on a pair of boots which he guessed belonged to the boilerman.

He spent a minute or so looking at his hands. The rope burns were healing, thanks to the foul-smelling mess (of Vadani origin, he'd heard somewhere) that the doctors had smeared all over them, and the edges of the torn blisters were hardening into opaque parchment. They were his souvenirs of the battle, his glorious and honorable scars. King Fashion had a certain amount to say about the proper presentation of scars honorably won in the hunt, and one could safely assume that the rules applied just as well to war. Ostentation was to be avoided; one should not, for example, order new shirts and doublets cut low so as to display scars to neck and shoulder, or shorten one's sleeves to reveal cut and gashes to the forearms. Where scars were visible in normal dress, however, it was permissible to choose lighter colors so that the scars stood out by contrast, and where a hat would otherwise be worn but would obscure a scar, it could be dispensed with.

Miel smiled at the thought. He doubted whether King Fashion had ever been rope-burned or blistered his hands in his life, unless you counted the little pinches between the fingertips that came from archery without a glove or a tab. Blisters and burns aside, he had nothing on the outside to show for the victory, unless you counted the scorpions themselves. They were, of course, the great trophies of the hunt, and they'd been displayed to the best possible advantage, where you couldn't help seeing them. He ought to feel proud, he supposed; the ambush had been his idea, and he'd commanded the army, at Orsea's insistence, because his friend felt he wasn't competent to carry out such a desperately important mission. He'd been right about that, of course, which only made it worse.

He thought about that, too. The plain fact was that Orsea wasn't up to this job, leading the people in a war to the death. He was too obsessed by fear of failure, of the consequences of a mistake on his part; he insisted that Miel should do everything, and at the same time resented him murderously for it. That made Miel feel guilty, because it was completely unfair, and the guilt led to further resentment. There was absolutely nothing he could do about that; but Veatriz had started to hate him now, because he was making Orsea so unhappy. She never even looked at him when they happened to meet, and if he spoke to her she snarled at him.

Thinking about that made him think of the letter. It had never been far from his thoughts, ever since he'd first intercepted and hidden it. He could feel it, like an arrowhead too deeply embedded to be cut out; his only act of treachery in a lifetime of dutiful service. Well, you could put it like that; but at the moment it was one burden on his mind too many. Just as they brought in the first jugs of hot water, he made up his mind to get rid of it for good. If he burned it, at least he'd be rid of the dilemma.

"I'll be right back," he said to the chambermaids, who stared at him as if he was some kind of wild animal, then curtsied and fled.

The final hiding place he'd chosen for the lethal packet of

parchment was, he couldn't help thinking, magnificently apt. A small crack between two stones in the wall in the upper solar, out of sight behind the extravagant tapestry (the unicorn hunt; three hundred years old, a late masterpiece of the last decadent phase of the primitive-realist school; absolutely priceless because only three other examples existed, all of them preserved here in the Ducas house since the day they'd been made); nobody ever came in here apart from the servants, who were absolutely forbidden to touch the tapestry. He'd only found out about the crack himself because he'd played in this room as a boy; he'd hidden behind the tapestry from Jarnac and the bigger boys, when he'd been the roebuck and they'd been the hounds. They'd found him, of course, by his faint tracks in the dust on the floor, but even they had never dared lift the tapestry to drag him out. He'd been safe there, because only the Ducas and his heir apparent would dare lay a fingertip on the unicorn tapestry. Now even he felt nervous to the point of trembling as he gently moved the heavy fabric away from the wall and stepped behind it.

Three paces in, collarbone height; his fingers traced the courses of stone until they found the narrow slot.

The letter wasn't there.

"You've got no idea," the woman said, "how hard it was getting it."

Vaatzes shrugged. "Couldn't have been that difficult," he said, "or you wouldn't have managed."

She didn't like that, but he didn't care. He knew she was just trying to justify the asking price, to which he'd already agreed without protest. It was a vast sum of money — seventy gold thalers, enough to buy a good house and three hundred acres of pasture complete with all live and dead stock. It was his share of the profit on sixty scorpions. He'd cheerfully have paid three times as much.

"The money," she said.

He reached in his desk drawer and pulled out the bag, dropping it on the desktop with a loud thump and resting his left hand on it. "You can count it," he said.

"I trust you," she replied disdainfully.

He shrugged. "Up to you," he said. "Let's see it, then."

She knelt down, lifted her basket up onto the desk, and started to empty it. Cabbage stalks, bean pods, pea helm, artichoke peel, carrot tops and a small square of parchment. He took it from her and carefully unfolded it. "Have you read it?" he said.

She shook her head. "Just what's on the outside," she said. She was lying, of course, but that didn't matter. He folded his arms on the desktop and leaned forward to decipher the tiny, awkward handwriting.

Valens Valentinianus to Veatriz Sirupati, greetings.

He lifted his head and looked at her. "If this is a fake," he said, "I'll kill you. Do you understand?"

She nodded, as though threats were a familiar part of her daily routine. Fleetingly, he wondered about her life, but it was none of his business.

"Thanks," he said, and lifted his hand off the money-bag.

"Pleasure's all mine," she said. The bag was too big for her to lift one-handed (she had small, plump paws, like a frog). "What do you want with it, anyhow?" she added.

"Do you really want me to tell you?"

She didn't answer. It was obvious she hated him, for a wide variety of reasons. "Don't you go making trouble for the master," she said. "He's a proper gentleman, the Ducas."

Vaatzes sighed. "Fine," he said. "In that case, you take it back and I'll have the money."

She scowled at him and took a step backward toward the door. He smiled.

"Go away," he said.

She hated him for another two seconds, then left the room. He heard her feet hammering on the spiral stone staircase, and a door slamming. He didn't move. He sat, with just the tips of his fingers resting lightly on the edges of the parchment, which smelled powerfully of decaying vegetables. The urge to read it was painful, but he restrained himself, to prolong the pleasure. All his adult life he'd made weapons, in the service of the Perpetual Republic; the frames and arms and springs and mechanisms of mighty engines, whose mechanical advantage was capable of magnifying the strength of the human arm into a force impossible to defend against. He knew a good weapon when he saw one, or touched its working components. He also knew a little about love-letters, particularly those that the beloved never gets to read. He'd made the connection long ago, and knew that love is the most destructive weapon of all, the only problem being how to contain and channel it into something that can be spanned, aimed and loosed.

With the tips of his forefingers, he lifted the letter off the desktop. It was faintly translucent, being old parchment, scraped several times. Like a butcher breaking the carcass of a bird, levering the breast up off the ribcage, he folded back the corners and opened it.

My chess-playing mind tells me that what you need is something to take your mind off your troubles: a story, an observation, a discussion about silk-painting or the use of nature imagery in the elegaics of Haut Bessamoges. You want me to open a hidden door in the wall and show you a room where you can hide for a little while. Instead, my mind is busy with cunning schemes—how can the Vadani take the heat off Orsea of Eremia, given that the two nations hate each other like poison?

Vaatzes smiled. A man after his own heart, Duke Valens, though he'd probably dislike him intensely if they ever met face to face. He both admired and resented the way he could put into words things that he himself could only feel. Presumably Cantacusene felt the same way when he'd been humiliated in his own workshop by a superior craftsman. He dismissed the resentment (after all, Valens was working for him now, just as Cantacusene was, and a good supervisor respects his valuable employees). It was most definitely a letter he couldn't have written himself; cut from solid instead of painstakingly pinned, brazed, fabricated out of scrounged components. No wonder she was in love with him.

(He closed his eyes and tried to recall the memory of her face, glimpsed briefly at the meet before the Duke's boar-hunt. Not beautiful; pretty in an everyday sort of way. He loved her too, of course, but only because she was his best and most effective weapon. She was going to smash open the gates of Mezentia for him; he'd walk into the city on a siege-mound of corpses she'd raised for him. In the circumstances, the very least he could do was love her. Also, she reminded him of someone who was with him all the time.)

He read the rest of the letter, folded it carefully and put it in his inside pocket. Until everything was ready and he needed it, it was only fitting that he should carry it next to his heart, as lovers are supposed to do.

It was some time before Miel Ducas remembered that he was still in his bathrobe, and the hot water was going cold. Not that that mattered—he was the Ducas, and he could do what he liked in his own house—but the last thing he wanted to do was make a scene. The eccentricities of the nobility were valuable commodities in the town. The usual fabricated variety commanded a high enough price in alcohol, entertainment or sexual favors; he didn't like to think about the market value of a genuine Ducas story. Needless to say, Orsea wouldn't set any store by tavern gossip, but he was probably the only person in the duchy who didn't.

He opened the solar door slowly and carefully, and walked out into a corridor crammed with servants, all of them standing perfectly still and looking at him. It was worse than the scorpion bombardment, far worse than facing the wounded boar, because all his princely qualities of valor and dash were useless; he couldn't grab a falchion off the wall and massacre the lot of them. All he could do was walk straight past them, pretending he hadn't seen them. As soon as he turned the corner, he broke into a run.

As he'd anticipated, his bathwater was cold. He lowered himself in, washed briskly, clambered out and scrubbed himself dry with the towel (he couldn't remember having seen it before; it was a pale orange color with embroidered lilies and snowdrops, one of the most revolting things he'd ever seen. He remembered that the Duchess had recently sent him some linen as a thank-you present for arranging the hunt, but he couldn't believe for an instant that she could deliberately have chosen to buy something like that. Thinking about Veatriz reminded him of the letter; he closed his eyes and shuddered, as though a surgeon was pulling an arrowhead out of his stomach).

There had to be a perfectly rational explanation. He'd considered hiding it there, but had changed his mind or never got round to doing it. It had fallen out of the crack and was lying on the floor, hidden by the hem of the tapestry. He'd put it there, but changed his mind, moved it, and forgotten he'd done so. It had been completely devoured by moths.

Or someone had found it and taken it. He noticed something strange, and experimented by holding his arm straight out in front of him. His hand was shaking.

Should've burned it; should've given it to Orsea straight away; should have given it to her. But he hadn't. He'd tethered it, it had slipped the hobbles and escaped, and now it was loose. He tried to think who might have taken it, but his mind couldn't grip on the question, like cartwheels on thick ice. Nothing ever disappeared in the Ducas house, even though it was jammed and constipated with the accumulated valuable junk of generations. A light-fingered servant could steal a fortune in gold and silver plate, fabrics, ornaments, and be over the border free and clear before anybody noticed, but it had never happened in living memory; so why should anybody steal a small piece of parchment? Half the servants couldn't even read (but if they'd been told what to look for, that didn't signify).

Maybe someone had taken it to light a fire (but why go looking for kindling behind the tapestry nobody was allowed to touch, when there was a cellar full of dried twigs and brush?). The truth had him at bay, and he had nowhere to run to. Someone had known what to look for and where to look. It was self-evident; but it was also impossible, because nobody else in the house knew about that place.

He could burn the house down; but it stood to reason that the thief would've got rid of the loot as quickly as possible, so that wouldn't achieve anything.

Without knowing what he was doing, he dressed in the clothes laid out for him. The only sensible course of action would be to go to Orsea, straight away, and tell him the whole story. But if Orsea hadn't been given the letter yet, he'd refuse to believe it; he'd fly into a rage and burst into tears, and everything would get worse. He should go to Veatriz (and what would he tell her? I intercepted your letter. Why did you do that, Miel?). He should leave Eremia tonight and defect to the Mezentines. It depressed him utterly to think that that was probably the best idea he'd had so far.

He realized he was looking in a mirror. It was an old one, spattered with patches of dark gray tarnish, and in it all he could see was the face of an idiot. But that was all very well. It was also a reasonably lifelike portrait of the Ducas; and if it came to his word against somebody else's, who was Orsea going to believe?

He looked away; because on any other subject there could be no possibility of a doubt, but where Veatriz was concerned, he had to admit that he simply didn't know. Orsea had a memory too; he could remember when it was unthinkable that the Sirupati heiress would marry anybody except the Ducas, and wasn't it a bizarre but wonderfully convenient coincidence that the Ducas should be completely besotted with the girl? He knew Orsea better than anybody else, far better than she did. It was highly unlikely that a day passed when Orsea didn't remember that.

Or he could kill himself, and slide out of the problem that way.

On balance, it'd be better than defecting to the enemy, but he didn't want to. Besides, what became of him really didn't matter; it wasn't nearly as simple as that. He couldn't think of escaping, by treachery or death or running away and joining a camel-train to the Cure Hardy, if it meant leaving her in mortal peril.

(Mortal peril; hero language again. He cursed himself for an idiot. Heroism wouldn't help here, because this wasn't a last-ditch battle against the forces of evil, it was a bloody stupid mess. You can't defeat messes with the sword, or by feats of horsemanship, endurance or strategy. You've got to slither your way out of them, and slithering simply wasn't part of his armory of skills.)

Or I could simply wait and see what happens; and as and when the letter shows up, I can tell the truth.

He stared at that thought for a long time; it was also a mirror, in which he saw himself. *I'm Miel Ducas. I tell the truth, because I'm too feckless to lie.* He shook his head; that was too easy, and he didn't believe it. *I can't lie in the same way a fish can't breathe air. I was bred to do the right thing, always.*

The right thing would be to tell Orsea the truth, if the letter comes into his hands. But the right thing would mean that the disaster falls on Veatriz, who did the wrong thing, and that can't be allowed to happen. I did the right thing concealing the letter — it'd have been wrong to burn it straight away, because that would have been a betrayal of Orsea. Bloody shame I hid it where someone could find it, but that's simply incompetence, not a moral issue.

I'm Miel Ducas, and for the first time in my life I don't know what to do.

She found him in the cartulary, of all places. He was standing on a chair, tugging at a parchment roll that had got wedged between two heavy books. If he tugged any harder, she could see, half the shelf would come crashing down.

"Orsea," she said.

He jumped, staggered and hopped sideways off the chair, which fell over. She wanted to laugh; he'd always had a sort of catlike grace-in-clumsiness, an ability to fall awkwardly off things and land on his feet. As he turned and saw her, he looked no older than sixteen.

"You startled me," he said.

"Sorry." She smiled; he grinned. He'd never quite understood why she seemed to like him most when he did stupid things. He felt like a buffoon, nearly falling off a chair, but her smile was as warm as summer. "What were you doing up there, anyway?"

He frowned. "Your father had a map of the Cleito range," he said. "I remember him showing it to me once, years ago. I thought it might be in here somewhere."

The Cleito; that was where Miel had ambushed the Mezentines. "It wouldn't be here," she replied. "Have you looked in the small council room? He always used to keep his maps there."

The expression on his face told her it hadn't occurred to him to do that. "Thanks," he said. "That's where it'll be. Good job you told me, or I'd have pulled the place apart looking for it."

That had come out sounding like an accusation rather than praise, but they both knew what he'd meant by it. She carried on smiling, but she was doing it deliberately now. "Have you got a moment?" she asked.

"Of course." As he looked at her his face was completely open; and she was planning on leading him—not into a trap exactly, but to a place he probably wouldn't want to go. For a brief moment she hated herself for it. "Let's go into the garden," he said, as she hesitated. "I think it's stopped raining."

He led the way down the single flight of stairs. He always scampered down stairs, there was no other word for it. A duke shouldn't scamper, of course. She smiled again, at the back of his head, without realizing she was doing it.

The garden glistened after the rain, and she could smell wet leaves. That was almost enough to choke her.

"So?" he asked briskly. "What's up?"

"Oh, nothing." The answer came out in a rush, instinctive as a fish lunging at a baited hook. "Only," she went on, rallying her forces into a reserve, and paused for effect. "Orsea, I'm worried. About the war."

The look on his face was unbearable; it was guilt, because he'd let war and death come close enough to her to be felt. He was going to say, "It's all right," but he didn't, because he didn't tell lies.

"Me too," he mumbled. "That's why I was looking for that stupid map. General Vasilisca thinks—"

The hell with General Vasilisca. "Orsea," she said (she used his name like a rap across the knuckles). "What's going to happen to us if they get past the scorpions?"

He took a deep breath, put on his serious face, which always annoyed her. "In order to do that," he said, slowly, looking away; he always looked so *pompous* doing that, "they'd have to mount a direct assault, with artillery support. But our artillery would take out their artillery before they could neutralize the walls, which means their infantry would have to attack in the face of a scorpion bombardment. Basically, we'd be killing them until we ran out of bolts. It'd be thousands, maybe tens of thousands—" He stopped. He looked like he wanted to be sick. "Their army wouldn't do it, for one thing. They're mercenaries, not fanatics. They'd simply refuse."

"Orsea," she said.

"And even if they were crazy enough to do it," he went on, ignoring her, "they'd still have to conduct a conventional assault— scaling ladders and siege towers, against a full garrison, and the best defensive position in the world. There's every likelihood that we'd beat them off, provided they don't have artillery control. It's simple arithmetic, actually, there's tables and formulas and stuff in the books; the proper ratio of attackers to defenders necessary for taking a defended city. I think it's five to one, at least. And of course, we've got much better archers than they have."

"Orsea," she said again, and the strength leaked out of him. "What'd happen to us, if they won?"

He looked away, and she knew he was beaten already, in his mind. Part of her was furious at him for being so feeble, but she knew him too well. He didn't believe they could win, because he was in command. In a secret part of her mind, she offered thanks to Providence for Miel Ducas, who was twice the man Orsea was, and who (on balance) she'd never loved. "I don't know," he said. "That's the really horrible thing about this war, I don't actually know why they're doing it. You'd think they might have the common good manners to let us know, but apparently not."

(He knew why, of course. The huntsman doesn't send heralds or formal declarations of war to the wolf, the bear or the boar. Their relationship is so close, there's no need to explain.)

She came closer to him, but there was no tenderness in it. Instead, she felt like a predator. "I want you to listen to me," she said.

He looked bewildered. "Sure," he said.

"If the war goes badly," she said, and stopped. Her mouth felt like it was full of something soft and disgusting. "If things go wrong, I don't want to stay here and be killed. I don't. I was a hostage all those years, because Father had to play politics to keep us going when the Vadani were closing in all the time, and every day when I woke up and realized where I was, I knew that if something went wrong, I could be killed and that'd be that. I was just a child, Orsea, and I had to live with that all the time. I was *frightened*. I can't stand being frightened anymore. It's not noble and strong to be brave when you can't fight and defend yourself. I was brave all those years, for Father and the Duchy, and I won't do it again. If the Mezentines are going to take the city, I don't want to be here. I want to run away, Orsea, do you understand? Me getting killed won't make anything better for anybody. I want to *escape*. Can you understand that?"

He was staring at her, and she thought of the old fairy tale where the handsome young hunter marries a strange, wild girl from outside the village, and on the wedding night she turns out to be a wolf-spirit disguised as a human. "You want to leave," he said, very quietly. "Fine."

Most of all she wanted to hit him, for being so annoying. "I want *us* to leave," she shouted at him. "You don't think I'd go without you? Don't be so stupid. I want *us* to get out of here before it's too late. Leave the Ducas and the Phocas and the great lords to defend the city, if they really feel they have to. I care about the people, of course I do, but there's nothing you or I can do to help them, and if we're killed, we're dead. That'd be *pointless*." She took a deep breath, ignoring the look on his face. "Orsea, I want you to care about us for once, for you and me. Two more dead bodies rotting in the sun won't make any difference to the world, but we could escape, go somewhere. I don't care about not being the Duchess anymore. I don't care what I do. But staying here just because—"

"Because it's the right thing to do," he said.

She closed her eyes, because she wanted to scream. "Fine," she said. "Just suppose we do the wrong thing, for once in our lives. Well, that'd be awful, wouldn't it? We might get into trouble for it, something bad might happen to us. Something worse than getting killed by the Mezentines."

She was losing control of herself, she could feel it, and he'd never seen her do that before. Of course not. He hadn't been there, the second time her father had sent her away, and they had had to drag her out of the house. She'd clung to the doors and the newel-post of the stairs with both hands; her nurse had had to prise her locked fingers apart.

"Where could we go?" he said, in a tiny voice, strained through bewilderment, horror and disgust. "There isn't anywhere. Nobody'd have us."

"They don't have to know it's us," she spat at him. "Come on, who the hell is going to recognize you and me? We could go..." She hesitated. "We could go to the Vadani. It's the last place anybody would think to look for us. I could get a red dress."

He grinned feebly. "You're too young to be a trader."

"My sister's a bloody trader," she said, far more forcefully than made sense. "She's over there now. She'll help us, she's got pots of money. Maybe even the Duke, Valens." A tiny hesitation, as though she had to think before she remembered his name. "I don't know, maybe it'd be expedient for him to shelter us. Doesn't matter. I'd rather sleep in doorways than be dead, wouldn't you?"

In the fairy tale, the young huntsman had loved his exotic bride very much; but when her lovely face melted and stretched and shrunk into the wolf's mask, he'd grabbed his falchion from the wall and cut off her head with one swift stroke. It had never occurred to him that he might be able to live with the wolf, who probably (on balance) loved him very much. That possibility hadn't occurred to her when she first heard the story; probably to nobody else who'd ever been told it. Not enough room in one cottage for two predators.

"Actually," he said, "no."

"Orsea!" (And she wanted to laugh, because she realized she sounded just like her mother.) "That's just posturing. Besides," she went on, trying to pull back out of the muzzle and the long ears and the round black eyes, "if you really want to do what's best for your people, you've got to stay alive. Once the Mezentines have gone away, they'll need you more than ever."

"The few that're left."

"Yes, that's right, the few that manage to hide or run away; but you can help them, you can't help the rest of them, they'll be dead." Her head was splitting; she could hardly hear herself think. And she wasn't putting the argument across terribly well. It had come too late, like cavalry returning from looting the enemy camp to find that the battle's been lost while they were away. "If you love me," she said.

He looked at her. He wasn't at bay anymore, he'd just given up. Sometimes an animal does that, according to King Fashion; he stands and looks at you, and that's the time to jump in and kill him. A heartbeat or so before she asked the question, the answer would have been yes (shouted so loud, with such furious intensity, they could've heard it in Mezentia). Now, because of the question, the answer would be, on balance, no.

"Fine," she said, and walked out.

Boiled down to productivity figures, which was how he liked it, things were going very well. Workforce increased by forty percent, productivity up sixty percent; they were actually turning out finished scorpions faster than the ordnance factory at home. Not that it could last, because pretty soon they'd run out of timber and quarter plate and spring steel and three-eighths rod — by his most recent calculations, ten days before the city fell — but that didn't matter. It wasn't as though he was planning on building a career here.

With three day shifts and two night shifts, the place was never quiet. That was something he missed, the peace and solitude of his room at the top of the tower, when everybody had gone home and he had the place to himself. There was a different kind of solitude now, but it had no nutritional value. Still, it wouldn't be for long.

Instead of the tower room (too many people knew to look for him there) he'd taken to hiding in the small charcoal store. Which was ludicrous; he was in charge of the place, it was his factory, he had no business hiding anywhere from anybody. But there were times when he needed to think, work out figures, deal with small modifications to the design, improvements or fixes. Also, he was sick to death of Eremians (so pale, so stupid).

After several false starts he'd contrived to smuggle a chair down there. He was working on a plan to get a table to go with it, and maybe even a better lamp, but it was still in its early stages. For now, he had the chair to sit in, and the wan light of a reed wick floating in thrice-reused tallow. Strip off the garbage, and what more could a man ask?

He knew the answer to that, and he was working on it (but all in good time). The immediate concern was the wire-drawing plates, which were going to have to be either refurbished or replaced within the next three days. It was a ridiculous, fatuous thing to have to think about. In the real world, in the City, all he'd need to do was send a requisition down to the stores for two eighteen-by-tens of inch plate. But there was no such thing as inch plate in Civitas Eremiae. Instead, he'd have to take six men off the forge and set them to bashing down a bloom of iron by hand. Six man-days wasted, and that was before they started trying to punch the holes.

If only we weren't at war with the Mezentines, we could send out for inch plate from the Foundrymen's; and in the City, when they said inch, they meant inch, not inch-and-a-thirty-second-in-places-and-twenty-nine-thirty-seconds-in-others. Really, he was doing the world a service, because a nation that can't read a simple caliper isn't fit to survive.

But... He scowled into the darkness. A wide tolerance, a whole sixteenth of an inch of abomination didn't actually matter in this case, because a wire-plate is just a primitive chunk of iron with a hole in it (he wanted it to matter, but it didn't). Even so, six man-days lost would cost the defenders a scorpion. One scorpion could loose twelve bolts a minute, seven hundred bolts an hour. At an estimated thirty percent efficiency rating, the wire-plates would save the lives of two hundred and thirty Mezentines —

He heard a boot scrape on the stairs, and looked up. Just when he'd thought he was safe, but apparently not. "I'm in here," he called out, "did you want me for something?" It seemed they didn't, because there was no reply. That was all right, then.

He tried to go back to his calculation, seven hundred divided by three, but he'd lost the thread. The lamp guttered. He pulled out his penknife and set off to trim the wick, crunching and staggering awkwardly on the piles of charcoal underfoot.

The wick was fine; must just have been a waft of air from somewhere. He straightened up, and heard another soft crunch, just like the ones he'd been making himself as he clambered over the charcoal heaps.

Of course, he had no time to shape a plan or design a mechanism. Instead, he stooped, grabbed the lamp and threw it as hard as he could. For a very short moment it was a tiny comet in the darkness, then a little ball of fire, then nothing. He heard the tinkle of the lamp breaking, and another noise, a soft grunt.

He had his penknife, one thin inch of export-grade Mezentine steel; and he had the darkness, and the sound of crushed charcoal. It wasn't much, but it would have to be everything.

If he moved, the hunter would hear him; and the other way round, of course, but the hunter presumably had fearsome weapons and great skill. He tried to think his way into the enemy's mind. He would have to be quick, both to hear and to act. He waited.

As soon as he heard the soft grinding, squashing noise of charcoal underfoot, he took a step—sideways, to the right, a random choice, but unpredictability was his best ally against the hunter's approach, which would be methodical and progressive. He reached out as far as he could with his left hand, keeping his right close to his body. Each time the hunter moved, he took a step of his own. The hardest part was controlling his breathing. Fear made him want to pant; instead he drew in air as smoothly as a good workman turning the lathe carriage handle to keep the cut fine, and let it go at precisely the same rate. That actually helped a little; the fog in his head started to clear, and he could see his thoughts, big and slow as a ship drifting in moonlight.

Now he could begin to work out the logical pattern. Someone must've told the hunter where to find him, so it was reasonable to assume the hunter knew the shape of the room. He recalled the dimensions, twenty feet by ten, with one door in the southwest corner. The pattern would therefore be from side to side. A man zigzagging down the length of the room with his arms outstretched would have a fair chance of touching another man in the dark, even if the prey was flat to the wall. Logical behavior for the prey would be to crouch and become as small as possible; logical meant predictable, and so that was what he couldn't do. Instead, his best course of action—

He'd moved too far, two steps to his enemy's one, because his own crunch wasn't echoed. He cringed at his own stupidity, caused by a failure to concentrate. Instinct yelled at him to make a charge, either to find and kill or to escape. He made an effort and wrestled the instinct down.

His best course of action was to become the hunter instead of the prey (because the first question the assassin would ask his inside source would be, *is he likely to be armed?* and the answer would've been *no*). It was unfortunate that he knew absolutely nothing about fighting; the last time he'd fought, he'd been nine, and he'd lost conclusively. Mezentines didn't fight. Of course, he wasn't a Mezentine anymore.

But he had the darkness on his side; also the fact that the last charcoal delivery had been late, and two night shifts had had to take their fuel from the reserve store. Obviously, they'd have loaded from nearest the door; but if they shoveled in a straight line, as reasonable men might be assumed to do, would there not be a clear, therefore silent path a shovel's breadth up the line of the southern wall? The enemy was between him and the door, there was no real chance of slipping by except by fluke, but if he could walk unheard...

Time was running low; he made a fair estimate of how long the pattern would take to execute, based on an average length of stride and his own progress. By now, both of them had to be fairly close to the middle of the room, but if he could make it across to the south wall, he'd have a little advantage, which would be all he'd need.

He moved with the crunch, and as his foot came down he heard another grunt. But it was in the wrong place, too far back. There were two of them.

Well, of course, there would be. The Perpetual Republic were no cheapskates, they wouldn't send only one man, like a lone hero charged with slaying a dragon. That made the south wall essential to his chances of survival, because the man on the door would be stationary; King Fashion would've called him the stop, while his colleague would be the beater. The crunch came and he moved with it, but his foot made no sound. He reached out with his right hand, a desperate risk but forced by necessity, and felt stone.

Now he had to stay still. If, by sheer bad luck, the hunter's pattern happened to bring him here, all he could hope for was the random advantage of the encounter. He wondered how perceptive the hunter was; would he notice the absence of the double footfall, and would he interpret it correctly? On balance, Vaatzes hoped his enemy was clever but not brilliant.

He heard two more steps, then a long pause. The missing sound had been noticed and was being duly considered. Because he was standing still, at last he could use his enemy's sound to place him. Excellent; he was nearer to the middle than the south wall, so the pattern should take him clear away, northeast or northwest didn't matter. Very carefully, as though he was scribing a line, Vaatzes began to edge down the south wall toward the door.

Tactically, of course, he was taking a substantial risk, now that he was in the middle between his two enemies. If he couldn't get through or past the stop quickly enough, the beater would be on him from the flank or the rear. He'd never read any military manuals so he was working from first principles, but he could see all too clearly how a clever plan badly or unluckily carried out must be worse than simple, stolid standing and fighting. Too late to be sensible now, though.

Four more crabbed paces, by his calculations; then he stooped, careful of his balance, and groped for a fair-sized chunk of charcoal. He found one and tossed it high in the air. The noise it made when it landed was all wrong, of course—it sounded like a lump of charcoal landing on a charcoal-covered floor—but all he needed to achieve was a moment's bewilderment.

A moment, of course, was all he had. He allowed enough time for the stop to turn and face the noise; that'd be instinct, and now he knew fairly well how his enemy would be standing, the direction his head and shoulders would be facing in. He took a long stride forward and another to the left, crunching his foot down hard in the murrain of charcoal beside the cleared path. Then he brought his right arm across in a wide, fast arc.

He felt an impact, and something hot and wet splashed in his face. It was all he could do not to shout in triumph, because he'd plotted it all out so precisely, inch-perfect, making the target turn so his neck-vein would be presented at the optimum angle to his sweeping cut, and here was his enemy's blood on his face to prove he'd got it right. No time for that now; with his left hand he reached out, grabbed, felt his fingers close on empty air, quickly recalculated allowing for the dying man falling to the ground, grabbed again and felt his fingertips snag in loose cloth. All the dying man's weight was pulling on his fingers, mechanical advantage was against him, but he managed to find the brute strength to haul the mass across and behind him. The knife was no good to him now. He opened his fingers and let it fall as his right hand groped for the door. He found the bar handle just as loud crunches behind him told him that the beater was coming for him. Now it was just running, something he'd never been any great shakes at.

As he wrenched the door open, the light burned him. The gap between door and frame was almost wide enough to give him clearance, but it wouldn't grow. He'd botched moving the body, and it was fouling the door. The urge was to glance over his shoulder and take a look at the beater's face but he hadn't got time. He crushed himself through the gap (like drifting a badly filed hole square with the big hammer), found the bottom step with his foot and pushed himself into a sprint. Breath was a problem, he'd squeezed too much of it out of himself getting through the doorway; his current plan was firmly based on yelling as loud as possible, so that people would come and rescue him before the beater could catch him. But the best he could manage was a soft woof, like a sleepy dog.

Best estimate was that the beater was in the doorway, while he was only four steps up the stairs; there were twelve steps, and if the beater grabbed his ankle and pulled him down, it'd all have been a waste of effort and ingenuity. He heard the beater say something—just swearing, probably—which suggested that luck had given him a little more time. He cleared the top step, filled his lungs, and yelled.

After the silence, where a soft crunch had been so loud, the echo of his voice in the stone stairwell made his head swim. But he felt fingertips brush the calf of his leg, gentle as a tentative lover. Even as he lunged toward the open air he was calculating: assuming the hunter had arms of average length and taking on trust his estimate of the length of his lower leg, from heel to knee-joint, he was safe from a dagger of no more than twelve inches, but a riding-sword, falchion, hanger or hand-axe would be the death of him.

He was in the courtyard; and here was where his plan foundered and crashed. He'd been working on the strict assumption that once he was clear of the stairwell he'd be safe, because the courtyard would be thronged with his stalwart employees, hurrying to answer his shout of distress. Accordingly, he hadn't troubled to plan beyond the threshold of the light. Foolish; here on the level, in the light, it was his ability to run against his enemy's. As if in confirmation, he felt a hand tighten on his shoulder like a clamp, drawing him back and slowing him down.

He hadn't expected to feel anything else, because the knife or the short sword would be properly sharp, and he'd be dead before his body could register the pain. Wrong; instead, he felt the buttons of his shirt give way, and the lapel pulling back over the ball of his shoulder. He could have laughed out loud for joy if he'd had time and breath. It was only a moral victory, of course. The courtyard was empty; they were all hard at work at their anvils and benches, as of course they should be. He'd trained them too well.

The next thing he registered mystified him. It was the paving-slabs of the courtyard floor rushing up to meet him, and the solid, painful contact of stone on his face. He'd fallen; he was lying face down on the ground. Not that it mattered, but...

He heard grunting, then a yell of pain, swearing, shouts, another yell, and the bump of a dead weight falling fairly close. He pushed at the ground with the palms of his hands, bounced himself upright and swung round.

He saw a face that was vaguely familiar, one of the carpenters, whose name there'd been no point using up memory on. The carpenter was kneeling on something; on a man's body, his knee was on the man's neck, and other men whose faces he couldn't see were bending or kneeling over the same body, trying to do something to it that called for effort and strength. "Are you all right?" the carpenter asked; he looked shocked and bewildered, and his face was cut. Vaatzes widened the scope of his vision and saw a short sword (to be precise, a Mezentine naval hanger) lying about a foot from the body's outstretched hand. Strange; more than twelve inches, so he ought to be dead. But (it occurred to him, as a flood of fear and shock swept through him) he wasn't.

"Don't kill him," he heard himself say, "I want him alive." At the same time, he rebuked himself for melodrama; also, what did he want with a Mezentine Compliance assassin? Nothing; correction, he wanted the names of his inside men, the ones who'd told him about the charcoal cellar. It was very important not to let those names get away.

One of the men whose faces he couldn't see mumbled an apology, and Vaatzes noticed that the assassin had stopped moving.

"Is he dead?" he asked.

"Fell on his own knife," someone replied. Knife? He'd had a knife as well as the hanger; a whole new variable he'd omitted to consider. Negligent. Really, he didn't deserve to be alive.

"What the fuck was all that about?" someone asked.

Later, sitting in the window of the main gallery recovering from a horrific bout of shaking and nausea, Vaatzes decided there couldn't have been a knife, because he'd felt the hunter's left hand grabbing at him on the stairs. That helped the world make sense again. He sent someone to fetch the man who'd answered his question. While he was waiting for him to arrive, he called half a dozen men off the bloom anvil and told them to form a half-circle facing him, about five yards back.

When he saw the man again, he recognized him. He even knew his name—Fesia Manivola, second foreman in the grinding shop. A pity, because he was a good worker.

"You wanted to see me?" Manivola was relaxed, inquisitive, friendly.

Vaatzes nodded; it was the cue for the six bloom-hammerers to close in behind Manivola. "You killed him, didn't you?" he said. "He didn't fall on his own knife like you said. You stabbed him so he couldn't give you away."

Manivola denied it, twice, and then one of the bloom-workers broke his neck. They dragged his body out into the yard, laid it next to the two assassins to wait for the arrival of the examining magistrate, who was needed for various formalities. Once they were over, the magistrate asked him the question he'd been asking himself: why did you have him killed straight away? For all you know, there could've been more than one.

"I know," he replied. "But that was enough. If there's more, they'll know they're safe now, but it's too dangerous to try again." He pulled a face. "I've already lost one key worker and there's a war on. If I found out the foundry chief and the foreman of the tempering shop were in on it as well, I'd have to close down a shift."

Either the magistrate saw the logic in that or he knew better than to argue with the man who made the scorpions that had won the great victory. He wrote things in his little book and went away. Shortly after dark a cart came for the bodies; according to the magistrate, they'd be tipped down a disused drain, and nobody need ever know.

In the middle of the first night shift, a messenger came to take him to see the Ducas. He'd been expecting that. He rode in a cart up to the shabby door of the Ducas house, and followed the messenger across courts, quadrangles and cloisters to a small room, by his calculations leading off the northeast corner of the great hall. He told Miel Ducas about Compliance, though he was fairly sure he knew the salient points already.

"The only surprise," he went on, "is that they waited so long. Usual procedure is to kill a defector as soon as possible."

Miel Ducas nodded. "How do you account for the delay?" he asked.

"Not sure," Vaatzes replied truthfully. "My guess is, once they heard about the scorpions we shot up the wagon train with and realized they were homemade, they knew they needed to put me out of action. But that doesn't explain why they haven't tried before."

The Ducas frowned. "So that's it, then. It's a mystery."

"Yes." Vaatzes smiled grimly. "And I'm not complaining. But I was very lucky indeed. I don't know anything about hand-to-hand combat, or any of that stuff."

"Maybe you should learn," the Ducas replied, as anticipated. Vaatzes acknowledged and moved on.

"We'll need guards now, obviously," he said. "It'll slow up loading and unloading, and it won't actually do any good. If they had Manivola helping them—"

"That's the accomplice?"

Vaatzes nodded. "Wouldn't have thought it of him," he said. "But we'll have guards anyway, just for the hell of it."

"All right. Do you want visitors searched for weapons?"

"In a factory?" Vaatzes laughed. "He could pick a tool off any bench that'd serve as well as any weapon; hammer, saw, whatever. And it'd take too much time. No, I was thinking of a different approach."

The Ducas waited, then said, "Well?"

Vaatzes said: "Normally, I'd make my own, but there isn't time. Do you happen to have such a thing as a brigandine coat?"

The Ducas dipped his head briskly. "Several," he said. "About three dozen, actually. Mine wouldn't fit you, but I'm sure I had a short ancestor at some point in the last three centuries. Wonderful how much useless junk you inherit; and of course we never throw anything away, because everything we acquire is nothing but the best, far too good to part with. I'll have it sent round as soon as possible."

"Thank you," Vaatzes said. "And nobody must know, of course, or there'd be no point."

"Naturally. And you really should find time for some simple lessons: single sword, sword and buckler, bare hand and dagger. My cousin Jarnac's sergeant-at-arms is the man you need. I'll talk to Jarnac when I've got a moment."

"That'd be kind of you," Vaatzes replied. He was looking hard for some sign in the Ducas' face, but what he saw there, in the eyes and the line of the mouth, could have been simple stress and fatigue from running a country at war. "You've been doing things for me ever since I came here. I'm grateful."

The Ducas shrugged. "It's thanks to you we've got a chance in this war," he said. "The scorpions..." He shook his head. "A chance," he repeated. "I don't know."

Vaatzes studied him for a moment, and saw a man in two minds. Half of him knew that Civitas Eremiae would inevitably fall; the other half couldn't see how it possibly could. Mostly, though, he saw a man who'd been tired for so long he was getting used to it. "The Republic's never lost a war," he said, "but there's always a first time. I think our best hope are the Potters and the Drapers; and the Foundrymen, of course."

It took the Ducas a moment to realize he was talking about Guilds. "Go on," he said.

"The Foundrymen are more or less in the ascendant at the moment," Vaatzes explained, "or at least they were when I left. There's never a deep underlying reason why one Guild gets to dominate. It's about personalities and political skill rather than fundamental issues; mostly, I think, because there's virtually nothing we don't all agree about. But the Foundrymen have been on top for longer than usual, and the Potters and Drapers have been trying to put them down for a while, and they're annoyed and upset because so far they've failed. The Foundrymen will have wanted this war because victory always makes the government popular, and we always win. But if we don't win, or at least not straight away, so it's costing lots of money and interfering with business, there's a good chance it'll bring down the Foundrymen. The Drapers and Potters will therefore want to make out that any major reverse is a genuine defeat—they'll say the Republic's been beaten for the first time in history, and it's all the Foundrymen's fault, and we should never have gone to war in the first place. Meanwhile the Foundrymen will be unhappy because they'll be taking men off civilian work to increase the production in the ordnance factory, so that'll be costing them money; they'll want to get rid of the present leadership and end the war so as to limit the damage before the Drapers and Potters have a chance to overthrow them. Also, the Drapers and Potters will have a fair degree of support, because most of the Guilds do a lot of export business with the old country, where the mercenaries come from. If thousands of mercenaries are killed in the war, it'll be very bad for their trade over there. It's possible to win this war, provided you can do as much damage as possible; kill as many men as you can, destroy as much equipment, cost them as much money as possible. As long as they want to fight you, they'll never give up; but if you can make them decide that the war isn't worth the cost and effort, you're in with a chance. It's not like your war with the Vadani, where you hated each other. Hate doesn't come into it with the Republic, that's the key as far as you're concerned. They make war for their own reasons. It's always all to do with them, not really anything about you. You're like the quarry in a hunt, rather than a mortal enemy; you don't hate the animals you hunt, you do it for the meat and the glory. When you're not worth hunting anymore, when you're more trouble than it's worth, they'll call it a day and go home."

Needless to say, the Ducas was as good as his word. The brigandine coat arrived the next morning, in a straw-filled barrel. The first thing Vaatzes looked for was a maker's mark, and he found it, in exactly the right place; the fifth rivet-head in from the armpit, right-hand side, second row down, was stamped with a tiny raised letter F, for Foundrymen. That meant it was Guild-made, and therefore complied exactly with the relevant specification.

The specification for a brigandine coat consists of two thousand, seven hundred and forty-six small, thin plates of best hard-ening steel, drawn to a spring temper. The plates are sandwiched, overlapping each other, between two layers of strong canvas, held in place by one-sixteenth-inch copper rivets; they're also wired and riveted to each other to make sure they move perfectly with every action of the wearer's body, so that at no time is it possible to drive the point of an ordinary sewing needle between the joints. The jacket is covered on the outside with middle-weight hard-wearing velvet, and lined inside with six layers of linen stuffed with lambs-wool and quilted into one-inch diamonds. The finished coat contains ten thousand, nine hundred and eighty-four rivets, weighs six pounds four ounces, will turn a cavalryman's lance or an arrow from a hundred-and-twenty-pound bow, should be as comfortable as a well-cut gentleman's doublet and shouldn't be noticeable when worn under an ordinary day-jacket. The Linen Armorers' Guild produces a hundred and twelve of them a year, of which ninety-six go for export.

Vaatzes lifted it out of the barrel, brushed away the straw, and held it out at arm's length. He'd never actually seen one before, al-though he knew the specification by heart. It was strange, here in this barbarous and unsatisfactory place, finally to find himself in the presence of perfection; as though a prophet or visionary had spent his whole life searching in the wilderness for enlightenment, only to find it, having abandoned the search, in a grubby market town, sitting on a toilet.

He laid it flat on the workbench in front of him, and ran his fingertips over the velvet before slowly unfastening the seventeen brass buttons. For one horrible moment, as he drew it across his shoulders, he was afraid it wouldn't fit. Once he was inside it, however, it closed in around him like water engulfing a diver. He could just feel a slight weight on his shoulders and chest, and a very gentle hug as he buttoned it up; just enough to let him know that he was now as perfectly safe as it's possible to be in an imper-fect world, his body's security guaranteed by the absolute wisdom and skill of the Perpetual Republic. He'd heard someone say once that a Guild coat would even turn a scorpion bolt; that was, of course, impossible, but there was a part of him deep down that was inclined to believe it. It wasn't the steel or the skill with which the rivets had been closed; it was the specification, the pattern that drew the thousands of plates together and made them move as one unbroken, unbreakable whole, like the City that had made them. The coat wouldn't protect him against scorpions, because even though the steel stayed unpierced, the shock would smash his bones to splinters and pulp his internal organs. That didn't matter, however, because it would be him that had failed rather than the coat. His own frailty in no way invalidated the consummate virtue of Specification; just as the death of one citizen doesn't kill a city.

He smiled. The irony was exact, precise, fitting as closely as the coat. His safety guaranteed by the City that was trying to kill him, he could now carry on unhindered with his design to bring that City to ruin, and all perfection with it. All he needed now was to be taught to kill by the Ducas family, and the symmetry would be complete.

20

Since the first army had unaccountably been exterminated, it was just as well that the second army arrived earlier than anticipated, thanks to an unusually strong tailwind. If it hadn't been for the defeat and the massacre, their arrival would have been a logistical disaster. There wouldn't have been nearly enough food, blankets, tents or equipment for twelve thousand men arriving a week ahead of schedule; there'd have been chaos, and the whole venture would've teetered on the edge of failure.

Thanks, however, to the Eremians and their homemade scorpions, the stores and magazines held ample supplies for seven thousand men who weren't going to be needing them after all. To the clerks and administrators of the Treasury and Necessary Evil, it was a source of quiet satisfaction that the crisis was averted and all that expensive food, clothing and equipment wouldn't go to waste after all. In the event, the only problem posed by the early arrival of the second army that didn't effectively solve itself was transport, and that was no big deal. Unlike other shipments of imported goods, mercenaries can transport themselves. They have legs, and can walk.

The commanding officer of the new army, Major-General Sthoe Melancton, didn't see it quite like that. He'd been promised ox-carts to shift his men and their gear from Lonazep to the City. It was in the contract, he pointed out, so it was his right; also, his men were in prime condition, ready for the long march up the mountains. An unscheduled route march to the capital would inevitably result in wear and tear on footwear, vehicles and equipment that had not been allowed for in the original agreement. Further, it would mean an extra four days' service, for which he wanted time and a half. The Republic replied by pointing out that by arriving early, he was in fundamental breach of contract, time inevitably being of the essence in any contract for services, and that the failure to provide the agreed transport was entirely the result of his own breach, therefore not the Republic's fault. If anybody had a right to compensation and damages, in fact, it was the Republic; however, they were prepared to waive their claim in the interests of friendly cooperation. General Melancton rejoined by pleading that the tailwind was an unpredictable outside agency, not party to the contract, and therefore not his responsibility or his fault. The Republic countered by citing precedents from mercantile and shipping case-law. Melancton refused to accept Mezentine precedents, arguing that the contract had been finalized in his own country, whose law therefore applied to it. That argument was easily defeated by reference to the document itself, which clearly stated that the agreement was governed by Mezentine law. Melancton gave way with a certain degree of grace. The soldiers marched.

They were met just outside the City by the artillery train. It was at this point that Melancton found out what had become of his compatriots in the first army. Afterward, it was generally agreed that he took the news better than had been expected. After a long moment of silent reflection, he told the representatives of Necessary Evil who'd broken the news to him that he was a man of his word and a professional, and he would do his job or else (here he was observed to dab a drop of sweat away from the side of his nose) die trying. He then asked a large number of detailed questions about the level of artillery support he could expect to receive, all of which the Mezentines were able to answer to his satisfaction.

He thanked them politely and withdrew to confer with his senior staff.

In accordance with the ancient and honorable traditions of their craft, the merchants stayed in Civitas Eremiae until almost the last moment; and when they left, they took with them substantial quantities of small, high-value goods which the more pessimistic citizens had been only too pleased to exchange at a loss for hard cash. The general feeling was that it was better, on balance, that the merchants had them for a song than to keep them for the looters to prise out of their dead fingers.

All but one of the merchant caravans headed for the Vadani border by the shortest possible road. The exception, however, turned in a quite unexpected direction, on a course that seemed likely to leave her stranded and dying of thirst in the great desert that formed the civilized world's only defense against the Cure Hardy. What became of her, nobody knew or cared much. It was assumed that she was headed that way because the Mezentines wouldn't be taking that road in a hurry. Those sufficiently curious to speculate about the subject guessed that she had a retreat somewhere on the edge of the desert, where she planned to hole up until the war was over and it was safe to come out. The last recorded sighting of her was, curiously enough, by a column of Cure Hardy light cavalry, heading north to offer their services to the Mezentines in the coming war. How they came to be there, nobody knew and nobody liked to ask. The official explanation was that they'd come the long way round, enduring months of hardship and privation threading their way through the mountain passes that would have defeated an army of significant size — they were, after all, only one squadron of two hundred men. If it occurred to anybody that if that were the case they'd had to have set off long before the Guild Assembly had even considered the possibility of a war, they kept their hypotheses to themselves.

*   *   *

The arrival of outriders from the Cure Hardy squadron was like rain on parched fields to Melancton and his liaison committee from Necessary Evil. Negotiations had broken down and been patched up over and over again, always foundering on the vexed issue of skirmishers. Melancton hadn't brought any with him, because the contract hadn't specified them; there had been an ample contingent with the first army, so there was no need. With the threat of a scorpion ambush hanging over him, he absolutely refused to move across the border without an advance guard of light, fast, expendable scouts, which the Mezentines were not in a position to provide. The Cure Hardy were perfectly suited to the role. They came as the answer to a prayer; which was why asking them how they came to be available at such short notice wasn't considered, or else was dismissed with pointed references to gift horses' teeth.

To those who could be bothered to ask, the newcomers de-clared that they were a privateer war-band from the Doce Votz, under the command of one Pierh Leal, an obscure off-relation of the ruling family. They were perfectly willing to ride ahead of the advancing army, keeping an eye out for scorpion emplacements (it was highly unlikely they had any idea what a scorpion looked like, but it was assumed they'd find out the hard way soon enough) and declared that their speed and agility would preserve them from anything the war machines could throw at them. Perhaps some of the members of the liaison committee felt a slight degree of unease at the speed with which the outriders returned with the rest of the squadron; it argued that the Cure Hardy were adept at moving very quickly through even the most hostile terrain. But their ar-rival meant that the second expeditionary force could at last set out, and that came as a relief in the City, particularly to the of-ficials of the Treasury. Melancton gave the Cure Hardy a day's start, then followed.

Much to his displeasure, he'd come to the conclusion after ex-haustive debate that he had no alternative but to follow the same route as his predecessors, up the Butter Pass and on to the main road as far as Palicuro. After that, he had options, or at least al-ternatives, but he declared that he intended to keep an open mind until he reached Palicuro. After a slow start, due in part to a brisk and unseasonable cloudburst, he picked up speed in the middle and late afternoon, and was on time for his first scheduled rendez-vous with the Cure Hardy at nightfall.

The scouts had very little to say for themselves. They claimed to have ridden a full day ahead of the edge of the search zone Me-lancton had assigned them, and to have seen no sign of the enemy, with or without war engines. Melancton was highly skeptical about these assertions, but had no choice but to rely on them and press on. The logistical support he'd insisted on before starting out was all in place, but he nevertheless wasn't inclined to dawdle and risk running short of supplies, thereby courting the same sort of disasters that had done for Beltista Eiconodoulus. Regrettably, this meant that he couldn't afford to wait for the artillery, which was making heavy weather of the road up the mountains and was believed to be at least half a day behind schedule. After a certain amount of soul-searching, he resolved to press on regardless. Artil-lery dismantled and packed on wagons wouldn't be any use to him if he was ambushed by scorpions in a narrow pass; in fact, they'd compound any disaster by falling into the hands of the Eremians. By keeping the artillery separate and behind him, he hoped to guard against that particular nightmare above all others.

The next two days proved that the Cure Hardy were reliable informants. For reasons best known to themselves, the enemy had failed to take advantage of two perfect locations for ambushes, both of them narrow bottle canyons through which Melancton had no option but to pass. This omission played on his nerves more than a clear sighting would have done; to an army already lacking in self-confidence, the enemy is never more unnerv-ing than when he's invisible. Resisting an almost overpowering urge to slow down, wait for the artillery and build redoubts to hide in until he found out exactly what the Eremians were up to, he pressed on. During the course of the next two days the scouts reported two possible sightings of lone Eremian horsemen, apparently watching the army from a distance of several miles. Of an army or scorpions, they'd seen no trace. The next day, they rode right up to the outskirts of Palicuro, and reported back that the village was apparently deserted.

Once again, they were proved right. In fact, Palicuro was more than deserted; overnight it had been burned to ash and charcoal and the village cistern had been fouled with the proceeds of the village's muckheaps and middens. Melancton had known better than to rely on being able to find food for his men and forage for his horses there, but he was disappointed nevertheless; as a result he'd have enough to get to Civitas Eremiae, but if the Mezentines wanted him to dig in under the walls for a siege, they'd have to send him a large supply train. Otherwise he risked the indignity of the well-fed defenders throwing their crusts and cabbage waste to his men out of pity.

Dispatches containing these observations arrived unexpectedly on the desk of Lucao Psellus early one morning, at a stage in his career when he'd pretty much convinced himself that his fellow commissioners believed he was dead, or had retired to the suburbs to grow sunflowers and keep bees. He'd given up trying to find out what was going on, or what they wanted him to do. Nobody was ever available to talk to him, his memos went unanswered, and copies of reports and minutes had stopped coming a long time ago. He nearly wept with joy to know they still remembered who he was.

With the dispatches was a curt note requiring him to expedite the supply train as requested. That he could do. It would involve a careful balancing of the three basic elements out of which all administration is ultimately formed: time, money and fear. Not many people, even full-time professional Guild officers, really understood the complex and fascinating interplay between these three monumental forces, but Psellus had been experimenting with them in different combinations and ratios for years, like a methodical alchemist. At last they'd given him a job he could do.

Of the unholy trinity, the most fundamental is money, since nothing can happen without it. Accordingly, he walked across two quadrangles and up and down six flights of stairs, and surprised his old friend Maniacis in the payments room, where he was working at his checkerboard.

It was, in its way, a beautiful thing; an enormous oak table, the sort that kings and barons in the barbarian countries would sit at to feast and drink, whose surface was inlaid with thousands of juxtaposed bone and ebony plates, all of them exactly the same size, about an inch and a half square. At the end of each row was a number, a multiple of ten. At the narrow end of the table sat Maniacis, a pile of wax tablets in front of him, a wooden pot at his elbow, a miniature rake with a long thin stem in his hand. Whenever he needed to make a calculation, he took small silver disks, like coins, from the pot and started laying them out on the squares of the bottom row to represent units. As soon as four squares were covered, he flicked them back with his rake, scooped them back into the pot and put one counter on the line between the bottom and the second row, to represent five units. The second row was tens, the third hundreds, while counters placed on the line dividing second and third were fifties. Mostly he would start a calculation slowly and carefully and gradually build up speed as he progressed, until his fingers were moving with extraordinary speed and the raked-back counters jingled and tinkled like a man running in scale armor. The counters were good silver, ninety parts fine, and stamped with the word TREASURY on one side and an inspiring scene from the history of the Republic on the other. New sets were issued every year, at which point the old sets were recalled and sent to be melted down, though the considerable number that reached the cabinets of avid counter-collectors suggested that the calling-in procedure wasn't absolutely watertight.

Psellus waited until his friend had his hand full of swept-up counters, then coughed. Maniacis dropped the counters, looked up and called him something.

"Now then," Psellus replied, and grinned. "You can't say that to me, I'm here in my official capacity."

"Is that right." Maniacis scowled at him. "In that case, triple what I said with spikes on. Your precious Necessary Evil's been running us ragged for weeks."

Psellus frowned. "Lucky you," he said. "They aren't even talking to me. I don't know what I've done to upset them, but they've cut me right out. I've been sitting counting the bricks in the wall."

"Oh." Maniacis looked at him thoughtfully. "So, what're you here bothering me for?"

Psellus perched on the edge of the table and picked up a counter. On the reverse, a nude fat woman of indeterminate age was presenting a muscle-bound warrior with a garland apparently woven from turnip-tops, while in the background smoke rose from a distant mountain. Underneath was the legend *The Eremian threat averted*. He raised an eyebrow and put it back where he'd found it. "A bit previous, surely," he said.

Maniacis shrugged. "Not pure silver, either. Don't suppose you noticed, but where it rubs on the table, like the edges of the laurel crown and the chubby bird's tits, the copper's starting to show through. Last year's issue were called in early and we got these instead, a week ago. They were supposed to go into service as part of the grand victory celebrations, but..." He shrugged. "That's how tight things are," he said. "We needed the silver, so we pulled the old ones early and put these ones out ahead of time. Tempting providence if you ask me, but there it is, there's a war on."

Psellus wasn't sure he liked the sound of that. "I had no idea things were so bad," he said.

"Oh, they aren't really," Maniacis said with a sigh. "Really, it's all to do with cashflow and housekeeping. The money's mostly there, but we're under orders to try and keep to within this year's budget. If we start breaking into next year's money, it looks very bad in Assembly. So, to tide things over, we're having to scratch about for loose change to bridge the gap."

"I see," Psellus said. "How's it going?"

Maniacis shook his head. "We lost the battle some time ago," he said. "So now we're having to borrow money from foreigners; the merchants, banks in the old country, even the Cure Doce. We'll pay it all back as soon as the new fiscal year starts, of course, but they'll screw us rotten for interest. That's politics for you. Your bloody Foundrymen, running scared of the Drapers."

"We didn't start it," Psellus replied automatically. "Well, anyway, I'm here to make things worse for you. We've got to expedite supplies for the new army, so I'm here on the scrounge."

Maniacis clicked his tongue. "Not sure I can help you," he said. "How much do you need?"

When Psellus told him, he opened his eyes wide and blinked.

"I know," Psellus said. "It's a lot of money."

Maniacis rested his chin on his fingertips and thought for a moment. "There's no way I can raise that much just by fiddling the books," he said. "Either we borrow it from the savages or you'll have to go to Assembly for a levy."

"Can't do that," Psellus said immediately. "For one thing it'd take too long. For another—like I said, I'm out of touch, but I can't see it getting through without blood on the floor."

"Quite so." Maniacis shook his head. "With so many workers taken out and put on war work, production generally's right down the drain. That's not all; all the available shipping's tied up ferrying men and supplies, so goods are piling up in the warehouses with no ships to carry them. If we don't deliver, we don't get paid. This war's bloody terrible for business, which is the exact opposite of how it was supposed to be. If I was a Foundryman, I'd be looking for heads to roll on my management committee."

"Be that as it may," Psellus said sharply, "looks like you'll need to raise a loan. How long's that going to take?"

Maniacis shrugged. "Not very long, actually," he said. "Just so happens, we've negotiated a line of credit with our new best friends, just in case things look like they're getting out of hand. Luckily they have plenty of money and their interest rates are not at all bad."

Psellus caught something in his friend's tone of voice. "There's a catch, isn't there?"

"Depends how you look at it," Maniacis replied, with a humorless grin. "The way we're viewing it in this department, there isn't a problem, but we can see how other people — you lot, for instance — might not like it very much. Which is why we haven't got around to telling anybody yet."

Something dropped into place, and Psellus winced, as though he'd turned his ankle or cut himself. "It's the Vadani, isn't it?" he said. "That's who you're borrowing all this extra money from."

Maniacis looked at him. "You're perfectly at liberty to speculate," he said. "I'm not saying anything. But if you want money for your grocery bill, I'd be obliged if you kept your face shut and your wild guesses to yourself." He looked away and said to the wall: "One thing the Vadani have got plenty of is silver. All they've got to do is dig it out of the sides of the mountains. The bad thing is, we've run projections of what the final cost is likely to be, once we've taken Civitas Eremiae and finished the mopping-up. I won't bore you with details, but it's going to be tight. So much so that I don't see us being able to pay back these emergency loans next year or any time soon. In fact, unless we get lucky and find treasuries stuffed with gold and silver in the ruins of Orsea's palace, we're going to be in hock to our new best friends for a very long time. Now I don't understand politics, I'm proud to say, so I don't have to bother my silly little head about the implications of that. Instead, I can leave it to the likes of you, so you can start planning ahead. I seem to remember an old proverb about holding a wild boar by its bollocks; holding on is no fun at all, but letting go would probably be worse." He sighed, leaned back, stretched. "Let me have a formal writ of requisition as soon as you can," he said. "While you're doing the paperwork, I'll talk to my bosses and we can get everything set up. You know," he added sourly, "if only your precious Guildsmen had put locks on your office windows, none of this mess would've happened in the first place."

General Melancton received the news that the supply train had been dispatched and was on its way with a mixture of relief and skepticism. He'd been taught in war school that fighting on two fronts is a bad thing, and of the two enemies he currently faced, the Mezentine Guilds worried him slightly more than the Eremians. He was, after all, allowed to kill the Eremians, assuming he could get close enough without being shot to ribbons by the artillery the Perpetual Republic had assured him he'd never have to face. Also, he felt confident that he could predict how they were likely to behave. The Guilds, on the other hand, were something he couldn't begin to understand. The one thing he knew about them was that if it suited them to do so, they'd strand him in the mountains without supplies or send him to his certain death without a second thought. It was a shame the savages were so poor; on balance, he'd far rather be fighting for them.

He sat in his tent studying the map. The ill-fated Captain Eiconodoulus had told him a few things about Mezentine cartography before they'd shipped him back home, and Melancton was inclined to take the captain's word over his employers'. This meant that he was obliged to rely increasingly on his scouts, the Cure Hardy light cavalry. He'd have preferred a company of properly trained surveyors from home, but there wasn't time to send for any; and the Cure Hardy, possibly because they were nomads and therefore used to constant and painstaking reconnaissance, seemed to be doing a perfectly adequate job. It didn't matter at all that he didn't like them much; and he only disliked them because he found them more or less impossible to understand, even though they spoke quite passable Mezentine. But he couldn't figure out what they wanted; why they were here, risking their lives on behalf of him and his employers. Money didn't seem to interest them, in the same way fish aren't interested in music. They weren't here for the glory, he was pretty sure of that. In his time in the military he'd come across men who went to the wars simply because they liked to fight, but the Cure Hardy took great and laudable pains to avoid the enemy. Therefore they remained a mystery, one of very many, and that bothered him, on the rare occasions when he had time and leisure to dwell on it.

Today, however, they had particularly interesting news. There was a path (maybe thirty years ago it could have been called a road, but a lot of heather can grow and a lot of dirt and rock can be washed away in thirty years) that appeared to lead round the side of the foothills of Civitas Mountain, bypassing the obvious place for a final pre-siege pitched battle; and as far as the scouts could see, this path was completely clear of the enemy. Melancton was a realist, with a healthy distrust of cleverness. Someone with pretensions to tactical genius would be thinking in terms of fooling the enemy into making a stand at the obvious place by feinting at it with cavalry and light infantry, while sending the bulk of his army round by the cunning path to take them from the rear and slaughter them like sheep. As far as he was concerned, that would be a first-class way to lose the war at a stroke; something would go wrong with timing or communications, he'd find himself losing the pitched battle through lack of numbers while his encirclement party walked straight into an ambush on the hidden path. He stroked his beard and scowled. He was getting too old to play games.

He looked up. His chief of staff, Tachista Pantocrator, had arrived with the duty roster, which meant it was noon already and he still hadn't made up his mind. "Tachista," he said, "if you were Duke Orsea, what'd you be most worried about?"

Pantocrator thought for a moment. "Losing," he said.

Not as silly an answer as it sounded. "What's the most likely way you'd lose?" he asked.

"Easy. Sheer weight of numbers."

Melancton nodded slowly. "So you'd be thinking it'd be nice

to even things up by slaughtering a few thousand of the bastards before they even get to the city."

"It wouldn't hurt."

"No. But we're contemplating what's losing you sleep."

"I see. Well, in that case, I'd be scared stiff of throwing away such advantages as I've got."

That made sense too. "And your best advantage?"

"Geography," Pantocrator replied immediately. "Superb defensive site, impregnable walls, and now I've got something approaching parity in artillery."

"So if you're smart," Melancton said, "what're you going to do?"

"Spend my time on the defenses of the city, and laying in as much food and materials as I can before the siege starts."

Melancton smiled. "And you're not going to risk wasting men in a field battle out in the open, when they'll be much harder to kill standing behind your wonderful city walls."

"I'd have to be stupid, wouldn't I?"

"Of course. In that case, tell the scouts to check out a day's march along the main road. I don't think they're going to come out to play. I think they'll stay in the city and wait for us until we're at the foot of their rotten hill. What do you think?"

Pantocrator shrugged. "That's what I'd do, probably," he said. "But then, I lack imagination. You said so in my last assessment."

"Fuck imagination," Melancton replied.

Hardening steel was the real problem. They'd run out of ordinary plain iron too, but the city was full of the stuff, in various shapes and forms. With the backing of the Ducas, Ziani had organized platoons of soldiers with nothing better to do into browsing parties, scouring the streets for frivolous and non-essential ironwork—door-hinges, gates, railings, lamp-standards, fire-dogs, boot-scrapers, sign-brackets, anything that could be drawn down, jumped up or hammer-welded together to make up bar stock.

Hardening steel, on the other hand, had always been a rare and expensive commodity. Cart springs were the obvious resource, but he'd already stripped the city bare of them; likewise pitchfork tines, spade and shovel blades, they were even prising perfectly good horseshoes off soundly shod hoofs just to feed the furnaces. As if that wasn't ridiculous enough, they were eking out the hardening steel by pattern-welding it into billets two to one with wrought iron, so that each twelve-by-three-by-three that went to be drawn through the plates into spring wire had been forge-welded, twisted, folded and welded again and again like the finest swords of ancient heroes. If you looked closely at the finished wire you could actually see the patterns—pool-and-eye, maidenhair, hugs and kisses. It was ludicrous and a truly desperate way of going about things, but they had no choice. Pattern-welded springs, though; if that wasn't an abomination, then the term had no meaning.

As he shuttled between the factory and the ramparts where the scorpions were being set up, Ziani felt like a newlywed wife getting ready to entertain her in-laws to dinner for the first time. He wanted everything to be perfect for the Mezentines when they arrived. Every scorpion had to be aligned exactly in its cradle and zeroed at each of the set distances, the dampening struts clamped down tight, the sliders and locks greased, every nut and wedge re-tightened after twenty trial shots. He had a team of four hundred volunteers doing nothing all day but retrieving shot bolts from the targets and bringing them back up to the wall. He wanted to be everywhere, doing everything himself; instead he had to watch half-trained, half-skilled Eremians doing each job more or less adequately, which was torture. Finally, he decided he'd had enough. If he had to watch one more thread being stripped or cradle-truss warped out of line, he'd go mad. With a tremendous effort he turned his back on the lot of them and walked slowly down the stairs to the street.

Someone was waiting for him; a tall, broad, bald man with a ferocious gray mustache. "You Vaatzes?" he asked.

It was too stupid a question to risk replying to, so he nodded. "Who're you?"

"Framea Orudino, sergeant-at-arms to the lesser Ducas," the bald man replied, puffing his chest out like a frog. "You wanted fencing lessons. I've been trying to find you all day, but nobody knew where you'd got to."

Ziani grinned. "You found me," he said. "Right, let's get to it. What do I have to do?"

Orudino studied him for a moment, as though he was a consignment of defective timber. "Follow me," he said.

Orudino led him down the inevitable tangle of narrow, messy streets, alleys and snickets until they reached a gray door in a sand-yellow brick wall. To Ziani's surprise, the door didn't open into a beautiful secret garden or a cool, fountain-strewn courtyard. Instead, they were inside a building that reminded him of all the warehouses he'd ever seen. The walls were bare brick, washed with lime. The floor was gray stone flags, recently swept. In one corner was a stout wooden rack, in which he saw about a dozen matching pairs of long, thin swords.

"Foils," Orudino explained. "The point's been blunted and wrapped in twine, so it can't hurt you, unless you get stuck in the eye. But I'm good enough not to hit where I don't want to, and you'll never be good enough to hit me unless I want you to, so there's no problem."

Ziani decided he didn't like Sergeant Orudino, but that hardly mattered. "What comes first?" he asked.

"We'll get you standing right," the sergeant said. "Now then. Over there, see, painted on the floor are two footprints. Put your feet on them, and that's your basic stance."

Orudino was bored, making the little speeches he'd made hundreds of times before, plodding through the stages of the lesson like a mule turning a flywheel. That was unfortunate, because Ziani found the whole business completely alien, and needed to have each step explained and demonstrated over and over again.

The footwork in particular he found almost impossible to master; it was almost as bad as dancing, and he'd never been able to dance. Maybe he could have managed it if he'd been able to look down and see where he was putting his feet, but the sergeant wouldn't let him, on the grounds that in a real fight he'd need to keep his eyes fixed on the other man's sword-point to the exclusion of everything else. So Ziani stumbled, blundered, tripped over his feet, fell over twice, with nothing to spur him on but his rapidly burgeoning hatred for the loud, pompous, bullying bald man with the bored voice and the supercilious grin. If anything, he loathed his condescending praise on the rare occasions when something went right more than his martyred patience with the bungles and mistakes. He kept himself going by chanting in his head, *if this shit-head can do it, so can I;* and slowly, gracelessly, he tightened up the tolerance, while his arms and legs and wrists and forearms and neck and back screamed pain at him, and the tip of the sergeant's foil stung him like a wasp.

He learned the four wards (high, side, low, middle); the steps ordinary and extraordinary; the advance, the retreat, the pass, the lunge; the wide and the narrow measure; the counter in time and double time; the disengage, the block, the beat; the mastery of the enemy sword and the slip-thrust, the stop-thrust, the tip-cut and the sidestep riposte in time. He learned to feint and to read feints, to wait and to watch, to move hand and foot together, to keep his kneecap over his toe in the lunge, to fend with his left hand and to close to disarm. Orudino killed him six dozen times, with thrusts to his throat, heart, stomach and groin, with draw-cuts and tip-cuts and the secret cut of the Ducas (a wrap with the false edge to sever the knee-tendon). Every death was a chore to the sergeant, and most of them were disappointments, because a child of twelve should have been able to master the relevant defense by now.

"You're thrashing about like a landed fish," the sergeant said, as Ziani lunged at him and missed. "It's no good if you can't land a thrust where it'll do some good. Come over here, I'll show you." He led Ziani to the middle of the floor, where a piece of string hung from a rafter. From his finger he pulled a heavy ring, brass with a little silver plate still clinging to it, and tied it to the string. Then, with a mild sigh, he lunged. The tip of his foil passed through the middle of the ring without touching it.

"Right," he said sadly. "You try."

Hopeless, of course. A couple of times he managed to swat the string, like a kitten batting at wool. Otherwise he missed outright. The sergeant laughed, took down the ring and replaced it with a small steel hoop about the size of an outstretched hand. "Come on," he said, "you ought to be able to hit that"; but Ziani tried and couldn't. The best he could do was slap into the string, setting the hoop swaying.

"Don't they practice fencing where you come from, then?" Orudino asked. Ziani shook his head.

"We aren't allowed to have weapons," he replied. "It's against the law."

The sergeant looked at him with contempt. "Doesn't stop you picking on the likes of us, though," he said. "Well, you aren't at home now. Concentrate. Fix your eyes on where you want to hit, and it should just come naturally."

Did it hell. After a long time and a great many attempts, the sergeant stopped him, took down the hoop and said, "Let's stick to the basic defenses for now. Right, high guard, sword-hand in First, watch what I'm doing and step in to block and push away."

The defenses were slightly better than the attacks, but they still weren't easy. At last, however, he grasped the idea of taking a step back or to the side to keep his distance. Try as he might, however, he couldn't organize himself well enough to counter each attack with a simultaneous attack of his own. *One thing at a time,* his brain insisted, *defend and then attack;* but by the time he'd blocked, deflected or avoided, there wasn't time to hit back. There was always another attack on the way, and pretty soon he found himself backed into a corner with nowhere to go.

"We're just not getting anywhere," the sergeant said. "I've been teaching fencing for twenty years, I've taught kids of ten and old men of sixty, and I've never had a complete failure, not till now. Sorry, but I don't think I can help you. Best thing you can do is buy yourself a thick padded coat or a breastplate, and try and stay out of trouble."

Ziani leaned against the wall. His legs were weak and shaky from the effort, his elbows and forearms hurt and he had a blinding headache. He hated the sergeant more than anybody he'd ever met. "Let's give it one more go," he said. "Don't try and teach me the whole lot. Let's just concentrate on one or two things."

The sergeant shrugged. "I've got nothing better to do," he said. "But I think you're wasting your time. All right, then, let's have a middle guard in Third. No, bring your back foot round more, and don't stick your right hand so far out, not unless you're trying to draw me in on purpose."

Slowly, bitterly, with extraordinary effort, Ziani learned to defend from the middle guard. "It's better than nothing," the sergeant told him. "Forget about countering for now, just concentrate on distance. If you aren't there, you can't be hit. Simple as that."

The sergeant wanted to leave it at that, but Ziani refused. "I want just one thing I can use," he said. "Like the hedgehog in the proverb."

"I don't know any proverbs about hedgehogs." The sergeant shrugged. "All right," he said, "we'll try the back-twist. Actually it's a pretty advanced move, but for anybody sparring with you, it'd come as a complete surprise. Now; middle guard in Third, like normal; and when I thrust at you on the straight line, you bring your back foot a long step behind your front foot, till you've almost turned away from me. That takes you right out of the way of my attack, and you can stab me where you like as I go past."

To the complete surprise of both of them, Ziani got it almost right on the third attempt. "It's like I always say," the sergeant told him, "if someone can't learn the easy stuff, teach him something difficult instead. You'd be surprised how often it works."

So they practiced the back-twist many, many times, until Ziani was doing it without thinking. "It's actually a good one to learn," the sergeant said, "because if you get it right, that's the fight over before it starts. It's half a circle instead of a straight line. All right, a couple more times and then I'm calling it a day."

It was a glorious relief to get away from him, out of his bare brick box into the open air. Ziani only had a very vague idea of where in the city he was, but he didn't care. He was content to wander, choosing turnings almost at random to see where they led. Almost perversely, he had no trouble finding a way home.

Cantacusene was in the main gallery, shouting at someone for ruining a whole batch of springs. He waited till he'd finished, then called him over.

"You know about swords and things," he said. "Where's the best place to buy one?"

Cantacusene frowned. "Depends," he said, predictably. "What do you want?"

"A side-sword," Ziani replied, "or a short rapier, preferably with a bit of an edge. Imported," he added quickly. "Nothing flashy, just something simple and sturdy."

Cantacusene told him a name, and where to find a particular stall in the market. "You can say I sent you if you like," he added. "She's my second cousin, actually."

"Thanks. What was that about a batch of springs, then?"

The next day, early, he went to the market and found Cantacusene's cousin; a tall, fat woman with a pleated shawl over her red bodice and gown. For some reason, she seemed to think he wanted something very expensive with a swept hilt, fluted pommel and ivory grip; it took him quite some time to convince her otherwise, but he managed it in the end and came away with a short rapier, slightly browned with age, in a battered scabbard. He left it propped against the wall of his tower room and went back to work.

Not long after midday, a messenger arrived, from Miel Ducas: could Vaatzes come immediately, please. He followed the messenger (he was getting tired of having to be led everywhere, like a blind man) to the Ducas house. Miel Ducas was waiting for him in a small room off the main cloister. He was sitting behind a table covered with maps, letters, lists and schedules, and he looked exhausted.

"Bad news," the Ducas said straight away. "They've bypassed the Barbuda gate — that's here," he added, jabbing his forefinger at some squiggle on a map, "and at the rate they're going, they'll be down there in the valley this time day after tomorrow. I'm taking three squadrons of cavalry to give them a bit of a hard time at a place I know, but really that's just to show willing. Fact is, the war's about to start. How ready can you be by then?"

Ziani shrugged. "I'm ready now," he said. "We've run out of hardening steel and we're nearly out of ordinary iron. I'm still making machines by bodging bits together, but I don't suppose I've got enough material for another full day's production. Really, we're as ready as we'll ever be. I've already got four hundred and fifty scorpions installed and ready; actually, it'd be a bit of a struggle to fit any more in on the wall."

"I see," the Ducas said. "Is that going to be enough?"

Ziani smiled. "No idea," he said. "When you're dealing with the Republic, there's no such thing as enough. It's like saying, how many buckets will I need to empty the sea? But," he went on, as the Ducas scowled at him, "they're going to need a bloody big army if they don't want to run out of men before we run out of scorpion bolts."

That seemed to cheer the Ducas up a little. He sighed, and nodded his head. "You've done very well," he said. "I'm grateful, believe me. If we get out of this ghastly mess in one piece, I'll see to it that you're not forgotten." He shrugged. "You know," he said, "there's a part of me that still doesn't really believe that all this can be happening. Try as I might, I can't understand why they're doing it. Doesn't make sense, somehow."

Ziani smiled wryly. "That's because you think it's about you," he said. "It isn't. It's really an internal matter; Guild politics, that sort of thing. I don't suppose that's any consolation."

The Ducas shook his head. "I don't imagine it'll be much

comfort to the poor bastards on the wrong end of your scorpion bolts," he said. "Tell me, what on earth possesses them to sign up, anyway? Isn't there any work for them back wherever they come from?"

"No idea," Ziani said. "All I know about the old country is that we came here to get away from them, a long time ago, and now we do a lot of business with them, mostly textiles, farm tools and domestic hardware. The general impression I've got over the years is that they're a practically inexhaustible supply of manpower, but I can't remember them ever getting slaughtered like sheep before. It's possible they may not want to keep coming if that happens."

"Well, quite." The Ducas grinned. "It's getting so difficult to find good help these days."

He didn't seem to want anything else, so Ziani made his excuses and took his leave. He felt a strong urge to look back over his shoulder, but he resisted it. Thanks to the Ducas, he'd learned a valuable lesson about compassion, and its deceptive relationship to love. With every step he took away from the place, he found it easier to bring to mind the fact that it was Duke Orsea who'd taken pity on him, on the day when he'd been dying in the mountains, and that the Ducas had been all in favor of having him quietly killed, or left to die. Not that it mattered, as things had turned out. The Ducas had paid him back many times over. Besides, compassion at first sight is generally like love at first sight; both of them are dangerous instincts, often leading to disaster.

He turned up the long, wide street whose name he could never remember (it was something to do with horses, not that that helped much) and followed it uphill toward the center of the city. At the lower crossroads he paused. If he turned right, he could go to his patron Calaphates' house. He hadn't spoken to his benefactor for a long time, let alone sent him any accounts, or a statement of his share of the profits. Calaphates had been kind to him, though largely out of self-interest; he owed him some consideration, the bare minimum required by good manners. Or he could turn left and take the wide boulevard lined with stunted cherry trees that led to the inner wall, and beyond that, the Duke's palace. If he owed a duty to his patrons, he certainly ought to make time to report to Duke Orsea, who'd shown him kindness even though he was an enemy, at a time when anybody would have forgiven him for doing the exact opposite. The thought made him smile, though part of him still regretted all of it, deeply and with true compassion. He went left. At the palace gatehouse he asked to see the chamberlain. After a shorter wait than he'd anticipated, he was seen and granted an interview with the Duke, at noon precisely, the day after tomorrow. It occurred to Ziani that if the Ducas was right, that would be the day before the Mezentine army was due to arrive. Couldn't be better, he decided.

After he'd seen Vaatzes, Miel Ducas spent an hour going over the plans for the cavalry raid one last agonizing time. He was sure there was at least one fatal flaw in his design, probably two or three, and that anybody with a faint trace of residual common sense would be able to spot it, or them, in a heartbeat. It was as though he could hear voices in the next room and knew they were discussing the disastrous failure of the coming raid, and how it had ultimately led to the fall of Eremia, but he couldn't quite make out what they were saying.

The same voices haunted him all evening. He took them with him when he went to bed (very early, since he had to be up well before dawn the next day) and they kept him awake until he was at the point where sleep would do him more harm than good. When the footman woke him up with hot water and a light breakfast he felt muzzy and cramped, with a tight feeling at the sides of his head that wanted to be a really nasty headache when it grew up.

It wasn't a good day for headaches; nor for stomach upsets, but he had one of them too. When he clambered awkwardly onto his horse, well behind schedule, he felt as though some malicious person was twisting his intestines tightly round a stick. Nerves, he promised himself; also he knew for a fact that there couldn't possibly be anything inside him left to come out.

As was only proper for the Ducas going to war, he wore a middleweight gambeson with mail gussets under a heavyweight coat of plates with full plate arm and leg defenses, right down to steel-soled sabatons on his feet. Because he was the commander in chief and therefore under an obligation to keep in touch with what was going on around him, he'd substituted an open sallet for the full great-helm, but someone had failed to check to see whether the Ducas crest (which was essential as a means of identification in the field) would fit the sallet's crest-holder. It didn't, so the sallet had to go back and the great-helm came out instead. Inside it, of course, he could barely see, hear or breathe; so he compromised by giving it to his squire to carry and going bare-headed.

He rode with only his squire for company as far as the Horse-fair, where he was joined by half a dozen mounted men in full armor, hurrying because they were running late. They slowed down when they saw it was him; one of them joked that he must've got the time wrong, because he was sure the muster had been set for half an hour earlier.

At the gate he found everybody else waiting for him. Cousin Jarnac had apparently assumed temporary command in his absence. Jarnac, of course, looked the part so much more than he did. The battle harness of the lesser Ducas was blued spring steel, with a single-piece placket instead of the coat of plates, and a bevored sallet with an eighteen-inch boiled leather crest in the form of a crouching boar. If he hadn't known better he'd have followed Jarnac unquestioningly; so, he suspected, would everybody else.

All told, the armored contingent numbered over four hundred; the rest of his army was made up of five hundred mounted archers and eight hundred lancers, middleweight-heavy cavalry in munition-grade black-and-white half-armor. Dawn was soaking through the dark blue sky, and a trace of mist hung round the main gate as, feeling horribly self-conscious about his appearance, horsemanship and perceived lack of any leadership ability whatsoever, Miel Ducas led the way out of the city and down the long road to the valley floor.

Because they were late starting, there was nothing for it but to take the old carters' road, Castle Lane, round the side of the hog's back crossed by the main road. That would save an hour, assuming it wasn't blocked by a landslide or fallen trees, and they'd come out five hundred yards from the fork where the Packhorse Drove branched off. The drove would take them down into the wooded combe that ran parallel to the road; at the Merebarton (assuming it wasn't a swamp after the late rain) they'd split into two and try and bottle the enemy up in the Blackwater Pass. Even if everything went perfectly they'd only be able to hold the two ends of the pass for a short while, but every Mezentine they killed today was one they wouldn't have to deal with later. At the council of war where the plan had been discussed, someone had described this approach as trying to empty a river with a tablespoon. Thinking about it, it had been Miel himself who said that, and nobody had contradicted him.

Castle Lane proved to be reasonably clear, and they made good time. Halfway down Packhorse Drove, however, they came almost within long bowshot of an enemy scouting party, who took one look at them and galloped away. Disaster; if the scouts got back to the main army, the whole plan would be ruined. Miel's first instinct was to send a half-squadron of lancers after them, but fortunately he didn't give in to it. God only knew how the enemy were managing to raise a gallop on the rock-and-mud surface of the drove; their horses must have iron hoofs and no bones in their legs. Trying to catch them or match their pace would be impossible for mere mortal horses, and the fewer men he sent charging around the landscape at this stage, the better. The only thing for it was to cut up diagonally across the rough to the road instead of taking the deer-trails he'd planned on using. That way, with luck, his men would stay between the scouts and their army, so they wouldn't be able to deliver their message. They'd come up a quarter-mile away from the gates of the canyon on the south side, but (with more luck) they'd be able to close that distance before the enemy got there. The northern wing would have to take its time getting into position. First screw-up of the day, Miel acknowledged sourly, and highly unlikely to be the last.

Cutting across the rough sounded fine when you said it, briskly and confidently, to your cool, eager staff officers. Putting the order into practice was something else entirely. Even the perfectly trained and schooled horses of the Ducas house weren't happy about leaving the path and crashing about through holly and briars; for the most part, the archers' and lancers' horses followed where the knights led, but it could only have been out of bewildered curiosity. Above all, they made a racket that surely could've been heard in the city. Only one man actually fell off and hurt himself, but he was the lesser Nicephorus, an enormous man in full plate, and the crash bounced about among the trees like a small bird trapped in a barn.

Coming out of the forest onto the road and into the light was a terrifying experience. Very reluctantly, but with duty forcing him on like a jailer, Miel led the way and was the first to break cover. He expected yells, movement, a flurry of arrows, but he had the road to himself. He reined in his horse and stood quite still for a moment or so, feeling as though he was the last man on earth. He could hear no birds singing, not even a bee or a horsefly, and it occurred to him that the enemy had already been and gone. But a glance at the road set his mind at rest; no hoofmarks, footprints, wheel-tracks to be seen.

Which reminded him. He turned in the saddle and waved his men on, then rode back to intercept one of the line officers, a man he trusted.

"Have the rearguard remembered to cut some branches?" he asked. He realized while he was saying it that the branch-cutting detail weren't this officer's responsibility; but he nodded and said yes, he'd watched them doing it, and did the Ducas want him to go back and make sure it was all done right?

Miel had absolute confidence in his subordinates, but even so he hung back and watched as the rearguard tied cut branches to the pommels of their saddles and dragged them behind as they rode on, sweeping away the column's hoofprints. The result didn't look right, but it was less obvious than the tracks of a thousand horses.

He remembered the canyon, though it was several years since the last time he'd been there, hunting late-season wolves with Jarnac and the Sphax twins. On that occasion the place had played cruelly on his nerves, because he hadn't yet got the hang of not being at war with the Vadani and therefore constantly at risk from maverick raiding parties, and because anybody with more imagination than a small rock could see it was a perfect place for an ambush. He started worrying; the enemy commander was by definition a professional soldier, trained from childhood to spot dangerous terrain. Surely he'd have recognized the risk from his scouts' reports. Either he wouldn't show up at all, which would be horribly embarrassing, or else he'd figured out an ingenious counter-ambush of his own that'd leave the Eremians trapped in their own snare. The more he thought about it, the more obvious it was that that was precisely what was about to happen. At any moment, archers would appear on the skyline, or the sun would disappear behind a curtain of falling scorpion bolts. Maybe he'd be lucky and die in the first volley, thereby spared the humiliating pain of knowing he'd led the flower of Eremian chivalry to a pointless, shameful death...

I'm turning into Orsea, he thought. *Maybe it's something that comes with being in charge.* As his men filed past, he scanned the top of the ridge on both sides. If there was an ambush waiting up there, they'd missed their chance. He'd got away with it after all.

Once they'd taken up position at the canyon neck, there was a great deal to be done. The lancers dismounted and started felling trees to build the roadblock, while the designated specialists in each unit unloaded and spread the caltrops and snagging wires they'd brought with them from the city. Miel couldn't recall offhand whose suggestion the caltrops had been, though he had a nasty feeling it'd been his. They were crude, put together in a hurry; a wooden ball the size of a large apple, with eight two-inch

spikes sticking out in all directions. Wouldn't it be the most delicate irony if the battle turned against him and those spikes ended
up buried in the frogs of his own horses' hoofs, as a painful lesson
in poetic justice to anybody who presumed to use weapons of in-
discriminate effect against the Mezentines?

Once the preparations had been made, he pulled all his men
back into cover, and settled down to wait. He knew this would be
the hardest part of the job, a lethal opportunity to shred his own
self-confidence to the point where he'd order the retreat sounded
the moment a single Mezentine appeared in the distance. He
almost wished he was the one being ambushed, since at least he
wouldn't have to cope with the anticipation.

When the enemy finally arrived, of course, he was looking the
other way. Worse; he was on foot, in a small holly grove, taking
a last pre-battle piss. He heard the creak of an axle, followed by
shouting; more shouting, as he fumbled numbly with his trousers
(no mean feat of engineering for a man wearing plate cuisses) and
battled his way out of the holly, stumbling on exposed roots and
fallen branches as he tried to get back to where he'd left his horse.
He mounted badly, twisting his ankle as he lifted into the saddle,
winding himself as he sat down. There were screams among the
shouts now, and a clattering of steel like blacksmiths trying to
work the metal too cold. For a split second his sense of direction
deserted him and he couldn't remember where the battle was.

His horse scrambled awkwardly out onto the road, and there
was nobody there; he turned his head in time to see the last of his
men joining in a full-blown charge. *They could've waited for me,* he
thought, unfairly and incorrectly; he followed them, a shamefaced
rearguard of one. Before he reached them he passed five dead men
and nine sprawled horses, all Eremians. Wonderful omen.

Immediately he saw what the problem was. Quite properly,
whoever had taken command while he was away urinating had
seen an opening in the enemy front and thrown a full charge at it.
Also quite reasonably, he hadn't expected the level of success that
in the event he'd achieved. The charge had gone home and then

gone too far, like an unbarred spear into a charging boar. The risk now was of being enveloped from the sides. Miel looked round in desperation for the horn-blower to sound the disengage. He found him almost straight away; lying on the ground, covered from the waist down by his fallen horse. He was dead, of course; and the horn lay beside him where he'd dropped it. At least one horse had trodden on it, crumpling it up like stiff paper.

Not so good, then. He sat still, frantically trying to decide what to do, painfully aware that the battle had slipped away from him, like a cat squirming out of a child's arms. Common sense urged him to stay out of the fighting, but he was the Ducas, and his place was in the thick of it. Muttering to himself, he pushed his horse into a half-hearted canter and, as something of an afterthought, drew his sword.

A horseman was closing on him; not an Eremian, therefore an enemy. He spurred forward to meet him, but the rider swerved away. Miel realized he was an archer, one of the Cure Hardy scouts. He pulled his horse's head round, determined to be at least a moving target, but the enemy was more concerned with getting away; he had his bow in his right hand and his left was on the reins. Before Miel could decide whether or not to do anything about him, the archer slumped forward on his horse's neck, dropped his bow and slid sideways out of the saddle. His foot snagged in his stirrup-leather just as his head hit the ground. His helmet came off and a tangle of long, dark hair flowed out like blood from a wound. He was being dragged. With each stride of the horse his head was jerked up, only to bump down again and bounce off a stone or the lip of a pothole. After a few yards, the horse slowed down; his foot came free from the stirrup, he rolled over a couple of times and came to rest. The side of his head was white with dust, like a fine lady's face-powder, blood blotting through it in a round patch, like blusher. The stub of a broken-off arrow stuck out of his neck, just above the rolled edge of his breastplate.

Miel looked up. He'd forgotten that, as he was moving into po- sition, he'd dismounted his own archers and sent them to command the tops of the ridges that flanked the road. His own tactical skill impressed him. His archers were already in position, and because the attacking cavalry had forced the enemy out of the way and over to the sides, they had a clear view with minimal risk of dropping stray shots into their own men. If he'd planned it that way, it would have been a clever and imaginative tactic. Planned or not, though, the archers had turned a potential disaster into the makings of a famous victory. The arrows were driving the enemy back into the center of the canyon, where they were coming up against the Eremian cavalry; crushed between arrows and lances, like ears of wheat between two grindstones, they were gradually being ground away. In the distance he heard louder, shriller yells, from which he gathered that battle had been joined on the other side of the canyon.

It is incumbent upon the Ducas always to fight in the front rank, always to be the best... Query, however: is the Ducas obliged to fight in the front rank even if nobody's watching? The battle was coming along very nicely without him, thanks to the timely intervention of the archers, and the sheer aggression of the horsemen. The charge had long since foundered and lost all its momentum. The knights and lancers were no longer moving. Instead they were standing in their stirrups, bashing down on the helmets and coats of plates of the enemy infantry, who were too tightly cramped together to be able to swing back at them with anything approaching lethal force. With a considerable degree of reluctance, he pushed his horse forward into the fighting.

It reminded him of a thrush cracking snail-shells against a stone. His fellow knights were whirling and swinging their swords, flattening their delicately honed edges against the cheap munitions plate of the enemy footsoldiers. Even the swords of the Phocas, the Suidas, the Peribleptus couldn't cut into sixteenth-inch domed iron sheet. Farm tools or hammers would probably have been more use, but noblemen didn't use such things. Instead, they tried to club the enemy to the floor with their light, blunt swords; it was perfectly possible, provided you hit hard enough and took pains to land your blows on the same spot. Cursing the aimless stupidity of it all, Miel Ducas dug his spurs into his horse's side and forced the poor creature into a clumsy, unwilling canter.

He saw the enemy. Things weren't going well with them. Tidemarks of dead bodies showed where they'd tried to scramble up the slope to get at the archers, only to find out by trial and error that it couldn't be done. Instead, they'd tried to go back, and that, presumably, was when they'd discovered that the other end of the canyon was blocked. There were thousands of them, all the scouts had agreed on that, but just now their vast weight of numbers was working against them. Jammed together as their flanks cringed away from the archers, most of them were useless to their commander; they were a traffic jam, obstructing the passage of orders and intelligence from one end of the canyon to the other. It occurred to Miel that if he'd only had another couple of thousand men, he could probably kill enough of them from this position to end the war. But that wasn't the case; and at any moment, the sheer pressure of men trying to get away from the spearhead of knights wedged into their center would explode up the canyon sides and flush away his archers, albeit with devastating loss of life...Entirely against his will and better judgment, he spared a moment to consider that. Ever since childhood he'd trained with weapons, as a nobleman should; he'd fought with the quintain and the pell, sparred with his instructors, shot arrows into targets both stationary and moving. In due course he'd put the theory into practice, against the Vadani, in what proved to be the last campaign of the war, and afterward in border skirmishes and police actions against brigands and free companies. All his life he'd learned to fight a target—a wooden post wrapped in sacking, a sack dangling from a swinging beam, a straw circle with colored rings painted on it, an exposed neck or forearm, the gap beside the armpit not covered by the armor plates. It hadn't ever worried him, until now. He paused to consider how deeply troubled he was, now that he was in command, and all these deaths and mutilations were by his order and decision. It troubled him, he discovered, but not enough.

Devastating loss of life; the sides of the canyon could be covered with dead men, packed close enough together that if it rained, the dust wouldn't get wet, and it'd still only be three thousand dead, maybe four, and that wouldn't be enough to end the war or even affect it significantly. It was an extraordinary thought; he could litter the landscape as far as the eye could see with the most grotesque obscenities he could imagine, and it wouldn't actually matter all that much, in the great scheme of things. He considered the duty of the Ducas, and the beneficial effect on morale that the sight of their commander in the thick of the fighting would have on his men, and thought, to hell with that. He'd had enough. What he needed most of all was a horn-blower.

What he got was a couple of Mezentines. Two infantrymen who'd squeezed and wriggled their way past, through, under, over the heaped corpses of their friends were running toward him, yelling what he assumed was abuse. Dispassionately, he assessed them from the technical point of view. Their defenses consisted of kettle-hats, mail collars and padded jacks reaching just below the waist. They were armed with some form of halberd (were those glaives or bardisches? He ought to know, but he always got them mixed up). Calm, determined and properly trained in the orthodox school of fencing they'd be formidable opponents, worthy of six pages of detailed drawings and explanatory text in the manual. As it was, they were a chore.

He rode at them, pulled left at the last moment, overshot the neck with a lazy thrust and severed the appropriate vein with a long, professional draw-cut. He felt blood on his face, which saved him the bother of turning his head to look. He could, of course, let the other man go, but that would be failing in his duty. He stopped his horse, dragged its head round and rode down the second man, hamstringing him with a delicate flick of the wrist as he passed him on the right. As chores went it hadn't exactly been arduous, but he felt annoyed, imposed upon; he was a busy man with a battle to stop, and he didn't have time for indulgences.

He found a horn-blower and ordered the disengage followed by the withdrawal in good order. The horn-blower looked at him before he blew. The effect was immediate. The archers vanished from the ridgetops, the knights and lancers wheeled and cantered away, leaving the butchered, stunned enemy staring after them. Pursuit, he knew, wouldn't be an issue. He asked the horn-blower if there was a recognized call for "back the way we came." Apparently there was.

Back into the cover of the trees, back down the deer-trails they should have taken the first time, back to the forest road, and they were safe. The archers joined them almost immediately. Their captain rode over and announced that his losses were fewer than twenty killed, a handful injured. Miel thanked him and rode on; he hadn't actually thought about it, or asked for a similar report from the captains of the knights and the lancers. That reminded him that he hadn't given any thought to the fate of the other half of his army, the men who'd blocked the far end of the canyon. Before he could ask anyone or send a scout, they appeared out of the trees in front of him. He could see riderless horses being led by their reins—how many? A dozen? Twenty? But their captain seemed in good spirits.

"How'd it go?" he asked.

"Wonderful," Jarnac replied, his voice comically muffled as he lifted off his helmet. "Couldn't have gone better if we'd rehearsed it with them beforehand. Your end?"

Miel nodded. "I think we should get out of here," he said. "I'm not inclined to push my luck any further today."

Jarnac grinned at him. "Quite right," he said. "It never does to be greedy, and the rest'll keep for another day. I couldn't see it all, of course, but I'm fairly sure our score's up into four figures. If only we'd brought another three squadrons, we could've had the lot."

Miel nodded and drew away from his cousin. He felt exhausted, angry and very sick. He cast his mind back to another massacre, when the scorpion bolts had curtained off the sun and it had been Eremians rather than Mezentines carpeting the dirt. That had been easier to bear, somehow.

The exuberance of his men had worn off by the time they reached the city; they were quiet as they rode in through the gate, too tired to care about much more than getting out of their armor, washing off the smell of blood and going to sleep. Even Jarnac (who'd insisted on riding beside him for much of the way) had stopped singing; instead he was whistling softly, and Miel couldn't make out the tune. There were a hundred and sixteen dead to own up to; mostly lancers, but of the twelve knights, one was the younger brother of the lesser Phocas (a brash, arrogant boy whom Miel had always disliked). The guilt of a victory is different from the guilt of a defeat, but no less depressing.

He gave the necessary orders to dismount, stand down and dismiss the army; a quick run-through his mental check-list, and he concluded that he'd done everything that was required of him and the rest of the day was his own. He went home; the streets were nearly empty, and there were only a few old women and drunks to stop and stare at the blood-spattered horseman in full armor, plodding up the cobbled street with his reins long and his horse's head drooping. Grooms were waiting at the gate to help him down and take the horse inside. The housekeeper and one of the gardeners helped him out of his armor.

"Where's Bucena?" the gardener asked; and Miel realized that he hadn't seen Bucena Joac, his squire, the head gardener's nephew, since shortly before the ambush. He didn't know whether the boy was alive or dead, so he couldn't answer the question. The two servants drew their own conclusions from his silence; they didn't say anything, which made for an awkward atmosphere. At any other time, Miel would've run out and looked to see if Bucena had come home; if not, he'd have found out what had become of him before stopping to shed his armor or wash his face. Instead, he told the housekeeper, "I need a bath. Soon as possible."

He fell asleep in his bath, and woke up shivering in the cold water. Someone was banging on the door, which wasn't a suitable level of behavior for the Ducas house. He demanded to know who was making that abominable noise.

It was the porter, and he had the butler, the sergeant and the housekeeper with him. Some men had come from the palace to talk to the Ducas. They had a piece of paper with a big red seal at the bottom. Apparently, they wanted to arrest him.

21

The debate that followed the attack on Melancton's expedition-ary force was unexpectedly subdued, as if neither major faction was sure what to make of it. Tactically, as the Drapers were quick to point out, it had been a disaster. Melancton had walked into a trap and been utterly humiliated; the enemy had come and gone with hardly a scratch. Strategically, as the Foundrymen immediately replied, it was something and nothing; the fact that the Eremians had committed so few men to the attack and had withdrawn so quickly, neglecting opportunities for slaughter that could have been exploited at affordable cost, argued that they had no stomach for the war and a deep-seated timidity that more or less guaranteed success to the invasion. The body-count could be taken either way. The Drapers said that Melancton had wasted three thousand lives through sheer fecklessness. The Foundry-men said that three thousand was still well within budget, given that the harrying attacks they'd anticipated as the army advanced through the hostile terrain of Eremia hadn't materialized; indeed, if the pre-invasion casualty estimates were compared with actual reported losses, the invasion was comfortably in credit. Further-more, the expeditionary force had been left in full possession of the field, and had resumed its march on Civitas Eremiae. By vir-tue of forced marches, Melancton had made up the lost time and was currently slightly ahead of schedule. Both sides were perfectly correct in their assertions, and neither faction even tried to dispute the other's arguments or statistics. A motion from the Clockmakers to dismiss Melancton wasn't even put to a vote, since (as Chairman Boioannes had pointed out in his opening remarks) there was no alternative candidate for overall command of the expedition who would be acceptable to the men themselves. A motion of censure was passed by a narrow majority, but it was agreed that it would be counterproductive and damaging to morale to publish it until the war was over and safely won, at which point it would be irrelevant; accordingly, it was agreed that it should lie on the file indefinitely.

Eventually she found him in a small room near the top of the old clock tower. When she burst in he was sitting facing the narrow window, a pile of papers on a small table beside him, a book open on his lap. She noticed that it was upside down.

"Orsea, you've got to do something," she said breathlessly, wondering as she said it why he hadn't turned his head to look at her. "There's this crazy rumor going around that Miel's been arrested and he's going to be executed or something. If people start believing that, there'll be panic and chaos and God knows what. You've got to tell them it's not true. Maybe the two of you could go out on the balcony and make a joint statement or something."

Still he didn't turn toward her. "Who says it's just a rumor?" she heard him say.

That didn't make sense. "Orsea," she said.

"Actually, the part about having him executed is a bit premature," he continued, in a voice that sounded like his, but very far away. "There'd have to be a trial first, and we can't allow that; at least, not till the war's over, assuming we survive it, and maybe not even then. In fact, definitely not. So no, we won't do that. Have to think up something else instead."

That was more cryptic gibberish than she could take. She lunged forward and grabbed at his shoulder; he avoided her, like a good fencer. "Are you completely out of your mind?" she said.

"He's just won a battle, for pity's sake. He's your best friend. You can't—"

Now he turned and looked at her, and she took a step back. He searched for something on the table, found it; a small square of closely folded parchment. He pointed it at her as though it was a weapon.

Oh, she thought.

"He had it," Orsea said. "At least, it was hidden in a room in the Ducas house, in a place only he knew about. And it so happens I can verify that myself, because when we were kids he stole my lucky penknife and hid it there—a little sort of crack in the wall, behind a tapestry; but I was watching through the keyhole, though he didn't know. It was his secret place. If he put it there, it was because he didn't want it found."

"How did you—?" Veatriz started to say. She cut the question short, but the damage was done.

"How did I find out?" Orsea laughed. There was something frightening in his voice. "Extraordinary thing. That Mezentine, Vaatzes, the one who builds the war engines; he scheduled a meeting with me, I thought it was just about production schedules, but as soon as we were alone he took it out of his pocket and handed it to me. I was stunned; I sat there staring at it, trying to figure out what the hell it was. I could read the words; but for ages I simply couldn't figure out what it could possibly mean. And also I kept thinking, why the hell would Miel be hiding a letter, written to you by the Duke of the bloody Vadani? How in God's name did you come into it? And then—"

"Orsea, don't," she heard herself say; but she might as well have been in the audience at a play, watching a drama written two hundred years ago. She could protest all she liked, but there was nothing she could do to alter the words that were due to come next.

"And then," Orsea went on, "I remembered that extraordinary speech of yours, about how we should run away and throw ourselves on the mercy of Duke Valens." He shook his head. "Really,

Triz, I don't know; have I been really stupid, not seeing the bloody obvious when it's right under my nose, or what? I didn't know you'd ever met him, even, let alone —"

"Once," she shouted. "Once, when we were kids, practically. I talked to him for five minutes at some horrible boring reception."

He looked at her and said nothing; his silence killed something inside her. "And Miel fits in, of course, I can see that now," he went on eventually. "He was always in love with you. You and he would've been married, only you had to marry me instead, because of politics. So of course he'd help you. The one thing I still can't figure out is who he's been betraying me to. I mean, this proves he's been working for the Vadani; then he goes and throws the battle, lets the bastards escape when he could've finished them off, so is he working for the Mezentines as well? Or is it just anything to screw me, because I took you off him?" He shrugged; big, melodramatic gesture. "I suppose I should care, because it matters politically, but I can't even be bothered to work it out. All I want is for the Mezentines to come quickly and finish us all off, before I find out anything else about what's been going on here."

She realized that her legs were giving way; she took two wobbly steps back and leaned against the wall. "It's not like that at all," she said. "Will you just listen to me?"

He looked at her. "I don't think so," he said. "It'll just make me feel worse if you lie to me."

That just made her feel murderously angry; if she'd had a knife, she'd have wanted to cut him with it. "Orsea," she said, "it was just letters. He wrote to me about something, or I wrote to him, I can't bloody remember which; and we just carried on, like friends. That's absolutely all it was, I swear. And God knows how Miel got hold of that letter, but he was nothing at all to do with it, I promise."

"You swear and you promise," Orsea said gravely. "There, now."

"Orsea, don't be —"

"Stop it, Triz," he said. "It's obvious. It's so obvious a bloody Mezentine who's only been in the country five minutes knows all about it; I suppose everybody knew but me. It's so *horrible*." He clenched his fists; it was a weak, petulant gesture, something a little boy might have done. "Would you please go away now," he went on. "I really don't want to talk to you anymore right now."

She tried to take a step toward him, but her feet wouldn't take her weight. "Orsea," she said. "Read the bloody letter. It's just harmless stuff, it's just *chat*. It doesn't—"

He laughed, and her mind was suddenly full of poison. "Just chat," he repeated. "Do you really think I'm so stupid? Well yes, apparently you do. Fine. I must be. Now would you please go away? I've got a war to run."

"Orsea. Will you please just listen?"

He shook his head. "No," he said. "Right now, if you told me my name I wouldn't believe you."

She wanted to fall on her knees and beg. She wanted to smash his face in. She couldn't do either. "At least talk to Miel," she said.

"No." He turned his back on her, sat down, picked up the book. It was *King Fashion and Queen Reason*. She could have burst out laughing. Instead, she leaned against the wall for balance and left the room.

The Mezentine army duly presented itself at the foot of the mountain road. Scouts reported that they numbered thirty thousand infantry, five hundred scorpions and a small garnish of light cavalry. They sat down and waited, like an actor waiting for his cue. Two days; nothing happened.

On the third morning, the baggage train arrived. It was suitably long and impressive; enough food and matériel for a long, thorough siege, enough plant and equipment for a devastating assault. Most of the machinery visible from the scouts' viewing point was so unfamiliar that they could only guess what it was supposed to be for; some reckoned it was heavy artillery for bashing down the walls, others were certain it was lifts and cranes for scaling ladders and siege towers, while a vocal minority insisted it was earth-moving equipment for undermining the main gate.

Just for the hell of it, Orsea sent an embassy under a flag of truce to ask why he was being invaded, and if there was anything he could do by way of reparation or apology. The embassy didn't come back. That, it was generally agreed inside the city, wasn't promising. On a more positive note, the Mezentine Vaatzes reported that all the scorpions were installed on the wall, fully operational, with good supplies of ammunition. If the enemy were stupid enough to come within range, he said, he could lay down a barrage that'd take out ten thousand of them before they had time to set up and load a single scorpion.

Certain death at the hands of an implacable and invincible enemy on the one hand; a stone-cold certain guarantee of victory on the other. Forced to choose between them, the Eremians in general made the obvious compromise and believed in both equally. It was easy enough to do; look down the valley at the enemy and abandon all hope, look up at the rows of war engines on the battlements and feel nothing but pity for the poor Mezentines, lambs to the pointless slaughter. Presumably the same ambivalence was what was keeping the enemy at a safe distance down in the valley; and there seemed to be no reason why they shouldn't stay there forever and ever.

As was only proper for such a noble and ancient house, there were plenty of precedents for the treatment and privileges of a Ducas arrested for high treason. It had been established over two centuries ago that he should be held in the East Tower of the inner keep, a substantial and self-contained space where he could enjoy the view out over the long cover, and the sun sparkling on the distant water of the Ribbon Lake. It was held that this would afford him peace and tranquillity in his darkest hour; further or in the alternative, it would remind him of the start of the falconry season, and by implication everything he'd forfeited by his foolish and presumptuous behavior. He should be brought food and fresh clothing three times a day direct from the Ducas house (tasting the food to make sure it wasn't poisoned was a special perquisite of the guard captain) together with books, writing materials, playing cards, chess sets and other basic necessities of civilized life. Each day two of his hounds should be brought to see him, so that the pack wouldn't pine for their master, and in the season he should be permitted to fly a peregrine falcon from his window at the doves roosting in the eaves of the bell-tower. His daily exercise should consist of a walk along the battlement of the curtain wall morning and evening, and shortly before noon either twelve ends of archery (with a child's bow and blunts) or sparring with wooden wasters in the courtyard behind the main guardhouse at the top of the tower. His valet should come to shave him at sunrise and sunset, under supervision of the guard captain. The Ducas steward, bailiff, treasurer, head chamberlain, private secretary, housekeeper, head keeper and huntsman were permitted to call at any time during the hours of daylight, or after dark when urgent business required the Ducas' attention; other visitors were at the guard captain's discretion and subject to review by a supervisor appointed directly by the Duke. In the event that the Ducas was unmarried, he should be permitted after thirty-eight consecutive months' detention, or if condemned to death, to marry a woman of good family nominated by the Duke solely for the purpose of begetting an heir. During any one calendar year, his personal expenditure was limited to sixty thousand thalers, and he was not permitted to buy land in excess of three hundred acres (except in completion of contracts entered into prior to his arrest) or participate in a mercantile venture to the value of more than two hundred and fifty thousand thalers (except for contracts for the supply of food, textiles or lumber to the army or the ducal household). He was permitted to stage a masque at midsummer and midwinter, employing no more than sixteen paid actors and thirty-six musicians, and to be staged in the main guardhouse; and to hold a banquet for no more than a hundred and twenty guests on the occasion of his birthday, the Duke's birthday and the anniversary of the Battle of Cantelac. He could have his portrait painted once every six months.

From the southern balcony of the East Tower, Miel could just see the extreme edge of the Mezentine camp: a section of the perimeter ditch, which they'd dug on the first night and second morning, a corner of the enclosure they'd built to pen up the wagon horses, and, if he leaned out and twisted his neck as far as it would go, the arms of the tallest of the giant long-range war engines that were being assembled from prefabricated components in a specially fortified stockade. Beyond that, he had to rely on observations made for him by members of his household; they told him about the arrival of the supply train, various comings and goings of auxiliaries and engineers, and the lack of any other significant activity.

In a curious way, much of the time he didn't feel like a prisoner. Running the everyday affairs of the Ducas — rent reviews, planting schedules, repairs and renovations to tenanted properties, adjudicating in tenants' disputes, all the duties he'd carried out all his adult life without a second thought — felt more or less the same, regardless of the fact that he was doing them in a slightly different setting. They'd brought up some of the tapestries and smaller paintings from the rent-room at the Ducas house, since it would've been unreasonable to expect the Ducas to receive his dependents and tenants in anything less than the proper surroundings; his sitting-room in the East Tower was, if anything, slightly larger than the rent-room, and not quite as drafty. *Once I've been acquitted,* he told his visitors, *I've got a good mind to ask Orsea if I can stay here.* Most of them smiled the first few times he said it.

He wrote to Orsea four times a day: once before breakfast, usually a quick, personal note asking for a meeting as soon as possible; a longer, more formal appeal composed during the morning; another similar during the afternoon; an expanded but more informal summary of all three, usually written in the early hours of the morning. All were delivered personally by his private secretary, all were read, none were answered. At least once a day he wrote to

Veatriz, between three and ten pages, all of which he burned once
he'd finished them. People brought him presents; mostly books
(Jarnac gave him a brand-new copy of *King Fashion,* profusely illuminated and illustrated by a leading artist) and fruit, as though
he was ill.

He didn't know what he was supposed to have done, or who had
accused him, or what evidence, if any, there was against him. The
general consensus of opinion among his visitors was that it was
something to do with the cavalry raid; it was cowardice or incompetence, or else deliberate collusion with the enemy, because he
could have killed far more of them from the position he'd been in
but had instead chosen to withdraw. His steward, a gloomy man
called Evech, reckoned it was all the Mezentine Vaatzes' fault;
he'd never forgotten how Miel had wanted to have him executed
as a spy, and now he was in a position of power and influence, he
was getting his revenge. Cousin Jarnac refused to offer any opinion whatsoever. He simply couldn't understand it, but Orsea had
refused to see him or answer his letters, so he could shed no light
on the matter. Miel's valet reckoned the Duke was after the family wealth, to help pay for the war. Nobody said anything about
Veatriz being involved in any way, but she hadn't been to see him
or written a letter. His housekeeper reckoned it was all a nasty plot
by the Phocas, whom she always blamed for everything.

"If you ask me," she said vehemently, "it's them bloody Phocas
who started this whole stupid war, just so they could do us down
and get the command. Nothing they wouldn't do to push us out
and be on top, only they know so long as you're around there's
no chance of that, so they start spreading their filthy lies, and of
course the Duke believes them, he'd believe any bloody thing—"

"You mustn't talk like that about the Duke," Miel said firmly.

She looked at him as if he was a martyred saint. "But look at
how he's treating you," she said, "his best friend and all. If I could
only get my hands on him—"

"That's enough," Miel said sharply; then he went on: "I mean,
it'd be no good if I got out of here to find my own housekeeper,

who's the only woman in the city who can run our house properly, is in jail for high treason. Fact is, you're far more important to the Ducas house than I am."

There were fat, soggy tears in her eyes; not just admiration and doglike devotion, but guilt as well. "You're making me feel dreadful," she said. "I wasn't going to tell you, not till you got out of here, but I can't keep it to myself anymore, it's like I'm betraying you when you need me most. For two pins I'd tell him to forget it, only everything's arranged now and I don't know if we'd be able to get the money back, and he's set his heart—"

"Hang on," Miel interrupted. "I think you may have missed a bit out. What can't you keep to yourself, and how are you betraying me?"

"Well," she said with a sniff, "me and Geratz—he's my husband, you know—"

"I've known him since I was six," Miel pointed out.

"Of course you have, I'm sorry. Anyway, we've come into a bit of money, a nice bit of money actually, and Geratz has always had his heart set on a farm, ever since he was a kid, his uncle being a smallholder out in the Crane valley and Geratz going there such a lot when he was a small boy—"

"You're buying a farm, then," Miel interrupted.

She nodded three times quickly. "Cousin of a friend of Geratz's aunt," she said, "got no kids of his own and he's getting on, the place is too big for him, but it's a good farm, there's sixty acres of pasture, a good vineyard, nice big plot for growing a bit of corn down by the river—that's the Mare's Tail, I expect you know it well, out west on the border, which would've put us off, of course, but now we're all friends with the Vadani there's really nothing to worry about—and there's a good road for taking the flock to market, and he wants next to nothing for it really, I think he just wants someone to look after it, make sure it doesn't all go to seed and ruin—well, you can understand that, after working all his life—"

"I'm delighted for you," Miel said firmly. "Truly I am. You deserve some luck, both of you."

She gazed at him as though her heart was breaking. "Yes, but leaving you, at a time like this, it just doesn't seem right..."

"Rubbish," Miel said. "The most important thing is to take your chances when you can. Now, as a token of my appreciation for all your hard work over the years I'd like to do something to help you set up. How about the live and dead stock? Is that included, or are you just buying the land?"

That had the effect of reducing her to tears, which was rather more than Miel could take. Besides, it was all completely fatuous; the Mezentines were camped at the foot of the mountain, and pretty soon all contracts, agreements, promises and plans would be null and void forever. It occurred to him to wonder whether she appreciated that. Absurd irony: to cherish an unthinkable ambition for a lifetime, to attain it through a small miracle (she hadn't said where the money had come from; a legacy, presumably) only to have it swept away by a huge, unexpected, illogical, ridiculous monstrosity of a war. Of course, he couldn't help thinking, here's my chance to be a hero; I could promise her any damn thing— five hundred prime dairy cows, a brand-new barn, a new plow and a team of twenty milk-white horses—and of course I'll never have to pay up, because in a very short time we'll all be dead. Oh, the temptation!

He spent the rest of her visit dealing with strictly domestic matters. Because of the siege, it wasn't possible for the steward of the home farm to send the usual supplies of provisions for the household up to the town house; it was therefore necessary to buy food for the staff, something that the Ducas hadn't done for generations. He authorized the extravagance with all due solemnity, and also agreed to a general washing and airing of curtains and bedlinen. ("Might as well get it all done while you're not at home," she'd said, "so it won't be a nuisance to you." He appreciated the thought, at any rate.) After a slight hesitation, she asked if she could take down the big tapestry, which she knew she shouldn't touch without express permission, but it had got in a dreadful state, with dust and all. There was a slight catch in her voice when she asked him that, but she was, after all, a rather emotional woman.

When she'd gone, he took a fresh sheet of paper (she'd brought a ream with her up from the house, since he was running low) and wrote his usual letters: to Orsea, conversational and slightly desperate; to Jarnac, asking him if he'd mind taking the riding horses to his stables for the time being, since he was concerned that they weren't getting enough exercise; to Veatriz, six pages, which he read over slowly before tearing them into small pieces and feeding them methodically into the fire. Not long after he'd finished that task, a guard told him he had another visitor: Vaatzes, the Mezentine, if he could spare a moment to see him.

"I think I might be able to fit him in," Miel replied gravely. The guard went away, and Miel got up to pour some wine from the jug into a decanter. There was a bowl of fresh apples, a new loaf and some seed-cakes, which the housekeeper had brought. The Ducas recipe for seed-cake was as old as the city itself and even more closely guarded; Miel had never liked it much.

Vaatzes looked tired, which was hardly surprising; he was thinner, and he grunted softly when he sat down. Then he yawned, and apologized.

"That's all right," Miel said. "I imagine they're keeping you busy right now."

Vaatzes nodded. "It sounds bad saying it," he replied, "but I'll almost be glad when the attack comes, and there's nothing else I can do. At the moment I keep thinking of slight modifications and improvements, which means breaking down four hundred sets of mountings just to put on an extra washer or slip in another shim. I know for a fact that all the artillery crews hate me. Don't blame them, either."

Miel shook his head. "You just wait," he said. "Once they attack, you'll have your work cut out."

"Not really," Vaatzes said. "I'm not a soldier, I'm just a mechanic. As soon as the bolts start flying I intend to find a deep, dark cellar and barricade myself in."

"Very wise," Miel said. "And you've done your bit already, God knows. But I suppose it's your war as much as ours, given the way they treated you. You want to get back at them, naturally."

Vaatzes frowned. "Not at all," he said. "I've got one hell of a grudge against a small number of officials in the Foundrymen's Guild and Compliance, but I love my city. What I want most in the whole world is to go home and carry on with my old life. That's not going to be possible, but it still doesn't mean I suddenly hate everybody I used to love, and that I've stopped believing in everything that I used to live by. No, I'm helping you because it's my duty, because you people rescued me when I was dying and gave me a home and a job to do; and because nobody else has a use for me. I'd have thought you of all people would've understood about duty."

"That old thing." Miel laughed. "It's actually one of our family's titles: the Ducas, Lord of the Mesogaea, Baron Hereditary of the Swan River, Master of the East Marches, Slave of Duty. Always made me laugh, that, but in fact it's true; the Ducas is the second most powerful man in this country, but everything he does every day, from getting up in the morning to going to bed at night, is pretty well dictated to him by duty. It's not something I ever think about, the way fish don't think about water."

Vaatzes studied him for a moment, as though making an assessment. "Duke Orsea's taken over running the war himself," he said. "Someone called the lesser Phocas is in charge of supplies and administration, and your cousin Jarnac's in command of the defense of the walls. There's a man called something Amyntas supposedly commanding the artillery, but I haven't met him yet. I think he's quite happy for me to get on with it; which is stupid, since I don't know the first thing about military science."

Miel grinned. "Neither does Tarsa Amyntas," he said. "He was famous for a week or so about fifteen years ago, when he killed a lot of Vadani in the war; hand-to-hand fighting in a forest, if I'm thinking about the right man. Since then, he's mostly spent his time composing flute-music and trying to grow strawberries in winter. Military command in this country goes according to birth, rank and position. It's a miracle we're still here."

"It seems to have worked," Vaatzes said mildly. "Take you, for instance. You won a battle."

"That seems to be a matter of opinion," Miel said.

"No, it's a fact. You were outnumbered—what, ten to one? It was something ridiculous like that. You outplanned and outfought the best professional commander money can buy. And I don't suppose it was just natural talent or beginner's luck," he added, with a small grin. "It's because you were born and brought up to do a particular job, just like sons follow their fathers in the Guilds. I'll bet you were learning about logistics and reading up old battles at an age when most kids are learning their times tables."

"Sort of," Miel said. "But I'm nothing special, believe me. It was just luck; and besides, I threw it all away by pulling back too early. At any rate, that seems to be what Orsea thinks, and the opinion of the Duke is the only thing that matters to the Ducas. Says so somewhere in the book of rules."

Vaatzes frowned at him. "Your family has a rule-book?" he said.

Miel laughed. "No, it's a figure of speech. Though, since you mention it, there is a Ducas code of honor, all properly written down and everything. The Five Transcendent Precepts, it's called. My great-great-"—he paused and counted on his fingers—"great-*great*-grandfather made it up and had it carved on a wall, on the left by the main hall door as you go in. I had to learn it by heart when I was eight."

"Really? What does it say?"

"Can't remember, to be honest with you. Not all of it, anyhow. Let's see: do your duty to your Duke, your family, your tenants and servants, your people and your country. That's one. Never question an order or give an order that deserves to be questioned, that's two. Three..." He closed his eyes, trying to visualize the chisel-cuts in the yellow stone. "Three is something like true courtesy dignifies the receiver and the giver. Four is, remember always that the acts of the Ducas live forever. Five—well, you get the general idea. Pretty intimidating stuff to force on an eight-year-old." He frowned slightly. "You're laughing," he said. "Which is fair enough, it's all pretty ridiculous stuff, but—"

"Actually," Vaatzes said, "I was thinking, that's something you and me have in common. Except when I was eight years old, I was learning the specifications of the Foundrymen and Machinists' Guild. At least all your rules of conduct make some sort of sense. The specifications are just a whole list of measurements and dimensions. But really they amount to the same thing; stuff you've got to live by, like it or not, because that's what we stand for. I can still remember them all, believe it or not. On my ninth birthday I had to go to the Guildhall along with all the other kids in my class and stand on a platform in the Long Gallery, and three scary old men tested us; it felt like hours, and we'd been told beforehand that if we got anything even slightly wrong, that'd be it—out of the Guild forever, which would've been the next best thing to a death sentence. Were we nervous? I can feel the sweat now, running down inside my shirt. And I was desperate for a pee—I'd gone about a dozen times while we were waiting in the lodge— but of course there was nothing I could do except stand with my legs crossed hoping nobody'd notice."

Miel laughed. "When I was that age I had to go up in front of everybody when we had company for dinner and recite poetry— Mannerist stuff, mostly, which I never could be doing with. If I did all right and remembered it all and didn't gabble, Father'd give me a present, like a new hood for my sparrowhawk or a new pair of riding gloves; but if I got it wrong and showed him up he'd be absolutely livid for days; wouldn't speak to me, just looked past me as though I didn't exist. I never could see the point of it, because the guests must've been bored stiff—who wants to hear a snot-nosed kid reciting sonnets about dew-spattered ferns?—and he'd be mortified if I wasn't absolutely perfect, and I hated it, of course. But apparently it was one of those things you had to do, so we all did it. Like you and your measurements, I suppose."

Vaatzes nodded. "There's a difference, though," he said. "To you it was all just a waste of time; a stupid, pointless chore but you did it out of duty. For me—I can honestly say, when I got off the platform and I realized I'd passed, it was the proudest moment of my life. I felt I belonged, you see; I'd earned my place."

"That's good," Miel said, after a light pause. "You were quite right to feel that way."

"I thought so," Vaatzes said. "It's like the story we were all told at school, about the man whose name was put forward for membership of General Council; there were twenty vacancies, and he'd been nominated by his co-workers, so he went along to the interview, feeling nervous as hell. Anyhow, that evening he comes home, and he's grinning like an idiot; so his wife looks at him and says, 'You got it, then,' and he grins a bit more and says, 'No.' 'So why're you smirking like that?' she says. 'I'm happy,' he replies. 'Happy? What're you happy about, you didn't make it.' And he beams at her and says, 'I'm happy for the City, because if I didn't get it, it means there's twenty men in Mezentia who're even more loyal and wise and clever than I am; isn't that fantastic?'"

Miel frowned. "That's supposed to be ironic, presumably."

"No," Vaatzes said.

"Ah." Miel shrugged. "Sorry. No disrespect. But even the Ducas never came up with anything as sappy as that."

"I think it's a good story," Vaatzes said. "Please, don't ever get me wrong. I haven't changed who I am, just because I'm in exile."

Miel sighed. "It's all very well you saying that," he said. "I mean, I'm the same as you. Orsea may have had me arrested and locked up in here, but he's still the Duke and my best friend, and if he honestly thinks this is where I should be, then fine. I happen to believe he's wrong, and once things are sorted out, we can go back to how we were. But in your case..." He shook his head. "What you did was absolutely harmless, there was nothing wrong about it, you hadn't hurt anybody, and they were going to kill you for it. You can't accept that, and you can't still have any faith in the society that was going to do that to you."

Vaatzes looked at him for a moment. "I was guilty," he said. "And they caught me, and I deserved to be punished. But there were other considerations, which meant I couldn't hold still and die. It wasn't up to me, the choice of whether or not to hold still and take what was coming to me. If I'd been a free agent..." He shook his head slowly. "If there hadn't been those other considerations, of course, I'd never have broken the law in the first place, so really it's a circular argument."

Miel, not surprisingly, didn't understand. "If that's really how you feel," he said, "what on earth prompted you to design and build all those war engines that're going to mow down your people in droves? No, don't interrupt; it's not like we came to you and asked you, let alone threatened you with torture if you refused. You offered. What's more, you offered and we refused, so you had to go to all the trouble of getting a private investor to put up the money and everything. That simply doesn't make any sense, does it?"

"Like I said," Vaatzes said quietly, "there are other considerations." He broke eye contact, looked out of the window. "If you're standing on a ledge and someone pushes you, it's not your fault that you fall. The whole thing has been out of my hands for a very long time now. It's a great shame, but there it is. You'd be doing the same as me, in my shoes."

Miel decided not to reply to that; when someone insists on willfully being wrong, it's bad manners to persist in correcting him. "Thank you for coming to see me," he said.

Vaatzes looked at him and grinned. "No problem," he said. "For what little it's worth, I'm absolutely positive you haven't done anything wrong. Also for what it's worth, I'd like to thank you for everything you've done to help me. Without you, I don't know what I'd have done. I wish I could repay you somehow, but I can't." He stood up. "I wish there was something I could do."

"Don't worry about it," Miel said.

Don't worry about it, he'd said; Ziani thought about that as he walked home. Technically, it was absolution, which was probably what he'd gone there to obtain. Query, however: is absolution valid if it's obtained through deceit, fraud and treachery?

Irrelevant; he didn't need the Ducas' forgiveness, any more than he'd have needed it if he'd been pushed off a ledge and fallen on him, breaking his arm or leg. In that case, he'd have been no more than a projectile, a weapon in the hand of whoever had pushed him. There are all sorts of ways in which people are made into weapons; what they do once they've been put to that use is not their fault. A man can't work in an arms factory unless he believes in the innocence of weapons.

As he cleared the lower suburbs and approached the wall, he became aware of a great deal of activity; a great many people walking fast or running, not aimlessly or in panic but with an obvious, serious purpose. Some of them were hurrying up the hill, toward the center of town and the palace. Most of them, however, were coming down the hill, heading for the wall or the gate. Fine, he thought; something's about to happen, we're about to get under way at last. He allowed himself a moment (there might not be another opportunity) to consider his feelings, which he'd learned to trust over the years. He realized that he felt, on balance, content. A great deal was wrong about what had happened and what was about to happen, but he was satisfied that he bore no blame for any of it. His part had been carried out with proper, in some respects elegant efficiency; and he was reasonably confident that it would all come out right, barring the unforeseen and the unforeseeable. He checked progress achieved against the overall schematic. There was still a long way to go, but he'd come a long way already. Most of all, everything was more or less under control. Suddenly, without expecting to, he laughed. The Eremian workers at the factory had an expression, *good enough for government work*, meaning something like, *by no means perfect, but who cares, it'll do*. It had always annoyed him when he'd heard them using it; right now, however, it was entirely appropriate. Very soon now, by the sound of it, there'd be plenty of government work on both sides of the city wall. He, of course, preferred to see things in terms of tolerances; what could and could not be tolerated in the context of the job that needed to be done. By those criteria, he'd passed the test and could go home with a quiet mind.

Orsea arrived at the wall expecting to see one of his nightmares. Instead, he found the seventh infantry drawn up in parade order, and the captain saluting him.

"What's happening?" he asked.

"They've started to climb the road," the captain told him. "Come and see for yourself."

Jarnac Ducas joined him on top of the gatehouse tower. Pre-occupied as Orsea was with thoughts of the end of the world, he couldn't help noticing that Jarnac's unerring dress sense had chosen exactly the right outfit for the occasion: a coat of plates backed in blue velvet over a shirt of flat, riveted mail; plain blued-steel arm and leg harness; an open-face bascinet with a mail aventail; simple mail chausses over strong shoes; workmanlike Type Fifteen sword in a plain leather scabbard. Is there, Orsea wondered, a book where you can look these things up: *Arms and Armor for Formal Occasions: A Guide for the Well-Dressed Warrior.* He wouldn't be the least surprised, he decided, if there was.

"Nothing either way as yet," Jarnac told him. "See down there, you can just make them out." (Jarnac pointed; Orsea couldn't see anything.) "That's their heavy artillery, the stuff we really don't know anything about. According to the Mezentine fellow, Vaatzes, they could have engines that could drop five-hundred-weight shot on the walls from about halfway up the road; which'd be a disaster, obviously, we'd have to send out a sortie to deal with them and that'd be simply asking for trouble. But, apparently, the platforms and carriages for that kind of engine are too wide or too fragile or something to be set up on the road—because of the gradient, presumably—so it's possible they won't be able to use them at all unless they stop halfway up and spend several days building a special platform. Nothing to stop them doing that, of course, unless we're brave enough or cocky enough to send out a night sortie. Alternatively, they could drag the heavy artillery round the back of the city and set it up roughly where the advance party of scorpions was supposed to be—where it would've been if we hadn't intercepted it, I mean. In fact, that's the only scenario we can think of which'd explain why they wanted to station scorpions there in the first place: to lay down a suppressing barrage to cover them while they get the heavy engines set up. Of course, you'd expect them to change the plan because of what happened, but you never know, they may decide to press on regardless. Basically, it's too early to say anything for certain."

That seemed to cover the situation pretty well, though Orsea felt he ought to be asking penetrating questions to display his perfect grasp of it. But the only thing he really wanted to know was whether, at some point between now and the start of the actual assault, Jarnac would be slipping off home to change into something else; or whether he'd got a full wardrobe of different armors laid out ready in the guard tower. He wished he didn't dislike Jarnac so much, particularly since he was going to have to rely on him; that made him think of Miel, which had the effect of freezing his mind. "Carry on," he heard himself say.

He toured the walls, of course, and anxious-looking officers whose names tended to elude him jumped up and saluted him wherever he went. They pointed things out to him, things he couldn't quite make out in the distance—high points where the enemy might put observers or long-range engines, patches of dead ground where a whole division could lurk unseen, secret mountain trails that could be useful for raids and sorties—and he knew that he ought to be taking it all in, building each component into a mechanism that would serve as a weapon against the enemy. But there was too much of everything for his mind to grasp. The only thing he knew for certain was that he was slowly seizing up, as fear, shock and pain coagulated and set inside him. The enemy would build their platform and their engines would grind down the walls at their leisure, smashing Vaatzes' hard-earned, expensive scorpions into rubbish before they'd had a chance to loose a single shot.

When that task had been completed to their perfect satisfaction, the enemy would advance, entirely safe, to the foot of the wall; their scorpions would clear away the last of Jarnac's defenders, the ladders would be raised, the enemy would surge in like a mighty white-fringed wave; and all the while, Miel (who could have saved the city) would watch from his tower window, and Veatriz would watch from hers; maybe they'd be watching when he was killed, maybe they'd see him fall and be unable to do anything...

Part of the torment was knowing that there was still enough time. He could send a runner to the captain of the East Tower; Miel could be here beside him in a few minutes, to forgive him and take over and make everything all right again. But he couldn't do that; because Miel had betrayed him, Miel and Veatriz — the truth was that he didn't know what it was they'd done, or how Duke Valens came into it; all he knew was that he could never trust either of them again, and without them he was completely useless, a fool in charge of the battle of life against death. It was like the nightmares he had now and again, where he was a doctor about to perform surgery, and he suddenly realized he didn't have the faintest idea what he was supposed to do; or he'd agreed to act in a play but he hadn't got round to learning his lines, and now he was due to go on in front of a hundred people. The officers carried on telling him things he ought to know, but it was as though they were speaking a foreign language. *We've had it,* he thought; and his mind started to fill up with images of the last time, the field of dead men and scorpion bolts. *It's all my fault,* he told himself, *I'm to blame for all of it; nobody else but me.*

Once the tour of inspection was over, he went back to Jarnac's tower and asked him what was happening. Jarnac pointed out the heavy engines — he could see them for himself now — being dragged up the slope by long trains of mules. Ahead of them trudged a dense mass of men; the work details, Jarnac explained, who'd be building the platform for the engines.

"I see," Orsea said. "So what should we be doing?"

He could see a flicker of concern in Jarnac's eyes, as if to say *what're you asking me for?* "Well," he said, "as I mentioned earlier, we have the option of launching a sortie. We can try and drive off the work details, or kill them, or capture or destroy the heavy engines. It's our only way of putting the engines out of action before they neutralize our defenses—assuming, of course, that they're capable of doing that. We've never seen them in action, or heard any accounts of what they can do, so we're guessing, basically. But if we launch the sortie, we'll be taking quite a risk. To put it bluntly, I don't think we'd stand any more of a chance than we did the last time we took on the Mezentines in the open. Our scorpions can't give us cover down there, and we'd be walking right up to theirs; and even if you leave the scorpions out of it completely, we'd be taking on their army in a pitched battle. I don't think that'd be a good idea."

Jarnac stopped talking and looked at him; so did a dozen or so other officers, waiting for him to decide. He could feel fear coming to life inside them (*the Duke hasn't got a plan, he can't make up his mind, he's useless, we're screwed*). He knew he had to say something, and that if he said the wrong thing it could easily mean the destruction of the city.

"Fine," he said. "No sortie. We'll just sit it out and wait and see."

The silence was uncomfortable, as though he'd just said something crass and tactless, or spouted gibberish at them. *I've lost them,* he thought, *but they'll obey my orders because I'm the Duke.* Their excellent loyalty would keep them from ignoring him and doing what they thought should be done, what they knew was the right course of action; they'd fail him by loyalty, just as Miel had failed him by treachery. Ah, symmetry!

But he'd given the order now; fatal to change his mind and trample down what little confidence in him they had left. Amusing thought: here was the entire Mezentine army coming up the mountain specially to kill him, well over thirty thousand men all hungering for his blood; even so, in spite of their multitudes, he was still his own worst enemy.

Jarnac cleared his throat. "If it's all right with you, I'd like to run the scorpion crews through a few more drills," he said. "We've got time, I'm fairly sure, and—"

"Yes, do that," Orsea snapped at him. "I'll get out of your way, you've got—" He didn't bother to finish the sentence. He headed for the stairs. People followed him; he ought to know who they all were, but he didn't. He had no clear idea of where he was going, or what he was going to do next.

In response to his urgent request for technical advice, they brought him a man called Falier, who was apparently the chief engineer of the state arms factory. It seemed logical enough. This Falier was in charge of building the machines, so presumably he'd know how they worked and what they were capable of doing.

Falier turned out to be younger than he'd expected; a nervous, good-looking, weak sort of man who'd probably agree with everything he said. General Melancton sighed, told him to sit down and offered him a drink.

"The heavy engines," he said. "The—what are they, the Mark Sixes. How far will they shoot?"

The man called Falier looked at him as if he didn't understand the question. "Well," he said slowly, "it all depends. I mean, for a start, how heavy a ball are you using?"

Expect the worst of people and you won't be disappointed. "I don't know," Melancton said with studied patience. "You tell me. What weight of ball will give me maximum range?"

Falier was doing sums in his head. "A two-hundredweight ball will carry six hundred yards," he said, "at optimum elevation, assuming the wind's not against you. But," he went on, "I can't guarantee it'd be effective against that sort of masonry; not at extreme range."

"I see." Melancton sighed. "So what weight of ball do I need to use?"

"Well," Falier said, "a five hundredweight'll go through pretty much anything."

"Excellent. And what's the extreme range of a five hundred-weight?"

Falier shrugged. "Two hundred yards," he said. "More if you've got a following wind, of course."

"That would be well inside scorpion range, from the city wall."

"Oh yes." Falier nodded enthusiastically. "Especially shot from the top of the wall there. Actually, it's quite a sophisticated calculation, where the point of release is higher up than the point of impact. It's all to do with the rate of decay of the bolt's trajectory, and the acceleration it builds up on its way down. The variables can make a hell of a difference, mind."

Falier, in other words, didn't know the answer to his question; so he thanked him and got rid of him, and resolved to build his siege platform at four hundred and fifty yards. If the balls dropped short at that range, they'd just have to move up a bit closer and build another platform. Embarrassing; but with any luck, all the witnesses to his embarrassment—the hostile ones at least—would be dead quite soon, and so it wouldn't really matter terribly much. He gave the order, then left his tent and walked a little way up the road so he could watch the building detail at work.

The mercenary infantry were, of course, too well trained and high-class to dig earth and carry it back and forth in baskets; so he'd sent to Mezentia for brute labor, and they'd sent him five hundred assorted Cure Doce, Paulisper, Cranace and Lonazep dockside miscellaneous, at three groschen a day. Twenty groschen to the Mezentine foreign thaler, and it's a sad fact of life that you get what you pay for. The Cure Doce dug and spitted with a kind of steadfast indifference; the Paulisper didn't mind heavy lifting, but were generally drunk by mid-afternoon; the Cranace picked fights with the Paulisper over matters of religion and spectator sport; the Lonazeppians worked hard but complained about everything (the food, the tents, the Cranace's singing). In the event, it took them four days and nights on a three-shift rotation to build the platform. Melancton's most optimistic forecast had been six. The Eremians made no effort to interfere in any way, which he found strange and faintly disturbing. In their position he'd have launched sorties; even if capturing or wrecking the engines proved too difficult, scaring the labor force into mass desertion would've been no trouble at all. An enemy who neglected such an obvious opportunity was either supremely confident or utterly resigned to defeat.

On the fifth morning, he went up to the platform with Syracoelus, his captain of artillery, the engineer Falier and a couple of pain-in-the-bum liaison officers from the Mezentine Guilds, who'd been sent up to find out why the war hadn't been won yet. The early mists had burned away in bright, harsh sunlight; the heavy engines had been hauled up overnight and were already dug in, aligned and crewed for action. Four hundred and fifty yards away, the enemy looked like roosting rooks behind their turrets and battlements, the noses of scorpions poking out from behind each crenellation.

Melancton and his party stood in silence for a while, looking up at the walls. Nobody seemed in any hurry to say anything, not even the usually unsilenceable Mezentines. Finally, Melancton said, "Well, I suppose we'd better get on with it." The engine crews hesitated, trying to figure out if that constituted a valid order to open fire. Melancton frowned, then nodded to Captain Syracoelus, who looked at the nearest engine-master and said, "Loose."

He was being somewhat premature, of course; first they had to span the huge windlass that dragged down the engine's throwing-arm against the tension of the nested, inch-thick leaf springs that powered it. In the silence the smooth snicks of the ratchet sounded horribly loud (it was as though the city was asleep, and Melancton was worried they'd wake it up). A louder, meatier snick told him the sear was engaged and the engine was ready to be loaded; a wheeled dolly was rolled under a derrick which lifted a three-hundredweight stone ball off a pile; the dolly ran on tracks that stopped under a short crane, which lifted the ball into the spoon on the end of the throwing-arm. Men with levers rolled it into place and jumped clear. Syracoelus repeated his order; someone pulled back a lever, and the arm reared up, sudden and violent as a punch. Melancton could hear the throbbing whistle the ball made as it spun; at first it climbed, almost straight, so far that he was sure they'd overshoot the city completely. At the top of its trajectory it hung for a split second, the sunlight choosing that moment to flare off it, like an unofficial moon. Then it began to fall, the decay of the cast seeming to draw it in as if there were chains attached to it. He lost sight of it against the backdrop of the walls; heard the dull thump as it bashed into the masonry, saw a puff of dust and steam lift into the air and drift for a moment before dispersing. "Elevation good," he heard someone say, "windage two minutes left"; another lever clicked and a sear rang like a bell, and that oscillating whistle again, followed by the thump and the round white ball of dust. The clicking of ratchets all round him was as busy as crickets in meadow-grass; men were straining at their windlasses, every last scrap of strength brought to bear on the long handles; voices were calling out numbers, six up, five left, two right; the distant thumps came so close together they melted into each other, and the whistles merged into a constant hum.

Compassion wasn't one of Melancton's weaknesses, but he couldn't help wondering what it must be like on the wall, as the shots landed; if the thumps were so heavy he could feel them through the soles of his feet four and a half hundred yards away, what did they feel like close to, as they butted into the stones of the wall? Melancton had never been on the wrong end of a bombardment like this; an earthquake, maybe, he thought, or the eruption of a volcano. "Keep it going for half an hour," he heard himself shouting over the extraordinary blend of noises, "and then we can see if we're doing any good." (Half an hour, he thought as he said it; how long would half an hour seem under the onslaught of the whistling stone predators, swooping in like a falcon on a partridge? He knew the fluffy white balls of cloud were steam because someone had explained it to him long ago; when the ball lands, the energy behind it is so great that for a split second it's burning hot, and any traces of moisture in the target are instantly boiled away into vapor. How could you be on the receiving end of something like that and not drop dead at once from sheer terror?)

The barrage didn't last half an hour; ten minutes at the very most, because by then all the shot had been used up, and it'd take at least an hour to replenish the stocks from the reserve supply. Syracoelus was quick to apologize; Melancton shrugged, having to make an effort not to admit that he was overjoyed that it was over; the clicking and ringing and the air full of that terrible humming noise, and the thuds of impacting shot a quarter-mile away as constant as the drumming of rain on a roof. He realized he'd been looking away, deliberately averting his eyes from the target. He looked up; and, to his considerable surprise, Civitas Eremiae was still there.

"Shit," someone said.

Syracoelus gave orders to his crews to stand by. "What's happening?" bleated one of the Mezentine liaisons. "I can't see from here." Someone else said, "Maybe we're just dropping them in the wrong place; how about if we concentrated the whole lot on the left-hand gatehouse tower?" Three people contradicted him simultaneously, drowning out each other's arguments as they competed for attention. "Hardly bloody scratched it," someone else said. "Fuck me, those walls must be solid."

Failure, then. Melancton felt like laughing out loud at the absurdity of it. The Mezentine heavy engines had been beaten, they weren't up to the job. Melancton caught himself on the verge of a grin; could it possibly be, he wondered, that he was beginning to *want* the Eremians to win?

"Wonderful," Syracoelus was saying. "Well, we can't possibly go in any closer, we'd be right under the noses of those scorpions on the wall. I suppose we could up the elevation to full and try the four-hundredweight balls, but I really don't think they'll get there, even."

"If we had a load of really strong pavises," someone else began to say; nobody contradicted him or shouted him down, but he didn't finish the suggestion.

It hadn't worked, then; or at least, not yet. There was still plenty of ammunition back at the supply train. He caught sight of Falier, the man from the ordnance factory, who hadn't contributed to the post-bombardment debate. He looked like he might throw up at any moment. "Is there any way to beef up the springs?" Melancton asked. He had to repeat the question a couple of times before he could get an answer, which was no, there wasn't. They were already on their highest setting, Falier explained, all the tensioners were done up tight.

"Any suggestions?" Melancton asked. "Come on, you produce the bloody things. Is there any kind of modification we could make?" Falier shuddered and shook his head. "Not allowed," he said.

Melancton looked at him. "Not allowed?"

"That's right," Falier replied. "Not without a dispensation from the Specifications directorate at the factory. Otherwise it'd be... I'd get into trouble."

Melancton smiled at him. "I'm giving you a direct order as commander in chief of the army," he said. "Now—"

"Sorry." Falier looked away. "I'm a civilian. You can't order me. If you threaten me, I'll have to report it. Anyhow," he went on, "it's all beside the point. We'd need to make new springs, and beef up the frames as well. Even if we got all the calculations right first time, it'd take weeks to have the springs made at the factory and sent up here. Have you got that much time?"

He's lying, Melancton realized. Of course he knew about Specifications, how they were sacrosanct and couldn't be altered on pain of death; he also knew that the arms factory was the one exception. As to the other argument (so neatly offered in the alternative), he had to take Falier's word for it, since he knew nothing about engineering or production times. He was fairly certain that Falier was exaggerating the timescale, but of course he couldn't prove it.

"Weeks," he repeated.

"And that's supposing we don't have setbacks," Falier said

quickly. "We can calculate the size and shape the spring'd have to be, up to a point, but in the end it'd be simple trial and error. Could be months, if we're unlucky."

Not so much a warning as a promise, Melancton suspected. For some reason, Falier didn't want to make any modifications to the engines. If forced to, he'd probably sabotage them, in some subtle, undetectable way. Melancton couldn't begin to understand why anybody would want to do that, but he'd been dealing with the Mezentines long enough to know that inscrutability was practically their defining characteristic. He might not be able to figure out what the reason was, but he had no trouble believing that there *was* a reason. He gave up; simple as that.

"Fine," he said. "So the long-range engines are useless, is that it?"

Falier shrugged. "If you could get them in closer," he said, "that'd be different. At this range, though..." He looked down at his hands. *For crying out loud*, Melancton thought.

"They're useless," he said. "Understood. Right, we'll have to find another way. Thank you so much for your help."

22

Melancton was a realist. He knew that he had no more chance of winning against the Perpetual Republic than the Eremians did. Just for the hell of it, however, he decided to persevere with the long-range engines for a little while. He had, after all, taken a great deal of pains to haul a large supply of ammunition for those engines; might as well use it up as let it go to waste, he thought. Even if it won't bring the walls tumbling down, it'll make life inside the city distinctly uncomfortable for a while. In war, every little helps.

So the bombardment resumed, as soon as the rest of the three-hundredweight balls had been lugged up from the valley. Melancton didn't hang around to watch, or listen; he left Syracoelus in charge and retired to his command center in the main camp. In his absence, the engines resumed their patient, unbearable rhythm.

Syracoelus was a straightforward man, not afflicted with gratuitous imagination. He ordered the engine crews to target four areas on the main gate towers, places where, in his experienced opinion, the structures would be most vulnerable to prolonged violent hammering. At the very least, he reckoned, he ought to be able to crack or weaken something. All it takes is a crack, sometimes.

It was hard to read anything, because of the dust. Each time one of the engine-stones bashed against the outside wall, a sprinkle floated down from the ceiling, where the two-hundred-year-old plaster moldings had cracked and were slowly being shaken apart. Dust covered the maps laid out on the long table, the dispatches and summaries and schedules. Orsea's mouth was full of it, and he kept licking his lips, like a cat.

The first bombardment had been all horror; ten minutes when he couldn't think because of the noise and the terrible shaking. But it had ended, and Jarnac had assured him that the walls had shrugged it off; the Mezentine engines hadn't done their job, he'd said; it was a miracle, he hadn't added, but there was no need. Quite unaccountably and contrary to all expectations, their invincible enemy had failed.

The second bombardment, he reckoned, was probably mostly just spite. The tempo was quite different. The engines were loosing their shots slowly, taking great pains to be accurate, to land each ball on precisely the same spot as its predecessor. Each time there'd be that unique, extraordinary swishing, humming whistle, followed by the thump you could feel in every part of your body, and then the little cloud of dust would shake out of the plaster and float down through the air. Then the interval, nearly a full minute; then, just when you were beginning to think that they'd given up and stopped, the whistle again.

"They're spinning it out," one of the councillors said, "making it last as long as they can."

"Let them," someone else said. "The chief mason says they can bash away at the towers till the snows come and they won't hurt anything. He reckons the stone those balls are made of is too soft; they're splitting and breaking up on impact, he says, and that's taking all the sting out of them. If that's the best they can do, we haven't got a lot to be worried about. They can't keep it up for too long, they'll run out of things to throw at us; and they can't sit down there and wait for fresh supplies, they haven't brought enough food with them. The plain fact is, they got it wrong, and they haven't got time to put it right."

"Even so," another voice said mildly, "it'll be nice when it stops. That row's making my teeth hurt."

Some people laughed; Orsea forced a smile, to show solidarity. It wasn't the thump, he'd realized, it was the whistle. He'd timed it by counting; one-two-three-four-five-*six*. When it came, he had no choice in the matter; his mind went blank and he counted. Anything else was blotted out, and once the thump came he had to start again from scratch. The constant jarring had given him a headache, which wasn't helping, either. He'd have given anything to be able to hit back, but he knew that was impossible. If he launched a sortie, just to shut the bloody things up, it could cost him the war, and the Eremians their lives. It was like being taunted by a bully; it kills you slowly, but you know that as soon as you respond, you've lost. Quite simply, there was nothing to be done. And here he was, doing it.

"Where's Jarnac?" someone asked.

"Went out to have a look," someone else replied. "I think he gets antsy, just sitting around. You know, man of action."

Scattered laughter; everybody knew Jarnac Ducas, of course. By the same token, everybody in the room was determinedly not looking at the vacant space where Miel Ducas should have been. They'd been not looking for hours. The strain was worse than the bombardment.

"How about a night sortie?" someone said. Silence. It wasn't the first time the suggestion had been made, and there was no reason to suppose that the many valid reasons against it had ceased to apply. "I was thinking of a small force, no more than a hundred men..."

Whoever it was bleated on for a minute or so, then shut up. Nobody could be bothered to say anything. They were waiting for the whistle; and when it came, they counted.

"The Duke's compliments," the man said, "and if it's convenient, we've got orders to move you to the ground floor."

Miel looked at him as though he was mad. "The ground floor?" he repeated.

The man nodded. "On account of the bombardment," he said.

"The Duke felt that if they were to bring engines round the side of the city, you might be in danger up here. Much better off on the ground floor."

Miel wanted to laugh. "That's very thoughtful," he said. "When would he like me out by?"

"As soon as you're ready," the man said. "No tearing hurry."

There were all manner of things that Miel wanted to ask, or say; but the man wouldn't know the answers to the questions, and it wouldn't do for him to hear the comments. "Send my valet up and we'll start packing," he said, with a faint smile. "Thank you."

Strange; the tower had become home. At least, it had become his customary environment, like a hawk's mews, a place where he perched and waited, hooded, until he was needed, or until someone came to pull his neck because he was no longer of any use. He wasn't sure he'd be able to cope as well, down at ground level.

It took a long time to put the proper state of the Ducas into bags and boxes (how can I have gathered so much *stuff* in such a short time? Miel wondered, as two more men staggered away down the stairs with their arms full). Eventually he was alone in a bare stone room, waiting for his keeper to take him down. Since he was on his honor (he was always on his honor), he hadn't even considered trying to slip away, bolt down the stairs while everyone was preoccupied with moving his possessions, try and run away. There was, after all, nowhere for him to go; he was the Ducas, everybody knew him by sight, and if he ran he'd have to leave being himself behind. That made him think, very briefly, of Ziani Vaatzes, who'd done just that. What on earth would that have felt like; jumping out of a window, he seemed to recall, and running like a doe or a boar flushed out of cover. And didn't he have a wife and children? I couldn't do that, Miel decided, I'd rather have stayed put and let them kill me.

The captain of the guard came to collect him; stood to one side to let him go first (due deference or a security precaution? Both, Miel decided; a happy coincidence of protocols). The tight coil of the spiral staircase made him feel slightly dizzy—always worse going down—and he had to stop for a moment and put his hand on the wall before they reached the bottom.

Just briefly they passed out into the open air. Miel stopped and looked up at the sky, then apologized for holding things up. It was time for his afternoon letter to Orsea.

"Can you tell me what's going on out there?" he asked the guard.

"Bombardment stopped about an hour ago," the captain replied. "We don't know yet if they've got any more stones to chuck at us, but it doesn't matter if they do. They just break up, like clods of dirt."

At that moment Miel felt a stab of bewilderment, as though he'd suddenly woken up in a strange place. If the city was being attacked, he ought to be on the wall or in the council room, doing whatever he could to help. It seemed ludicrous that he should be blinking in the sunlight on the wrong side of the city, dull-witted from prolonged idleness, about to settle down in another cozy, enclosed room with nothing useful to do. He tried to remember what it was that he'd done wrong, but he couldn't. *This is silly,* he thought. *I'll write a quick note to Orsea, he'll sort it all out.* Then he remembered; he'd already done that, many times, and for some reason it didn't seem to have worked. He turned to the captain, who seemed a decent enough sort.

"Excuse me," he said (because the Ducas is always polite). "Can I ask you something?"

The captain frowned, then nodded. "Of course."

"This sounds silly," Miel said, "but you wouldn't happen to know, would you, what it is I'm supposed to have done?"

The expression on the captain's face was hard to interpret. Surprise, definitely; incredulity, perhaps, or shock. "You mean..." he started to say, then hesitated for a moment. "You mean to say you don't know?"

"That's right," Miel said. "I mean, they arrested me and brought me here, but nobody seemed to want to tell me why. I've written to the Duke and everybody else I can think of, but they haven't seen fit…" He paused. *The Ducas doesn't criticize the Duke.* "I just wondered if you'd heard anything," he said.

"That's—" Again, the captain stopped himself. "If you haven't been told," he said, "it's got to be because there's a good reason. I'm sorry."

Miel looked at him. "So there is a reason?" he said. "You know what it is, but you won't tell me."

"I can't," the captain said.

Miel thought for a moment. "Let me ask you something," he said. "You know what it is I'm supposed to have done. Yes?"

The captain nodded slowly.

"Fine," Miel said. "And I suppose it must be something pretty bloody dreadful, if I've got to be locked up in here for it. So; do you think I'm guilty?"

The captain looked away. "It's not—"

"Do you think I did it or don't you?"

"Yes," the captain said. "Everybody knows about it, there was a letter—"

"A letter." Miel closed his eyes, just for an instant. "Right, thank you. I think I see now."

The captain was looking at him. "So it's true, then?" he said.

He tried not to, but he couldn't help laughing. "I don't bloody know, do I?" he said. "You won't tell me what the charges are."

There was an edge of anger to the captain's voice. "You were conspiring with the Vadani," he said. "You were plotting to get the Duke to escape, bugger off and leave us. You and—"

"That's not true," Miel said angrily. "What the hell have the Vadani got to do with it?" he added, because for a moment he'd forgotten who the letter had been from. He remembered as the captain replied.

"You're saying it's not true?" he said.

"I'd rather not discuss it," Miel said. "But for your information, because you're stuck with me and I don't want you thinking you're guarding some kind of evil monster, I've never had any dealings with the Vadani except as an accredited diplomat; I don't know

Duke Valens, I've never talked to him or written him a letter or had a letter from him. If this is about what I think it is, then it's just a private thing between Duke Orsea and me." He paused. "Do you believe me?"

The captain stared at him. "I don't know," he said.

"Oh come on," Miel said impatiently. "Either you do or you don't."

"You've got to go inside now," the captain said.

Miel breathed out slowly. "In case you're worried," he said, "I won't tell anybody about what you've just told me. If it comes up and they ask me how I knew, I'll say it was just some rumor my barber told me about. All right?"

The captain nodded gratefully. Evidently he was prepared to take the word of the Ducas. "All I know is what people have been saying," he said. "They found a letter hidden in your house, and apparently it links you to a conspiracy to lure the Duke out of the city; they're saying the idea was to persuade him to escape to the Vadani, and then Valens would hand him over to the Mezentines."

Miel nodded. "I see," he said. "Because the Vadani are really still our enemies."

"Partly. And partly…" The captain looked past him, as if the stairs they'd just come down were impossibly fascinating. "They say the Duchess is having an affair with Valens, and this is how they planned on getting Orsea out of the way."

Miel was silent for a moment. Then he said: "I think you'd better lock me up now. If you really believe all that, the least you can do is chain me to the wall. If I were you, I'd cut my throat right now."

Not surprisingly, the captain didn't reply. He led the way into the ground-floor apartment, which had already been furnished with the Ducas furniture and effects. The book he'd been reading was on the lectern, open at the right place. *The Perfect Mirror of the Chase;* Jarnac's choice, from his own library. Right now, Miel decided, he really wasn't in the mood. He flipped it shut and sat down in the window-seat, with his back to the world and the war.

On the table there was a stack of paper, his inkwell, pen, penknife, sand-shaker, seal and candle; they knew his routine.

Instead, he drew his knees up under his chin and stared at the wall. There was a tapestry there; he'd been staring at it for some time before he noticed it, because it was exactly where it should be, where it always had been in relation to where he was likely to be sitting. It was the tapestry that always hung on the back wall of his writing-room, back at the Ducas house. He smiled, though its presence hurt him, and for the first time in twenty years he took a moment to look at it.

He'd grown up with it, of course, because everything in the Ducas house had always been there, certainly as long as he could remember. It was relatively recent by Ducas standards, certainly no more than eighty years old; Neo-Classical Primitive, if you insisted on being technical, which meant the figures were lean and angular, their elbows and knees bent and pointed, their heads in profile, their lips curled in a frozen smile, their hands and feet unnaturally small. In the center, a unicorn was kneeling at the feet of a girl (she was flat-chested and her neck was freakishly long, which was the Neo-Classical Primitive way of telling you she was supposed to be pretty), while behind a nearby bush, half a dozen men lurked with spears and drawn bows. They weren't actually looking at the unicorn, because of artistic conventions, but it was pretty obvious what was going to happen next. Above and below the main scene ran borders crowded with running hounds—tiny heads, little stubby legs, stupidly long, thin bodies—in between exuberant growths of twisted, distorted flowers. He'd never really looked at it before, because if he had he'd have seen how terrifying it was, with its hideous, misshapen creatures and its message of treachery and death. It was supposed to be an allegory of courtly seduction; in Neo-Classicism, most things were. He wondered: which one is me, the girl or the hunters? The unicorn is Orsea, of course (it looked like a long, thin goat with a spike stuck in its head); I suppose I must be the girl, and the hunters in the bush are whoever's behind all this . . .

Somebody or other; he found he really wasn't interested in who it might be. Could be anybody, the Phocas, the Nicephorus, there were a dozen great families who traditionally sought to overthrow the Ducas at least once a generation. It was a pursuit without malice, carried out between natural enemies who respected each other; no apology given or sought. Nine of the greater Ducas had been executed for treason; according to family tradition, six of them had been innocent, falsely accused by rival houses. In return, the Ducas had contrived to bring down eight of the Phocas, six of the Perdicas, seven of the Tzimisces…It was a way of keeping score, like a championship or a league, with so many points for an execution, so many for a banishment and so on. It was one of those things, and you really couldn't feel resentful about it, just as the dove doesn't resent the falcon, though it does its very best to avoid it.

The letter, though; someone had found it (*they'd* found it, the captain had said; but he'd have known if the Duke's men had come to search the house). The whole point was that nobody knew about that hiding-place but him. The only possibility was a servant, someone who'd worked in the Ducas house for a long time, who'd come across it by accident while cleaning or tidying. That was a possibility he didn't want to think about; far better that it should be the Phocas than somebody he trusted. Besides, it didn't matter. As soon as he was able to talk to Orsea, he'd be able to explain everything; and besides, Orsea would know that ridiculous story the captain had told him couldn't possibly be true, because in order to believe it, Orsea would have to believe that Veatriz was part of the conspiracy, and that was, of course, impossible—

Veatriz. It hit him like a punch in the face. If, somehow, Orsea had persuaded himself or been persuaded that there was some kind of ridiculous plot, then he must think Veatriz was right at the heart of it—conspiring with her lover, the Vadani Duke, to lure him to his death. Only, Orsea couldn't be that stupid. Orsea would never believe anything like that.

Just as Orsea would never ignore letters from his best friend.

He was already on his feet before the idea had taken shape in his mind. His instincts were telling him, *you can't just sit here, you've got to get out and do something; rescue her, rescue both of them. It's your job, it's your duty.* He made himself sit down again. The Ducas doesn't break out of prison; for one thing it'd be dreadfully inconsiderate, since it'd be bound to cause trouble for servants and dependents, who'd be assumed to have arranged or assisted his escape. Instead, the Ducas writes a letter to the Duke, explaining all the silly misunderstandings; the Duke believes him, out of respect for the Ducas honor; everything is cleared up and put right. Unfortunately, the system presupposed a competent Duke, a man of intelligence and sound judgment, who wasn't pathetically insecure and morbidly jealous about his wife.

He sat down and wrote a letter.

Orsea—

This is ridiculous. I think I know what they've been telling you, and it simply isn't true. If you'll just come and see me for five minutes, I can prove it, and we can sort it all out. You owe me that.

He was about to sign it, but why bother? Nobody else on earth could have written that letter. He folded it, went to the door and called for a page. Nobody came, and that was a shock for the Ducas. Servants had always been there, all through his life. You didn't need to look; they'd be there, like component parts of a great machine. If the Ducas lifted up a plate, shut his eyes and dropped it, there'd be someone in the right place to catch it before it hit the floor. He called again, and waited. Eventually, a harassed-looking guard trotted up.

"Where is everybody?" Miel asked.

The soldier looked at him. "On the towers, or the roofs," he said. "Watching. Didn't anybody tell you? The Mezentines are attacking."

*   *   *

"Please," said Jarnac Ducas, with a hint of desperation. "Really, there's nothing you can do here, and I can't guarantee your safety. Please go back to the council room. That's where you're needed."

Don't lie to me, Orsea thought, *I've had enough lies from your family already.* "I'm the Duke," he said, "I should be here, on the front line. Where else should I be?"

Jarnac recognized the line; it was from a stirring speech made by Duke Tarsa IV, a hundred and seventy years ago. Probably Orsea didn't realize he was quoting. "Inside," he replied, "where it's safe. Look," he added, suddenly blunt, "if you're up here and you get killed or badly hurt, it'll totally fuck up our morale. If they get up on the wall I'll send for you; that's when you'll need to be seen. Just standing around dodging scorpion bolts, that's no bloody good to anybody."

And that's me told, Orsea thought rebelliously, but of course Jarnac was right. Not only did he sound right, he looked right, head to toe, in his no-nonsense open-face bascinet, brigandine coat over a light mailshirt, munitions arm and leg harness. You could believe in him, six foot five of lean muscle. He could've stepped straight off the pages of *The True Art of War,* or *A Discourse of Military Science.* He made Orsea feel about twelve years old.

"Fine," he said, "but you call me as soon as they get to the foot of the wall. That's an order."

"Understood," Jarnac said crisply; turned away, turned back impulsively. "There's one thing you can do," he said, in a voice more urgent and apprehensive than Orsea had ever heard him use before. "Something that'd really help."

"What?"

Jarnac stepped right up close, something the lesser Ducas had probably never done before in the history of the family. "You can release Miel and send him up here to take over from me," he said, with an edge to his voice that made Orsea step away. "He's the man you need, not me. He's good at this stuff."

He doesn't know, Orsea realized. "I can't," he said. "Look, I promise I'll explain; but it simply can't be done, you've got to believe me."

"I see." Jarnac's massive head drooped on his neck for a moment, and then he was himself again. "In that case, with your permission, I really must get back to the tower. I will send for you," he added, "you've got my word on that."

Once Orsea had gone, Jarnac bounded up the stairs to the top platform of the tower. His staff were waiting for him, anxious to point out things they'd noticed—a unit of archers previously misidentified as engineers, tenders full of scorpion ammunition, a banner that could be the enemy general staff. Jarnac pretended to listen and nodded appreciatively, but the buzzing swarm of detail didn't penetrate. He was staring at the enemy; a single swarming, crawling thing trudging unhappily up the steep road to his city, with the intention of killing him.

Jarnac Ducas had fought in seventeen military engagements; the first, when he was just turned sixteen, had been against the Vadani, a trivial cavalry skirmish on the borders that had sucked in infantry detachments that happened to be in the vicinity and had turned into a vicious, indecisive slogging-match; the most recent, Miel's raid against the Mezentines. He'd missed the scorpion-cloud and the massacre, and he'd felt bad about that ever since. He'd been reading approved military texts since he was ten, at which age he'd also started to train with weapons (the sword, the spear, the poll-axe, the bow, the halberd); ten hours a week of forms, four hours a week sparring. By his own estimation, he was eminently qualified to lead a full regiment of heavy cavalry, as befitted his place in the social order. Never in his worst dreams had he ever imagined himself in sole command of the defense of Civitas Eremiae. That was something that simply couldn't happen.

"Get the engines wound up," he said, not looking round to see who received the order. Whoever was responsible for doing it would know what to do. "They're good to three hundred and fifty yards, is that right?"

Someone assured him that it was, not that the information was necessary. Some weeks earlier, a party of workmen had hammered a row of white stakes into the ground in a straight line, precisely three hundred and forty-nine yards from the wall. As soon as the enemy crossed the staked line, the scorpion crews were going to loose their first volley. The engineers who installed the machines had carefully zeroed them to that range, so that the first cloud of bolts would land on the line, with a permitted tolerance of six inches either way. The enemy advance guard, marching purposefully up the hill in good order, were already as good as dead. It was the unit behind them Jarnac was thinking about.

The key would be the mobile scorpion batteries; he could see them, though the enemy had done their best to disguise them as ordinary wagons. If he could neutralize the Mezentine scorpions, he reckoned he could kill one man in three before they reached the base of the wall. Take away a third, and the enemy army wasn't strong enough to take the city; there were definitive tables of odds in the military manuals that told you the proportion by which the attackers needed to outnumber the defenders in order to secure victory. Jarnac had a copy of *A Discourse of Military Science* tucked inside the front of his brigandine, with a bookmark to help him find the place. The critical figure was one in three; simple arithmetic.

Now then, he thought. The skirmish line advances, I wipe them out; while our engines are rewinding, they push forward the mobile batteries so that they're in range. I loose a volley that gets rid of all their scorpion crews, but when we're all down again, they send up replacement crews to span and align their scorpions. If I'm quick, maybe I'll get those crews too, but there'll be a third wave, and a fourth. Sooner or later they'll get off their shot; I'll lose crewmen, which'll slow down my rate of fire as I replace them. Whoever runs out of scorpion crewmen first will lose the war. And that's all there is to it.

(He paused for a moment to consider the sheer scale of the enterprise he was committing himself to. Not tens of deaths but hundreds, not hundreds but thousands, not thousands but tens of thousands; each death caused by a wound, a tearing of flesh, smashing of bone, pouring out of blood, an experience of intense pain. He'd seen death several hundred times, the moment when the light went out in the eyes of an animal because of some action of his, at which point the shudders and twitches were simply mechanical, no longer controlled by a living thing. Each of those deaths he could justify in terms of meat harvested, crops preserved from damage, honor given and respectfully taken — there were times when he found it hard to believe any of those justifications, but he knew somehow that what he was doing was clean and legitimate. Now he was going to see death on a scale he couldn't begin to imagine, and the justification — which should have been self-evident — seemed elusive. Why kill ten thousand Mezentines, he asked himself, when the outcome is inevitable and the city is doomed to fall? Why should any human being kill another, given that the flesh and the hide are not used, and no trophy is taken? All he could find to shield himself with against these thoughts was a banal *they started it,* and the illogical, incredible fact that unless he killed them, all of them, they were going to wreck his city and murder his people. *Because there's no alternative;* it was a reason, not a justification, on a par with a parent's *because I say so,* something he had to obey but could neither understand nor respect. It was no job for a gentleman, even though it was the proper occupation of the lesser Ducas — but not to command, not to be in charge and accept responsibility. He hadn't been born to that; Miel had, and that was what he was there for. Except that he wasn't; why was that? he wondered.)

They were closing; they were only yards from the white posts; they were the quarry walking into the snare. Jarnac took a deep breath, sucked it in, found it impossible to let it go, because when he did so, he'd be saying the word, *loose,* that would kill all those people. Could he really do that, exterminate thousands of creatures with just one word, like a god or a magician in a story?

"Loose," he said, and the scorpions bucked all along the wall.

The sounds they made were the slider crashing home against the stop, a thump of steel on wood, and the hiss of the bolt forcibly parting the air. All around him, men were exploding into action, arching their backs as they worked frantically at windlasses, swirling and flickering like dancers as they picked up and loaded bolts, jumped clear as the sear dropped and the slider flew forward again. He pressed against the battlement and looked down, in time to see the cloud of bolts lift, a shimmering, insubstantial thing that fell like a net. The enemy were flattened like trampled grass, as if an invisible foot was stamping on them. They weren't people, of course; they were blades of grass, or ants, or bees swarming; not a thousand creatures who resembled him closely but one composite, collective thing, belonging to the species *enemy*. The bolt-cloud lifted again and blurred his view.

Something about it was wrong; at least, the enemy weren't acting in the way he'd been expecting. They'd sent forward another wave, but it was walking, scurrying right into the path of the bolts. He saw the invisible foot stamp it flat, and there wasn't another wave behind it. He realized what it meant: Vaatzes the Mezentine had improved the design of the windlasses, or something of the kind. These scorpions could be reloaded faster than the ones the Mezentines made, which meant their timings for their planned maneuvers were all wrong; accordingly, instead of sending their people into a neat, safe interval between volleys, they'd placed them right under the stamping foot. Jarnac felt sick; it was a wicked, treacherous thing to do, to trick the enemy into destroying his own people on such an obscene scale. He turned his head away, and saw an engineer hanging by his hands from a windlass handle, every ounce of bodyweight and every pound of strength compressed into desperate activity.

He forced himself to look back at the view below, as though it was a punishment he knew he deserved. They'd been moving their scorpions up; now they were trying to stop them before they vanished under a net of bolts. The enemy was a bubbling stream now, swirling and breaking around tiny black pebbles, swept against their will into a weir of flying pins. Most of all, it was an utterly ludicrous spectacle; and beyond it he could see the familiar copses, spinneys, chases and valleys of his home, places he knew down to the last deer-track and split tree. It was an impossibility; what was that word the Mezentine had used, to describe something that shouldn't be possible, outside any definition of tolerance? It was an abomination.

After a while he got used to it, or at least he blunted the significance of what he was watching. It took four abortive and costly experiments before the Mezentines figured out the timing of the Eremian scorpion winches; the fifth time they were successful. It was a strange kind of success—seconds after their scorpions had been advanced into position, every man in the moving party was dead—but it constituted a victory, because the rest of their army started cheering, a sound so incongruous that it took Jarnac several seconds to figure out what it was. The sixth wave managed to span and align the engines before they died. The seventh—

But Jarnac had been practicing for that. As soon as the sliders had slammed home, he raised both arms and yelled. Nobody could make out what he was saying, of course, but they'd been through the drill twenty times, anticipating this moment. As Jarnac dropped to his knees and shoved his shoulders tight against the rampart wall in front of him, he couldn't look round and see if the rest of his men were doing the same. He hoped they were; a heartbeat later he heard the swish, and that was when he closed his eyes. The clatter, as the enemy's scorpion bolts pitched all around him, was loud enough to force any kind of thought out of his head, and he forgot to give the next order. Fortunately, they didn't need to be told.

They got their next volley off just in time. Before his own bolt-cloud had pitched, a thin smear of enemy bolts sailed, peaked and dropped around him. He heard yells, a scream or two; he didn't look round, but couldn't help catching sight of a man with a bolt through his shoulder, in the hollow above the collarbone; he overbalanced and fell backward off the ledge. Jarnac leaned forward over the rampart—someone yelled at him but he took no notice—and saw confusion and an opportunity where the enemy scorpions were drawn up. It was an advantage; they'd have to bring up new crews now, and they'd run straight into the center ring of the target and be killed. Before they died, they'd have spanned the windlasses and loaded the bolts, so that their successors could slip the sears and launch the volley. *I'm killing men at an incredible rate,* Jarnac told himself, *but there's still too many of them.* As he watched the new crews run forward, work frantically and die, he knew he was wasting his time. Might as well fight the grass, he thought; you can fill a dozen barns with hay, and all you're doing is encouraging it to grow.

It was the twelfth wave that did the damage. He timed it as well as he could, but maybe the twelfth-wavers were faster or better-trained, or maybe his men were getting tired; just as he was about to yell, "Cover!" the bolts came down. It was like sea-spray breaking over a wall; and once he was up and on his feet again, he saw that half his crews were dead. The other half loosed their volley; he was leaning over the back edge of the walkway, yelling for fresh crewmen. They arrived in time to look up at a cloud of bolts. As the remaining engines returned fire he called again. The bolts overshot most of them as they scrambled into the cover of the wall, and they found engines spanned and ready to loose. *That's a thought,* Jarnac said to himself, and cursed his stupidity for not thinking of it before; loose alternately, in two shifts. He didn't need to give an order, they were doing it anyway. Another Mezentine volley pitched; he estimated that only a quarter of their engines were manned and operating. The trouble was, a quarter was plenty. Not only were they killing men, the bolts were stabbing into the timber frames of the engines, gouging out gobbets of splintered wood (the Mezentines, of course, made their frames out of steel). A return volley, and more men running up the stairs, jumping, vaulting over the piled-up dead, leaping at the windlass handles, ripping bolts out of nearby corpses to load the slider because it was quicker than stooping to load from the stack. Jarnac waited for the enemy reply. It didn't come.

He waited a little longer, then sprang to his feet and peered over the battlement. The main body of the enemy army was advancing, pouring round, past and over the line of engines, each with its grove of spitted dead men. Jarnac didn't understand; had they run out of artillerymen after all, or were they simply sick and tired of watching? It didn't matter; they were advancing into the killing zone — he heard the crash of the sliders, watched the enemy go down. He saw a whole line crumple and flatten, and the line behind them march on over them without stopping. The next volley pitched and slaughtered, but by then three other lines were out of the line of fire. Simple, when you thought about it. With his scorpions he could kill a quarter of the Mezentine army before they came within bowshot of the wall. But a quarter wouldn't be enough. He didn't need to open his copy of the *Discourse* and look it up on the table. He could do the sums in his head.

Someone, a junior staff officer of some kind, was standing a few yards away, gawping at the dead; half-witted, mouth open, arms dangling at his sides. Jarnac yelled to him but he didn't seem to hear, so he jumped up, grabbed his shoulder and shook him.

"Go to the palace," he said. "Fetch the Duke."

He had to repeat it twice, and then the man picked up his feet and ran, sliding in pooled blood, tripping on scorpion bolts and dead men's legs. That chore done and promise fulfilled, Jarnac turned back to the pointless task of killing ten thousand men.

At the foot of the wall, Melancton finally stopped and looked back over his shoulder. As he did so, he thought about the old fairy tale that says you mustn't look behind you in the kingdom of the dead, or the dead will get you. The hero, of course, gets as far as the gateway unscathed; but, because he's a tragic hero, he gives in at the very last moment, and is lost forever.

Best, therefore, not to think about the men who wouldn't be

joining him for the next phase of the operation. He leaned his head back and looked up at the wall. Above him, he couldn't see the enemy scorpions, but he could hear the crack of the sliders slamming home. He was safe from them here; the city wall sheltered him, which in itself was a pleasing irony. With a tremendous effort he cleared his mind of the images that clogged it, and tried to remember the next step.

If the defenses of Civitas Eremiae had a weakness, it was the main gate itself. The doors were strong—according to the reports he'd seen, six inches of cross-ply oak, reinforced with internal crossbeams—but they offered considerably more hope of success than the walls, and of course he had Mezentine ingenuity and craftsmanship to help him, provided he could move it the enormous distance of five hundred yards.

He glanced behind him again. Here it came; they'd listed it in the inventory as a battering-ram, but there was more to it than that. True, the first stage in its operation was simple enough, merely a beautifully engineered derivative of the crude old log-dangling-from-chains. Once it had been swung, however, and its two hardened and tempered beaks had pecked into the gate panels, it displayed hidden talents. At the heart of it was a windlass driving a worm. You could turn the windlass with one hand, but the power of mechanical advantage would force the two beaks apart, tearing the gate panels like rotten cloth. A point would be reached where the wretched timbers wouldn't be able to resist any longer. They'd be prised open, the frame of the gate would spring, and a sharp tug on the back of the ram would drag them out like a bad tooth. He had his employers' word on that, which was a comfort.

The ram edged forward. It was being pushed by fifty-odd men, who were sheltered from the scorpion bolts by eight-inch steel pavises mounted on the sides of the frame. An overimaginative observer with a tendency to romanticize might be put in mind of a wild boar beset by hounds; to Melancton it was a piece of equipment, and he bitterly resented having to pin his hopes on it. For all that, it came slowly; there were dead men and other obstacles under the wheels, which had to be either dragged out of the way or ridden over. There was a slight gradient to overcome as well. He could picture the machine's designers, shaking their heads and making excuses when they heard about how he'd failed. He could hear bones crunching and skin bursting under the wheels.

Of course, he hadn't failed yet. Men were crowding round it, partly to get what cover they could from the bolts, partly to add their weight and help it up the slope, over the obstructions. He saw a man pinned to a frame-timber by a scorpion bolt; he was still alive, and every jolt and bump twisted the steel pin in his ruptured intestines. A man shouldn't have to see things like that, he thought. Soldiers die in a battle, and each death is hideous and obscene, but a commander has to look past all that, so that he can see the pattern, the great shape of the mechanism. He scampered out of the way as the machine rumbled and crunched toward the gate. The noise was confusing, how could anyone think with that going on? There was a disgusting smell of sweat and urine, which he realized was his own.

He saw the beam sway backward, drawn by chains running on pulleys; trust the Mezentines to get a gear-train in somewhere. It hung in the air for a moment, and a slab of rock dropped from the battlement above, bounced off the wall as it fell, skipped out wildly and caught the side of a man's head. Melancton saw his legs and back collapse as he lurched sideways and fell in a heap, like discarded dirty laundry. The beam swung forward. He heard the splitting of wood. The beam had stopped dead, not a quiver in the chains. They were spanning the windlass now, he could hear the scream of the oak ply being levered apart. Shouting all around him, on all sides and above, where an Eremian officer was screaming at his men to lower the elevation on a scorpion as far as it would go. Not far enough, Melancton knew, and the panic in his enemy's voice delighted him. He lifted his head and saw a great wedge of daylight glowing through the wrecked panels of the door. The framing timbers were bent like the limbs of bows; it was shocking to see the torture of materials as the stress from the worm built up in them. It was impossible for solid oak bars to bend as far as that. They snapped, the ends a prickly mess of needle-pointed splinters running down the over-abused grain. He heard a voice give an order, though he couldn't make out the words. The beam jerked back; the doors popped out of their frame like a cork from a bottle.

Of course, he hadn't given much thought to what would happen after that. He'd sort of assumed that once the gate was open, that would be that; as though the gate was the enemy's neck, snap it and they die. Instead, a cloud flitted out of the open gateway, and in the fraction of a second it took to pass him by, he heard the hiss and recognized the flight of arrows.

The engine sheltered some of them, but not all. For a moment, long enough to count up to six, it was all perfectly still in the space in front of the gate, because nobody was left alive to move. The Eremians, he knew, were fumbling for arrows, nocking them, drawing. They'd be in time to meet the confused, furious charge with another volley. Melancton turned his head away until he heard the hiss. When he turned back, he saw his men charging.

The archers in the gateway changed their minds at the last moment, realizing they didn't have time for another volley. Just too late, they turned to run, and the infantry charge rammed them. Mostly they were simply knocked down and trampled on; there wasn't any room for using weapons, and no time. Melancton jumped up to join the charge. He was ready to go when he heard the slam of sliders.

They'd briefed him in great detail about the effective use of scorpions, with examples drawn from many campaigns against many different enemies. But they hadn't said anything about what would happen if a densely packed force of infantry received a scorpion volley at point-blank range. Given the proud thoroughness of Mezentine military intelligence, he could only presume that such a thing had never happened.

It had happened now. The men in the front of the scrum were

blown back as if by a blast of wind or an incoming breaker. Swept off their feet, they slammed into the men behind them, as the bolts plunged through them and out behind. Three men pinned together, unable to fall for a long moment, until they toppled sideways; the sheer crushing effect of so much force contained in such a crowded, fragile space. Melancton saw it all, and the images soaked into his mind. They would be there forever, like frescos painted on the inside of his eyelids. He noticed that he was stumbling toward the gateway, shoving his way in a jumble of calves, elbows, shoulders, backs. *What am I doing?* he wanted to know. *Why am I going there, it's dangerous.* He had no choice in the matter, apparently. He heard the hiss of arrows, and a soldier fell across him, treading on his kneecap as he sprawled to the ground. Three more paces brought him to a dead stop. Somehow it had turned into a pushing contest. His arms were jammed against his sides, so he shoved his shoulder into the back of the man trapped in front of him, and pushed with his back and legs. Someone else was doing the same to him. All the breath was forced out of his lungs, and he found he couldn't replace it. The panic of not being able to breathe suppressed every other thought for a moment, until the man behind him shifted a little and the pressure on his lungs eased up. He gobbled a deep pull of air, and was flattened against the man in front.

The Eremians loosed another volley from their scorpions.

By now, all the dead were too tightly wedged up to fall; they were a shield, a ram, something to push against. Melancton's mind evacuated all his remaining thoughts as pain rendered everything else irrelevant. He could hear his own voice screaming. Whatever was happening to him, it seemed to be going on forever. He could see the logic; he'd looked round on the threshold of death's kingdom, and now he would be here forever.

The Phocas were skeptical after the event. They maintained that in a crush like that, nobody could make a difference, no matter how strong they were, or how brave. But they kept their doubts to themselves, for fear of appearing ungracious. None of the other eye-witnesses agreed with them, in any event. The Bardanes and the Nicephorus both maintained that at the critical point of the battle in the gateway, Jarnac Ducas and his personal guard, recruited from his huntsmen and harborers, cut a path through the enemy with poll-axes and glaives, took their stand outside the gate and held their ground until all the Mezentines who'd spilled into the city had been killed, and the engineers had blocked the gateway with steel pavises propped up by scaffolding beams. Only Jarnac himself and one huntsman made it back, scrambling up over a pavise as it was being lifted into place and dropping down the other side. It was, the majority of those present agreed, the most extraordinary thing they'd ever seen.

The huntsman died ten minutes later—they counted twenty-one wounds on his body—but Jarnac was able to walk twenty yards to a mounting-block and sit down of his own accord before he passed out. The consensus was that he owed his life to the brigandine coat.

When he came round, half an hour later, he opened his eyes and asked what was going on. They told him that the attack had been driven back, with heavy losses. He didn't believe them, and passed out again.

It was Ziani Vaatzes who suggested dropping grappling-hooks from the gatehouse tower and simply lifting the battering-ram off the ground, using the portcullis winch. They did as he told them because he was a Mezentine, and therefore knew about such things. When the crisis was over and they wanted to lift him shoulder-high and salute him as the saviour of the city, he turned out not to be there. Meanwhile the ram dangled in the air like a dead spider, until someone thought of winching it up as far as it'd go and then slipping the winch. It fell thirty feet and smashed, and that was the end of it.

Duke Orsea arrived too late, of course. He'd run from the council room as soon as the messenger arrived, but the press of bodies was too thick and he couldn't get through. By the time he'd scrambled his way to the front of the scrum it was all over, and they were carrying the lesser Ducas home on a door. Everyone was convinced he was dead, until he appeared at his front gate, leaning on someone's shoulder. The cheering was as loud as the battle at the gate.

They spent the rest of the day and all the following night shoring up the barricades in the gateway and fixing or cannibalizing the damaged scorpions. Vaatzes reappeared to take charge of that side of it. Probably it was just stress and fatigue, but nobody was able to get a civil word out of him. He shouted at the workers, which wasn't how he usually behaved toward his men, and nobody seemed able to do anything right.

Some time after midnight, they finished counting the dead bodies and collating the casualty lists. Five hundred and seventeen killed, over nine hundred wounded; meanwhile, a work detail was struggling to get the dead Mezentines out of the gateway, so the masons could get in and block up the breach with bricks and rubble. Nobody could be bothered to count them, though there were inevitably a few jokes about saving some of the better heads for the lesser Jarnac's trophy collection. As and when there was time, the plan was to load them into ammunition derricks, winch them up to the top of the wall and throw them over. There wasn't enough space in the city to bury them, and burning such a monstrous quantity of material would have posed a fire hazard.

23

They waited until the surgeon had finished with him before they gave Melancton the casualty reports. It had taken an hour to dig the two arrowheads out of him — one in his stomach, the other in his shoulder — and he'd lost a lot of blood. His aides said the report could surely wait till morning (the dead would still be dead tomorrow, and possibly the day after, too), but the officer in charge pleaded an express order.

Seventeen thousand, four hundred and sixty-three dead. Lying in his tent, he looked at it as if it was a random squiggle on the scrap of parchment. Nobody could really understand a figure like seventeen thousand. A quick calculation — he'd always been good at mental arithmetic — told him that he'd lost slightly over half his men, and therefore, according to all the recognized authorities on the art of war, he now had insufficient forces at his disposal to carry the city. He'd failed.

Somehow, that hardly mattered. He was a mercenary, a skilled tradesman paid to do a job; they weren't going to behead him or lock him up, as they might well have done if he'd cost them that many citizens instead of mere migrant workers. He'd go home, unpaid, his career ruined, and that'd be that. Years ago he'd bought a reasonable-sized estate just outside the city where he'd been born, somewhere to retire to when his soldiering days were over. He'd been looking forward to it, in a vague sort of way.

Seventeen thousand. He remembered a story he'd heard years ago, about a man who owned a piece of land on which a great battle had been fought. He came back home a week after the battle to find the dead still lying. He was a fairly well-to-do farmer, with twenty men working for him; it had taken them weeks just to cart away the bodies and dump them in a disused quarry a couple of hundred yards from the battlefield. The land itself was ruined. Some of his neighbors put it down to malign influences, others reckoned the sheer quantity of blood that had drained into the soil had poisoned the ground. Plowing was next to impossible, because every few yards the share would jam on a helmet or a breastplate or some other piece of discarded junk. He tried a heavy mulch of manure for a couple of years, but nothing would grow except bindweed and nettles.

Seventeen thousand. As he stared at the tent roof, trying not to move (the doctor had given him all sorts of dire warnings about that), he made a few attempts at visualizing the number, but once he got past five thousand it all broke down.

The Mezentine liaisons came to see him around midday. For once, they didn't have much to say for themselves; he got the impression that they were preoccupied with what was likely to happen to them when they got home. One of them made a few half-hearted suggestions about a surprise attack by night; the other two ignored him.

"Can we at least say we've got enough men left to mount an effective siege?" another one asked him. "According to one set of reports, they probably outnumber us by now."

Melancton shrugged. "If they tried to make a sortie and chase us off, they'd be walking into our scorpions," he pointed out. "I'd love it if they tried, but I don't suppose they will. No, I think they'll sit tight and watch us use up our stocks of food. They're better supplied than we are. We weren't anticipating a siege."

One of the liaisons shifted uncomfortably. "How long can we stay here, then?" he asked.

Melancton grinned. "Well, we've got a lot fewer mouths to feed than we had this time yesterday, so we can probably stick it out for three weeks, assuming we want to. I can't see any point in that, though. They must have supplies for at least six months, probably more."

"Three weeks," the liaison repeated. "Well, it's possible that the reinforcements could get here by then. In the meantime, we'll send to the City for a supply train—"

"Reinforcements?" Melancton frowned, as though he didn't know what the word meant. "I don't understand."

"Fresh troops, from your country," the liaison explained. "Obviously we're going to have to raise another army before we try again. That's going to take time, naturally, so meanwhile our job will be to mount an effective siege—"

"Try again." Melancton couldn't think of any words for what he wanted to say. "You're going to try again?"

"Of course. The Republic never loses a war. As I was saying, time is going to be the key. Based on what we've just seen, we're going to have to make very substantial modifications to the long-range engines, and that'll probably mean shipping them back to the City for a complete refit. How long that'll take I simply don't know, but..."

Melancton paid no real attention to the rest of what they said. It wasn't any of his business anymore. Curiously, they'd spoken as though they assumed he'd still be in command when the reinforcements arrived; he thought about that. It was possible, of course, that the Mezentines wouldn't want to replace him, because that would be an acknowledgment of the disaster. Maybe they're just going to pretend it never happened, he thought; and of course, they could do that, it'd be possible. Getting another army from home— forty-five or fifty thousand this time—was also eminently feasible, given the time of year and the political situation. There'd be no shortage of recruits, assuming they had the common sense not to say anything about what had happened to the last expedition.

"Soon as you're up and about again," the liaison continued, making it sound as though he was getting over a nasty dose of flu, "we'll get you to come back with us to the City so you can brief Council on the sort of modifications needed to bring the engines up to the mark. The important thing," he added, "is to keep a sense of perspective."

They went away again shortly after that, and Melancton slid into a shallow doze. When he woke up, there was a man standing over him who looked vaguely familiar. Beside him was the day-officer, looking unhappy.

"Insists on seeing you," he said. "I told him you were asleep."

Falier; the name rose to the surface of his mind. Falier, the engineer from the ordnance factory. Presumably he was here to start mulling over those design modifications. "Tell him to go away," Melancton said.

"It's important." Falier was shouting, which surprised him. On the couple of occasions when they'd met, he'd formed an impression of a weak, scared little man whose main ambition was to be somewhere else. "I've got vital information, about the war."

Melancton raised an eyebrow. Melodrama. "Can't it wait?" he muttered.

"I know how to break into the city without a full assault."

That was almost worth sitting up for. "Is that right?" Melancton said.

"Yes. We can get in without them noticing, until it's too late."

It happened sometimes, after a serious disaster. You got people who suddenly declared they'd been visited by angels, or who'd just realized they were the Son of God. Usually the voices told them how to achieve total victory without further bloodshed. Occasionally, they decided they were some ancient warrior saint reincarnated, and they'd trot off on their own, sword drawn, yelling, toward the enemy, and be shot down by outlying archers. "You've found this out just now, I suppose," Melancton said wearily. "In a dream, or something."

"No." The little man was getting angry. "Look, it's all in here." He was holding out a silly little scrap of parchment, much folded. "It's a letter from Vaatzes, the traitor."

First, Melancton told the day-officer to get out, then, painfully, he raised himself just enough so he could reach the paper gripped in Falier's outstretched hand. "Give me that," he said. "What are you doing, getting letters from him?"

He remembered the answer before Falier gave it; there had been a footnote in his personnel file. "I knew him," Falier was saying. "I worked with him. We were friends."

The man's handwriting was atrocious; small, cramped, full of dots and needles. That made it frustrating, because there were several key words he couldn't make out. In the end he had to hand it back. "Read it to me," he said.

Falier cleared his throat, like a boy about to make a speech on Founder's Day.

Ziani Vaatzes to Falier Zenonis.

I hope you'll read this, Falier, rather than be all high-minded and burn it without breaking the seal — though if that's what you've done, I can't really blame you. After all, I'm entirely responsible for the terrible things that have happened over the last day or so.

Will you believe me, I wonder, when I say that I want to try and make amends? You'll have to form your own opinion. I hope you decide in my favor. It'll go badly with what's left of my conscience if you don't.

What I want you to do is take this letter to the military authorities, as high up the chain of command as you can possibly get. What follows are detailed instructions for capturing the city, easily, quickly and with minimal loss of life. I guess you could say I've had a change of heart; or maybe what I saw from the ramparts yesterday was more than even I could bear.

The key to it all is the city's water supply system. It's actually quite a remarkable thing. The mountain is honey-combed — I think that's the right word — with caves, tunnels and natural lakes. The Eremians have spent the last couple of centuries judiciously improving on nature. They can now store a year's supply of clean water, using nothing but the runoff from the eaves of their houses. Extraordinary piece of design; but it's also a glaring weak spot in the defenses. You see, in order to move around inside the mountain, so as to maintain and repair, they've enlarged or added to the cave network; there's a maze of tunnels and corridors under the mountain, wide enough to drive a cart along. And—this is where they were too smart by half—there's an entrance at the foot of the mountain, on the north side, one hundred and eighty degrees from the main gate. In fact, it's a drain plug. If there's unusually heavy rainfall and the cisterns get full up and there's a risk of backup and overflow, they open this plug and drain off the surplus water. Naturally it's a deadly secret, but these people aren't very good at secrecy.

You'll find the outside entrance to the drain directly under an outcrop of rock shaped like a parsnip. You'll know you've got the right place, because if you stand under it and look straight up, you'll see a watch-tower on the wall with a definite lean to it—six degrees or thereabouts.

Once you're inside, you'll find yourself in a long, straight tunnel. There are loads of turnings off it, but you need to keep going straight for six hundred yards, until you reach a fork. Take the left turning, and you'll be in a wide gallery, curving very slightly to the right all the time. You're actually following the line of the wall. Every fifty yards or so, you'll find a stairwell; the stairs go up to landings and then on again, right up to the level of the city floor, so to speak. Each stairwell is numbered; you keep going till you come to number 548. Go up the stairs, you'll find yourself on a landing or mezzanine, and then there'll be more stairs, another landing, and so on, till you've gone up eleven levels to a circular platform under a high stone ceiling. At that point, you're directly under the cistern for the guardhouse of the main gate. At roughly a hundred and ten degrees, you'll find a small passageway that leads to a heavy oak door. You'll need to smash your way through that; it's the failsafe plug, in case the cistern leaks. Get through that and you're in the cistern overflow, which is a sort of wellshaft leading right up into the guardhouse itself; there's an iron ladder bolted to the wall. You go up that, and you're no more than fifteen yards from the gate. After that, it's up to you.

You'll have noticed, I'm sure, that I'm giving you the information before I ask for something in return. Well, I never did have a head for business, and bargaining isn't my strong suit. What I'm asking for—well, let's be realistic. I know I can never go home. I've accepted that. I know if I struck a deal to give away this information in return for a pardon or whatever, they'd go back on their side of it as soon as they'd taken the city. The Perpetual Republic doesn't bargain with traitors and abominators, and isn't bound by its word when negotiating with them. Nor should it be. So, let's be realistic. This isn't an attempt to bargain, it's a simple plea for mercy. Please ask them to let Ariessa and Moritsa go; they've done nothing wrong, everything was my fault. I can't insist, I know; I can only beg, and try and set the score straight. I'm doing this because, in the final analysis, I've only ever loved my family and the Republic, and I've caused terrible harm to both of them. I can't go on living with that on my conscience, and simply killing myself without trying to make amends would only be another form of running away.

Well, Falier my dear old friend, that's all I've got to say for myself. If I survive the assault, I expect I'll be captured, taken home and killed in some flamboyant manner or other. That'd be no more than I deserve. I'm not brave enough to cut my own throat. I don't suppose I'll see you again. Please, please take care of Ariessa and Moritsa. I love them more than anything else. I've just got a lousy way of showing it, that's all.

* * *

Melancton looked up.

"That's his handwriting?" he said.

Falier nodded. "I can guarantee it," he said.

"You think he's telling the truth?"

"Yes," Falier said.

Melancton thought for a long time. "If he's lying," he said, "what would it achieve? At best, he'd have lured a couple of dozen of our men into a trap. Big deal, he's already killed seventeen thousand—" He broke off and grinned. "Hadn't you heard? That's the number, as far as we can make out. That's what your friend's got to answer for."

"I didn't know," Falier said quietly.

"Don't take it to heart." Melancton shrugged. "It's not like it's your fault. Doesn't make any odds, though. Whether or not the Guilds do as he asks and let the family go is political, nothing to do with me." He paused and frowned. "I believe him," he said. "Mostly because there's nothing to be gained by lying, in the position he's in. Tell me, you know him; is he screwed up enough to do something like this?"

Falier hesitated. "Yes," he said.

"Splendid." Melancton sighed, and let his head sink back onto the pillow. "It seems like he caused the mess and now he's going to put it right for us. Nobody need ever know, of course. As far as the folks back home are concerned, we found it out for ourselves. What about the family, by the way? What happened to them?"

"Nothing," Falier said. "The Republic doesn't do things like that, taking it out on innocent women and children. They're fine."

"Well then, that's all right," Melancton said bitterly. "He gets what he wants, and so do we. I may even be able to salvage my career from this godawful mess. Wouldn't that be nice? We'll give it a try; things can't get any worse if it doesn't work." He paused, scowling. "There's one thing, though. He talks about opening the gate, but that's out of the question. We smashed the gate in, and they've blocked the gateway up with rubble. Even if we get men inside, there's nothing much they can do."

Evidently Falier hadn't thought of that. "No," he said, "I see your point."

"It's a strange mistake to make," Melancton said. "He must know about the gate; I don't understand. But..." He closed his eyes. "I suppose that if we sent in, say, three dozen men, they might be able to make a breach before they're cut down. They must have beams and so forth shoring the blockage up from the inside; someone told me it's just bricks and rubble, they haven't had time to do a proper job. It's not as though I've got anything to lose, and what's three dozen men more or less?" He laughed out loud, for some reason. "Fine," he said. "Do me a favor, go and find my general staff, and we'll see what we can do about this. I wish I could see the point of this gate business, but there's always something. The bizarrely inexplicable is generally a factor in great events of world history — you know, the bridge unaccountably left unbroken, the sentry not posted because someone thought it was someone else's job." He yawned. "I'm rambling. I've had enough of this war."

Falier was glad to get out of the tent. He had the impression that whoever it was that the general had been talking to, it hadn't been him.

Find the general staff, he'd said. Of course, Falier had no idea how to go about something like that; so he stopped the first officer he came aross and told him to do it. The officer looked startled and bolted away like a rabbit.

Seventeen thousand, Falier thought. Of course, it didn't really matter, since they were only mercenaries, and there were proverbially plenty more where they'd come from. Nevertheless. He'd done exactly what Ziani had told him to do in his covering letter; it came naturally, doing what Ziani said, and he hadn't really thought about what the consequences might be. If he'd taken the letter to someone in authority straight away, as soon as he'd received it, things would be very different now. Before, he'd seen the situation only in terms of inevitabilities; it was inevitable that Civitas Eremiae would fall and that the Republic would prevail, that Ziani would be killed, and that he would be promoted to chief supervisor of the ordnance factory, in recognition of the part he'd played in bringing the war to a successful conclusion. He'd seen it all as one complex mechanism, designed by someone with a clearer eye than his, as complete and remote as a Guild Specification. Accordingly, he hadn't interfered (to alter Specification is an act of abomination, after all) and had relied instead on faith, as a good engineer should. In which case, his conscience was clear. Besides, they were all only foreigners.

He went back to his tent. Until yesterday he'd had to share it with an artillery captain, a loathsome man who snored, smelled of onions and stole things from his trunk. Now, however, he had it all to himself. His immediate reaction when they'd told him had been joy at the prospect of getting a good night's sleep; that wasn't good, he knew, but he really couldn't help it. There was, of course, a vast divide between failing to mourn the death of a nuisance and doing the sort of things Ziani had done, but even a vast divide is made up of small subdivisions of space, which add up to the whole.

They hadn't come for the artilleryman's things yet. Understandable; they were busy. The clutter of dirty clothes and boots was still there, but now at least he could brush them out of his way without any risk of being shouted at or hit. He cleared a space on the top of his trunk, opened it and took out his writing-set. The artilleryman had plundered six of his nine sheets of parchment; if he'd lived, he'd probably have had the other three before too long, so maybe everything had turned out for the best. He flipped the lid of the inkwell, dribbled in a few drops of water, stirred, and thought about what he was going to say.

My darling

Words on paper had never come easily to him. *I miss you, it's terrible being here without you, I don't know how much longer I can go on;* all perfectly true, but if he wrote that and sent it to her, she'd think he was cracking up, and he wasn't. He was unhappy, and being separated from her had a lot to do with that, but it wasn't the only thing. *This horrible war* ... Would they censor that? He didn't want to attract further attention to himself, given his links to the traitor, and the part he'd played in passing on his message. He knew what he wanted to say, but words were always difficult (he thought of Ziani, and his dreadful bad poetry; what had she made of it? he wondered. She'd never struck him as the poetic sort, somehow).

My darling, I wish I was back home with you instead of stuck here in this miserable place. I can't really say too much in a letter about how the war's going, but at present there's no real way of knowing how long it's likely to take.

He scowled. If the artilleryman hadn't been so free with his paper, he'd have screwed the sheet up and started again. He was, he knew, at a disadvantage in a situation like this, because he loved her so much more than she loved him. It was something he'd come to terms with, but it made him feel uncomfortably vulnerable when it came to expressing how he felt. Unfortunate; but there's no accounting for love.

If all goes well *[he could say that; he wasn't specifying how things might go well]* I may be home again fairly soon; I just don't know. You mustn't worry about money or anything like that, I've taken care of everything. If anything happens to me, I've seen to it you'll be all right. Not that I'm in any danger, I hasten to add. I'm just an engineer, after all, not a soldier.
    When I get home, I've got a surprise for you. I won't spoil it, but I think you'll like it.
    Anyway, that'll have to do for now, they're keeping me pretty busy. All my love, Falier.

Being used to a fairly active life, Miel Ducas found it hard to get to sleep after a day spent sitting around. Previously, before his arrest, his main problem had been staying awake; now he tended to spend the night lying on his back staring at the shadows cast on the ceiling by a single flickering candle. That was another recent development. He'd never been afraid of the dark when he was young, but lately—it wasn't fear, as such, but he felt uncomfortable unless there was light in the room. Maybe it was just the noise; his bedroom at home was perfectly, superbly quiet, but the wind sighed round the tower he was confined in, and he found it very hard not to notice it. The intrusion was worse in the dark, somehow; it made him feel as though people were whispering somewhere nearby, but he couldn't make out what they were saying.

Ever since the victory (everyone he'd talked to had called it that) he'd been hoping things would sort themselves out. If the Mezentines had really taken a beating, and the siege was on the point of being lifted, maybe Orsea would be able to find the time to come and see him, or at least answer his letters. A few minutes would be all it'd take; *Orsea, what on earth is all this in aid of?* he'd say; and Orsea would tell him, and then he'd explain, and that'd be that.

But in the dark, he tended to think about the letter, and the terrible things the guard captain had told him, and the possibility that Orsea wasn't ever going to come and let him out. That was as good a reason as any for burning a candle. It'd be nice, though, to have something to read, apart from the three books he'd read so often that he practically knew them by heart. Jarnac had promised to bring him some more books from home, but if what the guards had told him was true, Jarnac wouldn't be coming to visit for quite some time. Of course, Jarnac could have told his servant to bring them, but presumably the promise had slipped his mind, what with one thing and another.

It was ironic, therefore, that when he had finally managed to drift off to sleep, some fool should come along and wake him up. It turned out to be the night captain; a pleasant enough man, though not much of a conversationalist. He was standing in the doorway holding a lantern.

"Sorry to disturb you," he said. "But there's someone who wants to see you. Says it's very urgent."

"Really?" Miel sat up and yawned. "That doesn't sound likely. Who the hell is it?"

"It's the Mezentine," the captain said, frowning. "Engineer Vaatzes. I didn't like to tell him he'd have to come back in the morning."

Miel shrugged. "I suppose not," he said. "Well, you'd better show him in, and then we'll know what all this is about."

Vaatzes looked tired; more tired, Miel thought, than anyone he'd ever seen before in his life. He moved as if all his joints ached, and he grunted as he sat down. His clothes were filthy with brick-dust, sawdust and iron filings.

"You too?" Miel said.

"What?"

"You can't sleep either," Miel replied. "So you thought you'd come over here, and I could bore you to sleep with stories of the Ducas family through the ages."

Vaatzes grinned. "Oh, I could sleep all right," he said. "I could shut my eyes and fall over, and hitting the floor wouldn't wake me up. Too much to do, though."

"And here's me sitting idle all day," Miel said reproachfully. "I'd love to come and help you, even if it was just carrying your tools for you, only I don't think they'd let me."

"No." Vaatzes let his head loll forward onto his chest for a moment, then lifted it again. "I'll come to the point," he said. "Frankly, I'm too tired to dress it up, even if I wanted to. The fact is, I suppose I'm here to say I'm sorry."

Miel looked at him. "Sorry? What for?"

"For this." Vaatzes made a vague encircling gesture. "For being responsible for you ending up here. I suppose you could call it be-trayal."

Strange feeling; like walking into a tree, or putting your foot in a rabbit hole. "You?" Miel said stupidly.

"Me." Vaatzes nodded. "I got hold of Duke Valens' letter to

the Duchess and I gave it to Duke Orsea. And I told him where it came from."

"Oh." Miel was too amazed to be angry. He thought about getting up, but found he couldn't. "Why?"

"Long story."

Miel frowned. "Was it because I told Orsea I thought you were a spy, back when we found you?"

"No, certainly not," Vaatzes said. "Though in a way, I suppose, that was partly the cause of all your troubles. It showed you had good instincts." He grinned, like some kind of predator. "Your master is a dangerous fool, but you've always made up for that. And he trusted you far more than he trusted himself. Would you like me to tell you the long story, or at least the part of it that concerns you?"

"I suppose so," Miel said.

"Fine." Vaatzes yawned again. "Please excuse me," he said, "I'm dreadfully tired. We've been working on patching up the defenses for—what, seventy-two hours without a break. When I decided to make myself indispensable around here, I didn't realize how much hard work I'd be letting myself in for. Can I push my luck just a little further and beg a mouthful of whatever you've got in that jug?"

Miel smiled bleakly. "Help yourself," he said. "It's a rather pleasant sweet white wine from my estate in the Northfold."

"Very good," Vaatzes said, after he'd swallowed a cupful. "Though I have to say, I've got no taste in wine. We drink beer and cider in Mezentia, or water. Now then, I'm not quite sure where to start. There's a lot of background stuff that doesn't concern you, and it's quite personal, but you probably won't be able to follow the logic of the story unless I tell it to you."

Miel shrugged.

"Right," Vaatzes said. He poured out half a cup of wine and put it down on the floor by his feet. "You know why I was condemned to death back home?"

Miel pulled a face. "Sort of," he said. "Something about making changes to a design."

"Essentially, yes. It was a stupid thing to do. I knew it was wrong, but I thought I could get away with it. I didn't; someone betrayed me. I have no idea who it was, but it doesn't really matter. I committed a terrible crime, for which I should have been punished. Instead, I killed some innocent men and ran away—"

"Hang on," Miel interrupted—he was still feeling completely numb and vague from the astonishment Vaatzes' announcement had caused; he could hear himself talking calmly and pleasantly to this man, and he wondered why. Probably, he decided, because he didn't really believe him. "You make it sound like you—well, like you approve of what they were planning to do to you."

"You could put it like that."

"Fine. So why did you escape?"

Vaatzes smiled. "For a very basic, stupid reason. I'm in love with my wife, you see. If I die, I'll never see her again. So I had to stay alive. It's that simple."

Miel frowned. "But—sorry if I'm being a bit blunt—running away, coming here, and then building all the war engines so we could beat off the invasion. There's no way you'll ever be able to go home."

"We'll see about that," Vaatzes said mildly. "I rather believe I will, some day. But we're drifting away from the point. When I came here, it didn't take me long to realize how this country works. Basically, it's all rather haphazard. The people who rule this place aren't chosen because they're wise or talented, it goes entirely by what I believe is called the accident of birth. To make up for that, you noblemen are trained from birth to do the jobs you're born to; and you grow up having a code of duty and honor drilled into you, to the point where you aren't really in charge of your own actions. You do the right thing, instinctively." Vaatzes shrugged. "There are worse ways of running things," he said. "But I saw, straight away, that you're the man who the Duke listens to. And that's because he knows he's a bad leader and you're a better one; he's a fool, but clever enough to recognize a better man and let him run things. That's why I had to get rid of you; part of it, anyway, but the rest of it's a bit complicated. Anyway; I asked questions. I was sure that you must have a weak spot somewhere, a point where you'd be vulnerable, and it didn't take me long to find it. It's common knowledge that you were always supposed to marry Duchess Veatriz, because that was the best possible match for both of you, politically and socially. Also, you were more or less in love with her — not that it mattered, since the whole thing was a foregone conclusion."

Miel shifted uncomfortably and said nothing.

"Well," Vaatzes went on, "as soon as love came into it, I knew I'd found the weak point, something I could hammer a wedge into. Love's always the most dangerous thing; so much of the unhappiness and quite a lot of the evil in the world comes directly out of it. I guessed that you'd played the good loser, ever since Orsea married her, and that there'd never actually been anything between you and her after he won and you lost. Also, I reckoned it was extremely likely that, deep inside somewhere, Orsea would never really believe that she loves him and not you. Logical enough; he's a fool and you're a good man, everything he wishes he could be but can't. That was perfect, as far as I was concerned. Because you're innocent, you never had anything to hide, you never imagined you'd be vulnerable to attack on that front. All I had to do was find something wrong that I could involve the two of you in — you and her."

He paused and sipped his cup of wine. He looked so weary that Miel felt sorry for him, because he knew how it felt to be that tired.

"Instinct, I guess you could call it," Vaatzes went on. "Everything I heard about the Duchess led me to believe that she couldn't survive in a marriage with someone like Orsea unless she had an escape mechanism; a way of making up for everything he couldn't give her. I was pretty sure it wasn't just sex or anything as basic as that; I wasn't looking for torrid affairs with grooms and footmen. I was sure that somewhere the Duchess had — well, a friend. I talked to servants who'd known her family. She was always reading books when she was a child; alone most of the time, and then sent away to be a hostage, which must have been really horrible. But she survived; and she hadn't gone off the tracks and had affairs or anything like that. So she must have that escape mechanism somewhere, something or someone she could turn to when she desperately needed to be herself. I took the chance that there'd be something of the kind, and I set myself the job of finding out what it was."

"You seem to have a remarkable grasp of human nature," Miel said, "for an engineer."

Vaatzes shrugged. "I use the tools and materials available to me," he said. "If I can't use steel, I have to use flesh instead. Not what I'd have chosen, but you do your best with what you've got. People are easy enough to figure out, if you make an effort."

Miel shook his head but said nothing. Vaatzes went on: "The next step was to find out as much about her as I could. Servants were the obvious source, and one of her maids told me that she often spent time alone writing. That suggested either a diary or letters, but none of the servants had seen a diary, and it's the kind of thing they'd notice, or know about. Letters, then; and if so, who would she write to? Her sisters; well, that seemed reasonable enough, except I rather got the impression that there was something furtive, guilty even, about the way she went about writing these letters. Also, none of the servants could remember her making arrangements for letters to be sent or carried—well, a few, but not nearly enough to account for the time she spent writing them. Now that was significant, you see. If she writes more letters than get sent, it seems likely that she's carrying on a correspondence she doesn't want anybody to know about, and that the important letters are being carried secretly."

"What a clever man you are," Miel said quietly.

"I'm an engineer," Vaatzes said. "I study and understand mechanisms. This was purely a mechanical problem; more letters written than sent, so where are they going? I thought about who might be likely to carry these secret letters, and fairly soon I decided it must be the female merchants. They come and go freely, and they call on the Duchess regularly. She buys all sorts of stuff from them, the servants told me, but never wears any of it. In fact, most of what she buys is hideous rubbish, which struck the servants as odd because she's got such good taste."

"I never thought of that," Miel said.

"Why should you? You weren't actively looking for a mystery." Vaatzes shrugged. "By this point I'd set up my factory, and I had some dealings with the merchant women myself. I gambled on my theory being right and did a bit of gossiping with the ladies in red, making it sound like I knew what was going on, with the merchants carrying the Duchess' letters, and wasn't it an amusing little gobbet of scandal? I got some very odd looks until finally I was fortunate enough to find one who knew what I was talking about. She assumed I was in on the secret, that I was a courier in the secret correspondence myself. That was perfect. I found out who the letters were going to; and as soon as I knew that, everything slotted neatly into place. It was as though some kind friend had done half my work for me. Or you could say it was a gift from heaven, if you believe in a benign providence."

Vaatzes paused for a moment. Telling the story had made him rather more animated, but he still looked haggard and weak, a pitiful object.

"After that, it was a question of patient fieldwork. I arranged for servants to report the comings and goings of merchants to me; I worked out a pattern, the usual interval between incoming letters—from Valens—and her replies. Quite by chance—and this was almost enough to make me start believing in that benign providence—I also discovered that the merchants were carrying information back to agents of the Republic. Which was only to be expected, of course, but it made it delightfully easy for me to complete the circle, so to speak, and get you involved."

"I see," Miel said, and it was as though he'd just had a conjuring trick explained to him, or seen his opponent complete a complex gambit at chess. "It was you who informed on that merchant, the one we arrested for spying."

Vaatzes nodded. "The one who was carrying his letter," he said. "Which meant it came into your hands. And I knew exactly what you'd do. I felt sorry for you, torn between conflicting duties of terrible and equal force: your duty to Veatriz, your duty to Orsea. I knew you'd keep the letter and try to hide it. After that, it was a simple matter to find out where your own special hiding-place was; the one you thought only you knew about, but of course the servants had known about it for years. I had to pay a lot of money for it, the price of a good farm—"

"Oh," Miel said, and for the first time he felt angry. "So that's where she got the money from."

"Your housekeeper. She didn't realize the harm she was doing," Vaatzes said. "I made it sound like some trivial thing, a joke some friends wanted to play on you. There was no malice on her part."

"No," Miel said softly, "I don't suppose there was. So, it was all to destroy me, so you could deprive Orsea of my advice and bring down the city. I suppose I'm flattered."

"You can see it as a tribute to all your hard work for the people of Eremia."

"Yes," Miel said, "but it doesn't make any sense. I can see why you'd want to bring us down. If you could prove to your people that you'd helped win the war for them, maybe they'd forgive you and let you go home. But that's not what you've been doing. Exactly the opposite. You made it possible for *us* to win the war. You built the engines for us. Thanks to them, we killed thousands and thousands of the enemy's soldiers and drove them back; there's no way they can win now, they simply haven't got the manpower. And it's so totally obvious that it was you—nobody else could've built the scorpions—it must mean that you're the most evil man in the world, as far as they're concerned. They must hate you more than ever. You'll never be able to go home now."

Vaatzes shrugged. "That's another part of the mechanism," he said, "and I'm tired, and I haven't got the strength to go into it tonight. I think I'll go to bed now. I need to get some sleep; tomorrow's going to be a very hectic day, and it'll be an early start. Goodnight." He stood up. "For what it's worth, I'm sorry. You've been very kind to me, ever since we first encountered each other. I wish I'd had the time to figure out another mechanism that didn't involve hurting so many people. Regrettably—"

"I ought to kill you," Miel said. "For ruining my life, and hers, and Orsea's. I ought to break your neck right now."

But Vaatzes shook his head, as though they were discussing some abstraction, and he respectfully disagreed on some point. "I don't think so," he said. "After all, I haven't really done anything wrong, as far as you're concerned. I didn't betray Orsea; you did that. All I did was find out about it and tell him." He yawned again, mumbling an apology as he did so. "If you'd done the right thing and taken the letter to Orsea straight away, as soon as you got hold of it, you wouldn't be here now and my schemes would've failed. No, I'm sorry, you can't offload the blame on me. It was your decision. You chose her over him."

It was Miel's turn to shake his head. "I wasn't talking about that," he said. "I ought to kill you for what you did to her. And to Orsea, my best friend."

Vaatzes considered that. "You'd have a stronger case on those grounds, certainly," he said. "But that wouldn't be the real reason, just an excuse. No," he went on, getting painfully to his feet, "you won't do anything to me. For all sorts of reasons. Saving my life, for instance. That took some arranging, by the way."

Miel had thought he was beyond surprise by now. "Arranging?"

Vaatzes smiled and nodded. "On reflection," he said, "it was worth the effort. It got me into your house for an extended stay, which meant I was able to make contact with your housekeeper and various other members of the household. It was hard work, though; hours and hours reading those ridiculous books—*King*

Fashion and the *Mirror;* and teaching myself to shoot a bow and arrow. All that, just so I could talk to a few domestic servants without making them suspicious."

"I don't understand," Miel said weakly.

"What? Oh, right." Vaatzes leaned against the doorframe. "I read in one of the books, *King Fashion,* I think, about the dangers of boar-hunting. It said that a boar who's been shot in the back leg with an arrow is particularly dangerous; it can't run away, which is what its instincts tell it to, but it can still use its front legs to drag itself along and get at you, so you can pretty well guarantee it'll attack. So I made myself a bow and I practiced until I could hit a target the size of a boar's back leg every time. I knew there'd be no guarantee that the perfect opportunity would arise, but it was worth going along just in case it did. And I got lucky; and it all worked out perfectly after all. That benign providence again, I suppose. On balance, I'd have preferred it if you'd shown up about five seconds earlier; I'd have got away with some nasty cuts and bruises, and I could've faked broken bones and internal injuries instead of having to put up with the real things. But, like I said, it all came out just right. I got into your house like I wanted; also, because of your personal code of chivalry, it turned me into one of your responsibilities, someone you had to help and look out for thereafter. Naturally, that made my life much easier, by putting me above suspicion." He smiled slowly. "I won't deny I've had one or two really big slices of luck, but at least I've made the most out of them. A bit like a man killing a pig; nothing goes to waste, it all turns out to be useful."

Miel looked at him. "Get out," he said. "And if I ever set eyes on you again, I will kill you. For the reasons stated."

Vaatzes nodded, thanked him for the wine and left. He'd have liked to stay longer and explain further, but as always he was racing a deadline. Soon — he wasn't sure when, of course, he was basing all his timings on estimates, little more than guesses — soon the Mezentines would be creeping up through the maintenance tunnels, heading for the gate. That would be a problem, of course;

when he'd sent his letters to Falier, the first of them months ago, with the instructions enclosed, he hadn't foreseen the destruction and walling up of the gateway. It remained to be seen what effect it would have on the overall working out of the design; from here on, for a while, it was all out of his hands. He felt a degree of apprehension about that, quite naturally, and also a certain relief. He was far more tired than he'd anticipated he would be at this point, and that in itself was a reason to feel apprehensive.

Now, at least, he didn't have anything in particular to do. He daren't go back to his room at the factory and fall asleep; the factory was too near the gate, for one thing, and he would need to be fairly close to the palace. He didn't relish the prospect of wandering aimlessly about for an hour, or three hours, however long it was going to be. The sensible thing to do would be to find somewhere light and sheltered, and read the book he'd brought with him.

(Ludicrous, he thought; who else but me would remember to bring a book to read while waiting for a massacre to start? But, he reflected, all his life he'd had a peculiar horror of being bored, and he'd been saving this particular book for when he needed to take his mind off something. So; it was just a perfectly reasonable act of preparation.)

He wandered out into the courtyard, just below the tower. Since he was already inside the restricted area, and the guards knew who he was and why he was here, nobody was likely to bother him. They kept torches burning all night here — visibility was important, prisoners can escape better in the dark — and there was a bench he could sit on. Light to read by, and it wasn't uncomfortably cold, just fresh enough to help him stay awake. He sat down, curled his coat tails round his knees, and opened his book.

The candidate *[he read]* is not expected to understand the theoretical basis of perfection; nor is he encouraged to consider such matters in any further detail than that included in the syllabus. It is sufficient for him to be aware that, in a necessarily imperfect world, perfection is most immediately and tangibly represented in the various established specifications ordained by each Guild for its members.

However, some observations on the basic principles of this subject will prove useful to the candidate, and should be committed to memory. First, perfection can be expressed as the smallest degree of tolerance of error or divergence from Specification that can be obtained in the circumstances prevailing in each instance. Thus, a standard tolerance of one thousandth of an inch is allowed for in specifications of lathe work and most milling operations. In casting, a tolerance of ten thousandths is permitted; in general carpentry, twenty thousandths, although in fine joinery and cabinet-making this is reduced to ten thousandths.

None of these divergences can be taken to express perfection; a perfect artifact must conform to Specification exactly. Given the inevitability of error, however, the Guild recognizes the need for strictly regulated tolerance, and such tolerance is therefore included in the specification. The question arises, therefore, whether an artifact that is perfect, i.e. one that contains no error whatsoever, can be in accordance with Specification; since it differs from the prescribed form by omitting the permissible degree of error, is it not therefore out of Specification, and therefore an abomination?

This issue was addressed by the seventh extraordinary assembly of the united Guilds, who declared that a perfect artifact is permitted provided that in its creation there was no inherent intent to improve upon Specification by reducing error beyond permitted tolerance. Evidence of such intent would be, among other things, modification of other components to allow for or take advantage of perfection in any one component. Thus, if a mechanism is found to have only one perfect component, intent is not found; whereas if more than one component is perfect, and if the perfection of one component is ancillary to or dependent upon the perfection of another (for example, where two parts fit together), there is a rebuttable presumption of such intent, and the accused must prove beyond reasonable doubt that no such intent was in his mind when he produced the components.

He rested the book on his knees for a moment, then turned the page.

Perfection is most often attained, or, more usually, aspired to, through the destruction or removal of material. Such destroyed or discarded material is referred to as waste. Waste can be created by separation (for instance, by sawing off surplus material) or by attrition (e.g. filing, turning). The creation of waste can therefore be partly or wholly destructive. It is policy that wherever possible, partial destruction is preferred to total destruction, since surplus material that is only partially destroyed — offcuts, for example — can often be put to good use. However, this preference should not be allowed to interfere with the imperatives of precision. Thus, where a more exact result can be obtained by a wholly destructive process, e.g. filing or milling, than by a partially destructive one such as sawing or chain-drilling, total destruction is preferred. Acceptable levels of waste are, of course, allowed for in all Specifications, and any attempt to reduce waste beyond the specified levels is prohibited. As the report of the ninth general review committee puts it, waste is part and parcel of any properly conducted procedure; material is there to be cut and destroyed in the furtherance of the design.

He closed his eyes for a moment. There wasn't, as far as he was aware, a specification for the cutting and piercing of flesh, the bending and breaking of bone and sinew; there was no established tolerance through which perfection in this sphere could be expressed. In the absence of anything of the sort, it was impossible to establish what represented a permissible degree of waste. However, the basic rule must still apply: where a more exact result can be obtained by total destruction, it is preferred. He closed his hands around his face, and tried to find the absolution those words ought to bring. It was only logical. The mechanism he'd built wasn't some whim of his own. It was the only possible device that could be capable of achieving his only objective, and that objective had been forced on him by the men who'd taken him away from his house, his family, the only things in the world that mattered to him. So he'd followed the design to its logical end, accepting the inevitability of a high level of wholly destructive waste; in effect, he'd been following the design specified by the actions of his betters in the Guild, and it was the imperatives of precision that had destroyed Miel Ducas and Duchess Veatriz and Duke Orsea, and were even now threading their nervous way through the tunnels in the rock under his feet, heading for a gate that shouldn't have been blocked, with a view to the laying waste, by cutting and attrition, of an entire city.

He was glad that it was all outside his control for a while.

They had no idea what to expect as they lifted the heavy trapdoor. They weren't supposed to know that the whole plan was the work of the traitor-abominator Vaatzes, but the deputy chief of staff had felt obliged to tell them, just in case it was all a trap. It wasn't the sort of information that inspires confidence, particularly when taken together with the obvious mistake about the gate.

Nevertheless, a color-sergeant by the name of Pasargades lifted the trapdoor, took a deep breath and scrambled out of the tunnel into the sweet night air. He may have ducked his head involuntarily, as though anticipating a cut or a blow, but nothing like that happened. He jumped out, looked round quickly and dropped to his knees to help the next man out.

The first thing they noticed was how quiet it was. No voices, which was encouraging; no boots grinding on the cobbles, no scrape of heels or spear-butts. There was a certain degree of light, from a lantern hanging off a bracket five yards or so away. So far, the abominator had done them proud.

Thirty-six men followed Color-Sergeant Pasargades out of the tunnel: two infantry platoons, one squad of engineers and the commanding officer, Captain Boustrophedon. They were light enough on their feet—minimum armor, sidearms only, and the engineers' tools. All they had to do was breach the rubble blocking the gate. The army would do the rest.

The captain led the way, as was only right and proper. One platoon of infantry followed him, then the engineers, then the second infantry unit. They had a fair idea of where to go. The last Mezentine diplomat to visit the city had briefed them on the layout of the gatehouse, not that there was much to tell. Through the archway into a large empty room, and there was the gate.

Or there it wasn't. Instead, blocking a ragged-sided hole in the wall, there was a heap of wicker baskets, piled on top of each other, each one filled with rubble. In front of the heap someone had made a start on a brick wall, but as yet it was only three courses high. You could step over that without any bother. Propping up the heap of baskets were half a dozen beams—they looked like rafters, or something of the sort. Presumably the idea was that if there was another battering-ram attack, the beams would to some extent brace the baskets against the impact; either that, or the bricklayers were afraid that the heap was unsteady and might come crashing down on them at any moment. All in all, it was a fairly unconvincing piece of fortification. Once the brick wall was finished, of course, it'd be better, though not much. Not that it mattered. Even if the gate was wide open, the Mezentines didn't have the manpower for a direct assault, not if their entry was resisted.

Simple, thought Captain Boustrophedon: knock away the beams, get a grappling-hook into a few of those baskets, and pull. Of course, you wouldn't live to enjoy being a hero. The rubble would come down on you like a rockslide in the mountains, you'd be a bag full of splintered bones when you died.

Someone was calling out; an inquiry rather than a challenge, but it had to go unanswered. More voices, which meant choosing a course of action quickly and hoping it'd work. Well, the captain thought, if we can't have the rubble collapsing inward, we'll have to try pushing instead. He wasn't particularly happy about it, but there wasn't time to draw diagrams and calculate angles.

"Get hold of those beams and push," he ordered.

The back platoon were already engaged. He heard a shout or two, then a yell as someone got hurt — them or us, hardly matters. So long as this gateway's opened up in the next fifteen seconds.

They pushed. A couple of arrows skittered off the side wall, someone was yelling, "In there!" They pushed again, and in the split second it took for Boustrophedon to realize he'd made the wrong decision, the Eremian guards swept away the nine men of the back platoon who were still standing, and charged into the gatehouse.

Boustrophedon lived long enough to see the first gleam of light through the breach. He hardly noticed it, although it meant he'd succeeded; there was surprisingly little pain, but his sight was being squeezed into a narrow ring by encroaching darkness. The air was full of dust. He died, and a Mezentine soldier stumbling through the breach trod on his head before an Eremian shot him. That hardly mattered, in the grand scheme of things. There were plenty more where he'd just come from. What was left of the defenders was shoved out of the way as the assault party burst through. The Eremian night patrol, who might have made a difference if they'd arrived twenty seconds earlier, hardly slowed the attack up at all. The first objective, the square behind the main gate, was secured within a minute of the opening of the breach; five minutes, and the Mezentines were on the wall, racing along the ramparts to secure access to the whole city.

24

Miel Ducas had, remarkably enough, fallen asleep. He hadn't thought he'd be able to sleep, with Vaatzes' words rattling round inside his head like stones in a bucket. Nevertheless, when the guard captain burst in, he was flopped in his chair, eyes closed.

The captain was yelling at him. At first he thought, *he's come to kill me,* but it soon occurred to him that that wouldn't call for panic-stricken shouting, so he listened to what the man was saying.

"They're on the wall," he said, which didn't make sense. "We can't hold them. Come on, get out."

Get out he understood. "Hold on," he mumbled, "I'll get my things." But the captain grabbed him by the elbow and dragged him toward the door. He was too sleepy to resist.

"Head for the palace," the captain was saying, and that didn't make sense either.

"What's going on?" Miel asked.

"The Mezentines," the captain snapped back at him. "They're inside the city, and up on the wall. They'll be here any moment now. Head for the palace."

Still didn't make sense. We've won the war, how come there's Mezentines in the city? Miel knew better than to argue, however. The captain let go of his elbow and ran off, leaving him standing in the little courtyard. Well, Miel thought, I suppose I'm free.

If there really were Mezentines... He found it impossible to believe. How could they have got in? Surely there'd have been an alert, trumpets blasting and men shouting, war noises. Ridiculous. Even so; head for the palace. He could do that.

Someone jumped out in front of him. At first he thought it must be Vaatzes, because of his dark skin. Then he realized: Mezentine. Immediately he felt bloated with panic. The Mezentine soldier was coming at him, holding some kind of polearm, and he himself was empty-handed and defenseless. *Oh well,* he thought, but he sidestepped anyway, at the very last moment, and was pleasantly surprised as the soldier blundered past him, lunging ferociously at the patch of empty air he'd just left behind.

The drill he'd learned when he was twelve said that the sidestep is combined with a counterattack in time, either both hands round the throat or a stamping kick to the back of the knee. Miel, however, turned and ran.

Head for the palace. The courtyard archway opened into Coopers' Street; uphill, second left was Fourways, leading to Drapers' Lane, leading to Middle Walk. There he met the guards, running flat out; he flattened himself against a wall to let them pass. Up Middle Walk (he'd been cooped up in small rooms far too long, his legs were stiff and painful) to the Review Grounds, across the Horsefair and down the little alley that led to Fivesprings. Halfway down the alley was a narrow stair up the side of a house, which led to a passageway inside the palace wall, which let you into the Ducas' private entrance; assuming you had the key, which he didn't.

But the door was open; and the reason for that unexpected stroke of luck was Jarnac Ducas, struggling to do up the buckles on his brigandine coat left-handed as he pulled the key out of the lock with his right.

"Miel?" he said. "What are you doing here?"

Stupid question, as both of them realized as soon as he'd said it. "What's going on, Jarnac?" Miel asked. "They said the Mezentines are in the city, and I met—"

But Jarnac nodded. "Don't ask me how," he said. "Seems like

they came in through the gate, and now they've secured the walls, by the sound of it. We're falling back on the palace and the inner yards; if we can regroup, maybe we can push them back, I don't know. You coming?"

Another stupid question. Up onto the palace wall—they arrived at the same time as the guards, who told them that Duke Orsea was down below trying to drive the invaders out of the Horsefair. "Not going well when we left," one of the guards said. "He made a good start, but they came in from Long Lane and Halfacre, took him in flank. That's all I know."

Jarnac swore, and scrambled down the stairs into the palace. Miel followed; but by the time he made it to the long gallery that ran the length of the top floor, Jarnac had disappeared down one of the side passages. Miel stopped, leaned against the wall and caught his breath. This was ridiculous, he decided; I won't be any good to anybody, lost and out of breath.

He closed his eyes for a moment and thought. Something to fight with would be a good start, and then he supposed he ought to go and look for Orsea. There weren't any armories or guard stations on this floor, but there was a trophy of arms on the wall of the small reception chamber, fancy decorative stuff tastefully arranged in a sort of seashell pattern. He couldn't reach any of the swords or shields, but by standing on a chair he was able to pull down a finely engraved gilded halberd, which was going to have to do. Armor was out of the question, of course, and besides, he didn't have time to put it on.

Down five flights of stairs; people coming in both directions. Most of them gave him a startled look as he passed them, but nobody stopped or said anything. The front gate of the palace was open, though there was a platoon of guards standing by to close it as soon as the Duke managed to disengage and pull back. Assuming he was still alive.

As Miel ran through the gateway, the significance of what Jarnac had told him began to sink in. If Orsea had initially pushed through into the Horsefair, and then enemy units had come out from the alleys on either side, it was more than likely he'd been cut off, quite possibly encircled, depending on the numbers. It was exactly the sort of mess Orsea would get himself into (impulsive, brave, very stupid Orsea), and of course it was the hereditary duty of the Ducas to get him out of it.

That's right, he thought bitterly — the cobbles hurt his feet through his thin-soled slippers as he ran — *me in my shirtsleeves, with this stupid toy halberd.* This would be a good time to be excused duty, on grounds of having been imprisoned for high treason (can't get more excused than that). But he remembered, he was innocent. So that was no use.

North Parade was crowded with soldiers, some running forward toward the arch that led into the Horsefair, others scrambling through them, headed for the palace. The men coming back in had a dazed, bewildered look about them. Many were bloody, some were dragging wounded men along with them. One of them tried to grab his arm; he was shouting, *go back, get away, they're coming through.* Miel dodged him and kept going, but it didn't sound encouraging. All in all, it was a bad situation, he felt. Death in the defense of Duke and city was, naturally, a fitting and entirely acceptable end for the Ducas, but it was understood that somebody would be watching, taking notes, appreciating what he was doing with a view to making an appropriate entry in the family history. Death by massacre, blunder and shambles wasn't quite the same thing, but there wasn't anything he could do about it.

North Parade Arch was blocked by a crush of soldiers, filling the opening with their compressed bodies and limbs for want of anything better. No chance of getting through that; so he ran back along the wall, kicked open a doorway (side door of the Nicephorus house; he was sure they wouldn't mind) into a garden. The Nicephorus had their own private door opening into Horsefair — handy for the kitchenmaids going to market for spices and walnut oil. Assuming the enemy didn't know about it (they didn't, because the Nicephorus garden wasn't full of soldiers) he could use it to nip out into the battle, privileged to the last.

They'd bolted it, as they always did at night, but they hadn't locked it with the key. He shot the bolt, opened the door a crack and looked out. He could see people running, a bit of open space, and a big crowd on the north side, which presumably was the battle. Taking care to close the gate behind him, he slipped through.

Nobody took any notice of him, unless they were running and he got in their way, in which case they dodged round him or shoved him aside. It was still too dark to make out anything more than silhouettes and moving shadows in the distance, over on the north side of the Horsefair, where the fighting appeared to be. He walked rather than ran — why run to your death? he asked himself, it'll probably still be there in a minute or two. For the first time in a long while he was fully alert and focused. He knew what his job was — to save Orsea — and that it was most likely impossible, and that he'd die trying. Under other circumstances he'd be out of his mind with panic, but there didn't seem any call for that. As far as he could judge, the city was lost. Even if they managed to save it, his life as the Ducas was ruined, gone forever. Orsea, his best friend and his Duke, hated him as a traitor. There didn't seem to be much point in a life where everything he was had been taken away from him. If he couldn't be Miel Ducas anymore, he didn't want to play.

As he got closer to the fighting, he could hear the usual noises: shouts, yells, screams, thumps, scrapes, clangs, the shearing noise of cut meat. Take fear away and it was just noise; he approached it slowly and calmly, like a farmer walking up to a bull.

Something was going on directly in front of him; there was a commotion, and the movement seemed particularly intense. Remembering the silly gilded halberd he had in his hands, he quickened his pace a little. He had no idea where Orsea might be, assuming he was still alive, but here was as good a place to start as any.

The commotion turned out to be his cousin Jarnac. By the look of it, he was trying to cut his way into a dense wedge of the enemy. There was a handful of Eremians with him, but they were hanging back—probably, Miel guessed, because they didn't want to get too close to Jarnac while he was swinging his pole-axe.

It was an extraordinary sight. Every inch of Jarnac was on the move; as he dodged a spear-thrust, he pivoted, sidestepped, simultaneously jabbing, fending, hooking, hammering. There was a Mezentine right in front of him; he reversed the pole-axe and thrust the butt-spike into the man's stomach—there was eighteen-gauge steel plate in the way, but Jarnac's spike punched through it like tree-bark—then skipped side-and-back like a dancer to avoid another one; he jerked the spike out of the fallen man and tucked the hook inside the knee of his replacement; down that one went, Jarnac drove the spike through his helmet into his brain without bothering to look down, because his attention was fixed on another one, who got the axe-blade in his neck, in the gap between aventail and collarbone; Jarnac had moved again, diagonally forward so as to step in for a thrust in time into the face of the next Mezentine; he converted the pull that freed the blade into a backward thrust, piercing the skull of the man who was trying to get behind him; then he pushed forward and swung the pole-axe in a circle round his head to strike with every scrap of his strength; Miel couldn't see the man who was on the wrong end of that, but he heard the ring, clear and sharp as a hammer on an anvil. Every movement of hand and arm was mirrored in a step, forward, sideways or back; each step was combined with a twist or a turn that tensioned the muscles for the next thrust or cut. The only reason the Mezentines stood in his way was because they were too closely jammed together to get away; it was like watching a man dance his way through a tangle of briars. *What happened?* Miel asked himself. *What happened to turn my genial buffoon of a cousin into the angel of Death?*

As he watched, a Mezentine slipped past Jarnac on the left, got behind him and stabbed him in the back with a spear. Miel could feel his own heart suddenly stop, as though someone had reached down inside his chest and grabbed hold of it. Jarnac was dead; apparently not, because the spear didn't seem to want to go in. The attacker couldn't believe it. He froze, completely bewildered, and Jarnac spun on his heel and crushed his head with a monstrous overhand blow. Miel heard bone failing, and he remembered that when he'd met Jarnac in the passageway, he'd been climbing into a brigandine coat.

The dance stopped abruptly. Jarnac had run out of Mezentines for the time being, and exhaustion had caught up with him. He staggered, steadied himself against the axe-shaft, and stood still.

"Jarnac," Miel shouted. Jarnac lifted his head and frowned. A red wash from the rising sun bathed the side of his face, glittering off the splashed blood that coated his cheeks.

"Hello, Miel," Jarnac said quietly, and he grinned. "This is a fucking mess, isn't it?"

"Where's Orsea?" Miel asked.

Jarnac shook his head. "Search me," he said. "I caught sight of him a minute or so back, but then this lot here"—he jabbed the butt-spike in the vague direction of a dead man—"bust through our line and I got distracted." He frowned slightly. "I wouldn't bother going and looking for him, if I were you."

Miel shrugged. "I think I'd better have a go at it," he said.

"Bugger." Jarnac sighed. "Want me to come with you?"

"Thanks," Miel said, "but you'd better stay here. Someone's got to..." He couldn't say what he wanted to say. "You're needed," he went on, "I'm not. See you later."

"Take care," Jarnac said; and then he was moving again, and Miel darted through a gap between two dazed-looking Mezentines into a clear space. He wished he'd got a brigandine coat like Jarnac's, or even just a mailshirt or a padded jack.

A few steps brought him close enough to see what was happening. He saw the backs of a thin line of Eremians. They looked like they were walking backward, but they were being pushed, and every now and then one of them would trip and fall and be walked over. That, Miel realized, was all that was left of Orsea's gallant charge, the entire palace garrison. It was like watching a chick break out of an egg; the thin wall cracking, crumpling and breaking up, as something inside it flexed its strength to force its way out.

Never mind, Miel thought, and he lunged forward with his stupid halberd at some soldier or other who happened to be just inside his reach. The point slid off the man's gorget; he grabbed the shaft and pulled, ripping it out of Miel's hands, and threw it away. Miel let go and bundled sideways; collided awkwardly with someone he hadn't seen, tripped over his own feet and fell. His chin banged on the man's knee, jarring his neck and jaw. Too shocked to think, he dropped to the ground. A boot kicked his ribs—accident, not deliberate—and another slammed into the back of his head. *Am I dead?* he wondered, and then nothing.

All she could see was vague movement, like a river, or the swaying branches of trees. That moving thing, she knew, was the enemy, and it was coming closer. The logical conclusion was that the battle had been lost.

They wouldn't kill women though, would they? It stood to reason that Orsea was dead by now, but her mind was too preoccupied to consider the implications of that. *They wouldn't kill women; why would they want to do a thing like that?* She couldn't imagine a reason, but the same went for destroying a city. Why would anybody want to do such a thing?

No point in watching anymore. She turned and came in off the balcony, and saw someone standing and looking at her.

"I know you," she said. "You're Ziani Vaatzes."

Vaatzes nodded. He looked pathetically weary, and was wearing a heavy coat with big, bulging pockets. "We met at the hunt," he said awkwardly. The formality of it made her smile; it'd never do to be massacred in the company of a man to whom she hadn't been introduced. "What's happening?" he asked.

"I don't know," she said. "Come and see for yourself if you like."

"No thank you." He was frowning. "I think it might be a good idea if you were to leave now," he said.

That made her laugh. "Don't be silly," she said, "we can't leave. If we go out in the streets, we'll just get killed along with everybody else. There's no secret passages or anything like that."

"Actually," he said, and hesitated. "Actually," he repeated, "there's a way that'll take us right outside the city. Same way as they got in," he added.

There was something significant about that remark, but she couldn't spare the energy to figure out what it was. "No there isn't," she said. "I was born in this building, I know—"

"The maintenance tunnels for the water system," he interrupted. "They came in through them, but they'll be long gone by now. They're all out there," he said, pointing over her shoulder, "fighting the battle."

It occurred to her that he was quite right. She felt as though she'd just walked into a wall in the dark. Just when she'd made up her mind she was going to die, along came this funny little man with a viable alternative. "But I don't know how to get into them," she said, her voice suddenly creased with panic. "I've lived here all these years and—"

"I do," Vaatzes said. "You come with me and I'll show you. But I really think we should go now. It's quite a long way, and I'd rather we did the trip and got clear while the enemy's busy with other things, if you follow me."

She knew it was wrong even to think about escaping, deserting, when Orsea was lying out there dead and the city was about to fall. On the other hand, there was absolutely no reason why she should be killed, if it could be avoided. She nodded. "Give me a moment to change my shoes," she said. "I can't go running down maintenance tunnels in these things."

As she followed him, it did occur to her to ask why he'd come to save her. Everybody else seemed to have forgotten about her—her maids, her ladies-in-waiting, the guards, the chamberlains, the flower of Eremian nobility, theoretically sworn to defend her to the last drop of blood. They'd gone to the battle, or run off to hide, or simply melted away as though they'd never actually existed in the first place. Only this strange little brown-skinned man had thought of her, and by some lucky chance, he was also the only person in the city who'd thought of escaping through the water tunnels. Only a foreigner would've seen the possibility, she supposed; or something along those lines.

He'd already prised up a trapdoor in the little yard behind the cloister garden with the fountain. "I knew there'd be one around here somewhere," he said, with a faint smile. "Fountain — water."

"Yes, of course," she said. She'd never have thought of that.

"I'll go first, if you like," he said. He opened his coat and drew a sword. It looked ridiculous in his hand, somehow. "Give me a moment or so, then follow me."

"All right," she said. For some reason she trusted him completely. He took a deep breath, then walked down the steps, picking his way delicately like a still-wobbly foal. A few seconds later his head reappeared. "Seems to be all right," he said. He'd got a smear of cobweb in his hair, which made him look comical.

She should have been prepared for the darkness, once she was down in the tunnel, but she wasn't. The dark, the silence and the cold put her in mind of a grave. She couldn't see, and all she could hear was the soft patter of Vaatzes' feet somewhere up ahead of her. *This is ridiculous*, she thought; *I'm leaving my husband and my home and running out into the night in my third-best dinner gown; I've got no money and nothing to eat, and even if we survive and get outside the city, what the hell are we supposed to do then? Walk to —*

Walk to Civitas Vadani; the name slipped into her mind as neatly and unostentatiously as a cat jumping up on her lap on a winter evening. If Orsea was... She shied away from that; but if her old life was over, where else was there to go? *Yes,* she accused herself, *but now that I have thought of it, I want to go; because —*

"Stop." He'd said the word so softly she almost missed it, even in that dead silence. "Stay there."

There was an edge in that quiet voice that frightened her. She froze, with a half-drawn breath. Vaatzes hadn't been afraid earlier, she remembered, but now apparently that had changed. She had a feeling that anything capable of scaring him was likely to be very bad news indeed.

Then he was there, very close to her in the dark. "We can't go this way," he whispered intimately (she could feel his breath on her face). "I didn't think there'd be any of them down here, but—" He stopped. "I'm sorry," he said, and the apology in his voice, the admission of failure, left her weak with fear. "We'll have to go back and think of something else."

Of course; they'd go back, he'd think of something else. She still couldn't imagine why he'd apparently taken responsibility for her safety, but he had, and she still trusted him "Keep still," he went on, "I'll go past." She felt him brush past her, a tiny contact with the back of her hand, the faintest brush of a sleeve against her cheek. Once he was past, she followed, until they were back where they'd started. The sun was nearly up now, and on the cloister lawn, grossly incongruous in that green, formal space, lay the dead body of a man.

Vaatzes noticed it and frowned slightly, as if it was a loose bolt or a worn bearing. "Looks like they've been through here," he said. The dead man was an Eremian, a civilian; she didn't recognize him. "I'm not sure," Vaatzes continued. "Probably our best bet would be to go down the hill—against the flow, so to speak. Less likely to bump into them if we go where they've already been."

That was stupid, though; they were too conspicuous—him because of his dark face, her because of her aristocratic gown. "I don't think that'd be such a good idea," she said. It came out sounding different from what she'd intended.

"What did you have in mind?" he asked.

"I don't know," she mumbled. "I wish I knew what was happening."

To her surprise, he reacted as though she'd just said something very profound. "That's an idea," he said. "Probably best if we got up high—in one of the towers, maybe, except I'd rather not run into them on one of those narrow staircases. How about the Ducas house? Isn't there supposed to be a private entrance?"

She nodded. "But I don't know where it is."

"Forget that, then." He was shifting restlessly, as though the floor was painfully hot. "All I was thinking was, if we can get out into the Horsefair, and then straight down to the city gate; if the fighting's all done, there shouldn't be anybody much about right now. Or we could try hiding somewhere, if you can think of some place they wouldn't be likely to come looking."

Being offered a choice shocked her. It suggested that Vaatzes didn't have another plan to replace the one that had, apparently, failed; otherwise he'd simply have told her instead of asking her opinion.

Well," she said, "it's probably best if we don't stay here."

Vaatzes laughed at what she assumed was a private joke. "That's true enough," he said. "All right, we'll make for the Horsefair and see if we can get as far as the city gate. We'll just have to take it slow and steady, that's all."

Slow and steady was a nightmare. As Vaatzes had predicted, the streets where the enemy had already been were deserted, unless dead people counted as population, in which case they were crowded. Once they were out of the palace grounds, most of the bodies were Eremian soldiers, but there were civilians too, women and children as well as men. "They won't start setting fires till they've pulled out," Vaatzes said at one point. She hadn't even considered that possibility.

Very strange indeed to see the Horsefair so quiet. This time of day, it should've been packed—country people setting up stalls, staff from the big houses coming out to buy things for that evening's meal, horse-traders and merchants already doing business. She stepped over a man she knew slightly; she recognized him as a guardsman who often stood outside the palace gate. He'd been cut nearly in half by something, and the scowl on his face was pure anger.

"There's still a chance," Vaatzes was saying, "that we could duck down into the water tunnels somewhere else. To be honest, if we're going to play hide-and-seek, we'd stand a better chance in the dark than up here in the open."

She was about to say that she didn't really like that idea when she noticed he'd stopped. He was looking at something in the distance, on the far side of the fair. She looked, and saw men running, but she couldn't make out who they were, Mezentines or Eremians.

"I wonder what's got them so worked up," Vaatzes said.

A moment later he got an answer to his mystery. Through the archway came a party of horsemen, moving fast. In front of them, Mezentines were scattering, like poultry in a run when the fox has broken in. She saw, she could just about make out, a horseman riding one of them down. The rider came up behind the runner at a slow, contained canter, and she saw the runner throw up his arms and drop to the ground. More horsemen were spilling out now, a great many of them; as if in response, a large number of Mezentines coalesced, like bees forming into a swarm, from the edges and the walls. They were trying to get into some sort of formation, but it seemed as though they'd misjudged something, or left it too late. The horsemen rode through them while they were still scrambling about, and once the cavalry line had gone by, there didn't look to be any of them still standing.

"Who's that?" she heard herself ask. "They can't be ours, all our horses are stabled on the west side..."

Still more horsemen came in through the arch. A pattern was becoming visible. They were forming up to charge, in the direction of the palace. She looked round, and saw that Vaatzes was smiling, almost as though he'd been proved right about something.

"Excellent," he said. "Thank God for romance."

That was a very strange thing to say, as the unidentified cavalry—several hundred of them by now—burst into a fast canter, followed by a gallop, heading very close to where they were both standing. Vaatzes swore and grabbed her arm, pulling her behind him as he turned and ran. It took her a moment to understand; whoever they were, standing in their way wouldn't be a good idea.

They ran a short distance and stopped, and the cavalry flowed by like a lava stream; they were close enough to be more than just shapes now, and she made out men in armor, their faces visored, on tall, powerful horses. They didn't look like Eremians; she had no idea what Mezentian cavalry were supposed to look like. "Who are they?" she asked again, but the clatter of hoofs drowned her out.

Footsoldiers had appeared from somewhere—she hadn't been paying attention, so she didn't know where—and the cavalry plowed into them, so hard she could feel the impact through the soles of her feet. She tried to pull away and run, but Vaatzes was holding on to her, his fingers tight on her arm. She didn't know what to make of that; it felt like he wanted to keep her, as if she was some valuable thing he was determined to take with him. Now he came very close, and shouted in her ear, "Can you see him? I don't know what he looks like."

She shouted back, "Who?"

"Duke Valens."

She thought she'd misheard him; then she realized, as though she'd just been told the answer to a silly riddle a child could've guessed, who the horsemen were. Valens had come to rescue her.

It was a complete shambles, of course. Dead bodies everywhere, both the enemy and the Eremians scattered all over the place; he'd come expecting to fight a hopeless battle against ridiculous odds, but instead he'd turned up late, when it was all over; picked a fight with the Perpetual Republic, and all for nothing.

A footsoldier made the mistake of being in front of him. Valens twitched his left rein, urged his horse on with his heels and held his sword out just a little as he passed. No need to strike or anything like that; the sword's edge touched the man's neck, and momentum did the rest. Elegant; but he'd wanted to let off steam by hitting something hard.

All around him, his men were slaughtering the enemy like sheep, which wasn't what he was here for. Instead, he needed to find someone he could talk to; he needed to find her, and the fool Orsea, and then get out again as quickly as possible. Anything else he did here, such as killing Mezentines, was just making a bad situation worse.

Pull yourself together, he thought, *this is getting out of hand.* In front of him—while he'd been agonizing, the battle had overtaken him, proving once again that War has deplorable manners—his color squadron had surrounded a large unit of Mezentine infantry, jamming them close together so that they could hardly move, let alone fight back. He watched his men drive their horses tight up against the Mezentines' bodies, barging them back, while their riders hacked resignedly at heads and arms showing above an arbitrary line; it was like watching tired men cutting back a hedge, their hooks turning blunt, their dexterity worn down into mere flailing and bashing. It was a disgusting sight, and it had come about because the Vadani Duke was a hopeless romantic, who couldn't resist the thought of snatching his beloved out of the jaws of death. Busy as he was, and preoccupied with more practical matters, he had to stop and consider that. From the ugliness of his life he'd sought escape and redemption in pure and selfless love, and the upshot was lacerated flesh, cut and smashed bone, and the weariness of men worn out with the sheer hard work of killing.

Then he pulled himself together, as previously resolved, and forced himself to become the efficient, dispassionate professional. Thanks to surprise and his enemy's lack of imagination, he'd carried the field, for the time being. Such Mezentines as remained alive inside the Horsefair were penned up and harmless, but reinforcements would already be on their way from other parts of the city; his cavalry were good at attacking but not at being attacked, he lacked archers and infantry support, and he could expect no help from the shattered fragments of the Eremian forces. At best he had a quarter of an hour, in which he had to find her, and Orsea as well if possible. After that, he had to leave or face extermination. Fine.

It stood to reason she'd be in the palace; Orsea too, if he had any sense (but of course he hadn't). He could see the palace dead ahead of him, but he hadn't paid enough attention to the fine detail of how you got there from here. The map of Civitas Eremiae he'd studied earlier marked streets, gates and arches, but so far it had proved less than entirely reliable (should've known better than to trust a map he'd bought from a woman in a red dress). If, as he feared, there were narrow streets and alleys between here and the palace, it'd be a stupid risk to take horsemen in there. All in all, he was beginning to wish he'd stayed at home.

And then, unexpectedly, he saw her. She was quite close to him, no more than twenty yards away; there was a man with her, a brown-skinned man, therefore by implication a Mezentine or one of their mercenaries. He wasn't in armor, which suggested he was a diplomat or other civilian; not that it mattered. It was her, unmistakable, just the same as she'd been the one time they'd met, ten years ago.

He yanked his horse's head round and dug his heels in. Some fool of a footsoldier darted across his line of sight; probably only trying to get away, but for half a second he was inside Valens' reach, and that was the end of him. Valens didn't notice anything about him, wasn't entirely sure where the cut had landed. Out of the corner of his eye he saw him go down and his experience in such matters assured him that living men don't drop down at that angle. He felt a mild tingle of pain in his sword-arm, just above the elbow, where he'd abused the tendon.

She saw him approaching; froze for a moment in panic, then looked round for somewhere to run to. The fool with her had pulled out a sword (a short, single-edged huntsman's falchion, he noticed automatically; loot, presumably, and much good it'd do

him) and was trying to get between her and the presumed approaching danger. No time for that sort of thing; Valens swerved
left, leaned forward a little, smacked the falchion out of his hand
with the flat of his sword, and completed the engagement with a
short, stiff thrust to the heart.

He noticed in passing that the thrust was turned and didn't penetrate, but that was of no concern. The fool had fallen over, and
didn't matter anymore. She was standing quite still, her mouth
open in horror and no sound coming out. "It's all right," he yelled,
"it's me."

Of course, she didn't recognize him, even with his bevor up.
Why should she? It was ten years ago, and they'd only chatted for
a few minutes. "It's me," he howled, "it's Valens. I'm come to save
you." Melodrama, he thought; what a crass thing to say. "Please,
stay still, it's all right."

She was staring at him as though he had wings and a tail. She
said something but he couldn't hear. The hell with it, he thought,
and slid off his horse. He landed awkwardly, turning his ankle
over, and swore.

"Valens?" He heard her this time. "What are you—?"

Explanations; for crying out loud, no *time*. "Soon as I heard
about the assault," he said. He was lying; it had taken him a day,
a night and a morning before the pain had got too much for him
to bear and he'd ordered out the cavalry. "I came to get you. And
Orsea," he added, wishing it hadn't sounded such an obvious afterthought. "Where is he?"

She just looked at him. *Oh,* he thought, and he had enough conscience left to hate the part of him that added, *Well, never mind.*
"We can't hang around," he said, then remembered he'd forgotten
something; his manners. "Will you come with me?" he asked.

She didn't say anything for a very long time, maybe as long as a
third of a second. Then she nodded.

"Here, you take my horse," he said. He held out the reins. She
was looking at the horse; *how am I supposed to get up there?* He winced;

he really wasn't handling this very well, but seeing her made him feel seventeen and mortally awkward again. "Give you a leg-up," he said.

Her foot in his hand; a sharp stab of pain, as her weight aggravated the strained tendon. Then she was reaching down for the reins, as two of his captains rode up fast. Their faces told him they'd been looking for him, expecting not to find him alive. He turned to the nearest of them. "You," he said, "find me a horse. You, with me."

She was saying something, and he couldn't hear; the helmet-padding, probably. "What?" he asked.

"Orsea," she shouted back. "He led the counterattack, but I don't know what happened. You've got to—"

Valens knew perfectly well what he'd got to do without having to be told. "I know," he said. "Can you take me to where—?"

She shook her head; and then a voice somewhere behind him and to the right said, "I can." He looked round and saw the little brown-faced man, the one he hadn't managed to kill a moment ago. "I know where he fell," this incongruous man said, "I was watching from the tower. Before I came to find you," he added, to her. "I can show him."

She nodded rapidly and said, "Please"; and for a moment, Valens felt violently jealous. *For pity's sake*, he told himself. "All right," he said—the captain had come back with a riderless horse; quick service, he'd have to remember that—"you can take us there." He hopped into the saddle and grabbed the reins. "And then we really do have to leave," he shouted to her.

The little man looked up at him and sort of waved his hands—*what about me?*—at which the captain, clearly a man of initiative, reached down, grabbed him round the waist and pulled him up behind him on his horse. The other captain closed in behind them as they rode off, following the little man's pointing finger. *If he's lying*, Valens promised himself, *I'll have him gutted alive.*

It was delicate work, picking a way through the dead bodies. The horses didn't really want to tread on them, and stepped tentatively, like ladies in good shoes on a muddy track. Before they got to where the Mezentine was taking them, he sent the other captain to call off the attack and regroup the men, ready to leave as soon as they were through with looking for Orsea.

"Around here," the little man was saying—he wasn't used to riding; he was pointing with one hand and clinging grimly to the captain in front of him with the other. "I know I saw him go down; he was wearing a helmet with a white horsehair crest—"

"That's right," she said.

Valens was listening, but he was also looking at a big, tall man standing a few yards away. He'd been leaning on a pole-axe, a picture of complete exhaustion. There was so much blood on him that he glistened like a fish, and he appeared to be bewildered, almost in a daydream. He must have heard the horses' hoofs; he snapped upright and leveled the pole-axe in a high first guard; as he did so, a panel of his ruined brigandine flopped sideways and hung out at right-angles.

She screamed; she was calling out a name, which he didn't catch.

"Is that him?" he shouted.

"It's—" The name was Jar-something, Jarno or Jarnac. She urged her horse forward; the blood-covered man dropped his axe, stumbled and caught a handful of mane to hang from. "Jarnac, where is he?" she was yelling in his face. "Orsea; do you know—?"

The man said, "He's here," in a loud, clear voice. "He's alive."

Out of the corner of his eye, Valens noticed that there were a lot of dead men on the ground, all Mezentines, all horribly smashed and cut about. For some reason he thought of the boar at bay, and of the hound that won't leave its injured master. "Fine," he said loudly. "Let's get him and go home. Him too," he added, nodding at the man called Jarnac; because, by the look of it, he was too useful to waste. "Horses over here, quick."

She half-turned in the saddle to look at him. She didn't smile. He hadn't expected her to, it wasn't the time or the place for smiling;

but the expression on her face said, *It never even crossed my mind that you'd come for me, but I understand why you did; and yes, I accept the gift for what it is.* In that moment, Valens felt something he couldn't begin to identify, but which he'd never felt before, and he knew that it justified what he'd done, no matter how devastating and evil the consequences might be. Then she turned away from him. She was watching as two of his men lifted a bloody mess of a man's body onto a horse. He thought about that, too, and realized he couldn't lie to himself. He wished that Orsea had been dead when they found him, and he hoped he'd die, now or very soon, and he knew that he'd do everything in his power to keep him alive.

"Right," he said. "Now let's get out of here."

Miel Ducas lifted his head. He was alone.

He could see out of his left eye. His right eye was blurred and it stung. He closed it and wiped it with his right hand; just blood, that was all. Then the pain in his left arm started, or he noticed it for the first time. Under other circumstances it'd have monopolized his attention, but he couldn't afford the luxury. He was alive, for now, but everything else was pretty bad.

He was alone in the Horsefair, with a lot of dead people. His left arm was broken, and something bad had happened which had left a wet red patch on the left side of his shirt, hand-sized, just above his waist. He could hear hoofs clattering in one direction, and men yelling in another. Clearly not out of the woods yet, then.

He remembered. Orsea; he'd set out to find Orsea, death, or both. Instead, he'd been hit, fallen over his feet, blacked out. The city had fallen to the enemy, and presumably a massacre was in progress. All bad stuff; but for some reason he'd been left over, as though Death had declined to accept him. He grinned. For the first time in his life, the Ducas was apparently of no importance, finally—at the end of the world—relieved of duty.

I will no longer try and do anything beyond my capabilities. Other people's excessive expectations of me brought me to this pass, and I've had enough of them. Instead, let's see if I can stand up.

There'd be no commemorative fresco in the cloister of the Ducas house to celebrate it—would there still be a Ducas house, this time tomorrow?—but he achieved it, nonetheless; he pushed with his knees and straightened his back, and he was on his feet. He swayed dangerously, took a step forward to catch his balance. Let the word go out to every corner of the duchy. The Ducas was standing up.

Nobody seemed to have noticed, which was no bad thing. He staggered a couple of paces and stopped to rest. He couldn't bring himself to feel any sense of urgency, even though he knew time was short. Something had happened while he'd been lying on the ground, dead to the world; something important, and he'd missed it. Whatever it was, it had emptied the Horsefair of Mezentines, but he had a shrewd idea they'd be back soon enough. It would be nice to be somewhere else by then.

(Where? He had nowhere in the world to go. He thought about that. It also meant there was nowhere he had to go, no appointments made for him or obligations requiring him to be present anywhere. That was a very strange feeling indeed.)

There was a horse. It was standing about twenty yards away, its head neither up nor down, its reins tangled around its front nearside hoof. As he stared at it (come on, haven't you ever seen a horse before?), something snagged its attention and it started to walk away; but the movement tightened the rein and, being a well-schooled horse, it stopped. Miel grinned. Allegory, he thought; even at this late stage, the world puts on a moral fable for my benefit. A horse, on the other hand, could take him places, always assuming he could get up on its back.

Big assumption. Still, he wasn't busy. A yard at a time, nice and slow, conserving his meager strength and not startling the horse with sudden movements (an elegant economy of motivations), he approached it, until he was close enough to bend forward— that hurt surprisingly much—and tweak at the reins. Obligingly, the horse lifted its foot, releasing the tangle. Of course, it hadn't known to do it for itself. A fellow slave of duty.

He looked up at the saddle. Might as well ask him to climb a mountain on his knees. What he needed, of course, was a mounting block. He thought about that. He was in the Horsefair, which was called that for a reason. Over on the far east side there was a row of three dozen mounting blocks. If he could get there, he might be able to scramble up onto this horse's back and ride away, possibly even to the nebulous and unimaginable environment known as Safety. At the very least he could try. After all, if the world had wanted him to die here, it wouldn't have issued him with the horse.

A third of the way there his knees gave up. He hung for a quarter of a minute from the reins and a handful of the horse's mane, grabbed together in his right hand. He was too weak to pull himself upright by them, too contrary to let go and slide to the ground. In theory, he could call on rugged determination and force of character to spur him on to that last spurt of effort. Not in practice, though. The mane hairs were cutting into the side of his hand, and his bodyweight was pulling the curl out of his fingers. He knew that if he slumped to the ground, he wouldn't be able to get up again. It was a quiet, low-key way for the Ducas to fail. He was almost prepared to accept it.

At the last possible moment, the horse grunted, raised its head a few degrees and started to amble forward. It was only a very slight movement, but it was enough. The horse dragged him along, the toes of his slippers trailing on the ground; it had spotted the hay-nets that hung on the east wall, behind the row of mounting blocks.

On the neck of the pass that overlooked the road to Civitas Eremiae, Valens halted his men and looked back. Smoke was drifting up into the still air. It was mid-morning on a bright, warm day.

"What's happening?" asked one of his captains.

Valens narrowed his eyes against the glare. "They're burning the city," he said.

The captain thought about that. "Didn't take them long to evacuate the civilians," he said.

"I don't think they bothered with that," Valens replied.

It took the captain a moment to grasp what he'd heard. "So what are we going to do?" he said.

"Us?" Valens sighed. "We're going to go home, of course. We've done what we came for."

"I thought we came to save the Eremians."

"No." Valens shortened his reins into his left hand. "No, that'd be a mistake. Let's get moving."

He was glad to get over the pass, back onto the road that led to the border, where he couldn't see the smoke. He was pleased when they brought him the casualty report—twelve dead, seventeen injured, mostly minor cuts and grazes; his men had acquitted themselves extremely well under difficult circumstances. He could be proud of them. In fact, the only man who'd done badly in his small army, failed in his duty and brought disaster down on his comrades-in-arms and the entire Vadani people was himself. *My prerogative,* he thought; and he cast his mind back to when he'd first heard about Duke Orsea's insane idea of a preemptive strike against the Mezentines. Deliberately picking a fight with the most powerful, most ruthless nation on earth, people who never forgave, never forgot, took quiet pride in the total extermination of their enemies...Ordinary stupidity wouldn't be enough, you'd have to be actually deranged to do something like that.

Quite, he thought.

She was riding alongside the hastily improvised travois they'd rigged up for Orsea and his ferocious bodyguard whose name Valens had already forgotten. A travois was better than tying him onto a horse's back, but that was the best you could say for it. Every rut and pothole jarred him; he winced, cried, yelled with pain, while she watched and said nothing. The other one, the big, tall man, had passed out as soon as his head touched the cloth. He bumped and shifted and carried on sleeping, still and quiet as dead game carried home on a pole from the hunt. Behind the travois the little Mezentine trotted, clinging with both hands to the pommel of his saddle while a compassionate sergeant led his horse on a leading-rein. How exactly he'd come to acquire this oddity, Valens wasn't entirely sure. He'd trailed after Veatriz like a stray dog following you home from the market, and Valens couldn't see any particular reason to send him away. Besides, he was the man who'd built all those clever war engines, the ones that had slaughtered the Mezentines by the tens of thousands and still failed to preserve the city. Someone like that might come in useful if things went badly with the Perpetual Republic, as Valens was fairly sure they would.

There was an old story about a great conqueror who laid siege to a mighty city for ten years. Finally he took it by some cunning stratagem, burst in, looted everything worth taking, set fire to the buildings and withdrew. He had an army of fifty thousand men as he started the journey home; less than two hundred eventually crawled across the border, the only survivors of the plague they'd contracted from the rotting corpses of their enemies, unburied because their starved and emaciated countrymen lacked the strength. He'd remembered the story as a fine allegory of the hateful futility of war, destructive to losers and victors alike. *Wouldn't catch me doing something stupid like that,* the pompous voice of his thirteen-year-old self brayed inside his memory; *it can't really be a true story, because nobody'd be that clueless.*

She hadn't said more than a few words to him since they rode out of the gateway, but he'd made a point of keeping his distance (and besides, he had an army to lead, and they weren't out of danger yet, not by a long way); he was afraid of what she'd say to him, now that they were face to face at last and in this ghastly, impossible situation of his own making. Everything between them would be ruined, he knew that — that was another thing about the old stories, the ones where the knight-errant rescued the beautiful princess from the dragon or the ogre or the murderous stepfather; there was always a bland presumption of love, happiness-ever-

after, which was plainly absurd if you had even the slightest understanding of human nature. The next time Veatriz looked him
in the eyes, she'd see the man who'd risked his life and the lives of
his entire people to save her; if he hadn't done this stupid, insane
thing, she'd be dead; she'd see his love for her, and in it the ruin
of his duchy and the disastrous end of their friendship, which had
been the best thing in her life. *I've spoiled everything,* Valens realized,
*because I was too weak to bear the thought of losing her; and now, of course,
I've done exactly that.* He smiled; ride out to confront your worst fear,
as Orsea had done against the Mezentines, and you can be sure
you'll make it come true.

So; he wouldn't talk to her yet. Instead, he nudged his horse
along and fell in beside the Mezentine, who was still clinging desperately to his saddle and muttering. Valens took the leading-rein
from the sergeant and nodded to him to rejoin his troop.

"You're Vaatzes, right?" he said.

The Mezentine opened his eyes, saw the ground (too far away),
let go, wobbled alarmingly, nearly fell off, grabbed the saddle
again and said, "Yes."

Valens grinned. "The knack," he said, "is to sit up straight and
grip with your knees. All you're doing at the moment is loosening
the saddle. Carry on like that, it'll slip over one side and you'll
land on your head."

The Mezentine whimpered, but he knew how to follow instructions. "Like this?" he said.

"Better," Valens replied. "Try and keep the ball of your foot on
the stirrup-iron, with your heels pointing down. And stop jerking
on the reins, they're not handles for clinging on to."

"Right," the Mezentine said doubtfully. "Where I come from,
we don't go in for horses much. Sometimes we ride in carts, but
mostly we walk."

Valens looked at him. "Maybe you should've stayed there,"
he said.

"You know, I think you're right. Still, too late now. I'm sorry,"
he went on, "but I don't know who you are."

"I guessed that. My name's Valens."

"Ah." The Mezentine nodded. "Pleased to meet you. I'm Ziani Vaatzes."

"I know." In spite of himself, Valens was grinning. "I get the impression you don't go in much for formality in Mezentia either."

Vaatzes shrugged. "Forgive me," he said. "If you mean deferential language and conventional expressions of respect, no we don't. In theory, every Guildsman's as good as every other; so we don't learn all the right words, and foreigners think we're revoltingly arrogant. Which we are, but not the way you think. Maybe somebody could teach me the right things to say, and then I won't give offense."

"The Eremians didn't mind, then?"

"I expect they did, but nobody said anything, so I never got the opportunity to learn."

"It doesn't matter," Valens said. "Stuff like that annoys me, actually, it tends to get in the way, and that wastes time and effort and leads to confusion. By the sound of it, you plan on coming home with us."

Vaatzes dipped his head. "I was hoping to talk to somebody about that. Simple fact is, I haven't got anywhere else to go."

"You're straightforward, I'll say that for you. But you're bad luck, aren't you? Look what happened to the last lot who took you in."

Again, Vaatzes shrugged. "If you care to look at it from my point of view, I nearly saved them from the consequences of their own stupidity; I built war engines for them, and when I went to bed last night, we'd just won the war. Obviously something happened that I don't know about."

"Don't ask me," Valens replied. "We set out as soon as we heard the city was being assaulted. If you won the war—"

"We beat them back," Vaatzes said. "We killed thousands of them, mostly thanks to my engines, if the truth be known. How they got in and unblocked the gate I have no idea. That doesn't alter the fact that we beat the shit out of them."

Valens smiled. "Thanks to you."

"Thanks to me," Vaatzes said. "And if the Duke had listened to me when I first met him, and we'd started building war engines straight away instead of having to do it all in a desperate rush at the last minute, I'm prepared to bet we'd have seen them off for good. Still, it's too late now. You ask the Duchess, or Duke Orsea. They'll tell you."

"I will," Valens said. "So, you're a valuable asset. How much will you cost me?"

"That's up to you," Vaatzes said. "Assuming you can use me. But I believe you'll decide you can, after what's happened."

"After what's happened." Valens yawned; it was all starting to catch up with him. "After what I've gone and done, you mean."

"Yes. I won't ask you what you did it for..."

"Very sensible." Valens frowned. "Tell you what," he said. "When we get home and I've had a chance to calm down and get a grip on things, you come and tell me what you think you've got to offer, and I'll hear you out. Reasonable?"

"Entirely," Vaatzes said. "And I promise you, you won't regret it."

In due course, General Melancton presented himself before an extraordinary session of the Guilds council. In a prepared statement, which he read out in a clear, steady voice, he officially notified the assembly of the capture and destruction of Civitas Eremiae and the elimination of its inhabitants, pursuant to the requirements of council resolution composite 50773.

Before starting his account of the war, he drew the assembly's attention to the fact that he was deliberately omitting a certain amount of detail, since such matters would be heard separately in committee. He outlined the early stages of the campaign, including the unfortunate ambush of the artillery column that resulted in a substantial number of scorpion-class mobile war engines falling into the hands of the enemy. It was to these captured engines that he chiefly attributed the unexpectedly successful resistance mounted by the Eremians; however, there were other factors, in particular his own failure to make proper use of the long-range war engines with which he had been supplied, for which failure he was prepared to take full responsibility.

In the event, however, the setback had proved temporary. Factional strife inside the city had led one party to betray to him a means of entering the city by stealth. This approach proved entirely successful; the infiltration party were able to unblock the gateway and admit the bulk of the army, and the defenders were taken entirely by surprise and quickly suppressed. At the last moment, the conclusion of the assault was hindered by an unexpected and unprovoked attack by cavalry forces identified as belonging to Duke Valens of the Vadani. These aggressors were, however, quickly driven off and the final stage of the operation, the securing and burning of the city and the execution of surviving enemy military and civilian personnel, was successfully carried out without further hindrance.

Having thus achieved all the primary objectives set out in composite 50773, General Melancton had the honor to surrender his commission and return command of the armed forces of the Republic to the council, pending demobilization and repatriation.

Later, in a closed session of the select committee on security and defense, the general put his overall losses at twenty-three thousand killed, eleven thousand wounded to the point of permanent or temporary incapacitation. He had retrieved all the captured scorpions, together with almost three hundred of the copies made by the Eremians; the former had been restored to the Guilds, the latter destroyed.

With the city demolished and its people dead—questioned, he gave his opinion that the number of Eremians who were able to escape from the city before its destruction did not, at the worst possible estimate, exceed one hundred—the central district of Eremia was secure. In fact, it was deserted. The country people had left their homes before the city fell and had escaped into the mountains. Some of them remained there, carrying out a vigorous campaign of guerrilla activity against the Republic's forces of occupation; the rest had crossed the border, mostly into Vadani territory. Strenuous efforts would be required to dislodge them, and accordingly the general recommended that not only should the current army be retained, but substantial reinforcements recruited to supplement them. As to the whereabouts of Duke Orsea and the abominator Vaatzes, the general had no reliable information. Their bodies had not been recovered before the city was burned down; a search had been made, but given the situation, it had necessarily been perfunctory. A number of eye-witnesses reported that the Vadani cavalry had taken a number of Eremians with them, and it was entirely possible that Orsea and Vaatzes had been among them. Accordingly, Melancton concluded, the main objectives of the exercise had not been met, and for this shortcoming he held himself entirely responsible. Asked for his recommendations for further action, he advised that the first priority should be to secure the mountain regions and the Vadani border, since unless this was done it would be impossible to control the country in any meaningful sense. However, he noted, it was entirely possible that this would prove to be a lengthy and expensive process.

After the select committee's report had been received and considered by the council, it was resolved that the mercenary forces presently in the country should be retained temporarily to secure the borders and deal with insurgent activity in the few remaining pockets of resistance. Meanwhile, the council authorized the dispatch of ambassadors to the Vadani to demand the surrender of Duke Orsea, the abominator Vaatzes and Duke Valens—the last named to stand trial in respect of an unprovoked and illegal act of war against the Republic. Should these demands not be met within seven days, a formal declaration of war would be made, and preparations for the dispatch of an expeditionary force would be expedited.

In a closed meeting, a joint subcommittee of the Compliance and Security directorates interviewed Falier Zenonis of the ordnance factory and commended him for his part in bringing the operation against Civitas Eremiae to a satisfactory conclusion. The subcommittee pointed out that it was not possible for his contribution to be officially recognized; however, a formal commendation would be entered on his personnel record, and the subcommittee felt it was extremely likely that he would reap a tangible reward for his actions in due course. Closely questioned by Commissioner Psellus, Falier Zenonis stated that, in spite of his long acquaintance with the traitor Vaatzes, he could provide no convincing explanation for Vaatzes' conduct in the matter of the betrayal of the city; in his personal opinion, Zenonis added, Vaatzes acted as a result of deep-seated mental instability exacerbated by feelings of guilt resulting from the high level of casualties inflicted by the weapons he had made for the Eremians. Asked if he believed that Vaatzes was still alive, Zenonis replied that he was sure of it.

The Vadani refused to comply with the Republic's demands, as expressed in resolution composite 50979. Accordingly, a written declaration of war was drawn up and delivered to Duke Valens by special messenger.

She heard him; the click of the latch, the sigh of the curtain behind the door that kept out the draft, his boot-heel on the flagstones. She caught her breath for a moment.

"Falier?" she said.

"I'm home."

She stood up quickly and tucked the letter she'd been reading behind a cushion. He'd be tired after his journey; she could retrieve it once he'd gone to bed. She stirred the fire with the poker; it was dying down and the charcoal scuttle was empty.

"Come through and sit down," she said. "You must be worn out."

The door of the cramped back room opened, and he came in. He looked terrible. Exhaustion didn't suit him at all. He smiled wanly at her and dropped into the chair, still holding his hat in his left hand.

"Moritsa's asleep," she said. "She wanted to wait up for you but I said no, she's got school tomorrow."

He nodded. "We got held up on the road," he said.

"I thought that was what must've happened," she replied. "Can I get you anything?"

He pulled a face. "I'm too tired to eat," he said with a yawn.

"Get an early night," she said. "You can tell me all about it in the morning."

He yawned again. "I'll just sit here for a bit," he said. Then he added, "He got away."

She frowned. "Oh."

"We're pretty sure of it, anyway," he said. He paused. On the way home he'd made up his mind not to say anything about the letter, even to her. "The likeliest thing is that he escaped over the border."

"Good," she said. "It'll be better for us."

"Oh, they'll keep going after him," Falier said. "Still, there's nothing we can do about it, so the hell with it for now." He grinned lopsidedly. "Miss me?"

"Of course I missed you," she said. "Was it very bad?"

He nodded. "I hope I'm home for good now. There's going to be a lot of work on at the factory, they're going to need me here."

He'd started to mumble, and his chin was down on his chest; any moment now he'd slide into sleep, right on top of that stupid letter. She promised herself: first thing in the morning after he'd left for work, she'd put it on the fire, along with all the rest of them. It'd only cause trouble, no end of it, if he happened to find them. Besides, by now she knew all the good bits by heart, and she wouldn't miss the rest. Especially, she thought, the poetry.

From the sound of his breathing he was asleep. She sat down in the window-seat and looked at him for a while. Then she got slowly to her feet and raked the fire.

Acknowledgments

Much as I enjoy doing all my own stunts, I draw the line at picking fights with large, dangerous animals. I'm profoundly grateful, therefore, to Geoff Williams and Ian Farrington, for their insights into hunting the boar the hard way. My thanks are also due to Ken Funnell, for teaching me everything I know about machining; Tom Holt, for a crash course in cuir bouilli; and Tom Jennings and Ray Mullet, for the makings of the brigandine.

extras

orbit

meet the author

K. J. Parker is a pseudonym. Find more about the author at www.kjparker.com.

interview

Without giving too much away, can you give us some background to The Engineer Trilogy?

Basically, it's a love story, which is why tens of thousands die, cities are torched, nations overthrown, and everybody betrays everybody else at least once. It's also a story about a very ordinary man who's forced, through no real fault of his own, to do extraordinary things in order to achieve a very simple, everyday objective. Furthermore, it's an exploration of the nature of manufacture, artifice, and fabrication — the things we make, the reasons we make them, the ambivalence of everything we create, and the effects on other people of what we make. Ambitious, or what?

Your protagonist in *Devices and Desires*, Ziani Vaatzes, is not a typical fantasy hero in the traditional sense, is he? Was it a deliberate attempt to distance yourself from the default post-Tolkien fantasy formula that led you to choose an engineer rather than, say, a soldier?

I don't think so. Vaatzes couldn't be a traditional fantasy hero, because his motivation is completely mundane and unheroic; it's the lengths he has to go to in order to achieve it that both give him extraordinary stature and rob him of his humanity. I chose an engineer because I needed a catalyst figure, someone who sets in motion a mechanism that involves everybody around him. The man who designs and builds a space shuttle or a nuclear warhead isn't primarily an explorer or a mass murderer; he's an engineer. It's the use to which his artifact is put, usually by other people, that makes the difference. Vaatzes is both the maker of the machine and the man who uses it, and yet he's just a very ordinary man who's caught up in other mechanisms, not of his own making, that he can't control.

There seems to be a recurring theme in your work of a single warrior taking on a whole group of attackers at one go. Are you a secret martial arts film fan?

Martial arts films, no. Ever since I was too young to play with dangerous sharp objects, I've studied combat and war, in roughly the same way a doctor studies a disease she'd one day like to cure. In the course of my researches, I've learned the basics of the European medieval and Renaissance martial arts (which, I guiltily confess, was a whole lot of fun) as well as read every authentic account of duels and personal combats that I've been able to lay my paws on (most of my fight sequences are rehashes of accounts of genuine duels or encounters, at least as far as the moves are concerned; I believe that nothing gives that authentic feel quite as much as the genuine article with the serial numbers filed off). The overwhelming leitmotif that comes through all such accounts is that fights are lost through misjudgment, incompetence, or sheer bad luck rather than won by courage, skill, or Secret Ninja Combat Arts, and I hope this comes through in my descriptions.

How extensively do you plot your novels before you start writing them? Do you plot the entire trilogy/series before you start writing or do you prefer to let the story roam where it will?

I try to have the whole thing plotted out in some detail before I start. Sometimes the characters take over and lead me astray—in fact, they'd be pretty poor characters if they didn't—but usually a judicious combination of carrots and sticks gets them back in line before things get out of hand.

Some authors talk of their characters "surprising" them by their actions. Is this something that has happened to you?

Not really, because I try to map out their actions well in advance. The interesting bit, in which they often surprise me, is their *re*actions to the unpleasant experiences I put them through. Gorgas Loredan, for instance, completely won me over by the end of the Fencer books, and I must admit I can't wait to see how Valens handles the truly horrible stuff I have lined up for him in book two.

Do you see any particular trends in recent fantasy?

I confess I don't follow the genre closely enough to make an informed comment (and I'd like my pontifications in reply to the question below to be interpreted accordingly). This is because of the chameleon effect: if I admire a writer's work, subconsciously I'm tempted to indulge in the sincerest form of flattery.

Do you have any particular favorite authors who have influenced your work?

I have favorite authors, and I have authors who've influenced my work. For example, I don't much enjoy reading Iain M. Banks, simply because his worldview and mine don't coincide much, but I've learned an enormous amount from his masterful use of structure and language. Ditto J. K. Rowling, and her exquisite skill in developing an extended story line and designing characters who can go the distance.

Devices and Desires is the beginning of your third fantasy trilogy. Have you ever been tempted to write a longer series, George R. R. Martin– or Robert Jordan–style?

Temptation is always with us, but as a friend of mine is fond of saying, the difference between luck and a Land Rover is that luck doesn't work better if you push it. I'd like one day to acquire sufficient technical skill to write, say, a seven-part series. I'd also like to be president of the United States, but that's equally unlikely.

Finally, do you have a personal theory on why fantasy is so popular these days?

Evelyn Waugh said of P. G. Wodehouse (who was also, in his way, a writer of fantasy), "He has made a world for us to live in and delight in. He will continue to release future generations from a captivity that may be more irksome than our own." (Quoted from memory—something to that effect.) That's a large part of it, I guess. Because modern Western society is such a mess, we have a longing for simpler, better worlds—not necessarily places where everything is perfect, like in Tolkien's Shire, but places where the problems we have to confront in our daily lives are at least _soluble_ by, for example, defeating an evil overlord or throwing a ring into a volcano. The solution may be horrendously dangerous and strenuous, but it's straightforward; we can at least understand it, whereas real life in the twenty-first century is largely incomprehensible, and we feel powerless to do anything about it. In fantasy, we can believe in good and evil, whereas in real life both those concepts are increasingly nebulous.

By these criteria, of course, I don't write fantasy. . . . I prefer to create imaginary analogies to the bewildering, inescapable forces that govern real life, as a way of examining the ways in which we try and cope with them. Likewise I don't have heroes and villains for the same reason I don't have dragons and goblins; I believe that all four species are equally mythical. Which brings me kicking and screaming back to the question, I guess. Fantasy is popular because, since heroes and villains don't exist, it's absolutely necessary to our survival as a species to invent them.

introducing

If you enjoyed
DEVICES AND DESIRES,
look out for

EVIL FOR EVIL

Book Two of the Engineer Trilogy

by K. J. Parker

"The way to a man's heart," Valens quoted, drawing the rapier from its scabbard, "is proverbially through his stomach, but if you want to get into his brain, I recommend the eye socket."

He moved his right arm into the third guard, concentrated for a moment on the small gold ring that hung by a thread from the center rafter of the stable, frowned, and relaxed. Lifting the sword again, he tapped the ring gently on its side, setting it swinging like a pendulum. As it reached the upper limit of its swing and hung for a fraction of a second in the air, he moved fluently into the lunge. The tip of the rapier passed exactly through the middle of the ring without touching the sides. Valens grinned and stepped back. Not bad, he congratulated himself, after seven years of not practicing, and his poor ignorant student wasn't to know that he'd cheated.

"There you go," he said, handing Vaatzes the rapier. "Now you try." Vaatzes wasn't to know it was cheating, but Valens knew. The exercise he'd just demonstrated wasn't the one he'd so grudgingly learned, in this same stable, as a boy of fifteen. The correct form was piercing the stationary ring, passing the sword through the middle without making it move. He'd never been able to get it right, for all the sullen effort he'd lavished on it, so he'd cheated by turning it into a moving target, and he was cheating again now. The fact that he'd subverted the exercise by making it harder was beside the point.

"You made it look easy," Vaatzes said mildly. "It's not, is it?"

Valens smiled. "No," he said.

Vaatzes wrapped his hand around the sword hilt, precisely as he'd been shown—a quick study, evidently. It had taken Valens a month to master the grip when he was learning. The difference was, he reflected, that Vaatzes wanted to learn. That, he realized, was what was so very strange about the Mezentine. He wanted to learn *everything*.

"Is that right?"

"More or less," Valens replied. "Go on."

Vaatzes lifted the rapier and tapped the ring to set it swinging. He watched as it swung backward and forward, then made his lunge. He missed only by a hair, and the ring tinkled as the sword point grazed it on the outside.

"Not bad," Valens said. "And again."

Even closer this time; the point hit the edge of the ring, making it jump wildly on its thread. Vaatzes was scowling, though. "What'm I doing wrong?" he asked.

"Nothing, really. It's just a matter of practice," Valens replied. "Try again."

But Vaatzes didn't move; he was thinking. He looked stupid when he thought, like a peasant trying to do mental arithmetic. It was fortunate that Valens knew better than to go by appearances.

"Mind if I try something?" Vaatzes said.

Valens shrugged. "Go ahead."

Vaatzes stepped forward, reached up with his left hand, and steadied the ring until it was completely motionless. He stepped back, slipped into third guard like a man putting on his favorite jacket, and lunged. The rapier point passed exactly through the middle of the ring, which didn't move.

"Very good," Valens said.

"Yes." Vaatzes shrugged. "But it's not what you told me to do."

"No."

"I was thinking," Vaatzes said, "if I practice that for a bit, I can gradually work up to the moving target. Would that be all right?"

Valens had stopped smiling. "You do what you like," he said, "if you think it'd help."

For six days now it had rained; a heavy shower just before dawn, followed by weak sunshine mixed with drizzle, followed by a downpour at midmorning and usually another at noon. No earthly point trying to fly the hawks in this weather, even though it was the start of the season, and Valens had spent all winter looking forward to it. Today was supposed to be a hunting day; he'd cleared his schedule for it weeks in advance, spent hours deciding which drives to work, considering the countless variables likely to affect the outcome—the wind direction, the falcons' fitness at the start of the season, the quality of the grass in the upland meadows, which would draw the hares up and out of the newly mown valley. Carefully and logically, he'd worked through all the facts and possibilities and reached a decision, and it was raining. Bored and frustrated to the point of cold fury, Valens had remembered his offhand promise to the funny little Mezentine refugee who, for reasons Valens couldn't begin to fathom, seemed to want to learn how to fence.

"I think that's enough for today," Vaatzes said, laying the rapier carefully down on the bench, stopping it with his hands before it rolled off. "The meeting's in an hour, isn't it? I don't want to make you late."

Valens nodded. "Same time tomorrow," he said, "if it's still raining."

"Thank you," Vaatzes said. "It's very kind of you. Really, I never expected that you—"

Valens shrugged. "I offered," he said. "I don't say things unless I mean them." He yawned and slid the rapier back into its scabbard. "See you at the meeting, then. You know where it is?"

Vaatzes grinned. "No," he said. "You did tell me, but..."

"I know," Valens said. "This place is a bugger to find your way around unless you've lived here twenty years. Just ask someone. They'll show you."

After Vaatzes had gone, Valens drew the rapier once again and studied the ring for a long time. Then he lunged, and the soft jangle it made as the sword grazed it made him wince. He caught it in his left hand, pulled gently until the thread snapped, and put it back on his finger. All my life, he thought, I've cheated by making things harder. It's a habit I need to get out of, before I do some real damage. He glanced out the window; still raining. He could see pockmarks of rain in the flat puddles in the stable yard and slanting two-dimensional lines of motion made visible against the dark backdrop of the yard gate. He'd loved rain in late spring when he was a boy, partly because he'd loathed hunting when he was young, and rain meant his father wouldn't force him to go out with the hounds or the hawks, partly because the smell of it was so clean and sweet. Now, seven years after his father's death, he was probably the most ardent and skillful huntsman in the world, but the smell of rain was still a wonderful thing, almost too beautiful to bear. He put on his coat and pulled the collar up round his ears.

From the stable yard to the side door of the long hall was hardly any distance at all, but he was soaked to the skin by the time he shut the door behind him, and the smell was now the rich, heavy stench of wet cloth. Well, it was his meeting, so they'd have to wait for him. He climbed the narrow spiral staircase to the top of the middle tower. Clothes. Not something that interested him particularly. Perhaps that explained why he was so good at them. Slipping off the wet coat, shirt, and trousers, he swung open the chest and chose a dark blue brocade gown suitable for formal occasions. He took a minute or so to towel the worst of the damp out of his hair, couldn't be bothered to look in a mirror. One more glance through the window. Still raining. But he'd be dry, and everybody else at the meeting would be wet and uncomfortable, which would be to his advantage. That thought made him frown. Why was he allowing himself to think of his own advisers as the enemy?

He sighed. Today should have been a hunting day; or, if it was raining, it should've been a day for writing her a letter, or revising a first or second draft, or doing research for the reply to the next letter he received from her. But there weren't any letters anymore; she was here now, under the same roof as him, with her husband. On a whim he changed his shoes, substituting courtly long-toed poulaines for comfortable but sodden riding shoes. He hesitated, then looked in the mirror after all. It showed him a pale, thin young man expertly disguised as the Duke of the Vadani; a disguise so perfect, in fact, that only his father would've been able to see through it. Oh well, he thought, and went downstairs to face his loyal councillors.

As he ran down the stairs, he put words together in his mind—the question he'd have asked her in a letter, if they'd still been able to write letters to each other. Force of habit, but it was a habit he'd been dependent on for a very long time, until he'd reached the point where it was hard to think without it. *Suppose there was a conjuror, a professional sleight-of-hand artist, who hurt his wrist and couldn't do tricks anymore. Suppose he learned how to make things disappear and pull rabbits out of hats by using real magic. Would that be cheating?*

As he'd anticipated, the councillors were all wet and acting ashamed, as though getting rained on was a wicked and deliberate act. They stood up as he came in. Even now, it still rather surprised him when people did that.

He gave them a moment or so to settle down, looking round to see if anybody was missing. They seemed nervous, which he found faintly amusing. He counted to five under his breath and stood up. "First," he said, "my apologies for dragging you all up here in this foul weather. I'll try not to keep you any longer than necessary. We all know what the issues are, and I daresay we've all got our own opinions about what we should do. However," he went on, shifting his weight onto both feet like a fencer taking up a middle guard, "I've already reached my decision, so, really, it's not a case of what we're going to do so much as how we're going to do it."

He paused, looking for reactions, but they knew him well enough not to give anything away. He took a little breath and continued. "I've decided," he said, "to evacuate Civitas Vadanis. For what they're worth, you may as well hear my reasons. First, the war isn't going well. The latest reports I've seen — Varro, you may have better figures than me on this — put the Mezentine army at not far off thirty thousand men, not counting engineers, sappers and the baggage train. Now, we can match them for numbers, but we'd be kidding ourselves if we said we stood any sort of a chance in a pitched battle. So far we've avoided anything more than a few skirmishes; basically, we've been able to annoy them with cavalry raids and routine harassment, and that's all. It's fair to say we've got the better of them in cavalry and archers, but when it comes to the quality of heavy infantry needed to win a pitched battle, we're not in the same league, and that's not taking any account of their field artillery, which we all know is their greatest asset."

He paused to glance at Orsea and saw that the man was looking down at his feet, too ashamed to lift his head. As well he might be. Someone else who had trouble thinking straight. He wondered, before they were married, had Orsea ever written her a letter? He doubted it.

"That rules out a decisive battle in the open field," Valens went on. "By the same token, I don't like the idea of staying here and trying to sit out either an assault or a siege. We still don't really know what happened at Civitas Eremiae" — here he looked quickly across at Vaatzes, but as usual there was nothing to see in his face — "and I know some of you reckon it must have been treachery rather than any stroke of tactical or engineering genius on the Mezentines' part. The fact remains that the Mezentines won that round, and Eremia was supposed to be the best-defended city in the world. We haven't got anything like the position or the defenses that Orsea's people had, so the only way we could hope to win would be through overwhelming superiority in artillery. At Eremia, Vaatzes here had to work miracles just to give Orsea parity. I imagine I'm right in assuming you couldn't do the same for us."

Vaatzes considered for a moment before answering.

"I don't think so," he said. "With respect, there's nothing here for me to work with. There were just about enough smiths and armorers and carpenters at Eremia to give me a pool of competent skilled workers to draw on; all I had to do was train them, improvise the plant and machinery, and teach them how to build the existing designs. You simply don't have enough skilled men here; you don't have the materials or the tools. You've got plenty of money to buy them with, of course, but there's not enough time. Also, it's a safe bet that the Mezentines have been busy improving all their artillery designs since the siege of Eremia. I'm a clever man, but I can't hope to match the joint expertise of the Mezentine ordnance factory. Anything I could build for you would already be obsolete before the first bolt was loosed." He shook his head. "I'm sorry," he said, "but I don't think I can be much help to you."

Valens nodded. He knew all that already. "In that case," he said, "if we can't chase them away before they get here, and we can't hold them off when they come here, I believe our only option is to leave here and go somewhere else. In which case, the only question we're left with is, where do we go?"

He paused and looked round, but he knew that nobody was going to say anything, which was what he wanted, of course.

"As I see it," he went on, "the Mezentines are maintaining a large and very expensive mercenary army in hostile territory. Thanks to the efforts of Orsea's people, their lines of supply are painfully long and brittle, and living off the land isn't a realistic option. They need to finish this war quickly, before their own political situation gets out of hand. We know we can't fight them and win. Seems to me, then, that our best chance lies in not fighting, and the best way of doing that, I think, would be to keep moving. They can have the city and do what they like with it. We evacuate to the mountains, where we know the terrain and where their artillery train can't go. We dodge about, making them follow us until they get careless and give us a chance to bottle them up in a pass or a river valley. Meanwhile, our cavalry stays on the plains and makes life difficult for their supply wagons. Possibly we could also make trouble for the army of occupation in Eremia, just to give them something else to think about. It comes down to this: We can't beat the Mezentines; neither can Orsea's people or anybody else. The only people who can beat the Mezentines are the Mezentines themselves, by losing the will to carry on with this war. For them, it's a balance sheet. The point will come where the certain losses will outweigh the potential gains, and the political opposition will have gained enough strength to overthrow the current government. Our only hope is to hang on till that point is reached. I think evacuating, avoiding them, making life difficult, and costing them money is the best and safest way of going about it. Furthermore, I don't think we have an alternative strategy worth serious consideration. If I'm wrong and I've missed something obvious, though, I'd love to hear about it. Anybody?"

He sat down and waited. He had a pretty shrewd idea who'd be first. Sure enough, Orsea got to his feet. As usual, he looked nervous, as though he weren't quite sure whether he was allowed to speak or whether he needed to ask for permission.

"For what it's worth," he said, "I agree with Valens. I think I can honestly say I know the Mezentines better than any of you. I ought to, after all. It was my stupidity that got us all into this situation in the first place, and as a direct result of what I did, I've had to watch them invade my country, burn my city, and massacre my people. If it wasn't for Valens here, I'd be dead. Now, because Valens rescued us, you're facing the same danger. It's my fault that you've got to make this decision, and all I can say is, I'm sorry. That's no help, obviously." He hesitated, and Valens looked away. It pained him to see a grown man making a fool of himself, particularly someone who was his responsibility. "The point is," Orsea went on, "we mustn't let what happened at Civitas Eremiae happen again here. It's bad enough having to live with the destruction of my own people. If it happened to you as well—"

"Orsea," Valens said quietly, "it's all right. Sit down."

introducing

If you enjoyed DEVICES AND DESIRES,
look out for

WINTERBIRTH

Book One of the Godless World trilogy

by Brian Ruckley

Two years ago the warriors of Gyre had been one of the finest bodies
of fighting men in all the lands of the Kilkry Bloods, but the unremit-
ting carnage since then had consumed their strength as surely as a
fire loosed upon a drought-struck forest. In the end virtually every
able-bodied man—and many of the women—of the Black Road
had taken to the field at Kan Avor, drawn not just from Gyre but
from every Blood: still they had been outnumbered by more than
three to one. Now barely fifteen hundred men remained, a battered
rearguard for the flight of the Black Road into the north.

The man who rode up to join his Thane was as bruised and weary
as all the rest. His helm was dented, the ring mail on his chest stained
with blood, his round shield notched and half split where an axe had
found a lucky angle. Still, this man bore himself well and his eyes retained a glint of vigor. He nudged his horse through the crowds and
leaned close to Avann.

"Lord," he said softly, "it is Tegric."

Avann stirred, but did not raise his head or open his eyes.

"My scouts have come up, lord," the warrior continued. "The enemy draw near. Kilkry horsemen are no more than an hour or two adrift of us. Behind them, spearmen of Haig-Kilkry. They will bring us to bay before we are clear of the Vale."

The Thane of Gyre spat bloodily.

"Whatever awaits us was decided long ago," he murmured. His voice was thin and weak. "We cannot fear what is written in the Last God's book."

One of the Thane's shieldmen joined them, and fixed Tegric with a disapproving glare.

"Leave the Thane be," he said. "He must conserve his strength."

That at last raised Avann's head. He winced as he opened his eyes.

"My death will come when it must. Until then, I am Thane, not some sick old woman to be wrapped warm and fed broth. Tegric treats me as a Thane still; how much more should my own Shield?"

The shieldman nodded in acceptance of the reprimand, but stayed in close attendance.

"Let me wait here, lord," said Tegric softly. "Give me just a hundred men. We will hold the Vale until our people are clear."

The Thane regarded Tegric. "We may need every man in the north. The tribes will not welcome our arrival."

"There will be no arrival if our enemies come upon us here in the Vale. Let me stand here and I will promise you half a day, perhaps more. The cliffs narrow up ahead, and there is an old rockfall. I can hold the way against riders; spill enough of their blood that they will wait for their main force to come up before attempting the passage twice."

"And then you will be a hundred against what, five thousand? Six?" Avann grunted.

"At least," smiled Tegric.

An old man fell in the crowds that surrounded them. He cried out as a stone opened his knee. A gray-haired woman — perhaps his wife — hurried to help him to his feet, murmuring "Get up, get up." A score of people, including the Thane and Tegric, flowed past before she managed to raise him. She wept silently as the man hobbled onward.

"Many people have already died in defense of our creed," Avann oc Gyre said, lowering his head once more and closing his eyes. He seemed to shrink as he hunched forward in his saddle. "If you give us half a day—if it has been so written in the Last God's book—you and your hundred will be remembered. When the lands that have been taken from us are ours again, you will be named first and noblest amongst the dead. And when this bitter world is unmade and we have returned into the love of the Gods I will look for you, to give you the honor that will be your due."

Tegric nodded. "I will see you once again in the reborn world, my Thane."

He turned his horse and nudged it back against the current of humanity.

Tegric rested against a great boulder. He had removed his tunic, and was methodically stitching up a split seam. His mail shirt was neatly spread upon a rock, his shield and scabbarded sword lying beside it, his helm resting at his feet. These were all that remained to him, everything he had need of. He had given his horse to a lame woman who had been struggling along in the wake of the main column. His small pouch of coins had gone to a child, a boy mute from shock or injury.

Above, buzzards were calling as they circled lower, descending toward the corpses that Tegric knew lay just out of sight. His presence, and that of his hundred men, might deter the scavengers for a while longer, but he did not begrudge them a meal. Those who once dwelled in those bodies had no further need of them: when the Gods returned—as they would once all peoples of the world had learned the humility of the Black Road—they would have new bodies, in a new world.

From where he sat, Tegric could see down a long, sloping sweep of the Stone Vale. Every so often he glanced up from his stitching to cast his eyes back the way they had come. Far off in that direction lay

Grive, where he had lived most of his life: a place of soft green fields, well-fed cattle, as different from this punishing Vale of Stones as any place could be. The memory of it summoned up no particular emotion in him. The rest of his family had not seen the truth of the creed as he had. When Avann oc Gyre, their Thane, had declared for the Black Road they had fled from Grive, disappearing out of Tegric's life. In every Blood, even Kilkry itself, the blossoming of the Black Road had sundered countless families, broken ties and bonds that had held firm for generations. To Tegric's mind it was a cause for neither regret nor surprise. A truth as profound as that of the Black Road could not help but have consequences.

An old man, dressed in a ragged brown robe and leaning on a staff, came limping up the Vale. He was, perhaps, the very last of the fleeing thousands. Though they were close to the highest point of the pass, the sun, burning out of a cloudless sky, still had strength. The man's forehead was beaded with sweat. He paused before Tegric, resting all his weight upon his staff and breathing heavily. The warrior looked up at the man, squinting slightly against the sunlight.

"Am I far behind the rest?" the man asked between labored breaths.

Tegric noted the bandaged feet, the trembling hands.

"Some way," he said softly.

The man nodded, unsurprised and seemingly unperturbed. He wiped his brow with the hem of his robe; the material came away sweaty and dirty.

"You are waiting here?" he asked Tegric, who nodded in reply.

The man cast around, scanning the warriors scattered amongst the great boulders all around him.

"How many of you are there?"

"A hundred," Tegric told him.

The old man chuckled, though it was a cold and humorless kind of laugh.

"You have come to the end of your Roads then, you hundred. I had best press on, and discover where my own fate runs out."

"Do so," said Tegric levelly. He watched the man make his unsteady way along the path already trodden by so many thousands. There had been, in the gentle edges of his accent, no hint of the Gyre Blood or the Glas valley where Avann had ruled.

"Where are you from, old father?" Tegric called after him.

"Kilvale, in Kilkry lands," the man replied.

"Did you know the Fisherwoman, then?" Tegric asked, unable to keep the edge of wonder from his voice.

The old man paused and carefully turned to look back at the warrior.

"I heard her speak. I knew her a little, before they killed her."

"There will be a day, you know, when the Black Road marches through this pass again," Tegric said. "But then we will be marching out of the north, not into it. And we will march all the way to Kilvale and beyond."

Again the man laughed his rough laugh. "You are right. They've driven us from our homes, cast even your Thane out from his castle, but the creed survives. You and I are not fated to see it, friend, but the Black Road will rule in the hearts of all men one day, and all things will come to their end. This is a war that will not be done until the world itself is unmade."

Tegric gazed after the receding figure for a time. Then he returned to his sewing.

A while later, his hand paused in its rhythmic motion, the needle poised in mid-descent. There was something moving amongst the rocks, back down the pass to the south. He carefully set aside his tunic and half-rose, leaning forward on one knee.

"Kilkry," he heard one of his warriors muttering off to his left.

And the shape coalescing out of the rock and the bright light did indeed look to be a rider. Nor was it alone. At least a score of horsemen were picking their way up the Vale of Stones.

Tegric laid a hand instinctively on the cool metal of his chain vest. He could feel the dried blood, the legacy of a week's almost constant battle, beneath his fingertips. He was not afraid to die. That was one fear the Black Road lifted from a man's back. If he feared anything, it was that he should fail in his determination to face, both willingly and humbly, whatever was to come.

"Ready yourselves," he said, loud enough for only the few nearest men to hear. They passed the word along. Tegric snapped the needle from the end of its thread and slipped his tunic back on. He lifted his mail shirt above his head and dropped its familiar weight onto his shoulders. Like smoke rising from a newly caught fire, the line of riders below was lengthening, curling and curving its way up the pass.

The horsemen of Kilkry were the best mounted warriors to be found in all the Bloods, but their prowess would count for little where Tegric had chosen to make his stand. A titanic fall of rocks from the cliffs above had almost choked the Stone Vale with rubble. The riders would be greatly hampered, perhaps even forced to dismount. Tegric's swordsmen and archers would have the advantage here. Later, when the main body of the pursuing army came up, they would be overwhelmed, but that did not matter.

He glanced at the sun, a searingly bright orb in the perfectly blue sky. He could hear the buzzards and the ravens, could glimpse their dark forms gliding in effortless spirals. It did not seem a bad place, a bad day, to die. If, when he woke in the new world the Black Road promised him, this was his last memory of his first life, of this failed world, it would not displease him.

Tegric Wyn dar Gyre rose and buckled on his sword belt.